Wedding Cocktails

Cocktails for Three
and
The Wedding Girl

Also by Madeleine Wickham

The Tennis Party
A Desirable Residence
Swimming Pool Sunday
The Gatecrasher
Sleeping Arrangements

Madeleine Wickham

Wedding Cocktails

Cocktails for Three

and

The Wedding Girl

Thomas Dunne Books
St. Martin's Griffin
New York

THOMAS DUNNE BOOKS.
An imprint of St. Martin's Press.

WEDDING COCKTAILS: COCKTAILS FOR THREE. Copyright © 2000 by Madeleine Wickham. THE WEDDING GIRL. Copyright © 1999 by Madeleine Wickham. All rights reserved. Printed in the United States of America. For information, address St. Martin's Press, 175 Fifth Avenue, New York, N.Y. 10010.

www.thomasdunnebooks.com
www.stmartins.com

The Library of Congress Cataloging-in-Publication Data is available upon request.

ISBN 978-1-250-09141-3 (trade paperback)

Our books may be purchased in bulk for promotional, educational, or business use. Please contact your local bookseller or the Macmillan Corporate and Premium Sales Department at 1-800-221-7945, extension 5442, or by e-mail at MacmillanSpecialMarkets@macmillan.com.

Cocktails for Three and *The Wedding Girl* first published in Great Britain by Transworld Publishers

First Edition: June 2016

10 9 8 7 6 5 4 3 2 1

Cocktails *for* Three

Many thanks to my agent Araminta Whitley, to Linda Evans and Sally Gaminara and all at Transworld, for their constant enthusiasm and encouragement during the writing of this book. To my parents and sisters for their continual, cheerful support and to my friends Ana-Maria and George Mosley, for always being there with a cocktail shaker at the ready.

And finally to my husband Henry, without whom this book would have been impossible, and to whom it is dedicated.

Chapter One

Candice Brewin pushed open the heavy glass door of the Manhattan Bar and felt the familiar swell of warmth, noise, light and clatter rush over her. It was six o'clock on a Wednesday night and the bar was already almost full. Waiters in dark green bow ties were gliding over the pale polished floor, carrying cocktails to tables. Girls in slippy dresses were standing at the bar, glancing around with bright, hopeful eyes. In the corner, a pianist was thumping out Gershwin numbers, almost drowned by the hum of metropolitan chatter.

It was getting to be too busy here, thought Candice, slipping off her coat. When she, Roxanne and Maggie had first discovered the Manhattan Bar, it had been a small, quiet, almost secretive place to meet. They had stumbled on it almost by chance, desperate for somewhere to drink after a particularly fraught press day. It had then been a dark and old-fashioned-looking place, with tatty bar stools and a peeling mural of the New York skyline on one wall. The patrons had been few and silent – mostly tending towards elderly gentlemen with much younger female companions. Candice, Roxanne and Maggie had boldly ordered a round of cocktails and then several more – and by the end of the evening had decided, amid fits of giggles, that the place had a certain terrible charm and must be re-visited. And so the monthly cocktail club had been born.

But now, newly extended, relaunched and written up in every glossy magazine, the bar was a different place. These days a young, attractive after-work crowd came flocking in every evening. Celebrities had been spotted at the bar. Even the waiters all looked like models. Really, thought Candice, handing her coat to the coat-check woman and receiving an art deco silver button in return, they should find somewhere else. Somewhere less busy, less obvious.

At the same time, she knew they never would. They had been coming here too long; had shared too many secrets over those distinctive frosted martini glasses. Anywhere else would feel wrong. On the first of every month, it had to be the Manhattan Bar.

There was a mirror opposite, and she glanced at her reflection, checking that her short cropped hair was tidy and her make-up – what little there was of it – hadn't smudged. She was wearing a plain black trouser suit over a pale green T-shirt – not exactly the height of glamour, but good enough.

Quickly she scanned the faces at the tables, but couldn't see Roxanne or Maggie. Although they all worked at the same place – the editorial office of the *Londoner* – it was rare they made the walk to the bar together. For a start, Roxanne was a freelance, and at times only seemed to use the office to make long-distance calls, arranging the next of her foreign jaunts. And Maggie, as editor of the magazine, often had to stay for meetings later than the others.

Not today, though, thought Candice, glancing at her watch. Today, Maggie had every excuse to slip off as early as she liked.

She brushed down her suit, walked towards the tables and, spotting a couple getting up, walked quickly forward. The young man had barely made it out of his chair before she was sliding into it and smiling gratefully up at him. You couldn't hang about if you wanted a table at the Manhattan Bar. And the three of them always had a table. It was part of the tradition.

Maggie Phillips paused outside the doors of the Manhattan Bar, put down her bulky carrier bag full of bright, stuffed toys, and pulled unceremoniously at the maternity tights wrinkling around her legs. Three more weeks, she thought, giving a final tug. Three more weeks of these bloody things. She took a deep breath, reached for her carrier bag again and pushed at the glass door.

As soon as she got inside, the noise and warmth of the place made her feel faint. She grasped for the wall, and stood quite still, trying not to lose her balance as she blinked away the dots in front of her eyes.

'Are you all right, my love?' enquired a voice to her left. Maggie swivelled her head and, as her vision cleared, made out the kindly face of the coat-check lady.

'I'm fine,' she said, flashing a tight smile.

'Are you sure? Would you like a nice drink of water?'

'No, really, I'm fine.' As if to emphasize the point she began to struggle out of her coat, self-consciously aware of the coat-check lady's appraising gaze on her figure. For pregnancy wear, her black Lycra trousers and tunic were about as flattering as you could get. But still there it was, right in front her, wherever she moved. A bump the size of a helium balloon. Maggie handed over her coat and met the coat lady's gaze head on.

If she asks me when it's due, she thought, I swear I'll smother her with Tinky Winky.

'When's it due?'

9

'The 25th of April,' said Maggie brightly. 'Three weeks to go.'

'Got your bag packed?' The woman twinkled at her. 'Don't want to leave it too late, do you?' Maggie's skin began to prickle. What bloody business was it of anyone's whether she'd packed her bag or not? Why did everyone keep *talking* to her about it? A complete stranger had come up to her in the pub at lunchtime, pointed to her wine glass and said, 'Naughty!' She'd nearly thrown it at him.

'Your first, is it,' the lady added, with no hint of interrogation in her voice.

So it's that obvious, thought Maggie. It's that clear to the rest of the world that I, Maggie Phillips – or Mrs Drakeford as I'm known at the clinic – have barely ever touched a baby. Let alone given birth to one.

'Yes, it's my first,' she said, and extended her palm, willing the lady to hand over her silver coat-check button and release her. But the woman was still gazing fondly at Maggie's protruding belly.

'I had four myself,' she said. 'Three girls and a boy. And each time, those first few weeks were the most magical time of all. You want to cherish those moments, love. Don't wish it all away.'

'I know,' Maggie heard herself saying, her mouth in a false beam.

I don't know! she yelled silently. I don't know anything about it. I know about page layout and editorial ratios and commissioning budgets. Oh God. What am I doing?

'Maggie!' A voice interrupted her and she wheeled round. Candice's round, cheerful face smiled back at her. 'I thought I saw you! I've nabbed a table.'

'Well done!' Maggie followed Candice through the throng, aware of the path her unwieldy bulk created; the curious glances following her. No-one else in the bar was pregnant. No-one was even fat. Everywhere

10

she looked she could see girls with flat stomachs and stick legs and pert little breasts.

'OK?' Candice had reached the table and was carefully pulling out a chair for her. Biting back a retort that she wasn't ill, Maggie sat down.

'Shall we order?' said Candice. 'Or wait for Roxanne?'

'Oh, I dunno.' Maggie gave a grumpy shrug. 'Better wait, I suppose.'

'Are you OK?' asked Candice curiously. Maggie sighed.

'I'm fine. I'm just sick of being pregnant. Being prodded and patted and treated like a freak.'

'A freak?' said Candice in disbelief. 'Maggie, you look fantastic!'

'Fantastic for a fat woman.'

'Fantastic full stop,' said Candice firmly. 'Listen, Maggie – there's a girl across the road from me who's pregnant at the moment. I tell you, if she saw the way you look, she'd throw up in jealousy.'

Maggie laughed. 'Candice, I adore you. You always say the right things.'

'It's true!' Candice reached for the cocktail menu – tall green leather with a silver tassle. 'Come on, let's have a look, anyway. Roxanne won't be long.'

Roxanne Miller stood in the ladies' room of the Manhattan Bar, leaned forward and carefully outlined her lips in cinnamon-coloured pencil. She pressed them together, then stood back and studied her reflection critically, starting – as she always did – with her best features. Good cheekbones. Nothing could take away your cheekbones. Blue eyes a little bloodshot, skin tanned from three weeks in the Caribbean. Nose still long, still crooked. Bronzy-blond hair tumbling down from a beaded comb in her hair. Tumbling a little too wildly, perhaps. Roxanne reached into her bag for a hairbrush and began to smooth it down. She was dressed, as she so often was, in a white T-shirt. In her opinion, nothing in the world showed off a tan better than a plain white T-shirt. She put her hairbrush away and smiled, impressed by her own reflection in spite of herself.

Then, behind her, a lavatory flushed and a cubicle door opened. A girl of about nineteen wandered out and stood next to Roxanne to wash her hands. She had pale, smooth skin and dark sleepy eyes, and her hair fell straight to her shoulders like the fringe on a lampshade. A mouth like a plum. No make-up whatsoever. The girl met Roxanne's eyes and smiled, then moved away.

When the swing doors had shut behind her, Roxanne still stayed, staring at herself. She suddenly felt like a blowsy tart. A thirty-three-year-old woman, trying too hard. In an instant, all the animation disappeared from her face. Her mouth drooped downwards and the gleam vanished from her eyes. Dispassionately, her gaze sought out the tiny red veins marking the skin on her cheeks. Sun damage, they called it. Damaged goods.

Then there was a sound from the door and her head jerked round.

'Roxanne!' Maggie was coming towards her, a wide smile on her face, her nut-brown bob shining under the spotlights.

'Darling!' Roxanne beamed, and gaily thrust her make-up bag into a larger Prada tote. 'I was just beautifying.'

'You don't need it!' said Maggie. 'Look at that tan!'

'That's Caribbean sun for you,' said Roxanne cheerfully.

'Don't tell me,' said Maggie, putting her hands over her ears. 'I don't want to know. It's not even approaching fair. Why did I never do a single travel feature while I was editor? I must have been mad!' She jerked her head towards the door. 'Go and keep Candice company. I'll be out in a moment.'

As she entered the bar, Roxanne saw Candice sitting alone, reading the cocktail menu, and an involuntary smile came to her lips. Candice always looked the same, wherever she was, whatever she was wearing. Her skin always looked well scrubbed and glowing, her hair was always cut in the same neat crop, she always dimpled in the same place when she smiled. And she always looked up with the same wide, trusting eyes. No wonder she was such a good interviewer, thought Roxanne fondly. People must just tumble into that friendly gaze.

'Candice!' she called, and waited for the pause, the lift of the head, the spark of recognition and wide smile.

It was a strange thing, thought Roxanne. She could walk past scores of adorable babies in pushchairs and never feel a tug on her maternal instinct. But sometimes, while looking at Candice, she would, with no warning, feel a pang in her heart. An obscure need to protect this girl, with her round face and innocent, childlike brow. But from what? From the world? From dark, malevolent strangers? It was ridiculous, really. After all, what was the difference between them in years? Four or five at most. Most of the time it seemed like nothing – yet sometimes Roxanne felt a generation older.

She strode up to the table and kissed Candice twice.

'Have you ordered?'

'I'm just looking,' said Candice, gesturing to the menu. 'I can't decide between a Summer Sunset or an Urban Myth.'

'Have the Urban Myth,' said Roxanne. 'A Summer Sunset is bright pink and comes with an umbrella.'

13

'Does it?' Candice wrinkled her brow. 'Does that matter? What are you having?'

'Margarita,' said Roxanne. 'Same as usual. I lived on Margaritas in Antigua.' She reached for a cigarette, then remembered Maggie and stopped. 'Margaritas and sunshine. That's all you need.'

'So – how was it?' said Candice. She leaned forward, eyes sparkling. 'Any toyboys this time?'

'Enough to keep me happy,' said Roxanne, grinning wickedly at her. 'One return visit in particular.'

'You're terrible!' said Candice.

'On the contrary,' said Roxanne, 'I'm very good. That's why they like me. That's why they come back for more.'

'What about your—' Candice broke off awkwardly.

'What about Mr Married with Kids?' said Roxanne lightly.

'Yes,' said Candice, colouring a little. 'Doesn't he mind when you . . . ?'

'Mr Married with Kids is not allowed to mind,' said Roxanne. 'Mr Married with Kids has got his wife, after all. Fair's fair, don't you think?' Her eyes glinted at Candice as though to forbid any more questions, and Candice bit her lip. Roxanne always discouraged talk of her married man. She had been with him for all the time that Candice had known her – but she had resolutely refused to divulge his identity, or even any details about him. Candice and Maggie had jokingly speculated between themselves that he must be somebody famous – a politician, perhaps – and certainly rich, powerful and sexy. Roxanne would never throw herself away on someone mediocre. Whether she was really in love with him, they were less sure. She was always so flippant, almost callous-sounding about the affair – it was as though she were using him, rather than the other way around.

'Look, I'm sorry,' said Roxanne, reaching again for

14

her cigarettes. 'Foetus or no foetus, I'm going to have to have a cigarette.'

'Oh, smoke away,' said Maggie, coming up behind her. 'I'm sure it can't be worse than pollution.' As she sat down, she beckoned to a cocktail waitress. 'Hi. Yes, we're ready to order.'

As the fair-haired girl in the green waistcoat came walking smartly over, Candice stared curiously at her. Something about her was familiar. Candice's eyes ran over the girl's wavy hair; her snub nose; her grey eyes, shadowed with tiredness. Even the way she shook her hair back off her shoulders seemed familiar. Where on earth had she seen her before?

'Is something wrong?' said the girl, politely, and Candice flushed.

'No. Of course not. Ahm . . .' She opened the cocktail menu again and ran her eyes down the lists without taking them in. The Manhattan Bar served over a hundred cocktails; sometimes she found the choice almost too great. 'A Mexican Swing, please.'

'A Margarita for me,' said Roxanne.

'Oh God, I don't know what to have,' said Maggie. 'I had wine at lunchtime . . .'

'A Virgin Mary?' suggested Candice.

'Definitely not.' Maggie pulled a face. 'Oh, sod it. A Shooting Star.'

'Good choice,' said Roxanne. 'Get the kid used to a bit of alcohol inside its system. And now . . .' She reached inside her bag. 'It's present time!'

'For who?' said Maggie, looking up in surprise. 'Not for me. I've had *heaps* of presents today. Far too many. Plus about five thousand Mothercare vouchers . . .'

'A Mothercare voucher?' said Roxanne disdainfully. 'That's not a present!' She produced a tiny blue box and put it on the table. 'This is a proper present.'

'Tiffany?' said Maggie incredulously. 'Really? Tiffany?' She opened the box with clumsy, swollen fingers and carefully took something silver from its tiny bag. 'I don't believe it! It's a rattle!' She shook it, and they all smiled with childish delight.

'Let me have a go!' said Candice.

'You'll have the most stylish baby on the block,' said Roxanne, a pleased expression on her face. 'If it's a boy, I'll get him cufflinks to match.'

'It's wonderful,' said Candice, staring admiringly at it. 'It makes my present seem really . . . Well, anyway.' She put the rattle down and started to rummage in her bag. 'It's here somewhere . . .'

'Candice Brewin!' said Roxanne accusingly, peering over her shoulder. 'What's that in your bag?'

'What?' said Candice, looking up guiltily.

'More tea towels! And a sponge.' Roxanne hauled the offending items out of Candice's bag and held them aloft. There were two blue tea towels and a yellow sponge, each wrapped in cellophane and marked 'Young People's Cooperative'. 'How much did you pay for these?' demanded Roxanne.

'Not much,' said Candice, at once. 'Hardly anything. About . . . five pounds.'

'Which means ten,' said Maggie, rolling her eyes at Roxanne. 'What are we going to do with her? Candice, you must have bought their whole bloody supply, by now!'

'Well, they're always useful, aren't they, tea towels?' said Candice, flushing. 'And I feel so bad, saying no.'

'Exactly,' said Maggie. 'You're not doing it because you think it's a good thing. You're doing it because if you don't, you'll feel bad.'

'Well, isn't that the same thing?' retorted Candice.

'No,' said Maggie. 'One's positive, and the other's negative. Or . . . something.' She screwed up her face. 'Oh God, I'm confused now. I need a cocktail.'

'Who cares?' said Roxanne. 'The point is, no more tea towels.'

'OK, OK,' said Candice, hurriedly stuffing the packets back in her bag. 'No more tea towels. And here's my present.' She produced an envelope and handed it to Maggie. 'You can take it any time.'

There was silence around the table as Maggie opened it and took out a pale pink card.

'An aromatherapy massage,' she read out disbelievingly. 'You've bought me a massage.'

'I just thought you might like it,' said Candice. 'Before you have the baby, or after . . . They come to your house, you don't have to go anywhere—' Maggie looked up, her eyes glistening slightly.

'You know, that's the only present anyone's bought for me. For *me*, as opposed to the baby.' She leaned across the table and gave Candice a hug. 'Thank you, my darling.'

'We'll really miss you,' said Candice. 'Don't stay away too long.'

'Well, you'll have to come and see me!' said Maggie. 'And the baby.'

'In your country manor,' said Roxanne sardonically. 'Mrs Drakeford At Home.' She grinned at Candice, who tried not to giggle.

When Maggie had announced, a year previously, that she and her husband Giles were moving to a cottage in the country, Candice had believed her. She had pictured a quaint little dwelling, with tiny crooked windows and a walled garden, somewhere in the middle of a village.

The truth had turned out to be rather different. Maggie's new house, The Pines, had turned out to be situated at the end of a long, tree-lined drive. It had turned out to have eight bedrooms and a billiards room and a swimming pool. Maggie, it had turned out, was secretly married to a millionaire.

'You never told us!' Candice had said accusingly as they'd sat in the vast kitchen, drinking tea made on the equally vast Aga. 'You never told us you were rolling in it!'

'We're not rolling in it!' Maggie had retorted defensively, cradling her Emma Bridgwater mug. 'It just . . . looks bigger because it's in the country.' This remark she had never been allowed to forget.

'It just looks bigger . . .' Roxanne began now, snorting with laughter. 'It just *looks* bigger . . .'

'Oh, shut up, y'all,' said Maggie good-naturedly. 'Look, here come the cocktails.'

The blond-haired girl was coming towards them, holding a silver tray on the flat of her hand. Three glasses were balanced on it. One a Margarita glass, frosted round the rim, one a highball decorated with a single fanned slice of lime, and one a champagne flute adorned with a strawberry.

'Very classy,' murmured Roxanne. 'Not a cherry in sight.'

The girl set the glasses down expertly on their paper coasters, added a silver dish of salted almonds, and discreetly placed the bill – hidden inside a green leather folder – to one side of the table. As she stood up, Candice looked again at her face, trying to jog her memory. She knew this girl from somewhere. She was sure of it. But from where?

'Thanks very much,' said Maggie.

'No problem,' said the girl, and smiled – and as she did so, Candice knew, in a flash, who she was.

'Heather Trelawney,' she said aloud, before she could stop herself. And then, as the girl's eyes slowly turned towards her, she wished with all her soul that she hadn't.

Chapter Two

'I'm sorry,' began the girl puzzledly. 'Do I—' She stopped, took a step nearer and peered at Candice. Then suddenly her face lit up. 'Of course!' she said. 'It's Candice, isn't it? Candice . . .' She wrinkled her brow. 'Sorry, I've forgotten your last name.'

'Brewin,' said Candice in a frozen voice, barely able to utter the syllables. Her name seemed to rest in the air like a physical presence; a target, inviting attack. *Brewin*. As she saw Heather frowning thoughtfully, Candice flinched, waiting for the jolt of recognition, the anger and recriminations. Why had she not just kept her stupid mouth shut? What hideous scene was going to ensue?

But as Heather's face cleared, it was obvious that she recognized Candice as nothing but an old school acquaintance. Didn't she know? thought Candice incredulously. *Didn't she know?*

'Candice Brewin!' said Heather. 'That's right! I should have recognized you straight away.'

'How funny!' said Maggie. 'How do you two know each other?'

'We were at school together,' said Heather brightly. 'It must be *years* since we've seen each other.' She looked again at Candice. 'You know, I thought there was something about you, when I took your order. But

19

. . . I don't know. You look different, somehow. I suppose we've all changed since then.'

'I suppose so,' said Candice. She picked up her glass and took a sip, trying to calm her beating heart.

'And I know this is going to sound bad,' said Heather, lowering her voice, 'but after you've been waitressing for a while, you stop looking at the customers' faces. Is that awful?'

'I don't blame you,' said Maggie. 'I wouldn't want to look at our faces either.'

'Speak for yourself,' retorted Roxanne at once, and grinned at Maggie.

'You know, I once took an order from Simon Le Bon,' said Heather. 'Not here, at my old place. I took the order, and I didn't even notice who he was. When I got back to the kitchen, everyone was going "what's he like?" and I didn't know what they were talking about.'

'Good for you,' said Roxanne. 'It does these people good not to be recognized.'

Maggie glanced at Candice. She was staring at Heather as though transfixed. What the hell was wrong with her?

'So, Heather,' she said quickly, 'have you been working here long?'

'Only a couple of weeks,' said Heather. 'It's a nice place, isn't it? But they keep us busy.' She glanced towards the bar. 'Speaking of which, I'd better get on. Good to see you, Candice.'

She began to move off, and Candice felt a jolt of alarm.

'Wait!' she said. 'We haven't caught up properly.' She swallowed. 'Why don't you . . . sit down for a minute?'

'Well, OK,' said Heather after a pause. She glanced again at the bar. 'But I can't be long. We'll have to pretend I'm advising you on cocktails or something.'

20

'We don't need any advising,' said Roxanne. 'We *are* the cocktail queens.' Heather giggled.

'I'll just see if I can find a chair,' she said. 'Back in a tick.'

As soon as she had walked away, Maggie turned to Candice.

'What's wrong?' she hissed. 'Who is this girl? You're staring at her as though you've seen a bloody ghost!'

'Is it that obvious?' said Candice in dismay.

'Darling, you look as if you're practising to play Hamlet,' said Roxanne drily.

'Oh God,' said Candice. 'And I thought I was doing quite well.' She picked up her cocktail with a shaking hand and took a gulp. 'Cheers, everybody.'

'Never mind bloody cheers!' said Maggie. 'Who is she?'

'She's—' Candice rubbed her brow. 'I knew her years ago. We were at school together. She – she was a couple of years below me.'

'We know all that!' said Maggie impatiently. 'What else?'

'Hi!' Heather's bright voice interrupted them, and they all looked up guiltily. 'I found a chair at last.' She set it at the table and sat down. 'Are the cocktails good?'

'Wonderful!' said Maggie, taking a gulp of her Shooting Star. 'Just what the midwife ordered.'

'So – what are you up to now?' said Heather to Candice.

'I'm a journalist,' said Candice.

'Really?' Heather looked at her wistfully. 'I'd love to do something like that. Do you write for a newspaper?'

'A magazine. The *Londoner.*'

'I know the *Londoner*!' said Heather. 'I've probably even read articles you've written.' She looked around the table. 'Are you all journalists?'

'Yes,' said Maggie. 'We all work together.'

'God, that must be fun.'

'It has its moments,' said Maggie, grinning at Roxanne. 'Some better than others.'

There was brief silence, then Candice said, with a slight tremor in her voice, 'And what about you, Heather? What have you done since school?' She took another deep gulp of her cocktail.

'Oh well . . .' Heather gave a quick little smile. 'It was all a bit grim, actually. I don't know if you know – but the reason I left Oxdowne was my father lost all his money.'

'How awful!' said Maggie. 'What – overnight?'

'Pretty much,' said Heather. Her grey eyes darkened slightly. 'Some investment went wrong. The stock markets or something – my dad never said exactly what. And that was it. They couldn't afford school fees any more. Or the house. It was all a bit horrendous. My dad got really depressed over it, and my mum blamed him . . .' She broke off awkwardly. 'Well, anyway.' She picked up a paper coaster and began to fiddle with it. 'They split up in the end.'

Maggie glanced at Candice for a reaction, but her face was averted. She had a cocktail stirrer in her hand and was stirring her drink, round and round.

'And what about you?' said Maggie cautiously to Heather.

'I kind of lost it, too, for a bit.' Heather gave another quick little smile. 'You know, one minute I was at a nice fee-paying school with all my friends. The next, we'd moved to a town where I didn't know anyone, and my parents were arguing all the time, and I went to a school where they all gave me a hard time for talking posh.' She sighed, and let the coaster drop from her fingers. 'I mean, looking back, it was quite a good comprehensive. I should have just stuck it out and gone on to college . . . but I didn't. I left as soon as I was sixteen.' She pushed back her thick, wavy hair. 'My dad was living in London by then so I moved in with him and got a job in a wine bar. And that was it, really. I never did a degree, or anything.'

'What a shame,' said Maggie. 'What would you have done, if you'd stayed on?'

'Oh, I don't know,' said Heather. She gave an embarrassed little laugh. 'Done something like you're doing, maybe. Become a journalist, or something. I started a creative writing course once, at Goldsmiths', but I had to give it up.' She looked around the bar and shrugged. 'I mean, I do like working here. But it's not really . . . Anyway.' She stood up and tugged at her green waistcoat. 'I'd better get going, or André will kill me. See you later!'

As she walked away, the three of them sat in silence, watching her. Then Maggie turned to Candice, and said carefully,

'She seems nice.'

Candice didn't reply. Maggie looked questioningly at Roxanne, who raised her eyebrows.

'Candice, what's wrong?' said Maggie. 'Is there some history between you and Heather?'

'Darling, speak to us,' said Roxanne.

Candice said nothing, but continued stirring her cocktail, faster and faster and faster, until the liquid threatened to spill over the sides of the glass. Then she looked up at her friends.

'It wasn't the stock markets,' she said in a flat voice. 'It wasn't the stock markets that ruined Frank Trelawney. It was my father.'

Heather Trelawney stood at the corner of the bar, by the entrance to the kitchen, watching Candice Brewin's face through the crush of people. She couldn't take her eyes off the sight. Gordon Brewin's daughter, large as life, sitting at the table with her friends. With her nice haircut, and her good job, and money for cocktails

23

every night. Oblivious of what suffering her father had caused. Unaware of anything except herself.

Because she'd come out all right, hadn't she? Of course she had. Good-Time Gordon had been very clever like that. He'd never used his own money. He'd never put his own life on the line. Only other people's. Other poor saps, too greedy to say no. Like her poor reckless, stupid dad. At the thought, Heather's chin tightened, and her hands gripped her silver tray harder.

'Heather!' It was André, the head waiter, calling from the bar. 'What are you doing? Customers waiting!'

'Coming!' called back Heather. She put down her silver tray, shook out her hair and tied it back tightly with a rubber band. Then she picked up her tray and walked smartly to the bar, never once taking her eyes off Candice Brewin.

'They called him Good-Time Gordon,' said Candice in a trembling voice. 'He was there at every single party. Life and soul.' She took a gulp of her cocktail. 'And every school function. Every concert, every gym display. I used to think it was because – you know, he was proud of me. But all the time, he just wanted to pick up new contacts to do business with. Frank Trelawney wasn't the only one. He got to all our friends, all our neighbours . . .' Her hand tightened around her glass. 'They all started popping up after the funeral. Some had invested money with him, some had lent him money and he'd never paid it back . . .' She took a swig of her cocktail. 'It was horrendous. These people were our friends. And we'd had no idea.'

Roxanne and Maggie glanced at each other.

'So how do you know Heather's father was involved?' said Maggie.

'I found out when we went through the paperwork,' said Candice blankly. 'My mother and I had to go into his study and sort out the mess. It was . . . just awful.'

'How did your mum take it?' asked Maggie curiously.

'Terribly,' said Candice. 'Well, you can imagine. He'd actually told some people he needed to borrow money from them because she was an alcoholic and he wanted to put her through rehab.'

Roxanne snorted with laughter, then said,

'Sorry.'

'I still can't talk to her about it,' said Candice. 'In fact, I think she's pretty much persuaded herself it never happened. If I even mention it, she gets all hysterical . . .' She lifted a hand and began to massage her forehead.

'I had no idea about this,' said Maggie. 'You've never even mentioned any of this before.'

'Yes, well,' said Candice shortly. 'I'm not exactly proud of it. My father did a lot of damage.'

She closed her eyes as unwanted memories of that dreadful time after his death came flooding back into her mind. It had been at the funeral that she'd first noticed something wrong. Friends and relatives, clumped in little groups, had stopped talking as soon as she came near. Voices had been hushed and urgent; everyone had seemed to be in on one big secret. As she'd passed one group, she'd heard the words, '*How* much?'

Then the visitors had started arriving, ostensibly to pay their condolences. But sooner or later the conversation had always turned to money. To the five or ten thousand pounds that Gordon had borrowed. To the investments that had been made. No hurry, of course – they quite understood things were difficult . . . Even Mrs Stephens, their cleaning lady, had awkwardly brought up the subject of a hundred pounds, loaned some months ago and never repaid.

At the memory of the woman's embarrassed face,

Candice felt her stomach contract again with humiliation; with a hot, teenage guilt. She still felt as though she were somehow to blame. Even though she'd known nothing about it; even though there was nothing she could have done.

'And what about Frank Trelawney?' said Maggie. Candice opened her eyes dazedly, and picked up the cocktail stirrer again.

'He was on a list of names in the study,' she said. 'He'd invested two hundred thousand pounds in some venture capital project which folded after a few months.' She began to run the silver stirrer around the rim of her glass. 'At first I didn't know who Frank Trelawney was. It was just another name. But it seemed familiar . . . And then I suddenly remembered Heather Trelawney leaving school with no warning. It all made sense.' She bit her lip. 'I think that was the worst moment of all. Knowing that Heather had lost her place at school because of my father.'

'You can't just blame your father,' said Maggie gently. 'This Mr Trelawney must have known what he was doing. He must have known there was a certain risk.'

'I always used to wonder what happened to Heather,' said Candice, as though she hadn't heard. 'And now I know. Another life ruined.'

'Candice, don't beat yourself up about this,' said Maggie. 'It's not your fault. You didn't do anything!'

'I know,' said Candice. 'Logically, you're right. But it's not that easy.'

'Have another drink,' advised Roxanne. 'That'll cheer you up.'

'Good idea,' said Maggie, and drained her glass. She lifted her hand and, on the other side of the room, Heather nodded.

Candice stared at Heather as she bent down to pick up some empty glasses from a table and wipe it over, unaware she was being watched. As she stood up again, Heather gave a sudden yawn and rubbed her face with tiredness, and Candice felt her heart contract with emotion. She had to do something for this girl, she thought suddenly. She had to absolve her guilt for at least one of her father's crimes.

'Listen,' she said quickly, as Heather began to approach the table. 'They haven't got a new editorial assistant for the *Londoner* yet, have they?'

'Not as far as I know,' said Maggie in surprise. 'Why?'

'Well, what about Heather?' said Candice. 'She'd be ideal. Wouldn't she?'

'Would she?' Maggie wrinkled her brow.

'She wants to be a journalist, she's done creative writing . . . she'd be perfect! Oh, go on, Maggie!' Candice looked up, to see Heather approaching. 'Heather, listen!'

'Do you want some more drinks?' said Heather.

'Yes,' said Candice. 'But . . . but not just that.' She looked at Maggie entreatingly. Maggie gave her a mock-glare, then grinned.

'We were wondering, Heather,' she said, 'if you'd be interested in a job on the *Londoner*. Editorial assistant. It's pretty low-ranking, and the money's not great, but it's a start in journalism.'

'Are you serious?' said Heather, looking from one to the other. 'I'd love it!'

'Good,' said Maggie, and took out a card from her bag. 'This is the address, but it won't be me processing the applications. The person you need to write to is Justin Vellis.' She wrote the name on the card and handed it to Heather. 'Just write a letter about yourself, and pop in a CV. OK?'

Candice stared at her in dismay.

'Great!' said Heather. 'And . . . thanks.'

'And now I suppose we'd better choose some more

cocktails,' said Maggie cheerfully. 'It's a tough old life.'

When Heather had departed with their order, Maggie grinned at Candice and leaned back in her chair.

'There you are,' she said. 'Feel better now?' She frowned at Candice's expression. 'Candice, are you OK?'

'To be honest, no!' said Candice, trying to stay calm. 'I'm not! Is that all you're going to do? Give her the address?'

'What do you mean?' said Maggie in surprise. 'Candice, what's wrong?'

'I thought you were going to give her the job!'

'What, on the spot?' said Maggie, beginning to laugh. 'Candice, you must be joking.'

'Or an interview . . . or a personal recommendation, at least,' said Candice, flushing in distress. 'If she just sends in her CV like everyone else, there's no *way* Justin will give her the job! He'll appoint some awful Oxford graduate or something.'

'Like himself,' put in Roxanne with a grin. 'Some nice smarmy intellectual.'

'Exactly! Maggie, you know Heather hasn't got a chance unless you recommend her. Especially if he knows she's anything to do with me!' Candice flushed slightly as she said the words. It was only a few weeks since she had broken up with Justin, the features editor who was taking over from Maggie as acting editor. She still felt a little awkward, talking about him.

'But Candice, I can't recommend her,' said Maggie simply. 'I don't know anything about her. And neither, let's face it, do you. I mean, you haven't seen her for years, have you? She could be a criminal for all you know.'

Candice stared into her drink miserably, and Maggie sighed.

'Candice, I can understand how you feel, truly I can,'

she said. 'But you can't just leap in and procure a job for some woman you hardly know, just because you feel sorry for her.'

'I agree,' said Roxanne firmly. 'You'll be giving the tea towel girl a personal recommendation next.'

'And what would be wrong with that?' said Candice with a sudden fierceness. 'What's wrong with giving people a boost every so often if they deserve it? You know, we three have had it very easy, compared to the rest of the world.' She gestured round the table. 'We've got good jobs, and happy lives, and we haven't the first idea what it's like to have nothing.'

'Heather doesn't have nothing,' said Maggie calmly. 'She has good looks, she has a brain, she has a job, and she has every opportunity to go back to college if she wants to. It's not your job to sort her life out for her. OK?'

'OK,' said Candice after a pause.

'Good,' said Maggie. 'Lecture over.'

An hour later, Maggie's husband Giles arrived at the Manhattan Bar. He stood at the side of the room, peering through the throng – then spotted Maggie's face. She was clutching a cocktail, her cheeks were flushed pink and her head was thrown back in laughter. Giles smiled fondly at the sight, and headed towards the table.

'Man alert,' he said cheerfully as he approached. 'Kindly cease all jokes about male genitals.'

'Giles!' said Maggie, looking up in slight dismay. 'Is it time to go already?'

'We don't have to,' said Giles. 'I could stay for a drink or two.'

'No,' said Maggie after a pause. 'It's OK, let's go.'

It never quite worked when Giles joined the group. Not because the other two didn't like him – and not because he didn't make an effort. He was always genial

29

and polite, and conversation always flowed nicely. But it just wasn't the same. He wasn't one of them. Well – how could he be? thought Maggie. He wasn't a woman.

'I've got to go soon, anyway,' said Roxanne, draining her glass and putting her cigarettes away. 'I have someone to see.'

'Would that be Someone?' said Maggie with a deliberate emphasis.

'Possibly.' Roxanne smiled at her.

'I can't believe this is it!' said Candice, looking at Maggie. 'We won't see you again till you've had the baby!'

'Don't remind me!' said Maggie, flashing an over-cheerful smile.

She pushed back her chair and gratefully took the hand Giles offered. They all slowly made their way through the crowds to the coat-check, and surrendered their silver buttons.

'And don't think you're allowed to give up on the cocktail club,' said Roxanne to Maggie. 'We'll be round your bed in a month's time, toasting the babe.'

'It's a date,' said Maggie, and suddenly felt her eyes fill with easy tears. 'Oh God, I'm going to miss you guys.'

'We'll see you soon,' said Roxanne, and gave her a hug. 'Good luck, darling.'

'OK,' said Maggie, trying to smile. She suddenly felt as though she were saying goodbye to her friends for ever; as though she were entering a new world into which they wouldn't be able to follow.

'Maggie doesn't need luck!' said Candice. 'She'll have that baby licked into shape in no time!'

'Hey, baby,' said Roxanne, addressing Maggie's stomach humorously. 'You are aware that your mother is the most organized woman in Western civilization?' She pretended to listen to the bump. 'It says it wants to have someone else. Tough luck, kid.'

'And listen, Candice,' said Maggie, turning to her kindly. 'Don't let Justin lord it over you just because he's in charge for a few months. I know it's a difficult situation for you . . .'

'Don't worry,' said Candice at once. 'I can handle him.'

'Justin the bloody wunderkind,' said Roxanne, dismissively. 'You know, I'm glad we can all be rude about him now.'

'You always were rude about him,' pointed out Candice. 'Even when I was going out with him.'

'Well, he deserves it,' said Roxanne, unabashed. 'Anyone who comes to a cocktail bar and orders a bottle of claret is obviously a complete waste of space.'

'Candice, they can't seem to find your coat,' said Giles, appearing at Maggie's shoulder. 'But here's yours, Roxanne, and yours, darling. I think we should get going, otherwise it'll be midnight before we get back.'

'Right, well,' said Maggie in a shaky voice. 'This is it.'

She and Candice looked at each other, half grinning, half blinking back tears.

'We'll see each other soon,' said Candice. 'I'll come and visit.'

'And I'll come up to London.'

'You can bring the baby up for day trips,' said Candice. 'They're supposed to be the latest accessory.'

'I know,' said Maggie, giving a little laugh. She leaned forward and hugged Candice. 'You take care.'

'And you,' said Candice. 'Good luck with . . . everything. Bye, Giles,' she added. 'Nice to see you.'

Giles opened the glass door of the bar, and after one final backwards glance, Maggie walked out into the cold night air. Roxanne and Candice watched silently through the glass as Giles took Maggie's arm and they disappeared down the dark street.

'Just think,' said Candice. 'In a few weeks, they won't be a couple any more. They'll be a family.'

'So they will,' said Roxanne in indeterminate tones. 'A happy little family, all together in their huge, fuck-off happy house.' Candice glanced at her.

'Are you OK?'

'Of course I'm OK!' said Roxanne. 'Just glad it isn't me! The very thought of stretchmarks . . .' She gave a mock-shudder then smiled. 'I've got to shoot off, I'm afraid. Do you mind?'

'Of course not,' said Candice. 'Have a good time.'

'I always have a good time,' said Roxanne, 'even if I'm having a terrible time. See you when I get back from Cyprus.' She kissed Candice briskly on each cheek and disappeared out of the door. Candice watched her hailing a taxi and jumping in; after a few seconds, the taxi zoomed off down the street.

Candice waited until it had disappeared, counted to five – then, feeling like a naughty child, swivelled round to face the crowded bar again. Her stomach felt taut with expectation; her heart was thumping quickly.

'I've found your coat!' came the voice of the coat-check lady. 'It had fallen off its hanger.'

'Thanks,' said Candice. 'But I've just got to . . .' She swallowed. 'I'll be back in a moment.'

She hurried through the press of people, feeling light and determined. She had never felt so sure of herself in her life. Maggie and Roxanne meant well, but they were wrong. This time, they were wrong. They didn't understand – why should they? They couldn't see that this was the opportunity she'd unconsciously been waiting for ever since her father's death. This was her chance to make things right. It was like . . . a gift.

At first she couldn't see Heather, and she thought with a sinking heart that she was too late. But then, scanning the room again, she spotted her. She was behind the bar, polishing a glass and laughing with one

32

of the waiters. Fighting her way through the crowds, Candice made her way to the bar and waited patiently, not wanting to interrupt.

Eventually Heather looked up and saw her – and to Candice's surprise, a flash of hostility seemed to pass over her features. But it disappeared almost at once, and her face broke into a welcoming smile.

'What can I get you?' she said. 'Another cocktail?'

'No, I just wanted a word,' said Candice, feeling herself having to shout over the background hubbub. 'About this job.'

'Oh yes?'

'If you like, I can introduce you to the publisher, Ralph Allsopp,' said Candice. 'No guarantees – but it might help your chances. Come to the office tomorrow at about ten.'

'Really?' Heather's face lit up. 'That would be wonderful!' She put down the glass she was polishing, leaned forward and took Candice's hands. 'Candice, this is really good of you. I don't know how to thank you.'

'Well, you know,' said Candice awkwardly. 'Old school friends and all that . . .'

'Yes,' said Heather, and smiled sweetly at Candice. 'Old school friends.'

Chapter Three

As they reached the motorway, it began to rain. Giles reached down and turned on Radio Three, and a glorious soprano's voice filled the car. After a few notes, Maggie recognized the piece as 'Dove Sono' from *The Marriage of Figaro* – in her opinion, the most beautiful, poignant aria ever written. As the music soared over her, Maggie stared out of the rain-spattered windscreen and felt foolish tears coming to her eyes, in sympathy with the fictitious Countess. A good and beautiful wife, unloved by her philandering husband, sadly recalling moments of tenderness between them. *I remember . . .*

Maggie blinked a few times and took a deep breath. This was ridiculous. Everything was reducing her to tears at the moment. The other day, she'd wept at an advertisement on television in which a boy cooked supper for his two small sisters. She'd sat on the living-room floor, tears streaming down her face – and when Giles had come into the room, had had to turn away and pretend to be engrossed in a magazine.

'Did you have a good send-off?' asked Giles, changing lanes.

'Yes, lovely,' said Maggie. 'Heaps of presents. People are so generous.'

'And how did you leave it with Ralph?'

'I told him I'd call him after a few months. That's what I've told everybody.'

'I still think you should have been honest with them,' said Giles. 'I mean, you know you've no intention of going back to work.'

Maggie was silent. She and Giles had discussed at length whether she should return to work after the baby was born. On the one hand, she adored her job and her staff, was well paid, and felt that there were still things she wanted to achieve in her career. On the other hand, the image of leaving her baby behind and commuting to London every day seemed appalling. And after all, what was the point of living in a large house in the country and never seeing it?

The fact that she had never actually wanted to move to the country was something which Maggie had almost successfully managed to forget. Even before she'd become pregnant, Giles had been desperate for his future children to have the rough-and-tumble, fresh-air upbringing which he had enjoyed. 'London isn't healthy for children,' he had pronounced. And although Maggie had pointed out again and again that the London streets were full of perfectly healthy children; that parks were safer places to ride bicycles than country lanes; that nature existed even in cities, Giles had still not been persuaded.

Then, when he'd started applying for the details of country houses – glorious old rectories, complete with panelled dining rooms, acres of land and tennis courts – she'd found herself weakening. Wondering if it was indeed selfish to stay in London. On a wonderfully sunny day in June, they'd gone to look at The Pines. The drive had crackled under the wheels of their car; the swimming pool had glinted in the sun, the lawns had been mowed in light and dark green stripes. After showing them round the house, the owners had poured them glasses of Pimm's and invited them to sit under the weeping willow, then tactfully moved away. And Giles had looked at Maggie and said, 'This could be ours, darling. This life could be ours.'

And now that life was theirs. Except it wasn't so much a life yet as a large house which Maggie still didn't feel she knew very well. On working days, she barely saw the place. At the weekends, they often went away, or up to London to see friends. She had done none of the redecorations she had planned; in some strange way she felt as though the house wasn't really hers yet.

But things would be different when the baby arrived, she told herself. The house would really become a home. Maggie put her hands on her bump and felt the squirming, intriguing movements beneath her skin. A smooth lump rippled across her belly and disappeared as though back into the ocean. Then, with no warning, something hard jabbed into her ribs. A heel, perhaps, or a knee. It jabbed again and again, as though desperate to break out. Maggie closed her eyes. It could be any time now, her pregnancy handbook had advised her. The baby was fully matured; she could go into labour at any moment.

At the thought, her heart began to thump with a familiar panic, and she began quickly to think reassuring thoughts. Of course, she was prepared for the baby. She had a nursery full of nappies and cotton wool; tiny vests and blankets. The Moses basket was ready on its stand; the cot had been ordered from a department store. Everything was waiting.

But somehow – despite all that – she secretly still didn't feel quite ready to be a mother. She almost didn't feel *old* enough to be a mother. Which was ridiculous, she told herself firmly, bearing in mind she was thirty-two years old and had had an entire nine months to get used to the idea.

'You know, I can't believe it's really happening,' she

said. 'Three weeks away. That's nothing! And I haven't been to any classes, or anything . . .'

'You don't need classes!' said Giles. 'You'll be great! The best mother a baby could have.'

'Really?' Maggie bit her lip. 'I don't know. I just feel a bit . . . unprepared.'

'What's to prepare?'

'Well, you know. Labour, and everything.'

'One word,' said Giles firmly. 'Drugs.'

Maggie giggled. 'And afterwards. You know. Looking after it. I've never even *held* a baby.'

'You'll be fantastic!' said Giles at once. 'Maggie, if anyone can look after a baby, you can. Come on.' He turned and flashed a smile at her. 'Who was voted Editor of the Year?'

'I was,' she said, grinning proudly in spite of herself.

'Well then. And you'll be Mother of the Year, too.' He reached out and squeezed her hand, and Maggie squeezed gratefully back. Giles's optimism never failed to cheer her.

'Mum said she'd pop round tomorrow,' said Giles. 'Keep you company.'

'Oh good,' said Maggie. She thought of Giles's mother, Paddy – a thin, dark-haired woman who had, unaccountably, produced three huge, cheerful sons with thick, fair hair. Giles and his two brothers adored their mother – and it had been no coincidence that The Pines was in the next-door village to Giles's old family home. At first, Maggie had been slightly discomfited at the proximity of their new house to her in-laws. But, after all, her own parents were miles away, in Derbyshire and, as Giles had pointed out, it would be useful to have at least one set of grandparents around.

'She was saying, you'll have to get to know all the other young mums in the village,' said Giles.

'Are there many?'

'I think so. Sounds like one long round of coffee mornings.'

'Oh good!' said Maggie teasingly. 'So while you slave away in the City I can sip cappuccinos with all my chums.'

'Something like that.'

'Sounds better than commuting,' said Maggie, and leaned back comfortably. 'I should have done this years ago.' She closed her eyes and imagined herself in her kitchen, making coffee for a series of new, vibrant friends with cute babies dressed in designer clothes. In the summers they would hold picnics on the lawn. Roxanne and Candice would come down from London and they would all drink Pimm's while the baby gurgled happily on a rug. They would look like something from a lifestyle magazine. In fact, maybe the *Londoner* would run a piece on them. *Former editor Maggie Phillips and her new take on rural bliss.* It was going to be a whole new life, she thought happily. A whole wonderful new life.

The brightly lit train bounced and rattled along the track, then came to an abrupt halt in a tunnel. The lights flickered, went off, then went on again. A group of party-goers several seats down from Candice began to sing 'Why are we waiting', and the woman across from Candice tried to catch her eye and tut. But Candice didn't see. She was staring blindly at her shadowy reflection in the window opposite, as memories of her father which she had buried for years rose painfully through her mind.

Good-Time Gordon, tall and handsome, always dressed in an immaculate navy blazer with gilt buttons. Always buying a round, always everyone's friend. He'd been a charming man, with vivid blue eyes and a firm handshake. Everyone who met him had admired him. Her friends had thought her lucky to have such a fun-loving father – a dad who let her go to the pub; who bought her stylish clothes; who threw holiday brochures down on the table and said 'You choose' and meant it. Life had been endless entertainment. Parties, holidays, weekends away, with her father always at the centre of the fun.

And then he'd died, and the horror had begun. Now Candice could not think of him without feeling sick, humiliated; hot with shame. He'd fooled everybody. Taken them all for a ride. Every word he'd ever uttered now seemed double-edged. Had he really loved her? Had he really loved her mother? The whole of his life had been a charade – so why not his feelings, too?

Hot tears began to well up in her eyes, and she took a deep breath. She didn't usually allow herself to think about her father. As far as she was concerned he was dead, gone, excised from her life. In the midst of those dreadful days full of pain and confusion, she'd walked into a hairdresser's and asked to have all her long hair cropped off. As the lengths of hair had fallen onto the floor, she'd felt as though her connections with her father were, in some way, being severed.

But of course, it wasn't as easy as that. She was still her father's daughter; she still bore his name. And she was still the beneficiary of all his shady dealings. Other people's money had paid for her clothes and her skiing trips and the little car she'd been given for her seventeenth birthday. The expensive year off before university – history of art lessons in Florence followed by trekking in Nepal. Other people's hard-earned money had been squandered on her pleasure. The thought of it still made her feel sick with anger; with self-reproach. But how could she have known? She'd only been a child. And her father had managed to fool everybody. Until his car crash, halfway through her first year at university. His sudden, horrific, unexpected death.

Candice felt her face grow hot all over again, and tightly gripped the plastic armrests of her seat as, with a jolt, the train started up again. Despite everything, she still felt grief for her father. A searing, angry grief – not only for him, but for her innocence; her childhood. She grieved for the time when the world had seemed to make sense; when all she'd felt for her father was love and pride. The time when she'd happily held her head high and been proud of her name and family. Before everything had suddenly darkened and become coated in dishonesty.

After his death, there hadn't been nearly enough money left to pay everyone back. Most people had given up asking; a few had taken her mother to court. It had been several years before everyone was finally settled and silenced. But the pain had never been alleviated; the damage had never been properly repaired. The consequences to people's lives could not be settled so quickly.

Candice's mother Diana had moved away to Devon, where no-one had heard of Gordon Brewin. Now she lived in a state of rigid denial. As far as she was concerned, she had been married to a loving, honourable man, maligned after his death by evil rumours – and that was the end of it. She allowed herself no true memories of the past, felt no guilt; experienced no pain.

If Candice ever tried to bring up the subject of her father, Diana would refuse to listen, refuse to talk about it; refuse to admit – even between the two of them – that anything had happened. Several years after moving to Devon she had begun a relationship with a mild-mannered, elderly man named Kenneth – and he now acted as a protective buffer. He was always present when Candice visited, ensuring that conversation never ventured beyond the polite and inconsequential. And so Candice had given up trying

40

to get her mother to confront the past. There was no point, she had decided – and at least Diana had salvaged some happiness in her life. But she rarely visited her mother any more. The duplicity and weakness of the whole situation – the fact that Diana wouldn't admit the truth, even to her own daughter – slightly sickened Candice.

As a result, she had found herself shouldering the entire burden of memories herself. She would not allow herself the easy option, like her mother; she would not allow herself to forget or deny. And so she had learned to live with a constant guilt; a constant, angry shame. It had mellowed a little since those first nightmare years; she had learned to put it to the back of her mind and get on with her life. But the guilt had never quite left her.

Tonight, however, she felt as though she'd turned a corner. Perhaps she couldn't undo what her father had done. Perhaps she couldn't repay everyone. But she could repay Heather Trelawney – if not in money, then in help and friendship. Helping Heather as much as she possibly could would be her own private atonement.

As she got off the tube at Highbury and Islington, she felt light and hopeful. She briskly walked the few streets to the Victorian house where she had lived for the last two years, let herself in at the front door and bounded up the flight of stairs to her first-floor flat.

'Hey, Candice.' A voice interrupted her as she reached for her Yale key, and she turned round. It was Ed Armitage, who lived in the flat opposite. He was standing in the doorway of his flat, wearing ancient jeans and eating a Big Mac. 'I've got that Sellotape, if you want it back.'

'Oh,' said Candice. 'Thanks.'

'Give me a sec.' He disappeared into his flat, and

Candice leaned against her own front door, waiting. She didn't want to open her door and find him inviting himself in for a drink. Tonight, to be honest, she wasn't in the mood for Ed.

Ed had lived opposite Candice for as long as she'd lived there. He was a corporate lawyer at a huge City law firm, earned unfeasibly large amounts of money, and worked unfeasibly long hours. Taxis were frequently to be heard chugging outside the house for him at six in the morning, and didn't deliver him back home until after midnight. Sometimes he didn't come home at all, but caught a few hours' sleep on a bed at the office, then started again. The very thought of it made Candice feel sick. It was pure greed that drove him so hard, she thought. Nothing but greed.

'Here you are,' said Ed, reappearing. He handed her the roll of tape and took a bite of his Big Mac. 'Want some?'

'No thanks,' said Candice politely.

'Not healthy enough?' said Ed, leaning against the banisters. His dark eyes glinted at her as though he were enjoying his own private joke. 'What do you eat, then? Quiche?' He took another bite of hamburger. 'You eat quiche, Candice?'

'Yes,' said Candice impatiently. 'I suppose I eat quiche.' Why couldn't Ed just make polite small talk like everyone else? she thought. Why did he always have to look at her with those glinting eyes, waiting for an answer – as though she were about to reveal something fascinating? It was impossible to relax while talking to him. No idle comment could go unchallenged.

'Quiche is fucking cholesterol city. You're better off with one of these.' He gestured to his hamburger, and a piece of slimy lettuce fell onto the floor. To Candice's horror, he bent down, picked it up, and popped it in his mouth.

42

'See?' he said as he stood up. 'Salad.'

Candice rolled her eyes. Really, she felt quite sorry for Ed. He had no life outside the office. No friends, no girlfriend, no furniture even. She had once popped across to his flat for a drink in order to be neighbourly – and discovered that Ed possessed only one ancient leather chair, a wide-screen TV and a pile of empty pizza boxes.

'So, have you been sacked or something?' she said sarcastically. 'I mean, it's only ten p.m. Shouldn't you be hammering out some deal somewhere?'

'Since you ask, I'll be on gardening leave as from next week,' said Ed.

'What?' Candice looked at him uncomprehendingly.

'New job,' said Ed. 'So I get to spend three months doing sod-all. It's in my contract.'

'Three months?' Candice wrinkled her brow. 'But why?'

'Why do you think?' Ed grinned complacently and cracked open a can of Coke. 'Because I'm bloody important, that's why. I know too many little secrets.'

'Are you serious?' Candice stared at him. 'So you don't get paid for three months?' Ed's face creased in a laugh.

'Of course I get paid! These guys love me! They're paying me more to do nothing than I used to get working my arse off.'

'But that's . . . that's immoral!' said Candice. 'Think of all the people in the world desperate for a job. And you're getting paid to sit around.'

'That's the world,' said Ed. 'Like it or slit your wrists.'

'Or try to change it,' said Candice.

'So you say,' said Ed, taking a slurp of Coke. 'But then, we can't all be as saintly as you, Candice, can we?'

Candice stared furiously at him. How did Ed always manage to wind her up so successfully?

'I've got to go,' she said abruptly.

'By the way, your man's in there,' said Ed. 'Ex-man. Whatever.'

'Justin?' Candice stared at him, her cheeks suddenly flaming. 'Justin's in the flat?'

'I saw him letting himself in earlier,' said Ed, and raised his eyebrows. 'Are you two back together again?'

'No!' said Candice.

'Now, that's a shame,' said Ed. 'He was a really fun guy.' Candice gave him a sharp look. On the few occasions that Ed and Justin had met, it had been clear that the two had absolutely nothing in common.

'Well, anyway,' she said abruptly, 'I'll see you around.'

'Sure,' said Ed, shrugging, and disappeared back into his flat.

Candice took a deep breath, then opened her front door, her head whirling. What was Justin doing there? It was a good month since they'd split up. And more to the point, what the hell was he still doing with a key to her flat?

'Hi?' she called. 'Justin?'

'Candice.' Justin appeared at the end of the corridor. He was dressed, as ever, in a smart suit which verged on trendy, and holding a drink. His dark curly hair was neatly glossed back and his dark eyes glowed in the lamplight; he looked to Candice like an actor playing the role of a moody intellectual. 'A young Daniel Barenboim,' someone had once admiringly described Justin – after which, for several evenings, she had noticed him sitting casually in front of the piano, and sometimes even fingering the keys, despite the fact he couldn't play a note.

'I apologize for dropping in unannounced,' he said now.

'Glad to see you've made yourself at home,' said Candice.

'I expected you back earlier,' said Justin, in a slightly resentful tone. 'I won't be long – I just thought we should have a little chat.'

'What about?'

Justin said nothing, but solemnly ushered her down the corridor into the sitting room. Candice felt herself prickling with annoyance. Justin had a unique ability to make it seem as though he was always in the right and everyone else was in the wrong. At the beginning of their relationship, he had been so convincing that she too had believed he was always right. It had taken six months and a series of increasingly frustrating arguments for her to realize that he was just a self-opinionated pompous show-off.

When they'd first met, of course, he had dazzled her. He had arrived at the *Londoner* fresh from a year's experience on the *New York Times*, with the reputation of a huge intellect and a barrage of impressive connections. When he had asked her out for a drink she had felt flattered. She had drunk copious quantities of wine, and gazed into his dark eyes, and had listened admiringly to his views – half persuaded by everything he said, even when she would normally have disagreed. After a few weeks he had begun to stay the night at her flat every so often, and they had tentatively planned a holiday together. Then his flat-share in Pimlico had fallen apart, and he had moved in with her.

It was really then that things had gone wrong, thought Candice. Her hazy admiration had melted away as she saw him in close proximity – taking three times longer than herself to get ready in the mornings; claiming proudly that he couldn't cook and didn't intend to learn; expecting the bathroom to be clean but never once cleaning it himself. She had come to realize the full extent of his vanity; the strength of his arrogance and eventually – with a slight shock – that he considered her no intellectual match for himself. If she tried to argue intelligently with him he patronized her until she made a winning point, at which he grew sullen and angry. Never once would he admit defeat – his self-image simply would not allow it. For in his own mind, Justin was destined for great things. His ambition was almost frightening in its strength; it drove him like a steamroller, flattening everything else in his life.

Even now, Candice couldn't be sure which had been hurt most when she had ended the relationship – his feelings or his pride? He had almost seemed more sorrowful for her than anything else, as though she'd made a foolish mistake which he knew she would soon regret.

However, so far – a month on – she hadn't regretted her decision for an instant.

'So,' she said as they sat down. 'What do you want?'

Justin gave her a tiny smile.

'I wanted to come and see you,' he said, 'to make sure you're absolutely OK about tomorrow.'

'Tomorrow?' said Candice blankly. Justin smiled at her again.

'Tomorrow, as you know, is the day I take over as acting editor of the *Londoner*. Effectively, I'll be your boss.' He shook out his sleeves, examined his cuffs, then looked up. 'I wouldn't want any . . . problems to arise between us.' Candice stared at him.

'Problems?'

'I realize it may be a rather difficult time for you,' said Justin smoothly. 'My promotion coinciding with the break-up of our relationship. I wouldn't want you feeling at all vulnerable.'

'Vulnerable?' said Candice in astonishment. 'Justin, it was me who ended our relationship! I'm fine about it.'

'If that's the way you want to see it,' said Justin

kindly. 'Just as long as there are no bad feelings.'

'I can't guarantee that,' muttered Candice.

She watched as Justin swirled his glass of whisky, so that the ice-cubes in it clinked together. He looked as though he were practising for a television ad, she thought. Or a *Panorama* profile: 'Justin Vellis: the genius at home'. A giggle rose through her, and she clamped her lips together.

'Well, I mustn't keep you,' said Justin at last, and stood up. 'See you tomorrow.'

'Can't wait,' said Candice, pulling a face behind his back. As they reached the door she paused, her hand on the latch. 'By the way,' she said casually, 'do you know if they've appointed a new editorial assistant yet?'

'No they haven't,' said Justin, frowning. 'In fact, to tell you the truth, I'm a bit pissed off about that. Maggie's done absolutely nothing about it. Just disappears off into domestic bliss and leaves me with two hundred bloody CVs to read.'

'Oh dear, poor you,' said Candice innocently. 'Still, never mind. I'm sure someone'll turn up.'

Roxanne took another sip of her drink and calmly turned the page of her paperback. He had said nine-thirty. It was now ten past ten. She had been sitting in this hotel bar for forty minutes, ordering Bloody Marys and sipping them slowly and feeling her heart jump every time anyone entered the bar. Around her, couples and groups were murmuring over their drinks; in the corner, an elderly man in a white tuxedo was singing 'Someone to watch over me'. It could have been any bar in any hotel in any country of the world. There were women like her all over the globe, thought Roxanne. Women sitting in bars, trying to look lively, waiting for men who weren't going to show.

A waiter came discreetly towards her table, removed

her ashtray and replaced it with a fresh one. As he moved off, she sensed a flicker in his expression – sympathy, perhaps. Or disdain. She was used to both. Just as years of exposure to the sun had hardened her skin, so years of waiting, of disappointment and humiliation, had toughened her internal shell.

How many hours of her life had she spent like this? How many hours, waiting for a man who was often late and half the time didn't show up at all? There was always an excuse, of course. Another crisis at work, perhaps. An unforeseen encounter with a member of his family. Once, she'd been sitting in a London restaurant, waiting for their third anniversary lunch – only to see him entering with his wife. He'd glanced over at her with an appalled, helpless expression, and she'd been forced to watch as he and his wife were ushered to a table. To watch, with pain eating like acid at her heart, as his wife sat frowning at him, obviously bored by his company.

He'd later told her that Cynthia had bumped into him on the street and insisted on joining him for lunch. He'd told her how he'd sat in misery, unable to eat; unable to make conversation. The next weekend, to make up, he'd cancelled everything else and taken Roxanne to Venice.

Roxanne closed her eyes. That weekend had been an intoxication of happiness. She'd known a pure single-minded joy which she'd never since experienced; a joy she still desperately sought, like an addict seeking that first high. They had walked hand in hand through dusty ancient squares; along canals glinting in the sunshine; over crumbling bridges. They'd drunk Prosecco in Piazza San Marco, listening to Strauss waltzes. They'd made love in the old-fashioned wooden bed at their hotel, then sat on their balcony watching the gondolas ride past; listening to the sounds of the city travelling over the water.

They hadn't mentioned his wife or family once. For that weekend, four human beings simply hadn't existed. Gone, in a puff of smoke.

Roxanne opened her eyes. She no longer allowed herself to think about his family. She no longer indulged in wicked fantasies about car crashes and avalanches. Down that road lay pain; self-reproach; indecision. Down that road lay the knowledge that she would never have him to herself. That there would be no car crash. That she was wasting the best years of her life on a man who belonged to another woman; a tall and noble woman whom he had vowed to love and cherish for all his life. The mother of his children.

The mother of his fucking children.

A familiar pain seared Roxanne's heart and she drained her Bloody Mary, placed a twenty in the leather folder containing her bill and stood up in an unhurried motion, her face nonchalant.

As she made her way to the door of the bar, she almost bumped into a girl in a black Lurex dress, with thick make-up, over-dyed red hair and shiny gilt jewellery. Roxanne recognized her calling at once. There were women like this all over London. Hired as escorts for the evening from a fancy-named firm; paid to laugh and flirt and – for a fee – much more. Several steps up from the hookers at Euston; several steps down from the trophy wives in the dining room.

Once upon a time she would have despised such a person. Now, as she met the girl's eyes, she felt something like empathy pass between them. They'd both fallen out of the loop. Both ended up in situations which, if predicted, would have made them laugh with disbelief. For who on earth planned to end up an escort girl? Who on earth planned to end up the other woman for six long years?

A bubble, half sob, half laughter rose up in Roxanne's throat, and she quickly strode on past the escort girl, out of the bar and through the hotel foyer.

'Taxi, madam?' said the hotel doorman as she emerged into the cold night air.

'Thanks,' said Roxanne, and forced herself to smile brightly, hold her head high. So she'd been stood up, she told herself firmly. So what was new? It had happened before and it would happen again. That was the deal when the love of your life was a married man.

Chapter Four

Candice sat in the office of Ralph Allsopp, publisher of the *Londoner*, biting her nails and wondering where he was. She had hesitantly knocked on his door that morning, praying that he was in; praying that he wouldn't be too busy to see her. When he'd opened the door, holding a phone to his ear, and gestured her in, she'd felt a spurt of relief. First hurdle over. Now all she had to do was persuade him to see Heather.

But before she'd been able to launch into her little speech, he'd put the phone down, said, 'Stay there', and disappeared out of the room. That was about ten minutes ago. Now Candice was wondering whether she should have got up and followed him. Or perhaps said boldly, 'Where are you going – can I come too?' That was the sort of gumption Ralph Allsopp liked in his staff. He was famous for hiring people with initiative rather than qualifications; for admiring people not afraid to admit ignorance; for prizing and nurturing talent. He admired dynamic, energetic people, prepared to work hard and take risks. The worst crime a member of his staff could possibly commit was to be feeble.

'Feeble!' would come his roaring voice from the top floor. 'Bloody feeble!' And all over the building, people would pull their chairs in, stop chatting about the weekend, and begin typing.

But those who made the grade, Ralph treated with the utmost respect. As a result, staff tended to join Allsopp Publications and stay for years. Even those who left to become freelance or pursue other careers would keep in touch; pop in for a drink or do some photocopying and float their latest ideas past Ralph's enthusiastic ear. It was a sociable, relaxed company. Candice had been there five years and had never considered leaving.

She leaned back in her chair now and looked idly around Ralph's desk – legendary for its untidiness. Two wooden in-trays overflowed with letters and memos; copies of the company's publications competed for space with galley proofs covered in red ink; a telephone was perched on a pile of books. As she looked at it, the phone began to ring. She hesitated for a second, wondering if she ought to answer someone else's phone – then imagined Ralph's reaction if he came in to see her just sitting there, letting it ring. 'What's wrong, girl?' he'd roar. 'Afraid it'll bite you?'

Hastily she picked up the receiver.

'Hello,' she said in a businesslike voice. 'Ralph Allsopp's office.'

'Is Mr Allsopp there?' enquired a female voice.

'I'm afraid not,' said Candice. 'May I take a message?'

'Is this his personal assistant?' Candice glanced out of the office window at the desk of Janet, Ralph's secretary. It was empty.

'I'm . . . standing in for her,' said Candice. There was a pause, then the voice said, 'This is Mr Davies's assistant Mary calling from the Charing Cross Hospital. Please could you tell Mr Allsopp that Mr Davies is unfortunately unable to make the two o'clock appointment, and wondered if three would be convenient instead.'

'Right,' said Candice, scribbling on a piece of paper. 'OK. I'll tell him.'

She put the phone down and looked curiously at the message.

'So! My dear girl.' Ralph's breezy voice interrupted her, and she gave a startled jump. 'What can I do for you? Here to complain about your new editor already? Or is it something else?'

Candice laughed.

'Something else.'

She watched as he made his way round to the other side of the desk, and thought again what an attractive man he must have been when he was younger. He was tall – at least six foot three – with dishevelled greying hair and intelligent, gleaming eyes. He must be in his fifties now, she guessed – but still exuded a relentless, almost frightening energy.

'You just got this message,' she said almost unwillingly, handing him the bit of paper.

'Ah,' said Ralph, scanning it expressionlessly. 'Thank you.' He folded the note up and put it in his trouser pocket.

Candice opened her mouth to ask if he was all right – then closed it again. It wasn't her place to start enquiring about her boss's health. She had intercepted a private call; it was nothing to do with her. Besides, it occurred to her, it might be something minor and embarrassing that she didn't want to hear about.

'I wanted to see you,' she said instead, 'about the editorial assistant's job on the *Londoner*.'

'Oh yes?' said Ralph, leaning back in his chair.

'Yes,' said Candice, garnering all her courage. 'The thing is, I know somebody who I think would fit the bill.'

'Really?' said Ralph. 'Well, then, invite him to apply.'

'It's a girl,' said Candice. 'And the thing is, I don't think her CV is that spectacular. But I know she's talented. I know she can write. And she's bright, and enthusiastic . . .'

53

'I'm glad to hear it,' said Ralph mildly. 'But you know, Justin's the one you should be talking to.'

'I know,' said Candice. 'I know he is. But—' She broke off, and Ralph's eyes narrowed.

'Now, look,' he said, leaning forward. 'Tell me plainly – is there going to be trouble between you two? I'm quite aware of the situation between you, and if it's going to cause problems . . .'

'It's not that!' said Candice at once. 'It's just that . . . Justin's very busy. It's his first day, and I don't want to bother him. He's got enough on his plate. In fact . . .' She felt her fingers mesh tightly together in her lap. 'In fact, he was complaining yesterday about having to read through all the applications. And after all, he is only *acting* editor . . . So I thought perhaps—'

'What?'

'I thought perhaps you could interview this girl yourself?' Candice looked entreatingly at Ralph. 'She's downstairs in reception.'

'She's *where*?'

'In reception,' said Candice falteringly. 'She's just waiting – in case you say yes.'

Ralph stared at her, an incredulous look on his face, and for a dreadful moment Candice thought he was going to bellow at her. But suddenly his face broke into a laugh. 'Send her up,' he said. 'Since you've dragged her all this way, let's give the poor girl a chance.'

'Thanks,' said Candice. 'Honestly, I'm sure she'll be—' Ralph raised a hand to stop her.

'Send her up,' he said. 'And we'll see.'

Maggie Phillips sat alone in her magnificent Small-bone kitchen, sipping coffee and staring at the table and wondering what to do next. She had woken that morning at the usual early hour and had watched as Giles got dressed, ready for his commute into the City.

'Now, you just take it easy,' he'd said, briskly

knotting his tie. 'I'll try and be home by seven.'

'OK,' Maggie had said, grinning up at him. 'Give the pollution my love, won't you.'

'That's right, rub it in,' he'd retorted humorously. 'You bloody ladies of leisure.'

As she'd heard the front door slam, she'd felt a delicious feeling of freedom spread through her body. No work, she'd thought to herself. No work! She could do what she liked. At first, she'd tried to go back to sleep, closing her eyes and deliberately snuggling back under the duvet. But lying down was, perversely, uncomfortable. She was too huge and heavy to find a comfortable position. So after a few tussles with the pillows, she'd given up.

She'd come downstairs and made herself some breakfast and eaten it, reading the paper and admiring the garden out of the window. That had taken her until eight-thirty. Then she'd gone back upstairs, run a bath and lain in it for what seemed like at least an hour. When she emerged, she discovered she'd been in there for twenty minutes.

Now it was nine-thirty. The day hadn't even begun yet, but she felt as though she'd been sitting at her kitchen table for an eternity. How was it that time – such a precious, slipping-away commodity in London – seemed here to pass so slowly? Like honey dripping through an hourglass.

Maggie closed her eyes, took another sip of coffee and tried to think of what she was usually doing at this hour. Any number of things. Strap-hanging on the tube, reading the paper. Striding into the office. Buying a cappuccino from the coffee shop on the corner. Answering a thousand e-mails. Sitting in an early meeting. Laughing, talking, surrounded by people.

And stressed out, she reminded herself firmly, before the images became too positive. Buffeted by the crowds, choked by taxi fumes; deafened by the noise;

pressured by deadlines. Whereas here, the only sound was that of a bird outside the window, and the air was as clean and fresh as spring water. And she had no pressures, no meetings, no deadlines.

Except the big one of course – and that was utterly outside her own control. It almost amused her, the thought that she, who was so used to being boss, who was so used to running the show, was in this case utterly powerless. Idly, she reached for her pregnancy handbook and allowed it to fall open. 'At this point the pains will become stronger,' she found herself reading. 'Try not to panic. Your partner will be able to offer support and encouragement.' Hastily she closed the book and took another gulp of coffee. Out of sight, out of fright.

Somewhere at the back of her mind, Maggie knew she should have taken the midwives' advice and attended classes on childbirth. Each of her friendly, well-meaning midwives had pressed on her a series of leaflets and numbers, and exhorted her to follow them up. But didn't these women realize how busy she was? Didn't they appreciate that taking time off work for hospital appointments was disruptive enough – and that the last thing she and Giles felt like doing at the end of a busy day was trekking off to some stranger's house in order to sit on bean bags and talk about, frankly, quite private matters? She had bought a book and half watched a video – fast-forwarding through the gruesome bits – and that would have to be enough.

Firmly she pushed the book behind the breadbin, where she couldn't see it – and poured herself another cup of coffee. At that moment, the doorbell rang. Frowning slightly in surprise, Maggie heaved herself out of her chair and walked through the hall to the front door. There on the front step was her mother-in-law, dressed in a Puffa jacket, a stripy shirt and a blue corduroy skirt, straight to the knee.

'Hello, Maggie!' she said. 'Not too early, am I?'

'No!' said Maggie, half laughing. 'Not at all. Giles said you might pop round.' She leaned forward and awkwardly kissed Paddy, stumbling slightly on the step.

Although she had been married to Giles for four years, she still did not feel she had got to know Paddy very well. They had never once sat down for a good chat – principally because Paddy never seemed to sit down at all. She was a thin, energetic woman, always on the move. Always cooking, gardening, running someone to the station or organizing a collection. She had run the village Brownies for twenty-five years, sang in the church choir, and had made all Maggie's bridesmaids' dresses herself. Now she smiled, and handed Maggie a cake tin.

'A few scones,' she said. 'Some raisin, some cheese.'

'Oh, Paddy!' said Maggie, feeling touched. 'You shouldn't have.'

'It's no trouble,' said Paddy. 'I'll give you the recipe, if you like. They're terribly easy to rustle up. Giles always used to love them.'

'Right,' said Maggie after a pause, remembering her one disastrous attempt to make a cake for Giles's birthday. 'That would be great!'

'And I've brought someone to see you,' said Paddy. 'Thought you'd like to meet another young mum from the village.'

'Oh,' said Maggie in surprise. 'How nice!'

Paddy beckoned forward a girl in jeans and a pink jersey, holding a baby and clutching a toddler by the hand.

'Here you are!' she said proudly. 'Maggie, meet Wendy.'

As Candice tripped down the stairs to reception she felt elated with her success. Powerful, almost. It just

57

showed what could be achieved with a little bit of initiative, a little effort. She arrived at the foyer and walked quickly to the chairs where Heather was sitting, dressed in a neat black suit.

'He said yes!' she said, unable to conceal her triumph. 'He's going to see you!'

'Really?' Heather's eyes lit up. 'What, now?'

'Right now! I told you, he's always willing to give people chances.' Candice grinned with excitement. 'All you've got to do is remember everything I told you. Lots of enthusiasm. Lots of drive. If you can't think of an answer to the question, tell a joke instead.'

'OK.' Heather tugged nervously at her skirt. 'Do I look all right?'

'You look brilliant,' said Candice. 'And one more thing. Ralph is sure to ask if you've brought an example of your writing.'

'What?' said Heather in alarm. 'But I—'

'Give him this,' said Candice, suppressing a grin, and handed a piece of paper to Heather.

'What?' Heather gazed at it incredulously. 'What is it?'

'It's a short piece I wrote a few months ago,' said Candice. 'On how ghastly London transport is in summer. It was never used in the magazine, and the only other person who read it was Maggie.' A couple of visitors entered the foyer, and she lowered her voice. 'And now it's yours. Look – I've put your byline at the top.'

'"London's Burning",' read Heather slowly. '"By Heather Trelawney."' She looked up, eyes dancing. 'I don't believe it! This is wonderful!'

'You'd better read it over quickly before you go in,' said Candice. 'He might ask you about it.'

'Candice . . . this is so good of you,' said Heather. 'I don't know how I can repay you.'

'Don't be silly,' said Candice at once. 'It's a pleasure.'

'But you're being so kind to me. Why are you being

so kind to me?' Heather's grey eyes met Candice's with a sudden intensity, and Candice felt her stomach give a secret guilty flip. She stared back at Heather, cheeks growing hot and, for a heightened instant, considered telling Heather everything. Confessing her family background; her constant feeling of debt; her need to make amends.

Then, almost as she was opening her mouth, she realized what a mistake it would be. What an embarrassing situation she would put Heather – and herself – in by saying anything. It might make her feel better, it might act as a kind of catharsis – but to unburden herself would be selfish. Heather must never find out that her motives were anything but genuine friendship.

'It's nothing,' she said quickly. 'You'd better go up. Ralph's waiting.'

Paddy had insisted on making the coffee, leaving Maggie alone with Wendy. Feeling suddenly a little nervous, she ushered Wendy into the sitting room, and gestured to the sofa. This was the first fellow mother she'd met. And a neighbour, too. Perhaps this girl would become her bosom pal, she thought. Perhaps their children would grow up lifelong friends.

'Do sit down,' she said. 'Have you . . . lived in the village long?'

'A couple of years,' said Wendy, dumping her huge holdall on the floor and sitting down on Maggie's cream sofa.

'And . . . do you like living here?'

'S'all right, I suppose. Jake, leave that alone!'

Maggie looked up and, with a spasm of horror, saw Wendy's toddler reaching up towards the blue Venetian glass bowl Roxanne had given them as a wedding present.

'Oh gosh,' she said, getting to her feet as quickly as her bulk would allow. 'I'll just . . . move that, shall I?'

She reached the glass bowl just as Jake's sticky fingers closed around it. 'Thanks,' she said politely to the toddler. 'Ahm . . . would you mind . . .' His fingers remained tight around it. 'It's just that . . .'

'Jake!' yelled Wendy, and Maggie jumped in fright. 'Leave it!' Jake's face crumpled, but his grip obediently loosened. Quickly, Maggie withdrew the bowl from his grasp and placed it on top of the tallboy.

'They're monsters at this age,' said Wendy. Her eyes ran over Maggie's bump. 'When are you due?'

'Three weeks,' said Maggie, sitting back down. 'Not long now!'

'You might be late,' said Wendy.

'Yes,' said Maggie after a pause. 'I suppose I might.' Wendy gestured to the baby on her lap.

'I was two weeks late with this one. They had to induce me in the end.'

'Oh,' said Maggie. 'Still—'

'Then he got stuck,' said Wendy. 'His heartbeat started to fall and they had to pull him out with forceps.' She looked up and met Maggie's eye. 'Twenty-nine stitches.'

'Dear God,' said Maggie. 'You're joking.' Suddenly she thought she might faint. She took a deep breath, gripping the edge of her chair, and forced herself to smile at Wendy. Get off the subject of childbirth, she thought. Anything else at all. 'So – do you . . . work at all?'

'No,' said Wendy, staring at her blankly. 'Jake! Get off that!' Maggie turned, to see Jake balancing precariously on the piano stool. He gave his mother a murderous stare and began to bang on the piano keys.

'Here we are!' Paddy came into the room, carrying a tray. 'I opened these rather nice almond biscuits, Maggie. Is that all right?'

'Absolutely,' said Maggie.

'Only I know what it's like when you've planned all

your meals in advance, and then someone else comes and disrupts your store cupboard.' She gave a short little laugh, and Maggie smiled feebly back. She suspected that Paddy's idea of a store cupboard and her own were somewhat different.

'I've got some squash for Jake somewhere,' said Wendy. Her voice suddenly rose. 'Jake, pack it in or you won't get a drink!' She deposited the baby on the floor and reached for her holdall.

'What a pet!' said Paddy, looking at the baby wriggling on the floor. 'Maggie, why don't you hold him for a bit?' Maggie stiffened in horror.

'I don't think—'

'Here you are!' said Paddy, picking the baby up and putting him in Maggie's awkward arms. 'Isn't he a poppet?'

Maggie stared down at the baby in her arms, aware that the other two were watching her, and felt a prickling self-consciousness. What was wrong with her? She felt nothing towards this baby except distaste. It was ugly, it smelt of stale milk and it was dressed in a hideous pastel Babygro. The baby opened his blue eyes and looked at her, and she gazed down, trying to warm to him; trying to act like a mother. He began to squirm and chirrup, and she looked up in alarm.

'He might need to burp,' said Wendy. 'Hold him upright.'

'OK,' said Maggie. With tense, awkward hands, she shifted the baby round and lifted him up. He screwed up his face and for an awful moment she thought he was going to scream. Then his mouth opened, and a cascade of warm regurgitated milk streamed onto her jersey.

'Oh my God!' said Maggie in horror. 'He's thrown up on me!'

'Oh,' said Wendy dispassionately. 'Sorry about that. Here, give him to me.'

'Never mind,' said Paddy briskly, handing Maggie a muslin cloth. 'You'll have to get used to this kind of thing, Maggie! Won't she, Wendy!'

'Oh yeah,' said Wendy. 'You just wait!'

Maggie looked up from wiping her jersey to see Paddy and Wendy both looking complacently at her, as though in triumph. *We've got you*, their eyes seemed to say. Inside, she began to shiver.

'Wanta do a poo,' Jake announced, wandering over to Wendy's side.

'Good boy,' she said, putting down her cup. 'Just let me get the potty out.'

'Dear God, no!' cried Maggie, getting to her feet. 'I mean – I'll make some more coffee, shall I?'

In the kitchen she flicked on the kettle and sank into a chair, shaking, her jersey still damp with milk. She didn't know whether to laugh or cry. Was this really what motherhood was all about? And if so, what the hell had she done? She closed her eyes and thought, with a pang, of her office at the *Londoner*. Her organized, civilized office, full of grown-ups; full of wit and sophistication and not a baby in sight.

She hesitated, glancing at the door – then picked up the phone and quickly dialled a number.

'Hello?' As she heard Candice's voice, Maggie exhaled with relief. Just hearing those friendly, familiar tones made her relax.

'Hi, Candice! It's Maggie.'

'Maggie!' exclaimed Candice in surprise. 'How's it going? Are you all right?'

'Oh, I'm fine,' said Maggie. 'You know, lady of leisure . . .'

'I suppose you're still in bed, you lucky cow.'

'Actually,' said Maggie gaily, 'I'm hosting a coffee morning. I have a real-live Stepford mum in my living room.' Candice laughed, and Maggie felt a warm glow of pleasure steal over her. Thank God for friends, she thought. Suddenly the situation seemed funny; an entertaining anecdote. 'You won't *believe* what happened just now,' she added, lowering her voice. 'I'm sitting on the sofa, holding this pig-ugly baby, and he starts to wriggle. And the next minute—'

'Actually, Maggie,' interrupted Candice, 'I'm really sorry, but I can't really chat. Justin's holding some stupid meeting and we've all got to go.'

'Oh,' said Maggie, feeling a stab of disappointment. 'Well . . . OK.'

'But we'll talk later, I promise.'

'Fine!' said Maggie brightly. 'It doesn't matter at all. I was just calling on the off-chance. Have a good meeting.'

'I doubt that. Oh, but listen. Before I go, there's something I must tell you!' Candice's voice grew quieter. 'You remember that girl, Heather, we saw last night? The cocktail waitress?'

'Yes,' said Maggie, casting her mind back to the evening before. 'Of course I do.' Was it really only last night that they were all sitting in the Manhattan Bar? It seemed like a lifetime ago.

'Well, I know you told me not to – but I introduced her to Ralph,' said Candice. 'And he was so impressed, he offered her the job on the spot. She's starting as editorial assistant next week!'

'Really?' said Maggie in astonishment. 'How extraordinary!'

'Yes,' said Candice, and cleared her throat. 'Well, it turns out she's . . . she's very good at writing. Ralph was really impressed with her work. So he's decided to give her a chance.'

'Typical Ralph,' said Maggie. 'Well, that's great.'

'Isn't it fantastic?' Candice lowered her voice even further. 'Mags, I can't tell you what this means to me. It's as though I'm finally making amends for what my father did. I'm finally . . . doing something positive.'

63

'Then I'm really glad for you,' said Maggie more warmly. 'I hope it all works out well.'

'Oh, it will,' said Candice. 'Heather's a really nice girl. In fact, we're having lunch today, to celebrate.'

'Right,' said Maggie wistfully. 'Well, have fun.'

'We'll toast you. Look, Mags, I've got to run. Talk soon.' And the phone went dead.

Maggie stared at the receiver for a moment, then slowly replaced it, trying not to feel left out. Already, within twenty-four hours, office life had moved on without her. But of course it had. What did she expect? She gave a sigh, and looked up, to see Paddy standing in the doorway, watching her with a curious expression.

'Oh,' said Maggie guiltily. 'I was just talking to an old colleague about a . . . a work matter. Is Wendy all right?'

'She's upstairs, changing the baby's nappy,' said Paddy. 'So I thought I'd give you a hand with the coffee.'

Paddy went to the sink, turned on the hot tap, then turned round and smiled pleasantly.

'You know, you mustn't cling onto your old life, Maggie.'

'What?' said Maggie in disbelief. 'I'm not!'

'You'll soon find you put down roots here. You'll get to know some other young families. But it does require a bit of effort.' Paddy squirted washing-up liquid into the bowl. 'It's a different way of life down here.'

'Not that different, surely,' said Maggie lightly. 'People still have fun, don't they?' Paddy gave her a tight little smile.

'After a while, you may find you have less in common with some of your London friends.'

And more in common with Wendy? thought Maggie. I don't think so.

'Possibly,' she said, smiling back at Paddy. 'But I'll

make every effort to keep in touch with my old friends. There's a threesome of us who always meet up for cocktails. I'll certainly carry on seeing them.'

'Cocktails,' said Paddy, giving a short laugh. 'How very glamorous.'

Maggie stared back at her and felt a sudden stab of resentment. What business was it of hers who her friends were? What business of hers was it what kind of life she led?

'Yes, cocktails,' she said, and smiled sweetly at Paddy. 'My own personal favourite is Sex on the Beach. Remind me to give you the recipe some time.'

Chapter Five

The doorbell rang and Candice jumped, despite the fact that she'd been sitting still on the sofa, waiting for Heather's arrival, for a good twenty minutes. She glanced once more round the sitting room, making sure it was neat and tidy, then nervously headed towards the front door. As she opened it, she gasped in surprise, then laughed. All she could see was a huge bouquet of flowers. Yellow roses, carnations and freesias nestling in dark greenery, wrapped in gold-embossed cellophane and crowned with a large bow.

'These are for you,' came Heather's voice from behind the bouquet. 'Sorry about the hideous bow. They put it on before I could stop them.'

'This is so kind of you!' said Candice, taking the rustling bouquet from Heather and giving her a hug. 'You really shouldn't have.'

'Yes I should!' said Heather. 'And more.' Her eyes met Candice's earnestly. 'Candice, look at everything you're doing for me. A job, a place to stay . . .'

'Well, you know,' said Candice awkwardly, 'I do have two bedrooms. And if your other place was grim . . .'

It had been purely by chance that, during their lunch together, Heather had happened to start talking about the flat where she lived. As she had talked, making light of its awfulness, Candice had suddenly hit on the idea of asking Heather to move in with her – and to her delight, Heather had agreed on the spot. Everything was falling wonderfully into place.

'It was like a hovel,' said Heather. 'Six to a room. Utterly sordid. But this place . . .' She put down her suitcases and walked slowly into the flat, looking around incredulously. 'Is this all yours?'

'Yes,' said Candice. 'At least, I had a flatmate when I first moved in, but she moved out, and I never got round to—'

'It's a palace!' interrupted Heather, looking around. 'Candice, it's beautiful!'

'Thanks,' said Candice, flushing in pleasure. 'I . . . well, I like it.'

She was secretly rather proud of her attempts at home decoration. She'd spent a long time the previous summer stripping down the brown swirly wallpaper left by the previous occupant of the flat and covering the walls in a chalky yellow paint. The whole thing had taken rather longer than she'd imagined, and her arms had ached by the end of it, but it had been worth it.

'Look – the flowers I brought go perfectly with your walls,' said Heather, and her eyes danced a little. 'We obviously think alike, you and me. That's a good omen, don't you think?'

'Absolutely!' said Candice. 'Well, let's get your luggage in and you can . . .' She swallowed. 'You can see your room.'

She picked up one of Heather's cases and hefted it down the hall, then, with a slight tremor, opened the first bedroom door.

'Wow,' breathed Heather behind her. It was a large room, decorated simply, with lavender walls and thick cream-coloured curtains. In the corner was a huge, empty oak armoire; on the night-stand beside the

67

double bed was a pile of glossy magazines.

'This is fantastic!' said Heather. 'I can't believe this place.' She looked round. 'What's your room like? Is it this door?'

'It's . . . fine,' said Candice. 'Honestly . . .'

But Heather was too quick for her. She had already opened the door, to reveal a much smaller room, furnished with a single bed and a cheap pine wardrobe.

'Is this yours?' she said in puzzlement – then looked slowly back at the lavender-painted room. 'That one's yours, isn't it?' she said in surprise. 'You've given me your room!'

She seemed astonished – almost amused – and Candice felt herself flush with embarrassment. She had felt so proud of her little gesture; had hummed merrily the night before as she'd transferred all her clothes out of her own bedroom to make way for Heather. Now, looking at Heather's face, she realized it had been a mistake. Heather would, of course, insist on swapping back. The whole incident would bring an awkwardness to their arrangement.

'I just thought you'd want your own space,' she said, feeling foolish. 'I know what it's like, moving into someone else's home – sometimes you need to get away. So I thought I'd give you the bigger room.'

'I see,' said Heather, and looked again at the lavender room. 'Well – if you're quite sure.' She beamed at Candice and kicked one of her suitcases into the room. 'It's very good of you. I'll love being in here.'

'Oh,' said Candice, half relieved, half secretly discomfited. 'Right. Well . . . good. I'll leave you to unpack, then.'

'Don't be silly!' said Heather. 'I'll unpack later. Let's have a drink first.' She reached into her holdall. 'I brought some champagne.'

'Flowers *and* champagne!' Candice laughed. 'Heather, this is too much.'

'I always drink champagne on special occasions,' said Heather, and her eyes sparkled at Candice. 'And this occasion is very special indeed. Don't you agree?'

As Candice popped the champagne in the kitchen, she could hear the wooden floorboards of the sitting room creaking slightly as Heather moved about. She filled two champagne flutes – free gifts from a reception she'd once attended sponsored by Bollinger – then took them, together with the bottle, into the sitting room. Heather was standing by the mantelpiece, her blond hair haloed in the lamplight, gazing up at a framed photograph. As she saw her, Candice's heart began to thump. Why hadn't she put that photograph away? How could she have been so stupid?

'Here,' she said, handing Heather a glass of champagne and trying to draw her away from the mantelpiece. 'Here's to us.'

'To us,' echoed Heather, and took a sip. Then she turned back to the mantelpiece, picked up the photograph and looked at it. Candice took another gulp of champagne, trying not to panic. If she just acted naturally, she told herself, Heather would suspect nothing.

'This is you, isn't it?' said Heather, looking up. 'Don't you look sweet! How old were you there?'

'About eleven,' said Candice, forcing a smile.

'And are these your parents?'

'Yes,' said Candice, trying to keep her voice casual. 'That's my mother, and – ' she swallowed ' – and that's my father. He . . . he died a while back.'

'Oh, I'm sorry,' said Heather. 'He was a handsome man, wasn't he?' She stared at the picture again, then raised her head and smiled. 'I bet he spoiled you rotten when you were a kid.'

'Yes,' said Candice, and attempted a laugh. 'Well – you know what fathers are like . . .'

'Absolutely,' said Heather. She gave the photograph

one last look, then replaced it on the mantelpiece. 'Oh, this is going to be fun,' she said suddenly. 'Don't you think?' She came towards Candice and put her arm affectionately round her waist. 'The two of us, living together. It's going to be such fun!'

At midnight that night, after a four-course dinner and more than her fair share of a bottle of divine Chablis, Roxanne arrived back at her suite at the Aphrodite Bay Hotel, to find her bed turned down, the lights dimmed, and a message light blinking on her telephone. Kicking off her shoes, she sat down on the bed, pressed the message button and began to unwrap the chocolate mint which had been placed on her pillow.

'Hi, Roxanne? It's Maggie. Hope you're having a good time, you lucky cow – and give me a call some time.' Roxanne stiffened in excitement, and was about to pick up the phone, when the machine beeped again, indicating a second message.

'No, you dope, I haven't had the baby,' came Maggie's voice again. 'This is something else. Ciao.' Roxanne grinned, and stuffed the chocolate mint into her mouth.

'End of messages,' said a tinny voice. Roxanne swallowed the mint, reached for the phone and pressed three digits.

'Hello, Nico?' she said as the phone was answered. 'I'll be down in a minute. I just have to make a quick call.' She pointed her toes, admiring her tan against her pink-polished toenails. 'Yes, order me a Brandy Alexander. See you in a moment.' She replaced the receiver, then picked it up again and dialled Maggie's number from memory.

'Hello?' said a sleepy voice.

'Giles!' said Roxanne, and guiltily looked at her watch. 'Oh God, it's late, isn't it? Sorry! I didn't think. It's Roxanne. Were you asleep?'

70

'Roxanne,' said Giles blearily. 'Hi. Where are you?'

'Give it to me!' Roxanne could hear Maggie saying in the background, then, in a more muted voice, 'Yes, I know it's late! I want to talk to her!' There was a scuffling noise, and Roxanne grinned, imagining Maggie wrenching the phone determinedly from her husband's grasp. Then Maggie's voice came down the receiver. 'Roxanne! How are you?'

'Hi, Mags,' said Roxanne. 'Sorry I woke Giles up.'

'Oh, he's OK,' said Maggie. 'He's already fallen asleep again. So, how's life in Cyprus?'

'Bearable,' drawled Roxanne. 'A Mediterranean paradise of blazing sun, blue waters and five-star luxury. Nothing to speak of.'

'I don't know how you stand it,' said Maggie. 'I'd complain to the management if I were you.' Then her voice grew more serious. 'Listen, Roxanne, the reason I called – have you spoken to Candice recently?'

'Not since I came out here. Why?'

'Well, I rang her this evening,' said Maggie, 'just for a chat – and that girl was there.'

'Which girl?' said Roxanne, leaning back against the padded headrest of her bed. Through her uncurtained french windows, she could see fireworks from some distant revelry or other exploding into the night sky like coloured shooting stars.

'Heather Trelawney. The cocktail waitress in the Manhattan Bar, remember?'

'Oh yes,' said Roxanne, yawning slightly. 'The one Candice's father ripped off.'

'Yes,' said Maggie. 'Well, you know Candice got her the editorial assistant job on the *Londoner*?'

'Really?' said Roxanne in surprise. 'That was quick work.'

'Apparently she went to see Ralph the next morning, and made some special plea. God knows what she said.'

'Oh well,' said Roxanne easily. 'She obviously feels very strongly about it.'

'She must do,' said Maggie. 'Because now this girl's moved in with her.'

Roxanne sat up, frowning. 'Moved in with her? But, I mean, she hardly knows her!'

'I know,' said Maggie. 'Exactly. Don't you think it seems a bit . . .'

'Mmm,' said Roxanne. 'Sudden.'

There was silence down the line, punctuated by crackles and Giles coughing in the background.

'I just have a bad vibe about it,' said Maggie eventually. 'You know what Candice is like. She'll let anyone take advantage of her.'

'Yes,' said Roxanne slowly. 'You're right.'

'So I was thinking – maybe you could try and keep tabs on this girl? There's not much I can do . . .'

'Don't worry,' said Roxanne. 'As soon as I get back, I'll suss it out.'

'Good,' said Maggie, and exhaled gustily. 'I'm sure I'm just a bored pregnant woman worrying about nothing. It'll probably all turn out fine. But . . .' She paused. 'You know.'

'I do,' said Roxanne. 'And don't fret. I'm on the case.'

The next morning Candice woke to a sweet, mouth-watering smell wafting through the air. She rolled puzzledly over in bed, opened her eyes and found herself staring at an unfamiliar white wall. What was going on? she wondered blearily. What was she doing . . .

Then her brain clicked into place. Of course. She was in the spare room. Heather was living here. And from the smell of it, she was already up and cooking something. Candice swung her legs out of bed and sat up, groaning slightly at the heaviness of her head.

Champagne always got her like that. She stood up, put on a robe, and tottered down the hall to the kitchen.

'Hi!' said Heather, looking up from the stove, with a beam. 'I'm making pancakes. Do you want one?'

'Pancakes?' said Candice. 'I haven't had pancakes since . . .'

'Coming right up!' said Heather, and opened the oven. Candice stared in amazement, to see a pile of light, golden-brown pancakes, warming gently in the oven's heat.

'This is amazing,' she said, starting to laugh. 'You can stay.'

'You don't get pancakes every day,' said Heather, gazing at her in mock severity. 'Only when you've been good.'

Candice giggled. 'I'll make some coffee.'

A few minutes later, they sat down at Candice's marble bistro table, each with a pile of pancakes, sugar and lemon juice, and a steaming mug of coffee.

'We should have maple syrup, really,' said Heather, taking a bite. 'I'll buy some.'

'This is delicious!' said Candice, her mouth full of pancake. 'Heather, you're an utter star.'

'It's a pleasure,' said Heather, smiling modestly down at her plate.

Candice took another bite of pancake and closed her eyes, savouring the pleasure. To think she'd actually had some last-minute qualms about inviting Heather to live with her. To think she'd wondered if she was making a mistake. It was obvious that Heather was going to make a wonderful flat-mate – and a wonderful new friend.

'Well, I guess I'd better go and get ready.' Candice looked up to see a sheepish grin flash across Heather's face. 'Actually, I'm a bit nervous about today.'

'Don't be,' said Candice at once. 'Everyone's very friendly. And remember I'll be there to help you.' She

73

smiled at Heather, filled with a sudden affection for her. 'It'll all go fine, I promise.'

Half an hour later, as Candice brushed her teeth, Heather knocked on the bathroom door.

'Do I look OK?' she asked nervously, as Candice appeared. Candice gazed at her, feeling impressed and a little taken aback. Heather looked incredibly smart and polished. She was wearing a smart red suit over a white T-shirt and black high-heeled shoes.

'You look fantastic!' said Candice. 'Where's the suit from?'

'I can't remember,' said Heather vaguely. 'I bought it ages ago, when I had a windfall.'

'Well, it looks great!' said Candice. 'Just give me a sec, and we'll go.'

A few minutes later, she ushered Heather out of the flat and banged the door shut. Immediately Ed's front door swung open and he appeared on the landing, dressed in jeans and a T-shirt and clutching an empty milk bottle.

'Well, hello there!' he said, as though in surprise. 'Fancy bumping into you, Candice!'

'What a coincidence,' said Candice.

'Just putting the milk out,' said Ed unconvincingly, his eyes glued on Heather.

'Ed, we don't have a milkman,' said Candice, folding her arms.

'Not yet, we don't,' said Ed, and waved the milk bottle at Candice. 'But if I put this out as bait, maybe I can lure one this way. It works for hedgehogs. What do you think?'

He put the milk bottle down on the floor, looked at it consideringly for a moment, then moved it a little towards the stairs. Candice rolled her eyes.

'Ed, this is my new flat-mate, Heather. You may have heard her arrive last night.'

'Me?' said Ed innocently. 'No, I heard nothing.' He stepped forward, took Heather's hand and kissed it. 'Enchanted to meet you, Heather.'

'You too,' said Heather.

'And may I say how delightfully smart you look?' added Ed.

'You may,' said Heather, dimpling at him. She gave a satisfied glance at her own appearance and brushed a speck of dust off her immaculate red skirt.

'You know, you should take a few tips from Heather,' said Ed to Candice. 'Look – her shoes match her bag. Very chic.'

'Thanks, Ed,' said Candice. 'But the day I take sartorial tips from you is the day I give up wearing clothes altogether.'

'Really?' Ed's eyes gleamed. 'Is that a move you're planning in the near future?'

Heather giggled.

'What do you do, Ed?' she asked.

'He does nothing,' said Candice. 'And he gets paid for it. What is it today, Ed? Loafing around the park? Feeding the pigeons?'

'Actually, no,' said Ed. He leaned against the door frame of his flat and his eyes glinted in amusement. 'Since you ask, I'm going to go and look at my house.'

'What house?' said Candice suspiciously. 'Are you moving away? Thank God for that.'

'I've inherited a house,' said Ed. 'From my aunt.'

'Of course you have!' said Candice. 'Obviously. Some people inherit debts; Ed Armitage inherits a house.'

'Dunno what I'm going to do with it,' said Ed. 'It's down in Monkham. Bloody miles away.'

'Where's Monkham?' said Candice, wrinkling her brow.

'Wiltshire,' said Heather surprisingly. 'I know Monkham. It's very pretty.'

'I suppose I'll sell it,' said Ed. 'But then, I'm quite fond of it. I spent a lot of time there when I was a kid . . .'

'Sell it, keep it . . . who cares?' said Candice. 'What's an empty property here or there? It's not like there are people starving on the streets, or anything—'

'Or turn it into a soup kitchen,' said Ed. 'A home for orphans. Would that satisfy you, St Candice?' He grinned, and Candice scowled at him.

'Come on,' she said to Heather. 'We'll be late.'

The editorial office of the *Londoner* was a long, large room with windows at each end. It held seven desks – six for members of editorial staff and one for the editorial secretary, Kelly. At times it could be a loud and noisy place to work; on press day it was usually mayhem.

As Candice and Heather arrived, however, the room was full of the usual mid-month, Monday morning lethargy. Until the eleven o'clock meeting, no real work would be done. People would open their post, exchange stories about the weekend, make pots of coffee and nurse their hangovers. At eleven o'clock they would all cluster into the meeting room and report on the progress of the June issue; at twelve o'clock they would all emerge feeling motivated and energetic – and promptly go off for lunch. It was the same every Monday.

Candice stood at the door to the room, grinned encouragingly at Heather, and cleared her throat.

'Everybody,' she said, 'this is Heather Trelawney, our new editorial assistant.'

A murmur of hungover greetings went round the room, and Candice smiled at Heather.

'They're very friendly really,' she said. 'I'll introduce you properly in a moment. But first we should try to find Justin . . .'

'Candice,' came a voice behind her, and she jumped. She turned round to see Justin standing in the corridor. He was dressed in a dark purple suit, holding a cup of coffee and looking harassed.

'Hi!' she said. 'Justin, I'd like you to . . .'

'Candice, a word,' interrupted Justin tersely. 'In private. If I may.'

'Oh,' said Candice. 'Well . . . OK.'

She glanced apologetically at Heather, then followed Justin to the corner by the photocopying machine. Once upon a time, she thought, he would have been leading her off into the corner to whisper in her ear and make her giggle. But now, as he turned round, the expression on his face was distinctly unfriendly. Candice folded her arms and stared back at him defiantly.

'Yes?' she said, wondering if she'd made some horrendous gaffe in the magazine without realizing. 'Is something wrong?'

'Where were you on Friday?'

'I took the day off,' said Candice.

'In order to avoid me.'

'No!' said Candice, rolling her eyes. 'Of course not! Justin, what's wrong?'

'What's wrong?' echoed Justin, as though he could barely believe her effrontery. 'OK, tell me this, Candice. Did you or did you not go over my head to Ralph last week – *deliberately* undermining my credibility – simply in order to secure a job for your little friend?' He jerked his head towards Heather.

'Oh,' said Candice, taken aback. 'Well, not on purpose. It just . . . happened that way.'

'Oh yes?' A tense smile flickered across Justin's face. 'That's funny. Because the way I heard it was that after our discussion the other night, you went straight up to Ralph Allsopp, and told him I was too busy to process the applications for editorial assistant. Is that what you told him, Candice?'

'No!' said Candice, feeling herself colouring. 'At least . . . I didn't mean anything by it! It was just—'

She broke off, feeling slightly uncomfortable. Although – of course – she'd been acting primarily to help Heather, she couldn't deny that it had given her a slight *frisson* of pleasure to have outwitted Justin. But that hadn't been the *main* reason she'd done it, she thought indignantly. And if Justin were just a bit less arrogant and snobbish, maybe she wouldn't have had to.

'How do you think that makes me look?' hissed Justin furiously. 'How do you think Ralph rates my management skills now?'

'Look, it's no big deal!' protested Candice. 'I just happened to know someone who I thought would be good for the job, and you'd said you were busy—'

'And you happened to see a neat way to sabotage my position on day one,' said Justin, with a little sneer.

'No!' said Candice in horror. 'God, is that the way you think my mind works? I would never do anything like that!'

'Of course you wouldn't,' said Justin.

'I *wouldn't*!' said Candice, and glared at him. Then she sighed. 'Look, come and meet Heather – and then you'll see. She'll be an excellent editorial assistant. I promise.'

'She'd better be,' said Justin. 'We had two hundred applicants for that job, you know. Two *hundred*.'

'I know,' said Candice hurriedly. 'Look, Justin, Heather'll be great. And I didn't mean to undermine you, honestly.'

There was a tense silence, then Justin sighed.

'OK. Well, perhaps I over-reacted. But I'm having problems enough as it is today.' He took a sip of coffee and scowled. 'Your friend Roxanne hasn't helped.'

'Oh really?'

'She described some new hotel as a "vulgar

78

monstrosity" in the last issue. Now I've got the company on the phone, demanding not only a retraction, but a free full-page advertisement. And where's the woman herself? On some bloody beach somewhere.'

Candice laughed.

'If she said it's a monstrosity, it probably is.' She felt a movement at her arm and looked up in surprise. 'Oh, hello, Heather.'

'I thought I'd come and introduce myself,' said Heather brightly. 'You must be Justin.'

'Justin Vellis, Acting Editor,' said Justin, holding out his hand in a businesslike fashion.

'Heather Trelawney,' said Heather, shaking it firmly. 'I'm so delighted to be working for the *Londoner.* I've always read it, and I look forward to being part of the team.'

'Good,' said Justin shortly.

'I must just also add,' said Heather, 'that I love your tie. I've been admiring it from afar.' She beamed at Justin. 'Is it Valentino?'

'Oh,' said Justin, as though taken aback. 'Yes, it is.' His fingers reached up and smoothed the tie down. 'How . . . clever of you.'

'I love men in Valentino,' said Heather.

'Yes, well,' said Justin, flushing very slightly. 'Good to meet you, Heather. Ralph's told me about the high quality of your writing, and I'm sure you're going to be an asset to the team.'

He nodded at Heather, glanced at Candice, then strode away. The two girls looked at each other, then started to giggle.

'Heather, you're a genius!' said Candice. 'How did you know Justin had a thing about his ties?'

'I didn't,' said Heather, grinning. 'Just call it instinct.'

'Well, anyway, thanks for rescuing me,' said

79

Candice. 'You got me out of a tight corner there.' She shook her head. 'God, Justin can be a pain.'

'I saw you arguing,' said Heather casually. 'What was the problem?' She looked at Candice, and a curious expression came over her face. 'Candice, you weren't arguing about . . . me, were you?' Candice felt herself flush red.

'No!' she said hastily. 'No, of course we weren't! It was . . . something else completely. It really doesn't matter.'

'Well — if you're sure,' said Heather, and gazed at Candice with luminous eyes. 'Because I'd hate to cause any trouble.'

'You're not causing trouble!' said Candice, laughing. 'Come on, I'll show you your desk.'

Chapter Six

Maggie was in her large, cool bedroom, sitting by the rain-swept window and staring out at the muddy green fields disappearing into the distance. Fields and fields, as far as the eye could see. Proper, old-fashioned English countryside. And twenty acres of it belonged to her and Giles.

Twenty whole acres – vast by London standards. The thought had thrilled her beyond measure in those first exhilarating months after they'd decided to move. Giles – used to his parents' paddocks and fields full of sheep – had been pleased to acquire the land, rather than excited. But to Maggie, after her own suburban upbringing and the tiny patch of land they'd called a garden in London, twenty acres had seemed like a country estate. She'd imagined striding around her land like a gentleman farmer, getting to know every corner, planting trees; picnicking in her favourite shady spot.

That first October weekend after they'd moved in, she'd made a point of walking to the furthest point of the plot and looking back towards the house – greedily taking in the swathe of land that now belonged to her and Giles. The second weekend it had rained, and she'd huddled inside by the Aga. The third weekend, they'd stayed up in London for a friend's party.

Since then, the thrill of ownership had somewhat paled. Admittedly, Maggie still liked to drop her twenty acres into the conversation. She still liked to think of herself as a landowner and talk carelessly about buying a horse. But the thought of going and actually trudging through her own muddy fields exhausted her. It wasn't as if they were particularly beautiful or interesting. Just fields.

The phone rang and she looked at her watch. It would be Giles, wanting to know what she had been doing with herself. She had told herself – and him – that she would go up to the attic bedrooms today and plan their redecoration. In fact, she had done nothing more than go downstairs, eat some breakfast and come back upstairs again. She felt heavy and inert; slightly depressed by the weather; unable to galvanize herself into action.

'Hi, Giles?' she said into the receiver.

'How are you doing?' said Giles cheerily down the line. 'It's lashing it down here.'

'Fine,' said Maggie, shifting uncomfortably in her chair. 'It's raining here, too.'

'You sound a bit down, my sweet.'

'Oh, I'm OK,' said Maggie gloomily. 'My back hurts, it's pissing with rain and I haven't got anyone to talk to. Apart from that, I'm doing great.'

'Did the cot arrive?'

'Yes, it's here,' said Maggie. 'The man put it up in the nursery. It looks lovely.'

Suddenly she felt a tightening across the front of her stomach, and drew in breath sharply.

'Maggie?' said Giles in alarm.

'It's OK,' she said, after a few seconds. 'Just another practice contraction.'

'I would have thought you'd had enough practice by now,' said Giles, and laughed merrily. 'Well, I'd better shoot off. Take care of yourself.'

'Wait,' said Maggie, suddenly anxious for him not to disappear off the line. 'What time do you think you'll be home?'

'It's bloody frantic here,' said Giles, lowering his voice. 'I'll try and make it as early as I can – but who knows? I'll ring you a bit later and let you know.'

'OK,' said Maggie disconsolately. 'Bye.'

After he'd rung off she held the warm receiver to her ear for a few minutes more, then slowly put it down and looked around the empty room. It seemed to ring with silence. Maggie looked at the still telephone and felt suddenly bereft, like a child at boarding school. Ridiculously, she felt as though she wanted to go home.

But this was her home. Of course it was. She was Mrs Drakeford of The Pines.

She got to her feet and lumbered wearily into the bathroom, thinking that she would have a warm bath to ease her back. Then she must have some lunch. Not that she felt very hungry – but still. It would be something to do.

She stepped into the warm water and leaned back, just as her abdomen began to tighten again. Another bloody practice contraction. Hadn't she had enough already? And why did nature have to play such tricks, anyway? Wasn't the whole thing bad enough as it was? As she closed her eyes, she remembered the section in her pregnancy handbook on false labour. 'Many women,' the book had said patronizingly, 'will mistake false contractions for the real thing.'

Not her, thought Maggie grimly. She wasn't going to have the humiliation of summoning Giles from the office and rushing excitedly off to the hospital, only to be told kindly that she'd made a mistake. You think *that's* labour? the silent implication ran. Ha! You just wait for the real thing!

Well, she would. She'd wait for the real thing.

Roxanne reached for her orange juice, took a sip and leaned back comfortably in her chair. She was sitting at a blue and green mosaic table on the terrace of the Aphrodite Bay Hotel, overlooking the swimming pool and, in the distance, the beach. A final drink in the sunshine, a final glimpse of the Mediterranean, before her flight back to England. Beside her on the floor was her small, well-packed suitcase, which she would take onto the plane as hand luggage. Life was far too short, in her opinion, to spend waiting by airport carousels for suitcases of unused clothes.

She took another sip and closed her eyes, enjoying the sensation of the sun blazing down on her cheeks. It had been a good week's work, she thought. She had already written her two-thousand-word piece for the *Londoner* on holidaying in Cyprus. She had also visited enough new property developments to be able to write a comprehensive survey for the property pages of one of the national newspapers. And for one of their rivals, under a pseudonym, she would pen a light-hearted diary-type piece on living in Cyprus as an expatriate. The *Londoner* had funded half the cost of her trip – with these extra pieces of work she would more than pay for the rest of it. Nice work if you can get it, she thought idly, and began to hum softly to herself.

'You are enjoying the sun,' came a voice beside her and she looked up. Nico Georgiou was pulling a chair out and sitting down at the table. He was an elegant man in his middle years, always well dressed; always impeccably polite. The quieter, more reserved of the two Georgiou brothers.

She had met them both on her first trip to Cyprus, when she had been sent to cover the opening of their new hotel, the Aphrodite Bay. Since then, she had never stayed anywhere else in Cyprus, and over the years, had got to know Nico and his brother Andreas well. Between them, they owned three of the major hotels on the island, and a fourth was currently under construction.

'I adore the sun,' said Roxanne now, smiling. 'And I adore the Aphrodite Bay.' She looked around. 'I can't tell you how much I've enjoyed my stay here.'

'And we have, as always, enjoyed having you,' said Nico. He lifted a hand, and a waiter came rushing to attention.

'An espresso, please,' said Nico, and glanced at Roxanne. 'And for you?'

'Nothing else, thanks,' said Roxanne. 'I have to leave soon.'

'I know,' said Nico. 'I will drive you to the airport.'

'Nico! I've booked a taxi.'

'And I have unbooked it,' said Nico, smiling. 'I want to talk to you, Roxanne.'

'Really?' said Roxanne. 'What about?'

Nico's coffee arrived and he waited for the waiter to retreat before he spoke again.

'You have been to visit our new resort, the Aphrodite Falls.'

'I've seen the construction site,' said Roxanne. 'It looks very impressive. All those waterfalls.'

'It will be impressive,' said Nico. 'It will be unlike anything previously seen in Cyprus.'

'Good!' said Roxanne. 'I can't wait till it opens.' She grinned at him. 'If you don't invite me to the launch party you're in trouble.' Nico laughed, then picked up his coffee spoon and began to balance it on his cup.

'The Aphrodite Falls is a very high-profile project,' he said, and paused. 'We will be looking for a . . . a dynamic person to run the launch and marketing of the resort. A person with talent. With energy. With contacts in journalism . . .' There was silence, and Nico looked up. 'Someone, perhaps, who enjoys the

Mediterranean way of life,' he said slowly, meeting Roxanne's eyes. 'Someone, perhaps, from Britain?'

'Me?' said Roxanne disbelievingly. 'You can't be serious.'

'I am utterly serious,' said Nico. 'My brother and I would be honoured if you would join our company.'

'But I don't know anything about marketing! I don't have any qualifications, any training—'

'Roxanne, you have more intelligence and flair than any of these so-called qualified people,' said Nico, gesturing disparagingly. 'I have hired these people. The training seems to dull their wits. Young people go into college with ideas and enthusiasm, and come out with only flip-charts and ridiculous jargon.'

Roxanne laughed. 'You do have a point.'

'We would provide accommodation for you,' said Nico, leaning forward. 'The salary would be, I think, generous.'

'Nico—'

'And, of course, we would expect you to continue with a certain amount of travel, to other comparable resorts. For . . . research purposes.' Roxanne looked at him suspiciously.

'Has this job been tailor-made for me?'

A smile flickered over Nico's face. 'In a way . . . perhaps yes.'

'I see.' Roxanne stared into her glass of orange juice. 'But . . . why?'

There was silence for a while – then Nico said in a deadpan voice, 'You know why.'

A strange pang went through Roxanne and she closed her eyes, trying to rationalize her thoughts. The sun was hot on her face; in the distance she could hear children shrieking excitedly on the beach. 'Mama!' one of them was calling, 'Mama!' She could live here all year round, she thought. Wake up to sunshine every day. Join the Georgiou family for long, lazy celebration meals – as she once had for Andreas's birthday.

And Nico himself. Courteous, self-deprecating Nico, who never hid his feelings for her – but never forced them on her either. Kind, loyal Nico; she would die rather than hurt him.

'I can't,' she said, and opened her eyes to see Nico gazing straight at her. The expression in his dark eyes made her want to cry. 'I can't leave London.' She exhaled sharply. 'You know why. I just can't—'

'You can't leave him,' said Nico, and, in one movement, drained his espresso.

Something was ringing in Maggie's mind. A fire alarm. An alarm clock. The doorbell. Her mind jerked awake and she opened her eyes. Dazedly, she glanced at her watch on the side of the bath and saw to her astonishment that it was one o'clock. She'd been in her bath for almost an hour, half dozing in the warmth. As quickly as she could, she stood up, reached for a towel, and began to dry her face and neck before getting out.

Halfway out of the bath another practice contraction seized her and in slight terror she clung onto the side of the bath, willing herself not to slip over. As the painful tightness subsided, the doorbell rang again downstairs, loud and insistent.

'Bloody hell, give me a minute!' she yelled. She wrenched angrily at a towelling robe on the back of the door, wrapped it around herself and padded out of the room. As she passed the mirror on the landing she glanced at herself and was slightly taken aback at her pale, strained reflection. Hardly a picture of blooming health. But then, in the mood she was in, she didn't care what she looked like.

She headed for the front door, already knowing from the thin shadowy figure on the other side of the frosted glass that her visitor was Paddy. Barely a day went by without Paddy popping in with some excuse or other

– a knitted blanket for the baby, a cutting from the garden, the famous recipe for scones, copied onto a flowery card. 'She's keeping bloody tabs on me!' Maggie had complained, half jokingly, to Giles the night before. 'Every day, like clockwork!' On the other hand, Paddy's company was better than nothing. And at least she hadn't brought Wendy back for a visit.

'Maggie!' exclaimed Paddy, as soon as Maggie opened the door. 'So glad to have caught you in. I've been making tomato soup, and, as usual, I've made far too much. Can you use some?'

'Oh,' said Maggie. 'Yes, I should think so. Come on in.' As she stood aside to let Paddy in, another contraction began – this one deeper and more painful than the others. She gripped the door, bowing her head and biting her lip, waiting for it to pass – then looked up at Paddy, a little out of breath.

'Maggie, are you all right?' said Paddy sharply.

'Fine,' said Maggie, breathing normally again. 'Just a practice contraction.'

'A what?' Paddy stared at her.

'They're called Braxton-Hicks contractions,' explained Maggie patiently. 'It's in the book. Perfectly normal in the last few weeks.' She smiled at Paddy. 'Can I make you a cup of coffee?'

'You sit down,' said Paddy, giving Maggie an odd look. 'I'll do it. Are you *sure* you feel all right?'

'Really, Paddy, I'm fine,' said Maggie, following Paddy into the kitchen. 'Just a bit tired. And my back aches a bit. I'll take some paracetamol in a minute.'

'Good idea,' said Paddy, frowning slightly. She filled the kettle, switched it on and took two mugs down from the dresser. Then she turned round.

'Maggie, you don't think this could be it?'

'What?' Maggie stared at Paddy and felt a little plunge of fear. 'Labour? Of course not. I'm not due for another two weeks.' She licked her dry lips. 'And I've been having practice contractions like this all week. It's . . . it's nothing.'

'If you say so.' Paddy reached inside a cupboard for the jar of coffee, then stopped.

'Shall I run you up to the hospital, just to make sure?'

'No!' said Maggie at once. 'They'll just tell me I'm a stupid woman and send me home again.'

'Isn't it worth being on the safe side?' said Paddy.

'Honestly, Paddy, there's nothing to worry about,' said Maggie, feeling the tightness begin again inside her. 'I'm just . . .' But she couldn't manage the rest of her sentence. She held her breath, waiting for the pain to pass. When she looked up, Paddy was standing up and holding her car keys.

'Maggie, I'm no expert,' she said cheerfully, 'but even I know that wasn't a practice contraction.' She smiled. 'My dear, this is it. The baby's coming.'

'It can't be,' Maggie heard herself say. She felt almost breathless with fright. 'It can't be. I'm not ready.'

It was raining, a soft slithery rain, when Roxanne emerged from London Underground at Barons Court. The skies were dark with clouds, the pavements were wet and slimy, and an old Mars Bar wrapper was floating in a puddle next to a pile of *Evening Standards*. It felt, to Roxanne, like the middle of winter. She picked up her case and began to walk briskly along the street, wincing as a passing lorry spattered her legs with dirty water. It seemed hardly believable that only a few hours ago she'd been sitting in the blazing heat of the sun.

Nico had driven her to the airport in his gleaming Mercedes. He had, despite her protestations, carried her suitcase into the airport terminal for her, and had ensured that everything was in order at the check-in desk. Not once had he mentioned the job at the

Aphrodite Bay. Instead he had talked generally, about politics and books, and his planned trip to New York – and Roxanne had listened gratefully, glad of his tact. Only as they'd been about to bid farewell to one another at the departure desk had he said, with a sudden vehemence, 'He is a fool, this man of yours.'

'You mean I'm a fool,' Roxanne had responded, trying to smile. Nico had shaken his head silently, then taken her hands.

'Come back to visit us soon, Roxanne,' he'd said in a low voice. 'And . . . think about it? At least think about it.'

'I will,' Roxanne had promised, knowing that her mind was already made up. Nico had scanned her face, then sighed and kissed her fingertips.

'There is no-one like Roxanne,' he'd said. 'Your man is very lucky.'

Roxanne had smiled back at him, and laughed a little, and waved cheerfully as she went through the departure gate. Now, with rain dripping down her neck and buses swooshing by every few seconds, she felt less cheerful. London seemed a grey unfriendly place, full of litter and strangers. What was she living here for, anyway?

She reached her house, ran up the steps to the front door and quickly felt inside her bag for her keys. Her tiny little flat was on the top floor, with what estate agents described as far-reaching views over London. By the time she reached the top of the stairs, she was out of breath. She unlocked the door to her flat, pushed it open, and stepped over a pile of post. The air was cold and unheated and she knew her hot water would be off. Quickly she went into the little kitchen and switched on the kettle, then wandered back into the hall. She picked up her mail and began to flip through it, dropping all the uninteresting bills and circulars back onto the floor. Suddenly, at a handwritten white envelope, she stopped. It was a letter from him.

With cold hands, still wet from the rain, she tore it open and sank her eyes into the few lines of writing.

My darling Rapunzel

As many apologies as I can muster for Wednesday night. Will explain all. Now as my deserved punishment – must wait jealously for your return. Hurry home from Cyprus. Hurry, hurry.

The letter ended, as ever, with no name but a row of kisses. Reading his words, she could suddenly hear his voice; feel his touch on her skin; hear his warm laughter. She sank to the floor and read the letter again, and again, devouring it greedily with her eyes. Then eventually she looked up, feeling in some strange way restored. The truth was, that there was no conceivable alternative. She couldn't stop loving him; she couldn't just move to a new country and pretend he didn't exist. She needed him in her life, just as she needed food and air and light. And the fact that he was rationed, the fact that she could not have him properly, simply made her crave him all the more.

The phone rang and, with a sudden lift of hope, she reached for the receiver. 'Yes?' she said lightly, thinking that if it was him, she would get in a taxi and go to him straight away.

'Roxanne, it's Giles Drakeford.'

'Oh,' said Roxanne in surprise. 'Is Maggie all—'

'It's a girl,' said Giles, sounding more emotional than she'd ever heard him. 'It's a girl. Born an hour ago. A perfect little girl. Six pounds eight. The most beautiful baby in the world.' He took a deep, shuddering breath. 'Maggie was . . . fantastic. She was so quick, I only just made it in time. God, it was just the most amazing experience. Everyone cried, even the midwives. We've decided we're going to call her Lucia. Lucia Sarah Helen. She's . . . she's perfect. A perfect little daughter.' There was silence. 'Roxanne?'

'A daughter,' said Roxanne, in a strange voice. 'Congratulations. That's . . . that's wonderful news.'

'I can't talk long,' said Giles. 'To be honest, I'm bloody shattered. But Maggie wanted you to know.'

'Well, thanks for calling,' said Roxanne. 'And congratulations again. And s-send all my love to Maggie.'

She put the phone down, and looked at it silently for a minute. Then, with no warning at all, she burst into tears.

Chapter Seven

The next day dawned bright and clear, with the smell of summer and good spirits in the air. On the way to the office, Roxanne stopped off at a florist and chose an extravagantly large bunch of lilies for Maggie from an illustrated brochure entitled 'A New Arrival'.

'Is it a boy or a girl?' enquired the florist, typing the details into her computer.

'A girl,' said Roxanne, and beamed at the woman. 'Lucia Sarah Helen. Isn't that pretty?'

'LSH,' said the florist. 'Sounds like a drug. Or an exam.' Roxanne gave the woman an annoyed glance, and handed her a Visa card. 'They'll go out this afternoon,' added the woman, swiping the card. 'Is that all right?'

'Fine,' said Roxanne, and imagined Maggie sitting up like one of the women in the brochure, in a crisp white bed, rosy-cheeked and serene. A tiny sleeping baby in her arms, Giles looking on lovingly and flowers all around. Deep inside her she felt something tug at her heart, and quickly she looked up with a bright smile.

'If you could just sign there,' said the florist, passing a slip of paper to Roxanne, 'and write your message in the box.' Roxanne picked up the biro and hesitated.

'Can't wait to mix Lucia her first cocktail,' she wrote

eventually. 'Much love and congratulations to you both from Roxanne.'

'I'm not sure that'll fit on the card,' said the florist doubtfully.

'Then use two cards,' snapped Roxanne, suddenly wanting to get away from the sickly scent of flowers; the brochure full of winsome photographs of babies. As she strode out of the shop, a petal fell from a garland onto her hair like confetti, and she brushed it irritably away.

She arrived at the editorial office a little after nine-thirty, to see Candice sitting cross-legged on the floor sketching something out on a piece of paper. Sitting next to her, head also bent over the piece of paper, was the blond-haired girl from the Manhattan Bar. For a few moments Roxanne gazed at them, remembering Maggie's phone call. Was this girl really trouble? Was she really using Candice? She looked outwardly innocuous, with her freckled snub nose and cheerful smile. But there was also, Roxanne noticed, a firmness to her jaw when she wasn't smiling, and a curious coolness to her grey eyes.

As she watched, the blond girl looked up and met Roxanne's gaze. Her eyes flickered briefly, then she smiled sweetly.

'Hello,' she said. 'You probably don't remember me.'

'Oh yes I do,' said Roxanne, smiling back. 'It's Heather, isn't it?'

'That's right.' Heather's smile became even sweeter. 'And you're Roxanne.'

'Roxanne!' said Candice, looking up, eyes shining. 'Isn't it wonderful news about the baby?'

'Fantastic,' said Roxanne. 'Did Giles call you last night?'

'Yes. He sounded absolutely overwhelmed, didn't you think?' Candice gestured to the piece of paper. 'Look, we're designing a card for the Art Department to make up. Then we'll get everyone to sign it. What do you think?'

'It's an excellent idea,' said Roxanne, looking fondly at her. 'Maggie'll love it.'

'I'll take it down to the studio,' said Candice, standing up. Then she looked a little hesitantly from Heather to Roxanne. 'You remember Heather, don't you, Roxanne?'

'Of course,' said Roxanne. 'Maggie told me all about Heather joining the team. That certainly was quick work.'

'Yes,' said Candice, colouring slightly. 'It's . . . it's all worked out really well, hasn't it?' She glanced again at Heather. 'Right, well – I'll just pop down with this card. I won't be long.'

When she'd gone, there was silence between them. Roxanne gave Heather an appraising look and Heather stared back innocently, twisting a lock of hair around her finger.

'So, Heather,' said Roxanne at last, in a friendly tone. 'How are you enjoying the *Londoner*?'

'It's wonderful,' said Heather, gazing at her earnestly. 'I feel so lucky to be working here.'

'And I gather you're living with Candice now.'

'Yes, I am,' said Heather. 'She's been so incredibly kind.'

'Has she?' said Roxanne pleasantly. 'Well, you know, that doesn't surprise me at all.' She paused thoughtfully. 'Candice is a very kind, generous person. She finds it very difficult to say no to people.'

'Really?' said Heather.

'Oh yes. I'm surprised you haven't picked that up.' Roxanne nonchalantly examined her nails for a moment. 'In fact, her friends – including myself – sometimes get quite worried about her. She's the sort of person it would be so easy to take advantage of.'

'Do you think so?' Heather smiled sweetly at

Roxanne. 'I would have thought Candice could take pretty good care of herself. How old is she now?'

Well, thought Roxanne, almost impressed. She certainly gives as good as she gets.

'So,' she said, abruptly changing the subject, 'I gather you've never worked on a magazine before.'

'No,' said Heather unconcernedly.

'But you're a very good writer, I hear,' said Roxanne. 'You obviously impressed Ralph Allsopp tremendously at your interview.'

To her surprise, a faint pink flush began to creep up Heather's neck. Roxanne stared at it with interest until it faded away again.

'Well, Heather,' she said. 'Lovely to meet you again. We'll be seeing lots of each other, I'm sure.'

She watched as Heather sauntered away, into Justin's office, noticing that Justin looked up with a smile as Heather entered. Typical male, she thought acidly. He'd clearly already been seduced by Heather's sweet smile.

Roxanne stared through the window at Heather's cute, snub-nosed profile, trying to work her out. She was young, she was pretty, and probably talented to some degree. She was charming – on the surface. At face value, a lovely girl. So why did she make Roxanne's hackles rise? The consideration passed through Roxanne's mind that she might simply be jealous of Heather – and immediately she dismissed it.

As she stood, staring, Candice came back into the office, holding a colour page proof.

'Hi!' said Roxanne, smiling warmly at her. 'Listen – fancy a quick drink after work?'

'I can't,' said Candice regretfully. 'I promised Heather I'd go shopping with her. I'm going to find a present for Maggie.'

'No problem,' said Roxanne lightly. 'Another time.'

She watched as Candice went into Justin's office, grinned at Heather and started talking. Justin immediately began to gesture, frowning, at the page proof – and Candice nodded earnestly and began to gesture herself. As they both stared, engrossed, at the proof, Heather slowly turned and met Roxanne's eyes coolly through the window. For a moment, they simply stared at each other – then Roxanne abruptly turned away.

'Roxanne!' Justin was looking up and calling. 'Can you come and have a look at this?'

'In a minute!' called Roxanne and strode out of the office. She didn't wait for the lift but hurried, with a sudden rush of adrenalin, up the stairs and straight along the corridor to Ralph Allsopp's office.

'Janet!' she said, stopping at his elderly secretary's desk. 'Can I see Ralph for a moment?'

'He's not in, I'm afraid,' said Janet, looking up from her knitting. 'Not in at all today.'

'Oh,' said Roxanne, subsiding slightly. 'Damn.'

'He does know about Maggie's baby, though,' said Janet. 'I told him when he rang in this morning. He was thrilled. Such a lovely name, too. Lucia.' She gestured to her knitting. 'I'm just running her up a little matinée jacket.'

'Really?' said Roxanne, looking at the bundle of lemon wool as though it were a curiosity from another land. 'That's very clever of you.'

'It takes no time, really,' said Janet, clicking briskly with her needles. 'And she doesn't want to be dressing the little thing in shop-bought cardigans.'

Doesn't she? thought Roxanne in puzzlement. Why on earth not? Then she shook her head impatiently. She wasn't here to talk about baby clothes.

'Listen, Janet,' she said. 'Can I ask you something?'

'You can ask,' said Janet, picking up her knitting again and beginning to click. 'Doesn't mean you'll get.'

Roxanne grinned, and lowered her voice slightly.

'Has Ralph said anything to you about this new editorial assistant, Heather?'

'Not really,' said Janet. 'Just that he was giving her the job.'

Roxanne frowned. 'But when he interviewed her. He must have said something.'

'He thought she was very witty,' said Janet. 'She'd written a very funny article about London Transport.'

'Really?' Roxanne looked at her in surprise. 'Was it really any good?'

'Oh yes,' said Janet. 'Ralph gave a copy of it to me to read.' She put down her knitting, leafed through a pile of papers on her desk and produced a piece of paper. 'Here. You'll like it.'

'I doubt that,' said Roxanne. She glanced at the piece of paper, then put it in her bag. 'Well, thanks.'

'And do give my love to Maggie when you speak to her,' added Janet fondly, shaking out the little yellow matinée jacket. 'I do hope motherhood isn't too much of a shock for her.'

'A shock?' said Roxanne in surprise. 'Oh no. Maggie'll be fine. She always is.'

A voice calling her name dragged Maggie from a vivid, frenzied dream in which she was running after something nameless and invisible. She opened her eyes in a flurry of panic and blinked a few times disorientatedly at the bright overhead light.

'Maggie?' Her eyes snapped into focus, and she saw Paddy, standing at the end of her hospital bed, holding an enormous bunch of lilies. 'Maggie, dear, I wasn't sure if you were asleep. How are you feeling?'

'Fine,' said Maggie in a scratchy voice. 'I'm fine.' She tried to sit up, wincing slightly at her aching body, and pushed her hair back off her dry face. 'What time is it?'

'Four o'clock,' said Paddy, looking at her watch,

'just gone. Giles will be along any moment.'

'Good,' whispered Maggie. Giles, along with all the other visitors, had been ejected from the ward at two o'clock so that the new mothers could catch up on some rest. Maggie had lain tensely awake for a while, waiting for Lucia to cry, then had obviously drifted off to sleep. But she didn't feel rested. She felt bleary and unfocused; unable to think straight.

'And how's my little granddaughter?' Paddy looked into the plastic cradle beside Maggie's bed. 'Asleep like a lamb. What a good little baby! She's been an angel, hasn't she?'

'She was awake quite a lot of the night,' said Maggie, pouring herself a glass of water with shaking hands.

'Was she?' Paddy smiled fondly. 'Hungry, I expect.'

'Yes.' Maggie looked through the glass of the crib at her daughter. A little bundle in a cellular blanket, her tiny, screwed-up face just visible. She didn't seem real. None of it seemed real. Nothing had prepared her for what this would be like, thought Maggie. Nothing.

The birth itself had been like entering another, alien world, in which her body responded to some force she had no control over. In which her dignity, her ideals, her self-control and self-image were obliterated; in which none of the rules of normal life applied. She had wanted to object; to call a halt to the whole proceedings. To produce some last-minute get-out clause. But it had been too late. There was no get-out clause; no escape route. No alternative but to grit her teeth and do it.

Already the hours of pain were fading from her memory. In her mind the whole event seemed to have kaleidoscoped around those last few minutes – the bright white lights and the arrival of the paediatrician and the actual delivery of the baby. And that, thought Maggie, had been the most surreal moment of all. The delivery of another, living, screaming human being from inside her. Looking around the maternity ward at the faces of the other mothers, she could not believe how calmly they seemed to be taking this momentous, extraordinary event; how they seemed able to chat about brands of nappies and plots of soap operas, as though nothing of any importance had happened.

Or perhaps it was just that they'd all done it before. None of the other women on the ward was a first-time mother. They all dandled their little bundles with accustomed ease. They could simultaneously breast-feed and eat their breakfasts and talk to their husbands about redecorating the spare room. During the night, she had heard the girl in the bed next to hers joking with the midwife on duty about her baby.

'Greedy little bugger, isn't he?' she'd said, and laughed. 'Won't leave me alone.' And Maggie, on the other side of the floral curtain, had felt tears pouring down her face as, once again, she tried to persuade Lucia to feed. What was wrong with her? she had thought frantically, as, yet again, Lucia sucked for a few seconds, then opened her mouth in a protesting shout. As the baby's squawls had become louder and louder, a midwife had appeared, looked at Maggie and pursed her lips with disapproval.

'You've let her get too wound up,' she'd said. 'Try to calm her down first.'

Flushed with distress and humiliation, Maggie had tried to soothe a flailing, wailing Lucia. She had once read in an article that a newborn baby already knew its mother's smell; that a baby even a few hours old could be calmed by hearing its mother's voice. The article had concluded that the bond between mother and child was one that could not be paralleled. But as Maggie had rocked her own newborn baby, Lucia's screams had only become louder and louder. With a sigh of impatience, the midwife had eventually reached for her. She had laid the baby on the bed, wrapped her up tightly in a blanket, and lifted her up again. And almost immediately, Lucia's cries had ceased. Maggie had stared at her own baby, peaceful and quiet in someone else's arms, and had felt cold with failure.

'There,' the midwife had said more kindly. 'Try again.' Stiff with misery, Maggie had taken the baby from her, fully expecting Lucia to protest. She had held Lucia to her breast and, almost magically, the baby had begun to feed contentedly.

'That's more like it,' the midwife had said. 'You just need a bit of practice.'

She had waited a few minutes, then had looked more closely at Maggie's red-rimmed eyes. 'Are you OK? Not feeling too down?'

'Fine,' Maggie had said automatically, and forced herself to smile brightly at the midwife. 'Honestly. I just need to get to grips with it.'

'Good,' the midwife had said. 'Well, don't worry. Everyone has trouble at first.'

She'd glanced at Lucia, then left the flowery cubicle. As soon as she'd gone, tears had begun to pour down Maggie's face again. She'd stared straight ahead at the end of her bed, feeling the hot wetness on her cheeks, but not daring to move or make a sound lest she disturbed Lucia – or even worse, was heard by one of the other mothers. They would think her a freak, to be crying over her baby. Everybody else in the ward was happy. She should be happy, too.

'These lilies arrived for you just as I was leaving,' Paddy was saying now. 'Shall we find another vase here, or shall I take them back to the house?'

'I don't know,' said Maggie, rubbing her face. 'Did . . . did my mother call?'

'Yes,' said Paddy, beaming. 'She's coming down tomorrow. Unfortunately she couldn't take today off. Some crucial meeting.'

'Oh,' said Maggie, trying not to let her disappointment show on her face. After all, she was a grown
woman. What did she need her mother for?

'And look, here's Giles!' said Paddy brightly. 'I'll go
and fetch us all a nice cup of tea, shall I?' She laid the
lilies carefully on the bed and walked off briskly.
Where she was going to find a nice cup of tea, Maggie
had no idea. But then, Paddy was that kind of woman.
Abandoned in the middle of the jungle with nothing
but a penknife, she would still, no doubt, be able to
rustle up a nice cup of tea – and probably a batch of
scones as well.

Maggie watched as mother and son greeted each
other. Then, as Giles approached her bed, she tried to
compose her features into light-hearted friendliness; a
suitable expression for a happy, loving wife. The truth
was, she felt dissociated from him, unable to com-
municate on anything but a surface level. In a matter of
twenty-four hours she had moved into a new world
without him.

She had not intended it to be that way. She had
wanted him there beside her; with her in every sense.
But by the time the message had got to him at work,
she had been well into the throes of labour. He had
arrived just in time for the last half-hour, by which
time she had barely been aware of his existence. Now,
although he could claim to have been present at his
daughter's birth, she felt that he had seen the denoue-
ment without experiencing any of the build-up; that he
would never fully understand what she had been
through.

As she had stared, shocked and silent at her new
daughter, he had cracked jokes with the nurses and
poured glasses of champagne. She had craved some
time alone together; a moment or two of quiet in which
to gather her thoughts. A chance for the two of them to
acknowledge the unbelievable nature of what had just

passed. A chance for her to talk honestly, without putting on an act. But after what seemed like only a few minutes, a midwife had come and gently told Giles it was time for all visitors to leave the maternity ward and that he could return in the morning. As he'd gathered his belongings, Maggie had felt her heart start to thud with panic. But instead of letting him see her fear, she'd smiled cheerfully as he'd kissed her good-bye, and even managed a crack about all the other women waiting for him at home. Now she smiled again.

'You took your time.'

'Did you have a nice sleep?' Giles sat down on the bed and stroked Maggie's hair. 'You look so serene. I've been telling everyone how wonderful you were. Everyone sends their love.'

'Everyone?'

'Everyone I could think of.' He looked at the crib. 'How is she?'

'Oh, fine,' said Maggie lightly. 'She hasn't done much since you left.'

'Nice flowers,' said Giles, looking at the lilies. 'Who are they from?'

'I haven't even looked!' said Maggie. She opened the little envelope and two embossed cards fell out. 'Roxanne,' she said, laughing. 'She says she's going to mix Lucia her first cocktail.'

'Typical Roxanne,' said Giles.

'Yes.' As Maggie stared down at the message, she could hear Roxanne's husky, drawling voice in her mind, and to her horror, felt the treacherous tears pricking her eyes again. Hurriedly she blinked, and put the cards down on the bedside table.

'Here we are!' came Paddy's voice. She was carrying a tray of cups and accompanied by a midwife Maggie didn't recognize. Paddy put the tray down and beamed at Maggie. 'I thought perhaps, after your tea, you could give Lucia her first bath.'

103

'Oh,' said Maggie, taken aback. 'Yes, of course.'

She took a sip of tea and tried to smile back at Paddy, but her face was red with embarrassment. It hadn't even occurred to her that Lucia would need a bath. It hadn't even occurred to her. What was wrong with her?

'Has she fed recently?' said the midwife.

'Not since lunchtime.'

'Right,' said the midwife cheerfully. 'Well, maybe you'd like to feed her now. Don't want to leave her too long. She's only a little thing.'

A renewed stab of guilt went through Maggie's chest and her face flushed even brighter.

'Of course,' she said. 'I'll . . . I'll do it now.'

Aware of everyone's eyes on her she reached into the crib, picked up Lucia and began to unwrap the tiny cellular blanket.

'Let me hold her for a moment,' said Giles suddenly. 'Let me just look at her.' He picked Lucia up, nestling her comfortably into the crook of his arm. As he did so, she gave an enormous yawn, then her tiny screwed-up eyes suddenly opened. She stared up at her father, her little pink mouth open like a flower.

'Isn't that the most beautiful sight?' said Paddy softly.

'Can I have a little look?' said the midwife.

'Of course,' said Giles. 'Isn't she perfect?'

'Such a healthy colour!' said Paddy.

'That's what I was wondering about,' said the midwife. She placed Lucia on the bed and briskly unbuttoned her sleepsuit. She stared at Lucia's chest, then looked up at Maggie. 'Has she always been this colour?'

'Yes,' said Maggie, taken aback. 'I . . . I think so.'

'She's got a tan,' said Giles, and laughed uncertainly.

'I don't think so,' said the midwife, and frowned. 'Someone should have picked this up. I think she's got jaundice.'

The unfamiliar word hung in the air like a threat. Maggie stared at the midwife and felt the colour drain from her cheeks; felt her heart begin to thump. They'd lied to her. They'd all lied. Her baby wasn't healthy at all.

'Is it very serious?' she managed.

'Oh no! It'll clear up in a few days.' The woman looked up at Maggie's face and burst into laughter. 'Don't worry, sweetheart. She'll live.'

Ralph Allsopp sat on a bench outside the Charing Cross Hospital, watching as a man with a broken leg painfully made his way past on crutches; as two nurses greeted each other and began to chatter animatedly. On his lap was a greetings card he had bought from the hospital shop, depicting a crib, a bunch of flowers and a winsome, grinning baby. 'My dear Maggie,' he had written shakily inside the card. Then he had stopped and put the pen down, unable to write any more.

He felt ill. Not from the disease itself: that had crept up quietly, unnoticed, like a friendly confidence trickster. It had slipped one silent toe inside him, and then another – and then had spread quickly about his body with the assurance of a welcome guest. Now it had squatter's rights. It could do as it pleased; could not be dislodged. It was stronger than him. And perhaps because of that fact – because it knew its own power – it had, until now, treated him with relative kindness. Or maybe that was all part of its strategy. It had tiptoed around him, setting up camp wherever it could find a foothold, letting him remain unaware of its presence until it was too late.

Now, of course, he was no longer unaware. Now he knew it all. He had had his disease explained to him carefully by three separate doctors. Each had apparently been concerned that he should understand every single detail completely, as though he were entering an exam on the subject. Each had looked him straight in the eye with a practised, compassionate expression; had mentioned counselling and hospices and Macmillan Nurses – then, after a pause, his wife. It had been taken for granted that his wife and family would be told; that his staff would be told; that the world would be told. It had been taken for granted that this dissemination of information was his task; his choice; his responsibility.

And it was this responsibility which made Ralph feel ill; which made him feel a coldness up and down his spine, a nausea in the pit of his stomach. The responsibility was too much. Whom to tell. What to tell. How many boats to rock at once. For the moment the words were out of his lips, everything would change. It seemed to him that he would immediately become public property. His life – his limited, diminishing life – would no longer be his own. It would belong to those he loved. And therein lay the problem; the heartache. To whom did those last months, weeks, days, belong?

By speaking now, he would grant the rest of his life to his wife, to his three children, to the closest of his friends. And so it should be. But to include was also to exclude; to reveal was also to attract scrutiny. By speaking now, it seemed to him, his last months would at once be placed under a giant magnifying glass, allowing no secrets; no intruders; no unexpected elements. He would be obliged to play out the remainder of his life in conventional, noble fashion.

For, after all, cancer patients were not adulterers, were they?

Ralph closed his eyes and massaged his brow wearily. Those doctors thought they owned the sum of the world's knowledge, with their graphs and scans and statistics. What they didn't know was that outside the consulting room, life was more complicated than that. That there were factors they knew nothing about. That the potential for hurt and misery was enormous.

He could, of course, have told them everything. Offered them his dilemma as he had offered his body; watched them whispering and conferring and consulting their textbooks. But what would have been the point? There was no solution, just as there was no cure to his illness. All ways forward would be painful; the most he could hope was to minimize the pain as much as possible.

Feeling a sudden shaft of determination, he picked up his pen again. 'A new little light in the world,' he wrote in the baby card. 'With many congratulations and love from Ralph.' He would buy a magnum of champagne, he suddenly decided, put the card in with that and send the whole lot by special delivery. Maggie deserved something special.

He sealed the envelope, stood up stiffly, and looked at his watch. Half an hour to go. Half an hour to rid his pockets of all leaflets, all pamphlets, all evidence; to rid his nostrils of that cloying hospital smell. To turn from a patient back into an ordinary person. A taxi was cruising slowly along the street and he hurried forward to hail it.

As it moved off through the thick evening traffic, he stared out of the window. People were bad-temperedly barging past one another as they crossed the road and he gazed at them, relishing the normality of their expressions after the guarded looks of the doctors. He would hold on to that normality for as long as possible, he thought fiercely. He would hold on to that easy, wonderful disregard for the miracle of human existence. People weren't designed to roam the earth constantly and gratefully aware of their healthy functioning bodies. They were designed to strive, to love, to fight and bicker; to drink too much and eat too much and lie too long in the sun.

He got out of the taxi at a corner and walked slowly along the street to the house in which she lived. As he looked up he could see all her windows lit up and uncurtained in a brilliant, defiant blaze. The sight seemed suddenly to have a strange poignancy. His unwitting Rapunzel in her tower, unaware of what the future held. A dart of pain went through his heart and for a moment, he desperately wanted to tell her. To tell her that very night; to hold her tight and weep with her into the small hours.

But he would not. He would be stronger than that. Taking a deep breath, he quickened his pace and arrived at her front door. He pressed the buzzer and after a few moments the front door was released. Slowly he climbed the stairs, arrived at the top and saw her waiting at her front door. She was wearing a white silk shirt and a short black skirt and the light from behind was burnishing her hair. For a few moments he just stared at her.

'Roxanne,' he said eventually. 'You look . . .'

'Good,' she said, and her mouth curved in a half-smile. 'Come on in.'

Chapter Eight

The gift shop was small and quiet and sweetly scented – and, although the rest of the shopping mall seemed to be crowded with people, practically empty. Candice walked around, listening to her own footsteps on the wooden floor and looking doubtfully at sampler cushions and mugs saying 'It's a Girl!' She stopped by a shelf of stuffed toys, picked up a teddy bear and smiled at it. Then she turned it over to look at the price and, as she saw the ticket, felt herself blanch.

'How much?' said Heather, coming up behind her.

'Fifty pounds,' said Candice in an undertone, and hastily stuffed the bear back onto the shelf.

'Fifty quid?' Heather stared at the teddy incredulously, then began to laugh. 'That's outrageous! It hasn't even got a nice face. Come on. We'll go somewhere else.'

As they walked out of the shop, Heather unselfconsciously took Candice's arm in hers, and Candice felt herself blush slightly with pleasure. She could hardly believe it was only a week since Heather had moved in with her. Already they felt like old friends; like soulmates. Every night, Heather insisted on cooking a proper supper and opening a bottle of wine; every night she had another entertainment planned. One evening she had given Candice a facial, another evening she'd brought home videos and popcorn; the next, she'd brought home an electric juicer and announced she was setting up a juice bar in the kitchen. By the end of that evening their hands had been raw from peeling oranges and they'd produced approximately one glass of warm, unappealing juice – but they'd both been in fits of giggles. Even now, remembering it, Candice felt a giggle rising.

'What?' said Heather, turning towards her.

'The juicer.'

'Oh God,' said Heather. 'Don't remind me.' She paused by the entrance to a big department store. 'Here, what about in here? There must be a baby department.'

'Oh, that's a good idea,' said Candice.

'In fact, I'm just going to slip off,' said Heather. 'I've got something I need to buy. So I'll see you in the baby department.'

'OK,' said Candice, and headed for the elevator. It was seven o'clock at night, but the shop was as crowded and bustling as though it were the middle of the day. As she arrived at the baby department she felt a sudden slight selfconsciousness, but forced herself to walk forward, among all the pregnant women staring at prams. A row of little embroidered dresses took her eye and she began to leaf through the rack.

'Here you are!' Heather's voice interrupted her and she looked up.

'That was quick!'

'Oh, I knew what I wanted,' said Heather, and flushed slightly. 'It's . . . actually, it's for you.'

'What?' Puzzled, Candice took the paper bag Heather was holding out to her. 'What do you mean, it's for me?'

'A present,' said Heather, gazing earnestly at her. 'You've been so good to me, Candice. You've . . . transformed my life. If it weren't for you, I'd be . . . well. Something quite different.'

110

Candice stared back at her wide grey eyes and felt suddenly shamefaced. If Heather only knew. If she only knew the real reason for Candice's generosity; knew the trail of guilt and dishonesty that lay behind their friendship. Would she still be standing there, looking at Candice with such candid, friendly eyes?

Feeling suddenly sick at her own deceit, Candice ripped the bag open and drew out a slim silver pen.

'It's not much,' said Heather. 'I just thought you'd like it. For when you're writing up your interviews.'

'It's beautiful,' said Candice, feeling tears coming to her eyes. 'Heather, you really shouldn't have.'

'It's the least I can do,' said Heather. She took Candice's arm and squeezed it. 'I'm so glad I ran into you, that night. There's something really . . . special between us. Don't you think? I feel as if you're my closest friend.' Candice looked at her, then impetuously leaned forward and hugged her. 'I know your other friends don't like me,' came Heather's voice in her ear. 'But . . . you know, it doesn't matter.'

Candice withdrew her head and looked at Heather in surprise.

'What do you mean, my other friends don't like you?'

'Roxanne doesn't like me.' Heather gave a quick little smile. 'Don't worry about it. It doesn't matter.'

'But this is awful!' exclaimed Candice, frowning. 'Why don't you think she likes you?'

'I might have got it wrong,' said Heather at once. 'It was just a look she gave me . . . Honestly, Candice, don't hassle about it. I shouldn't have said anything.' She flashed a quick grin. 'Come on, choose one of these dresses, and then let's go and try on some proper clothes.'

'OK,' said Candice. But as she began to pick up the baby dresses again, her face was creased in a frown.

'Look, now I feel terrible!' said Heather. 'Please,

111

Candice, forget I said anything.' She lifted a thumb and ran it slowly down the crease in Candice's forehead. 'Forget about Roxanne, OK? I'm probably just sensitive. I probably got it all wrong.'

Roxanne lay happily on the sofa in a T-shirt, listening to low, jazzy music and, in the background, the sounds of Ralph cooking in the kitchen. He always cooked the supper – partly because he claimed to enjoy it, and partly because she was useless at it. She associated some of their happiest moments together with meals that he had cooked, after sex. Those were the times she cherished the most, she thought. The times when she could almost believe that they lived together; that they were a normal couple.

Of course, they weren't a normal couple. Perhaps they never would be. Automatically – and almost dispassionately – Roxanne's thoughts flicked to Ralph's youngest son Sebastian. Sweet little Sebastian, the afterthought. The blessing. The accident, let's face it. And still only a child; still only ten years old. Ten years, five months and a week.

Roxanne knew Sebastian Allsopp's age to the minute. His older brother and sister were in their twenties, safely off in their own lives. But Sebastian lived at home, went to school, brushed his teeth and still had a teddy bear. Sebastian was too young to bear the turmoil of a divorce. Not until he was eighteen, Ralph had said once after a few brandies. Eighteen. Another seven years, six months and three weeks. In seven years she would be forty.

For the sake of the children. It was a phrase which had once meant nothing to her. Now it seemed burnt into her soul with a branding iron. For the sake of Sebastian. He'd been four years old that night when she and Ralph had first danced together. A poppet in pyjamas, sleeping in his bed, while she looked into his

112

father's eyes and realized with a sudden urgency that she wanted more of them. That she wanted more of him. She'd been twenty-seven, then. Ralph had been forty-six. Anything in the world had seemed possible.

Roxanne closed her eyes, remembering. It had been at the first night of a star-laden visiting production of *Romeo and Juliet* at the Barbican. Ralph had been sent two complimentary tickets and, at the last minute, had wandered into the editorial office of the *Londoner,* looking for a second taker. When Roxanne had jumped at the chance, his face had registered slight surprise, which he had tactfully hidden. He had, he'd later confessed, always thought of her as a glossy, materialistic girl – bright and talented but with no real depth. When he turned to her at the end of the play to see her still staring forward, her face streaked unashamedly with tears, he'd felt a lurch of surprise, and an unexpected liking for her. Then, when she'd pushed her hair back off her brow, wiped her eyes and said, with her customary spirit, 'I'm bloody parched. How about a cocktail?' he'd thrown back his head and laughed. He'd produced two invitations for the post-performance party – which he hadn't been intending to use – had called his wife and told her that he would be a little later than he'd thought.

He and Roxanne had stood at the edge of a party full of strangers, drinking Buck's Fizz, talking about the play and inventing stories about all the other guests. Then a jazz band had struck up, and the floor had crowded with couples. And after hesitating a second, Ralph had asked her to dance. As soon as she'd felt his arms around her and looked up into his eyes, she'd known. She'd simply known.

A familiar spasm, half pain, half joy, went through Roxanne at the memory. She would always remember that night as one of the most magical in her life. Ralph had disappeared off to make a phone call which she

113

hadn't allowed herself to think about. Then he had returned to the table at which she was sitting, trembling with excitement. He had sat down opposite her, had met her eyes and said slowly, 'I was thinking about going on somewhere from here. A hotel, perhaps. Would you . . . care to join me?' Roxanne had stared at him silently for a few seconds, then had put down her drink.

She had intended to play it cool; to maintain a sophisticated reserve for as long as possible. But the moment they had got into their taxi, Ralph had turned to her, and she had found herself gazing back with an almost desperate longing. As their lips met she had thought, with a brief flash of humour, Hey, I'm kissing the boss. And then his kiss had deepened and her eyes had closed and her mind had lost its capacity for coherent thought. A capacity which had only returned in the morning, as she woke up in a Park Lane hotel with an adulterous man nineteen years her senior.

'Glass of wine?' Ralph's voice interrupted her and she opened her eyes to see him gazing fondly down at her. 'I could open the bottle I brought.'

'Only if it's properly cold,' she said suspiciously. 'If it's warm, I'm sending it back.'

'This one is cold,' said Ralph, smiling. 'I put it in the fridge when I got here.'

'It'd better be,' said Roxanne. She sat up and hugged her knees as he went back out to the kitchen. A minute later Ralph returned with two glasses full of wine.

'Why weren't you in the office today, by the way?' said Roxanne. She lifted her glass. 'Cheers.'

'Cheers,' replied Ralph. He took a long sip, then looked up and said easily, 'I had a meeting with my accountant all morning and into lunch. It didn't seem worth coming in.'

'Oh, right,' said Roxanne, and took a sip of wine. 'Slacker.'

A half-smile flickered across Ralph's face and he lowered himself slowly into a chair. Roxanne stared at him and frowned slightly.

'Are you OK?' she said. 'You look knackered.'

'Bit of a late night last night,' said Ralph, and closed his eyes.

'Oh well,' said Roxanne cheerfully. 'In that case, you don't get any sympathy from me.'

Candice took another swig of wine and gazed around the packed restaurant.

'I can't believe how full it is!' she said. 'I had no idea late-night shopping was such a big thing.'

Heather laughed. 'Have you never been shopping in the evening before?'

'Of course. But I didn't realize what a . . . party atmosphere there was here.' She took another swig of wine and looked around again. 'You know, I might suggest to Justin that we do a piece on it. We could come down, interview some people, take some photographs . . .'

'Good idea,' said Heather, and sipped at her wine. In front of her was a paper menu and a pen which their waiter had left behind, and Heather idly picked it up. She began to doodle on the menu: spiky starlike creations with far-reaching glittering rays. Candice watched her, slightly mesmerized, slightly drunk. They had had to wait half an hour for a table, during which time they had consumed a gin and tonic each and half a bottle of wine. Somehow she seemed to be drinking more quickly than Heather, and on an empty stomach the alcohol seemed stronger than usual.

'It's funny, isn't it?' said Heather, looking up suddenly. 'We're so close, and yet we don't really know each other.'

'I suppose not,' said Candice, and grinned. 'Well, what do you want to know?'

'Tell me about Justin,' said Heather after a pause. 'Do you still like him?'

'No!' said Candice, then laughed. 'I suppose I can stand him as an editor. But I don't have any . . . feelings for him. I think that was all a huge mistake.'

'Really?' said Heather lightly.

'He impressed me when I first met him. I thought he was incredibly clever and articulate and wonderful. But he's not. Not when you actually listen to what he's saying.' She took another gulp of wine. 'He just likes the sound of his own voice.'

'And there's no-one else on the horizon?'

'Not at the moment,' said Candice cheerfully. 'And I can't say I mind.'

A waiter appeared at the table, lit the candle between them and began to lay out knives and forks. Heather waited until he'd gone, then looked up again, her face glowing in the candlelight.

'So . . . men aren't important to you.'

'I don't know,' said Candice, laughing a little. 'I suppose the right one would be.' She watched as Heather picked up the bottle of wine, replenished Candice's glass then looked up, her eyes shining with a sudden intensity.

'So what is?' she asked softly. 'What means most to you in the world? What do you . . . treasure?'

'What do I treasure?' Candice repeated the question thoughtfully, staring into her glass. 'I don't know. My family, I suppose. Although my mother and I aren't that close any more. And my friends.' She looked up with a sudden certainty. 'I treasure my friends. Roxanne and Maggie especially.'

'Your friends.' Heather nodded slowly. 'Friends are such important things.'

'And my job. I love my job.'

'But not for the money,' probed Heather.

'No! I don't care about money!' Candice flushed

slightly, and took a gulp of wine. 'I hate materialism. And greed. And . . . dishonesty.'

'You want to be a good person.'

'I want to try.' Candice gave an embarrassed little laugh and put her wine glass down. 'What about you? What do you treasure?'

There was a short silence, and a curious expression flitted across Heather' s face.

'I've learned not to treasure anything much,' she said eventually, and gave a quick smile. 'Because you can lose it all overnight, with no warning. One minute you have it, the next you don't.' She snapped her fingers. 'Just like that.'

Candice stared at her in guilty misery, suddenly wanting to talk more; perhaps even reveal the truth.

'Heather . . .' she said hesitantly. 'I've . . . I've never—'

'Look!' interrupted Heather brightly, gesturing behind Candice. 'Here comes our food.'

Roxanne took a last mouthful of pasta, put down her fork and sighed. She was sitting opposite Ralph at her tiny folding dining table, the lights were dim and Ella Fitzgerald was crooning softly in the background.

'That was bloody delicious.' Roxanne hugged her stomach. 'Aren't you eating yours?'

'Go ahead.' Ralph gestured to his half-full plate, and, wrinkling her brow slightly, Roxanne pulled it towards her.

'No appetite?' she said. 'Or is it still your hang-over?'

'Something like that,' said Ralph lightly.

'Well, I'm not going to let it go to waste,' said Roxanne, plunging her fork into the pasta. 'You know, I always miss your cooking when I go away.'

'Do you?' said Ralph. 'What about all those five-star chefs?'

Roxanne pulled a face. 'Not the same. They can't do pasta like you.' She tilted her dining chair back so that it rested against the sofa, took a sip of wine and comfortably closed her eyes. 'In fact, I think it's very selfish of you not to come and cook me pasta every night.' She took another sip of wine, then another.

Then, as the silence continued, she opened her eyes. Ralph was gazing speechlessly at her, a curious expression on his face.

'I am selfish,' he said at last. 'You're right. I've treated you appallingly selfishly.'

'No you haven't!' said Roxanne, giving a little laugh. 'I'm only joking.' She reached for the bottle of wine, replenished both their glasses, and took a gulp. 'Nice wine.'

'Nice wine,' echoed Ralph slowly, and took a sip.

For a while they were both silent. Then Ralph looked up and, almost casually, said, 'Suppose in a year's time you could be doing anything. Anything at all. What would it be?'

'In a year's time,' echoed Roxanne, feeling her heart start to beat a little more quickly. 'Why a year?'

'Or three years,' said Ralph, making a vague gesture with his wine glass. 'Five years. Where do you see yourself?'

'Is this a job interview?' said Roxanne lightly.

'I'm just interested, I suppose,' said Ralph, shrugging. 'Idle fantasies.'

'Well, I . . . I don't know,' said Roxanne, and took a sip of wine, trying to stay calm.

What was going on? She and Ralph, by tacit agreement, never discussed the future; never discussed any part of life that might cause hurt or resentment. They talked about work, about films, food and travel. They gossiped about colleagues and speculated about Roxanne's dubious-looking downstairs neighbour. They watched television soap operas together and, in fits of laughter, ridiculed the wooden-faced acting. But, even when they were staring at adultery on the screen, they never talked about their own situation.

In the early days, she had tearfully insisted on hearing about his wife, about his family; about every last detail. She had shaken with misery and humiliation each time he'd left; had thrown accusations and ultimatums at him to no avail. Now she behaved almost as though each evening, each night spent in his arms, were a one-off; a self-contained bubble. It was simple self-preservation. That way disappointment could creep up on her less easily. That way she could pretend – at least to herself – that she was conducting the relationship on her own terms; that this was what she'd wanted all along.

She looked up, to see Ralph still waiting for an answer and, as she saw his expression, felt her stomach give a little flip. He was staring straight at her, his eyes glistening slightly, as if her answer really mattered to him. She took a gulp of wine, playing for time, then pushed her hair back and forced herself to smile unconcernedly.

'In a year's time?' she said lightly. 'If I could be anywhere, I think I'd like to be lying on a white beach somewhere in the Caribbean – with you, naturally.'

'Glad to hear it,' said Ralph, his face crinkling into a smile.

'But not just you,' said Roxanne. 'A posse of attentive waiters in white jackets would see to our every need. They'd ply us with food and drink and witty stories. Then, as if by magic, they would discreetly disappear, and we'd be left on our own in the magical sunset.'

She broke off, and took a sip of wine, then, after a short silence, looked up. As she met Ralph's eyes, her heart was thumping. Does he realize, she thought, that what I have just described is a honeymoon?

Ralph was staring at her with an expression she'd never seen in his eyes before. Suddenly he took hold of her hands and drew them up to his lips.

'You deserve it,' he said roughly. 'You deserve it all, Roxanne.' She gazed at him, feeling a hotness growing at the back of her throat. 'I'm so sorry for everything,' he muttered. 'When I think what I've put you through . . .'

'Don't be sorry.' Roxanne blinked hard, feeling tears smarting at her eyes. She drew him close across the table and kissed his wet eyes, his cheeks, his lips. 'I love you,' she whispered, and felt a sudden swell of painful, possessive happiness inside her. 'I love you, and we're together. And that's all that counts.'

Chapter Nine

The hospital was a large, Victorian building, with well-tended gardens at the front and a fenced area for children to play in. As Roxanne and Candice got out of the car and began to walk along the path towards the main entrance, Roxanne started laughing.

'Typical Maggie,' she said, looking around the pleasant scene. 'Even the hospital's a bloody picture postcard. She couldn't have her baby in some grim London hell-hole, could she?'

'What do we want?' said Candice, squinting at a colour-coded signpost with arrows pointing in all directions. 'Gynaecology. Labour suite.' She looked up. 'We don't want that, do we?'

'You can visit the labour suite if you like,' said Roxanne, giving a little shudder. 'As far as I'm concerned, ignorance is bliss.'

'Neo-natal. Pre-natal. Maternity,' read Candice, and wrinkled her brow. 'I can't work this out at all.'

'Oh, come on,' said Roxanne impatiently. 'We'll find her.'

They strode into the spacious reception area and spoke to a friendly woman at a desk, who tapped Maggie's name into a computer.

'Blue Ward,' she said, looking up with a smile.

'Follow the corridor round as far as you can go, then take the lift to the fifth floor.'

As they walked along the corridors, Candice glanced around at the beige walls and pulled a face.

'I hate the smell of hospitals,' she said. 'Horrible places. I think if I ever had a baby, I'd have it at home.'

'Of course you would,' said Roxanne. 'With pan pipes playing in the background and aromatherapy candles scenting the air.'

'No!' said Candice, laughing. 'I'd just . . . I don't know. Prefer to be at home, I suppose.'

'Well, if I ever have a baby, I'll have it by Caesarean,' said Roxanne drily. 'Full anaesthesia. They can wake me up when it's three years old.'

They arrived at the lift and pressed the fifth-floor button. As they began to rise, Candice glanced at Roxanne. 'I feel nervous!' she said. 'Isn't that weird?'

'I feel a bit nervous, too,' said Roxanne, after a pause. 'I suppose it's just that one of us has finally grown up. Real life has begun. The question is – are we ready for it?' She raised her eyebrows, and Candice gazed at her critically.

'You look tired, actually,' she said. 'Are you feeling OK?'

'I'm great,' said Roxanne at once, and tossed her hair back. 'Never better.'

But as they rose up in the lift, she stared at her tinted reflection in the lift doors and knew that Candice was right. She did look tired. Since that night with Ralph she had found it difficult to sleep; impossible to wrench her mind away from their conversation and what it had meant. Impossible to stop hoping.

Of course, Ralph had said nothing definite. He had made no promises. After that one short conversation, he had not even referred to the future again. But something was going on; something was different. Thinking back, she'd realized there had been something different about him from the moment he stepped in the door. Something different in the way he looked at her, and talked to her. As they'd said goodbye he'd stared at her for minutes without speaking. It was as though inside, behind his eyes, he was coming to the hardest decision of his life.

She knew it was a decision that couldn't be hurried; that couldn't be arrived at in a snap. But the stress of this constant uncertainty was unbearable. And they were both suffering because of it – Ralph looked more tired and strained these days than she'd ever seen him. She'd glimpsed him the other day at the office, and had realized with a shock that he was actually losing weight. What mental hell he must be going through. And yet if he would only make up his mind and take courage, the hell would be over for good.

Once again, a surge of painful hope rose through her, and she clasped her bag more tightly. She shouldn't allow herself to think like this. She should return to her former, disciplined state of mind. But it was too hard. After six frugal years of refusing to hope or even think about it, her mind was now gorging itself on fantasy. Ralph would leave his wife. They would both, finally, be able to relax; to enjoy each other. The long hard winter would be over; the sun would come out and shine. Life would begin again for both of them. They would set up house together. Perhaps they would even—

There she stopped herself. She could not let herself go that far; she had to keep some control on herself. After all, nothing had been said. Nothing was definite. But surely that conversation had meant something? Surely he was at least thinking about it?

And she deserved it, didn't she? She bloody well deserved it, after everything she'd been through. An unfamiliar resentment began to steal over her, and she forced herself to breathe slowly and calmly. Over the past few days, having let her mind break out into fantasy land, she had discovered that beneath the joyous hope there was a darker flip-side. An anger that she had suppressed for too many years. Six whole years of waiting and wondering and grabbing moments of happiness where she could. It had been too long. It had been a prison sentence.

The lift doors opened and Candice looked up at Roxanne.

'Well, here we are,' she said, and gave a little smile. 'At last.'

'Yes,' said Roxanne, and exhaled sharply. 'At last.'

They walked out of the lift and towards a swing door marked 'Blue Ward'. Candice glanced up at Roxanne, then hesitantly pushed the door open. The room was large, but divided into cubicles by unnamed floral curtains. Candice raised her eyebrows at Roxanne, who shrugged back. Then a woman in a dark blue uniform, holding a baby, approached them.

'Are you here to visit?' she said, smiling.

'Yes,' said Roxanne, staring down at the baby in spite of herself. 'Maggie Phillips.'

'No, it'll be Drakeford, won't it?' said Candice. 'Maggie Drakeford.'

'Oh yes,' said the woman pleasantly. 'In the corner.'

Roxanne and Candice glanced at each other, then advanced slowly down the ward. Slowly, Candice pushed back the curtain of the final cubicle, and there she was, Maggie, looking familiar but unfamiliar, sitting up in bed with a tiny baby in her arms. She looked up, and for a still moment none of them said anything. Then Maggie gave a wide smile, held up the baby to face them and said, 'Lucia, meet the cocktail queens.'

*   *   *

Maggie had had a good night. As she watched Roxanne and Candice advance hesitantly towards the bed, eyes glued on Lucia's tiny face, she allowed herself to feel a warm glow of contentment. A bit of sleep, that was all. A bit of sleep every night, and the world changed.

The first three nights had been hell. Utter misery. She had lain stiffly in the darkness, unable to relax; unable to sleep while there was even the smallest chance that Lucia might wake. Even when she had drifted off to sleep, every snuffle from the tiny crib would wake her. She would hear cries in her dreams and jerk awake in a panic, only to find Lucia peacefully asleep and some other baby wailing. Then she would fear that the other baby's cries would wake Lucia – and she would tense up with apprehension, unable to fall asleep again.

On the fourth night, at two in the morning, Lucia had refused to go back to sleep. She had cried when Maggie tried to place her in her cot, thrashed about when Maggie tried to feed her, and screamed protestingly when, in desperation, Maggie began to sing. After a few minutes, a face had appeared round Maggie's floral curtain. It was an elderly midwife on night duty whom Maggie had not met before, and at the sight of Lucia, she shook her head comically.

'Young lady, your mother needs her sleep!' she'd said, and Maggie's head had jerked up in shock. She had expected a lecture on demand feeding or mother-baby bonding. Instead, the midwife had advanced inside Maggie's cubicle, looked at her shadowed face and sighed. 'This is no good! You look exhausted!'

'I feel a bit tired,' Maggie had admitted in a wobbly voice.

'You need a break.' The midwife had paused, then said, 'Would you like me to take her to the nursery?'

'The nursery?' Maggie had stared at her blankly. Nobody had told her about any nursery.

'I can keep an eye on her, and you can have a sleep. Then, when she needs feeding, I can bring her back.'

Maggie had stared at the midwife, wanting to burst into tears with gratitude.

'Thank you. Thank you . . . Joan,' she had managed, reading the woman's name-badge in the dim light. 'I . . . will she be all right?'

'She'll be fine!' Joan had said reassuringly. 'Now, you get some rest.'

As soon as she had left the cubicle, wheeling Lucia's crib, Maggie had fallen into the first relaxed sleep she'd had since Lucia's birth. The deepest, sweetest sleep of her life. She had woken at six, feeling almost restored, to see Lucia back in the cubicle again, ready for feeding.

Since then, Joan had appeared at Maggie's bedside each night, offering the services of the nursery – and Maggie had found herself guiltily accepting every time.

'No need to feel guilty,' Joan had said one night. 'You need your sleep to produce milk. No good wearing yourself out. You know, we used to keep mothers in for two weeks. Now, they shoo you all off after two days. Two days!' She clucked disapprovingly. 'You'd be home already if it weren't for the baby's jaundice.'

But despite Joan's reassuring comments, Maggie did feel guilty. She felt she should be with Lucia twenty-four hours a day, as all the books recommended. Anything less was failure. And so she hadn't mentioned Joan to Giles or to Paddy – or, in fact, to anyone.

Now she smiled at Roxanne and Candice and said, 'Come on in! Sit down. It's so good to see you!'

'Mags, you look wonderful!' said Roxanne. She embraced Maggie in a cloud of scent, then sat down on the edge of the bed. She was looking thinner and more glamorous than ever, thought Maggie. Like an exotic bird of paradise in this room full of dopey-eyed mother ducks. And for an instant, Maggie felt a twinge of jealousy. She'd imagined that straight after the birth she would regain her old figure; that she would slip back into her old clothes with no problem. But her stomach, hidden under the bedclothes, was still frighteningly flabby, and she had no energy to exercise it.

'So, Mags,' drawled Roxanne, looking around the ward. 'Is motherhood all it's cracked up to be?'

'Oh, you know.' Maggie grinned. 'Not too bad. Of course, I'm an old hand now.'

'Maggie, she's beautiful!' Candice looked up with shining eyes. 'And she doesn't look ill at all!'

'She's not, really,' said Maggie, looking at Lucia's closed-up, sleeping face. 'She had jaundice, and it's taken a while to clear up. It just meant we had to stay in hospital a bit longer.'

'Can I hold her?' Candice held out her arms and, after a pause, Maggie handed the baby over.

'She's so light!' breathed Candice.

'Very sweet,' said Roxanne. 'You'll be making me broody in a moment.'

Maggie laughed. 'Now, that *would* be a miracle.'

'Do you want to hold her?' Candice looked up at Roxanne, who rolled her eyes comically.

'If I must.'

She had held scores of babies before. Little bundles belonging to other people, that aroused in her no feeling other than tedium. Roxanne Miller did not coo over babies – she yawned over them. She was famous for it. Whether she was genuinely uninterested, or whether this was a defensive response deliberately cultivated over the years, she had never allowed herself to consider.

But as she looked into the sleeping face of Maggie's baby, Roxanne felt her defences begin to crumble;

found herself thinking thoughts she had never let herself think before. She wanted one of these, she found herself thinking. Oh God. She actually wanted one. The thought frightened her; exhilarated her. She closed her eyes and, without meaning to, imagined herself holding her own baby. Ralph's baby. Ralph looking fondly over her shoulder. The picture made her almost sick with hope – and with fear. She was treading on forbidden ground, allowing her mind to venture into dangerous places. And on what basis? On the basis of one conversation. It was ridiculous. It was foolhardy. But, having started, she couldn't seem to stop.

'So, what do you reckon, Roxanne?' said Maggie, looking at her amusedly. Roxanne stared at Lucia a few seconds longer, then forced herself to look up with a nonchalant expression.

'Very nice, as babies go. But I warn you, she'd better not pee on me.'

'I'll take her back,' said Maggie, smiling, and a ridiculous thud of disappointment went through Roxanne.

'Here you are then, Mummy,' she drawled, handing the bundle back.

'Oh, Maggie, I brought you these,' said Candice, rescuing the bouquet of flowers which she'd deposited on the floor. 'I know you'll have heaps already . . .'

'I did have,' said Maggie. 'But they're all dead. They don't last five minutes in here.'

'Oh good! I mean—'

'I know what you mean,' said Maggie, smiling. 'And they're lovely. Thank you.'

Candice looked around the cubicle. 'Have you got a vase?'

Maggie pulled a doubtful face.

'There might be one in the corridor. Or one of the other wards.'

'I'll find one.' Candice put the flowers down on the bed and headed out of the ward. When she'd gone, Maggie and Roxanne smiled at each other.

'So – how are you?' asked Maggie, stroking Lucia's cheek gently with the tip of her finger.

'Oh, fine,' said Roxanne. 'You know, life goes on . . .'

'How's Mr Married with Kids?' asked Maggie cautiously.

'Still got kids,' said Roxanne lightly. 'Still married.' They both laughed, and Lucia stirred slightly in her sleep. 'Although . . . you never know,' Roxanne couldn't resist adding. 'Changes may be afoot.'

'Really?' said Maggie in astonishment. 'You're not serious!'

'Who knows?' A smile spread over Roxanne's face. 'Watch this space.'

'You mean we might actually get to meet him?'

'Oh, I don't know about that.' Roxanne's eyes flashed in amusement. 'I've got used to him being my little secret.'

Maggie glanced at her, then looked around for her watch.

'What time is it? I should offer you a cup of tea. There's an urn in the day room . . .'

'Don't worry,' said Roxanne, suppressing a shudder at the idea. 'I've brought a little liquid refreshment. We can have it when Candice gets back.' She looked around the maternity ward, trying to find something polite to say about it. But it seemed, to her, an over-heated floral hell. And Maggie had been here for well over a week. How could she bear it? 'How much longer are you in here for?' she asked.

'I go home tomorrow. The paediatrician has to check Lucia over – and then we're out of here.'

'I bet you're relieved.'

'Yes,' said Maggie, after a pause. 'Yes, of course I am. But . . . but let's not talk about hospitals.' She smiled at

129

Roxanne. 'Tell me about the outside world. What have I been missing?'

'Oh God, I don't know,' said Roxanne lazily. 'I never know the gossip. I'm always away when things happen.'

'What about that girl of Candice's?' said Maggie, suddenly frowning. 'Heather Whatsername. Have you met her again?'

'Yes, I saw her at the office. Didn't exactly warm to her.' Roxanne pulled a face. 'Bit sickly sweet.'

'I don't know why I got so worked up about her,' said Maggie ruefully. 'Pregnancy paranoia. She's probably a lovely girl.'

'Well, I wouldn't go that far. But I tell you what – ' Roxanne sat up and reached for her bag. 'She can certainly write.'

'Really?'

'Look at this.' Roxanne pulled a sheet of paper from her bag. 'I got it from Janet. It's actually very funny.'

She watched as Maggie read the first two lines of the piece, frowned, then scanned further down to the end.

'I don't believe it!' she exclaimed as she looked up. 'Did she really get a job at the *Londoner* on the strength of this piece?'

'I don't know,' said Roxanne. 'But you've got to admit, it's on the nail.'

'Of course it is,' said Maggie drily. 'Everything Candice writes is on the nail.'

'What?' Roxanne stared at her.

'Candice wrote this for the *Londoner*,' said Maggie, hitting the piece of paper with her hand. 'I remember it. Word for word. It's her style and everything.'

'I don't believe it!'

'No wonder Ralph was impressed,' said Maggie, rolling her eyes. 'God, Candice can be an idiot sometimes.'

*   *   *

Candice had taken longer than she had expected to find a vase, and had struck up a conversation with one of the midwives on another ward. As she finally made her way, humming, back into the ward, she saw Roxanne and Maggie staring at her, ominous expressions on their faces.

'So,' said Roxanne as she neared the bed. 'What do you have to say for yourself?'

'What?' said Candice.

'This,' said Maggie, producing the piece of paper with a flourish. Candice stared at it in bewilderment – then, as her gaze focused on the text, realized what it was. A flush spread over her cheeks and she looked away.

'Oh, that,' she said. 'Well . . . Heather didn't have any examples of her writing. So I—' She broke off awkwardly.

'So you thought you'd supply her with an entire portfolio?'

'No!' said Candice. 'Just one little piece. Just . . . you know.' She shrugged defensively. 'Something to get her started. For God's sake, it's no big deal.'

Maggie shook her head.

'Candice, it's not fair. You *know* it's not fair. It's not fair on Ralph, it's not fair on all the other people who applied for the job . . .'

'It's not fair on Heather, come to that,' put in Roxanne. 'What happens when Justin asks her to write another piece just like that one?'

'He won't! And she's fine. You know, she has got talent. She can do the job. She just needed a chance.' Candice looked from Roxanne to Maggie, feeling a sudden impatience with them both. Why couldn't they see that in some cases the ends more than justified the means? 'Come on, be honest,' she exclaimed. 'How many jobs are got through nepotism? How many people drop names and use contacts and pretend

131

they're better than they are? This is just the same.'

There was silence – then Maggie said, 'And she's living with you.'

'Yes.' Candice looked from face to face, wondering if she'd missed something. 'What's wrong with that?'

'Is she paying you rent?'

'I . . .' Candice swallowed. 'That's our business, don't you think?'

She had not yet mentioned rent to Heather – nor had Heather ever brought the subject up. In her heart she had always assumed that Heather would offer to pay something, at least – but then even if she didn't, Candice thought with a sudden fierceness, what was the big deal? Some people paid rent to their friends, and some people didn't. And it wasn't as if she was desperate for the money.

'Of course it is,' said Roxanne mildly. 'As long as she isn't using you.'

'*Using* me?' Candice shook her head disbelievingly. 'After what my father did to her family?'

'Candice—'

'No, listen to me,' said Candice, her voice rising a little. 'I owe her one. OK? I owe her one. So maybe I got her this job under slightly false pretences, and maybe I'm being more generous to her than I normally would. But she deserves it. She deserves a break.' Candice felt her face growing hot. 'And I know you don't like her, Roxanne, but—'

'What?' said Roxanne in outrage. 'I've barely spoken to her!'

'Well, she has the impression you don't like her.'

'Maybe she doesn't like *me*. Had you thought of that?'

'Why wouldn't she like you?' retorted Candice indignantly.

'I don't know! Why wouldn't I like her, for that matter?'

'This is ridiculous!' cut in Maggie. 'Stop it, both of you!'

At her raised voice, Lucia gave a sudden wriggle and began to wail, plaintively at first, then more lustily.

'Now look what you've done!' said Maggie.

'Oh,' said Candice, and bit her lip. 'Sorry. I didn't mean to lose it like that.'

'No,' said Roxanne. 'Neither did I.' She put a hand out and squeezed Candice's. 'Don't get me wrong. I'm sure Heather's a great girl. We just . . . worry about you.'

'You're too blinking nice,' put in Maggie, then winced. The others turned and, in appalled fascination, watched her putting Lucia to her breast.

'Does it *hurt*?' said Candice, watching Maggie's face involuntarily screw up in pain.

'A bit,' said Maggie. 'Just at first.' The baby began to suck and gradually her face relaxed. 'There. That's better.'

'Bloody hell,' said Roxanne, staring blatantly at Maggie's breast. 'Rather you than me.' She pulled a face at Candice, who gave a sudden giggle.

'She likes a drink, anyway,' she said, watching Lucia greedily sucking.

'Like her mother,' said Roxanne. 'Speaking of which . . .' She reached into her bag and, after some rummaging, produced a large silver cocktail shaker.

'No!' exclaimed Maggie in disbelief. 'You haven't!'

'I told you we'd toast the baby with cocktails,' said Roxanne.

'But we can't!' said Maggie, giggling. 'If somebody sees us, I'll get thrown out of the Good Mother club.'

'I thought of that, too,' said Roxanne. With a completely straight face, she reached into the bag again and produced three little baby bottles.

'What—'

'Wait.'

133

She unscrewed each of the bottles, placed them in a row on the bedside table, picked up the cocktail shaker and gave it a good shake as the other two watched in amazement. Then she removed the lid of the cocktail shaker and solemnly poured a thick white liquid into each of the bottles.

'What is it?' said Candice, staring at it.

'Not milk, surely?' said Maggie.

'Pina Colada,' said Roxanne airily.

At once, Candice and Maggie exploded into giggles. Pina Colada was a standing joke between them – ever since that first uproarious night at the Manhattan Bar, when Roxanne had announced that if anyone ordered Pina Colada she was disowning them.

'I mustn't!' wailed Maggie, trying not to shake. 'I mustn't laugh. Poor Lucia.'

'Cheers,' said Roxanne, handing her a baby bottle.

'To Lucia,' said Candice.

'Lucia,' echoed Roxanne, holding her bottle up.

'And to you two,' said Maggie, smiling at Roxanne and Candice. She took a gulp and closed her eyes in delight. 'God, that's good. I haven't tasted proper alcohol for weeks.'

'The thing is,' said Candice, taking a slurp, 'that actually, Pina Colada is bloody delicious.'

'It's not bad, is it?' said Roxanne, sipping thoughtfully. 'If they could just call it something classier . . .'

'Talking of alcohol, Ralph Allsopp sent us a magnum of champagne,' said Maggie. 'Wasn't that nice of him? But we haven't opened it yet.'

'Great minds think alike,' said Roxanne lightly.

'Mrs Drakeford?' A man's voice came from outside the floral curtains and the three looked guiltily at each other. The next moment, a doctor's cheerful head popped round the side of the curtain and grinned at them all. 'Mrs Drakeford, I'm one of the paediatricians. Come to check up on little Lucia.'

'Oh,' said Maggie weakly. 'Ahm . . . come in.'

'I'll take your . . . milk, shall I?' said Roxanne help-fully, and reached for Maggie's baby bottle. 'Here. I'll leave it on your bedside table for later.'

'Thanks,' said Maggie. Her mouth was tight; she was obviously trying not to laugh.

'Maybe we'd better go,' said Candice.

'OK,' whispered Maggie.

'See you soon, babe,' said Roxanne. She downed her Pina Colada in one and thrust the empty bottle back into her bag. 'Nothing like a nice healthy drink of milk,' she said to the paediatrician, who nodded in surprise.

'Lucia's gorgeous,' said Candice, and bent over the bed to kiss Maggie. 'And well see you soon.'

'At the Manhattan Bar,' put in Roxanne. 'First of the month. You think you'll be able to make it, Maggie?'

'Absolutely,' said Maggie, and grinned at her. 'I'll be there.'

Chapter Ten

As Candice arrived home that evening her cheeks were flushed with happiness, and she still felt giggles rising whenever she thought of the baby bottles full of Pina Colada. She also felt more emotional than she had been expecting to. The sight of Maggie and her baby – a new little person in the world – had stirred her deep inside; more than she had been aware at the time. Now she felt overflowing with affection for both her friends.

The only awkward moment between the three of them had been over Heather – and that, thought Candice, was because they didn't understand. After all, how could they? Maggie and Roxanne had never felt her secret, constant guilt – so they couldn't know what it was like to feel that guilt alleviated. They couldn't understand the lightness she had felt inside over the past few weeks; the sheer pleasure it gave her to see Heather's life falling into place.

Besides which, neither of them had really met Heather properly. They had no idea what a warm and generous person she was; how quickly the friendship between them had developed. Perhaps she had started out thinking of Heather primarily as victim; perhaps her initial generosity had been spurred by guilt rather than anything else. But now there was a genuine bond between them. Maggie and Roxanne behaved as though having Heather living in her flat were a huge disadvantage. In fact, the opposite was true. Now that she had a flat-mate, Candice couldn't imagine living again without one. How had she spent the evenings before Heather? Sipping cocoa on her own, instead of snuggled up with Heather on the sofa in pyjamas, reading out horoscopes in fits of laughter. Heather wasn't a disadvantage, thought Candice affectionately. She was a life-enhancer.

As she closed the front door behind her, she could hear Heather's voice in the kitchen. She sounded as though she might be on the phone, and Candice advanced cautiously down the corridor, not wanting to disturb Heather's privacy. A few feet before she reached the kitchen, she stopped in slight shock.

'Don't give me any of your grief, Hamish!' Heather was saying, in a low, tense voice so far from her usual bubbling tones that Candice barely recognized it. 'What the fuck is it to you?' There was a pause, then she said, 'Yeah, well maybe I don't care. Yeah well, maybe I will!' Her voice rose to a shout and there was the sound of the phone slamming down. Out in the hall, Candice froze in panic. Please don't come out, she thought. Please don't come out and see me.

A moment later, she heard Heather putting the kettle on, and the sound seemed to jolt her into action. Feeling absurdly guilty, she tiptoed a few feet back down the hall, opened the front door again, then banged it shut.

'Hi!' she called brightly. 'Anyone in?'

Heather appeared at the kitchen door and gazed at Candice appraisingly, without smiling.

'Hi,' she said at last. 'How was it?'

'Great!' said Candice enthusiastically. 'Lucia's gorgeous! And Maggie's fine . . .' She tailed off, and Heather leaned against the door frame.

'I was on the phone,' she said. 'I expect you heard.'

'No!' said Candice at once. 'I've only just got in.' She felt herself flushing and turned her head away, pretending to fiddle with the sleeve of her jacket.

'Men,' said Heather after a pause. 'Who needs them?' Candice looked up in surprise.

'Have you got a boyfriend?'

'Ex-boyfriend,' said Heather. 'Utter bastard. You really don't want to know.'

'Right,' said Candice awkwardly. 'Well – shall we have some tea?'

'Why not?' said Heather, and followed her back into the kitchen.

'By the way,' said Heather, as Candice reached for the tea-bags, 'I needed some stamps, so I got some from your dressing table. You don't mind, do you? I'll pay you back.'

'Don't be silly!' said Candice, turning round. 'And of course I don't mind. Help yourself.' She laughed. 'What's mine is yours.'

'OK,' said Heather casually. 'Thanks.'

Roxanne arrived back at her flat cold and hungry, to see a cardboard box waiting outside the front door. She stared at it, bewildered, then opened the door and gave it little shoves with her foot until it was inside. She shut the front door, flicked on the lights then crouched down and looked at the box more closely. The postmark was Cyprus, and the writing on the label was Nico's. The sweetheart. What had he sent her this time?

Smiling a little, Roxanne ripped open the box, to see row upon row of bright orange tangerines, still with their green leaves attached to the stalks. She picked one up, closed her eyes, and inhaled the sweet, tangy, unmistakable scent. Then she reached for the handwritten sheet lying on top of the tangerines.

My dearest Roxanne. A small reminder of what you

are missing, here in Cyprus. Andreas and I are still hoping you will reconsider our offer. Yours as ever, Nico.

For a moment, Roxanne was quite still. Then she looked at the tangerine consideringly, threw it into the air and caught it. Bright and sweet, sunny and appealing, she thought. Another world altogether; a world she'd almost forgotten about.

But her world was here. Here in the soft London rain, with Ralph.

After all the visitors had left the ward, the lights had been turned down and Lucia had settled to sleep, Maggie lay awake, staring up at the high, white, institutional ceiling, trying to quell her feelings of panic.

The paediatrician had been very complimentary about Lucia's progress. The jaundice had completely gone, she was putting on weight well, and all was as it should be.

'You can go home tomorrow,' he'd said, making a mark on his white form. 'I expect you're sick of this place.'

'Absolutely,' Maggie had said, and had smiled weakly at him. 'I can't wait to get home.'

Later, Giles had arrived to visit – and when she'd told him the good news, had whooped with delight.

'At last! What a relief. You must be thrilled. Oh, darling, won't it be great, having you home again?' He'd leaned forward and hugged her so tightly she could hardly breathe, and her spirits had, for a moment, lifted to something near euphoria.

But now, lying in the dark, she could feel nothing but fear. In ten days, she had become used to the rhythm of life in hospital. She had become used to three meals a day; to the friendly chatter of the midwives; to the cups of tea which appeared on trolleys at four o'clock. She had become used to the feeling of security: the knowledge that, if disaster struck, there was always a button to press, a nurse to summon. She had become used to Joan wheeling Lucia off at two in the morning and returning at six.

To her shame, she had secretly almost been relieved when Lucia's jaundice had responded more slowly than expected to phototherapy. Every extra night in hospital was putting off the day when she would have to leave the safety, familiarity and camaraderie of the maternity ward for her empty, chilly house. She thought of The Pines – her home – and tried to summon up some feeling of affection for it. But the strongest emotion she had ever felt for the house was pride in its grandeur – and somehow that no longer appealed to her. What was the point of all that cold, open space? She was used to her warm, cosy floral cell, with everything within arm's reach.

Giles, of course, would never understand that. He adored the house in a way she feared she would never be able to.

'I've been so looking forward to having you home,' he'd said that afternoon, holding her hand. 'You and the baby, home at The Pines. It'll be . . . just as I always imagined it.' And a twinge of surprise had gone through her. Of envy, almost. Giles so obviously had a clear vision in his mind of what life at home with a baby would be like. Whereas she still could hardly believe it was actually happening.

Throughout her pregnancy, she had been unable to picture herself with a child. She had known in her logical mind that there would be a baby; had occasionally tried to imagine herself pushing the smart Mamas and Papas pram or rocking the Moses basket. She had looked at the piles of new white sleeping suits and had told herself that a living, breathing child would soon be inhabiting them. But despite everything she'd said to herself, none of it had felt quite real.

And now, the thought of herself alone at home with Lucia seemed just as unreal. She exhaled sharply, then switched on her night light, glanced at Lucia's sleeping face, and poured herself a glass of water.

'Can't sleep?' A young midwife poked her head round the curtain. 'I expect you're excited about going home.'

'Oh yes,' said Maggie again, forcing a smile onto her dry face. 'Can't wait.'

The midwife disappeared and she stared miserably into her glass of water. She couldn't tell anyone how she really felt. She couldn't tell anyone that she was scared of returning to her own home, with her own baby. They would think she was absolutely mad. Perhaps she was.

Late that night, Candice woke with a start, and stared into the darkness of her room. For a moment she couldn't think what had woken her. Then she realized that a sound was coming from the kitchen. Oh my God, she thought: a burglar. She lay quite still, heart thumping in panic – then slowly and silently she got out of bed, wrapped a dressing gown around herself and cautiously opened the door of her room.

The kitchen light was on. Did burglars usually put lights on? She hesitated, then quickly padded out into the corridor. As she reached the kitchen, she stopped and stared in shock. Heather was sitting at the table, cradling a cup of coffee, surrounded by page proofs of the *Londoner*. As Candice stared, she looked up, her face drawn and anxious.

'Hi,' she said, and immediately looked back at the sheets of paper.

'Hi,' said Candice, staring at her. 'What are you doing? You're not working, surely?'

'I forgot all about it,' said Heather, staring down at the page proofs. 'I completely forgot.' She rubbed her red eyes, and Candice gazed at her in alarm. 'I brought these pages home to work on over the weekend, and I forgot to do them. How can I be so *stupid*?'

'Well . . . don't worry!' said Candice. 'It's not the end of the world!'

'I've got to redo five pages by tomorrow!' said Heather, a note of desperation in her voice. 'And then I've got to put all the corrections onto the computer by the time Alicia arrives! I promised they'd be ready!'

'I don't understand,' said Candice, sinking onto a chair. 'Why have you got so much work?'

'I got behind,' said Heather. She took a sip of coffee and winced. 'Alicia gave me a load of stuff to do, and I . . . I don't know, maybe I'm not as quick as everyone else. Maybe everyone else is cleverer than me.'

'Rubbish!' said Candice at once. 'I'll have a word with Alicia.' She had always liked Alicia, the earnest chief sub-editor; at one time they had even considered sharing a flat.

'No, don't,' said Heather at once. 'She'll just say—' She stopped abruptly and there was silence in the little kitchen, broken only by the ticking of the electric clock.

'What?' said Candice. 'What will she say?'

'She'll say I should never have got the job in the first place,' said Heather miserably.

'What?' Candice laughed. 'Alicia wouldn't say that!'

'She already has,' said Heather. 'She's said it several times.'

'Are you serious?' Candice stared at her in disbelief. Heather gazed back at her, as though debating whether to carry on, then sighed.

'Apparently a friend of hers applied for the job, too. Some girl with two years' experience on another magazine. And I got it over her. Alicia was a bit annoyed.'

'Oh.' Candice rubbed her nose, discomfited. 'I had no idea.'

'So I can't let her know I'm slipping behind. I've just got to somehow . . . manage.' Heather pushed her hair back off her shadowed face and took another sip of coffee. 'Go back to bed, Candice. Honestly.'

'I can't just leave you!' said Candice. She picked up a page proof covered in coloured corrections, then put it down again. 'I feel terrible about this. I had no idea you were being worked so hard.'

'It's fine, really. Just as long as I get it all done by tomorrow morning . . .' Heather's voice shook slightly. 'I'll be all right.'

'No,' said Candice, with a sudden decisiveness. 'Come on, this is silly! I'll do some of this work. It won't take me nearly as long.'

'Really? Would you?' Heather looked up at her entreatingly. 'Oh, Candice . . .'

'I'll go in early and do the work straight onto the computer. How's that?'

'But . . .' Heather swallowed. 'Won't Alicia know you've been helping me?'

'I'll send the pages over to your terminal when I've finished them. And you can print them out.' Candice grinned at her. 'Easy.'

'Candice, you're a star,' said Heather, sinking back into her chair. 'And it'll just be this once, I promise.'

'No problem,' said Candice, and grinned at her. 'What are friends for?'

The next day she went into work early and sat, patiently working through the pages Heather had been given to correct. It took her rather longer than she had expected, and it was eleven o'clock before she had perfected the final proof. She glanced over at Heather, gave her the thumbs-up, and pressed the button that would send the page electronically to Heather's computer terminal. Behind her she could hear Alicia saying, 'This page is fine, too. Well done, Heather!'

Candice grinned, and reached for her cup of coffee. She felt rather like a schoolchild, outwitting the teachers.

'Candice?' She looked up at Justin's voice and saw him standing at the door of his office, looking as polished as ever. His brows were knitted together in a thoughtful frown – which he'd probably been practising in the bathroom mirror, she thought with an inward grin. After having lived with Justin and seen his little vanities close at hand, she couldn't take his studied facial expressions seriously any more. Indeed, she could barely take him seriously as an editor at all. He could be as pompous as he liked and throw as many long words as he liked around at meetings, but he would never be half the editor Maggie was. He might have a large vocabulary and he might know the name of the maître d' at Boodles, but he didn't have the first idea about people.

Once again she felt a flicker of astonishment that, for a while, she had fallen for Justin's gloss; that she had actually believed that she might love him. It just showed, she thought, what an insidious influence good looks could have on one's judgement. If he'd been less attractive physically, she might have paid attention to his character from the start and realized sooner what a selfish person he was, underneath all the eloquent, superficial charm.

'What is it?' she said, reluctantly getting out of her seat and going towards his office. That was another thing which, in her opinion, made Justin inferior to Maggie. If Maggie had to say something, she came and said it. But Justin seemed to enjoy holding court in his little office, watching the staff of the magazine run in and out like faithful lackeys. Roll on Maggie's return, she thought wistfully.

'Candice, I'm still waiting for the profile list you promised me,' said Justin as she sat down. He had retreated behind his desk and was gazing moodily out of the window as though being photographed for a fashion shoot.

'Oh yes,' she said, and felt herself flush with annoyance. Trust Justin to catch her out. She'd meant to type up the list that morning, but Heather's pages had taken priority. 'I'm onto it,' she said.

'Hmm.' He swivelled round so he was facing her. 'This isn't the first piece of work you've been late with, is it?'

'Yes it is!' said Candice indignantly. 'And it's only a list. It's not exactly front-page editorial.'

'Hmm.' Justin looked at her thoughtfully and Candice felt herself stiffen with irritation.

'So, how are you enjoying being acting editor?' she said, to change the subject.

'Very much,' said Justin, nodding gravely. 'Very much indeed.' He put his elbows on the desk and carefully placed his fingertips together. 'I see myself rather as—'

'Daniel Barenboim,' said Candice before she could stop herself, and stifled a giggle. 'Sorry,' she whispered.

'As a troubleshooter,' said Justin, shooting her a look of annoyance. 'I intend to institute a series of spot checks in order to locate problems with the system.'

'What problems?' said Candice. '*Are* there problems with the system?'

'I've been analysing the running of this magazine since I took power—'

Power! thought Candice scornfully. Next he'd be calling himself the Emperor.

' – and I've noticed several glitches which, frankly, Maggie just didn't pick up on.'

'Oh, really?' Candice folded her arms and gave him the least impressed look she could muster. 'So, you think, after a few weeks, you're a better editor than Maggie.'

145

'That's not what I said.' Justin paused. 'Maggie has, as we all know, many wonderful talents and qualities—'

'Yes, well, Ralph obviously thinks so,' put in Candice loyally. 'He sent her a magnum of champagne.'

'I'm sure he did,' said Justin, and leaned comfortably back in his chair. 'You know he's retiring in a couple of weeks' time?'

'What?'

'I just heard it this morning. Wants to spend more time with his family, apparently,' said Justin. 'So it looks like we're all going to have a new boss. It seems one of his sons is going to take over. He's coming in to meet us all next week.'

'Gosh,' said Candice, taken aback. 'I had no idea that was on the cards.' She frowned. 'Does Maggie know about this?'

'I doubt it,' said Justin, carelessly. 'Why should she? She's got other things to think about.' He took a sip of coffee, then glanced over her shoulder through the window at the editorial office. 'That friend of yours is doing well, by the way.'

'Who, Heather?' said Candice, with a glow of pride. 'Yes, she is good, isn't she? I told you she would be.' She turned to follow Justin's gaze, met Heather's eye and smiled.

'She came to me with an excellent idea for a feature the other day,' said Justin. 'I was impressed.'

'Oh yes?' said Candice, turning back interestedly. 'What's the idea?'

'Late-night shopping,' said Justin. 'Do a whole piece on it.'

'What?' Candice stared at him.

'We'll run it in the lifestyle section. Take a photographer down to a shopping mall, interview some customers . . .' Justin frowned at her flabbergasted expression. 'What's wrong? Don't you think it's a good idea?'

'Of course I do!' exclaimed Candice, feeling herself grow hot. 'But . . .' She broke off feebly. What could she say without looking as though she wanted to get Heather into trouble?

'What?'

'Nothing,' said Candice slowly. She turned round again and glanced out of the window, but Heather had vanished. 'It's . . . it's a great idea.'

Heather stood by the coffee machine with Kelly, the editorial secretary. Kelly was a sixteen-year-old girl with long bony legs and a thin, bright-eyed face, always eager for the latest gossip.

'You were working hard this morning,' she said, pressing the button for hot chocolate. 'I saw you, typing hard!' Heather smiled, and leaned against the coffee machine. 'And sending lots of things to Candice, weren't you?' added Kelly.

Heather's head jerked up.

'Yes,' she said carefully. 'How could you tell that?'

'I heard your e-mail pinging away!' said Kelly. 'The two of you, pinging away all morning!' She laughed merrily, and picked up her polystyrene cup full of hot chocolate.

'That's right,' said Heather after a pause. 'How observant of you.' She pressed the button for white coffee. 'You know what all that e-mail was?' she said in a lower voice.

'What?' said Kelly interestedly.

'Candice makes me send all my work to her to be checked,' whispered Heather. 'Every single word I write.'

'You're joking!' said Kelly. 'Why does she do that?'

'I don't know,' said Heather. 'I suppose she thinks I'm not up to scratch, or something . . .'

'Bloody nerve!' said Kelly. 'I wouldn't stand for it.' She blew on her hot chocolate. 'I've never liked that Candice very much.'

'Really?' said Heather and moved casually nearer. 'Kelly – what are you doing at lunchtime?'

Roxanne sat opposite Ralph at her little dining table and looked accusingly at him across her mound of beef stroganoff.

'You've got to stop cooking me such nice food!' she said. 'I'm going to be fat now.'

'Rubbish,' said Ralph, taking a sip of wine and running a hand down Roxanne's thigh. 'Look at that. You're perfect.'

'That's easy for you to say,' said Roxanne. 'You haven't seen me in a bikini.'

'I've seen you in a lot less than a bikini.' Ralph grinned at her.

'On the beach, I mean!' said Roxanne impatiently. 'Next to all the fifteen-year-olds. There were scores of them in Cyprus. Horrible skinny things with long legs and huge brown eyes.'

'Can't stand brown eyes,' said Ralph obligingly.

'You've got brown eyes,' pointed out Roxanne.

'I know. Can't stand them.'

Roxanne laughed and leaned back in her chair, lifting up her feet so that they nestled in Ralph's lap. As he reached down and began to massage them, she felt again the light tripping sensation in her heart; the lift of hope, of excitement. Ralph had arranged this meeting as an unexpected extra treat; a few days ago he had surprised her with a bouquet of flowers. It wasn't her imagination – he was definitely behaving differently. Ever since she'd got back from Cyprus he'd been different. A sudden fizz of hope rose through Roxanne like sherbet in a glass of lemonade and she felt a smile spread across her face.

'How did the trip go, by the way?' he added, stroking her toes. 'I never asked. Same old thing?'

'More or less,' said Roxanne. She reached for her wine and took a deep sip. 'Oh, except you'll never guess what. Nico Georgiou offered me a job.'

'A job?' Ralph stared at her. 'In Cyprus?'

'At the new resort he's building. Marketing manager or something.' Roxanne shook back her hair and looked provocatively at Ralph. 'He's offering a very good deal. What do you think? Shall I take it?'

Over the years, she had often teased him like this. She would mention job opportunities in Scotland, in Spain, in America – some genuine, some fabricated. The teasing was partly in fun – and partly from a genuine need to make him realize that she was choosing to be with him; that she was not staying with him simply by default. If she was utterly honest with herself, it had also, in the past, been from a need to see him hurt. To see his face fall; to see him experience, just for a second, the feeling of loss that she felt every time he left her.

But today, it was almost a test. A challenge. A way of getting him to talk about the future again.

'He even sent me a box of tangerines,' she added, gesturing to the fruit bowl, where the tangerines were piled up in a shiny orange pyramid. 'So he must be serious. What do you think?'

What she expected was for him to grin, and say, 'Well, he can sod off' as he usually did. What she wanted was for him to take her hands and kiss them and ask again what she wanted to be doing in a year's time. But Ralph did neither. He stared at her as though she were a stranger – then, eventually, cleared his throat and said, 'Do you want to take it?'

'For God's sake, Ralph!' said Roxanne, disappointment sharpening her voice. 'I'm only joking! Of course I don't want to take it.'

149

'Why not?' He was leaning forward, looking at her with an odd expression on his face. 'Wouldn't it be a good job?'

'I don't know!' exclaimed Roxanne. 'Since you ask, I expect it would be a marvellous job.' She reached for her cigarettes. 'And naturally they're *desperate* to have me. You know they'd even provide me with a house?' She lit her cigarette and looked at him through the smoke. 'I haven't noticed anyone at Allsopp Publications offering me any real estate.'

'So – what did you say to them?' said Ralph, meshing his hands together as though in prayer. 'How did you leave it?'

'Oh, the usual,' said Roxanne. 'Thanks but no thanks.'

'So you turned it down.'

'Of course I did!' said Roxanne, giving a little laugh. 'Why? Do you think I should have said yes?'

There was silence, and Roxanne looked up. At Ralph's tense expression she felt a sudden coldness inside her.

'You're joking,' she said, and tried to smile. 'You think I should have said yes?'

'Maybe it's time for you to move on. Take one of these opportunities up.' Ralph reached for his glass of wine with a trembling hand and took a sip. 'I've held you back far too long. I've got in your way.'

'Ralph, don't be stupid!'

'Is it too late to change your mind?' Ralph looked up. 'Could you still go to them and say you're interested?'

Roxanne stared at him in shock, feeling as though she'd been slapped.

'Yes,' she said eventually. 'I suppose I could, in theory . . .' She swallowed, and pushed her hair back off her face, scarcely able to believe they were having this conversation. 'Are you going to tell me I should?

Do you . . . do you *want* me to take this job?' Her voice grew more brittle. 'Ralph?'

There was silence, then Ralph looked up.

'Yes,' he said. 'I do. I think you should take it.'

There was silence in the room. This is a bad dream, thought Roxanne. This is a fucking bad dream.

'I . . . I don't understand,' she said at last, trying to stay calm. 'Ralph, what's going on? You were talking about the future. You were talking about Caribbean beaches!'

'I wasn't, you were.'

'You *asked* me!' said Roxanne furiously. 'Jesus!'

'I know I did. But that was . . . dreaming. Idle fantasies. This is real life. And I think if you have an opportunity in Cyprus, then you should take it.'

'Fuck the opportunity!' She felt close to tears, and swallowed hard. 'What about you and me? What about that opportunity?'

'There's something I need to tell you,' said Ralph abruptly. 'There's something which will . . . make a difference to you and me.' He stood up, walked to the window, then, after a long pause, turned round. 'I'm planning to retire, Roxanne,' he said without smiling. 'To the country. I want to spend more time with my family.'

Roxanne stared at his straight brown eyes. At first she didn't comprehend what he was saying. Then, as his meaning hit her, she felt a stabbing pain in her chest.

'You mean it's over,' she whispered, her mouth suddenly dry. 'You mean you've had your fun. And now you're off to . . . to play happy families.'

There was silence.

'If you want to put it that way,' said Ralph eventually, 'then yes.' He met her eye, then looked away quickly.

'No,' said Roxanne, feeling her whole body starting to shake. 'No. I won't let you. You can't.' She flashed a desperate smile at him. 'It can't be over. Not just like that.'

'You'll go to Cyprus,' said Ralph, a slight tremor in his voice. 'You'll go to Cyprus and you'll make a wonderful new life for yourself. Away from all . . . all this.' He lifted a hand to his brow and rubbed it. 'It's for the best, Roxanne.'

'You don't want me to go to Cyprus. You don't mean it. Tell me you don't mean it.' She felt out of control, almost dizzy. In a minute she would start grovelling on the floor. 'You're joking.' She swallowed. 'Are you joking?'

'No, Roxanne. I'm not joking.'

'But you love me!' Her smile grew even wider; tears began to drip down her cheeks. 'You love me, Ralph.'

'Yes,' said Ralph in a suddenly choked voice. 'I do. I love you, Roxanne. Remember that.'

He stepped forward, took her hands and squeezed them hard against his lips. Then, without saying anything he turned, picked up his coat from the sofa and left.

Through a sea of pain, Roxanne watched him go; heard the front door shut. For a second she was silent, white-faced, quivering slightly, as though waiting to vomit. Then with a trembling hand she reached for a cushion, held it up to her face with both hands and screamed silently into it.

Chapter Eleven

Maggie leaned against a fence and closed her eyes, breathing in the clean country air. It was mid-morning, the sky was bright blue and there was a feel of summer about the air. In her previous life, she thought, she would have felt uplifted by the weather. She would have felt energized. But today, standing in her own fields, with her baby asleep in the pram beside her, all she could feel was exhausted.

She felt pale and drained through lack of sleep; edgy and constantly on the verge of tears. Lucia was waking every two hours, demanding to be fed. She could not breastfeed her in bed, because Giles, with his demanding job, needed to sleep. And so she seemed to be spending the whole night sitting in the rocking chair in the nursery, falling into a doze as Lucia fed, then waking with a start as the baby began to wail again. As the greyness of morning approached, she would rouse herself, pad blearily into the bedroom, holding Lucia in her arms.

'Good morning!' Giles would say, beaming sleepily from the big double bed. 'How are my girls?'

'Fine,' Maggie said every morning, without elaborating. For what was the point? It wasn't as if Giles could feed Lucia; it wasn't as if he could make her sleep. And she felt a certain dogged triumph at her own refusal to complain; at her ability to smile and tell Giles that everything was going wonderfully, and see him believe her. She had heard him on the phone, telling his friends, in tones of pride, that Maggie had taken to motherhood like a duck to water. Then he would come and kiss her warmly and say that everyone was amazed at how competent she was; at how everything had fallen into place so quickly. 'Mother of the Year!' he said one evening. 'I told you so!' His delight in her was transparent. She couldn't spoil it all now.

So she would simply hand Lucia to him and sink into the warm comfort of the bed, almost wanting to cry in relief. Those half-hours every morning were her salvation. She would watch Giles playing with Lucia and meet his eyes over the little downy head, and feel a warm glow creep over her; a love so strong, it was almost painful.

Then Giles would get dressed and kiss them both, and go off to work, and the rest of the day would be hers. Hours and hours, with nothing to do but look after one small baby. It sounded laughably easy.

So why was she so tired? Why did every simple task seem so mountainous? She felt as if she would never shift the fog of exhaustion that had descended on her. She would never regain her former energy, nor her sense of humour. Things that would have seemed mildly irritating before the birth now reduced her to tears; minor hitches that would once have made her laugh now made her panic.

The day before, she had taken all morning to get herself and Lucia dressed and off in the car to the supermarket. She had stopped halfway to feed Lucia in the Ladies', then had resumed and joined the queue – at which point Lucia had begun to wail. Maggie had flushed red as faces had begun to turn, and tried to soothe Lucia as discreetly as she could. But Lucia's cries had grown louder and louder until it seemed the whole shop was looking at her. Finally the woman in front had turned round and said knowledgeably, 'He's hungry, poor little pet.'

To her own horror, Maggie had heard herself snapping, 'It's a she! And she's not! I've just fed her!' Almost in tears, she had grabbed Lucia from the trolley and run out of the shop, leaving a trail of astonished glances behind her.

Now, remembering the incident, she felt cold with misery. How competent a mother could she be if she couldn't even manage a simple shopping trip? She saw other mothers coolly walking along the streets, chatting unconcernedly to their friends; sitting in cafés with their babies quietly sleeping beside them. How could they be so relaxed? She herself would never dare enter a café for fear that Lucia would start screaming: for fear of those irritated, judgmental glances from those trying to enjoy a quiet coffee. The sorts of glances she had always given mothers with squalling babies.

A memory of her old life rose in her mind – so tantalizing it made her want to sink down on the ground and weep. And immediately, as if on cue, Lucia began to cry; a small, plaintive cry, almost lost in the wind. Maggie opened her eyes and felt the familiar weariness steal over her. That piercing little cry dogged her every hour: she heard it in her dreams, heard it in the whine of the electric kettle, heard it in the running of the taps when she attempted to take a bath. She could not escape it.

'OK, my precious,' she said aloud, smiling down into the pram. 'Let's get you back inside.'

It was Giles who had suggested that she take Lucia outside for a walk that morning, and, seeing the cloudless blue sky outside, she had thought it a good idea. But now, pushing the pram back through resistant layers of thick mud, the countryside seemed nothing but a battleground. What was so superior about manure-scented air, anyway? she thought, shoving at the pram as it got stuck in a patch of brambles. Inside, Lucia began to wail even more piteously at the unaccustomed jolting movement.

'Sorry!' said Maggie breathlessly. She gave one final push, freeing the wheel, and began to march more quickly towards the house. By the time she arrived at the back door, her face was drenched in sweat.

'Right,' she said, taking Lucia out of the pram. 'Let's get you changed, and feed you.'

Did talking to a four-week-old baby count as talking to oneself? she wondered as she sped upstairs. Was she going mad? Lucia was wailing more and more lustily, and she found herself running along the corridor to the nursery. She placed Lucia on the changing table, unbuttoned her snow suit and winced. Lucia's little sleeping suit was sodden.

'OK,' she crooned. 'Just going to change you . . .' She pulled at the snowsuit and quickly unbuttoned the sleeping suit, cursing her fumbling fingers. Lucia's wails were becoming louder and louder, faster and faster, with a little catch of breath in between. Tears appeared at the tiny creases of her eyes, and Maggie felt her own face flush scarlet with distress.

'I've just got to change you, Lucia,' she said, trying to stay calm. She quickly pulled apart Lucia's wet nappy, threw it on the floor and reached for another one. But the shelf was empty. A jolt of panic went through her. Where were the nappies? Suddenly she remembered taking the last one off the shelf before setting off for her walk; promising herself to open the box and restock the shelf. But of course, she hadn't.

'OK,' she said, pushing her hair back off her face. 'OK, keep calm.' She lifted Lucia off the changing table and placed her on the safety of the floor. Lucia's screams became incomparably loud. The noise seemed to drive through Maggie's head like a drill.

'Lucia, please!' she said, feeling her voice rise dangerously. 'I'm just getting you a new nappy, OK? I'll be as quick as I can!'

She ran down the corridor to the bedroom, where she had dumped the new box of nappies, and began to rip hastily at the cardboard. At last she managed to get the box open – to find the nappies snugly encased in plastic cocoons.

'Oh God!' she said aloud, and began to claw frenziedly at the plastic, feeling like a contestant on some hideous Japanese game of endurance. Eventually her fingers closed over a nappy and she pulled it out, panting slightly. She ran back down the corridor to find Lucia in wailing paroxysms.

'OK, I'm coming,' said Maggie breathlessly. 'Just let me put your nappy on.' She bent down over Lucia and fastened the nappy around her as quickly as she could – then, with the baby in one arm, scrambled to the rocking chair in the corner. Every second seemed to count, with the noise of Lucia growing louder and louder in her ears. She reached with one hand under her jumper to unfasten her bra, but the catch was stuck. With a tiny scream of frustration, she placed Lucia on her lap and reached with the other hand inside her jumper as well, trying to free the catch; trying to stay calm. Lucia's screams were getting higher and higher, faster and faster, as though the frequency on the record had been turned up.

'I'm coming!' cried Maggie, jiggling hopelessly at the catch. 'I'm coming as quick as I can, OK!' Her voice rose to a shout. 'Lucia, be quiet! Please be quiet! I'm coming!'

'There's no need to scream at her, dear,' came a voice from the door.

Maggie's head jerked up in fright – and as she saw who it was, she felt her face drain of colour. There, watching her, lips tight with disapproval, was Paddy Drakeford.

157

*　　*　　*

Candice stood, holding a cup of coffee, peering at her computer screen over the shoulder of the computer engineer and trying to look intelligent.

'Hmm,' said the engineer eventually, and looked up. 'Have you ever had any virus screening programs installed?'

'Ahm . . . I'm not sure,' said Candice, and flushed at his glance. 'Do you think that's what it is, a virus?'

'Hard to tell,' said the engineer, and punched a few keys. Candice surreptitiously looked at her watch. It was already eleven-thirty. She had called out a computer engineer believing he would fix her machine in a matter of minutes, but he had arrived an hour ago, started tapping and now looked like he was settled in for the day. She had already called Justin, telling him she would be late, and he had 'Hmm'd' with disapproval.

'By the way, Heather says, can you bring in her blue folder,' he'd added. 'Do you want to have a word with her? She's right here.'

'No, I've . . . I've got to go,' Candice had said hastily. She had put down the phone, exhaled with relief, and sat down, her heart thudding slightly. This was getting ridiculous. She had to sort her own mind out; to rid herself of the tendrils of doubt that were growing inside her over Heather.

Outwardly, she and Heather were as friendly as ever. But inside, Candice had started to wonder. Were the others right? Was Heather using her? She had still paid no rent, neither had she offered to. She had barely thanked Candice for doing that large amount of work for her. And she had – Candice swallowed – she had blatantly stolen Candice's late-night shopping feature idea and presented it as her own.

A familiar twinge went through Candice's stomach and she closed her eyes. She knew that she should

158

confront Heather on the matter. She should bring the subject up, pleasantly and firmly, and listen to what Heather had to say. Perhaps, reasoned a part of her brain, it had all been a misunderstanding. Perhaps Heather simply hadn't realized that it wasn't done to take credit for someone else's idea. It was no big deal – all she had to do was mention it to Heather and see what the response was.

But she couldn't quite bring herself to. The thought of appearing to accuse Heather – of perhaps descending into an argument over it – filled her with horror. Things had been going so well between them – was it really worth risking a scene just over one little idea?

And so for more than a week she had said nothing, and had tried to forget about it. But there was a bad feeling inside her stomach which would not go away.

'Do you ever download from the Internet?' said the computer engineer.

'No,' said Candice, opening her eyes. Then she thought for a second. 'Actually, yes. I tried to once, but it didn't really work. Does that matter?'

The engineer sighed, and she bit her lip, feeling foolish. Suddenly the door bell rang, and she breathed out in relief.

'Excuse me,' she said. 'I'll be back in a minute.'

Standing in the hall was Ed, wearing an old T-shirt, shorts and espadrilles.

'So,' he said with no preamble. 'Tell me about your flat-mate.'

'There's nothing to tell,' said Candice, flushing defensively in spite of herself. 'She's just . . . living with me. Like flat-mates do.'

'I know that. But where's she from? What's she like?' Ed sniffed past Candice. 'Is that coffee?'

'Yes.'

'Your flat always smells so nice,' said Ed. 'Like a

coffee shop. Mine smells like a shit-heap.'

'Do you ever clean it?'

'Some woman does.' He leaned further into the flat and sniffed longingly. 'Come on, Candice. Give me some coffee.'

'Oh, all right,' said Candice. 'Come in.' At least it would be an excuse not to return to the computer engineer.

'I saw your friend leaving this morning without you,' said Ed, following her into the kitchen, 'and I thought – aha. Coffee time.'

'Don't you have any plans today?' said Candice. 'Properties to visit? Daytime TV to watch?'

'Don't rub it in!' said Ed. He reached for the salt cellar and tapped it on his palm. 'This bloody gardening leave is driving me nuts.'

'What's wrong?' said Candice unsympathetically.

'I'm bored!' He turned the salt cellar upside down and wrote 'Ed' in salt on the table. 'Bored, bored, bored.'

'You obviously don't have any inner resources,' said Candice, taking the salt cellar from his fingers.

'No,' said Ed. 'Not a one. I went to a museum yesterday. A *museum*. Can you believe it?'

'Which one?' said Candice.

'I dunno,' said Ed. 'One with squashy chairs.' Candice gazed at him for a moment, then rolled her eyes and turned away to fill the kettle. Ed grinned, and began to mooch about the kitchen.

'So, who's this kid?' he said, looking at a photograph tacked up on the pinboard.

'That's the Cambodian child I sponsor,' said Candice, reaching for the coffee.

'What's his name?'

'Pin Fu. Ju,' she corrected herself. 'Pin Ju.'

'Do you send him Christmas presents?'

'No. It's not considered helpful.' Candice shook

coffee into the cafetière. 'Anyway, he doesn't want some Western tat.'

'I bet he does,' said Ed. 'He's probably dying for a Darth Vader. Have you ever met him?'

'No.'

'Have you ever spoken to him on the phone?'

'No. Don't be stupid.'

'So how you do you know he exists?'

'What?' Candice looked up. 'Of course he exists! There he is.' She pointed at the photograph and Ed grinned wickedly at her.

'You're very trusting, aren't you? How do you know they aren't sending all you saps the same picture? Call him a different name each time; hive off the money for themselves. Does Pin Ju send you a personal receipt?'

Candice rolled her eyes dismissively. Sometimes Ed wasn't even worth responding to. She poured hot water into the cafetière and a delicious smell filled the kitchen.

'So, you haven't told me about Heather,' said Ed, sitting down. At the name, Candice felt a spasm inside her stomach, and looked away.

'What about her?'

'How do you know her?'

'She's . . . an old friend,' said Candice.

'Oh yeah? Well, if she's such an old friend, how come I never saw her before she moved in?' Ed leaned forward with an inquisitive gaze. 'How come you never even mentioned her?'

'Because . . . we lost touch, all right?' said Candice, feeling rattled. 'Why are so you interested, anyway?'

'I don't know,' said Ed. 'There's something about her that intrigues me.'

'Well, if she intrigues you so much, why don't you ask her out?' said Candice curtly.

'Maybe I will,' said Ed, grinning.

There was a sharp silence in the kitchen. Candice

handed Ed his cup of coffee and he took a sip. 'You wouldn't mind, would you, Candice?' he added, eyes gleaming slightly.

'Of course not!' said Candice at once, and shook her hair back. 'Why should I mind?'

'Ahem.' The voice of the computer engineer interrupted them, and they both looked up.

'Hi,' said Candice. 'Have you found out what's wrong?'

'A virus,' said the engineer, pulling a face. 'It's got into everything, I'm afraid.'

'Oh,' said Candice in dismay. 'Well – can you catch it?'

'Oh, it's already long gone,' said the engineer. 'These viruses are very slick. In and out before you know it. All I can do now is try to repair the damage it's left behind.' He shook his head reprovingly. 'And in future, Miss Brewin, I suggest you try to protect yourself a little better.'

Maggie sat at her kitchen table, stiff with humiliation. At the Aga, Paddy lifted the kettle and poured scalding water into the teapot, then turned round and glanced at the Moses basket by the window.

'She seems to be sleeping nicely now. I expect all that screaming wore her out.'

The implied criticism was obvious, and Maggie flushed. She couldn't bear to look Paddy in the eye; couldn't bear to see that disapproving look again. You try! she wanted to scream. You try keeping calm after nights and nights of no sleep. But instead she stared silently down at the table, tracing the pattern of the wood round and round with her finger. Just keep going, she told herself, and clenched her other hand in her lap. Keep going till she's gone.

After arriving on the scene in the nursery, Paddy had left her alone to breastfeed and she had sat in misery, feeling like a punished child. She arrived downstairs, holding Lucia, to find that Paddy had tidied the kitchen, stacked the dishwasher and even mopped the floor. She knew she should have felt grateful – but instead she felt reproved. A good mother would never have let her kitchen descend into such a sordid state. A good mother would never have gone out without wiping down the kitchen surfaces.

'Here you are,' said Paddy, bringing a cup of tea over to the table. 'Would you like some sugar in it?'

'No thanks,' said Maggie, still staring downwards. 'I'm trying to keep tabs on my weight.'

'Really?' Paddy paused, teapot in hand. 'I found I needed to eat twice as much when I breastfed, otherwise the boys would have gone hungry.' She gave a short little laugh and Maggie felt a spasm of irrational hatred for her. What was she saying now? That she wasn't feeding Lucia properly? That there was something inferior about her breast milk? A hot lump suddenly appeared in her throat and she swallowed hard.

'And how are the nights going?' said Paddy.

'Fine,' said Maggie shortly, and took a sip of tea.

'Is Lucia settling into a routine?'

'Not particularly,' said Maggie. 'But actually, these days they don't recommend bullying babies into routines.' She looked up and met Paddy's gaze square-on. 'They recommend feeding by demand and letting the baby settle into its own pattern.'

'I see,' said Paddy, and gave another short laugh. 'It's all changed since my day.'

Maggie took another gulp of tea and stared fixedly out of the window.

'It's a shame your parents couldn't visit for a little longer,' said Paddy. A spasm of pain went through Maggie and she blinked hard. Did the woman have to twist *every* knife? Her parents had visited for two days

163

while Maggie was in hospital – then, reluctantly, had had to leave. Both still worked, after all – and the drive from Derbyshire to Hampshire was a long one. Maggie had smiled brightly as they'd left, had promised she would be all right and would visit soon. But in truth their parting had hit her harder than she'd expected. The thought of her mother's kindly face could still sometimes reduce her to tears. And here was Paddy, reminding her of the fact.

'Yes, well,' she said, without moving her head, 'they're busy people.'

'I expect they are.' Paddy took a sip of tea and reached into the tin for a biscuit. 'Maggie—'

'What?' Reluctantly, Maggie turned her head.

'Have you thought about having any help with the baby? A nanny, for example.'

Maggie stared at her, feeling as though she'd been hit in the face. So Paddy really did think she was an unfit mother; that she couldn't care for her own child without paid help.

'No,' she said, giving a laugh that was nearer tears. 'Why, do you think I should?'

'It's up to you,' said Paddy, 'of course—'

'I'd rather look after my child myself,' said Maggie in a trembling voice. 'I may not do it perfectly, but . . .'

'Maggie!' said Paddy. 'Of course I didn't mean—' She broke off, and Maggie looked stiffly away. There was silence in the kitchen, broken only by Lucia's sleeping snuffles.

'Perhaps I should go,' said Paddy eventually. 'I don't want to get in your way.'

'OK,' said Maggie, giving a tiny shrug.

She watched as Paddy gathered her things together, shooting Maggie the odd anxious glance.

'You know where I am,' she said. 'Bye bye, dear.'

'Bye,' said Maggie, with careless indifference.

She waited as Paddy walked out of the kitchen and

let herself out of the front door; waited as the car engine started and the gravel crackled under the wheels. And then, when the car had disappeared completely and she could hear nothing more, she burst into sobs.

Chapter Twelve

Roxanne sat on a wooden bench, her shoulders hunched and her face muffled in a scarf, staring across the road at Ralph Allsopp's London home. It was a narrow house in a quiet Kensington square with black railings and a blue front door. A house that she'd seen the outside of too many times to count; a house that she'd cursed and wept at and stared at for hours – and never once stepped inside.

At the beginning, years ago, she had secretly used to come and sit outside the house for hours. She would station herself in the square garden with a book and stare at the façade behind which Ralph and his family lived, as though trying to memorize each brick; each stone in the path, wondering if today she would catch a glimpse of her, or of him, or of any of them.

For at that time, Cynthia had still spent most of her time in London – and Roxanne had quite often seen her coming up or down the steps with Sebastian, both dressed in exemplary navy blue overcoats. (From Harrods, probably, judging by the number of times Harrods delivery vans arrived at the front door.) The front door would open, and Roxanne would stiffen, and put down her book. Then Cynthia would appear. Cynthia Allsopp, with her elegant, oblivious face. And her little son Sebastian, with his innocent Christopher

Robin haircut. Roxanne would sit and stare at them as they came down the steps and got into the car or walked off briskly down the road. She would take in every new addition to Cynthia's wardrobe, every new hairstyle, every overheard word, every possible detail. The sight never failed to appal her; to fascinate her – and, ultimately, to depress her. Because Cynthia was his wife. That elegant, soulless woman was his wife. And she, Roxanne, was his mistress. His tawdry, tacky mistress. That initial excitement of seeing them – the feeling of power, almost – had always given way to a kind of emptiness; a black, destructive devastation.

And yet she'd been unable to stop coming back – unable to resist the draw of that blue front door – until the heart-stopping day when Ralph had come down the steps, holding a box full of books, glanced towards the garden square, and had seen her. She'd immediately hunched down, heart pounding, praying that he wouldn't give her away; that he would remain cool. To his credit, he had done. But he had not been cool on the phone that evening. He had been angry – more angry than she'd ever known him. She'd pleaded with him, reasoned with him; promised never to set foot in the square again. And she'd kept that promise.

But now she was breaking it. Now she didn't give a fuck who saw her. Now she *wanted* to be seen. She reached into her pocket for her cigarettes and took out her lighter. The irony was, of course, that now, years later, it didn't matter. The windows were dim; the house was empty. Cynthia didn't even live in the bloody house now. She'd decamped to the country manor, and only came up for the Harrods sale. And Sebastian rode his little ponies, and everyone was happy. And that was the life Ralph was choosing over her.

Roxanne inhaled deeply on her cigarette and exhaled with a shudder. She wasn't going to cry any more. She'd ruined enough fucking make-up already. For the past two weeks, she'd sat at home, drinking vodka and wearing the same pair of leggings every day, and staring out of her window, sometimes crying, sometimes shaking, sometimes silent. She'd left the answer machine on and listened to messages mount up like dead flies – irrelevant, stupid messages from people she couldn't be interested in. One, from Justin, had been to invite her to Ralph's retirement drinks party – and she'd felt a pain shoot through her like an electric shock. He was really doing it, she'd thought, tears welling up yet again. He was really fucking doing it.

Candice had left countless messages, and so had Maggie – and she had almost been tempted to phone back. Of all people, those were the ones she'd wanted to talk to. She'd even picked up the receiver once and begun to dial Candice's number. And then she had stopped, shaking in terror, unable to think of what she would say; how she would even start. How she would halt the flow once she'd begun. It was too big a secret. Easier – so much easier – to say nothing. She'd had six years' practice, after all.

They, of course, had assumed she was abroad. 'Or perhaps you're with Mr Married,' Maggie had said on one of her messages, and Roxanne had actually found herself half laughing, half crying. Dear Maggie. If she only knew. 'But we'll see you on the first,' Maggie had continued anxiously. 'You will be there, won't you?'

Roxanne looked at her watch. It was the first of the month. It was six o'clock. In half an hour's time they would be there. The two faces – at this moment – dearest to her in the world. She stubbed out her cigarette, stood up and faced Ralph Allsopp's house square-on.

'Fuck you,' she said out loud. 'Fuck you!' Then she turned and strode away, her heels clicking loudly on the wet pavement.

*　　*　　*

Ralph Allsopp lifted his head from the chair he was sitting in and looked towards the window. Outside, the sky was beginning to darken, and the street lights of the square were beginning to come on. He reached for a lamp and switched it on, and immediately the dim room brightened.

'Is there a problem?' said Neil Cooper, glancing up from his papers.

'No,' said Ralph. 'I just thought I heard something. Probably nothing.' He smiled. 'Carry on.'

'Yes,' said Neil Cooper. He was a young man, with a severe haircut and a rather nervous manner. 'Well, as I was explaining, I think your easiest option, in this instance, is to add a short codicil to the will.'

'I see,' said Ralph. He stared at the panes of the window, wet with London rain. Wills, he thought, were like family life itself. They started off small and simple – then expanded over the years with marriage and children; grew even more complex with infidelity; with accumulated wealth; with divided loyalties. His own will was now the size of a small book. A conventional family saga.

But his life had not been a mere conventional family saga.

'A romance,' he said aloud.

'I'm sorry?' said Neil Cooper.

'Nothing,' said Ralph, shaking his head as though to clear it. 'A codicil. Yes. And can I draw that up now?'

'Absolutely,' said the lawyer, and clicked his pen expectantly. 'If you give me, first of all, the name of the beneficiary?'

There was silence. Ralph closed his eyes, then opened them and exhaled sharply.

'The beneficiary's name is Roxanne,' he said, and his hand tightened slightly around the arm of his chair. 'Miss Roxanne Miller.'

*   *   *

Maggie sat at a plastic table in a Waterloo café and took another sip of tea. Her train had arrived in London an hour ago, and originally she had thought she might take the opportunity to go shopping. But, having made her way off the train, the very thought of shops and crowds had exhausted her. Instead, she had come in here and ordered a pot of tea and had sat, immobile, ever since. She felt shell-shocked by the effort it had taken to get herself here; could scarcely believe she had once made that long journey every single day.

She picked up the glossy magazine she'd bought at a kiosk, then put it down, unable to focus. She felt light-headed; almost high with fatigue. Lucia had been awake for most of the night before, with what she could only suppose was colic. She had paced up and down the bedroom furthest from Giles, trying to soothe the baby's cries, eyes half shut, almost sleeping on her feet. Then Giles had left for work, and instead of crawling back into bed, she had spent the entire remainder of the day preparing for her evening out. An occasion which, once upon a time, would have required no thought whatsoever.

She had decided to wash her hair, hoping the blast of the shower would wake her up. Lucia had woken up as she had started to dry it and she had been forced to carry on whilst simultaneously rocking Lucia's bouncy chair with her foot. For once, the situation had struck her as comical, and she had made up her mind to tell the other two about it that evening. Then she had opened her wardrobe, wondering what to wear – and her spirits had immediately sunk. She still fitted into none of her pre-pregnancy clothes. A whole wardrobe of designer clothes was hanging in front of her – and they might as well not have existed.

It had been her own decision not to buy any new

clothes in her larger size, as Giles had suggested. For one thing, it would be admitting defeat – and for another, she had seriously believed that within a month or so she would be slim again. Her handbook had assured her that she would lose weight from breastfeeding, and she had taken this to mean that within a few weeks she would be back to normal.

Seven weeks after the birth, however, she was still nowhere near. Her stomach was flabby, her hips were huge, and her breasts, full of milk, were even vaster than they had been during pregnancy. As she'd stared at herself in the mirror – large, dumpy and pale-faced with fatigue – she'd suddenly felt like cancelling the whole thing. How could she walk into the Manhattan Bar looking like that? People would laugh at her. She sank down onto the bed and buried her head in her hands, feeling easy tears rising.

But after a while, she looked up, and wiped her face and told herself not to be silly. She wasn't going up to London to pose. She was going to be with her two best friends. They wouldn't care what she looked like. Taking a deep breath, she stood up and approached her wardrobe again. Averting her eyes from all her old clothes, she assembled a well-worn outfit in unadventurous black, and placed it on the bed, ready to put on at the last moment. She didn't want to risk any spillages from Lucia.

At two o'clock, Paddy rang the doorbell and Maggie let her in with a polite greeting. Ever since that day when Paddy had interrupted her, there had been a certain distance between them. They were courteous to one another but nothing more. Paddy had offered to babysit for Maggie's evening out, and Maggie had politely accepted – but no warmth of feeling had flowered between them.

As Paddy came into the house she scanned Maggie's face with a frown, then said, 'My dear, you look very

171

tired. Are you sure you want to go all the way up to London, just for a few cocktails?'

Count to ten, Maggie told herself. Count to ten. Don't snap.

'Yes,' she said eventually, and forced herself to smile. 'It's . . . it's quite important to me. Old friends.'

'Well, you look to me as if you'd do better with an early night,' said Paddy, and yet again gave that short little laugh. Immediately, Maggie had felt herself tense up all over.

'It's very kind of you to babysit,' she'd said, staring fixedly at the banisters. 'I do appreciate it.'

'Oh, it's no trouble!' Paddy had said at once. 'Anything I can do to help.'

'Right.' Maggie had taken a deep breath, trying to stay calm; to be pleasant. 'Well, let me just explain. The expressed milk is in bottles in the fridge. It needs to be warmed up in a saucepan. I've left it all in the kitchen for you. If she cries, she might need her colic drops. They're on the—'

'Maggie.' Paddy had lifted her hand with a little smile. 'Maggie, I've raised three children of my own. I'm sure I can manage little Lucia.'

Maggie had stared back, feeling snubbed; wanting to make some retort, but unable to.

'Fine,' she'd said at last, in a trembling voice. 'I'll just get ready.' And she'd run upstairs, suddenly not wanting to go to London at all. Wanting to tell Paddy to go away and to spend the evening alone, rocking her baby.

Of course she had done nothing of the sort. She had brushed her hair, put on her coat, imagining that she could already hear Lucia crying; telling herself not to be so foolish. But as she had come downstairs, the crying had got louder. She had run into the kitchen and felt her heart stop as she saw a wailing Lucia being comforted in Paddy's no-nonsense arms.

172

'What's wrong?' she'd heard herself say breathlessly as the doorbell rang.

'Nothing's wrong!' Paddy had said, laughing a little. 'That'll be your taxi. Now you go off and have a nice time. Lucia will calm down in a minute.'

Maggie had stood, stricken, staring at her daughter's red, crumpled face.

'Maybe I'll just take her for a moment—' she'd begun.

'Honestly, dear, she'll be fine! No point hanging about and confusing her. We'll go for a nice walk around the house in a moment, won't we, Lucia? Look, she's cheering up already!'

And sure enough, Lucia's cries had tailed off into silence. She gave a huge yawn and stared at Maggie with blue, teary eyes.

'Just go,' Paddy had said gently. 'While she's quiet.'

'OK,' Maggie had said numbly. 'OK, I'll go.'

Somehow she'd made herself walk out of the kitchen, through the hall to the front door. As she'd closed it behind her she'd thought she could hear Lucia sobbing again. But she hadn't gone back. She'd forced herself to keep going, to get in the taxi and ask for the station; she'd even managed to smile brightly at the ticket officer as she'd bought her ticket. It was only as the train to Waterloo pulled out of the station that tears had begun to fall down her cheeks, ruining her carefully applied make-up and falling on the pages of her glossy magazine.

Now she rested her head in her palms, listening to the railway Tannoy in the distance, and thought, with disbelief, how much things had changed in her life. There was no point even attempting to convey to Candice and Roxanne quite how much physical and emotional effort it had taken for her to be here this evening. No-one who was not herself a mother would comprehend; would believe what she had gone through. And so, in some way, that meant they would

173

never quite understand how highly she prized their friendship. How important their little threesome was to her.

Maggie sighed, and reached into her bag for a compact to check her reflection, wincing at the dark shadows under her eyes. Tonight, she decided, she would have as much fun as she possibly could. Tonight would make up for it all. Tonight she would talk and laugh with her dearest friends, and return – perhaps – to something like her former self.

Candice stood in front of the mirror in the Ladies', applying her make-up for the evening. Her hand shook slightly as she applied her mascara, and her face looked gaunt in the bright overhead light. She should have been looking forward to the evening out – a chance to see Maggie and Roxanne again; a chance to relax. But she felt unable to relax while she was still so confused about Heather. Another week had gone by, and still she had said nothing. She had not mentioned any of the matters troubling her, and neither had Heather. And so the unresolved situation remained and the niggling feeling remained in her stomach.

On the surface, of course, she and Heather were still the best of friends. She was sure that Heather suspected nothing was amiss – and certainly nobody else at the office had picked anything up. But Maggie and Roxanne were sharper than that. They would see the tension in her face; they would realize that something was wrong. They would quiz her until she admitted the truth – and then berate her for having ignored their advice. Half of her wanted to duck out of the meeting altogether.

The door opened, and she looked up to see Heather coming in, dressed smartly in a violet-coloured suit.

'Hi, Heather,' she said, and flashed an automatic little smile.

'Candice.' Heather's voice was full of distress. 'Candice, you must hate me. I feel so awful!'

'What about?' said Candice, half laughing. 'What are you talking about?'

'About your idea, of course!' said Heather, and looked at her with earnest grey eyes. 'Your late-night shopping feature!'

Candice stared at her and felt a thud of shock. She pushed back her hair and swallowed.

'Wh-what do you mean?' she said, playing for time.

'I've just seen the features list for July. Justin's put down that feature as though it was my idea.' Heather took hold of Candice's hands and grasped them tightly. 'Candice, I told him it was your idea in the first place. I don't know where he got the thought that it was mine.'

'Really?' Candice gazed at Heather, her heart thumping.

'I shouldn't even have said anything about it,' said Heather apologetically. 'But I just happened to mention it over a cup of coffee, and Justin got really enthusiastic. I told him it was your idea – but he can't have been listening.'

'I see,' said Candice. She felt hot with shame; with a drenching guilt. How could she have doubted Heather so readily? How could she have leapt to the wrong conclusion without even checking the facts. It was Maggie and Roxanne, she thought with a sudden flicker of resentment. They'd turned her against Heather

'You know, I could tell something was wrong,' said Heather, blinking a little. 'I could tell there was bad feeling between us. But I had no idea what it was. I thought maybe I'd done something in the flat to annoy you, or you were just getting tired of me . . . And then I saw the list and I realized.' Heather met Candice's eyes steadily. 'You thought I'd stolen your idea, didn't you?'

'No!' said Candice at once, then flushed. 'Well, maybe . . .' She bit her lip. 'I didn't know what to think.'

175

'You have to believe me, Candice. I would never do that to you. Never!' Heather leaned forward and hugged Candice. 'You've done everything for me. I owe you so much . . .' When she pulled away, her eyes were glistening slightly, and Candice felt her own eyes well up in sympathy.

'I feel so ashamed,' she whispered. 'I should never have suspected you. I might have known it was bloody Justin's fault!' She gave a shaky laugh and Heather grinned back.

'Let's go out tonight,' she said. 'Friends again.'

'Oh, that would be great,' said Candice. She wiped her eyes, and grinned ruefully at her smeared reflection. 'But I'm meeting the others at the Manhattan Bar.'

'Oh well,' said Heather lightly. 'Another time, perhaps . . .'

'No, listen,' said Candice, seized by a sudden fierce affection for Heather. 'Come with us. Come and join the gang.'

'Really?' said Heather cautiously. 'You don't think the others would mind?'

'Of course not! You're my friend – so you're their friend too.'

'I'm not sure about that,' said Heather. 'Roxanne—'

'Roxanne loves you! Honestly, Heather.' Candice met her gaze. 'Please come. It would mean a lot to me.' Heather pulled a doubtful face.

'Candice, are you sure about this?'

'Of course!' Candice gave Heather an impetuous hug. 'They'll love to see you.'

'OK.' Heather beamed. 'I'll see you downstairs, shall I? In about . . . fifteen minutes?'

'Fine,' smiled Candice. 'See you then.'

Heather stepped out of the Ladies' and looked around. Then she headed straight for Justin's office and knocked.

'Yes?' he said.

'I wondered if I could see you for a moment,' said Heather.

'Oh yes?' Justin smiled. 'Any more wonderful ideas for the magazine?'

'No, not this time.' Heather pushed back her hair and bit her lip. 'Actually . . . it's a bit of an awkward matter.'

'Oh,' said Justin in surprise, and gestured to a chair. 'Well, come on in.'

'I don't want to make a fuss,' said Heather apologetically, sitting down. 'In fact, I'm embarrassed even mentioning it. But I had to talk to somebody . . .' She rubbed her nose and gave a little sniff.

'My dear girl!' said Justin. 'What's wrong?' He got up from his chair, walked round behind Heather and shut the door. Then he walked back to his desk. Behind him, in the window, the reflected lights of the office shone back: a curved series of bright lozenges against the darkness.

'If you've got any kind of problem, I want to know,' said Justin, leaning back. 'Whatever it is.' He picked up a pencil and held it between his two hands, as though measuring something. 'That's what I'm here for.'

There was silence in the little office.

'Can this remain completely confidential?' said Heather at last.

'Of course!' said Justin. 'Whatever you say will remain between these four walls – ' he gestured ' – and our two selves.'

'Well . . . OK,' said Heather doubtfully. 'If you're absolutely sure . . .' She took a deep shuddering breath, pushed back her hair again and looked up beseechingly at Justin. 'It's about Candice.'

Chapter Thirteen

The Manhattan Bar was holding a Hollywood Legends night, and the glass door was opened for Maggie by a beaming Marilyn Monroe lookalike. Maggie walked into the foyer a few paces, staring at the vibrant scene before her, then closed her eyes and let the atmosphere just pour over her for a second. The buzz of people chatting, the jazzy music in the background, the scent of sizzling swordfish steaks, of cigarette smoke and designer fragrances wafting past. Snatches of overheard conversation, a sudden shriek of laughter – and filtering through her closed eyelids, the brightness, the glitter, the colour. Metropolitan people enjoying themselves. As she opened her eyes, a happiness that was almost tearful began to well up inside her. She had not realized quite how much she'd missed it all. After the silence and mud of the fields, after the constant wearying wailing of Lucia, this warm noisy bar was like coming home.

She surrendered her coat to the coat check, took her silver button and turned towards the throng. At first she thought she must be the first to arrive. But then, suddenly, she spotted Roxanne. She was sitting alone at a table in the corner, a drink already in front of her. As she turned her head, unaware she was being watched, Maggie's stomach gave a small lurch.

Roxanne looked terrible. Her face was shadowed, her eyes looked bloodshot, and there was a weary downward crease to her mouth. A hangover, Maggie would have thought, or jetlag – had it not been for the expression in Roxanne's eyes. Those bright snappy eyes, usually so full of wit and verve, were tonight dull and unseeing, as though nothing around her interested her. As Maggie watched, Roxanne picked up her glass and took a deep gulp. Whatever was in it was obviously strong, thought Maggie, and she felt a slight pang of alarm.

'Roxanne!' she called, and began to make her way to the table, threading through the crowds of people. 'Roxanne!'

'Maggie!' Roxanne's face lit up and she stood up, holding her arms out. The two women embraced for slightly longer than usual; as Maggie pulled away, she saw that Roxanne's eyes were glistening with tears.

'Roxanne, are you OK?' she said cautiously.

'I'm fine!' said Roxanne at once. She flashed a bright smile and reached into her bag for her cigarettes. 'How are *you*? How's the babe?'

'We're all fine,' said Maggie slowly. She sat down, staring at Roxanne's trembling hands as she scrabbled for her lighter.

'And Giles? How's he enjoying being a father?'

'Oh, he loves it,' said Maggie drily. 'All ten minutes a day of it.'

'Not exactly a New Man, then, our Giles?' said Roxanne, lighting up.

'You could say that,' said Maggie. 'Roxanne—'

'Yes?'

'Are you OK? Seriously.'

Roxanne looked at her through a cloud of smoke. Her blue eyes were full of pain; she seemed to be struggling to keep control.

'I've been better,' she said eventually. 'Thanks for all your messages, by the way. They really kept me going.'

'Kept you going?' Maggie stared at her, aghast. 'Roxanne, what's going on? Where have you been?'

'I haven't been anywhere.' Roxanne gave a wobbly smile and dragged on her cigarette. 'I've been at home, drinking lots of vodka.'

'Roxanne, what the hell's happened?' Maggie's eyes sharpened. 'Is it Mr Married?'

Roxanne looked for a moment at the still-burning end of her cigarette, then stubbed it out with a suddenly vicious movement.

'You know I said watch this space? Well, you needn't have bothered.' She looked up. 'Mr Married is out of the picture. His choice.'

'Oh my God,' whispered Maggie. She reached for Roxanne's hands across the table. 'God, you poor thing. The bastard!'

'Hello there!' A cheery voice interrupted them and they both looked up. Scarlett O'Hara was smiling at them, notebook in hand. 'May I take your order?'

'Not yet,' said Maggie. 'Give us a few minutes.'

'No, wait,' said Roxanne. She drained her glass and gave it to Scarlett. 'I'd like another double vodka and lime.' She smiled at Maggie. 'Vodka is my new best friend.'

'Roxanne—'

'Don't worry! I'm not an alcoholic. I'm an alcohol-lover. There's a difference.'

Scarlett disappeared, and the two friends looked at each other.

'I don't know what to say,' said Maggie, and her hands clenched the table. 'I feel like going over to wherever he lives, and—'

'Don't,' cut in Roxanne. 'It's . . . it's fine, really.' Then, after a pause, she looked up with a glint in her eye. 'What, out of interest?'

'Scraping his car,' said Maggie fiercely. 'That's where it hurts them.' Roxanne threw back her head and roared with laughter.

'God, I've missed you, Maggie.'

'You too,' said Maggie. 'Both of you.' She sighed, and looked around the humming bar. 'I've been looking forward to this evening like a little kid. Counting off the days!'

'I would have thought there was no room in your grand country life for us any more,' said Roxanne, grinning slyly at her. 'Aren't you too busy going to hunt balls and shooting things?' Maggie gave her a wan smile, and Roxanne frowned. 'Seriously, Maggie. Is it all OK? You look pretty beat-up.'

'Thanks a lot.'

'You're welcome.'

'Here you are!' The voice of Scarlett O'Hara interrupted them. 'One double vodka with lime.' She put the glass down and smiled at Maggie. 'And can I get you anything?'

'Oh, I don't know,' said Maggie, picking up the cocktail menu and putting it down again. 'I was going to wait until we were all here.'

'Where is Candice, anyway?' said Roxanne, lighting another cigarette. 'She is definitely coming?'

'I suppose so,' said Maggie. 'Oh, come on, I can't wait any longer.' She looked up at the waitress. 'I'll have a Jamaican Rumba, please.'

'And a Margarita for me,' said Roxanne. 'Can't have you starting on the cocktails without me,' she added, at Maggie's look. As the waitress retreated, she leaned back in her chair and looked appraisingly at Maggie. 'So, come on. What's it like, being Mummy Drakeford of The Pines?'

'Oh, I don't know,' said Maggie, after a pause. She picked up a silver coaster and stared at it, twisting it round and round in her fingers. Part of her yearned to confide in someone. To share her feelings of weariness and loneliness; to describe her deteriorating relationship with Giles's mother; to try and paint a picture of the monotonous drudgery that her life seemed, overnight, to have become. But another part of her couldn't bring herself to admit such defeat, even to such a close friend as Roxanne. She was used to being Maggie Phillips: editor of the *Londoner*, clever and organized and always on top of things. Not Maggie Drakeford, a pale, fatigued, disillusioned mother who couldn't even bring herself to go shopping.

And how could she begin to explain how these feelings of weariness and depression were bound up inextricably with a love; a joy so intense it could leave her feeling faint? How could she describe the wonderment every time she saw the flash of recognition in Lucia's eyes; every time those tiny wrinkled features broke into a smile? How could she convey the fact that during some of her happiest moments she was, nevertheless, in tears of exhaustion?

'It's different,' she said eventually. 'Not quite how I imagined it.'

'But you're enjoying it.' Roxanne's eyes narrowed. 'Aren't you?'

There was silence. Maggie put the coaster down on the table and began to trace circles on it with her finger.

'I'm enjoying it, of course I am,' she began after a while. 'Lucia's wonderful, and . . . and I love her. But at the same time . . .' She broke off and sighed. 'Nobody can have any idea what it's—'

'Look, there's Candice,' interrupted Roxanne. 'Sorry, Maggie. Candice!' She stood up and peered through the throng. 'What's she doing?'

Maggie turned in her seat and followed Roxanne's gaze.

'She's talking to someone,' she said, wrinkling her

182

brow. 'I can't quite see who . . .' She broke off in dismay. 'Oh no.'

'I don't believe it,' said Roxanne slowly. 'I don't believe it! She's brought that bloody girl.'

As Candice picked her way through the crowd of people to the table where Maggie and Roxanne were sitting, she felt Heather tugging at her sleeve, and turned back.

'What's wrong?' she said, looking at Heather's anxious expression in surprise.

'Look, Candice, I'm not sure about this,' said Heather. 'I'm not sure I'm going to be welcome. Maybe I'd better just go.'

'You can't go!' said Candice. 'Honestly, they'll be delighted to see you. And it'll be nice for you to meet them properly.'

'Well . . . OK,' said Heather after a pause.

'Come on!' Candice smiled at Heather and took her hand, pulling her forward. She felt buoyant tonight; overflowing with good spirits and affection. Towards Heather, towards Maggie and Roxanne; even towards the waitress dressed as Doris Day who crossed their path, forcing them to stop. 'Isn't this fun?' she said, turning to Heather. 'Just think, a few weeks ago it would have been you, dressing up.'

'Until you rescued me from my sad waitressing life,' said Heather, squeezing Candice's hand. 'My own Princess Charming.' Candice laughed, and pushed on through the crowds.

'Hi!' she said, arriving at the table. 'Isn't it busy tonight!'

'Yes,' said Roxanne, looking at Heather. 'Overpopulated, one might say.'

'You remember Heather, don't you?' said Candice cheerfully, looking from Roxanne to Maggie. 'I thought I'd ask her along.'

'Evidently,' muttered Roxanne.

'Of course!' said Maggie brightly. 'Hello, Heather. Nice to see you again.' She hesitated, then moved her chair round to make space at the little table.

'Here's another chair,' said Candice. 'Plenty of room!' She sat down and smiled at her two friends. 'So, how are you both? How's life, Roxanne?'

'Life's just fine,' said Roxanne, after a pause, and took a gulp of her vodka.

'And you, Maggie? And the baby?'

'Yes, fine,' said Maggie. 'Everything's fine.'

'Good!' said Candice.

There was an awkward silence. Maggie glanced at Roxanne, who was sipping her vodka, stony-faced. Candice smiled encouragingly at Heather, who grinned nervously back. Then, in the corner of the bar, the jazz band began to play 'Let's Face the Music' and suddenly a man in top hat and tails appeared, leading a woman in a white Ginger Rogers dress. As the crowd cleared a space for them, the two began to dance, and a round of applause broke out. The noise seemed to bring the group back to life.

'So, are you enjoying working for the *Londoner*, Heather?' said Maggie politely.

'Oh yes,' said Heather. 'It's a great place to work. And Justin's a wonderful editor.' Roxanne's head jerked up.

'That's what you think, is it?'

'Yes!' said Heather. 'I think he's fantastic!' Then she looked at Maggie. 'Sorry, I didn't mean—'

'No,' said Maggie, after a pause. 'Don't be silly. I'm sure he's doing marvellously.'

'Congratulations on the birth of your baby, by the way,' said Heather. 'I gather she's very sweet. How old is she?'

'Seven weeks,' said Maggie, smiling.

'Oh right,' said Heather. 'And you've left her at home, have you?'

'Yes. With my mother-in-law.'

'Is it OK to leave them that young?' Heather spread her hands apologetically. 'Not that I know anything about babies, but I once saw a documentary saying you shouldn't leave them for the first three months.'

'Oh, really?' Maggie's smile stiffened a little. 'Well, I'm sure she'll be fine.'

'Oh, I'm sure she will!' Heather blinked innocently. 'I don't know anything about it, really. Look, here comes a waiter. Shall we order?' She picked up her cocktail menu, looked at it for a second, then lifted her eyes to meet Roxanne's.

'And what about you, Roxanne?' she said sweetly. 'Do you think you'll ever have children?'

By the time the others were all ordering their second cocktails, Roxanne was on her fifth drink of the evening. She had eaten nothing since lunchtime, and the potent combination of vodka and Margaritas was beginning to make her head spin. But it was either keep drinking, and try somehow to alleviate the tension inside her, or scream. Every time she looked up and met Heather's wide-eyed gaze she felt acid rising in her stomach. How could Candice have fallen for her smooth talk? How could Candice – one of the most sensitive, observant people she knew – be so utterly blind in this case? It was crazy.

She glanced up, met Maggie's eye over her cocktail and rolled her eyes ruefully. Maggie looked about as cheerful as she felt. What a bloody disaster.

'I don't actually think much of this place,' Heather was saying dismissively. 'There's a really great bar in Covent Garden I used to go to. You should try it.'

'Yes, why not?' said Candice, looking around the table. 'We could probably do with a change.'

'Maybe,' said Maggie, and took a sip of her cocktail.

'That reminds me!' said Heather, suddenly bubbling

over with laughter. 'Do you remember that school trip to Covent Garden, Candice? Were you on it? Where we all got lost and Anna Staples got her shoulder tattooed.'

'No!' said Candice, her face lighting up. 'Did she really?'

'She had a tiny flower done,' said Heather. 'It was really cute. But she got in terrible trouble. Mrs Lacey called her in, and she'd put a plaster over it. So then Mrs Lacey said, "Is something wrong with your shoulder, Anna?"' Heather and Candice both dissolved into giggles, and Roxanne exchanged disbelieving looks with Maggie.

'Sorry,' said Candice, looking up with bright eyes. 'We're boring you.'

'Not at all,' said Roxanne. She took out a packet of cigarettes and offered it to Heather.

'No thanks,' said Heather. 'I always think smoking ages the skin.' She smiled apologetically. 'But that's just me.'

There was silence as Roxanne lit up, blew out a cloud of smoke and looked through it at Heather with dangerously glittering eyes.

'I think I'll go and check on Lucia,' said Maggie, and pushed her chair back. 'I won't be a minute.'

The quietest place to call from was the foyer. Maggie stood by the glass door looking out onto the street, watching as a group of people in black tie hurried past. She felt flushed, hyped up by the evening and yet exhausted. After all the preparation, all the effort, she was not enjoying herself as much as she had hoped. Partly it was that Candice had ruined the cosy familiar threesome by bringing along her awful friend. But partly it was because she herself felt frighteningly brain-dead; as though she could not keep up with the conversation. Several times she had found herself groping for the right word and having to give up. She, who was supposed to be an intelligent, articulate person. As she leaned against the wall and took out her mobile phone, she caught a glimpse of herself in the mirror opposite, and felt a jolt of shock at how fat she looked; how grey her face looked, despite the make-up she had carefully put on. Her eyes looked miserably back at her, and suddenly she found herself wishing she were at home, away from Candice's hateful friend and her insensitive comments, away from the bright lights and the pressure to sparkle.

'Hello?'

'Hi! Paddy, it's Maggie.' A group of people entered the foyer and Maggie turned away slightly, covering her ear with one hand. 'I just thought I'd see how things were going.'

'All's well,' said Paddy briskly. Her voice sounded thin and tinny, as though she were miles away. Which of course she is, thought Maggie miserably. 'Lucia's been coughing a little, but I'm sure it's nothing to worry about.'

'Coughing?' said Maggie in alarm.

'I wouldn't worry,' said Paddy. 'Giles will be back soon, and if there's any problem, we can always send for the doctor.' A thin cry came from the background; a moment later, Maggie felt a telltale dampness inside her bra. Oh shit, she thought miserably. Shit shit.

'Do you think she's OK?' she asked, a perilous wobble in her voice.

'Really, dear, I wouldn't worry. You just enjoy yourself.'

'Yes,' said Maggie, on the verge of tears. 'Thanks. Well, I'll call later.' She clicked off the phone and leaned back against the wall, trying to breathe deeply; trying to gain some perspective. A cough was nothing to worry about. Lucia was fine with Paddy. This was her one night off; she was entitled to enjoy herself and forget about her responsibilities.

187

But suddenly it all seemed irrelevant. Suddenly the only person she wanted to be with was Lucia. A single tear ran down her face and she brushed it away roughly. She had to get a grip on herself. She had to go back in there and make an effort to be entertaining company.

Perhaps if it had just been the three of them, she thought miserably, she would have confided in the others. But she couldn't with Heather there. Heather with her smooth young skin and her innocent eyes and those constant snide little comments. She made Maggie feel slow-witted and middle-aged; the frump among the glamour girls.

'Hi!' A voice interrupted her and her head jerked up in shock. Heather was standing in front of her, an amused look on her face. 'Baby OK?'

'Yes,' muttered Maggie.

'Good.' Heather shot her a patronizing smile and disappeared into the Ladies'. God, I hate you, thought Maggie. I *hate* you, Heather Trelawney.

Oddly enough, the thought made her feel a little better.

As soon as Heather had disappeared to the Ladies', Roxanne turned to Candice and said, 'What the hell did you have to bring her for?'

'What do you mean?' said Candice in surprise. 'I just thought it would be fun for us all to get together.'

'Fun? You think it's fun listening to that bitch?'

'What?' Candice stared at her incredulously. 'Roxanne, are you drunk?'

'Maybe I am,' said Roxanne, stubbing out her cigarette. 'But to steal a phrase, she'll still be a bitch in the morning. Didn't you *hear* her? "I always think smoking ages the skin. But that's just me." ' Roxanne's voice rose in savage mimicry. 'Stupid little cow.'

'She didn't mean anything by it!'

188

'Of course she did! Jesus, Candice, can't you see what she's like?'

Candice rubbed her face and took a few deep breaths, trying to stay calm. Then she looked up.

'You've had it in for Heather from day one, haven't you?'

'Not at all.'

'You have! You told me not to get involved with her, you gave her a nasty look at the office . . .'

'Oh, for God's sake,' said Roxanne impatiently.

'What's she ever done to you?' Candice's voice rose shakily above the chatter. 'You haven't even *bothered* to get to know her . . .'

'Candice?' Maggie arrived at the table and looked from face to face. 'What's wrong?'

'Heather,' said Roxanne.

'Oh,' said Maggie, and pulled a face. Candice stared at her.

'What, so you don't like her either?'

'I didn't say that,' said Maggie at once. 'And that's beside the point, anyway. I just think it would have been nice if the three of us could have . . .' She was interrupted by Roxanne coughing.

'Hi, Heather,' said Candice miserably.

'Hi,' said Heather pleasantly, and slid into her seat. 'Everything all right?'

'Yes,' said Candice, her cheeks aflame. 'I think I'll just . . . go to the loo. I won't be a minute.'

When she'd gone, there was silence around the table. In the corner, Marilyn Monroe had stepped up to the microphone and was singing a husky 'Happy Birthday' to a delighted-looking man with a sweating face and paunch. As she reached his name, the crowd around him cheered, and he punched the air in a victory salute.

'Well,' said Maggie awkwardly. 'Shall we all order another cocktail?'

189

'Yes,' said Roxanne. 'Unless you think cocktails age the skin, Heather?'

'I wouldn't know,' said Heather politely.

'Oh, really?' said Roxanne, her voice slightly slurred. 'That's funny. You seem to know about everything else.'

'Is that so?'

'Anyway,' said Maggie hastily. 'There's a full one here.' She picked up a highball, filled with crushed ice and an amber-coloured liquid and decorated with frosted grapes. 'Whose is this?'

'I think it was supposed to be mine,' said Heather. 'But I don't want it. Why don't you have it, Roxanne?'

'Have your lips touched the glass?' said Roxanne. 'If so, no thanks.'

Heather stared at her for a tense moment, then shook her head, almost laughing.

'You really don't like me, do you?'

'I don't like users,' said Roxanne pointedly.

'Oh, really?' said Heather, smiling sweetly. 'Well, I don't like sad old lushes, but I'm still polite to them.'

Maggie gasped and looked at Roxanne.

'What did you call me?' said Roxanne very slowly.

'A sad old lush,' said Heather, examining her nails. She looked up and smiled. 'A sad – old – lush.'

For a few seconds, Roxanne stared at her, shaking. Then, very slowly and deliberately, she picked up the highball full of amber liquid. She stood up and held the glass up to the glittering light for a moment.

'You wouldn't,' said Heather scathingly, but a flicker of doubt passed over her face.

'Oh yes she would,' said Maggie, and folded her arms. There was a moment of still tension as Heather stared disbelievingly up at Roxanne – then, with a sudden flick of the wrist, Roxanne up-ended the cocktail over Heather's head. The icy drink hit her straight in the face and she gasped, then spluttered

190

furiously, brushing crushed ice out of her eyes.

'Jesus Christ!' she spat, getting to her feet. 'You're a fucking . . . nutcase!' Maggie looked at Roxanne and broke into giggles. At the next table, people drinking cocktails put them down and began to nudge each other.

'Hope I haven't aged your skin,' drawled Roxanne, as Heather angrily pushed past. They both watched as Heather disappeared out of the door, then looked at each other and burst into laughter.

'Roxanne, you're wonderful,' said Maggie, wiping her eyes.

'Should have done it at the beginning of the evening,' said Roxanne. She surveyed the disarray on the table – empty glasses, puddles of liquid and crushed ice everywhere – then raised her head and met Maggie's eyes. 'Looks like the party's over. Let's get the bill.'

Candice was washing her hands when Heather burst into the Ladies'. Her hair and face were drenched, the shoulders of her jacket were stained, and she had a murderous expression on her face.

'Heather!' said Candice, looking up in alarm. 'What's happened?'

'Your bloody friend Roxanne, that's what!'

'What?' Candice, stared at her. 'What do you mean?'

'I mean,' said Heather, her jaw tight with anger, 'that Roxanne tipped a whole fucking cocktail over my head. She's crazy!' She headed towards the brightly lit mirror, reached for a tissue and began to blot her hair.

'She tipped a *cocktail* over your head?' said Candice disbelievingly. 'But why?'

'God knows!' said Heather. 'All I said was, I thought she'd had enough to drink. I mean, how many has she had tonight? I just thought maybe she should move onto the soft stuff. But the moment I suggested it, she went berserk!' Heather stopped blotting for a moment and met Candice's eye in the mirror. 'You know, I reckon she's an alcoholic.'

'I can't believe it!' said Candice in dismay. 'I don't know what she can have been thinking of. Heather, I feel awful about this! And your poor jacket . . .'

'I'll have to go home and change,' said Heather. 'I'm supposed to be meeting Ed in half an hour.'

'Oh,' said Candice, momentarily distracted. 'Really? For a . . .' She swallowed. 'For a date?'

'Yes,' said Heather, throwing a piece of sodden tissue into the bin. 'God, look at my face!' Heather stared at her dishevelled reflection, then sighed. 'Oh, I don't know, maybe I was tactless.' She turned round and met Candice's gaze. 'Maybe I should have kept my mouth shut.'

'No!' exclaimed Candice, feeling fresh indignation on Heather's behalf. 'God, don't blame yourself! You made every effort, Heather. Roxanne just—'

'She's taken against me all along,' said Heather, looking at Candice with distressed eyes. 'I've done my best to be friendly . . .'

'I know,' said Candice, her jaw firming. 'Well, I'm going to have a little word with Roxanne.'

'Don't argue!' said Heather, as Candice strode towards the door of the Ladies'. 'Please don't argue over me!' But her words were lost as the door closed behind Candice with a bang.

Out in the foyer, Candice saw Roxanne and Maggie at the table, standing up. They were leaving! she thought incredulously. Without apologizing, without making any effort whatsoever . . .

'So,' she said, striding towards them. 'I hear you've been making Heather feel welcome in my absence.'

'Candice, she had it coming,' said Maggie, looking up. 'She really is a little bitch.'

'Waste of a good drink, if you ask me,' said Roxanne.

192

She gestured to the green leather bill on the table. 'Our share's in there. I've paid for the three of us. Not for her.'

'I don't believe you, Roxanne!' said Candice furiously. 'Aren't you sorry? Aren't you going to apologize to her?'

'Is she going to apologize to me?'

'She doesn't have to! It was you who poured the drink over her! Bloody hell, Roxanne!'

'Look, just forget it,' said Roxanne. 'Obviously you can see nothing wrong in your new best friend—'

'Well, maybe if you'd made more of an effort with her, and hadn't just taken against her for no good reason—'

'No good reason?' exclaimed Roxanne in an outraged voice. 'You want to hear all the reasons, starting with number one?'

'Roxanne, don't,' said Maggie. 'There's no point.' She sighed, and picked up her bag. 'Candice, can't you understand? We came to see you. Not her.'

'What, so we're a little clique, are we? No-one else can enter.'

'No! That's not it. But—'

'You're just determined not to like her, aren't you?' Candice stared at them with a trembling face. 'I don't know why we bother to meet up, if you can't accept my friends.'

'Well, I don't know why we bother to meet up if you're going to sit chatting about school all night to someone we don't know!' said Maggie, with a sudden heat in her voice. 'I made huge sacrifices to be here, Candice, and I've hardly spoken a word to you all evening!'

'We can talk another time!' said Candice defensively. 'Honestly—'

'I can't!' cried Maggie. 'I don't *have* another time. This *was* my time!'

'Well, maybe I'd talk to you a bit more if you weren't

so bloody gloomy!' Candice heard herself snapping. 'I want to have fun when I go out, not just sit like a misery all night!'

There was an aghast silence.

'See you,' said Roxanne remotely. 'Come on, Maggie.' She took Maggie's arm and, without looking again at Candice, led her away.

Candice watched them walk through the noisy crush of people and felt a cold shame spread through her. Shit, she thought. How could she have said such an awful thing to Maggie? How could the three of them have ended up yelling so aggressively at each other?

Her legs suddenly felt shaky, and she sank down onto a chair, staring miserably at the wet table, the chaos of ice and cocktail glasses and – like a reprimand – the bill in its green folder.

'Hi there!' said a waitress dressed as Dorothy from *The Wizard of Oz*, stopping at the table. She briskly wiped the table and removed the debris of glasses, then smiled at Candice. 'Can I take your bill for you? Or haven't you finished?'

'No, I've finished, all right,' said Candice dully. 'Hang on.' She opened her bag, reached for her purse and counted off three notes. 'There you are,' she said, and handed the bill to the waitress. 'That should cover it.'

'Hi, Candice?' A voice interrupted her, and she looked up. It was Heather, looking clean and tidy, with her hair smoothed down and her make-up reapplied. 'Have the others gone?'

'Yes,' said Candice stiffly. 'They . . . they had to leave.' Heather looked at her closely.

'You had a falling-out, didn't you?'

'Kind of,' said Candice, and attempted a smile.

'I'm really sorry,' said Heather. 'Truly.' She squeezed Candice's shoulder, then looked at her watch. 'I've got to go, I'm afraid.'

194

'Of course,' said Candice. 'Have a good time. And say hello to Ed,' she added as Heather walked off, but Heather didn't seem to hear.

'Your bill,' said the waitress, returning the green folder.

'Thanks,' said Candice. She pocketed the slip of paper and got up from the table, feeling weary with disappointment. How could everything have gone so wrong? How could the evening have ended like this?

'Have a safe trip home and come back soon,' beamed the waitress.

'Yes,' said Candice dispiritedly. 'Maybe.'

Chapter Fourteen

The next morning, Candice woke with a cold feeling in her stomach. She stared up at the ceiling, trying to ignore it, then turned over, burying her head in the duvet. But the chill persisted; would not leave her. She had argued with Maggie and Roxanne, her brain relentlessly reminded her. Her two best friends had walked out on her. The thought sent a dripping coldness down her spine; made her want to hide under her duvet for ever.

As recollections of the evening began to run through her head, she squeezed her eyes tight shut and blocked her ears with her hands. But she could not avoid the images – the iciness in Roxanne's eyes; the shock in Maggie's face. How could she have behaved so badly? How could she have let them leave without sorting it out?

At the same time, as pieces of the evening resurfaced in her head, she felt a lingering resentment begin to lift itself off the lining of her mind. A slow self-justification began to pervade her body; a self-justification which grew warmer the more she remembered. After all, what crime had she really committed? She had brought along a friend, that was all. Perhaps Heather and Roxanne had not hit it off, perhaps Maggie had wanted to have a cosy tête-à-tête. But was she to blame for all that? If things had gone the other way – if they had all warmed to Heather and adopted her as a new chum – wouldn't they now be ringing Candice, and congratulating her on having such a nice friend? It wasn't her fault things hadn't worked out. She shouldn't have snapped at Maggie – but then, Maggie shouldn't have called Heather a bitch.

With a small surge of annoyance, Candice swung her legs out of the bed and sat up, wondering if Heather had already had her shower. And then it hit her. The flat was completely silent. Candice bit her lip and walked to the door of her little room. She pushed it open and waited, listening for any sounds. But there were none – and Heather's bedroom door was ajar. Candice walked towards the kitchen, and as she passed Heather's room, casually glanced in. It was empty, and the bed was neatly made. The bathroom was empty, too. The whole flat was empty.

Candice glanced at the clock on the kitchen wall. Seven-twenty. Heather could have got up extremely early, she told herself, putting on the kettle. She could have suffered from insomnia, or instituted a rigorous new regime.

Or she could have stayed out all night with Ed.

An indeterminate spasm went through Candice's stomach, and she shook her head crossly. It was none of her business what Ed and Heather did, she told herself firmly. If he wanted to ask her out, fine. And if Heather was desperate enough to want to spend the evening with a man who thought 'gourmet' meant three pizza toppings, fine again.

She walked briskly back into the bathroom, peeled off her nightshirt and stepped under the shower – noticing, in spite of herself, that it hadn't been used that morning. Quickly she lathered herself with a rose-scented gel marked 'Uplifting', then turned the shower on full hot blast to wash away the bubbles, the cold feeling in her stomach, her curiosity about Heather and Ed. She wanted to rinse it all away; to emerge refreshed and untroubled.

By the time she came back into the kitchen in her towelling robe, there was a pile of post on the mat and the kettle had boiled. Very calmly, she made herself a cup of camomile tea as recommended by the detox diet that had run in the *Londoner* the month before, and began to open her letters, deliberately keeping till last the mauve envelope at the bottom of the pile.

A credit card bill – higher than usual. Heather's arrival had meant more treats, more outings, more expenditure. A bank statement. Her bank balance also seemed rather higher than usual and she peered at it, puzzled, for a while, wondering where the extra money had come from. Then, shrugging, she stuffed it back into its envelope and moved on. A furniture catalogue in a plastic wrapper. A letter exhorting her to enter a prize draw. And then, at the bottom, the mauve envelope; the familiar loopy handwriting. She stared at it for a moment, then ripped it open, knowing already what she would find.

Dear Candice, wrote her mother. *Hope all is well with you. The weather is moderately fine here. Kenneth and I have been on a short trip to Cornwall. Kenneth's daughter is expecting another baby . . .*

Quietly, Candice read to the end of the letter, then put it back into the envelope. The same anodyne words as ever; the same neutral, distancing tone. The letter of a woman paralysed by fear of the past; too cowardly to reach out even to her own daughter.

A familiar flame of hurt burned briefly within Candice, then died. She had read too many such letters to let this one upset her. And this morning she felt clean and quiet; almost numb. *I don't care*, flashed through her head as she put the letters in a neat pile on the counter. *I don't care.* She took a sip of camomile tea, then another. She was about to take a third when the doorbell rang, startling her so much that her tea spilled all over the table.

She pulled her robe more tightly around her, cautiously walked to the front door and opened it.

'So,' said Ed, as though continuing a conversation begun three minutes ago, 'I hear one of your friends tipped a cocktail over Heather last night.' He shook his head admiringly. 'Candice, I never knew you ran with such a wild set.'

'What do you want?' said Candice.

'An introduction to this Roxanne character for a start,' said Ed. 'But a cup of coffee would do.'

'What's wrong with you?' said Candice. 'Why can't you make your own bloody coffee? And anyway, where's Heather?' Immediately the words were out of her mouth, she regretted them.

'Interesting question,' said Ed, leaning against the door frame. 'The implication being – what? That Heather should be making my coffee?'

'No!' snapped Candice. 'I just—' She shook her head. 'It doesn't matter.'

'You just wondered? Well . . .' Ed looked at his watch. 'To be honest, I have no idea. She's probably on her way to work by now, wouldn't you think?' He raised his eyes and grinned innocently.

Candice stared back at him, then turned on her heel and walked back into the kitchen. She flicked the kettle on, wiped down the tea-sodden table, then sat down and took another sip of camomile tea.

'I have to thank you, by the way,' said Ed, following her in. 'For giving me such sound advice.' He reached for the cafetière and began to spoon coffee into it. 'You want some?'

'No thank you,' said Candice coldly. 'I'm detoxing. And what did I give you advice about?'

199

'Heather, of course. You were the one who suggested I ask her out.'

'Yes,' said Candice. 'So I was.'

There was silence as Ed poured water into the cafetière and Candice stared into her cup of unappealing, lukewarm camomile tea. Don't ask, she told herself firmly. Don't ask. He's only come round to brag.

'So – how was it?' she heard herself saying.

'How was what?' said Ed, grinning. Candice felt a flush come to her cheeks.

'How was the evening?' she said in deliberate tones.

'Oh, the *evening*,' said Ed. 'The evening was lovely, thank you.'

'Good.' Candice gave an uninterested shrug.

'Heather's such an attractive girl,' continued Ed musingly. 'Nice hair, nice clothes, nice manner . . .'

'Glad to hear it.'

'Barking mad, of course.'

'What do you mean?' said Candice bad-temperedly. Typical bloody Ed. 'What do you mean, barking mad?'

'She's screwy,' said Ed. 'You must have noticed.'

'Don't be stupid.'

'Being her oldest friend and all,' said Ed, taking a sip of his coffee and looking at Candice quizzically over the rim of his mug. 'Or perhaps you hadn't noticed.'

'There's nothing to notice!' said Candice.

'If you say so,' said Ed, and Candice stared at him in frustration. 'And of course, you know her better than I do. But I have to say, in my opinion—'

'I'm not interested in your opinion!' cut in Candice. 'God, what do you know about people, anyway? All you care about is . . . is fast food and money.'

'Is that so?' said Ed, raising his eyebrows. 'The Candice Brewin Analysis. And in what order do I rate these two staples of life? Do I put money above fast food? Fast food above money? Even stevens?'

'Very funny,' said Candice sulkily. 'You know what I mean.'

'No,' said Ed after a pause. 'I'm not sure I do.'

'Oh, forget it,' said Candice.

'Yes,' said Ed, a curious look on his face. 'I think I will.' He put his coffee mug down and walked slowly towards the door, then stopped. 'Just let me tell you this, Candice. You know about as much about me as you do about your friend Heather.'

He strode out of the kitchen and down the hall, and, in slight dismay, Candice opened her mouth to say something; to call him back. But the front door banged closed, and she was too late.

As she arrived at work a couple of hours later, Candice paused at the door of the editorial office and looked at Heather's desk. It was empty and her chair was still tucked in. Heather had obviously not turned up yet.

'Morning, Candice,' said Justin, walking past towards his office.

'Hi,' said Candice absently, still staring at Heather's desk. Then she looked up. 'Justin, do you know where Heather is?'

'Heather?' said Justin, stopping. 'No. Why?'

'Oh, no reason,' said Candice at once. 'I was just wondering.' She smiled at Justin, expecting him to smile back or make some further conversational remark. Instead he frowned at her.

'You keep pretty close tabs on Heather, don't you, Candice?'

'What?' Candice wrinkled her brow. 'What's that supposed to mean?'

'You supervise a lot of her work, is that right?'

'Well,' said Candice, after a pause. 'I suppose I some-times . . . check things for her.'

'Nothing more than that?'

Candice stared back at him and felt herself flush a guilty red. Had Justin realized that she'd been doing most of Heather's work for her? Perhaps he'd recognized her style of subbing; perhaps he'd seen her working on the articles Heather was supposed to have done; perhaps he'd noticed her constant e-mailing of documents to Heather.

'Maybe a bit more,' she said eventually. 'Just a helping hand occasionally. You know.'

'I see,' said Justin. He looked at her appraisingly, running his eyes across her face as though searching for typographical errors. 'Well, I think Heather can probably do without your little helping hand from now on. Would you agree?'

'I . . . I suppose so,' said Candice, taken aback by his harsh tone. 'I'll leave her to it.'

'I'm glad to hear it,' said Justin, and gave her a long look. 'I'll be watching you, Candice.'

'Fine!' said Candice, feeling rattled. 'Watch me all you like.'

A phone began to ring in Justin's office and, after a final glance at Candice, he strode off. Candice watched him go, feeling a secret dismay rising inside her. How had Justin worked out that she'd been helping Heather so much? And why was he so hostile about it? All she'd been trying to do, after all, was help. She frowned, and began to walk slowly towards her own desk. As she sat down and stared at her blank computer screen, a new, worrying thought came to her. Was her own performance suffering as a result of helping Heather? Was she genuinely spending too much time on Heather's work?

'People.' Justin's voice interrupted her thoughts and she swivelled round in her chair. He was standing at the door to his little office, looking round the editorial room with a strange expression on his face. 'I have some rather shocking news for you all.' He paused and waited for everyone in the office to turn away from what they were doing and face him. 'Ralph Allsopp is extremely ill,' he said. 'Cancer.'

There was silence, then someone breathed,

'Oh my God.'

'Yes,' said Justin. 'It's a bit of a shock for everyone. Apparently he's had it for a while, but no-one else knew. And now it's . . .' He rubbed his face. 'It's quite advanced. Quite bad, in fact.'

There was another silence.

'So . . . so that's why he retired,' Candice heard herself saying, in a faltering voice. 'He knew he was ill.' As she said the words, she suddenly remembered the message she'd once taken from Charing Cross Hospital, and a coldness began to drip down her spine.

'He's gone into hospital,' said Justin. 'But apparently it's spread everywhere. They're doing all they can, but . . .' He tailed off and looked around the stunned room. He appeared genuinely distressed by the news, and Candice felt a sudden flash of sympathy with him. 'I think a card would be nice,' he added, after a pause, 'signed by us all. Cheerful, of course . . .'

'How long do they think he's got?' asked Candice awkwardly. 'Is it . . .' She halted, and bit her lip.

'Not long, apparently,' said Justin. 'Once these things take hold, it's—'

'Months? Weeks?'

'I think . . .' He hesitated. 'I think from what Janet said, it'll be a matter of weeks. Or even . . .' He broke off.

'Jesus Christ!' said Alicia shakily. 'But he looked so . . .' She broke off and buried her head in her hands.

'I'll phone Maggie and let her know,' said Justin soberly. 'And if you can all think of anyone else who would like to be informed . . . Freelancers, for example. David Gettins will want to know, I'm sure.'

'Roxanne,' said somebody.

'Exactly,' said Justin. 'Maybe somebody should phone Roxanne.'

*　　*　　*

Roxanne flipped over on her sun lounger, stretched out her legs and felt the heat of the evening sun warm her face like a friendly smile. She had arrived at Nice airport at ten that morning and had immediately taken a taxi to the Paradin Hotel. Gerhard, the general manager, was an old friend and, after a quick call to the hotel group's publicity department, had managed to find her a spare room at a vastly reduced rate. She didn't want much, she had insisted. A bed, a shower, a place by the pool. A place to lie with her eyes closed, feeling the healing, warming sun on her body. A place to forget about everything.

She had lain all day on a sun-bed under the blistering sunshine, oiling herself sporadically and taking sips from a pitcher of water. At six-thirty she looked at her watch and felt a lurch of amazement that only twenty-four hours before, she'd been in the Manhattan Bar, about to descend into the evening from hell.

If she closed her eyes, Roxanne could still summon up the thrill she'd felt as she'd seen the first piece of crushed ice hit that little bitch in the face. But it was a faded thrill; an excitement that even at the time had been overshadowed by disappointment. She had not wanted to argue with Candice. She had not wanted to end up in the cold evening air, drunk and alone and miserable.

Maggie had abandoned her. After the two of them had walked out of the bar, both flushed and still buoyed up with adrenalin from the argument, Maggie had looked at her watch and said reluctantly, 'Roxanne . . .'

'Don't go,' Roxanne had said, the beginnings of panic in her voice. 'Come on, Maggie. This evening's been so shitty. We've got to redeem it somehow.'

'I've got to get back,' Maggie had said. 'It's already late—'

'It's not!'

'I have to get back to Hampshire.' Maggie had sounded genuinely upset. 'You know I do. And I have to feed Lucia, otherwise I'll burst.' She'd reached for Roxanne's hand. 'Roxanne, I'd stay if I could—'

'You could if you wanted to.' There had been a childish wobble in Roxanne's voice; she'd felt a sudden cold fear of being left alone. First Ralph, then Candice. Now Maggie. Turning to others in their lives. Their friends; their families. Preferring other people to her. She'd looked down at Maggie's warm hand clasping hers, adorned with its huge engagement sapphire and had felt a surge of jealousy. 'OK then, go,' she'd said savagely. 'Go back to hubby. I don't care.'

'Roxanne,' Maggie had said pleadingly. 'Roxanne, wait.' But Roxanne had wrenched her hand away and tottered down the street, muttering curses under her breath; knowing that Maggie would not run after her. Knowing in her heart of hearts that Maggie had no choice.

She had slept for a few hours, woken at dawn and made a snap decision to leave the country; to go anywhere as long as it had sunshine. She didn't have Ralph any longer. Perhaps she didn't even have her friends any longer. But she had freedom and contacts and a good figure for a bikini. She would stay here as long as she felt like it, she thought, then move on. Perhaps even further afield than Europe. Forget Britain, forget it all. She wouldn't pick up her messages, she wouldn't even file her monthly copy. Let Justin sweat a little. Let them all sweat a little.

Roxanne sat up on her sun lounger, lifted her hand and watched in pleasure as a white-jacketed waiter came walking over. That was service for you, she thought with pleasure. Sometimes she thought she would like to spend her whole life in a five-star hotel.

'Hello,' she said, beaming up at him. 'I'd like a club sandwich, please. And a freshly squeezed orange juice.' The waiter scribbled on his pad, then moved off again, and she sank comfortably back onto her sun lounger.

Roxanne stayed at the Paradin for two weeks. The sun shone every day, and the pool glistened, and her club sandwich arrived fat and crisp and delicious. She did not vary her routine, did not talk to her fellow guests and did not venture beyond the hotel portals more than once. The days passed by like beads on a string. She felt dispassionate; remote from everything but the sensation of sun and sand and the sharp tang of the first Margarita of the evening. Somewhere in England, all the people she knew and loved were going about their daily lives, but they seemed shadowy in her mind, almost like people from the past.

Only occasionally would flashes of pain descend upon her, so great that she could do nothing but close her eyes and wait for them to pass. One night, as she sat at her corner table in the bar, the band struck up a song that she used to listen to with Ralph – and with no warning she felt a stabbing in her chest that brought tears to her eyes. But she sat quietly, allowing the tears to dry on her cheeks rather than rub them away. And then the song ended, and another began, and her Margarita arrived. And by the time she'd finished it, she was thinking of something else completely.

After two weeks she woke up and strode to her window and felt the first stirrings of ennui. She felt energetic and restless; suddenly the confines of the hotel seemed narrow and limited. They had provided security, but now they were prison-like. She had to get away, she thought suddenly. Much further away. Without pausing to reconsider, she reached for her suitcase and began to pack. She didn't want to allow herself to sit still and think about her options.

Thinking brought pain. Travelling brought hope and excitement.

By the time she kissed Gerhard farewell in the hotel foyer, she had booked herself a seat on a flight to Nairobi and called her friends at the Hilton. A week at half-rate and concessions on a two-week safari. She would write the whole thing up for the *Londoner* and as many others as she could. She would take photographs of elephants and watch the sun rise over the horizon. She would sink her eyes into the vastness of the African plains and lose herself completely.

The flight was only half full, and after some discussion with the girl at the check-in desk, Roxanne managed to get herself an upgrade. She strode onto the plane with a satisfied smirk on her face and settled comfortably into her wide seat. As the flight attendants demonstrated the safety procedures, she reached for a complimentary copy of the *Daily Telegraph* and began to read the front-page stories, letting the familiar names and references fall onto her parched mind like rain. It seemed like a lifetime since she'd been in England. She flicked over a few pages and stopped at a feature about holiday fashions.

They were on the runway now, and moving more quickly; the roar of the engines was getting louder, almost deafening. The plane picked up speed until it seemed that it couldn't go any faster – and then, with a tiny jolt, lifted into the air. At that moment Roxanne turned the page again, and felt a mild surprise. Ralph was staring back at her, in stark black and white. Automatically, her mind skimmed over any acquisitions he'd been planning; over any newsworthy event he might have been involved with.

Then, as she realized what page she was on, her face grew rigid with disbelief.

Ralph Allsopp, read the obituary title. *Publisher who brought life to defunct magazine the 'Londoner'.*

'No,' said Roxanne in a voice that didn't sound like hers. 'No.' Her hands were shaking so much, she could barely read the text.

Ralph Allsopp, who died on Monday . . .

'No,' she whispered, searching the page desperately for a different answer, a punchline.

He left a wife, Cynthia, and three children.

Pain hit Roxanne like a hammer. She stared at his picture and felt herself start to shudder, to retch. With useless hands, she began to tug at her safety strap. 'No,' she heard herself saying. 'I've got to go.'

'Madam, is everything all right?' A stewardess appeared in front of her, smiling frostily.

'Stop the plane,' said Roxanne to the stewardess. 'Please. I've got to go. I have to go back.'

'Madam—'

'No! You don't understand. I have to go back. It's an emergency.' She swallowed hard, trying to keep outwardly calm. But something was bubbling up uncontrollably inside her, taking hold of her body.

'I'm afraid—'

'Please. Just turn the plane round!'

'We can't do that, I'm afraid,' said the stewardess, smiling slightly.

'Don't you fucking laugh at me!' Roxanne's voice rose to a roar; suddenly she couldn't keep control of herself any more. 'Don't laugh at me!' Tears began to course down her face in hot streams.

'I'm not laughing!' said the stewardess in surprise. She glanced at the crumpled page in Roxanne's hand and her face changed. 'I'm not laughing,' she said gently. She crouched down and put her arms around Roxanne. 'You can fly back from Nairobi,' she said quietly into Roxanne's hair. 'We'll sort it out for you.' And as the plane soared higher and higher into the clouds, she knelt on the floor, ignoring the other passengers, stroking Roxanne's thin, sobbing back.

Chapter Fifteen

The funeral was nine days later, at St Bride's, Fleet Street. Candice arrived early, to find groups of people clustering outside, exchanging the same numb, disbelieving looks they'd been exchanging all week. The whole building had been silenced by the news that Ralph had died only two weeks after being admitted into hospital. People had sat blankly at their computers, unable to believe it. Many had wept. One nervous girl, on hearing the news, had laughed – then burst into mortified tears. Then, while they were all still shell-shocked, the phones had started ringing and the flowers had started to arrive. And so they had been forced to put on brave faces and start dealing with the messages pouring in; the expressions of sympathy; the curious enquiries about the future of the company, veiled in layers of concern.

Ralph's son Charles had been glimpsed a few times, pacing the corridors with a stern look on his face. He had been at the company for such a short time, no-one knew what he was like, beneath the good looks and the expensive suit. His face was familiar, from the rows of photographs on Ralph's wall, but he was still a stranger. As he had toured the offices directly after his father's death, there had been a chorus of murmured sympathy; shy comments about what a wonderful man

Ralph had been. But no-one dared approach Charles Allsopp one-to-one; no-one dared to ask him what his plans for the company were. Certainly not until after the funeral. And so business had carried on as usual, with heads down and voices low and a feeling of slight unreality.

Candice shoved her hands in her pockets and went to sit alone on a bench. The news of Ralph's death had brought back her own father's death with a painful vividness. She could still remember the disbelief she'd felt; the shock, the grief. The hope every waking morning that it had all been a bad dream. The sudden realization she'd had, looking at her mother one morning, that their family unit was now down to two – that instead of expanding, it was prematurely closing in on itself. She could remember feeling suddenly alone and very vulnerable. What if her mother died, too, she'd thought? What if she was left all alone in the world?

And then, just as she'd felt she was levelling out and beginning to cope, the descent into nightmare had begun. The discoveries; the humiliation. The realization that the beloved husband and father had been a swindler, a conman. Roughly, Candice brushed a tear from her eye and stared at the ground, blinking hard. There was no-one she could share these memories and emotions with. Her mother would change the subject immediately. And Roxanne and Maggie – the only other two who knew the story – were out of the picture. Nobody had heard from Roxanne for weeks. And Maggie . . . Candice winced. She had tried to call Maggie, the day after the announcement of Ralph's death. She had wanted to apologize; to make friends again; to share the shock and grief. But as she'd said, falteringly, 'Hi, Maggie, it's Candice', Maggie had snapped back, 'Oh, I'm interesting now, am I? I'm worth talking to, am I?'

'I didn't mean . . .' Candice had begun helplessly. 'Maggie, please . . .'

'Tell you what,' Maggie had said. 'You wait until Lucia's eighteen, and call me then. OK?' And the phone had been slammed down.

Candice flinched again at the memory, then forced herself to look up. It was time to forget her own problems; to concentrate on Ralph. She glanced about the milling crowd for familiar faces. Alicia was standing alone, looking glum; Heather was in a corner comforting a weeping Kelly. There were lots of people she half recognized and even a few mildly famous ones. Ralph Allsopp had made many friends over the years, and had lost few.

Candice stood up, brushed down her coat and prepared to walk over to Heather. Then, as her gaze passed over the gates, she stopped. Coming in, looking more suntanned than ever, her bronzy-blond hair cascading down over a black coat, was Roxanne. She was wearing dark glasses and walking slowly, almost as though she were ill. At the sight of her, Candice's heart contracted, and tears suddenly stung her eyes. If Maggie wouldn't make up, Roxanne would.

'Roxanne,' she said, hurrying forward, almost tripping over herself. She reached her and looked up breathlessly. 'Roxanne, I'm so sorry about the other night. Can we just forget it ever happened?'

She waited for Roxanne to agree; for the two of them to hug and shed a few sentimental tears. But Roxanne was silent, then in a husky voice – as though with a huge effort – said, 'What are you talking about, Candice?'

'At the Manhattan Bar,' said Candice. 'We all said things we didn't mean—'

'Candice, I don't give a shit about the Manhattan Bar,' said Roxanne roughly. 'You think that's important now?'

211

'Well – no,' said Candice, taken aback. 'I suppose not. But I thought . . .' She broke off. 'Where've you been?'

'I went away,' said Roxanne. 'Next question?' Her face was inscrutable, unfriendly almost, behind her shades. Candice stared at her, discomfited.

'How . . . how did you hear the news?'

'I saw the obituary,' said Roxanne. 'On the plane.' With a quick, jerky gesture, she opened her bag and reached for her cigarettes. 'On the fucking plane.'

'God, that must have been a shock!' said Candice.

Roxanne looked at her for a long while, then simply said, 'Yes. It was.' With shaking hands, she tried to light her cigarette, flicking and flicking as the flame refused to catch light. 'Stupid thing,' she said, her breaths coming more quickly. 'Fucking bloody . . .'

'Roxanne, let me,' said Candice, taking the cigarette from her. She felt taken aback by Roxanne's obvious lack of composure – Roxanne, who normally took all of life's downs with a grin and a sparky comment. On this occasion, she seemed almost worse affected than anyone. Had she been very close to Ralph? She had known him for a while – but then, so had everybody. Candice looked puzzled as she lit the cigarette and handed it back to Roxanne.

'Here you are,' she said, then stopped. Roxanne was gazing transfixed at a middle-aged woman with a neat blond bob and a dark coat who had just got out of a black mourner's car. A boy of around ten got out and joined her on the pavement, then a young woman and, after a moment, Charles Allsopp.

'Oh,' said Candice curiously. 'That must be his wife. Yes, of course it is. I recognize her.'

'Cynthia,' said Roxanne. 'And Charles. And Fiona. And little Sebastian.' She put her cigarette to her lips and took a deep puff. On the pavement, Cynthia briskly brushed down Sebastian's coat and inspected his face.

'How old is he?' said Candice, gazing at them. 'The little one?'

'I don't know,' replied Roxanne, and gave an odd little laugh. 'I've . . . I've stopped counting.'

'Poor little thing,' said Candice, biting her lip. 'Imagine losing your father at that age. It was bad enough . . .' She broke off, and took a deep breath.

The Allsopps turned, and, led by Cynthia and Charles, began to head towards the church. As they passed Roxanne, Cynthia's gaze flickered towards her, and Roxanne stuck her chin out firmly.

'Do you know her?' said Candice curiously, when they'd gone by.

'I've never spoken to her in my life,' said Roxanne.

'Oh,' said Candice, and lapsed into a puzzled silence. Around them, people were beginning to file into the church. 'Well . . . shall we go in?' said Candice eventually. She looked up. 'Roxanne?'

'I can't,' said Roxanne. 'I can't go in there.'

'What do you mean?'

'I can't do it.' Roxanne's voice was a whisper and her chin was shaking. 'I can't sit there. With all of them. With . . . her.'

'With who?' said Candice. 'Heather?'

'Candice,' said Roxanne in a trembling voice, and pulled off her sunglasses. 'Will you get it through your bloody head that I don't care one way or the other about your stupid little friend?'

Candice stared back at her in pounding shock. Roxanne's eyes were bloodshot and there were dark grey shadows beneath them, unsuccessfully concealed by a layer of bronze make-up.

'Roxanne, what is it?' she said desperately. 'Who are you talking about?' She followed Roxanne's stare and saw Cynthia Allsopp disappearing into the church. 'Are you talking about *her*?' she said, wrinkling her brow in incomprehension. 'You don't want to sit with Ralph's wife? But I thought you said – you said . . .' Candice tailed off, and looked slowly at Roxanne's haggard face. 'You're not . . .' She stopped. 'No.'

She took a step backwards and rubbed her face, trying to steady her breath, to calm her thoughts; to stop herself leaping to ridiculous conclusions.

'You can't mean . . .' She raised her eyes to meet Roxanne's and, as she saw the expression in them, felt her stomach flip over. 'Oh my God.' She swallowed. 'Ralph.'

'Yes,' said Roxanne, without moving. 'Ralph.'

Maggie sat on the sofa in her sitting room, watching the health visitor scribbling in Lucia's little book. The others would all be at the funeral now. Ralph's funeral. She couldn't quite believe it. This had to be one of the worst periods in her life, she thought dispassionately, watching as the health visitor carefully recorded Lucia's weight on a graph. Ralph was dead. And she had fallen out with both her best friends.

She could hardly bear to remember that evening at the Manhattan Bar. So many hopes had been pinned on it – and it had ended so terribly. She still felt raw whenever she remembered Candice's cruel remarks. After all the effort she'd made, after all the sacrifice and all the guilt – to be told she wasn't interesting enough to bother with. To be – effectively – dismissed. She had travelled back to Hampshire that evening drained with exhaustion and in tears. When she'd arrived home it had been to find Giles holding a fretful Lucia, clearly at his wits' end, and Lucia frantic for a feed. She felt as though she'd failed them both; failed everybody.

'So, how was it?' Giles had said as Lucia started

214

ravenously feeding. 'Mum said you sounded as though you were having a good time.' And Maggie had stared at him numbly, unable to bring herself to tell the truth; to admit that the evening she'd been pinning all her hopes on had been a disaster. So she'd smiled, and said, 'Great!' and had sunk back in her chair, grateful to be home again.

Since then, she had been out only infrequently. She was getting used to her own company; was starting to watch a great deal of soothing daytime television. On the day she'd heard the news about Ralph she'd sat and wept in the kitchen for a while, then reached for the phone and dialled Roxanne's number. But there was no reply. The next day, Candice had rung, and she'd found herself lashing out angrily; not wanting to, but unable to stop herself retaliating with some of the hurt she still felt. Humiliation still burned in her cheeks when she remembered Candice's comments. Obviously Candice thought she was a miserable, boring frump. Obviously Candice preferred Heather's exciting, vibrant company to hers. She had slammed down the receiver on Candice and felt a moment of powerful adrenalin. Then, a moment later, the tears had begun to fall. Poor Lucia, thought Maggie. She lives in a constant shower of salt water.

'Solids at four months,' the health visitor was saying. 'Baby rice is widely available. Organic if you prefer. Then move on to apple, pear, anything simple. Cooked well and puréed.'

'Yes,' said Maggie. She felt like an automaton, sitting and nodding and smiling at regular intervals.

'And what about you?' said the health visitor. She put down her notebook and looked directly at Maggie. 'Are you feeling well in yourself?' Maggie stared at the woman, and felt her cheeks flame scarlet. She had not expected any questions about herself.

'Yes,' she said eventually. 'Yes, I'm fine.'

215

'Is husband nice and supportive?'

'He does his best,' said Maggie. 'He's . . . he's very busy at work, but he does what he can.'

'Good,' said the health visitor. 'And you – are you getting out much?'

'A . . . a fair bit,' said Maggie defensively. 'It's difficult, with the baby . . .'

'Yes,' said the health visitor. She smiled sympathetically, and took a sip of the tea Maggie had made her. 'What about friends?'

The word hit Maggie like a bolt. To her horror, she felt tears starting at her eyes.

'Maggie?' said the health visitor, leaning forward in concern. 'Are you all right?'

'Yes,' said Maggie, and felt the tears yet again begin to course down her face. 'No.'

A pale spring sun shone as Roxanne and Candice sat in the courtyard of St Bride's, listening to the distant strains of 'Hills of the North, Rejoice'. Roxanne gazed ahead, unseeingly, and Candice stared up at the gusting clouds, trying to work out whether she and Maggie had been incredibly blind, or Roxanne and Ralph had been incredibly discreet. Six years. It was unbelievable. Six years of complete and utter secrecy.

What had shocked Candice the most, as Roxanne had told her story, was how much the two had obviously loved each other. How deep their relationship had been, beneath all Roxanne's jokes, all her flippancy, her apparent callousness. 'But what about all your toyboys?' Candice had faltered at one point – to be rewarded with a searing blue gaze. 'Candice,' Roxanne had said, almost wearily, 'there *weren't* any toyboys.'

Now, in the stillness, she inhaled deeply on her cigarette and blew a cloud of smoke into the air.

'I thought he didn't want me any more,' she said,

without moving her head. 'He told me to go to Cyprus. To have a new life. I was utterly . . . devastated. All that bullshit about retiring.' She stubbed out her cigarette. 'He must have thought he was doing me a favour. He must have known he was dying.'

'Oh, he knew,' said Candice without thinking.

'What?' Roxanne turned and stared at her. 'What do you mean?'

'Nothing,' said Candice, wishing she'd kept her mouth shut. Roxanne stared at her.

'Candice, what do you mean? Do you mean . . .' She paused, as though trying to keep control of herself. 'Do you mean you knew Ralph was ill?'

'No,' said Candice, not quite quickly enough. 'I . . . I took a message once, from Charing Cross Hospital. It was meaningless. It could have been anything.'

'When was this?' asked Roxanne in a trembling voice, as, inside the church, the hymn came to a final chord. 'Candice, when was this?'

'I don't know,' said Candice, feeling herself flush. 'A while ago. A couple of months.' She looked up at Roxanne and flinched under her gaze.

'And you said nothing,' said Roxanne disbelievingly. 'You didn't even mention it to me. Or Maggie.'

'I didn't know what it meant!'

'Didn't you guess?' Roxanne's voice harshened. 'Didn't you *wonder*?'

'I . . . I don't know. Maybe I wondered a bit—'

Candice broke off and ran a hand through her hair. From inside the church came a rumble of voices in prayer.

'You knew Ralph was dying and I didn't.' Roxanne shook her head distractedly as though trying to sort out a welter of confusing facts.

'I didn't know!' said Candice in distress. 'Roxanne—'

'You knew!' cried Roxanne. 'And his wife knew. And the whole world knew. And where was I when he

217

died? In the fucking south of France. By the fucking pool.'

Roxanne gave a little sob and her shoulders began to shake. Candice gazed at her in horrified silence.

'I should have known,' said Roxanne, her voice thick with tears. 'I could see something was wrong with him. He was thin, and he was losing weight, and he . . .' She broke off, and wiped her eyes roughly. 'But you know what I thought? I thought he was stressed out because he was planning to leave his wife. I thought he was planning to set up house with me. And all the time he was dying. And . . .' She paused disbelievingly. 'And you knew.'

In dismay, Candice tried to put her arm around her, but Roxanne shrugged it off.

'I can't stand it!' she said desperately. 'I can't stand that everyone knew but me. You should have told me, Candice.' Her voice rose like a child's wail. 'You should have told me he was ill!'

'But I didn't know about you and Ralph!' Candice felt tears pricking her own eyes. 'How could I have known to tell you?' She tried to reach for Roxanne's hand, but Roxanne was standing up, moving away.

'I can't stay,' she whispered. 'I can't look at you. I can't take it – that you knew, and I didn't.'

'Roxanne, it's not my fault,' cried Candice, tears running down her face. 'It's not my fault!'

'I know,' said Roxanne huskily. 'I know it's not. But I still can't bear it.' And without looking Candice in the eyes, she walked quickly off.

Maggie wiped her eyes and took a sip of hot, fresh tea.

'There you are,' said the health visitor kindly. 'Now don't worry, a lot of new mothers feel depressed to begin with. It's perfectly natural.'

'But I've got nothing to be depressed about,' said Maggie, giving a little shudder. 'I've got a loving husband and a great big house, and I don't have to work. I'm really lucky.'

She looked around her large, impressive sitting room: at the grand piano covered in photographs, the fireplace stacked with logs; the french windows leading out onto the lawn. The health visitor followed her gaze.

'You're quite isolated out here, aren't you?' she said thoughtfully. 'Any family nearby?'

'My parents live in Derbyshire,' said Maggie, closing her eyes and feeling the hot steam of the tea against her face. 'But my mother-in-law lives a few miles away.'

'And is that helpful?'

Maggie opened her mouth, intending to say Yes.

'Not really,' she heard herself say instead.

'I see,' said the health visitor tactfully. 'You don't get on particularly well?'

'We do . . . but she just makes me feel like such a failure,' said Maggie, and as the words left her mouth she felt a sudden painful relief. 'She does everything so well, and I do everything so . . .' Tears began to stream down her face again. 'So badly,' she whispered.

'I'm sure that's not true.'

'It is! I can't do anything right!' Maggie gave a little shudder. 'I didn't even know I was in labour. Paddy had to *tell* me I was in labour. I felt so . . . so stupid. And I don't keep the house tidy, and I don't make scones – and I got rattled changing Lucia's nappy, and Paddy came in and saw me shouting at her . . .' Maggie wiped her eyes and gave a huge sniff. 'She thinks I'm a terrible mother.'

'I'm sure she doesn't—'

'She does! I can see it in her eyes every time she looks at me. She thinks I'm useless!'

'I don't think you're useless!' Maggie and the health visitor both started, and looked round. Paddy was standing at the door of the sitting room, her face

219

flushed. 'Maggie, where did you get such a dreadful idea?'

Paddy had arrived at the house meaning to ask Maggie if she wanted anything from the shops, and had found the door on the latch. As she'd walked through the hall, she'd heard Maggie's voice, raised in emotion and, with a sudden jolt of shock, had heard her own name. She had told herself to walk away – but instead had drawn nearer the sitting room, unable to believe what she was hearing.

'Maggie, my darling girl, you're a wonderful mother!' she said now, in a trembling voice. 'Of course you are.'

'I'm sure it's all just a misunderstanding,' said the health visitor soothingly.

'No-one understands!' said Maggie, wiping her blotchy face. 'Everyone thinks I'm bloody super-woman. Lucia never sleeps . . .'

'I thought you said she was sleeping well,' said the health visitor with a frown, consulting her notes.

'I know!' cried Maggie in sudden anguish. 'I said that because everyone seems to think that's what she should be doing. But she's not sleeping. And I'm not sleeping either. Giles has no idea . . . no-one has any idea.'

'I've tried to help!' said Paddy, and glanced defensively at the health visitor. 'I've offered to babysit, I've tidied the kitchen . . .'

'I know,' said Maggie. 'And every time you tidy it you make me feel worse. Every single time you come round . . .' She looked at Paddy. 'Every time, I'm doing something else wrong. When I went up to London you told me I should have an early night instead.' Tears began to pour down her face again. 'My one night off.'

'I was worried about you!' said Paddy, her face

reddening in distress. 'I could tell you were exhausted; I didn't want you to make yourself ill!'

'Well, that's not what you said.' Maggie looked up miserably. 'You made me feel like a criminal.' Paddy stared at her for a few silent moments, then sank heavily down onto a chair.

'Perhaps you're right,' she said slowly. 'I didn't think.'

'I'm grateful for everything you've done,' muttered Maggie. 'I am, really. But . . .'

'It sounds like you could do with more emotional support,' said the health visitor, looking from Paddy to Maggie. 'You say your husband's got a very demanding job?'

'He's very busy,' said Maggie, and blew her nose. 'It's not fair to expect him . . .'

'Nonsense!' cut in Paddy crisply. 'Giles is this baby's father, isn't he? Then he can share the burden.' She gave Maggie a beady look. 'Anyway, I thought all you women were into New Men these days.' Maggie gave a shaky laugh.

'I am, in principle. It's just that he works so hard—'

'And so do you! Maggie, you must stop expecting miracles of yourself.'

Maggie flushed. 'Other women manage,' she said, staring at the floor. 'I just feel so inadequate . . .'

'Other women manage *with help*,' said Paddy. 'Their mothers come to stay. Their husbands take time off. Their friends rally round.' She met the health visitor's eye. 'I don't think any husband ever died from losing a night's sleep, did he?'

'Not to my knowledge,' said the health visitor, grinning.

'You don't have to do it all,' said Paddy to Maggie. 'You're doing marvellously as it is. Much better than I ever did.'

'Really?' said Maggie, and raised a shaky smile. 'Even though I don't make scones?'

Paddy was silent. She looked down at little Lucia, sleeping in her basket, then raised her eyes to meet Maggie's.

'I make scones because I'm a bored old woman,' she said. 'But you've got a lot more in your life than that. Haven't you?'

As people began to pour out of the church, Candice looked up. Her limbs felt stiff; her face felt dry and salty from tears; she felt internally bruised from Roxanne's powerful anger. She didn't want to see anyone, she thought, and quickly got up to leave. But as she was walking away, Justin suddenly appeared from nowhere and tapped her on the shoulder.

'Candice,' he said coldly. 'A word, please.'

'Oh,' said Candice, and rubbed her face. 'Can't it wait?'

'I'd like you to come and see me tomorrow. Nine-thirty.'

'OK,' said Candice. 'What's it about?'

Justin gave her a long look, then said, 'Let's just speak tomorrow, shall we?'

'All right,' said Candice, puzzled. Justin nodded curtly, then walked on into the crowds.

Candice stared after him, wondering what on earth he was talking about. The next moment, Heather appeared at her side.

'What did Justin want?' she said casually.

'I've no idea. He wants to see me tomorrow. Very serious about something or other.' Candice rolled her eyes. 'He was very cloak and dagger about it. Probably his latest genius idea about something.'

'Probably,' said Heather. She looked at Candice consideringly for a moment, then grinned and squeezed her waist. 'Tell you what, let's go out tonight,' she said. 'Have some supper somewhere nice. We could do with some fun after all this misery. Don't you think?'

'Absolutely,' said Candice in relief. 'I feel pretty wrung out, to tell you the truth.'

'Really?' said Heather thoughtfully. 'I saw you and Roxanne, earlier. Another row?'

'Kind of,' said Candice. An image of Roxanne's haggard face passed through her mind and she winced. 'But it . . . it doesn't matter.' She looked at Heather's wide, friendly smile and suddenly felt uplifted; warmed and encouraged. 'It really doesn't matter.'

Chapter Sixteen

The next morning, as Candice got ready for work, there was no sign of Heather. She smiled to herself as she made a cup of coffee in the kitchen. They had sat in a restaurant until late the night before, eating pasta and drinking mellow red wine and talking. There was an ease between the two of them; a natural, understated affection, which Candice treasured. They seemed to see life in exactly the same way; to hold the same values; to share the same sense of humour.

Heather had drunk more than Candice and, as their bill had arrived, had almost tearfully thanked Candice once again for everything she'd done for her. Then she'd rolled her eyes and laughed at herself. 'Look at me, completely out of it as usual. Candice, if I don't wake up in the morning, just leave me. I'll need the day off to recover!' She'd taken a sip of coffee and looked at Candice over her cup, then added, 'And good luck with your meeting with Justin. Let's hope it's something nice!'

It had been a healing evening, thought Candice. After the grief and drama of Ralph's funeral, it had been an evening to absorb the events of the day, to take stock and move on. She still felt raw from her parting with Roxanne; still felt a disbelieving shock whenever she thought about her and Ralph. But this morning she felt a new strength; an ability to look ahead and focus on other things in her life. Her friendship with Heather; her love of her job.

Candice finished her coffee, tiptoed to Heather's room and listened. There was no sound. She grinned, picked up her bag and left the flat. It was a crisp morning, with the feel of summer in the air, and she walked along briskly, wondering what Justin wanted to see her about.

As she arrived at work she saw that his office was empty. She went to her desk and immediately switched on her computer – then, validated, turned round to chat with whoever was about. But Kelly was the only one in the office, and she was sitting at her desk, furiously typing, not looking up for a second.

'I saw you at the funeral,' said Candice in friendly tones. 'It seemed very moving.' Kelly looked up and gave Candice a strange look.

'Yeah,' she said, and carried on typing.

'I didn't make it to the actual service,' continued Candice. 'But I saw you going in with Heather.'

To her surprise, a pink tinge spread over Kelly's face.

'Yeah,' she said again. She typed for a bit longer, then abruptly stood up. 'I've just got to . . .' she said, bit her lip and walked out of the room. Candice watched her go in puzzlement, then turned back to her computer. She tapped idly, then turned round again. There wasn't any point beginning work if she was seeing Justin at nine-thirty.

Again, she wondered what he wanted to see her about. Once upon a time she might have thought he was going to ask her advice on something, or at least her opinion. But since he'd taken over the running of the magazine, Justin had become more and more his own master, and behaved as though Candice – along with all the rest of the staff – was no longer his equal.

She would have resented it, had she not found it so ridiculous.

At nine twenty-five, Justin appeared at the door of the editorial office, still in conversation with someone in the corridor.

'OK, Charles,' he was saying. 'Thanks for that. Much appreciated. Yes, I'll keep you posted.' He lifted his hand in farewell, then came into the room and met Candice's eye.

'Right,' he said. 'In you come.'

He ushered Candice to a chair, then closed the door behind her and snapped the window blind shut. Slowly he walked round his desk, sat down and looked at her.

'So, Candice,' he said eventually, stopped, and gave a sigh. 'Tell me, how long have you been working for the *Londoner*?'

'You know how long!' said Candice. 'Five years.'

'That's right,' said Justin. 'Five years. And you've been happy here? You've been well treated?'

'Yes!' said Candice. 'Of course I have. Justin—'

'So you'd think, wouldn't you, that in all that time, a degree of . . . trust would have built up. You'd think that a satisfied employee would have no need to resort to . . . dishonesty.' Justin shook his head solemnly and Candice stared at him, half wanting to laugh at his gravitas, trying to work out what he was getting at. Had someone broken into the office? Or been pick-pocketing?

'Justin,' she said calmly. 'What are you talking about?'

'God, Candice, you're making this bloody difficult for me.'

'What?' said Candice impatiently. 'What are you talking about?' Justin stared at her as though in disbelief, then sighed.

'I'm talking about expenses, Candice. I'm talking about claiming false expenses.'

'Really?' said Candice. 'Who's been doing that?'

'You have!'

The words seemed to hit Candice in the face like a slap.

'What?' she said, and heard herself give an incongruous giggle. 'Me?'

'You think it's funny?'

'No! Of course not. It's just . . . ridiculous! Are you serious? You're not serious.'

'Oh, come on!' said Justin. 'Stop this act. You've been caught, Candice.'

'But I haven't done anything!' said Candice, her voice coming out more shrilly than she had intended. 'I don't know what you're talking about!'

'So you don't know about these?' Justin reached into his desk drawer and produced a pile of expense claim forms with receipts attached. He flicked through it and, with a slight lurch, Candice caught a glimpse of her name. 'Haircut at Michaeljohn,' he read from the top form. 'Are you telling me that's a legitimate editorial expense?'

'What?' said Candice, flabbergasted. 'I didn't submit that! I would never submit that!' Justin was turning to the next page. 'A beauty morning at Manor Graves Hotel.' He turned again. 'Lunch for three at the Ritz.'

'That was Sir Derek Cranley and his publicist,' said Candice at once. 'I had to give them lunch to get an interview. They refused to go anywhere else.'

'And Manor Graves Hotel?'

'I've never even been to Manor Graves Hotel!' said Candice, almost laughing. 'And I wouldn't claim something like that! This is a mistake!'

'So you didn't sign this hotel receipt and fill in this claim form.'

'Of course not!' said Candice incredulously. 'Let me see.'

She grabbed the piece of paper, looked at it and felt her stomach flip over. Her own signature stared up at her from a receipt she knew she'd never signed. An expenses claim form was neatly filled in – in what looked exactly like her handwriting. Her hands began to tremble.

'A total of one hundred and ninety-six pounds,' said Justin. 'Not bad, in a month.'

Suddenly a cold feeling came over Candice. Suddenly she remembered her bank statement; the extra money which had seemed to come out of nowhere. The extra money – which she hadn't bothered to question. She looked quickly at the date on the hotel receipt – a Saturday, six weeks ago – and again at the signature. It looked like hers, but it wasn't. It wasn't her signature.

'Perhaps it doesn't seem like a big deal to you,' said Justin. Candice looked up to see him standing by the window, facing her. The light from the window silhouetted his face so she couldn't see his expression, but his voice was grave. 'Fiddling expenses.' He made a careless gesture. 'One of those little crimes that doesn't matter. The truth is, Candice, it does matter.'

'I know it matters!' spat Candice in frustration. 'Don't bloody patronize me! I know it matters. But I didn't do it, OK?'

She took a deep breath, trying to keep calm – but her mind felt like a fish on the deck, thrashing back and forth in panic, trying to work it out.

'So what are these?' Justin pointed to the expense forms.

'Someone else must have filled them in. Forged my signature.'

'And why would they do that?'

'I . . . I don't know. But look, Justin! It isn't my handwriting. It just looks like it!' She flipped quickly through the pages. 'Look at this form compared to . . . this one!' She thrust the pages at Justin but he shook his head.

'You're saying somebody – for a reason we have yet to ascertain – forged your signature.'

'Yes!'

'And you knew nothing about it.'

'No!' said Candice. 'Of course not!'

'Right,' said Justin. He sighed as though disappointed by her reply. 'So when the expenses came through a week ago – expenses you say you knew nothing about – and you found a load of unexplained money in your account, you naturally pointed out the mistake and returned it straight away.'

He looked at her evenly and Candice stared back dumbly, feeling her cheeks flame bright red. Why hadn't she queried the extra money? Why hadn't she been honest? How could she have been so . . . so stupid?

'For God's sake, Candice, you might as well admit it,' said Justin wearily. 'You tried to fleece the company and you got caught.'

'I didn't!' said Candice, feeling a sudden thickness in her throat. 'Justin, you *know* I wouldn't do something like that.'

'To be honest, Candice, I feel at the moment as though I don't know you very well at all,' said Justin.

'What's that supposed to mean?'

'Heather's told me all about your little power trips over her,' said Justin, a sudden hostile note in his voice. 'To be honest, I'm surprised she didn't make an official complaint.'

'What?' said Candice in astonishment. 'Justin, what the hell are you talking about?'

'All innocent again?' said Justin sarcastically. 'Come on, Candice. We even spoke about it the other day. You admit you've been insisting on supervising all

229

Heather's work. Using your power over her to intimidate her.'

'I've been *helping* her!' said Candice in outrage. 'My God! How can you—'

'It probably made you feel pretty big, didn't it, getting a job for Heather?' Justin folded his arms. 'Then she started to make progress, and you resented it.'

'No! Justin—'

'She told me how badly you treated her after she presented her feature idea to me.' Justin's voice harshened. 'You just can't stand the fact that she's got talent, is that it?'

'Of course not!' said Candice, flinching at his voice. 'Justin, you've got it all wrong! It's twisted! It's—'

Candice broke off, and gazed at Justin, trying to marshal her flying thoughts. Nothing was making sense. Nothing was making—

She stopped, as something hit her. The receipt for the Michaeljohn haircut. That was hers. Her own private receipt, from her own pile of papers on the dressing table in her bedroom. Her own bedroom, in her own flat. No-one else could have—

'Oh my God,' she said slowly.

She picked up one of the expense forms, gazed at it again and slowly felt herself grow cold. Now that she looked closely, she could see the hint of another handwriting beneath the veneer of her own. Like a mocking wave, Heather's handwriting was staring up at her. She looked up, feeling sick.

'Where's Heather?' she said in a trembling voice.

'On holiday,' said Justin. 'For two weeks. Didn't she tell you?'

'No,' said Candice. 'No, she didn't.' She took a deep breath, and pushed her hair back off her damp face. 'Justin, I think . . . I think Heather forged these claims.'

'Oh really?' Justin laughed. 'Well, there's a surprise.'

'No.' Candice swallowed. 'No, Justin, really. You have to listen to me—'

'Candice, forget it,' said Justin impatiently. 'You're suspended.'

'What?' Utter shock drained Candice's face of colour.

'The company will carry out an internal investigation, and a disciplinary hearing will be held in due course,' said Justin briskly, as though reading lines from a card. 'In the meantime, until the matter is resolved, you will remain at home on full pay.'

'You . . . you can't be serious.'

'As far as I'm concerned, you're lucky not to be fired on the spot! Candice, what you did is fraud,' said Justin, and raised his chin slightly. 'If I hadn't instituted random spot-checks of the expenses system, it might not even have been picked up. Charles and I had a little chat this morning, and we both feel that this kind of thing has to be cracked down on firmly. In fact, we're going to be using this as an opportunity to—'

'Charles Allsopp.' Candice stared at him in sudden comprehension. 'Oh my God,' she said softly. 'You're doing this to impress bloody Charles Allsopp, aren't you?'

'Don't be stupid,' said Justin angrily, and flushed a deep red. 'This is a company decision based on company policy.'

'You're really doing this to me.' Candice's eyes suddenly smarted with disbelieving, angry tears. 'You're treating me like a criminal, after . . . everything. I mean, we lived together for six months, didn't we? Doesn't that count for *anything*?'

At her words, Justin's head jerked up and he gave her an almost triumphant look.

He's been waiting for me to say that, thought Candice in horrified realization. He's been waiting for me to grovel.

'So you think I should make an exception for you

231

because you used to be my girlfriend,' said Justin. 'You think I might do you a special favour and turn a blind eye. Is that it?'

Candice stared at him, feeling sickened.

'No,' she said, as calmly as she could manage. 'Of course not.' She paused. 'But you could . . . trust me.'

There was silence as the two stared at each other and, for an instant, Candice thought she saw the old Justin looking at her – the Justin who would have believed her; possibly even defended her. Then, as though coming to, he turned and reached into his desk drawer.

'As far as I'm concerned,' he said coldly, 'you've forfeited my trust. And everybody else's. Here.' He looked up and held out a black plastic bin liner. 'Take what you want and go.'

Half an hour later, Candice stood on the pavement outside the glass doors, holding her bin liner and flinching at the curious gazes of passers-by. It was ten o'clock in the morning. For most people the day was just beginning. People were hurrying to their offices; everyone had somewhere to go. Candice swallowed and took another step forward, trying to look as though she was standing here on the pavement with a bin bag on purpose. But she could feel her calm face slipping; could feel raw emotion threatening to escape. She had never felt so vulnerable; so frighteningly alone.

As she'd come back into the editorial office, she'd managed to maintain a modicum of dignity. She'd managed to hold her head up high and – above all – had refused to look guilty. But it had been difficult. Everyone obviously knew what had happened. She could see heads looking up at her, then quickly looking away; faces agog with curiosity; with relief that it wasn't them. With a new member of the Allsopp family in charge of the company, the future was uncertain

232

for everybody. At one point she'd caught Alicia's eye and saw a genuine flash of sympathy before Alicia, too, looked away. Candice didn't blame her. No-one could afford to take any chances.

She'd shaken the bin bag open with trembling fingers, sickened by its slithery touch. She had never felt so sordid; so humiliated. Around the room, everyone was working silently at their computers, which meant they were all listening. Almost unable to believe she was doing it, Candice had opened her top desk drawer and looked at its familiar contents. Notebooks, pens, old disks, a box of raspberry tea-bags.

'Don't take any disks,' Justin had said, passing by. 'And don't touch the computer. We don't want any company information walking out with you.'

'Just leave me alone!' Candice had snapped savagely, tears coming to her eyes. 'I'm not going to *steal* anything.'

Now, standing outside on the hard pavement, a hotness rose to her eyes again. They all believed she was a thief. And why shouldn't they? The evidence was convincing enough. Candice closed her eyes. She still felt dizzy at the idea that Heather had fabricated evidence about her. That Heather had, all the time, been plotting behind her back. Her mind scurried backwards and forwards, trying to think logically; trying to work it all out. But she could not think straight while she was fighting tears; while her face was flushed and her throat blocked by something hard.

'All right, love?' said a man in a denim jacket, and Candice's head jerked up.

'Yes thanks,' she muttered, and felt a small tear escape onto her cheek. Before he could say anything else she began walking along the pavement, not knowing where she was going, her mind skittering wildly about. The bin liner banged against her legs, the plastic was slippery in her grasp; she imagined that

233

everyone she passed looked at it with a knowing glance. In a shop window she glanced at her reflection and was shocked at the sight. Her face was white, and busy with suppressed tears. Her suit was already crumpled; her hair had escaped from its smooth fastening. She had to get home, she thought frantically. She would take off her suit, take a bath, hide away mindlessly like a small animal in a hole until she was feeling able to emerge.

At the corner she reached a telephone box. She pulled open the heavy door and slipped inside. The interior was cool and quiet; a temporary haven. Maggie, she thought frantically, picking up the receiver. Or Roxanne. They would help her. One of them would help her. Roxanne or Maggie. She reached to dial, then stopped.

Not Roxanne. Not after the way they'd parted at Ralph's funeral. And not Maggie. Not after the things she'd said to her; not after that awful phone call.

A cold feeling ran down Candice's spine and she leaned against the cool glass of the kiosk. She couldn't call either of them. She'd lost them both. Somehow she'd lost her two closest friends in the world.

Suddenly a banging on the glass of the telephone box jolted her, and she opened her eyes in shock.

'Are you making a call?' shouted a woman holding a toddler by the hand.

'No,' said Candice dazedly. 'No, I'm not.'

She stepped out of the telephone box onto the street, shifted her bin liner to the other hand and looked around confusedly, as though resurfacing from a tunnel. Then she began to walk again in a haze of misery, barely aware of where she was going.

As Roxanne came up the stairs, holding a loaf of bread and a newspaper, she heard the telephone ringing inside her flat. Let it ring, she thought. Let it ring.

There was no-one she wanted to hear from. Slowly she reached for her key, inserted it into the lock of the front door and opened it. She closed the door behind her, put down the loaf of bread and the newspaper, and stared balefully at the phone, still ringing.

'You don't bloody give up, do you?' she said, and reached for the receiver. 'Yes?'

'Am I speaking to Miss Roxanne Miller?' said a strange male voice.

'Yes,' said Roxanne. 'Yes, you are.'

'Good,' said the voice. 'Let me introduce myself. My name is Neil Cooper and I represent the firm of Strawson and Co.'

'I don't have a car,' said Roxanne. 'I don't need car insurance. And I don't have any windows.'

Neil Cooper gave a nervous laugh. 'Miss Miller, I should explain. I am a lawyer. I'm telephoning you in connection with the estate of Ralph Allsopp.'

'Oh,' said Roxanne. She stared at the wall and blinked furiously. Hearing his name unexpectedly on other people's lips still took her by surprise; still sent shock-waves through her body.

'Perhaps I could ask you to come into the office?' the man was saying, and Roxanne's mind snapped into focus. Ralph Allsopp. The estate of Ralph Allsopp.

'Oh God,' she said, and tears began to run freely down her face. 'He's gone and left something to me, hasn't he? The stupid, sentimental bastard. And you're going to give it to me.'

'If we could just arrange a meeting . . .'

'Is it his watch? Or that crappy ancient typewriter.' Roxanne gave a half-laugh in spite of herself. 'That stupid bloody Remington.'

'Shall we say half-past four on Thursday?' the lawyer said, and Roxanne exhaled sharply.

'Look,' she said. 'I don't know if you're aware, but Ralph and I weren't exactly . . .' She paused. 'I'd rather stay out of the picture. Can't you just send whatever it is to me? I'll pay the postage.'

There was silence down the line, then the lawyer said, more firmly, 'Half-past four. I'll expect you.'

Candice became aware that her steps were, unconsciously, taking her towards home. As she turned into her street she stopped at the sight of a chugging taxi outside her house. She stood still, staring at it, her mind ticking over – then stiffened as Heather appeared, coming out of the front door. She was wearing jeans and a coat and carrying a suitcase. Her blond hair was just as bouncy as ever, her eyes just as wide and innocent – and as Candice stared at her she felt herself falter in confusion.

Was she really accusing Heather – this cheery, warmhearted friend – of deliberately setting her up? Logically, the facts drew her to that conclusion. But as she gazed at Heather talking pleasantly to the taxi driver, everything in her resisted it. Could there not be some other plausible explanation? she thought frantically. Some other factor she knew nothing about?

As she stood transfixed, Heather turned as though aware of Candice's gaze, and gave a slight start of surprise. For a few moments the two girls stared at each other silently. Heather's gaze ran over Candice, taking in the bin bag; her flustered face, her bloodshot eyes.

'Heather.' Candice's voice sounded hoarse to her own ears. 'Heather, I need to talk to you.'

'Oh yes?' said Heather calmly.

'I've just been . . .' She paused, barely able to say the words aloud. 'I've just been suspended from work.'

'Really?' said Heather. 'Shame.' She smiled at Candice, then turned and got into the taxi.

Candice stared at her and felt her heart begin to pound.

'No,' she said. 'No.' She began to run along the pave-

236

ment, her breath coming quickly, her bin bag bouncing along awkwardly behind her. 'Heather, I . . . I don't understand.' She reached the taxi door just as Heather was reaching to close it, and grabbed hold of it.

'Let go!' snapped Heather.

'I don't understand,' said Candice breathlessly. 'I thought we were friends.'

'Did you?' said Heather. 'That's funny. My father thought your dad was his friend, too.'

Candice's heart stopped. She stared at Heather and felt her face suffuse with colour. Her grip on the door weakened and she licked her lips.

'When . . . when did you find out?' Her voice was strangled; something like cotton wool seemed to be blocking her airway.

'I didn't have to find out,' said Heather scathingly. 'I knew who you were all along. As soon as I saw you in that bar.' Her voice harshened. 'My whole family knows who you are, Candice Brewin.'

Candice stared at Heather speechlessly. Her legs were trembling; she felt almost dizzy with shock.

'And now you know how I felt,' said Heather. 'Now you know what it was like for me. Having everything taken away, with no warning.' She gave a tiny, satisfied smile and her gaze ran again over Candice's dishevelled appearance. 'So – are you enjoying it? Do you think it's fun, losing everything overnight?'

'I trusted you,' said Candice numbly. 'You were my friend.'

'And I was fourteen years old!' spat Heather with a sudden viciousness. 'We lost everything. Jesus, Candice! Did you really think we could be friends, after what your father did to my family?'

'But I tried to make amends!' said Candice. 'I tried to make it up to you!' Heather shook her head, and wrenched the taxi door out of Candice's grasp. 'Heather, listen!' said Candice in panic. 'Don't you

237

understand?' She leaned forward, almost eagerly. 'I was trying to make it up to you! I was trying to help you!'

'Yes, well,' said Heather coldly. 'Maybe you didn't try hard enough.'

She gave Candice one final look, then slammed the door.

'Heather!' said Candice through the open window, her heart thumping. 'Heather, wait! Please. I need my job back.' Her voice rose in desperation. 'You have to help me! Please, Heather!'

But Heather didn't even turn round. A moment later the taxi zoomed away up the street.

Candice watched it go in disbelief, then sank shakily down onto the pavement, the bin bag still clutched in her hand. A couple passing by with their dog looked at her curiously, but she didn't react. She was oblivious of the outside world, oblivious of everything except her own thudding shock.

Chapter Seventeen

There was a sound behind her and Candice looked up. Ed was standing at the door of the house, gazing at her, for once without any glint of amusement in his eye. He looked serious, almost stern.

'I saw her getting all her stuff together,' he said. 'I tried to call you at work, but they wouldn't put me through.' He took a couple of steps towards her, and looked at the bin liner lying in a crumpled heap on the ground. 'Does that mean what I think it does?'

'I've been . . . suspended,' said Candice, barely able to manage the words. 'They think I'm a thief.'

'So – what went wrong?'

'I don't know,' said Candice, rubbing her face wearily. 'I don't know what went wrong. You tell me. I just . . . All I wanted, all along, was to do the right thing. You know?' She looked up at him. 'I just wanted to . . . do a good deed. And what happens?' Her voice began to thicken dangerously. 'I lose my job, I lose my friends . . . I've lost everything, Ed. Everything.'

Two tears spilled onto her cheeks, and she wiped them away with the sleeve of her jacket. Ed looked at her consideringly for a moment.

'It's not so bad,' he said. 'You haven't lost your looks. If that's of any interest to you.' Candice stared at him, then gave a shaky giggle. 'And you haven't lost—' He broke off.

'What?'

'You haven't lost me,' said Ed, looking straight at her. 'Again – if that's of any interest to you.'

There was a taut silence.

'I . . .' Candice swallowed. 'Thanks.'

'Come on.' Ed held out his hand. 'Let's get you inside.'

'Thanks,' whispered Candice, and took his hand gratefully. 'Thanks, Ed.'

They trudged up the stairs in silence. As she arrived at the front door of her flat Candice hesitated, then pushed it open. Immediately she had a feeling of emptiness. Heather's coat was gone from the stand in the hall; her message pad had disappeared from the little phone table; her bedroom door was ajar and the wardrobe visibly empty.

'Is everything still there?' said Ed behind her. 'If she's stolen anything we can call the police.'

Candice walked a few steps into the sitting room and looked around.

'I think everything's still here,' she said. 'Everything of mine, anyway.'

'Well, that's something,' said Ed. 'Isn't it?'

Candice didn't reply. She walked over to the mantelpiece and looked silently at the photograph of herself, her mother and her father. Smiling into the sun, innocently happy, before any of it happened. Her breath began to come more quickly; something hot seemed to rise through her, burning her throat, her face, her eyes.

'I feel so . . . stupid,' she said. 'I feel so completely stupid.' Tears of humiliation began to run down her cheeks and she buried her face in her hands. 'I believed every bloody thing she said. But she was lying. Everything she said was . . . lies.'

Ed leaned against the door frame, frowning.

'So – what – she had it in for you?'

'She had it in for me all along.' Candice looked up and wiped her eyes. 'It's a . . . it's a long story.'

'And you had no idea.'

'I thought she liked me. I thought we were best friends. She told me what I wanted to hear, and I . . .' A fresh wave of humiliation passed through Candice. 'And I fell for it.'

'Come on, Candice,' said Ed. 'You can't just blame yourself. She fooled everyone. Face it, she was good.'

'You weren't fooled by her though, were you?' retorted Candice, looking up with a tearstained face. 'You told me you thought she was mad.'

'I thought she was a bit weird,' said Ed, shrugging. 'I didn't realize she was a fucking psycho.'

There was silence. Candice turned away from the mantelpiece and took a few steps towards the sofa. But as she reached it she stopped, without sitting down. The sofa no longer seemed welcoming. It no longer seemed hers. Everything in the flat suddenly seemed tainted.

'She must have been plotting all along,' she said, and began to pick distractedly at the fabric of the sofa. 'From the moment she walked in the door with all those flowers. Pretending to be so grateful.' Candice closed her eyes, feeling a sharp pain run up her body. 'Always so sweet and grateful. Always so . . .' She swallowed hard. 'In the evenings, we used to sit on this sofa together watching the telly. Doing each other's nails. I'd be thinking what a great friend she was. I'd be thinking I'd found a soulmate. And what was Heather thinking?' Candice opened her eyes and looked bleakly at Ed. 'What was she really thinking?'

'Candice—'

'She was sitting there, hating me, wasn't she? Wondering what she could do to hurt me.' Fresh tears began to fall down Candice's face. 'How could I have been so *stupid*? I did all her bloody work for her, she never paid me a penny rent . . . and I kept thinking I still owed her! I kept feeling guilty about her. Guilty!' Candice wiped her streaming nose. 'You know what she told them at work? She said I was bullying her.'

'And they believed her?' said Ed incredulously.

'Justin believed her.'

'Well,' said Ed. 'That figures.'

'I tried to tell him,' said Candice, her voice rising in distress. 'I tried to explain. But he wouldn't believe me. He just looked at me as though I was a . . . criminal.'

She broke off into a shuddering silence. Outside in the distance, a siren gave a long wail, as though in imitation of her voice, then broke into whoops and faded away.

'You need a stiff drink,' said Ed finally. 'Have you got any drink in the house?'

'Some white wine,' said Candice after a pause. 'In the fridge.'

'White wine? What is it with women and white wine?' Ed shook his head. 'Stay here. I'm going to get you a proper drink.'

Roxanne took a sip of cappuccino and stared blankly out of the café window at a group of lost tourists on the street. She had told herself that today she would spring back into action. She'd had, in all, nearly a month off. Now it was time to get back on the phone, start working again; start leading her former life.

But instead, here she was, sitting in a Covent Garden café, sipping her fourth cappuccino, letting the morning slip past. She felt unable to concentrate on anything constructive; unable to pretend to herself that life was anything like back to normal. Grief was like a grey fog that permeated every move, every thought;

that made everything seem pointless. Why write any more articles? Why make the effort? She felt as if everything she had ever done over the last few years had been in relation to Ralph. Her articles had been written to entertain him, her trips abroad had been to provide anecdotes that would make him laugh; her clothes had been bought because he would like them. She had not realized it at the time, of course. She'd always thought herself completely, ferociously independent. But now he was gone – and the point seemed to have gone out of her life.

She reached in her bag for her cigarettes and, as she did so, her fingers came across the scrap of paper bearing the name of Neil Cooper and an address. Roxanne looked at the paper for a few steady seconds, then thrust it away from her, feeling sick. She had been thrown by the lawyer's call; still felt shaky when she remembered it. In her memory, his voice seemed to have had a patronizing note. A smooth, oh-so-discreet knowingness. A firm like his probably dealt with dead clients' mistresses every day. There was probably a whole bloody department dedicated to them.

Tears stung Roxanne's eyes and she flicked her lighter savagely. Why had Ralph had to tell a fucking *lawyer* about the two of them? Why had he had to tell anyone? She felt exposed; vulnerable at the idea that an entire plushy office was laughing at her. She would walk in and they would smile behind their hands; eye her outfit and hairstyle; suppress a giggle as they asked her to sit down. Or, even worse, stare at her with blatant disapproval.

For they were on Cynthia's side, weren't they? These lawyers were all part of that secure, established life Ralph had enjoyed with his wife. A union that had been legitimized by a marriage certificate, by children, by solid shared property; that had been buttressed by family friends, by distant cousins, by accountants and lawyers. An entire support system, dedicated to propping up and validating the joint entity of Ralph and Cynthia.

And what had she and Ralph had in comparison? Roxanne drew on her cigarette, feeling the acrid smoke burning her lungs. What had she and Ralph had? Mere ephemera. Fleeting experiences, memories, stories. A few days here, a few days there. Furtive embraces; secretly whispered endearments. Nothing public, nothing solid. Six whole years of wishes and whimsy.

A tree falls in the forest, thought Roxanne, staring bleakly out of the window. A man tells a woman he loves her. But if no-one is present to hear it – does he really make a sound? Did it really happen?

She sighed, and stubbed out her cigarette. Forget Neil Cooper, she thought, draining her cappuccino. Forget the meeting on Thursday. Forget. That was all she wanted to do.

Candice sat silently on the sofa, head buried in her hands, her eyes closed and her mind a whirl of images and memories. Heather's innocent smile and gushing words. Heather leaning forward in the candlelight and asking her what meant most to her in the world. Heather squeezing her waist affectionately. And her own pride and delight in her new friend; her idealistic belief that she was atoning for her father's crimes.

The memories made her wince in pain; in mortification. How could she ever have believed that life was that easy; that people were that accepting? How could she have seen things so simplistically? Her attempt to make amends now suddenly seemed laughable; her trust in Heather almost criminally naive.

'I was a fool,' she muttered aloud. 'A gullible, stupid—'

'Stop talking to yourself,' came Ed's voice from above her, and her head jerked up. 'And get that inside you,' he added, holding out a glass of transparent liquid.

'What is it?' she said suspiciously, taking it.

'Grappa. Wonderful stuff. Go on.' He nodded at the glass and she took a gulp, then gasped as the fiery liquid hit her mouth.

'Bloody hell!' she managed, her mouth tingling with pain.

'Like I said.' Ed grinned. 'Wonderful stuff. Go on, have some more.'

Candice braced herself, and took another gulp. As the alcohol descended inside her, a warm glow began to spread through her body, and she found herself smiling up at Ed.

'There's plenty more,' said Ed, replenishing her glass from the bottle in his hand. 'And now,' he added, reaching for the phone, 'before you get too comfortable, you've got a call to make.' He plonked the phone in her lap and grinned at her.

'What?' said Candice, confused.

'Phone Justin. Tell him what Heather said to you – and that she's scarpered. Prove she's a nutcase.' Candice gazed up at him and, gradually, realization descended on her.

'Oh my God,' she said slowly. 'You're right! That changes everything, doesn't it? He'll have to believe me!' She took another gulp of grappa, then picked up the receiver. 'OK. Let's do it.' Briskly she dialled the number and, as she heard the ringing tone, felt a surge of excitement.

'Hello,' she said, as soon as she got through, 'I'd like to speak to Justin Vellis, please.'

'I'll just check for you,' said the receptionist. 'May I say who's calling?'

'Yes,' said Candice. 'It's . . . it's Candice Brewin.'

'Oh yes,' said the receptionist, in tones which might have been scorn or merely indifference. 'I'll just try the line for you.'

As she heard Justin's phone ringing, Candice felt a pang of apprehension. She glanced at Ed, leaning against the arm of the sofa, and he gave her the thumbs-up.

'Justin Vellis.'

'Hi, Justin,' said Candice, winding the telephone cord tightly around her fingers. 'It's Candice.'

'Yes,' said Justin. 'What do you want?'

'Listen, Justin.' Candice tried to speak quickly but calmly. 'I can prove that what I said in your office was true. Heather's admitted she set me up. She's got a vendetta against me. She yelled at me in the street!'

'Oh, really?' said Justin.

'Yes! And now she's cleared out of the flat with all her stuff. She's just . . . disappeared!'

'So what?'

'So, isn't that a bit suspicious?' said Candice. 'Come on, think about it!'

There was a pause, then Justin sighed. 'As I recall, Candice, Heather's gone on holiday. Hardly suspicious.'

'She hasn't gone on holiday!' cried Candice in frustration. 'She's gone for good! And she admitted she'd got me into trouble on purpose.'

'She actually said that she'd forged your handwriting?'

'No,' said Candice after a pause. 'Not exactly in those words. But she said—'

'Candice, I'm afraid I don't have time for this,' interrupted Justin coolly. 'You'll have an opportunity to state your case at the hearing. But please don't telephone me again. I'll be telling reception not to put through your calls.'

'Justin, how can you be so bloody obtuse?' yelled Candice. 'How can you—'

'Goodbye, Candice.' The phone went dead and Candice stared at it in disbelief.

'Let me guess,' said Ed, taking a gulp of grappa. 'He apologized and offered you a pay rise.'

'He doesn't believe me,' said Candice. 'He doesn't bloody well believe me!' Her voice rose in outrage. 'How can he believe her over me? How *can* he?'

She rose to her feet, letting the phone fall to the ground with a crash, and strode to the window. She was shaking with anger, unable to keep still.

'Who the hell does he think he is, anyway?' she said. 'He gets a bit of temporary power, and suddenly he thinks he's running the whole bloody company. He spoke to me as if I was some bloody . . . shopfloor worker, and he was the president of some huge corporation. It's pathetic!'

'Tiny dick, obviously,' said Ed.

'Not tiny,' said Candice, still staring out of the window. 'But fairly meagre.' She turned round, met Ed's eyes, and gave a bursting gasp of laughter. 'God, I can't believe how furious I am.'

'Neither can I,' said Ed in impressed tones. 'Angry Candice. I like it.'

'I feel as though—' She shook her head mutely, smiling tightly as though suppressing more laughter. Then a tear ran quickly down her face.

'So what do I do now?' she said more quietly. She wiped the tear away and exhaled. 'The hearing won't be for another two weeks, apparently. At least. So what do I do in the meantime?' She pushed a hand through her dishevelled hair. 'I can't even get back into the building. They took my security card away.'

There was silence for a few seconds, then Ed put down his glass of grappa and stood up.

'Come on,' he said. 'Let's get out of here. Go to my aunt's house.'

'What?' Candice looked at him uncertainly. 'The house you inherited?'

'Change of scene. You can't stick in this flat all day.'

'But . . . it's miles away, isn't it? Wiltshire or some-where.'

'So what?' said Ed. 'Plenty of time.' He looked at his watch. 'It's only eleven.'

'I don't know.' Candice rubbed her face. 'I'm not sure it's such a great idea.'

'Well, what else are you going to do all day? Sit around and go crazy? Sod that.'

There was a long pause.

'You're right,' said Candice eventually. 'I mean, what else am I going to do?' She looked up at Ed and felt a smile licking across her face; a sudden euphoria at the thought of escaping. 'You're right. Let's go.'

Chapter Eighteen

At midday, Giles knocked on the bedroom door and waited until Maggie sleepily lifted her head.

'Someone to see you,' he said softly. Maggie rubbed her eyes and yawned as he advanced into the room, holding Lucia in his arms. The room was bright with sunshine and she could smell coffee in the air. And she didn't feel tired. She grinned, and stretched her arms high above her head, enjoying the sensation of the cotton sheets against her well-rested limbs. What a wonderful place bed was, she thought happily.

'Oh, I feel good!' she said, and sat up, leaning against a mound of pillows. She gave a huge yawn, and smiled at Giles. 'I feel fantastic. Except I'm bursting with milk . . .'

'I'm not surprised,' said Giles, handing Lucia to her and watching as Maggie unbuttoned her nightshirt. 'That's fourteen hours you've been asleep.'

'Fourteen hours,' said Maggie wonderingly, as Lucia began to feed. 'Fourteen hours! I can't remember the last time I slept for more than . . .' She shook her head. 'And I can't believe I didn't wake up!'

'You've been a noise-free zone,' said Giles. 'I turned all the phones off and took Lucia out for a walk. We only got back a few minutes ago.'

'Did you?' Maggie looked down at Lucia's little face

249

and smiled, with a sudden tenderness. 'Isn't she pretty?'

'She's gorgeous,' said Giles. 'Like her mother.'

He came and sat down on the bed, and watched them both in silence. After a while, Maggie looked up at him.

'And how was she during the night? Did you get much sleep?'

'Not much,' said Giles ruefully. 'She doesn't seem to like that cot much, does she?' His gaze met Maggie's. 'Is that what it's been like, every night?'

'Pretty much,' said Maggie after a pause.

'I don't understand why you never told me.' Giles pushed a hand back through his rumpled hair. 'We could have got help, we could have—'

'I know.' Maggie bit her lip and looked out of the window at the blue sky. 'I just . . . I don't know. I couldn't face admitting how awful it was.' She hesitated. 'You thought I was doing so well, and you thought Lucia was so perfect, and you were so proud of me . . . If I'd told you it was a nightmare . . .'

'I would have said sod the baby, let's send it back,' said Giles promptly and Maggie giggled.

'Thanks for taking her last night,' she said.

'Maggie, don't *thank* me!' said Giles, almost impatiently. 'She's my child too, isn't she? I've got just as much right to curse her at three o'clock in the morning as you have.'

'Bloody baby,' said Maggie, smiling down at her.

'Bloody baby,' echoed Giles. 'Bloody silly Mummy.' He shook his head in mock-disapproval. 'Lying to the health visitor. I don't know. You could get put in prison for that.'

'It wasn't lying,' said Maggie, transferring Lucia to the other breast. 'It was . . .' She thought for a moment. 'It was spin.'

'Good PR, you mean.'

'Exactly,' said Maggie, giving a self-mocking smile. '"Life with my new baby is utter bliss," commented Ms Phillips. "Yes, she is an angel, and no, I have encountered no problems. For I am Supermum."' She stared at Lucia's tiny, sucking face, then looked up seriously at Giles. 'I thought I had to be like your mother. But I'm nothing like your mother.'

'You're not as bossy as my mother,' said Giles, pulling a face. 'She gave me a real earful about my responsibilities. I felt as if I was about ten years old again. She can be pretty fearsome when she wants to, my mum.'

'Good,' said Maggie, grinning.

'Which reminds me,' said Giles. 'Would Madam like breakfast in bed?'

'Madam would *adore* breakfast in bed.'

'And what about Mademoiselle? Shall I take her with me or leave her?'

'You can leave Mademoiselle,' said Maggie, stroking Lucia's head. 'I'm not sure she's quite finished her own breakfast.'

When Giles had gone she lay back comfortably against the pillows, staring out of the window at the fields beyond the garden. From that distance, no mud was visible; no brambles could be seen. A bright sun was beating down and wind was ruffling the long green grass; a small bird fluttered out of one of the hedges. The countryside at its most idyllic. The kind of backdrop she'd imagined for her fantasy rustic picnics.

'What do you think?' she said, looking down at Lucia. 'You like rustic? You like cows and sheep? Or you like cars and shops? Cows and sheep or cars and shops. You choose.'

Lucia looked at her intently for a moment, then screwed up her tiny face in a yawn.

'Exactly,' said Maggie. 'You don't really give a toss, do you?'

'Voilà!' Giles appeared at the door holding a tray on which reposed a glass of orange juice, a cafetière full of steaming coffee, a plate of warm croissants and a pot of Bonne Maman Apricot Conserve. He looked at Maggie silently for a second, then put the tray down on a table.

'You look beautiful,' he said.

'Yeah, right,' said Maggie, flushing slightly.

'You do.' He came towards the bed, plucked Lucia from Maggie's arms and placed her carefully on the floor. He sat down on the bed and stroked Maggie's hair, her shoulder; then, very gently, her breast. 'Any room in that bed for me, do you think?'

Maggie stared back at him and felt her well-rested body respond to his touch. Remembered sensations began to prickle at her skin; her breath began to come slightly more quickly.

'Could be,' she said, and smiled self-consciously.

Slowly Giles leaned forward and kissed her. Maggie closed her eyes in delight and wrapped her arms around his body, losing herself in delicious sensation. Giles's lips found her earlobe, and she gave a little moan of pleasure.

'We could make number two,' came Giles's voice in her ear. 'Wouldn't that be lovely?'

'What?' Maggie stiffened in horror. 'Giles . . .'

'Joke,' said Giles. She pulled away, to see him laughing at her. 'Joke.'

'No!' said Maggie, her heart still thudding. 'That's not a joke! That's not even . . . not even half-funny. It's . . . It's . . .' Suddenly she found herself giggling. 'You're evil.'

'I know,' said Giles, and nuzzled her neck. 'Aren't you glad you married me?'

Ed's car was a navy blue convertible. As he bleeped it open, Candice stared at it in disbelief.

'I didn't know you had a . . . what is this?'

'BMW,' said Ed.

'Wow,' said Candice. 'So how come I've never seen you in it?'

Ed shrugged. 'I don't drive a lot.'

Candice wrinkled her brow.

'So then – why have you got a flash car like this if you never drive?'

'Come on, Candice.' He grinned disarmingly. 'I'm a boy.'

Candice laughed in spite of herself, and got into the car. Immediately she felt ridiculously glamorous. As they drove off, her hair began to blow about her face. The sun glinted on the windscreen and the shiny chrome of the wing mirrors. They stopped at a traffic light and Candice watched a girl of about her own age cross the road. She was dressed smartly and obviously hurrying back to the office. Back towards a secure job; a trusting environment; a secure future.

At the beginning of the day she'd been just like that girl, thought Candice. Oblivious and trusting, completely unaware of what was about to happen. And in a matter of hours it had all changed.

'I'll never be the same again,' she said, without quite meaning to. Ed swivelled in his seat and looked at her.

'What do you mean?'

'I'll never be so . . . trusting. I was a stupid, gullible fool.' She rested her elbow on the door, supporting her head with her hand. 'What a bloody disaster. What a bloody . . .'

'Candice, don't get like that,' said Ed. Candice turned her head to look at him.

'What?' she said sarcastically. 'Don't blame myself?'

Ed shrugged. 'Don't tear yourself to bits. What you did, helping Heather – it was a . . . a generous, positive thing to do. If Heather'd been a different person, maybe it would have worked out fine.'

'I suppose so,' muttered Candice after a pause.

253

'It wasn't your fault she was a nutter, was it? She didn't arrive with a sign round her neck.'

'But I was so bloody . . . idealistic about the whole thing.'

'Of course you were,' said Ed. 'That's what makes you . . . you.'

There was a sudden stillness between them. Candice gazed back into Ed's dark, intelligent eyes and felt a faint tinge in her cheeks. Then, behind them, a horn sounded. Without speaking, Ed put the car into gear and drove off, and Candice sat back in her seat and closed her eyes, her heart thumping.

When she opened her eyes again, they were on the motorway. The sky had clouded over a little and the wind had become too strong to allow talking. Candice struggled up to a sitting position and looked about. There were fields, and sheep, and a familiar country smell. Her legs felt stiff and her face dry from the wind, and she wondered how much further away it was.

As though reading her mind, Ed signalled left and turned off the motorway.

'Are we nearly there?' shouted Candice. He nodded, but said nothing more. They passed through a village and she peered with interest at the cottages and houses, wondering what Ed's house might be like. He had said nothing about it; she didn't know if it was large or small, old or new. Suddenly the car was swinging off the main road up a narrow track. They bumped along for two miles or so, then Ed turned in at a gate. The car crackled down a sloping drive, and Candice gazed ahead of her in disbelief.

They were approaching a low, thatched cottage, turned slightly away from them as though too shy to show its face. The walls were painted a soft apricot; the window frames were turquoise; from inside a window she caught a splash of lilac. Around the corner she could see several brightly painted pots clustering outside the wooden front door.

'I've never seen anything like it,' Candice said in astonishment. 'It's like a fairytale.'

'What?' said Ed. He switched the engine off and looked around with a suppressed gleam. 'Oh yes. Didn't I say? She was a painter, my aunt. Liked a bit of colour.' He opened the car door. 'Come on. Come and see inside.'

The front door opened onto a low hall; a bunch of dried flowers hung from a low beam.

'That's to warn tall bastards,' said Ed. He glanced at Candice, who was peering into the flagstoned kitchen. 'What do you think? You like it?'

'I love it,' said Candice. She took a few steps into the warm red kitchen and ran her hand over the wooden table. 'When you said a house, I imagined . . . I had no idea.'

'I stayed here quite a bit,' said Ed. 'When my parents were splitting up. I used to sit in front of that window, playing with my trains. Sad little git, really.'

'How old were you?' said Candice.

'Ten,' said Ed. 'The next year, I went away to school.'

He turned away, staring out of the window. Somewhere in the house, a clock was still ticking; outside was a still, country silence. Over Ed's shoulder, through the glass, Candice could see a bird pecking anxiously in a pink-painted flowerpot.

'So,' said Ed, turning to face her. 'What do you reckon I'd get for it?'

'You're not going to sell it!' said Candice in horror.

'No,' said Ed, 'I'm going to become a bloody farmer and live in it.'

'You wouldn't have to live in it all the time. You could keep it for—'

'Weekends?' said Ed. 'Drive down every Friday rush

hour to sit and freeze? Give me a break, Candice.'

'Oh well,' said Candice. 'It's your house.' She looked at a framed sampler on the wall. *Absence makes the heart grow fonder.* Next to it was a charcoal drawing of a shell, and below that a child's painting of three fat geese in a field. Looking more closely, Candice saw the name 'Edward Armitage' written in a teacher's hand in the bottom left-hand corner.

'You never told me it was like this,' she said, turning round. 'You never told me it was so . . .' She spread her hands helplessly.

'No,' said Ed. 'Well, you never asked.'

'So what happened to my breakfast,' murmured Maggie, lying in the crook of Giles's arm. Lazily he shifted, and opened one eye.

'You want breakfast, *too*?'

'You bet I do. You don't get off that lightly.' Maggie sat up to allow Giles to move, then flopped back on the pillows and watched as he sat up and reached for his T-shirt. Halfway through putting it on, he stopped.

'I don't believe it!' he whispered. 'Look at this!' Maggie sat up and followed his gaze. Lucia was fast asleep on the carpet, her little hands curled into fists.

'Well, we obviously didn't disturb her,' she said with a giggle.

'How much did that cot cost?' said Giles ruefully. He tiptoed past Lucia, lifted the tray of breakfast off the table and presented it to Maggie.

'Madam.'

'Fresh coffee, please,' she said at once. 'This is lukewarm.'

'The management is devastated,' said Giles. 'Please accept this complimentary glass of orange juice and array of fine croissants with our humblest apologies.'

'Hmmm,' said Maggie, taking a doubtful sip. 'Plus a meal for two at the restaurant of my choice?'

'Absolutely,' agreed Giles. 'It's the least the management can do.'

He took the cafetière and headed out of the room. Maggie sat up, pulled open a croissant and spread it thickly with the amber-coloured conserve. She took a huge bite and then another, savouring the buttery taste, the sweetness of the jam. Simple food had never tasted so delicious. She felt as though her taste buds, along with everything else, had been temporarily dulled and then sprung back to life.

'This is more like it,' said Giles, coming back into the room with fresh coffee. He sat down on the bed, and smiled at Maggie. 'Isn't it?'

'Yes,' said Maggie, and took a gulp of tangy orange juice. Sunlight glinted off the glass as she put it back down on the tray and took another bite of apricot croissant. Warm colours, sweet and light, like heaven in her mouth. She looked out of the window again at the green fields, shining in the sunshine like an English paradise, and felt a momentary pull towards them.

Brambles and weeds, she reminded herself. Mud and manure. Cows and sheep. Or cars and shops and taxis. Bright lights. People.

'I think,' she said casually, 'I might go back to work.' She took a sip of grainy, delicious coffee and looked up at Giles.

'Right,' he said cautiously. 'To your old job? Or . . .'

'My old job,' said Maggie. 'Editor of the *Londoner*. I was good at it, and I miss it.' She took another sip of coffee, feeling pleasurably in command of the situation. 'I can still take a few months more maternity leave, and then we can hire a nanny, and I can go back.'

Giles was silent for a few minutes. Cheerfully, Maggie finished her first croissant and began to spread jam on the second.

'Maggie . . .' he said eventually.

'Yes?' She smiled at him.

'Are you sure about this? It would be hard work.'

'I know. And so is being a full-time mother.'

'And you think we could find a nanny . . . just like that?'

'Thousands of families do,' said Maggie. 'I don't see why we should be any different.'

Giles frowned. 'It would be a very long day. Up on the train, all day at work, back again . . .'

'I know. It would if we carried on living here.' Maggie looked at Giles and her smile broadened. 'And that's why we're going to have to move back to London.'

'What?' Giles stared at her. 'Maggie, you're not serious.'

'Oh yes I am. Lucia agrees, too, don't you, sweetheart? She wants to be a city girl, like me.' Maggie glanced fondly over at Lucia, still fast asleep on the floor.

'Maggie . . .' Giles swallowed. 'Darling, aren't you over-reacting just a tad? All our plans have always been—'

'Your plans,' put in Maggie mildly.

'But with my mother so close, and everything, it seems absolutely crazy to—'

'Your mother agrees with me.' Maggie smiled. 'Your mother, in case you didn't know, is a star.'

There was silence as Giles gazed at her in astonishment. Then, suddenly, he threw his head back and laughed.

'You women! You've been bloody plotting behind my back, haven't you?'

'Maybe.' Maggie smiled wickedly.

'You'll be telling me next you've sent for house details in London.'

'Maybe,' said Maggie after a pause, and Giles guffawed.

'You're unbelievable. And have you spoken to them at work?'

'Not yet,' said Maggie. 'But I'll phone the new chap today. I want to catch up with what's been going on, anyway.'

'And do I have any function in any of this?' said Giles. 'Any role whatsoever?'

'Hmmm.' Maggie looked at him consideringly. 'You could make some more coffee, if you like.'

Candice and Ed sat outside in the sunshine, side by side on the front doorstep, drinking instant coffee out of oddly shaped pottery mugs. Beside them was a plate of elderly digestive biscuits, found in a tin and abandoned after the first bite.

'You know the really stupid thing?' said Candice, watching a squirrel dart across the top of the barn roof. 'I still feel guilty. I still feel guilty towards her.'

'Heather?' said Ed in amazement. 'You're joking. After everything she did?'

'Almost *because* of everything she did. If she could hate me that much . . .' Candice shook her head. 'What does that mean about what my father did to her family? He must have utterly ruined their lives.' She looked soberly at Ed. 'Every time I think about it I feel cold all over.'

There was silence. In the distance a peewit called shrilly and flapped out of a tree.

'Well, I don't know a lot about guilt,' said Ed at last. 'Being a lawyer.' He took a sip of coffee. 'But one thing I do know is that you have nothing to feel bad about. You didn't rip off Heather's family. Your father did.'

'I know. But . . .'

'So. You can feel sorry about it – like you feel sorry about an earthquake. But you can't feel guilty about it. You can't blame yourself.' He looked directly at her. 'It wasn't you, Candice. It wasn't you.'

259

'I know,' said Candice after a pause. 'You're right. In my head, I know you're right. But . . .' She took a sip of coffee and sighed miserably. 'I've got everything wrong, haven't I? It's as if I've been seeing everything upside down.' Carefully she put down her coffee cup and leaned back against the painted door frame. 'I mean, these last few weeks, I was so happy. I really thought Heather and I were . . .'

'In love with each other?'

'Almost that.' Candice gave a shamefaced laugh. 'We just got on so well . . . And it was silly things. Like . . .' She gave a little shrug. 'I don't know. One time she gave me a pen.'

'A pen?' said Ed, grinning.

'Yes,' said Candice defensively. 'A pen.'

'Is that all it takes to win your heart? A pen?' Ed put down his coffee and reached into his pocket.

'No! Don't be—' Candice stopped as Ed produced a scruffy old biro.

'Here you are,' he said, presenting it to her. 'Now do you like me?'

'Don't laugh at me!' said Candice, feeling a flush come to her cheeks.

'I'm not.'

'You are! You think I'm a fool, don't you?' she said, and felt an embarrassed flush suffuse her face. 'You think I'm just a stupid . . .'

'I don't think you're stupid.'

'You despise me.'

'You think I despise you.' Ed looked at her without the glimmer of a smile. 'You really think I despise you, Candice.'

Candice raised her head and looked up into his dark eyes. And as she saw his expression, she felt a sliding sensation, as though the ground had fallen away from beneath her; as though the world had swung into a different focus. She stared silently at Ed, unable to speak;

scarcely able to breathe. A leaf blew into her hair, but she was barely aware of it.

For an endless, unbearable time, neither of them moved. Then, very slowly, Ed leaned towards her, his eyes still pinned on hers. He raised one finger and ran it down her cheek. He touched her chin and then, very gently, the corner of her mouth. Candice gazed back, transfixed by a longing so desperate it was almost fear.

Slowly he leaned closer, touched her earlobe, softly kissed her bare shoulder. His lips met the side of her neck and Candice shuddered, unable to control herself, unable to stop herself wanting more. And then, finally, he bent his head and kissed her, his mouth first gentle, then urgent. They paused, and looked at each other, not speaking; not smiling. As he pulled her, determinedly, to her feet and led her into the house, up the stairs, her legs were as staggery as those of a new-born calf.

She had never made love so slowly; so intensely. The world seemed to have dwindled to Ed's two dark eyes, staring into hers, mirroring her own hunger; her own gradual, unbelieving ecstasy. As she'd come to orgasm, she'd cried out in tears, at the relief of what seemed like a lifetime's tension. Now, sated, she lay in his arms, gazing up at the ceiling, in a room whose details she was only now beginning to notice. Plain white walls; simple blue and white curtains; an old oak bed. A surprising haven of tranquillity after the riot of colour downstairs. Her gaze shifted to the window. In the distance she could see a flock of sheep hurrying down a hill, jostling each other as though afraid of being late.

'Are you asleep?' said Ed after a while. His hand caressed her stomach and she felt a fresh, undeserved delight run through her body.

'No.'

'I've wanted you ever since I've known you.'

There was a pause, then Candice said, 'I know.' Ed's hand moved slowly up to her breast and she felt a renewed *frisson* of self-consciousness; of strangeness at being so close to him.

'Did you . . . want me?' he said.

'I want you now,' said Candice, turning towards him. 'Is that enough?'

'It'll do,' said Ed, and pulled her down to kiss him.

Much later, as the evening sun crested the hills, they wandered downstairs.

'There should be some wine somewhere,' said Ed, going into the kitchen. 'See if you can find some glasses on the dresser.'

Yawning slightly, Candice went into the little adjoining parlour. A pine dresser in the corner was covered with colourful crockery, postcards of paintings and thick, bubbled glasses. As she went towards it, she passed a writing desk, and glanced down as she did so. A handwritten letter was poking out of the tiny drawer, beginning, 'Dear Edward'.

Edward, she thought hazily. Ed. Dear Ed.

Curiosity overwhelmed her. She struggled with herself for a few moments – then glanced back at the door and pulled the letter out a little further.

Dear Edward, she read quickly. *Your aunt was so pleased to see you last week; your visits do her the power of good. The last cheque was much appreciated and so generous. I can hardly believe—*

'Found them?' Ed's voice interrupted Candice, and she hastily stuffed the letter away.

'Yes!' she said, grabbing two glasses off the dresser. 'Here we are.' As Ed entered the room she looked at him anew.

'You must miss your aunt,' she said. 'Did you . . . visit her much?'

262

'A fair bit.' He shrugged. 'She was a bit gaga by the end. Had a nurse living in, and everything.'

'Oh, right,' said Candice casually. 'That must have been pretty expensive.'

A faint colour came to Ed's cheeks.

'The family paid,' he said, and turned away. 'Come on. I've found some wine.'

They sat outside, sipping wine, watching as the sun grew lower and a breeze began to blow. As it got chillier, Candice moved closer to Ed on the wooden bench, and he put an arm round her. The silence was complete, thought Candice. Unlike anything in London. Her mind floated absently for a while, landed on Heather and quickly bounced away again, before the flash of pain could catch light from her thoughts. No point thinking about it, she told herself. No point reliving it all.

'I don't want to go back,' she heard herself saying.

'Then let's not. Let's stay the night,' said Ed.

'Really?'

'It's my house,' said Ed, and his arm tightened around Candice's shoulders. 'We can stay as long as we like.'

Chapter Nineteen

It was three days later that Maggie got round to ringing Charles Allsopp about coming back to work. She waited until Paddy arrived for morning coffee, then handed Lucia to her, together with a load of house details.

'I want to sound businesslike,' she explained. 'No wailing babies in the background.'

'Good idea,' said Paddy cheerfully. 'Are these more London houses?'

'Arrived this morning. I've put red crosses on the ones I think are possibles.'

Maggie waited until Paddy had carried Lucia carefully off to the sitting room, then dialled the number of Allsopp Publications.

'Hello, yes,' she said, as soon as the phone was answered. 'Charles Allsopp, please. It's Maggie Phillips.' Then she beamed in pleasure. 'Yes, I'm fine, thanks, Doreen. Yes, she's fine, too. An absolute poppet.'

Paddy, from inside the sitting room, caught Maggie's eye and gave her an encouraging smile. This, she thought, as she dangled a pink furry octopus in front of Lucia's waving hands, this is what the real Maggie was like. Confident and cheerful and in command. Thriving on a challenge.

'I'll miss you,' she murmured to Lucia, letting the

baby grasp her finger and tug at it. 'I'll miss you. But I think you'll be happier. Don't you?' Paddy reached for one of the estate agents' house details and began to read the description, trying to conceal her shock at the pitiful size of the garden and the enormous figure printed in bold black and white at the top of the page. For that money around here . . . she found herself thinking – then smiled at herself. For that money around here you could buy The Pines. And look what a success that had been.

'Yes, I look forward to it, too, Charles,' she could hear Maggie saying in the kitchen. 'And I'll be in contact with Justin. Oh, could you? Well, thank you. And I look forward to our meeting. Yes. Bye.' She looked up, caught Paddy's eye and gave the thumbs-up. 'He seems really nice!' she hissed. 'He even suggested I have a computer set up at home, so I can . . . Oh, hello, Justin,' she said in a louder voice. 'Just wondering how it's all going?'

'Shall we get you a computer?' said Paddy, smiling down at Lucia. 'Would you like that?' She tickled Lucia's little tummy and watched in pleasure as the baby began to chortle. 'Are you going to be clever like your mummy? Are you going to be—'

'What?' Maggie's voice came ripping out of the kitchen, and both Paddy and Lucia jumped. 'You did *what*?'

'Goodness,' said Paddy. 'I wonder . . .'

'And she didn't have any explanation?' Maggie stood up and began to pace furiously about the kitchen. 'Oh, she did. And you followed that up, did you?' Maggie's voice grew colder. 'I see. And nobody thought to consult me?' There was a pause. 'No, I'm not angry, Justin. I'm livid.' There was another pause. 'Justin, I don't give a fuck about your spot-checks!'

'Goodness!' said Paddy again, and glanced nervously at Lucia.

'Yes, I am challenging your authority!' shouted Maggie. 'To be frank, you don't deserve any!' She thrust the phone down and said angrily, 'Wanker!' Then she picked up the phone again and jabbed in a number.

'Oh dear,' said Paddy faintly. 'I wonder what—'

'Come on,' said Maggie in the kitchen, drumming her nails on the wooden table. 'Come on, answer the phone. Candice, where the hell are you?'

Candice was lying in the garden of the cottage, staring up at the leaves above her. The early summer sun was warm on her face and she could smell the sweet scent of lavender on the breeze. But she was cold inside as thoughts she had tried to put from her mind during the last few days came crowding in.

She had been suspended from work. She had been publicly branded dishonest. And she had ruined the two friendships that meant most to her in the world. A sharp wave of pain went through Candice and she closed her eyes. How long ago was it that the three of them had been sitting in the Manhattan Bar, innocently ordering their cocktails, unaware that the girl in the green waistcoat standing at their table was about to enter their lives and ruin everything? If only she could rewind and play the scene again, thought Candice miserably. If only Heather hadn't been serving that night. If only they'd gone to a different bar. If only . . . A sickening self-reproach went through Candice and she sat up, trying to escape her thoughts, wondering what Ed was doing. He had disappeared mysteriously off that morning, muttering something about a surprise. As long as it wasn't more hideous local cider, she thought, and raised her face, enjoying the warm breeze on her cheeks.

They had been down at the cottage for four days now, but it felt as though it could have been weeks.

They had done little but sleep and eat and make love, and lie on the grass in the early summer sun. Their only forays into the local village had been to buy essentials: food, soap and toothbrushes. Neither had brought any spare clothes – but in the spare room, Ed had found a pile of colourful extra-large T-shirts advertising a screen-printing exhibition, and, for Candice, a wide-brimmed straw hat decorated with a bunch of cherries. They had not spoken to a soul, had not even read a paper. It had been a haven; a place for sanctuary and healing.

But although her body was well rested, thought Candice, her mind was not. She could push the thoughts from her brain, but they only came rushing back in when she wasn't expecting it. Emotions would suddenly hit her, causing pain to spread through her body and tears to start to her eyes. She felt bruised, humiliated; full of shame. And her mind constantly circled around Heather.

Heather Trelawney. Blond hair, grey eyes, snub nose. Warm hands which had held Candice's affectionately; bubbling infectious laughter. Thinking back, Candice felt sickened, almost violated. Had every single moment of their friendship been an act? She could hardly believe it.

'Candice!' Ed's voice interrupted her thoughts and she stood up, shaking out her stiff legs. He was coming towards her, a strange look in his eye. 'Candice,' he said, 'don't get angry – but I've got someone to see you.'

'What?' Candice stared at him. 'What do you mean, someone to see me?' Her gaze shifted over his shoulder but she could see no-one.

'He's in the house,' said Ed. 'Come on.'

'Who is?' said Candice, her voice truculent. Ed turned and looked at her steadily. 'Someone I think you need to speak to,' he said.

267

'Who?' She followed him with hasty legs, stumbling with nerves. 'Who is it? Oh God, I know who it is,' she said at the door, her heart pounding. 'It's Justin, isn't it?'

'No,' said Ed, and pushed the door open.

Candice peered into the gloom and saw a young man of about twenty standing by the dresser in the kitchen. He looked up apprehensively and pushed a hand back through his long fair hair. Candice stared at him in puzzlement. She had never seen him before in her life.

'Candice,' said Ed, 'this is Hamish.'

'Hamish,' said Candice wrinkling her brow. 'You're . . .' She stopped as a memory surfaced in her mind like a bubble. 'Oh my God. You're Heather's ex-boyfriend, aren't you?'

'No, I'm not,' said Hamish, and looked at her with steady grey eyes. 'I'm her brother.'

Roxanne sat in the office of Strawson and Co., sipping tea out of a bone china cup and wishing that her hand wouldn't shake every time she put it down. There was a smooth, thickly carpeted silence about the place; an air of solid opulence and respectability which made her feel flimsy and cheap, even though she was wearing one of the most expensive, sober outfits she possessed. The room she was sitting in was small but grand – full of heavy oak bookcases and a muted atmosphere, as though the very walls themselves were aware of the confidential nature of their contents.

'I'm so glad you decided to come,' said Neil Cooper.

'Yes, well,' said Roxanne shortly. 'Curiosity won in the end.'

'It often does,' said Neil Cooper, and picked up his own cup to take a sip.

He was much younger than Roxanne had expected, and had an earnest, guarded expression on his face, as though he didn't want to disappoint her. As though he didn't want to let down the hopes of the gold-digging mistress. A flash of humiliation passed through Roxanne and she put down her cup.

'Look,' she said, more aggressively than she'd intended. 'Let's just get this over with, shall we? I wasn't expecting anything, so whatever it is, I'll just sign for it and leave.'

'Yes,' said Neil Cooper carefully. 'Well, it's not quite as simple as that. If I can just read to you a codicil which the late Mr Allsopp added to his will shortly before dying . . .'

He reached for a black leather folder, opened it and shuffled some papers together, and Roxanne stared at his calm, professional face in sudden realization.

'Oh God,' she said, in a voice which shook slightly. 'He really has left something to me, hasn't he? Something serious. What is it? Not money.'

'No,' said Neil Cooper, and looked up at her with a tiny smile. 'Not money.'

'We're fine for money,' said Hamish, taking a sip of tea from the mug Ed had made. 'In fact, we're pretty loaded. After my parents split up, my mum remarried this guy Derek. He's . . . well, he's stinking. He gave me my car . . .' He gestured out of the window, to where a new Alfa Romeo was sitting smartly on the gravel next to Ed's BMW. 'He's been really good to us. Both of us.'

'Oh,' said Candice. She rubbed her face, trying to marshal her thoughts; trying to let yet another astonishing fact sink in. She was sitting across the table from Hamish, and every time she looked up at him she could see Heather in his face. Heather's little brother. She hadn't even known Heather had a brother. 'So . . . so why was Heather working as a cocktail waitress?'

'It's the kind of thing she does,' said Hamish. 'She starts something like an art course or a writing course and then she drops out and takes some crummy job so we all feel bad.'

'Oh,' said Candice again. She felt slow and very stupid, as though her brain had overloaded on information.

'I knew she'd gone to live with you,' said Hamish. 'And I thought she might do something stupid. I told her the two of you should just talk about it. You know – work it out. But she wouldn't listen.' He paused, and looked at Candice. 'I really didn't think she'd go as far as . . .' He broke off, and took another sip of tea.

'So . . . she really hated me,' said Candice, managing to keep her voice low and calm.

'Oh God,' said Hamish, exhaling sharply. 'This is . . .' He was silent for a few moments, then looked up. 'Not you,' he said. 'Not you as a person. But . . .'

'But what I represented.'

'You have to understand. What your dad did – it split up our family. My dad was wrecked. He went a bit crazy. And my mum couldn't cope with it, so . . .' Hamish broke off for a few moments. 'And it was easy to blame your dad for everything. But now I look back – I think maybe it would have happened anyway. It wasn't like my parents had such a great marriage.'

'But Heather didn't agree?' said Candice tentatively.

'Heather never saw the whole picture. She was away at school, so she didn't see my parents rowing the whole time. She thought they had the perfect set-up. You know, big house, perfect marriage . . . Then we lost all our money and they split up. And Heather couldn't deal with it. She went a bit . . . screwy.'

'So when she saw me in the Manhattan Bar . . .' Candice rested her head in her hands.

'Candice, let me get this straight,' said Ed, leaning forward. 'Both of you knew about what your dad had done – but neither of you ever mentioned it?'

'Heather behaved as if she had no idea!' said Candice defensively. 'And I didn't say anything to her because I didn't want her to think I was helping her out of pity. I wanted to . . .' She flushed slightly. 'I really wanted to be her friend.'

'I know,' said Hamish. He met Candice's eyes. 'For what it's worth, I think you were probably the best friend she ever had. But of course she wouldn't have seen that.'

There was silence in the kitchen, then Candice said apprehensively, 'Do you know where she is now?'

'No idea,' said Hamish. 'She disappears for weeks. Months. But she'll turn up eventually.'

Candice swallowed. 'Would you . . . would you do me a favour?'

'What?'

'Come and tell Justin, my boss, what Heather's really like? Tell him that she set me up?'

There was a long pause.

'No,' said Hamish at last. 'No, I won't. I love my sister, even if she is a bit—' He broke off. 'I'm not going to go into some office and tell them she's a conniving, crazy bitch. I'm sorry.' He looked at Candice, then pushed his chair back with a scraping sound. 'I have to get going.'

'Yes,' said Candice. 'Well . . . thanks for coming.'

'I hope everything works out,' said Hamish, shrugging slightly.

Ed followed him out, then after a few minutes came back into the kitchen as the Alfa Romeo disappeared up the track. Candice stared at him, then said incredulously, 'How did you find him?'

'Heather told me her family lived in Wiltshire. I looked them up and paid them a visit.' Ed gave a rueful grin. 'To be honest, I was half hoping to find her there, too. Catch her out.'

Candice shook her head. 'Not Heather.'

Ed sat down beside Candice and took her hand.

'But anyway. Now you know.'

'Now I know. Now I know I was harbouring a

psychopath.' Candice smiled at him, then buried her head in her hands. Tears began to ooze out of the corners of her eyes.

'What?' said Ed in alarm. 'Oh, Jesus. I'm sorry. I should have warned you. I shouldn't have just—'

'It's not that.' Candice looked up and wiped her eyes. 'It's what Hamish said about me being a good friend.' She stared straight ahead, her face trembling slightly. 'Roxanne and Maggie were the best friends I ever had. They tried to warn me about Heather. And what did I do?' She took a deep, shuddering breath. 'I got angry with them. I argued with them. I was so . . . *besotted* with Heather, I would rather lose them than hear the truth.'

'You haven't lost them!' said Ed. 'I'm sure you haven't.'

'I said some unforgivable things, Ed. I behaved like a . . .'

'So call them.'

'I tried,' said Candice miserably. 'Maggie put the phone down on me. And Roxanne is furious with me. She thinks I was keeping Ralph's illness a secret from her, or something . . .'

'Well, it's their loss,' said Ed. 'It's their bloody loss.'

'It's not, though, is it?' said Candice, as tears began to roll down her face again. 'It's mine.'

Roxanne stared at Neil Cooper, feeling a whooshing in her head, a pounding in her ears. The walls of the office seemed to be closing in on her; for the first time in her life, she thought she might faint.

'I . . . that can't be right,' she managed. 'It can't be right. There must be . . .'

'To Miss Roxanne Miller,' repeated Neil Cooper deliberately, 'I leave my London house. 15 Abernathy Square, Kensington.' He looked up from his leather folder. 'It's yours. To live in, sell – whatever you prefer.

272

We can provide you with advice on the matter if you like. But obviously there's no hurry to decide. In any case, it will all take a while to go through.'

Roxanne stared back at him, unable to speak; unable to move. Ralph had left her his house. He'd sent a message to her – and to the world – that she had meant something. That she hadn't been a nothing. He'd almost . . . legitimized her.

Something hot and powerful began to rise up inside her body; she felt as though she was going to be sick.

'Would you like another cup of tea?' said Neil Cooper.

'I . . .' Roxanne stopped, and swallowed hard against the lump in her throat. 'I'm sorry,' she gulped, as tears suddenly began to stream down her face. 'Oh God. It's just I never expected . . .'

Sobs were overtaking her; she was powerless to stop them. Furiously she scrabbled for a tissue, trying to control herself, aware of Neil Cooper's politely sympathetic gaze.

'It's just . . .' she managed eventually '. . . a bit of a shock.'

'Of course it is,' said Neil Cooper diplomatically, and hesitated. 'Do you . . . know the property?'

'Only the outside,' said Roxanne, wiping her eyes. 'I know every blasted brick of the outside. But I've never been inside.'

'Well. If you would like to visit it, that can be arranged.'

'I . . . No. I don't think so. Not yet.' Roxanne blew her nose, and watched as Neil Cooper made a note on the pad in front of him.

'What about . . .' she began, then stopped, almost unable to say the words. 'The . . . the family. Do they know?'

'Yes,' said Neil Cooper. 'Yes, they do.'

'Are they . . .' Roxanne broke off, and took a deep breath. 'Do they hate me?'

'Miss Miller,' said Neil Cooper earnestly, 'there's no need for you to concern yourselves with the other members of the Allsopp family. Let me just reassure you that Mr Allsopp's will was very generous to all parties concerned.' He paused, and met her gaze. 'But his bequest to you is between you and him.'

There was a pause, then Roxanne nodded.

'OK,' she said quietly. 'Thanks.'

'If you have any further questions . . .'

'No,' said Roxanne. 'No thanks. I think I'd just like to go and . . . digest it all.' She stood up and met the young man's eyes. 'You've been very kind.'

As they walked to the panelled door, she caught a glimpse of herself in a wall mirror and winced at her bloodshot eyes. It was obvious she'd been crying – but then, that was probably pretty standard for a family law firm, she thought with a half-grin.

Neil Cooper adroitly opened the door for her and stood aside, and Roxanne walked into the hall to see a man in a navy blue overcoat standing at the reception desk.

'I'm sorry,' he was saying. 'I am rather early . . .'

Roxanne stopped in her tracks. Beside her, she was aware of Neil Cooper giving a small start of shock. At the desk, Charles Allsopp looked up, saw Roxanne and froze.

There was an instant of silence, as they stared at each other – then Roxanne turned quickly away, trying to keep calm.

'Well, thank you very much,' she said to Neil Cooper in a voice which trembled with nerves. 'I'll . . . I'll be in touch. Thanks very much.' And without looking him in the eye she began to walk towards the exit.

'Wait.' Charles Allsopp's voice halted her in her tracks. 'Please.'

Roxanne stopped and very slowly turned round, aware that her cheeks were flushed; that her mouth was lipstickless and reddened; that her legs were still shaking. But she didn't care. And suddenly, as she met his gaze, she wasn't nervous. Let him say what he liked. He couldn't touch her.

'Are you Roxanne Miller?'

'I really think,' said Neil Cooper, hurrying forward protectively, 'that for all parties concerned . . .'

'Wait,' said Charles Allsopp, and lifted a hand. 'All I wanted was to introduce myself. That's all.' He hesitated – then slowly held out his hand. 'How do you do. My name's Charles Allsopp.'

'Hello,' said Roxanne after a pause, and cleared her throat. 'I'm Roxanne.'

Charles nodded gravely and Roxanne found herself wondering how much he knew about her; whether Ralph had said anything to his eldest son before he died.

'I hope they're looking after you,' said Charles, glancing towards Neil.

'Oh,' said Roxanne, taken aback. 'Yes. Yes, they are.'

'Good,' said Charles Allsopp, and looked up at an elderly lawyer descending the stairs into the hall. 'Well, I must go,' he said. 'Goodbye.'

'Goodbye,' said Roxanne awkwardly, watching as he walked towards the stairs. 'And . . . and thanks.'

Outside, on the pavement, she leaned against a wall and took a few deep breaths. She felt confused; euphoric; shattered with emotion. Ralph had left her his house: the house she'd spent obsessive hours staring at. It was hers. A house worth a million pounds was hers. The thought made her feel tearful, almost sick.

She hadn't expected Ralph to leave her anything. She hadn't expected Charles Allsopp to behave so politely to her. The world was suddenly being nice to her, and she didn't know how to react.

Roxanne reached inside her bag for her cigarettes, and as she did so, felt again the vibrating motion of her mobile phone. She'd noticed it several times during the meeting; someone was trying to contact her. She hesitated, then took the phone out and half reluctantly put it to her ear.

'Hello?'

'Roxanne! Thank God.' Maggie's voice crackled urgently down the line. 'Listen, have you spoken to Candice recently?'

'No,' said Roxanne. 'Is something wrong?'

'That little twerp Justin has suspended her from work. Some nonsense about expenses.'

'*What?*' exclaimed Roxanne, her mind snapping back into focus.

'And she's disappeared off the face of the earth. No-one knows where she is. She isn't answering her phone . . . she could be dead in a ditch somewhere.'

'Oh my God,' said Roxanne, her heart beginning to thump. 'I had no idea.'

'Hasn't she called you, either? When did you last speak to her?'

'At the funeral,' said Roxanne. She paused. 'To be honest, we didn't part very well.'

'The last time I spoke to her was when she phoned up to apologize,' said Maggie miserably. 'I snapped at her and put the phone down.'

There was a subdued silence.

'Anyway,' said Maggie. 'I'm coming up to London tomorrow. Breakfast?'

'Breakfast,' agreed Roxanne. 'And let me know if you hear anything.' She switched off her phone and began to walk on, her face clouded with sudden worry.

Chapter Twenty

At eleven o'clock the next morning, Maggie and Roxanne stood outside Candice's front door, fruitlessly ringing the bell. After a while, Maggie bent down and peered through the letterbox into the communal hall.

'There's a load of letters piled up on the table,' she reported.

'Addressed to Candice?'

'I can't see. Possibly.' Maggie dropped the letterbox flap, stood up and looked at Roxanne. 'God, I feel shitty.'

'I feel awful,' agreed Roxanne. She sank down onto the front step, and Maggie sat down beside her. 'I gave her such a hard time at Ralph's funeral. I was just . . . oh, I don't know. Beside myself.'

'Of course you were,' said Maggie at once. 'It must have been a terrible time.'

Her voice was sympathetic, but again she felt a *frisson* of shock at the idea of Roxanne and Ralph as lovers. Roxanne had, haltingly, told her everything on the journey from Waterloo to Candice's flat, and for at least five minutes Maggie had been utterly unable to speak. How could two people be friends for such a long time and one of them have a secret as big as that? How could Roxanne have talked about Ralph so normally, without once giving their relationship away?

How could she have let Maggie moan on to her so many times about Ralph's annoying little ways without somehow warning her that they were talking about her lover? Of course it was understandable, of course she hadn't had any choice – but even so, Maggie felt hurt; as though she would never look at Roxanne in quite the same way.

'It was as if I'd finally found someone to blame,' said Roxanne, staring bleakly ahead. 'So I took it all out on her.'

'It's a natural reaction,' said Maggie after a pause. 'You feel grief, you need a scapegoat.'

'Perhaps it is,' said Roxanne. 'But Candice, of all people . . .' She closed her eyes briefly. 'Candice. How could I have blamed Candice?'

'I know,' said Maggie shamefacedly. 'I feel the same. I can't believe I slammed the phone down on her. But I just felt so hurt. Everything seemed so awful . . .' She looked at Roxanne. 'I can't tell you what these last few weeks have been like. I honestly think I lost it for a bit.'

There was a short silence. A car drove by and its occupants looked curiously out of the window at the pair of them.

'I had no idea,' said Roxanne eventually. 'You always looked so . . . in control. It all seemed so perfect.'

'I know,' said Maggie, staring at the pavement. 'I was stupid. I couldn't bear to admit how terrible I felt to anyone. Not to Giles, not to anyone.' She paused in sudden recollection. 'Actually that's not true. I was going to tell you about it once. That night at the Manhattan Bar. But we got interrupted. And then . . .' She gave a rueful smile. 'You know, that night has to be one of the worst in my life. I felt fat, I was exhausted, I was guilty at leaving Lucia . . . Then we all end up arguing with each other. It was . . .' She gave a short laugh. 'It was one to forget.'

'God, I feel terrible.' Roxanne looked miserably at Maggie. 'I should have realized you were depressed. I should have called. Visited.' She bit her lip. 'Some friend I've been. To both of you.'

'Come on,' said Maggie. 'You've had it worse than either of us. Much worse.'

She put an arm round Roxanne's shoulders and squeezed them. For a while they were both silent. A postman arrived, looked at them oddly, then reached past them to post a bundle of letters through the letter-box.

'So, what do we do now?' said Roxanne finally.

'We go and put Justin on the spot,' said Maggie. 'He's not going to get away with this.' She stood up and brushed down her skirt. 'Let's find a taxi.'

'That's a nice suit, by the way,' said Roxanne, looking up at her. Then she frowned. 'In fact, now I come to think of it, you're looking very good all over.' She surveyed Maggie's silk, aubergine-coloured suit; her simple white T-shirt; her gleaming nut-brown hair. 'Have you just had your hair cut?'

'Yes,' said Maggie, a half-smile coming to her face. 'This is a whole new me. New hair, new clothes, new lipstick. I went shopping yesterday afternoon. Spent a bloody fortune, I might add.'

'Good for you,' said Roxanne approvingly. 'That's a fantastic colour on you.'

'I just have to avoid hearing any crying babies,' said Maggie, pulling Roxanne to her feet. 'Or I'll leak milk all over the jacket.'

'Oooh.' Roxanne pulled a face. 'You didn't have to tell me that.'

'The joys of motherhood,' said Maggie cheerfully, and began to stride ahead to the corner. If someone had told her a few weeks ago, she thought, that she'd be *laughing* about breastfeeding, she just wouldn't have believed them. But then, neither would she have believed that she'd be wearing a suit two sizes bigger than normal and feeling good in it.

As they got out of a chugging taxi outside the Allsopp Publications building, Maggie tilted her head back and stared at it. The building where she'd spent most of her working life looked as familiar as ever – and yet different. In just a few weeks it seemed, almost imperceptibly, to have changed.

'This is so strange,' she murmured as Roxanne swiped her security card and pushed open the glass doors to reception. 'I feel as if I've been away for years.'

'Ditto,' muttered Roxanne. 'In fact, I'm surprised my card still works.' She looked at Maggie. 'Ready?'

'Absolutely,' said Maggie. The two grinned at each other, then, side by side, walked into the foyer.

'Maggie!' exclaimed Doreen at the reception desk. 'What a surprise! Don't you look well? But where's the baby?'

'At home,' said Maggie, smiling. 'With my mother-in-law.'

'Oh! What a shame! You should have brought her in! Little pet.' Doreen nudged the girl sitting next to her at the desk – a shy-looking redhead whom Maggie didn't recognize. 'This is Maggie who I was telling you about,' she said to the girl. 'Maggie, this is Julie. Just started on reception yesterday.'

'Hello, Julie,' said Maggie politely. 'Doreen—'

'And is she a good little baby? I bet she's as good as gold.'

'She's . . . she's great,' said Maggie. 'Actually, Doreen, I'm here to see Justin. Could you give him a quick call?'

'I don't think he's in,' said Doreen in surprise. 'He and Mr Allsopp have gone off somewhere together. I'll just check.' She pressed a button and said, 'Hello, Alicia? Doreen here.'

'Damn!' said Maggie, and looked at Roxanne. 'It didn't even occur to me he wouldn't be in.'

'Back in about an hour, apparently,' said Doreen, looking up. 'They've gone to a design presentation.' Maggie stared at her.

'What for? What design presentation?'

'Don't ask me, dear.'

Maggie's jaw tightened and she glanced at Roxanne.

'Nice of them to keep me informed,' she said. 'They're probably redesigning the whole bloody magazine without telling me.'

'So what do we do?' said Roxanne.

'We wait,' said Maggie firmly.

An hour later, Justin was still not back. Maggie and Roxanne sat on leather chairs in the foyer, leafing through old copies of the *Londoner* and looking up every time the door opened. Some of those entering were visitors who gave them polite, interested looks; others were members of staff who came over to greet Maggie warmly and ask where the baby was.

'The next time someone asks me that,' Maggie muttered to Roxanne, as a group of marketing executives walked off to the lifts, 'I'm going to say it's in my briefcase.'

Roxanne didn't answer. She was transfixed by a photograph of Candice she had just come across in an old issue of the *Londoner. Staff writer Candice Brewin investigates the plight of the elderly in London's hospitals,* read the caption. And next to it, Candice's round face stared out, eyebrows slightly raised, as though surprised. Roxanne gazed down at the familiar picture as though for the first time, and felt a pain in her chest at the innocence of Candice's expression. She didn't look like a hard-hitting reporter. She looked like a child.

'Roxanne?' said Maggie curiously. 'Are you OK?'

'We should have seen it coming,' said Roxanne in a trembling voice. She put the magazine down and looked at Maggie. 'We knew that little bitch was up to no good. We should have . . . I don't know.' She rubbed her face. 'Warned Candice, or something.'

'We tried, remember?' said Maggie. 'Candice kept defending her.'

'But we could have done *something*. Tried to protect her, instead of standing back and letting her walk right into it . . .'

'What could we have done?' said Maggie reasonably. 'We didn't know anything. I mean, let's face it, it was nothing more than instinct. We just didn't like the girl.'

There was silence. A couple of businessmen came into the foyer, glanced at Maggie and Roxanne, then headed for the reception desk.

'Where do you think she is?' said Roxanne, and looked up at Maggie with a sober face. 'It's been days. People don't just disappear for days.'

'I . . . I don't know,' said Maggie. 'I'm sure she's fine. She's probably . . . having a holiday or something,' she added unconvincingly.

'We should have been there for her,' said Roxanne in a low, fierce voice. 'I'll never forgive myself for shutting her out. Or you, for that matter.' She looked up at Maggie. 'I should have been there for you when you were feeling down.'

'You weren't to know,' said Maggie awkwardly. 'How could you have known?'

'But that's my point!' said Roxanne urgently. 'We shouldn't keep secrets . . . or . . . or put on acts for each other. None of us should ever feel we have to struggle through on our own.' She gazed at Maggie with blue eyes suddenly glittering with tears. 'Maggie, ring me next time. If it's the middle of the night, or . . . whenever it is, if you're feeling low, ring me. I'll come straight over and take the baby for a walk. Or Giles. Whichever one you want off your hands.' She grinned, and Maggie gave a giggle. 'Please,' said Roxanne seriously. 'Ring me, Maggie. Don't pretend everything's fine when it isn't.'

'I won't,' said Maggie, blinking away her own tears. 'I'll . . . I'll ring you, I promise. Maybe even when things *aren't* bad.' She smiled briefly, then hesitated. 'And next time you have a six-year-long affair with the boss – you tell me too, all right?'

'It's a deal.' Impulsively, Roxanne leaned forward and hugged Maggie tightly. 'I've missed you,' she murmured. 'Come back to London soon.'

'I've missed you too,' said Maggie, her throat blocked with emotion. 'God, I've missed you all. I feel as though—'

'Shit,' said Roxanne, staring over her shoulder. 'Shit. Here they come.'

'What?' Maggie swivelled round and saw Justin walking along the pavement towards the glass doors of the building. He was dressed in a dark green suit, talking enthusiastically and gesturing to Charles Allsopp at his side. 'Oh God!' she said in dismay and turned back to Roxanne. She gave a huge sniff and lifted her hands to her eyes. 'Quickly. Do I look all right? Has my make-up run?'

'A bit,' said Roxanne, leaning forward and quickly wiping away a smudge of eye-liner. 'How about mine?'

'It looks fine,' said Maggie, peering intently at her face. 'All intact.'

'That's waterproof mascara for you,' said Roxanne lightly. 'Copes with sea, sand, strong emotions . . .' She broke off as the glass doors swung open. 'Oh fuck,' she murmured. 'Here they are. What are we going to say?'

'Don't worry,' said Maggie. 'I'll do the talking.' She stood up, smoothing her skirt down, and took a deep breath. 'Right,' she said, glancing nervously at Roxanne. 'Here goes. Justin!' she exclaimed, raising her voice and taking a step forward. 'How are you?'

Justin turned at the sound of Maggie's voice as

though he'd been scalded. As he saw her, his face fell spectacularly – then, just as spectacularly, repositioned itself in an expression of delight.

'Maggie!' he said, opening his arms wide as though to hug her. 'What a charming surprise.'

'I thought I'd just pop in and see how things were going,' said Maggie, smiling back and making no effort to mirror his gesture.

'Great!' said Justin with a forced enthusiasm. 'What a . . . marvellous idea!'

'So this is the famous Maggie Phillips,' said Charles Allsopp, giving her a friendly smile and extending his hand towards her. 'Maggie, I'm Charles Allsopp. Congratulations on the birth of your baby. It must be a very exciting time for you.'

'Thank you,' said Maggie pleasantly. 'And, yes it is.'

'I have to say though, not a day goes by without my being asked when you're coming back to the *Londoner.*'

'Really?' said Maggie, allowing herself a tiny, satisfied glance at Justin's crestfallen face. 'Well, I'm very glad to hear it. And let me tell you, I'm intending to return to work in a matter of weeks.'

'Good!' said Charles Allsopp. 'Glad to hear it.'

'Charles, this is Roxanne Miller,' said Justin in a loud, attention-seeking voice. 'One of our regular freelancers.'

'Miss Miller and I have already met,' said Charles after a tiny pause, and gave Roxanne a friendly little smile. 'Now, may I offer the two of you a cup of tea? A drink?'

'Very kind,' said Maggie in a businesslike manner. 'But I'm afraid this visit isn't social. I'm actually here on an unfortunate matter. The suspension of Candice Brewin. I was a little perturbed to hear about it.'

'Ah,' said Charles Allsopp, and glanced at Justin. 'Justin?'

'It was completely justified,' said Justin defensively. 'The fact is, Candice has been found to be defrauding the company. If you don't think that's a serious offence, Maggie—'

'Of course I do,' said Maggie calmly. 'But I can't believe Candice is capable of doing such a thing.'

'I've got the evidence in my office,' said Justin. 'You can see it with your own eyes if you like!'

'Fine,' said Maggie, and gestured towards the lifts. 'Let's see it.'

As Maggie strode through the door of the editorial office, she felt suddenly proprietorial. Here was her magazine; here was her team. It was almost as though she were coming home.

'Hi, Maggie,' said Alicia casually as she walked past, then double-took. 'Maggie! How are you! Where the hell's that bump gone?'

'Damn,' said Maggie in mock-alarm. 'I knew I was missing something.' There was a giggle round the office. Bright-eyed faces looked up from desks, glanced at Justin and back to Maggie.

'I'm just popping in briefly,' said Maggie, looking around the room. 'Just a quick hello.'

'Well, good to see you,' said Alicia. 'Bring the baby next time!'

'Will do,' said Maggie cheerily, then turned and walked into Justin's office where he, Charles and Roxanne were waiting. She pulled the door shut behind her and for a few moments there was silence.

'I have to say,' said Charles eventually to Maggie, 'I'm a little unclear as to why you're here. The evidence against Candice seems, I'm afraid, fairly strong. And she will, of course, be given a chance at the hearing . . .'

'Hearing!' said Maggie impatiently. 'You don't need a hearing to sort this out!'

285

'Here we are,' said Justin, producing from a drawer a pile of photocopied forms, each headed with Candice's name. His voice sharpened slightly with triumph. 'What do you make of these?'

Maggie ignored him. 'Did you hear her explanation?' she asked Charles.

'Some story about being set up by one of her colleagues?' He wrinkled his brow. 'It seems a little fanciful.'

'Well, frankly, the idea that Candice Brewin is capable of fraud is even more fanciful!' exclaimed Roxanne.

'You're her friend,' said Justin scathingly. 'You would defend her.'

'Correct me if I'm wrong,' retorted Roxanne, 'but you're her ex-boyfriend. You *would* get rid of her.'

'Really?' said Charles in surprise. He frowned, and looked at Justin. 'You didn't tell me that.'

'It's irrelevant!' said Justin, flushing. 'I behaved in a completely fair and impartial way.'

'On the contrary,' said Maggie in her calm, competent voice. 'If you ask me, you behaved in a completely high-handed and irresponsible way. You took the word of Heather Trelawney – a girl who has been at the company for a matter of weeks – over that of Candice, who's worked here for, what, five years? You fell for this ridiculous story of office bullying – did you ever actually see it going on with your own eyes? You took at face value these expenses claims –' Maggie picked one up and dropped it dismissively on the desk. 'But I'm a hundred per cent sure that if they were analysed, they would be shown to be an imitation of Candice's handwriting, not the real thing.' She paused, letting her words sink in. 'I would say, Justin, that not only have you shown a partisan and improper haste to get rid of a talented employee, but that your lack of judgement has cost the company substantially in terms

286

of lost time, disruption and damaged morale.'

There was silence. Roxanne glanced at Charles Allsopp and gave an inward grin. He was staring at Maggie open-mouthed.

'There were witnesses to the bullying,' said Justin, leafing through his papers. 'There was definitely a . . . Yes.' He pulled out a sheet of paper. 'Kelly Jones.' He stood up, stalked to the door and called, 'Kelly? Could you step in here a moment please? Our secretary,' he added, in a lower voice to Charles. 'Heather said she had witnessed some instances of Candice's unpleasant behaviour.'

'Unpleasant behaviour?' said Roxanne. 'Oh, for God's sake, Justin. Can't you wake up and smell the bullshit?'

'Let's just hear what Kelly has to say, shall we?' said Justin coolly.

As the sixteen-year-old girl came into the office, a hot pink blush spread over her face. She stood by the door, her legs wound awkwardly around each other, her gaze steadily fixed on the floor.

'Kelly,' said Justin, adopting a smooth, patronizing tone. 'I'd like to ask you about Candice Brewin – who, as you know, has been suspended from the company – and Heather Trelawney.'

'Yes,' whispered Kelly.

'Did you ever see any unpleasantness between them?'

'Yes,' said Kelly after a pause. 'I did.'

Justin shot a pleased glance around the room.

'Could you tell us a little more?' he said.

'I feel really bad about it now,' added Kelly miserably, twisting her hands together. 'I was going to come and say something before. But I didn't want to . . . you know. Cause trouble.'

'Never mind that,' said Justin kindly. 'What were you going to say?'

'Well, just that . . .' Kelly hesitated. 'Just that Heather hated Candice. Really . . . hated her. And she knew Candice was going to get in trouble, even before it happened. It was expenses, wasn't it?' Kelly looked up nervously. 'I think maybe Heather had something to do with it.'

Roxanne looked at Justin's face, gave a snort of laughter and clamped her hand to her mouth.

'I see,' said Charles Allsopp heavily and looked at Justin. 'I would say, at the very least, this matter could have done with a little further investigation before action. What do you think, Justin?'

There was a short, still silence.

'I . . . I . . . I utterly agree,' said Justin finally, in a furious, stammering voice. 'Obviously there has been some . . . some gross misrepresentation of the facts . . .' He shot an angry look at Kelly. 'Perhaps if Kelly had come to me sooner . . .'

'Don't blame *her*!' said Roxanne. 'It's you who got rid of Candice!'

'I think what we need in this case is a . . . a full and thorough investigation,' said Justin, ignoring her. 'Clearly some errors have been made . . .' he swallowed, 'and clearly some . . . some clarification of the situation is needed. So what I suggest, Charles, is that as soon as Heather gets back—'

'She isn't coming back,' said Kelly.

'What?' said Justin, impatient at the interruption.

'Heather's not coming back.' Kelly twisted her hands even harder. 'She's gone to Australia.'

Everyone stared at her.

'For good?' said Justin, his voice rising in disbelief.

'I don't know,' said Kelly, flushing. 'But she's not coming back here. She . . . she gave me a goodbye present.'

'The sweetheart,' said Roxanne.

Charles Allsopp shook his head disbelievingly.

'This is ludicrous,' he said. 'Utterly—' He stopped himself and nodded at the blushing girl. 'Thank you, Kelly. You can go now.'

As the door closed behind her, he looked at Maggie.

'What we must do, straight away, is contact Candice and arrange a meeting. Could you do that, Maggie? Ask her to come in as soon as possible. Tomorrow, perhaps.'

'I would do,' said Maggie. 'But we don't know where she is.'

'What?' Charles stared at her.

'She's disappeared,' said Maggie soberly. 'She isn't answering the phone, her letters are all piled up in her hallway . . . We're actually rather alarmed.'

'Christ!' said Charles in dismay. 'This is all we need. Has anyone called the police?'

'Not yet,' said Maggie. 'But I think perhaps we should.'

'Jesus God,' said Charles, lifting a hand to his brow. 'What a bloody fiasco.' For a moment or two he was silent. Then he turned to Justin, his face stern. 'Justin, I think the two of us need to have a little talk.'

'Ab-absolutely,' said Justin. 'Good idea.' He reached for his desk planner with a trembling hand. 'Ahm . . . when were you thinking of?'

'I was thinking of now,' said Charles curtly. 'Right now, upstairs in my office.' He turned to the others. 'If you'll excuse me . . .'

'Absolutely,' said Maggie.

'Go right ahead,' said Roxanne, and grinned maliciously at Justin.

When the two of them had left, Roxanne and Maggie sank heavily onto chairs and looked at each other.

'I feel absolutely . . . shattered,' said Maggie. She lifted her hands to her head and began to rub her temples.

'I'm not surprised!' said Roxanne. 'You were fantastic. I've never seen anything like it.'

'Well, I think I made my point,' said Maggie, giving a satisfied smile.

'Made your point? I tell you, after your performance, Charles will be welcoming Candice back with the whole red carpet treatment.' Roxanne stretched out her legs in front of her and kicked off her shoes. 'He'll probably give her a pay rise on the spot. Flowers on her desk every day. E-mails to the whole company, extolling her virtues.' Maggie began to giggle, then stopped.

'If we find her,' she said.

'If we find her,' echoed Roxanne, and looked soberly at Maggie. 'Were you serious about calling the police?'

'I don't know.' Maggie sighed. 'To be honest, I'm not sure the police can actually do anything. They'll probably tell us to mind our own business.'

'So what can we do?' said Roxanne.

'God knows,' said Maggie, and rubbed her face. 'Call her mother?'

'She won't have gone there,' said Roxanne, shaking her head. 'She can't stand her mother.'

'She hasn't got anyone, has she?' said Maggie, sudden tears starting to her eyes. 'Oh shit, I can't bear to think about it. She must have felt so completely alone.' She looked miserably at Roxanne. 'Think about it, Roxanne. She's been let down by us, by Heather . . .'

There was a sound at the door, and she stopped midstream. Outside the glass panel of the door, the new receptionist Julie was peering in anxiously. As Maggie beckoned, she cautiously opened the door.

'Sorry to bother you,' she said, looking from face to face.

'That's OK,' said Maggie, dabbing at her eyes. 'What is it?'

'There's somebody downstairs to see Justin,' said

Julie nervously. 'Doreen wasn't sure if he was in a meeting or not.'

'He is, I'm afraid,' said Maggie.

'And he may be some time,' added Roxanne. 'At least, we hope he will.'

'Right.' Julie paused doubtfully. 'So what should I say to the person?'

'What do you think?' said Maggie, glancing at Roxanne. 'Shall I see them myself?'

'I don't see why you should,' said Roxanne, stretching her arms above her head. 'You're not here to work. You're on maternity leave, damn it.'

'I know,' said Maggie. 'But even so . . . it might be important.'

'You're too conscientious,' said Roxanne. 'Nothing's that important.'

'Maybe you're right,' said Maggie after a pause, then pulled a face. 'Oh, I don't know.' She looked at Julie. 'Do you happen to know what the name was?'

There was a pause as Julie consulted her little piece of paper.

'She's called . . . Candice Brewin.' Julie looked up. 'Apparently she used to work here or something?'

Candice stood by the reception desk, trying desperately to fight the impulse to run out of the door and never return. Her legs were trembling in their brand new tights, her lips were dry, and every time she thought of having to face Justin she felt as if she might vomit. But at the same time, there was a determination inside her like a thin steel rod; a determination which kept her trembling legs pinned to the floor. I have to do this, she told herself yet again. If I want my job back, my integrity back – I have to do this.

That morning at the cottage, she had awoken feeling a strange lightness inside her. A sense of release, almost. For a while she had stared silently up at the ceiling, trying to place this new sensation; trying to work out what had happened.

And then it had hit her. She didn't feel guilty any more.

She didn't feel guilty any more. It was as though she'd been absolved; as though she had been cured. As though a burden that she'd unconsciously been carrying for years had been lifted – and suddenly she was able to stretch her shoulders; to enjoy the sensation of freedom; to move in any way she liked. The guilt she'd been carrying for her father's crimes was gone.

Deliberately she had tested herself by bringing Heather to the forefront of her mind; waiting – amid all the anger and humiliation – for the flash of guilt. That spark of shame that she always felt; the twinge in her stomach as she remembered her father's misdemeanours. It was such an automatic reaction, she had got used to it over the years. But this morning there had been nothing. A new absence inside her. A numbness.

She had lain still and silent, marvelling at her transformation. Now she was able to view Heather with uncluttered eyes; to view the whole relationship between them in a different way. She had owed Heather nothing. Nothing. As Ed shifted beside her in bed, Candice had felt clear-headed and cool.

'Morning,' he'd murmured sleepily and leaned over to kiss her.

'I want my job back,' she'd replied, staring straight at the ceiling. 'I'm not waiting for any hearing. I want my job back, Ed.'

'Good,' he'd said, and kissed her ear. 'Well, go and get it.'

They'd eaten breakfast and packed up the cottage almost silently, as though to chat would be to destroy the mood; the focus. As they'd driven back to London, Candice had sat tensely, her hand gripping the top of the door, staring straight ahead. Ed had taken her home, waited while she changed into the smartest outfit she possessed, then had driven her here. Somehow she'd managed to stride confidently into the foyer and ask for Justin. Somehow she'd got that far.

But now, standing on the marble floor, flinching under Doreen's curious gaze, her confidence was evaporating. What exactly was she going to say to Justin? How was she going to change his mind? She felt suddenly vulnerable beneath her veneer, as though the slightest confrontation would blow away her poise completely. The clear-headedness she'd felt that morning was now clouded; her chest was beginning to heave with a renewed humiliation.

What if Justin wouldn't listen? What if he simply had her ejected from the building? What if he called her a thief again? She had rehearsed her story, had planned exactly what she would say – but now it seemed unconvincing in her own mind. Justin would simply dismiss her explanation and order her to leave. Candice felt her cheeks burn in mortification and she swallowed hard.

'Yes,' said Doreen, looking up. 'It's as I thought. Justin is in a meeting at the moment.'

'Oh,' said Candice in a trembling voice. 'I see.'

'But you've been asked to wait here,' said Doreen coldly. 'Someone will be down presently.'

'What – what for?' said Candice, but Doreen merely raised her eyebrows.

Candice felt her heart pound with fright. Perhaps they were going to charge her. Perhaps they were going to bring the police in. What had Justin said to them? Her face began to burn harder than ever; her breaths were shallow and nervous. She should never have come back, she thought frantically. She should never have come.

At the back of the foyer, there was a ping as the lift

arrived at the ground floor. Candice felt her stomach lurch in panic. She took a deep breath, steeling herself for the worst. Then the lift doors opened, and her face went numb with shock. It couldn't be. She blinked several times, feeling giddy; wondering if she was hallucinating. There, in front of her, was Maggie, coming out of the lift, her hazel eyes looking ahead anxiously. And, behind her, Roxanne, her face taut, almost stern with worry.

They stopped as they saw Candice and there was a tense silence as the three gazed at each other.

'It's you,' whispered Candice at last.

'It's us,' said Roxanne, nodding. 'Isn't it, Maggie?'

Candice stared at her friends' unsmiling faces through a haze of fear. They hadn't forgiven her. They were never going to forgive her.

'I . . . Oh God. I'm so sorry.' Tears began to stream down her face. 'I'm so sorry. I should have listened to you. I was wrong and you were right. Heather was . . .' She swallowed desperately. 'She was a . . .'

'It's OK,' said Maggie. 'It's OK, Candice. Heather's gone.'

'And we're back,' said Roxanne, and started to walk towards Candice with glittering eyes. 'We're back.'

Chapter Twenty-One

The grave was plain and white; almost anonymous-looking amongst the rows in the suburban, functional cemetery. Perhaps it was a little untidier than most – overgrown with grass, its gravel scattered around the plot. But it was the plainly engraved name which differentiated it; which turned it from a meaningless slab of stone into a memorial of a life. She stared at it, chiselled into the stone in capital letters. The name she'd been ashamed of for all her adult life. The name she'd come, over the years, to dread hearing.

Candice clutched her bunch of flowers more tightly, and walked towards her father's grave. She hadn't been to visit it for years. Neither, judging by its state, had her mother. Both of them too consumed by anger, by shame, by denial. Both wanting to look ahead; to forget the past.

But now, staring at the overgrown stone, Candice felt a sense of release. She felt as though, in the last few weeks, she had handed all the blame, all the guilt, back to her father. It was his again, every last drop of it; her shoulders were light again. And in return she was beginning to be able to forgive him. After years of feeling nothing for him but shame and hatred, she was beginning to recall her father in a different light; to remember all those good qualities which she'd almost forgotten. His wit, his warmth. His ability to put people at their ease; to singlehandedly entertain a whole table full of dullards. His generosity; his impulsiveness. His sheer enjoyment of the good things in life.

Gordon Brewin had caused a lot of misery in his life. A lot of pain and a lot of suffering. But he had also given a lot of people a great deal of pleasure. He had brought light and laughter; treats and excitement. And he had given her a magical childhood. For nineteen unsullied years, right up until his death, she had felt loved, secure and happy. Nineteen years of happiness. That was worth something, wasn't it?

With shaky legs, Candice took a step nearer the grave. He hadn't been an evil man, she thought. Only a man with flaws. A happy, dishonest, generous man with too many flaws to count. As she stared at his name, etched in the stone, hot tears came to her eyes and she felt again a childish, unquestioning love for him. She bent down, placed the flowers on his grave and brushed some of the spilled gravel back onto the plot, tidying the edges of the grave. She stood up and stared at it silently for a few moments. Then she turned abruptly and walked away, back to the gates where Ed was waiting for her.

'Where's the other godmother?' said Paddy, bustling up to Maggie in a rustle of blue flowery crêpe. 'She's not going to be late, is she?'

'On her way, I'm sure,' said Maggie calmly. She fastened a final button on Lucia's christening robe and held her up to be admired. 'What do you think?'

'Oh, Maggie!' said Paddy. 'She looks an angel.'

'She does look rather fine, doesn't she?' said Maggie, surveying the frothing trail of silk and lace. 'Roxanne, come in here! See your god-daughter!'

'Let's have a look,' said Roxanne, and sauntered into the room. She was wearing a tightly fitted black and white suit, and a stiff, wide-brimmed hat with a curling ostrich feather. 'Very nice,' she said. 'Very nice indeed. Although I'm not sure about that bonnet affair. Too many ribbons.' Maggie gave a little cough.

'Actually,' she said, 'Paddy very kindly made this bonnet, especially to match the christening robe. And I . . . I rather like the ribbons.'

'All my boys wore that robe when they were christened,' put in Paddy proudly.

'Hmm,' said Roxanne, looking the robe up and down. 'Well, that explains a lot.' She met Maggie's eye and, without meaning to, Maggie gave a snort of laughter.

'Paddy,' she said, 'do you think the caterers have brought napkins, or should we have provided them?'

'Oh dear,' said Paddy, looking up. 'Do you know, I'm not sure. I'll just pop down and check, shall I?'

When she'd left the bedroom, there was silence for a while. Maggie popped Lucia under her baby gym on the floor and sat down at the dressing table to do her make-up.

'Budge up,' said Roxanne presently, and sat down next to her on the wide stool. She watched as Maggie hastily brushed shadow onto her eyelids and stroked mascara onto her lashes, checking her appearance peremptorily after each stage.

'Glad to see you still take your time with your maquillage,' she said.

'Oh absolutely,' said Maggie, reaching for her blusher. 'We mothers enjoy nothing more than spending an hour in front of the mirror.'

'Slow down,' said Roxanne, and reached for a lip pencil. 'I'll do your lips. Properly.' She swivelled Maggie's face towards her and carefully began to outline her mouth in a warm shade of plum. She finished the outline, studied her work, then reached for a lipstick and a lip brush.

'Listen here, Lucia,' she said as she brushed the colour on. 'Your mother needs time to put on her lipstick, OK? So you just give her time. You'll realize why it's important when you're a bit bigger.' She finished, and handed Maggie a tissue. 'Blot.'

Maggie pressed her lips slowly on the tissue, then drew it away from her mouth and looked at it.

'God, I'm going to miss you,' she said. 'I'm really going to . . .' She exhaled sharply and shook her head. 'Cyprus. I mean, *Cyprus*. Couldn't it have been . . . the Isle of Wight?'

Roxanne laughed. 'Can you see me living on the Isle of Wight?'

'Well, I can't see you living in Cyprus!' retorted Maggie. There was a long pause, then she said reluctantly, 'Well – perhaps I can. If I try hard.'

'I'll be back at least every month,' said Roxanne. 'You won't know I'm gone.' Her blue gaze met Maggie's in the mirror. 'And I meant what I said, Maggie. I still stand by it. If you ever feel down, if you're ever depressed – ring me. Whatever time it is.'

'And you'll fly back,' said Maggie, laughing.

'I'll fly back,' said Roxanne. 'That's what you do for family.'

As Ed turned into the drive of The Pines, he gave an impressed whistle.

'So this is the house she's *selling*? What the hell's wrong with it?'

'She wants to live in London again,' said Candice. 'They're going to live in Ralph's house. Roxanne's house. Whatever.' She looked anxiously in the mirror. 'Do I look all right?'

'You look bloody fantastic,' said Ed without turning his head.

'Should I have worn a hat?' She stared at herself. 'I hate hats. They make my head look stupid.'

'No-one wears hats to christenings,' said Ed.

'Yes they do!' As they approached the house, Candice gave a wail. 'Look, there's Roxanne. And she's wearing a hat. I knew I should have worn one.'

'You look like a cherub.' Ed leaned over and kissed her. 'Babyface.'

'I'm not supposed to be the baby! I'm supposed to be the godmother.'

'You look like a godmother, too.' Ed opened his door. 'Come on. I want to meet your friends.'

As they crunched over the gravel, Roxanne turned and beamed at Candice. Then her gaze shifted to Ed and her eyes narrowed appraisingly.

'Jesus Christ,' muttered Ed to Candice. 'She's checking me out with her bloody X-ray vision.'

'Don't be silly! She loves you already.' Candice strode breathlessly towards Roxanne and hugged her. 'You look fantastic!'

'And so do you,' said Roxanne, standing back and holding Candice by the shoulders. 'You look happier than you have for a long time.'

'Well . . . I feel happy,' said Candice, and glanced shyly at Ed. 'Roxanne, this is—'

'This is the famous Ed, I take it.' Roxanne's gaze swivelled and her eyes gleamed dangerously. 'Hello, Ed.'

'Roxanne,' replied Ed. 'Delighted to meet your hat. And you, of course.' Roxanne inclined her head pleasantly and surveyed Ed's face.

'I have to say, I thought you'd be better looking,' she said eventually.

'Yup. Easy mistake to make,' said Ed, unperturbed. 'A lot of people make it.' He nodded confidentially at Roxanne. 'Don't let it worry you.'

There was a short silence, then Roxanne grinned.

'You'll do,' she said. 'You'll do nicely.'

'Hey, godmothers!' came Maggie's voice from the

front door. 'In here! I need to give you this sheet on what your duties are.'

'We have duties?' said Roxanne to Candice, as they walked together across the gravel. 'I thought we just had to be able to pick out silver.'

'And remember birthdays,' said Candice.

'And wave our magic wands,' said Roxanne. 'Lucia Drakeford, you *shall* go to the ball. And here's a pair of Prada shoes to go in.'

The church was thick-walled and freezing, despite the heat of the day outside, and Lucia wailed lustily as the unheated water hit her skin. When the ceremony was over, Candice, Roxanne and Lucia's godfather – an old university friend of Giles – posed together for photographs in the church porch, taking turns to hold her.

'I find this very stressful,' muttered Roxanne to Candice through her smile. 'What if one of us drops her?'

'You won't drop her!' said Candice. 'Anyway, babies bounce.'

'That's what they say,' said Roxanne ominously. 'But what if they forgot to put the indiarubber in this one?' She looked down at Lucia's face and gently touched her cheek. 'Don't forget me,' she whispered, so quietly that not even Candice could hear. 'Don't forget me, little one.'

'OK, that's enough pictures,' called Maggie eventually, and looked around the crowd of milling guests. 'Everybody, there's champagne and food at the house.'

'Well, come on then!' said Roxanne. 'What are we waiting for?'

Back at The Pines, a long trestle table had been laid out on the lawn and covered with food. A pair of ladies from the village were serving champagne and offering canapés, and a Mozart overture was playing from two speakers lodged in trees. Roxanne and Candice collected their drinks, then wandered off, a little way from the main crowd.

'Delicious!' said Candice, taking a sip of icy cold champagne. She closed her eyes and let the warm summer sun beat down on her face, feeling herself expand in happiness. 'Isn't this lovely? Isn't it just . . . perfect?'

'Nearly perfect,' said Roxanne, and gave a mysterious grin. 'There's just one more thing we have to do.' She raised her voice. 'Maggie! Bring your daughter over here!'

As Candice watched in puzzlement, she reached into her chic little bag, produced a miniature of brandy and emptied it into her champagne glass. Then she produced a sugar lump and popped that in, too.

'Champagne cocktail,' she said, and took a sip. 'Perfect.'

'What is it?' Maggie joined them, holding Lucia, her eyes bright and her cheeks flushed with pleasure. 'Didn't it all go well? Wasn't Lucia good?'

'It was beautiful,' said Candice, squeezing her shoulder. 'And Lucia was an angel.'

'But it's not quite over,' said Roxanne. 'There's one more vital ceremony that needs to be performed.' Her voice softened slightly. 'Come here, Lucia.'

As the others looked on in astonishment, Roxanne dipped her finger into the champagne cocktail and wetted Lucia's brow.

'Welcome to the cocktail club,' she said.

For a few moments there was silence. Maggie stared down at her daughter's tiny face, then looked up at the others. She blinked hard a few times, then nodded. Then, without speaking, the three turned and slowly walked back across the grass to the party.

THE END

THE WEDDING GIRL

For Hugo, who arrived in the middle

PROLOGUE

A group of tourists had stopped to gawp at Milly as she stood in her wedding dress on the registry office steps. They clogged up the pavement opposite while Oxford shoppers, accustomed to the yearly influx, stepped round them into the road, not even bothering to complain. A few glanced up towards the steps of the registry office to see what all the fuss was about, and tacitly acknowledged that the young couple on the steps did make a very striking pair.

One or two of the tourists had even brought out cameras, and Milly beamed joyously at them, revelling in their attention; trying to imagine the picture she and Allan made together. Her spiky, white-blond hair was growing hot in the afternoon sun; the hired veil was scratchy against her neck, the nylon lace of her dress felt uncomfortably damp wherever it touched her body. But still she felt light-hearted and full of a euphoric energy. And whenever she glanced up at Allan—at her husband—a new, hot thrill of excitement coursed through her body, obliterating all other sensation.

She had only arrived in Oxford three weeks ago. School had finished in July—and while all her friends had planned trips to Ibiza and Spain and Amsterdam, Milly had been packed off to a secretarial college in Oxford. 'Much more useful than some silly holiday,' her mother had announced firmly. 'And just think what an advantage you'll have over the others when it comes to job-hunting.' But Milly didn't want an advantage over the others. She wanted a suntan and a boyfriend, and beyond that, she didn't really care.

So on the second day of the typing course, she'd slipped off after lunch. She'd found a cheap hairdresser and, with a surge of exhilaration, told him to chop her hair short and bleach it. Then, feeling light and happy, she'd wandered around the dry, sun-drenched streets of Oxford, dipping into cool cloisters and chapels, peering behind stone arches, wondering where she might sunbathe. It was pure coincidence that she'd eventually chosen a patch of lawn in Corpus Christi College; that Rupert's rooms should have been directly opposite; that he and Allan should have decided to spend that afternoon doing nothing but lying on the grass, drinking Pimm's.

She'd watched, surreptitiously, as they sauntered onto the lawn, clinked glasses and lit up cigarettes; gazed harder as one of them took off his shirt to reveal a tanned torso. She'd listened to the snatches of their conversation which wafted through the air towards her and found herself longing to know these debonair, good-looking men. When, suddenly, the older one addressed her, she felt her heart leap with excitement.

'Have you got a light?' His voice was dry, American, amused.

'Yes,' she stuttered, feeling in her pocket. 'Yes, I have.'

'We're terribly lazy, I'm afraid.' The younger man's eyes met hers: shyer; more diffident. 'I've got a lighter; just inside that window.' He pointed to a stone mullioned arch. 'But it's too hot to move.'

'We'll repay you with a glass of Pimm's,' said the American. He'd held out his hand. 'Allan.'

'Rupert.'

She'd lolled on the grass with them for the rest of the afternoon, soaking up the sun and alcohol; flirting and giggling; making them both laugh with her descriptions of her fellow secretaries. At the pit of her stomach was a feeling of anticipation which increased as the afternoon wore on: a sexual frisson heightened by the fact that there were two of them and they were both beautiful. Rupert was lithe and golden like a young lion; his hair a shining blond halo; his teeth gleaming white against his smooth brown face. Allan's face was crinkled and his hair was greying at the temples, but his grey-green eyes made her heart jump when they met hers, and his voice caressed her ears like silk.

When Rupert rolled over onto his back and said to the sky, 'Shall we go for something to eat tonight?' she'd thought he must be asking her out. An immediate, unbelieving joy had coursed through her; simultaneously she'd recognized that she would have preferred it if it had been Allan.

But then Allan rolled over too, and said 'Sure thing.' And then he leaned over and casually kissed Rupert on the mouth.

The strange thing was, after the initial, heart-stopping shock, Milly hadn't really minded. In fact, this way was almost better: this way, she had the pair of them to herself. She'd gone to San Antonio's with them that night and basked in the jealous glances

of two fellow secretaries at another table. The next night they'd
played jazz on an old wind-up gramophone and drunk mint juleps
and taught her how to roll joints. Within a week, they'd become
a regular threesome.

And then Allan had asked her to marry him.

Immediately, without thinking, she'd said yes. He'd laughed,
assuming she was joking, and started on a lengthy explanation of
his plight. He'd spoken of visas, of Home Office officials, of out-
dated systems and discrimination against gays. All the while, he'd
gazed at her entreatingly, as though she still needed to be won
over. But Milly was already won over, was already pulsing with
excitement at the thought of dressing up in a wedding dress, holding a bouquet; doing something more exciting than she'd ever
done in her life. It was only when Allan said, half frowning, 'I can't
believe I'm actually asking someone to break the law for me!' that
she realized quite what was going on. But the tiny qualms which
began to prick her mind were no match for the exhilaration pounding through her as Allan put his arm around her and said quietly
into her ear, 'You're an angel.' Milly had smiled breathlessly back,
and said, 'It's nothing,' and truly meant it.

And now they were married. They'd hurtled through the vows:
Allan in a dry, surprisingly serious voice; Milly quavering on the
brink of giggles. Then they'd signed the register. Allan first, his
hand quick and deft, then Milly, attempting to produce a grown-
up signature for the occasion. And then, almost to Milly's surprise,
it was done, and they were husband and wife. Allan had given Milly
a tiny grin and kissed her again. Her mouth still tingled slightly
from the touch of him; her wedding finger still felt self-conscious
in its gold-plated ring.

'That's enough pictures,' said Allan suddenly. 'We don't want to be too conspicuous.'

'Just a couple more,' said Milly quickly. It had been almost impossible to persuade Allan and Rupert that she should hire a wedding dress for the occasion; now she was wearing it, she wanted to prolong the moment for ever. She moved slightly closer to Allan, clinging to his elbow, feeling the roughness of his suit against her bare arm. A sharp summer breeze had begun to ripple through her hair, tugging at her veil and cooling the back of her neck. An old theatre programme was being blown along the dry empty gutter; on the other side of the street the tourists were starting to melt away.

'Rupert!' called Allan. 'That's enough snapping!'

'Wait!' said Milly desperately. 'What about the confetti!'

'Well, OK,' said Allan indulgently. 'I guess we can't forget Milly's confetti.'

He reached into his pocket and tossed a multicoloured handful into the air. At the same time, a gust of wind caught Milly's veil again, this time ripping it away from the tiny plastic tiara in her hair and sending it spectacularly up into the air like a gauzy plume of smoke. It landed on the pavement, at the feet of a dark-haired boy of about sixteen, who bent and picked it up. He began to look at it carefully, as though examining some strange artefact.

'Hi!' called Milly at once. 'That's mine!' And she began running down the steps towards him, leaving a trail of confetti as she went. 'That's mine,' she repeated clearly as she neared the boy, thinking he might be a foreign student; that he might not understand English.

'Yes,' said the boy, in a dry, well-bred voice. 'I gathered that.'

He held out the veil to her and Milly smiled self-consciously at him, prepared to flirt a little. But the boy's expression didn't change; behind the glint of his round spectacles, she detected a slight teenage scorn. She felt suddenly aggrieved and a little foolish, standing bare-headed, in her ill-fitting nylon wedding dress.

'Thanks,' she said, taking the veil from him. The boy shrugged. 'Any time.'

He watched as she fixed the layers of netting back in place, her hands self-conscious under his gaze. 'Congratulations,' he added.

'What for?' said Milly, without thinking. Then she looked up and blushed. 'Oh yes, of course. Thank you very much.'

'Have a happy marriage,' said the boy in deadpan tones. He nodded at her and before Milly could say anything else, walked off.

'Who was that?' said Allan, appearing suddenly at her side.

'I don't know,' said Milly. 'He wished us a happy marriage.'

'A happy divorce, more like,' said Rupert, who was clutching Allan's hand. Milly looked at him. His face was glowing; he seemed more beautiful than ever before.

'Milly, I'm very grateful to you,' said Allan. 'We both are.'

'There's no need to be,' said Milly. 'Honestly, it was fun!'

'Well, even so. We've bought you a little something.' Allan glanced at Rupert, then reached in his pocket and gave Milly a little box. 'Freshwater pearls,' he explained as she opened it. 'We hope you like them.'

'I love them!' Milly looked from one to the other, eyes shining. 'You shouldn't have!'

'We wanted to,' said Allan seriously. 'To say thank you for being a great friend—and a perfect bride.' He fastened the necklace around Milly's neck, and she flushed with pleasure. 'You look beautiful,' he said softly. 'The most beautiful wife a man could hope for.'

'And now,' said Rupert, 'how about some champagne?'

They spent the rest of that day punting down the Cherwell, drinking vintage champagne and making extravagant toasts to each other. In the following days, Milly spent every spare moment with Rupert and Allan. At the weekends they drove out into the countryside, laying sumptuous picnics out on checked rugs. They visited Blenheim, and Milly insisted on signing the visitors' book, Mr and Mrs Allan Kepinski. When, three weeks later, her time at secretarial college was up, Allan and Rupert reserved a farewell table at the Randolph, made her order three courses and wouldn't let her see the prices.

The next day, Allan took her to the station, helped her stash her luggage on a rack, and dried her tears with a silk handkerchief. He kissed her goodbye, and promised to write and said they would meet in London soon.

Milly never saw him again.

CHAPTER ONE

Ten Years Later

The room was large and airy and overlooked the biscuity streets of Bath, coated in a January icing of snow. It had been refurbished some years back in a traditional manner, with striped wallpaper and a few good Georgian pieces. These, however, were currently lost under the welter of bright clothes, CDs, magazines and make-up piled high on every available surface. In the corner a handsome mahogany wardrobe was almost entirely masked by a huge white cotton dress carrier; on the bureau was a hat box; on the floor by the bed was a suitcase half full of clothes for a warm-weather honeymoon.

Milly, who had come up some time earlier to finish packing, leaned back comfortably in her bedroom chair, glanced at the clock, and took a bite of toffee apple. In her lap was a glossy magazine, open at the problem pages. 'Dear Anne,' the first began. 'I have been keeping a secret from my husband.' Milly rolled her eyes. She didn't even have to look at the advice. It was always the same. Tell the truth. Be honest. Like some sort of secular catechism, to be learned by rote and repeated without thought.

Her eyes flicked to the second problem. 'Dear Anne. I earn much more money than my boyfriend.' Milly crunched disparagingly on her toffee apple. Some problem. She turned over the page to the homestyle section, and peered at an array of expensive waste-paper baskets. She hadn't put a waste-paper basket on her wedding list. Maybe it wasn't too late.

Downstairs, there was a ring at the doorbell, but she didn't move. It couldn't be Simon, not yet; it would be one of the bed and breakfast guests. Idly, Milly raised her eyes from her magazine and looked around her bedroom. It had been hers for twenty-two years, ever since the Havill family had first moved into 1 Bertram Street and she had unsuccessfully petitioned, with a six-year-old's desperation, for it to be painted Barbie pink. Since then, she'd gone away to school, gone away to college, even moved briefly to London—and each time she'd come back again; back to this room. But on Saturday she would be leaving and never coming back. She would be setting up her own home. Starting afresh. As a grown-up, bona fide, married woman.

'Milly?' Her mother's voice interrupted her thoughts, and Milly's head jerked up. 'Simon's here!'

'What?' Milly glanced in the mirror and winced at her dishevelled appearance. 'He can't be.'

'Shall I send him up?' Her mother's head appeared round the door and surveyed the room. 'Milly! You were supposed to be clearing this lot up!'

'Don't let him come up,' said Milly, looking at the toffee apple in her hand. 'Tell him I'm trying my dress on. Say I'll be down in a minute.'

Her mother disappeared, and Milly quickly threw her toffee apple into the bin. She closed her magazine and put it on the floor, then, on second thoughts, kicked it under the bed. Hurriedly she peeled off the denim-blue leggings she'd been wearing and opened her wardrobe. A pair of well-cut black trousers hung to one side, along with a charcoal grey tailored skirt, a chocolate trouser suit and an array of crisp white shirts. On the other side of the wardrobe were all the clothes she wore when she wasn't going to be seeing Simon: tattered jeans, ancient jerseys, tight bright miniskirts. All the clothes she would have to throw out before Saturday.

She put on the black trousers and one of the white shirts, and reached for the cashmere sweater Simon had given her as a Christmas present. She looked at herself severely in the mirror, brushed her hair—now buttery blond and shoulder-length—till it shone, and stepped into a pair of expensive black loafers. She and Simon had often agreed that buying cheap shoes was a false economy; as far as Simon was aware, her entire collection of shoes consisted of the black loafers, a pair of brown boots, and a pair of navy Gucci snaffles which he'd bought for her himself.

Sighing, Milly closed her wardrobe door, stepped over a pile of underwear on the floor, and picked up her bag. She sprayed herself with scent, closed the bedroom door firmly behind her and began to walk down the stairs.

'Milly!' As she passed her mother's bedroom door, a hissed voice drew her attention. 'Come in here!'

Obediently, Milly went into her mother's room. Olivia Havill was standing by the chest of drawers, her jewellery box open.

'Darling,' she said brightly, 'why don't you borrow my pearls for this afternoon?' She held up a double pearl choker with a diamond clasp. 'They'd look lovely against that jumper!'

'Mummy, we're only meeting the vicar,' said Milly. 'It's not that important. I don't need to wear pearls.'

'Of course it's important!' retorted Olivia. 'You must take this seriously, Milly. You only make your marriage vows once!' She paused. 'And besides, all upper-class brides wear pearls.' She held the necklace up to Milly's throat. 'Proper pearls. Not those silly little things.'

'I like my freshwater pearls,' said Milly defensively. 'And I'm not upper class.'

'Darling, you're about to become Mrs Simon Pinnacle.'

'Simon isn't upper class!'

'Don't be silly,' said Olivia crisply. 'Of course he is. His father's a multimillionaire.' Milly rolled her eyes.

'I've got to go,' she said.

'All right.' Olivia put the pearls regretfully back into her jewellery box. 'Have it your own way. And, darling, do remember to ask Canon Lytton about the rose petals.'

'I will,' said Milly. 'See you later.'

She hurried down the stairs and into the hall, grabbing her coat from the hall stand by the door.

'Hi!' she called into the drawing room, and as Simon came out into the hall, glanced hastily at the front page of that day's *Daily Telegraph*, trying to commit as many headlines as possible to memory.

'Milly,' said Simon, grinning at her. 'You look gorgeous.' Milly looked up and smiled.

'So do you.' Simon was dressed for the office, in a dark suit which sat impeccably on his firm, stocky frame, a blue shirt and a purple silk tie. His dark hair sprang up energetically from his wide forehead and he smelt discreetly of aftershave.

'So,' he said, opening the front door and ushering her out into the crisp afternoon air. 'Off we go to learn how to be married.'

'I know,' said Milly. 'Isn't it weird?'

'Complete waste of time,' said Simon. 'What can a crumbling old vicar tell us about being married? He isn't even married himself.'

'Oh well,' said Milly vaguely. 'I suppose it's the rules.'

'He'd better not start patronizing us. That *will* piss me off.'

Milly glanced at Simon. His neck was tense and his eyes fixed determinedly ahead. He reminded her of a young bulldog ready for a scrap.

'I know what I want from marriage,' he said, frowning. 'We both do. We don't need interference from some stranger.'

'We'll just listen and nod,' said Milly. 'And then we'll go.' She felt in her pocket for her gloves. 'Anyway, I already know what he's going to say.'

'What?'

'Be kind to one another and don't sleep around.' Simon thought for a moment.

'I expect I could manage the first part.'

Milly gave him a thump and he laughed, drawing her near and planting a kiss on her shiny hair. As they neared the corner he reached in his pocket and bleeped his car open.

'I could hardly find a parking space,' he said, as he started the engine. 'The streets are so bloody congested.' He frowned. 'Whether this new bill will really achieve anything . . .'

'The environment bill,' said Milly at once.

'That's right,' said Simon. 'Did you read about it today?'

'Oh yes,' said Milly. She cast her mind quickly back to the *Daily Telegraph*. 'Do you think they've got the emphasis quite right?'

And as Simon began to talk, she looked out of the window and nodded occasionally, and wondered idly whether she should buy a third bikini for her honeymoon.

Canon Lytton's drawing room was large, draughty and full of books. Books lined the walls, books covered every surface, and teetered in dusty piles on the floor. In addition, nearly everything in the room that wasn't a book, looked like a book. The teapot was shaped like a book, the firescreen was decorated with books; even the slabs of gingerbread sitting on the tea-tray resembled a set of encyclopaedia volumes.

Canon Lytton himself resembled a sheet of old paper. His thin, powdery skin seemed in danger of tearing at any moment; whenever he laughed or frowned his face creased into a thousand lines. At the moment—as he had been during most of the session—he was frowning. His bushy white eyebrows were knitted together, his eyes narrowed in concentration and his bony hand, clutched around an undrunk cup of tea, was waving dangerously about in the air.

'The secret of a successful marriage,' he was declaiming, 'is trust. Trust is the key. Trust is the rock.'

'Absolutely,' said Milly, as she had at intervals of three minutes for the past hour. She glanced at Simon. He was leaning forward, as though ready to interrupt. But Canon Lytton was not the sort of speaker to brook interruptions. Each time Simon had taken a breath to say something, the clergyman had raised the volume of his voice and turned away, leaving Simon stranded in frustrated but deferential silence. He would have liked to take issue with much of what Canon Lytton was saying, she could tell. As for herself, she hadn't listened to a word.

Her gaze slid idly over to the glass-fronted bookcases to her left. There she was, reflected in the glass. Smart and shiny; grown-up and groomed. She felt pleased with her appearance. Not that Canon Lytton appreciated it. He probably thought it was sinful to spend money on clothes. He would tell her she should have given it to the poor instead.

She shifted her position slightly on the sofa, stifled a yawn, and looked up. To her horror, Canon Lytton was watching her. His eyes narrowed, and he broke off mid-sentence.

'I'm sorry if I'm boring you, my dear,' he said sarcastically. 'Perhaps you are familiar with this quotation already.'

Milly felt her cheeks turn pink.

'No,' she said, 'I'm not. I was just . . . um . . .' She glanced quickly at Simon, who grinned back and gave her a tiny wink. 'I'm just a little tired,' she ended feebly.

'Poor Milly's been frantic over the wedding arrangements,' put in Simon. 'There's a lot to organize. The champagne, the cake . . .'

'Indeed,' said Canon Lytton severely. 'But might I remind you that the point of a wedding is not the champagne, nor the cake; nor is it the presents you will no doubt receive.' His eyes flicked around the room, as though comparing his own dingy things with the shiny, sumptuous gifts piled high for Milly and Simon, and his frown deepened. 'I am grieved,' he continued, stalking over to the window, 'at the casual approach taken by many young couples to the wedding ceremony. The sacrament of marriage should not be viewed as a formality.'

'Of course not,' said Milly.

'It is not simply the preamble to a good party.'

'No,' said Milly.

'As the very words of the service remind us, marriage must not be undertaken carelessly, lightly, or selfishly, but—'

'And it won't be!' Simon's voice broke in impatiently; he leaned forward in his seat. 'Canon Lytton, I know you probably come across people every day who are getting married for the wrong reasons. But that's not us, OK? We love each other and we want to spend the rest of our lives together. And for us, that's a serious matter. The cake and the champagne have got nothing to do with it.'

He broke off and for a moment there was silence. Milly took Simon's hand and squeezed it.

'I see,' said Canon Lytton eventually. 'Well, I'm glad to hear it.' He sat down, took a sip of cold tea and winced. 'I don't mean to lecture you unduly,' he said, putting down his cup. 'But you've no idea how many unsuitable couples I see coming before me to get married. Thoughtless young people who've barely known each other five minutes; silly girls who want an excuse to buy a nice dress . . .'

'I'm sure you do,' said Simon. 'But Milly and I are the real thing. We're going to take it seriously. We're going to get it right. We know each other and we love each other and we're going to be very happy.' He leaned over and kissed Milly gently, then looked up at Canon Lytton, as though daring him to reply.

'Yes,' said Canon Lytton. 'Well. Perhaps I've said enough. You do seem to be on the right track.' He picked up his folder and began to rifle through it. 'There are just a couple of other matters . . .'

'That was beautiful,' whispered Milly to Simon.

'It was true,' he whispered back, and gently touched the corner of her mouth.

'Ah yes,' said Canon Lytton, looking up. 'I should have mentioned this before. As you will be aware, Reverend Harries neglected to read your banns last Sunday.'

'Did he?' said Simon.

'Surely you noticed?' said Canon Lytton looking beadily at Simon. 'I take it you were at morning service?'

'Oh yes,' said Simon after a pause. 'Of course. Now you mention it, I thought something was wrong.'

'He was most apologetic—they always are.' Canon Lytton gave a tetchy sigh. 'But the damage has been done. So you will have to be married by special licence.'

'Oh,' said Milly. 'What does that mean?'

'It means, among other things,' said Canon Lytton, 'that I must ask you to swear an oath.'

'Zounds damnation,' said Milly.

'I'm sorry?' He looked at her in puzzlement.

'Nothing,' she said. 'Carry on.'

'You must swear a solemn oath that all the information you've given me is true,' said Canon Lytton. He held out a Bible to Milly, then passed her a piece of paper. 'Just run your eyes down it, check that it's all correct, then read the oath aloud.'

Milly stared down at the paper for a few seconds, then looked up with a bright smile.

'Absolutely fine,' she said.

'Melissa Grace Havill,' said Simon, reading over her shoulder. 'Spinster.' He pulled a face. 'Spinster!'

'OK!' said Milly sharply. 'Just let me read the oath.'

'That's right,' said Canon Lytton. He beamed at her. 'And then everything will be, as they say, above board.'

By the time they emerged from the vicarage, the air was cold and dusky. Snowflakes were falling again; the street lamps were already on; a row of fairy lights from Christmas twinkled in a window opposite. Milly took a deep breath, shook out her legs, stiff from sitting still for so long, and looked at Simon. But before she could speak, a triumphant voice came ringing from the other side of the street.

'Aha! I just caught you!'

'Mummy!' exclaimed Milly.

'Olivia,' said Simon. 'What a lovely surprise.'

Olivia crossed the street and beamed at them both. Snowflakes were resting lightly on her smartly cut blond hair and on the shoulders of her green cashmere coat. Nearly all of Olivia's clothes were in jewel colours—sapphire blue, ruby red, amethyst purple—accented by shiny gold buckles, gleaming buttons and gilt-trimmed shoes. She had once secretly toyed with the idea of turquoise-tinted contact lenses but had been unable to reassure herself that she wouldn't become the subject of smirks behind her back. And so instead she made the most of her natural blue by pasting a bright gold on her eyelids and visiting a beautician once a month to have her lashes dyed black.

Now her eyes were fixed affectionately on Milly.

'I don't suppose you asked Canon Lytton about the rose petals, did you?' she said.

'Oh!' said Milly. 'No, I forgot.'

'I knew you would!' exclaimed Olivia. 'So I thought I'd better pop round myself.' She smiled at Simon. 'Isn't my little girl a scatterhead?'

'I wouldn't say so,' said Simon in a tight voice.

'Of course you wouldn't! You're in love with her!' Olivia smiled gaily at him and ruffled his hair. In high heels she was very slightly taller than Simon, and he'd noticed—though nobody else had—that since he and Milly had become engaged, Olivia wore high heels more and more frequently.

'I'd better be going,' he said. 'I've got to get back to the office. We're frantic at the moment.'

'Aren't we all!' exclaimed Olivia. 'There are only four days to go, you know! Four days until you walk down that aisle! And I've a thousand things to do!' She looked at Milly. 'What about you, darling? Are you rushing off?'

'Not me,' said Milly. 'I took the afternoon off.'

'Well then, how about walking back into town with me? Perhaps we could have . . .'

'Hot chocolate at Mario's,' finished Milly.

'Exactly.' Olivia smiled almost triumphantly at Simon. 'I can read Milly's mind like an open book!'

'Or an open letter,' said Simon. There was a short, tense pause.

'Right, well,' said Olivia eventually, in clipped tones. 'I won't be long. See you this evening, Simon.' She opened Canon Lytton's gate and began to walk quickly up the path, skidding slightly on the snow.

'You shouldn't have said that,' said Milly to Simon, as soon as she was out of earshot. 'About the letter. She made me promise not to tell you.'

'Well, I'm sorry,' said Simon. 'But she deserves it. What makes her think she's got the right to read a private letter from me to you?' Milly shrugged.

'She did say it was an accident.'

'An accident?' exclaimed Simon. 'Milly, you must be joking. It was addressed to you and it was in your bedroom!'

'Oh well,' said Milly good-naturedly. 'It doesn't really matter.' She gave a sudden giggle. 'It's a good thing you didn't write anything rude about her.'

'Next time I will,' said Simon. He glanced at his watch. 'Look, I've really got to go.'

He took hold of her chilly fingers, kissed them gently one by one, then pulled her towards him. His mouth was soft and warm on hers; as he drew her gradually closer to him, Milly closed her eyes. Then, suddenly he let go of her, and a blast of cold snowy air hit her in the face.

'I must run. See you later.'

'Yes,' said Milly. 'See you then.'

She watched, smiling to herself, as he bleeped open the door of his car, got in and, without pausing, zoomed off down the street. Simon was always in a hurry. Always rushing off to do; to achieve. Like a puppy, he had to be out every day, either doing something constructive or determinedly enjoying himself. He couldn't bear wasting time; didn't understand how Milly could spend a day happily doing nothing, or approach a weekend with no plans made. Sometimes he would join her in a day of drifting indolence, repeating several times that it was nice to have a chance to relax. Then, after a few hours, he would leap up and announce he was going for a run.

The first time she'd ever seen him, in someone else's kitchen, he'd been simultaneously conducting a conversation on his mobile phone, shovelling crisps into his mouth, and bleeping through the news headlines on Teletext. As Milly had poured herself a glass of wine, he'd held his glass out too and, in a gap in his conversation, had grinned at her and said, 'Thanks.'

'The party's happening in the other room,' Milly had pointed out.

'I know,' Simon had said, his eyes back on the Teletext. 'I'll be along in a minute.' And Milly had rolled her eyes and left him to it, not even bothering to ask his name. But later on that evening, when he'd rejoined the party, he'd come up to her, introduced himself charmingly, and apologized for having been so distracted.

'It was just a bit of business news I was particularly interested in,' he'd said.

'Good news or bad news?' Milly had enquired, taking a gulp of wine and realizing that she was rather drunk.

'That depends,' said Simon, 'on who you are.'

'But doesn't everything? Every piece of good news is someone else's bad news. Even . . .' She'd waved her glass vaguely in the air. 'Even world peace. Bad news for arms manufacturers.'

'Yes,' Simon had said slowly. 'I suppose so. I'd never thought of it like that.'

'Well, we can't all be great thinkers,' Milly had said, and had suppressed a desire to giggle.

'Can I get you a drink?' he'd asked.

'Not a drink,' she'd replied. 'But you can light me a cigarette if you like.'

He'd leaned towards her, cradling the flame carefully, and she'd registered that his skin was smooth and tanned, and his fingers strong, and he was wearing an aftershave she liked. Then, as she'd inhaled on the cigarette, his dark brown eyes had locked into hers, and to her surprise a tingle had run down her back, and she'd slowly smiled back at him.

Later on, when the party had turned from bright, stand-up chatter into groups of people sitting on the floor and smoking joints, the discussion had turned to vivisection. Milly, who had happened to see a *Blue Peter* special on vivisection the week before while at home with a cold, had produced more hard facts and informed reasoning than anyone else, and Simon had gazed at her in admiration.

He'd asked her out to dinner a few days later and talked a lot about business and politics. Milly, who knew nothing about either subject, had smiled and nodded and agreed with him; at the end of the evening, just before he kissed her for the first time, Simon had told her she was extraordinarily perceptive and understanding. When, a bit later on, she'd tried to tell him that she was woefully ignorant on the subject of politics—indeed, on most subjects— he'd chided her for being modest. 'I saw you at that party,' he'd said, 'destroying that guy's puerile arguments. You knew exactly what you were talking about. In fact,' he'd added, with darkening eyes, 'it was quite a turn-on.' And Milly, who'd been about to admit to her source of information, had instead moved closer so that he could kiss her again.

Simon's initial impression of her had never been corrected. He still told her she was too modest; he still thought she liked the same highbrow art exhibitions he did; he still asked her opinion on topics such as the American presidency campaign and listened carefully to her answers. He thought she liked sushi; he thought she had read Sartre. Without wanting to mislead him, but without wanting to disappoint him either, she'd allowed him to build up a picture of her which—if she were honest with herself—wasn't quite true.

Quite what was going to happen when they started living together, she didn't know. Sometimes she felt alarmed at the degree to which she was being misrepresented; felt sure she would be exposed as a fraud the first time he caught her crying over a trashy novel. At other times, she told herself that his picture of her wasn't so inaccurate. Perhaps she wasn't quite the sophisticated woman he thought she was—but she could be. She would be. It was simply a matter of discarding all her old clothes and wearing only the new ones. Making the odd intelligent comment—and staying discreetly quiet the rest of the time.

Once, in the early days of their relationship, as they lay together in Simon's huge double bed at Pinnacle Hall, Simon had told her that he'd known she was someone special when she didn't start asking him questions about his father. 'Most girls,' he'd said bitterly, 'just want to know what it's like, being the son of Harry Pinnacle. Or they want me to get them a job interview or something. But you . . . you've never even mentioned him.'

He'd gazed at her with incredulous eyes, and Milly had smiled sweetly and murmured an indistinct, sleepy response. She could hardly admit that the reason she'd never mentioned Harry Pinnacle was that she'd never heard of him.

'So—dinner with Harry Pinnacle tonight! That should be fun.' Her mother's voice interrupted Milly's thoughts, and she looked up.

'Yes,' she said. 'I suppose so.'

'Has he still got that wonderful Austrian chef?'

'I don't know,' said Milly. She had, she realized, begun to imitate Simon's discouraging tone when talking about Harry Pinnacle. Simon never prolonged a conversation about his father if he could help it; if people were too persistent he would change the subject abruptly, or even walk away. He had walked away from his future mother-in-law plenty of times as she pressed him for details and anecdotes about the great man. So far she had never seemed to notice.

'The really lovely thing about Harry,' mused Olivia, 'is that he's so normal.' She tucked Milly's arm cosily under her own and they began to walk down the snowy street together. 'That's what I say to everybody. If you met him, you wouldn't think, here's a multimillionaire tycoon. You wouldn't think, here's a founder of a huge national chain. You'd think, what a charming man. And Simon's just the same.'

'Simon isn't a multimillionaire tycoon,' said Milly. 'He's an ordinary advertising salesman.'

'Hardly ordinary, darling!'

'Mummy . . .'

'I know you don't like me saying it. But the fact is that Simon's going to be very wealthy one day.' Olivia's arm tightened slightly around Milly's. 'And so are you.' Milly shrugged.

'Maybe.'

'There's no point pretending it's not going to happen. And when it does, your life will change.'

'No it won't.'

'The rich live differently, you know.'

'A minute ago,' pointed out Milly, 'you were saying how normal Harry is. He doesn't live differently, does he?'

'It's all relative, darling.'

They were nearing a little parade of expensive boutiques; as they approached the first softly lit window, they both stopped. Inside the window was a single mannequin, exquisite in heavy white velvet.

'That's nice,' murmured Milly.

'Not as nice as yours,' said Olivia at once. 'I haven't seen a single wedding dress as nice as yours.'

'No,' said Milly slowly. 'Mine is nice, isn't it?'

'It's perfect, darling.'

They lingered a little at the window, sucked in by the rosy glow of the shop; the clouds of silk, satin and netting lining each wall; the dried bouquets and tiny embroidered bridesmaids' shoes. At last Olivia sighed.

'All this wedding preparation has been fun, hasn't it? I'll be sorry when it's all over.'

'Mmm,' said Milly. There was a little pause, then Olivia said, as though changing the subject, 'Has Isobel got a boyfriend at the moment?'

Milly's head jerked up.

'Mummy! You're not trying to marry Isobel off, too.'

'Of course not! I'm just curious. She never tells me anything. I asked if she wanted to bring somebody to the reception . . .'

'And what did she say?'

'She said no,' said Olivia regretfully.

'Well then.'

'But that doesn't prove anything.'

'Mummy,' said Milly. 'If you want to know if Isobel's got a boyfriend, why don't you ask her?'

'Maybe,' said Olivia in a distant voice, as though she wasn't really interested any more. 'Yes, maybe I will.'

An hour later they emerged from Mario's Coffee House, and headed for home. By the time they got back, the kitchen would be filling up with bed and breakfast guests, footsore from sightseeing. The Havills' house in Bertram Street was one of the most popular bed and breakfast houses in Bath: tourists loved the beautifully furnished Georgian townhouse; its proximity to the city centre; Olivia's charming, gossipy manner and ability to turn every gathering into a party.

Tea was always the busiest meal in the house; Olivia adored assembling her guests round the table for Earl Grey and Bath buns. She would introduce them to one another, hear about their days, recommend diversions for the evening and tell them the latest gossip about people they had never met. If any guest expressed a desire to retreat to his own room and his mini-kettle, he was given a look of disapproval and cold toast in the morning. Olivia Havill despised mini-kettles and tea-bags on trays; she only provided them in order to qualify for four rosettes in the *Heritage City Bed and Breakfast Guide*. Similarly she despised, but provided, cable television, vegetarian sausages and a rack of leaflets about local theme parks and family attractions—which, she was glad to note, rarely needed replenishing.

'I forgot to say,' said Olivia, as they turned into Bertram Street. 'The photographer arrived while you were out. Quite a young chap.' She began to root around in her handbag for the doorkey.

'I thought he was coming tomorrow.'

'So did I!' said Olivia. 'Luckily those nice Australians have had a death in the family, otherwise we wouldn't have had room. And speaking of Australians . . . look at this!' She put her key in the front door and swung it open.

'Flowers!' exclaimed Milly. On the hall stand was a huge bouquet of creamy white flowers, tied with a dark green silk ribbon bow. 'For me? Who are they from?'

'Read the card,' said Olivia. Milly picked up the bouquet, and reached inside the crackling plastic.

' "To dear little Milly," ' she read slowly. ' "We're so proud of you and only wish we could be there at your wedding. We'll certainly be thinking of you. With all our love from Beth, Scott and Adrian." ' Milly looked at Olivia in amazement.

'Isn't that sweet of them! All the way from Sydney. People are so kind.'

'They're excited for you, darling,' said Olivia. 'Everyone's excited. It's going to be such a wonderful wedding!'

'Why, aren't those pretty,' came a pleasant voice from above. One of the bed and breakfast guests, a middle-aged woman in blue slacks and sneakers, was coming down the stairs. 'Flowers for the bride?'

'Just the first,' said Olivia, with a little laugh.

'You're a lucky girl,' said the middle-aged woman to Milly.

'I know I am,' said Milly and a pleased grin spread over her face. 'I'll just put them in some water.'

Still holding her flowers, Milly pushed open the door to the kitchen, then stopped in surprise. Sitting at the table was a young man wearing a shabby denim jacket. He had dark brown hair and round metal spectacles and was reading the *Guardian*.

'Hello,' she said politely. 'You must be the photographer.'

'Hi there,' said the young man, closing his paper. 'Are you Milly?'

He looked up, and as she saw his face, Milly felt a jolt of recognition. Surely she'd met this guy before somewhere?

'I'm Alexander Gilbert,' he said in a dry voice, and held out his hand. Milly advanced politely and shook it.

'Nice flowers,' he said, nodding to her bouquet.

'Yes,' replied Milly, staring curiously at him. Where on earth had she seen him before? Why did his face feel etched into her memory?

'That's not your wedding bouquet, though.'

'No, it's not,' said Milly. She bent her head slightly and inhaled the sweet scent of the flowers. 'These were sent by some friends in Australia. It's really thoughtful of them, considering—'

Suddenly she broke off, and her heart began to beat faster.

'Considering what?' said Alexander.

'Nothing,' said Milly, backing away. 'I mean—I'll just go and put them away.'

She moved towards the door, her palms sweaty against the crackling plastic. She knew where she'd seen him before. She knew exactly where she'd seen him before. At the thought of it, her heart gave a terrified lurch and she gritted her teeth, forcing herself to stay calm. Everything's OK, she told herself as she reached for the door handle. Everything's OK. As long as he doesn't recognize me . . .

'Wait.' His voice cut across her thoughts as though he could read her mind. Feeling suddenly sick, she turned round, to see him staring at her with a slight frown. 'Wait a minute,' he said. 'Don't I know you?'

CHAPTER TWO

Sitting in a traffic jam on his way home that night, watching the endlessly falling snow and rhythmic sweeping of his windscreen wipers, Simon reached for his phone to dial Milly's number. He pressed the first two digits, then changed his mind and switched the phone off. He had only wanted to hear her voice; make her laugh; picture her face as she spoke. But she might be busy, or she might think him ridiculous, phoning on a whim with nothing to say. And if she was still out, he might find himself talking to Mrs Havill, instead.

Her mother was the only thing about Milly that Simon would have changed if he could. Olivia was a pleasant enough woman, still attractive, charming and amusing; he could see why she was a popular figure at social events. But the way she treated Milly irritated him intensely. She seemed to think Milly was still a six-year-old—helping her choose her clothes, telling her to wear a scarf, wanting to know exactly what she was doing, every minute of every day. And the worst thing was, Simon thought, that Milly didn't seem to mind. She allowed her mother to smooth her hair and say, 'Good little girl'; she telephoned dutifully when she thought she might be late home. Unlike her older sister Isobel, who had long ago bought her own flat and moved out, Milly seemed to have no natural desire for independence.

The result was that her mother continued to treat her like a child, instead of the mature adult she really was. And Milly's father and sister Isobel were nearly as bad. They laughed when Milly expressed views on current issues, they joked about her career, they discussed important matters without consulting her. They refused to see the intelligent, passionate woman he saw; refused to take her seriously; refused to elevate her to grown-up status.

Simon had tried to talk to Milly about her family; tried to make her see how they patronized and limited her. But she had simply shrugged and said they weren't so bad, and when he'd strengthened his attack on them, had got upset. She was too good-natured and affectionate a creature to see any faults in them, thought Simon, turning off the main road out of Bath, towards Pinnacle Hall. And he loved her for it. But things would have to alter when they were married, when they set up their own home together. Milly's focus would have to change, and her family would have to respect that. She would be a wife; maybe some day a mother. And the Havills would just have to realize that she was no longer their little girl.

As he approached Pinnacle Hall he pressed the security code on his bleeper, then sat, waiting impatiently for the gates to swing open—heavy, iron gates, with the word 'Pinnacle' wrought into the design. Lights were blazing from every window of the house; cars were parked in the allocated spaces and the office wing was still buzzing. His father's red Mercedes was parked bang in front of the house; a big, shiny, arrogant car. Simon loathed it.

He parked his own Golf in an unobtrusive spot and crunched over the snow-covered gravel towards Pinnacle Hall. It was a large, eighteenth-century house which had been a luxury hotel during the eighties, complete with a leisure complex and a tastefully added wing of extra bedrooms. Harry Pinnacle had bought it when the owners had gone bust and turned it back into a private home, with his company headquarters housed in the extra wing. It suited him, he would tell visiting reporters, to be out of London. He was, after all, getting old and past it. There would be a beat of silence—then everyone would laugh, and Harry would grin, and press the bell for more coffee.

The panelled hall was empty and smelt of beeswax. From his father's study came a light; Simon could hear his voice, muffled behind the door, then a burst of low laughter. Resentment, never far from the surface, began to prickle at Simon's skin, and his hands clenched tightly inside his pockets.

For as long as he could remember, Simon had hated his father. Harry Pinnacle had disappeared from the family home when Simon was three, leaving his mother to bring up Simon alone. His mother had never elaborated on exactly why the marriage had broken down, but Simon knew it had to be the fault of his father. His overbearing, arrogant, obnoxious father. His driven, creative, incredibly successful father. It was the success that Simon hated the most.

The story was well known by all. In the year that Simon had

turned seven, Harry Pinnacle had opened a small juice bar called Fruit 'n Smooth. It served healthy drinks at chrome counters and was an instant hit. The next year, he opened another, and the year after that, another. The year after that, he began selling franchises. By the mid-eighties, there was a Fruit 'n Smooth in every town and Harry Pinnacle was a multimillionaire.

As his father had grown in wealth and stature, as he'd leapt from the inside business pages to the front-page headlines, the young Simon had watched his progress with fury. Cheques arrived every month, and his mother always exclaimed over Harry's generosity. But Harry never appeared in person, and Simon hated him for it. And then, when Simon was nineteen, his mother had died and Harry Pinnacle had come back into his life.

Simon frowned, and felt his nails digging into the flesh of his hands as he remembered the moment, ten years ago, when he'd seen his father for the first time. He'd been pacing the corridor outside his mother's hospital room, desperate with grief, with anger, with tiredness. Suddenly he'd heard a voice calling his name, and he'd looked up to see a face which was familiar from a thousand newspaper photographs. Familiar—and yet strange to him. As he'd stared at his father in silent shock, he'd realized for the first time that he could see his own features in the older man's face. And in spite of himself he'd felt emotional tentacles reaching out; instinctive feelers like a baby's. It would have been so easy to fall on his father's neck, to allow the burden to be shared, to accept his overtures and make him a friend. But even as he'd felt himself beginning to soften, Simon had stamped on his feelings and ground them back into himself. Harry Pinnacle didn't deserve his love, and he would never have it.

After the funeral, Harry had welcomed Simon into his house.

He'd given him his own room, his own car; taken him on expensive holidays. Simon had accepted everything politely. But if Harry had thought that by showering him with expensive gifts he would buy his son's affection, he had thought wrong. Although Simon's adolescent fury had soon simmered down, there had arisen in its place a determination to outdo his father on every front. He would run a successful business and make money—but, unlike his father, he would also marry happily; bring up his children to love him; become the figurehead of a contented, stable family. He would have the life that his father had never had—and his father would envy and hate him for it.

And so he'd begun, by launching his own little publishing company. He'd started with three specialist newsletters, a reasonable profit and high expectations. Those expectations had never been realized. After three years of struggle his profits were down to nothing; at the end of the fourth year he went into liquidation.

Humiliation still burned through Simon as he remembered the day he'd had to admit to his father that his business had gone bust; the day he'd had to accept his father's offer, sell his flat and move back into Pinnacle Hall. His father had poured him a deep glass of whisky, had uttered clichés about the rough and the smooth, had offered him a job with Pinnacle Enterprises. Simon had immediately turned it down with a few muttered words of thanks. He could barely look his father in the eye; could barely look anyone in the eye. At that low point he'd despised himself almost as much as he despised his father. His whole being was wrought with embarrassed disappointment.

At last he'd found himself a job selling advertising on a small, low-profile business magazine. He'd winced as Harry congratulated him; winced as he watched his father leafing through the drab little publication and trying to find some words of praise. 'It's not much of a job,' he'd said defensively. 'But at least I'm in work.' At least he was in work, at least the days were filled, at least he could begin to pay off his debts.

Three months after starting on the magazine, he'd met Milly. A year later he'd asked her to marry him. His father had again congratulated him; had offered to help out with the engagement ring. But Simon had refused his offer. 'I'll do this my way,' he'd said, and looked his father straight in the eye with a new confidence, almost a challenge. If he couldn't beat his father at business, then he would beat him at family life. He and Milly would have a perfect marriage. They would love each other, help each other, understand each other. Worries would be discussed; decisions would be made jointly; affection would be expressed freely. Children would enhance the bliss. Nothing was allowed to go wrong. Simon had experienced failure once; he never wanted to experience it again.

Suddenly his thoughts were interrupted by another burst of laughter from inside his father's room, a mumble of conversation, and then the sharp ping which meant his father had replaced the old-fashioned receiver of his private-line telephone. Simon waited a minute or two, then took a deep breath, approached his father's door and knocked.

As Harry Pinnacle heard the knock at his door he gave an uncharacteristic start. Quickly he put the tiny photograph he was holding into the desk drawer in front of him and closed it. Then, for good measure, he locked the drawer. For a few moments he sat, staring at the drawer key, lost in thoughts.

There was another knock, and he looked up. He swivelled his chair away from the desk and ran his hands through his silvering hair.

'Yes?' he said and watched the door open.

Simon came in, took a few paces forward and looked angrily at his father. It was always the same. He would knock on his father's door and would be kept waiting outside, like a servant. Never once had Harry exhorted him not to knock; never once had he even looked pleased to see Simon. He always looked impatient, as though Simon were interrupting crucial business. But that's bullshit, thought Simon. You're not in the middle of crucial business. You're just an arrogant bastard.

His heart was beating quickly; he was in the mood for a confrontation. But he couldn't bring himself to say any of the words of attack circling his mind.

'Hi,' he said in a tense voice. He gripped the back of a leather chair and glared at his father, somehow hoping to provoke a reaction. But his father simply stared back at him. After a few moments he sighed, and put down his pen.

'Hello,' he said. 'Good day?' Simon shrugged and looked away. 'Feel like a whisky?'

'No. Thanks.'

'Well, I do.'

As he got up to pour himself a drink, Harry caught a glimpse of his son's unguarded face: tense, miserable, angry. The boy was full of anger; he'd been carrying the same anger around ever since Harry had first seen him, standing outside his mother's hospital room. That day he'd spat at his father's feet and stalked away before Harry could say anything. And a wretched guilt had begun to grow inside Harry, a guilt which stabbed him every time the boy looked at him with his mother's blasted eyes.

'Good day?' he said, lifting the whisky glass to his lips.

'You already asked that.'

'Right. So I did.' Harry took a slug of the fiery liquid and immediately felt a little better. He took another.

'I came,' said Simon, 'to remind you about dinner tonight. The Havills are coming.'

'I remember,' said Harry. He put down his glass and looked up. 'Not long now till the big day. Are you nervous?'

'No, not at all,' said Simon at once. Harry shrugged.

'It's a big commitment.'

Simon stared at his father. He could feel a string of words forming at his lips; pent-up words which he'd carried around for years like a constant weight.

'Well,' he found himself saying, 'you wouldn't know much about commitment, would you?'

A flash of anger passed across his father's face, and Simon felt a sudden fearful thrill. He waited for his father to shout at him, winding himself up to an even angrier response. But as suddenly as it had appeared, the animation vanished from his father's face and he walked away, towards the huge sash windows. Simon felt himself tense up with frustration.

'What's wrong with commitment?' he shouted. 'What's wrong with loving one person all your life?'

'Nothing,' said Harry, without turning.

'Then why . . .' began Simon, and stopped. There was a long silence, punctuated only by the crackles of the fire. Simon gazed at his father's back. Say something, he thought desperately. Say something, you fucker.

'I'll see you at eight,' said Harry at last.

'Fine,' said Simon, in a voice scored with hurt. 'See you then.' And without pausing, he left the room.

Harry gazed at the glass in his hand and cursed himself. He hadn't meant to upset the boy. Or maybe he had. He couldn't trust his own motives any more, couldn't keep tabs on his feelings. Sympathy so quickly turned into irritation; guilt so quickly transformed into anger. Good intentions towards his son disappeared the minute the boy opened his mouth. Part of him couldn't wait for the moment when Simon married; left his house; became swallowed up by another family; finally gave him some peace. And part of him dreaded it; didn't even want to think about it.

Frowning, Harry poured himself another whisky and went back to his desk. He reached for the phone, dialled a number and listened impatiently to the ringing tone. Then, with a scowl, crashed the receiver down again.

Milly sat at the kitchen table with a thumping heart, wishing she could run away and escape. It was him. It was the boy from Oxford. The boy who had seen her marrying Allan; who had picked up her wedding veil and handed it back to her. He was older now. His face was harder and there was stubble over his chin. But his round metal spectacles were just the same, and so was his arrogant, almost scornful expression. Now he was leaning back in his chair, staring at her curiously. Just don't remember, thought Milly, not daring to meet his gaze. For God's sake don't remember who I am.

'Here we are,' said Olivia, coming over to the table. 'I've arranged your flowers for you, darling. You can't just dump them and forget about them!'

'I know,' muttered Milly. 'Thanks.'

'Now, would you like some more tea, Alexander?'

'Yup,' said the boy, holding out his cup. 'Thanks very much.' Olivia poured the tea, then sat down and smiled around the table.

'Isn't this nice,' she said. 'I'm starting to feel as though this wedding is really happening!' She took a sip of tea, then looked up. 'Milly, have you shown Alexander your engagement ring?'

Slowly, feeling her insides clenching, Milly held out her left hand to Alexander. His gaze passed inscrutably over the antique diamond cluster, then he raised his eyes to hers.

'Very nice,' he said and took a sip of tea. 'You're engaged to Harry Pinnacle's son. The heir to Fruit 'n Smooth. Is that right?'

'Yes,' said Milly reluctantly.

'Quite a catch,' said Alexander.

'He's a sweet boy,' said Olivia at once, as she always did when anyone referred to Simon's money or family background. 'Quite one of us, now.'

'And what does he do?' Alexander's voice was faintly mocking. 'Work for his father?'

'No,' said Milly. Her voice felt awkward and unfamiliar. 'He sells advertising.'

'I see,' said Alexander. There was a pause. He took another sip of tea and frowned at Milly. 'I'm still sure I recognize you from somewhere.'

'Do you really?' said Olivia. 'How funny!'

'Well, I'm afraid I don't recognize you,' said Milly, trying to sound light-hearted.

'Yes, darling,' said Olivia, 'but you're not very good with faces, are you?' She turned to Alexander. 'Now, I'm just the same as you, Alexander. I never forget a face.'

'Faces are my business,' said Alexander. 'I spend my life looking at them.' His eyes ran over Milly's face and she felt herself flinching. 'Have you always had your hair like that?' he suddenly asked. Milly's heart lurched in fright.

'Not always,' she said, and gripped her cup tightly. 'I . . . I once dyed it red.'

'Not a success,' said Olivia emphatically. 'I told her to go to my salon, but she wouldn't listen. And then of course—'

'That's not it,' said Alexander, cutting Olivia off. He frowned again at Milly. 'You weren't at Cambridge, were you?'

'No,' said Milly.

'But Isobel was,' said Olivia triumphantly. 'Perhaps you're thinking of her!'

'Who's Isobel?' said Alexander.

'My sister,' said Milly, gripped by sudden hope. 'She . . . she looks just like me.'

'She read modern languages,' said Olivia. 'And now she's doing *terribly* well. Flies all over the world, interpreting at conferences. You know, she's met all the world leaders. Or at least . . .'

'What does she look like?' said Alexander.

'That's a picture of her there,' said Olivia, pointing to a photograph on the mantelpiece. 'You and she should really meet before the wedding,' she added lightly, watching Alexander scan the picture. 'I'm sure you've got lots in common!'

'It wasn't her,' said Alexander, turning back to Milly. 'She looks nothing like you.'

'She's taller than Milly,' said Olivia, then added thoughtfully,

'You're quite tall, aren't you, Alexander?' He shrugged, and stood up.

'I've got to go. I'm meeting a friend in town.'

'A friend,' said Olivia. 'How nice. Someone special?'

'An old mate from school,' said Alexander, looking at Olivia as though she were mad.

'Well, have fun!' said Olivia.

'Thanks,' said Alexander. He paused by the door. 'I'll see you tomorrow, Milly. I'll take a few informal shots and we can have a little chat about what you want.' He nodded at her, then disappeared.

'Well!' exclaimed Olivia, as soon as he had gone. 'What an interesting young man.'

Milly didn't move. She stared straight at the table, hands still clenched round her cup, her heart beating furiously.

'Are you all right, darling?' said Olivia, peering at her.

'Fine,' said Milly. 'I'm fine.' She forced herself to smile at her mother and take a sip of tea. It was OK, she told herself firmly. Nothing had happened. Nothing was going to happen.

'I was looking at his portfolio earlier on,' said Olivia. 'He's really very talented. He's won awards, and everything!'

'Really,' said Milly in a dry voice. She picked up a biscuit, looked at it and put it down again, feeling a sudden swoop of fear. But what if it came back to him? What if he remembered—and told someone exactly what he'd seen her doing ten years ago? What if it all came out? Her stomach curdled at the thought; she felt suddenly ill with panic.

'He and Isobel really should meet each other,' Olivia was saying. 'As soon as she gets back from Paris.'

'What?' Milly's attention was momentarily drawn. 'Why?'

She stared at Olivia, who gave a tiny shrug. 'Mummy, no! You don't mean it!'

'It's just a thought,' said Olivia defensively. 'What chance has poor Isobel got to meet men, stuck in dreary conference rooms all day?'

'She doesn't want to meet men. Not your men!' Milly gave a tiny shudder. 'And especially not him!'

'What's wrong with him?' said Olivia.

'Nothing,' said Milly quickly. 'He's just . . . not Isobel.'

An image of her sister came into Milly's mind—clever, sensible Isobel. Suddenly she felt a surge of relief. She would talk to Isobel. Isobel always knew what to do. Milly looked at her watch.

'What time is it in Paris?'

'Why? Are you going to make a call?'

'Yes,' said Milly. 'I want to speak to Isobel.' Suddenly she felt desperate. 'I need to speak to Isobel.'

Isobel Havill arrived back at her hotel room at eight o'clock to find the message light on her telephone furiously blinking. She frowned, rubbed a weary hand over her brow, and opened the minibar. The day had been even more draining than usual. Her skin felt parched from the dry atmosphere of the conference room; her mouth tasted of coffee and cigarette smoke. She had spent all day listening, translating and speaking into her microphone in the low, measured tones that made her so highly sought after. Now her throat felt sore and her mouth incapable of further speech; her head was still a maelstrom of furious, multilingual discussion.

Holding a glass of vodka, she went slowly into the white marble bathroom, switched on the light and looked for a few silent seconds at her red-rimmed eyes. She opened her mouth to say something, then feebly closed it again. She felt unable to think; unable to initiate a single idea of her own. For too many hours, her brain had been acting as nothing but a high-powered conduit of information. She was still geared up only to channel words back and forth; not to interrupt the flow with her own thoughts; not to sully the translation with her own opinions. She had operated immaculately all day, never flagging, never losing her cool. And now she felt like a dried-out, empty shell.

She drained her glass of vodka and put it down on the glass bathroom shelf. The clinking sound made her wince. In the mirror, her reflection stared back at her with an apprehensive expression. All day, she'd managed to put this moment from her mind. But now she was alone and her work was finished, and there was no longer any excuse. With a trembling hand she reached into her bag and pulled out a crackly pharmacist's bag; took out a little oblong box. Inside was a leaflet bearing instructions printed in French, German, Spanish and English. Her eyes flicked impatiently over each of them, noticing that the Spanish paragraph was poorly constructed and there was a discrepancy in the German version. But all seemed agreed on the short time span of the test. Only one minute. *Une minute. Un minuto.*

She carried out the test, scarcely able to believe what she was doing, then left the little phial on the edge of the bath and went back into the bedroom. Her jacket was still lying on the huge hotel bed; the telephone was still furiously bleeping. She pressed the button for messages, went to the minibar and poured herself another vodka. Thirty seconds to go.

'Hi, Isobel. It's me.' A man's low voice filled the room, and Isobel flinched. 'Call me if you have time. Bye.'

Isobel looked at her watch. Fifteen seconds to go.

'Isobel, it's Milly. Listen, I really need to speak to you. Please, please can you call me back as soon as you get this? It's really really urgent.'

'Isn't it always urgent?' said Isobel aloud.

She looked at her watch, took a deep breath and strode towards the bathroom. The little blue stripe was visible before she even reached the door. Suddenly she felt sick.

'No,' she whispered. 'I can't be.' She backed away from the pregnancy test, as though from something contaminated, and shut the bathroom door. She took a deep, shuddering breath, and reached automatically for her glass of vodka. Then, in sudden realization, her hand stopped. A lonely dismay crept over her.

'Isobel?' the machine was saying brightly. 'It's Milly again. I'll be at Simon's tonight, so maybe you could call me there?'

'No,' shouted Isobel, and she felt a sudden pricking of tears. 'I couldn't, all right?' She picked up the vodka, drained it in one, and crashed the glass defiantly down on the bedside table. But suddenly more tears were filling her eyes, suddenly she was unable to control her breath. Like a wounded animal, she crawled into bed, buried her head in her hotel pillow. And as the telephone rang again, she silently began to cry.

CHAPTER THREE

At eight-thirty, Olivia and Milly arrived at Pinnacle Hall. They were met at the door by Simon and shown into the large baronial drawing room.

'Well,' said Olivia, wandering over to the crackling fire. 'Isn't this nice!'

'I'll get some champagne,' said Simon. 'Dad's still on the phone.'

'Actually,' said Milly faintly, 'I think I'll try Isobel again. I'll use the phone in the games room.'

'Can't it wait?' said Olivia. 'What do you want to speak to her about?'

'Nothing,' said Milly at once. 'Nothing. I just . . . need to talk to her.' She swallowed. 'I won't be long.'

When they'd gone, Olivia settled herself into a chair, admiring the portrait above the fireplace. It was a grandly framed oil paint-ing which looked as though it could have been bought along with the house; in fact it was a picture of Harry's grandmother as a girl. Harry Pinnacle was so famous as a self-made man that it was widely assumed he'd started from nothing. The fact that he'd at-tended an expensive public school only spoiled the story, as did the hefty parental loans which had got him started—so these were generally brushed over by everyone, including Harry himself.

The door opened, and a pretty blond girl in a smart trouser suit entered, holding a tray of champagne glasses.

'Simon's just coming,' she said. 'He just remembered a fax he had to send.'

'Thank you,' said Olivia, taking a glass and giving a small, re-gal smile.

The girl left the room, and Olivia took a sip of champagne. The fire was warm on her face; her chair was comfortable; clas-sical music was playing pleasantly through concealed speakers. This, she thought, was the life. A pang went through her—part delight, part envy—at the knowledge that soon her daughter would be entering this kind of existence. Milly was already as much at home at Pinnacle Hall as she was at 1 Bertram Street. She was used to dealing easily with Harry's staff; was used to sitting alongside Si-mon at grand dinner parties. Of course she and Simon could main-tain that they were just like any other young couple, that the money wasn't theirs—but who were they kidding? They would be rich one day. Fabulously rich. Milly would be able to have anything she wanted.

Olivia clenched her hand more tightly around her glass. When the engagement had first been announced, she'd been overcome by an astonished, almost giddy delight. For Milly to have any kind of connection with the son of Harry Pinnacle was good enough. But for them to be marrying—and so quickly—was unasked-for bliss. As the wedding plans had progressed and become more concrete, she'd prided herself on keeping her triumph concealed; on treating Simon as casually as any other young beau; on playing down—to herself as much as anyone else—the significance of the match.

But now, with only a few days to go, her heart was beginning to beat quickly again with jubilation. In only a few days the whole world would see her daughter marrying one of the most eligible bachelors in the country. All her friends—indeed, everyone she had ever known—would be forced to admire as she presided over the biggest, glitziest, most romantic wedding any of them had ever seen. This was an event which Olivia felt as though she had been building up to all her life; an event surpassing even her own wedding. That had been a modest, anonymous little affair. Whereas this occasion would be crammed with important, influential, wealthy people, all forced to take a back seat as she—and of course Milly—strolled prominently, centre stage.

In just a few days' time she would be donning her designer outfit and smiling at massed rows of cameras and watching as all her friends and acquaintances and jealous relatives goggled at the lavishness of Milly's reception. It would be a beautiful day, a day they would all carry in their thoughts for ever. Like some wonderful movie, thought Olivia happily. Some wonderful, romantic Hollywood movie.

James Havill arrived at the front door of Pinnacle Hall and tugged at the heavy wrought-iron bell-pull. As he waited for an answer he looked around and frowned. The place was too beautiful, too perfect. It was a cliché of opulence, more like some ghastly Hollywood movie than a real place. If this is what money can buy, he thought dishonestly, then you can keep it. I'd rather have real life.

The front door was, he realized, slightly ajar, and he pushed it open. A fire was blazing cheerily in a huge fireplace and the chandeliers were all lit up, but no one was about. He gazed cautiously around, trying to distinguish the panelled doors from each other. One of these doors was the huge drawing room with the deers' heads. He remembered it from previous visits. But which was it? For a few seconds he dithered, then, suddenly irritated with himself, he stepped towards the nearest door and pushed it open.

But he'd got it wrong. The first thing he saw was Harry. He was sitting at an enormous oak desk, listening intently to a phone conversation. He raised his silvery head at the sound of the door opening, narrowed his eyes, then waved James away in irritation.

'Sorry,' said James quietly, backing out.

'Mr Havill?' came a low voice behind him. 'I'm sorry I didn't answer the door more quickly.' James turned to see a blond girl he recognized as one of Harry's assistants behind him. 'If you'd like to come with me . . .' she said, tactfully guiding him out of the room and closing the study door.

'Thank you,' said James, feeling patronized.

'The others are in the drawing room. Let me take your coat.'

'Thank you,' said James again.

'And if you need anything else,' said the girl pleasantly, 'just ask me. All right?' In other words—thought James resentfully—don't go wandering about. The girl gave him a smooth smile, opened the door of the drawing room and ushered him in.

Olivia's pleasant dreamworld was interrupted as the door suddenly opened. She quickly smoothed down her skirt and looked up with a smile, expecting to see Harry. But it was the pretty blond girl again.

'Your husband's here, Mrs Havill,' she said, and stepped aside.

Into the room walked James. He'd come straight from the office; his dark grey suit was crumpled and he looked tired.

'Been here long?' he said.

'No,' said Olivia with a forced cheerfulness. 'Not very.'

She rose from her seat and walked towards James, intending to greet him with a kiss. Just before she reached him, the girl tactfully withdrew, and closed the door.

Olivia stopped in her tracks, suddenly feeling self-conscious. Physical contact between herself and James had, over the last few years, become something which only happened in front of other people. Now she felt awkward, standing this close to him without an audience; without a reason. She looked at him, hoping he would help her out, but his face was blank; she couldn't read it. Eventually she leaned forward, flushing slightly, and gave him a peck on the cheek—then immediately stepped backwards and took a gulp of champagne.

'Where's Milly?' said James in an expressionless voice.

'She's popped off to make a telephone call.'

Olivia watched as James helped himself to a glass of champagne and took a deep swig. He walked over to the sofa and sat down, stretching his legs out comfortably in front of him. Olivia gazed down at his head. His dark hair was damp from the snow but neatly combed, and she found herself running her eyes idly along his side parting. Then, as he turned his head, she quickly looked away.

'So,' she began—then stopped and took a sip of champagne. She wandered over to the window, pulled open the heavy brocade curtain and looked out into the snowy night. She could barely remember the last time she'd been alone in a room with James; certainly couldn't recall the last time they'd talked together naturally. Topics of conversation passed through her mind like shrink-wrapped food on a conveyor belt, each as unappealing and difficult to get into as the next. If she told James the latest piece of Bath gossip, she would have to begin by reminding him who all the main characters were. If she told him about the wedding shoe fiasco, she would first have to explain the difference between duchesse satin and slub silk. Nothing she could think of to say seemed quite worth the effort of starting.

Once, long ago, their conversation had flowed like a seamless length of ribbon. James had listened to her stories in geniune amusement; she'd laughed at his dry wit. They'd entertained each other, had fun together. But these days all his jokes seemed tinged with a bitterness she didn't understand, and a tense boredom crept over his face as soon as she began to speak.

So they remained in silence, until finally the door opened and Milly came in. She gave James a brief, strained smile.

'Hello, Daddy,' she said. 'You made it.'

'Did you get through to Isobel?' said Olivia.

'No,' said Milly shortly. 'I don't know what she can be doing. I had to leave another message.' Her eye fell on the tray. 'Oh good. I could do with a drink.'

She took a glass of champagne and raised it. 'Cheers.'

'Cheers!' echoed Olivia.

'Your good health, my darling,' said James. All three drank; there was a little silence.

'Did I interrupt something?' said Milly.

'No,' said Olivia. 'You didn't interrupt anything.'

'Good,' said Milly without really listening, and walked over to the fire, hoping no one would talk to her.

For the third time, she'd got through to Isobel's message machine. As she'd heard the tinny tones she'd felt a spurt of anger, an irrational conviction that Isobel was there and just wasn't answering. She'd left a brief message, then remained staring at the phone for a few minutes, biting her lip, hoping desperately that Isobel would call back. Isobel was the only one she could talk to—the only one who would listen calmly; who would think of a solution rather than lecturing.

But the phone had remained silent. Isobel hadn't called back. Now Milly's hand tightened around her champagne glass. She couldn't stand this niggling, secret panic. On the way over to Pinnacle Hall she'd sat silently in the car, gathering reassuring thoughts around herself like sandbags. Alexander would never remember, she'd told herself again and again. It had been a two-minute encounter, ten years ago. He couldn't possibly remember that. And even if he did, he wouldn't say anything about it. He would just keep quiet and get on with his job. Civilized people didn't deliberately cause trouble.

'Milly?' Simon's voice interrupted her thoughts and she jumped guiltily.

'Hi,' she said. 'Did you send your fax all right?'

'Yes.' He took a sip of champagne and looked more closely at her. 'Are you OK? You're looking tense.'

'Am I?' She smiled at him. 'I don't feel it.'

'You're tense,' persisted Simon, and he began to massage her shoulders gently. 'Worrying about the wedding. Am I right?'

'Yes,' said Milly.

'I knew it.'

Simon sounded satisfied and Milly said nothing. Simon liked to think that he was in tune with her emotions; that he knew her likes and dislikes; that he could predict her moods. And she'd got into the habit of agreeing with him, even when his assertions were wildly inaccurate. After all, it was sweet of him to have a go. Most men wouldn't have bothered.

And to have expected him to get it right all the time would have been unreasonable. Most of the time she herself was unsure exactly how she was feeling. Emotions shaded her mind like colours on a palette—some lingering, some momentary, but all blended together in an inseparable wash. Whereas Simon's moods seemed to march through him, distinct and uniform, like a row of children's building blocks. When he was happy, he smiled. When he was angry, he frowned.

'Let me guess what you're thinking,' murmured Simon against her hair. 'You're wishing it was just the two of us tonight.'

'No,' said Milly honestly. She turned round and looked straight up at him, breathing in his musky, familiar scent. 'I was thinking how much I love you.'

It was nine-thirty before Harry Pinnacle strode into the room. 'My apologies,' he said. 'This is unforgivable of me.'

'Harry, it's utterly forgivable!' exclaimed Olivia, who was by now on her fifth glass of champagne. 'We know what it's like!'

'I don't,' muttered Simon.

'And I'm sorry about earlier,' said Harry to James. 'It was an important call.'

'That's quite all right,' said James stiffly. There was a slight pause.

'Well, let's not hang about,' said Harry. He turned politely to Olivia. 'After you.'

They slowly made their way across the hall, into the dining room.

'All right, sweetheart?' said James to Milly as they sat down round the magnificent mahogany dining table.

'Fine,' she said, and gave him a taut smile.

But she wasn't, thought James. He'd watched her knocking back glasses of champagne as though she were desperate; watched her jump every time the phone rang. Was she having second thoughts? He leaned towards her.

'Just remember, darling,' he said in an undertone. 'You don't have to go through with it if you don't want to.'

'What?' Milly's head jerked up as though she'd been stung, and James nodded reassuringly.

'If you change your mind about Simon—now, or even on the day itself—don't worry. We can call the whole thing off. No one will mind.'

'I don't want to call the whole thing off!' hissed Milly. Suddenly she looked close to tears. 'I want to get married! I love Simon.'

'Good,' said James. 'Well, that's fine then.'

He sat back in his chair, glanced across the table at Simon and

felt unreasonably irritated. The boy had everything. Good looks,
a wealthy background, an annoyingly calm and balanced person-
ality. He quite obviously adored Milly; he was polite to Olivia; he
was thoughtful towards the rest of the family. There was nothing
to complain about. And tonight, James admitted to himself, he was
in a mood for complaint.

He'd had a grisly day at work. The engineering firm in whose
finance department he worked had undergone restructuring in
recent months. Endless rumours had that day culminated in the
announcement that there would have to be four junior redundan-
cies in his department. The news was supposed to be confidential
but it had obviously spread: as he'd left the office, all the younger
members of the team had still been hunched dutifully over their
desks. Some had kept their heads down; others had looked up
with scared eyes as he passed. Every single one of them had a
family and a mortgage. None of them could afford to lose their
job. None of them deserved to.

By the time he'd arrived at Pinnacle Hall he'd felt unspeakably
depressed by the whole thing. As he had parked his car he had
made up his mind that when Olivia asked how his day had been,
he would, for once, tell her the truth. Perhaps not everything
straight away, but enough to make her concerned; enough to make
her realize what a burden he was struggling with. But she had not
asked—and a certain pride had stopped him from volunteering his
story; from admitting to her his vulnerability. He didn't want his
wife turning her mind to him as if he were just another one of her
charity projects. Abandoned ponies, handicapped children, a miserable husband.

He should, thought James, be used to Olivia by now. He should
be used to the fact that she was not very interested in him; that

her life was full enough of other concerns; that she paid more attention to the problems of her chattering girlfriends than she ever did to him. After all, they had managed to carve out a stable, workable life together. If they weren't soul-mates there was at least some sort of symbiosis between them. She had her life and he had his—and where they overlapped they were always perfectly amicable. James had resigned himself to this arrangement long ago, had thought it would be all that he ever needed. But it wasn't. He needed more; he wanted more. He wanted a different life, before it was too late.

'I'd like to propose a toast.'

Harry's voice interrupted James's thoughts and he looked up, frowning slightly. There he was. Harry Pinnacle, one of the most successful men in the country, and his own daughter's prospective father-in-law. James was aware that this alliance made him the envy of his peers and knew that he should be pleased at Milly's future financial security. But he refused to rejoice in the fact of his daughter becoming a Pinnacle; refused to bask, as his wife did, in the fascinated curiosity of their friends. He'd heard Olivia on the phone, dropping Harry's name into the conversation, assuming an intimacy with the great man that he knew she did not have. She was milking the situation for all it was worth—and her behaviour made him curl up with shame. There were days when he wished Milly had never met the son of Harry Pinnacle.

'To Milly and Simon,' declaimed Harry, in the gravelly voice which made all his utterances sound more significant than everyone else's.

'To Milly and Simon,' echoed James, and picked up the heavy Venetian glass in front of him.

'Simply delicious wine,' said Olivia. 'Are you a wine expert as well as everything else, Harry?'

'Christ, no,' replied Harry. 'I rely on people with taste to tell me what to buy. It's all the same to me.'

'Now, I don't believe that! You're too modest,' exclaimed Olivia. James watched in disbelief as she reached over and patted Harry intimately on the hand. Just who did she think she was? He turned away, slightly sickened, and caught Simon's eye.

'Cheers, James,' he said, and raised his glass. 'Here's to the wedding.'

'Yes,' said James, and took a huge gulp of wine. 'To the wedding.'

As he watched everyone drinking his father's wine, Simon felt a sudden tightening in his throat. He coughed and looked up.

'There's someone missing here tonight,' he said. 'And I'd like to propose a toast to her.' He raised his glass. 'To my mother.'

There was a slight pause and he was aware of eyes darting towards the head of the table. Then Harry raised his glass.

'To Anne,' he said gravely.

'To Anne,' echoed James and Milly.

'Was that her name?' said Olivia, looking up with flushed cheeks. 'I always thought it was Louise.'

'No,' said Simon. 'Anne.'

'Oh well,' said Olivia, 'if you say so.' She raised her glass. 'To Anne. Anne Pinnacle.' She drank from her glass, then looked at Milly, as though struck by a sudden thought. 'You're not planning to keep your own name, are you, darling?'

'I don't think so,' said Milly. 'Although I might stay as Havill for work.'

'Oh no!' exclaimed Olivia. 'Too confusing. Just be Pinnacle through and through!'

'I think it's a good idea,' said James. 'Keep your independence. What do you think, Simon? Would you mind if Milly stayed Havill?'

'To be honest,' said Simon, 'I'd prefer it if we shared a name. We'll be sharing everything else.' He turned towards Milly and smiled. 'But I'll be sad to lose Milly Havill, too. After all, it was Milly Havill I fell in love with.'

'Very touching,' said James.

'Would you consider changing your name to Havill?' said Harry, from the end of the table. Simon looked at him steadily.

'Yes I would,' he said. 'If Milly really wanted it.'

'No!' exclaimed Olivia. 'You don't, do you, darling?'

'I don't suppose you would have changed your name for Mum, would you, Dad?' said Simon.

'No,' said Harry. 'I wouldn't.'

'Yes well,' said Simon tautly, 'the difference is that I'm prepared to put my marriage before everything else.'

'The difference is,' Harry said, 'that your mother's maiden name was Parry.' Olivia laughed and Simon shot her a furious look.

'The point is,' he said loudly, 'names are irrelevant. It's people that make a marriage work. Not names.'

'And you, of course, are an expert on marriage,' said Harry.

'I'm more of an expert than you! At least I haven't screwed mine up yet!' There was a short silence. The Havills all looked at their plates. Simon gazed at his father, breathing hard. Then Harry shrugged.

'I'm sure you and Milly will be very happy,' he said. 'We can't all be so lucky.'

'It's not a matter of luck,' retorted Simon angrily. 'Luck doesn't come into it!' He looked at James and Olivia. 'What would you say makes a successful marriage?'

'Money,' said Olivia, then laughed brightly. 'Only joking!'

'It's communication, isn't it?' said Simon. He leaned forward earnestly. 'Sharing, talking; knowing each other inside out. Wouldn't you agree, James?'

'I'll take your word for it,' said James, and took a swig of wine.

'You're absolutely right, Simon,' said Olivia. 'I was actually going to say communication.'

'I'd put sex above communication,' said Harry. 'Good sex, and plenty of it.'

'Well, I wouldn't know much about that, either,' said James drily.

'James!' exclaimed Olivia, and gave a tinkling laugh. Simon gave James a curious look, then glanced at Milly. But she didn't seem to be listening to the conversation at all.

'What about you, Harry?' Olivia was saying, gazing up at him through her lashes.

'What about me?'

'Aren't you ever tempted to marry again?'

'I'm too old to marry,' said Harry shortly.

'Nonsense!' exclaimed Olivia gaily. 'You could easily find yourself a lovely wife.'

'If you say so.'

'Of course you could.' Olivia took another sip of wine. 'I'd marry you myself!' She gave a little laugh.

'Very kind of you,' said Harry.

'Oh no,' said Olivia, waving her glass in the air. 'It would be a pleasure. Really.'

There was a choice of puddings.

'Oh!' said Olivia, looking from lemon mousse to chocolate torte and back again. 'Oh dear, I can't decide.'

'Then have both,' said Harry.

'Really? Would that be all right? Is anyone else going to have both?' Olivia looked around the table.

'I'm not going to have any,' said Milly, pleating her napkin nervously between her fingers.

'You're not slimming, are you?' said Harry.

'No,' said Milly. 'I'm just not very hungry.' She managed a smile at Harry and he nodded pleasantly back. He was basically a kind man, thought Milly. She could see it, even if Simon couldn't.

'You're as bad as Isobel!' said Olivia. 'Isobel eats like a little bird.'

'She's too busy to eat,' said James.

'How is she?' asked Harry politely.

'She's great!' said James with sudden animation. 'Forging ahead with her career, travelling the world . . .'

'Does she have a boyfriend?'

'Oh no,' James laughed. 'She's too busy doing her own thing. Isobel's always been an independent spirit. She's not going to get tied down in a hurry.'

'She might,' objected Olivia. 'She might meet someone tomorrow! Some nice businessman.'

'God help us,' said James. 'Can you really see Isobel settling down with some dreary businessman? Anyway, she's far too young still.'

'She's older than me,' said Milly.

'Yes,' said James, 'but the two of you are very different.'

'How?' said Milly. She looked at her father. The tensions of the day were throbbing unbearably inside her head; she felt suddenly on edge. 'How are we different? Are you saying I'm too stupid to do anything but get married?'

'No!' said James. He looked shocked. 'Of course not! All I mean is that Isobel's a bit more adventurous than you. She likes taking risks.'

'I've taken risks in my time!' cried Milly. 'I've taken risks you know nothing about!' She broke off, and stared at her father, breathing hard.

'Milly, don't get upset,' said James. 'All I'm saying is that you and Isobel are different.'

'And I prefer you,' whispered Simon to Milly. She gave him a grateful smile.

'Anyway, James, what's wrong with businessmen?' said Olivia. 'You're a businessman, aren't you, and I married you.'

'I know, my love,' said James tonelessly. 'But I'm hoping Isobel might do a little better than someone like me.'

Later on, as the pudding plates were being removed, Harry cleared his throat for attention.

'I don't want to make a big thing of this,' he said. 'But I've got a bit of a present for the happy couple.'

Simon looked up defensively. He'd bought a present of his own to give Milly this evening and had planned to spring it on her while they were all drinking coffee. But whatever Harry had bought, it would undoubtedly be more expensive than the ear-rings he'd chosen. Surreptitiously he felt for the small leather box, safely in his pocket, and wondered whether to leave it for another day— a day without competition from his father. But then a small wave of indignation rose through him. Why should he be ashamed? Perhaps his father could afford to spend a bit more than him—but then, what did everyone expect?

'I've got a present too,' he said, trying to sound casual. 'For Milly.'

'For me?' said Milly confusedly. 'But I haven't got anything for you. At least, not anything to give you tonight.'

'This is something extra,' said Simon.

He leaned over and gently pushed Milly's blond hair back behind her shoulders, exposing her little pink ears. As he did so, the gesture seemed suddenly erotic; and as he stared at her flawless skin, breathing in her sweet, musky scent, a proud desire surged through him. Sod the rest of them, he thought—Olivia with her unbearable smugness, Harry with all his cash. He had Milly's divine body all to himself, and that was all that counted.

'What is it?' said Milly.

'Dad first,' said Simon, feeling magnanimous. 'What have you got us, Dad?'

Harry felt in his pocket, and for a mad moment, Simon thought he was going to produce an identical pair of ear-rings. But instead, Harry dropped a key on the table.

'A key?' said Milly. 'What's it for?'

'A car?' said Olivia in incredulous tones.

'Not a car,' said Harry. 'A flat.'

There was a unanimous gasp. Olivia opened her mouth to speak, then closed it again.

'You're joking,' said Simon. 'You've bought us a flat?'

Harry pushed the key across the table.

'All yours.'

Simon stared at his father, feeling all the wrong emotions rise to the surface. He tried to locate a feeling of gratitude, but all he could feel was shock—and the beginnings of a defensive, smarting anger. He glanced at Milly. She was gazing at Harry with shining eyes. Simon felt a sudden despair.

'How . . .' he began, trying to summon the correct, grateful tones, but only managing to sound peevish. 'How do you know we'll like it?'

'It's the one you wanted to rent.'

'The one in Marlborough Mansions?'

Harry shook his head.

'The one you *wanted* to rent. The one you couldn't afford.'

'The flat in Parham Place?' whispered Milly. 'You *bought* it for us?'

Simon stared at his father, and felt like punching him. Fuck him for being so thoughtful.

'This is very good of you, Harry,' said James. 'Incredibly generous.' Harry shrugged.

'One less thing for them to worry about.'

'Oh darling!' said Olivia, clasping Milly's hand. 'Won't it be lovely? And you'll be so near us.'

'Well now, there's a plus,' said Simon, before he could stop himself. James glanced at him, and cleared his throat tactfully.

'And now,' he said, 'what about Simon's present?'

'Yes,' said Milly. She turned to Simon and touched his hand gently. 'What is it?'

Simon reached into his pocket and silently presented her with the little box. Everyone watched as she opened it to reveal two tiny, twinkling diamond studs.

'Oh Simon,' said Milly. She looked at him, her eyes suddenly glittering with unshed tears. 'They're beautiful.'

'Pretty,' said Olivia dismissively. 'Oh Milly! Parham Place!'

'I'll put them on,' said Milly.

'You don't have to,' said Simon, trying to control himself. His heart pounded with a raw, hurt anger; it seemed to him that everyone was laughing at him. Even Milly. 'They're nothing very special.'

'Of course they are,' said Harry gravely.

'No they're not!' Simon found himself shouting. 'Not compared with a piece of fucking real estate!'

'Simon,' said Harry calmly, 'no one is making that comparison.'

'Simon, they're lovely!' said Milly. 'Look.' She smoothed her hair back and the little diamonds sparkled in the candlelight.

'Great,' said Simon without looking up. He was making things worse, he knew, but he could not help himself. He felt like a small, humiliated schoolboy.

Harry caught James's eye, then rose to his feet.

'Let's have coffee,' he said. 'Nicki will have put it in the drawing room.'

'Absolutely,' said James, taking his cue. 'Come on, Olivia.'

The three parents moved out of the dining room, leaving Milly and Simon together in silence. After a few moments Simon looked up, to see Milly gazing at him. She wasn't laughing, she wasn't pitying. Suddenly he felt ashamed.

'I'm sorry,' he muttered. 'I'm being a complete prick.'

'I haven't said thank you for my present yet,' said Milly.

She leaned forward and kissed him with warm, soft lips. Simon closed his eyes and cupped her face, feeling nothing but sweet sensation. Gradually, his father receded from his thoughts; his soreness began to lessen. Milly was all his—and nothing else really mattered.

'Let's elope,' he said suddenly. 'Sod the wedding. Let's just go and do it on our own in a registry office.' Milly pulled away.

'Do you really want to?' she said. Simon stared back at her. He had been only half-serious, but she was staring at him intently. 'Shall we, Simon?' she said, and there was a slight edge to her voice. 'Tomorrow?'

'Well,' he said, feeling a little taken aback. 'We could do. But wouldn't everyone get a bit pissed off? Your mother would never forgive me.' Milly stared at him for a moment, then bit her lip.

'You're right,' she said. 'It's a stupid idea.' She pushed her chair back and stood up. 'Come on. Are you ready to be grateful to your father yet? He's very kind, you know.'

'Wait,' said Simon. He reached out and grasped her hand tightly. 'Would you really elope with me?'

'Yes,' said Milly simply. 'I would.'

'I thought you were looking forward to the wedding. The dress, and the reception, and all your friends . . .'

'I was,' said Milly. 'But . . .' She looked away and shrugged slightly.

'But you'd give it all up and elope,' said Simon in a shaking voice. 'You'd give it all up.' He gazed at Milly and thought he'd never known such love, such generosity of spirit. 'No other girl would do that,' he said, his voice thick with emotion. 'God, I love you. I don't know what I've done to deserve you. Come here.'

He pulled her down onto his knee and began kissing her neck; feeling for her bra strap; tugging urgently at the zip of her skirt.

'Simon . . .' began Milly.

'We'll close the door,' he whispered. 'Put a chair under the door handle.'

'But your father . . .'

'He made us wait for him,' said Simon, against Milly's warm, scented skin. 'And now he's going to wait for us.'

CHAPTER FOUR

The next morning, Milly woke feeling refreshed. The rich food, wine and conversation from the night before seemed to have disappeared from her system; she felt light and energetic.

As she went into the kitchen for breakfast, a couple of guests from Yorkshire, Mr and Mrs Able, looked up from their coffee and nodded pleasantly.

'Morning, Milly!' said her mother, looking up from the phone. 'There's another special delivery for you.' She pointed to a large cardboard box on the floor. 'And someone's sent you a bottle of champagne. I've put it in the fridge.'

'Champagne!' said Milly in delight. 'And what's this?' She poured herself a cup of coffee, sat down on the floor and began to rip open the cardboard.

'It looks exciting,' said Mrs Able encouragingly.

'And Alexander says he'll meet you at ten-thirty,' said Olivia. 'To take some shots and have a little chat.'

'Oh,' said Milly, suddenly feeling sick. 'Good.'

'You'd better put on some make-up first,' said Olivia. She looked critically at Milly. 'Darling, is something wrong?'

'No,' said Milly. 'Of course not.'

'Ah, Andrea,' said Olivia, turning to the phone. 'Yes, I got your message. And, frankly, it perturbed me.'

Milly began to tug at the plastic wrapping with shaky hands, feeling bubbles of panic rise inside her. She didn't want to see him. She wanted to run away like a child and block him out of her mind.

'Well then, perhaps Derek will have to *buy* a morning suit,' Olivia was saying sharply. 'Andrea, this is a society wedding. Not some dismal affair in a church hall. No, a good lounge suit certainly would not do.' She rolled her eyes at Milly. 'What is it?' she mouthed, gesturing to the present.

Silently, Milly pulled out a pair of Louis Vuitton travel bags and stared at them. Another sumptuous gift. She tried to smile, tried to look pleased. But all she could think of was the thudding fear growing inside her. She didn't want to feel his scrutinizing eyes on her face again. She wanted to hide herself until she was safely married to Simon.

'Well!' said Olivia.

'I've never seen anything like it,' said Mrs Able. 'Geoffrey! Just look at that for a wedding gift. Who are they from, dear?'

Milly looked at the card. 'Someone I've never even heard of.'

'One of Harry's friends, I expect,' said Olivia, putting down the phone.

'I've never known a wedding like this,' said Mrs Able, shaking her head. 'The stories I'm going to tell when I get back home!'

'I told you about the procession, didn't I?' said Olivia complacently going over to the Aga. 'We're having an organist specially flown in from Geneva. He's the best, apparently. And three trumpeters are going to play a fanfare as Milly arrives at the church.'

'A fanfare!' said Mrs Able to Milly. 'You'll feel like a princess.'

'Darling, have an egg,' said Olivia.

'No thanks,' said Milly. 'I'll just have coffee.'

'Still a little fragile after last night,' said Olivia airily, cracking eggs into a pan. 'It was a wonderful dinner, wasn't it, Milly?' She smiled at Mrs Able. 'I have to say, Harry's a wonderful host.'

'I've heard his business dinners are quite something,' said Mrs Able.

'I'm sure they are,' said Olivia. 'But of course, it's different when it's just us.' She gave a reminiscent little smile. 'We never have any of that stuffy formality—we just all enjoy ourselves. We eat, we drink, we talk . . .' She glanced over at Mr and Mrs Able to make sure they were listening. 'After all, Harry is one of our closest friends. And soon he'll be family.'

'Think of that,' said Mr Able. 'Harry Pinnacle, part of your family. And you just running a bed and breakfast house.'

'An *upmarket* bed and breakfast,' snapped Olivia. 'There's a difference!'

'Geoff!' whispered Mrs Able crossly. 'You must dine with him often,' she said quickly to Olivia. 'Being such close friends.'

'Oh well . . .' said Olivia in mollified tones. She waved her egg-slice vaguely in the air.

Twice, thought Milly. You've been twice.

'It really depends,' said Olivia, smiling kindly at Mrs Able. 'We don't have any hard and fast arrangements. Sometimes he'll be out of the country for weeks—then he'll come back and just want to spend a quiet few days with friends.'

'Have you visited his London home?' asked Mrs Able.

'No, I haven't,' said Olivia regretfully. 'Milly has, though. And his villa in France. Haven't you, darling?'

'Yes,' said Milly tightly.

'Quite a jump for you, love,' said Mr Able. 'Joining the jet set overnight.' Olivia bridled.

'It's hardly as though Milly comes from a deprived family,' she exclaimed. 'You're used to mingling with all sorts of people, aren't you, darling? At Milly's school,' she added, giving Mr Able a satisfied glance, 'there was an Arab princess. What was her name, now?'

'I've got to go,' said Milly, unable to bear any more. She stood up, leaving her coffee undrunk.

'That's right,' said Olivia. 'Go and put some make-up on. You want to look your best for Alexander.'

'Yes,' said Milly faintly. She paused by the kitchen door. 'Isobel hasn't called for me this morning, has she?' she asked casually.

'No,' said Olivia. 'I expect she'll ring you later.'

At ten-forty, Alexander appeared at the door of the drawing room.

'Hi, Milly,' he said. 'Sorry I'm a bit late.'

Milly felt a sickening thud of nerves, as though she were being called for an exam or the dentist.

'It doesn't matter,' she said, putting down the copy of *Country Life* she had been pretending to read.

'That's right,' said Olivia, following in behind Alexander. 'By the window, do you think, Alexander, or by the piano?'

'Just where you are, I think,' said Alexander, looking critically at Milly's position on the sofa. 'I'll need to put up a couple of lights . . .'

'Would anyone like a cup of coffee?' said Olivia.

'I'll make it,' said Milly quickly and, without looking back, scuttled out of the room. On the way into the kitchen she glanced at herself in the mirror. Her skin was dry, her eyes had a frightened look in them; she looked nothing like a happy bride. Digging her nails into her palms, she forced herself to smile brightly at her reflection. Everything would be fine. If she could just force herself to act confidently, everything would be fine.

By the time she got back, the room had been transformed into a photographer's studio. A white cloth was draped on the floor and white umbrellas and light stands surrounded the sofa on which Olivia sat, smiling self-consciously at Alexander's camera.

'I'm being your stand-in, darling!' she said brightly.

'Nervous?' said Alexander to Milly.

'Not at all,' she said coolly.

'Let me see your nails, darling,' said Olivia, standing up. 'If we're going to see your engagement ring . . .'

'They're fine,' snapped Milly, whipping her hands away from her mother's grasp. She picked her way over the white cloth, sat down on the sofa and looked up at Alexander with all the calmness she could muster.

'That's right,' said Alexander. 'Now just relax. Sit back a bit.

Loosen your hands.' He stared critically at her for a while. 'Could you sweep your hair back, off your face?'

'That reminds me!' exclaimed Olivia. 'Those photographs I was telling you about. I'll fetch them.'

'OK,' said Alexander absently. 'Now, Milly, I want you to lean back a little and smile.'

Without intending to, Milly found herself obeying his commands. As she smiled, she felt her body relax; felt herself sink into the cushions of the sofa. Alexander seemed utterly preoccupied with his camera. Any suggestion that they'd met before seemed to have been forgotten. She'd been worrying over nothing, she told herself comfortably. Everything was going to be all right. She glanced at her ring, sparkling prettily on her hand, and shifted her legs slightly, to a more flattering position.

'Here we are!' said Olivia, bustling up beside Alexander with a photograph album. 'These are of Isobel, just before she graduated. Now, we thought they were marvellous shots—but then, we don't have the expert's eye. What do you think?'

'Nice,' said Alexander, glancing briefly down.

'Do you really think so?' said Olivia, pleased. She flipped the page backwards. 'Here she is again. And again.' She flipped the pages back further. 'And this is one of Milly at around the same time. It must be ten years ago, now. Just look at her hair!'

'Nice,' said Alexander automatically. He turned his head to look, then, as his eyes fell on the picture of Milly, stopped still. 'Wait,' he said. 'Let me see that.' He took the album from Olivia, stared for a few seconds at the photograph, then looked incredulously at Milly.

'She cut all her hair off and bleached it without telling us!' Olivia was saying brightly. 'She was quite a wild little thing back then! You'd never believe it, looking at her now, would you?'

'No,' said Alexander. 'You'd never believe it.' He gazed down, mesmerized, at the album. 'The wedding girl,' he said softly, as though to himself.

Milly felt her insides turn to ice. She stared at him helplessly, feeling sick with fright, not daring to move a muscle. He remembered. He remembered who she was. But if he would just keep his mouth shut, everything could still be all right. If he would just keep his mouth shut.

'Well,' said Alexander, finally looking up. 'What a difference.' He looked at Milly with a small, amused smile and she stared back, her stomach churning.

'It's the hair,' said Olivia eagerly. 'That's all it is. If you change your hairstyle, everything else seems to change too. You should have seen me with a beehive!'

'I don't think it's just the hair,' said Alexander. 'What do you think, Milly? Is it just the hair? Or is it something else completely?'

He met her eyes and she gazed at him in terror.

'I don't know,' she managed eventually.

'It's a mystery, isn't it?' said Alexander. He gestured to the album. 'There you are, ten years ago . . . and here you are, now, a different woman completely.' He paused, loading film into his camera. 'And here I am.'

'Here's a super picture of Isobel in her school play,' said Olivia, holding the album out to Alexander. He ignored her.

'By the way, Milly,' he said conversationally. 'I never asked you. Is this your first marriage?'

'Of course it's her first marriage!' exclaimed Olivia, laughing slightly. 'Does Milly look old enough to be on her second marriage?'

'You'd be surprised,' said Alexander, adjusting something on the camera. 'These days.' A sudden white flash went off, and Milly flinched as though she were being attacked. Alexander looked up at her.

'Relax,' he said, and the flicker of a smile passed across his face. 'If you can.'

'You look lovely, darling,' said Olivia, clasping her hands together.

'I only asked,' continued Alexander, 'because I seem to do a lot of second marriages these days.' He paused, and surveyed Milly over his camera. 'But that's not you.'

'No,' said Milly in a strangled voice. 'That's not me.'

'Interesting,' said Alexander.

Milly glanced at her mother apprehensively. But Olivia had on her face the same look of polite incomprehension which appeared when business guests started discussing computer software or the yen. As she caught Milly's eye she nodded and started backing deferentially away.'

'I'll see you later, shall I?' she whispered.

'That's good,' said Alexander. 'Now turn your head to the left. Lovely.' The room flashed again. In the corner the door closed softly behind Olivia.

'So, Milly,' said Alexander. 'What have you done with your first husband?'

The room swam around Milly's head; every muscle in her body tightened. She stared fixedly at the camera lens without speaking.

'Loosen your hands,' instructed Alexander. 'They're gripping too tightly. Try to relax.' He took another couple of shots. 'Come on, Milly. What's the story?'

'I don't know what you're talking about,' said Milly in a dry voice. Alexander laughed.

'You're going to have to do better than that.' He reached across and adjusted one of the white umbrellas. 'You know exactly what I'm talking about. And it's obvious no one knows about it except me. I'm intrigued. Try crossing your legs,' he added, looking at her through the lens. 'Left hand on your knee so we can see the ring. And the other under your chin.'

The white flash went off again. Milly stared desperately ahead, trying to frame in her mind a reply, a put-down, a witty riposte. But her thoughts were inarticulate and feeble, as though her brain-power had been sapped by panic. She felt pinned to the sofa by fear, unable to do anything but follow his commands.

'A first marriage isn't against the law, you know,' observed Alexander. 'So what's the problem? Would your bridegroom dis-approve? Or his father?' He took another few shots, then loaded a new reel of film. 'Is that why you're keeping it secret?' He eyed her thoughtfully. 'Or maybe there's a bit more to the story.' He lowered his eye to the lens. 'Can you come slightly forward?'

Milly edged forward. Her stomach was tense, her skin felt prickly.

'I've still got an old photograph of you, by the way,' said Alexander. 'In your wedding dress, on the steps. It made a good shot. I almost framed it.'

The room flashed again. Milly felt giddy with fright. Her mind scurried back to that day in Oxford; to the crowd of tourists who had taken photographs of her and Allan on the steps, as she prinked and smiled and encouraged them. How could she have been so stupid? How could she have . . .

'Of course, you look very different now,' said Alexander. 'I nearly didn't recognize you.'

Milly forced herself to look up and meet his eye.

'You didn't recognize me,' she said. A tiny note of pleading entered her voice. 'You didn't recognize me.'

'Well, I don't know about that,' said Alexander, shaking his head. 'Keeping secrets from your future husband, Milly. Not a good sign.' He peeled off his jersey and threw it into a corner. 'Doesn't the poor guy deserve to know? Shouldn't someone tell him?'

Milly moved her lips to speak but no sound came out. She had never felt so scared in all her life.

'That's great,' said Alexander, looking into the camera again. 'But try not to frown.' He looked up at her and grinned. 'Think happy thoughts.'

After what seemed like hours, he came to an end.

'OK,' he said. 'You can go now.' Milly got up from the sofa and stared at him speechlessly. If she appealed to him—told him everything—he might relent. Or he might not. A tremor ran through her. She couldn't risk it.

'Did you want something?' said Alexander, looking up from his camera case.

'No,' said Milly. For an instant her eyes met his and a bolt of fear went through her. 'Thank you,' she added.

She walked to the door as quickly as she could without looking rushed, forced herself to turn the door knob calmly, and slipped out into the hall. As the door closed behind her, she felt almost tearful with relief. But what should she do now? She closed her eyes for a second, then opened them and reached for the phone. By now she knew the number off by heart.

'Hello,' came a voice. 'If you would like to leave a message for Isobel Havill, please speak after the tone.'

Milly crashed the receiver back down in frustration and stared at it. She had to talk to someone. She couldn't stand this any more. Then a sudden note of inspiration hit her, and she picked up the phone again.

'Hello?' she said, as it was answered. 'Esme? It's Milly. Can I come and see you?'

Milly's godmother lived in a large, elegant house to the north of the city, set back from the road and enclosed in a walled garden. As Milly walked up the path to her house, Esme opened the door and her two lean, pale whippets bounded out into the snow, jumping up at Milly and placing their paws lightly on her chest.

'Get down, you brutes,' exclaimed Esme, from the doorway. 'Leave poor Milly alone. She's feeling sensitive.' Milly looked up.

'Is it that obvious?'

'Of course it isn't,' said Esme. She inhaled on her cigarette and leaned against the door frame. Her dark eyes met Milly's appraisingly. 'But you don't normally ring me in the middle of the day with requests for immediate meetings. I imagine something must be wrong.'

Milly looked into Esme's scrutinizing eyes and suddenly felt shy.

'Not exactly,' she said. She rubbed the dogs' heads absently. 'I just felt like talking to someone, and Isobel's away . . .'

'Talking about what?'

'I don't know really,' said Milly. She swallowed. 'All sorts of things.' Esme puffed again at her cigarette.

'All sorts of things. I'm intrigued. You'd better come in.'

A fire was crackling in the drawing room and a jug of mulled wine was sending fragrant steam into the air. As Milly gave Esme her coat and sank down gratefully into the sofa, she found herself marvelling again that such an urbane, sophisticated woman could be related to her own dull father.

Esme Ormerod was the second half-cousin of James Havill. She had been brought up in London by a different, wealthier side of the family, and James had never known her well. But then, at around the time Milly was born, she had moved to Bath, and had made courteous contact with James. Olivia, impressed by this new, rather exotic relation of James's, had immediately asked her to be Milly's godmother, thinking that this might promote some intimacy between the two women. It had not done so. Esme had never become intimate with Olivia; she was not, as far as Milly knew, intimate with anyone particularly. Everyone in Bath knew of the beautiful Esme Ormerod. Many had attended parties in her house, admired her unusual clothes and the constantly changing collection of *objets* strewn around her rooms, but few could boast that they knew Esme well. Even Milly, who was closest to her of all the Havills, was often at a loss to know what she was thinking or what she might say next.

Neither did she know quite how Esme made her money. Although Esme's branch of the family was wealthy, it was generally agreed that it couldn't be wealthy enough to have fully funded Esme's easy existence for all these years. The few paintings which Esme occasionally sold were, as Milly's father put it, not even enough to keep her in velvet scarfs; apart from that she had no obvious income. The subject of Esme's money was the source of much speculation. One of the latest rumours circulating Bath was that she travelled to London once a month to perform unspeakable sexual acts with an ageing millionaire, who paid her a handsome allowance in return. 'Honestly, what rubbish,' Olivia had said when she'd heard the rumour—then, in the next breath, 'But I suppose it's possible . . .'

'Have one of these.' Esme passed Milly a plate of biscuits, each a beautifully made, individual creation.

'Gorgeous,' said Milly, hovering between one dusted with swirls of cocoa powder and another strewn with almond flakes. 'Where did you get these from?'

'A little shop I know,' said Esme. Milly nodded, and bit into the cocoa swirls; a heavenly, chocolatey taste immediately filled her mouth. Esme seemed to buy everything from tiny, unnamed shops—the opposite of her mother, who preferred large establishments with names that everyone recognized. Fortnum and Mason. Harrods. John Lewis.

'So, how are the wedding preparations going?' said Esme, sitting on the floor in front of the fire and pushing back the sleeves of her grey cashmere sweater. The opal pendant which she always wore glowed in the firelight.

'Fine,' said Milly. 'You know what it's like.' Esme shrugged noncommittally, and it occurred to Milly that she hadn't seen or talked to her godmother for weeks, if not months. But that was not unusual. Their relationship had always gone in phases, ever since Milly was a teenager. Whenever things had gone badly at home, Milly would head straight for Esme's house. Esme always understood her; Esme always treated her like an adult. Milly would spend days in her godmother's company, soaking up her thoughts, adopting her vocabulary, helping her prepare interesting meals filled with ingredients of which Olivia had never heard. They would sit in Esme's drawing room drinking pale, chilled wine, listening to chamber music. Milly would feel grown-up and civilized, and vow to live more like Esme in future. Then, after a day or two, she would return home and pick up her old life exactly where she had left off— and Esme's influence would amount to little more than the odd new word or bottle of cold-pressed olive oil.

'So, darling,' Esme was saying. 'If it's not the wedding, then what is it?'

'It is the wedding,' said Milly. 'But it's a bit complicated.'

'Simon? Have you argued?'

'No,' said Milly at once. 'No. I just . . .' She exhaled sharply and put her biscuit down. 'I just need some advice. Some . . . hypothetical advice.'

'Hypothetical advice?'

'Yes,' said Milly desperately. She met Esme's eyes. 'Hypothetical.'

There was a little pause, then Esme said, 'I understand.' She gave Milly a catlike smile. 'Continue.'

At one o'clock a call came through to Simon's desk from Paris.

'Simon? It's Isobel.'

'Isobel! How are you?'

'Do you know where Milly is? I've been trying to ring her.' Isobel's voice sounded ridiculously distant and tinny, thought Simon. She was only in Paris, for God's sake.

'Isn't she at work?' said Simon.

'Apparently not. Listen, have you two had a row? She's been trying to call me.'

'No,' said Simon, taken aback. 'Not that I know of.'

'Must be something else then,' said Isobel. 'I'll try at home. OK, well, I'll see you when I get back.'

'Wait!' said Simon suddenly. 'Isobel—I want to ask you something.'

'Yes?' She sounded suspicious. Or maybe that was just his paranoia. Simon always found Isobel a little tricky to deal with. For a start, she always said so little. Whenever he spoke to her he ended up feeling self-conscious under her intelligent scrutiny, and wondering what on earth she thought of him. Of course he was fond of her—but he also found her very slightly scary.

'It was a favour, actually,' he said. 'I wondered if you would pick me up a present for Milly.'

'What sort of present?' said Isobel.

If it had been Milly, thought Simon, she would have cried 'Of course I will!' straight away—and then asked for details.

'I want to get her a Chanel bag.' He swallowed. 'So maybe you could choose her one.'

'A Chanel bag?' said Isobel incredulously. 'Do you know how much they cost?'

'Yes,' said Simon.

'Hundreds.'

'Yes.'

'Simon, you're mad. Milly doesn't want a Chanel bag.'

'Yes she does!'

'It's not her style.'

'Of course it is,' retorted Simon. 'Milly likes elegant, classic pieces.'

'If you say so,' replied Isobel drily. Then she sighed. 'Simon, is this about your father buying you a flat?'

'No!' said Simon. 'Of course not.' He hesitated. 'How did you know about that?'

'Mummy told me. And she told me about the ear-rings.' Isobel's voice softened. 'Look, I can guess it wasn't an easy moment for you. But that's no reason to go and spend all your money on an expensive bag.'

'Milly deserves the best.'

'She's got the best. She's got you!'

'But—'

'Look, Simon. If you really want to buy Milly something, buy something for the flat. A sofa. Or a rug. She'd love that.'

There was silence.

'You're right,' said Simon eventually.

'Of course I'm right.'

'It's just . . .' Simon exhaled. 'My fucking father!'

'I know,' said Isobel. 'But what can you do? He's a generous millionaire. It's a bummer.' Simon winced.

'God, you're harsh, aren't you? I think I prefer your sister.'

'Fine by me. Look, I've got to go. I've got a plane to catch.'

'OK. Listen, thanks, Isobel. I'm really grateful.'

'Yeah, yeah. I know. Bye.' And she was gone before Simon could say anything more.

'All right,' said Milly. She hunched her shoulders up, staring away from Esme, into the flickering fire. 'Suppose there was a person. And suppose that person had a secret.'

'A person,' said Esme, looking at her quizzically. 'And a secret.'

'Yes,' said Milly, still staring at the fire. 'And suppose she'd never told anyone about it. Not even the man she loved.'

'Why not?'

'Because he didn't need to know,' said Milly defensively. 'Because it was just some stupid, irrevelant thing which happened ten years ago. And if it came out, it would ruin everything. Not just for her. For everybody.'

'Ah,' said Esme. 'That kind of secret.'

'Yes,' said Milly. 'That kind of secret.' She took a deep breath. 'And suppose . . .' She bit her lip. 'Suppose someone came along who knew about the secret. And he started threatening to say something.'

Esme exhaled softly.

'I see.'

'But she didn't know if he was serious or not. She thought he might just be joking.'

Esme nodded.

'The thing is,' said Milly, 'what should she do?' She looked up. 'Should she tell the . . . the partner? Or should she just keep quiet and hope that she'd get away with it?'

Esme reached for her cigarette case.

'Is it really a secret worth keeping?' she said. 'Or is it just some silly little indiscretion that no one would mind about? Might this person be overreacting?'

'No,' said Milly, 'she's not overreacting. It's a very big secret. Like a . . .' She paused. 'Like a previous marriage. Or something.'

Esme raised her eyebrows.

'That *is* a big secret.'

'Or something,' repeated Milly. 'It doesn't matter what it is.' She met Esme's eyes steadily. 'The point is, she's kept it secret for ten years. No one's ever known about it. No one needs to know.'

'Yes,' said Esme. 'I see.' She lit a fresh cigarette and inhaled deeply.

'So what would you do, if you were that person?' said Milly. Esme blew out a cloud of smoke thoughtfully.

'What is the risk of this other character giving her away?'

'I don't know,' said Milly. 'Quite small at the moment, I think.'

'Then I would say nothing,' said Esme. 'For the moment. And I would try to think of a way of keeping the other one quiet.' She shrugged. 'Perhaps the whole thing will quietly fade away.'

'Do you think so?' Milly looked up. 'Do you really think so?' Esme smiled.

'Darling, how many times have you tossed and turned at night, worried about something, only to find in the morning that there was nothing to fear? How many times have you rushed in with an excuse for some misdemeanour, only to find no one realized you'd done anything wrong?' She took a deep drag on her cigarette. 'Nine times out of ten, it's better to say nothing and keep your head down and hope that everything will proceed smoothly. And no one need ever know.' She paused. 'Hypothetically speaking, of course.'

'Yes, of course.'

There was silence, broken only by the crackle and spitting of the fire. Outside, it had begun to snow again, in thick, blurry flakes.

'Have some more mulled wine,' suggested Esme. 'Before it gets cold. And another biscuit.'

'Thanks,' murmured Milly. She picked up a disc of smooth

clementine fondant and gazed at it. 'You don't think I . . . the person should be honest with her partner.'

'Why should she?'

'Because . . . because she's going to marry him!' Esme smiled.

'Darling, it's a nice idea. But a woman should never try to be honest with a man. It's quite impossible.'

Milly looked up. 'What do you mean, impossible?'

'Of course, one can try,' said Esme. 'But essentially, women and men speak different languages. They have . . . different senses. Put a man and a woman in exactly the same situation and they'll perceive it entirely differently.'

'So?'

'So, they're foreign to each other,' said Esme. 'And the truth is, you can't be completely honest with someone you don't properly understand.'

Milly thought for a few moments.

'People who've been happily married for years understand each other,' she said at last.

'They muddle through,' said Esme, 'with a mixture of sign language and goodwill and the odd phrase picked up over the years. But they don't understand each other. They don't have access to the rich depths of each other's spirits. The common language simply isn't there.' She inhaled on her cigarette again. 'And there aren't any interpreters. Or at least, very few.'

Milly stared at her. 'So you're saying there's no such thing as a happy marriage.'

'I'm saying there's no such thing as an honest marriage,' said Esme. 'Happiness is something else.' She blew out a cloud of smoke.

'I suppose you're right,' said Milly doubtfully, and glanced at her watch. 'Esme, I've got to go.'

'So soon?'

'We're having a wedding present given to us at Simon's work.'

'I see.' Esme tapped her cigarette ash into a mother of pearl dish. 'Well, I hope I've been some help with your little problem.'

'Not really,' said Milly bluntly. 'If anything, I'm more confused than before.' Esme smiled amusedly.

'Oh dear. I'm sorry.' She surveyed Milly's face. 'So—what do you think your . . . hypothetical person will do?'

There was silence.

'I don't know,' said Milly eventually. 'I really don't know.'

James Havill had left the office at lunchtime that day and headed for home. As he let himself in, the house was steeped in a midday quiet, silent apart from the odd creak. He stood for a few moments in the hall, listening for voices. But the house seemed as empty as he had hoped it would be. At this time of day, the guests would be out, sightseeing. Milly would still be at work; the daily woman would have finished. The only person in the house now would be Olivia.

He climbed the stairs as soundlessly as possible. As he rounded the corner to the second floor his heart began to beat in anticipation. He had planned this encounter all morning; had sat in meetings thinking of nothing except what he would say to his wife that afternoon. What he would say—and how he would say it.

The door to her room was closed. James stared for a moment at the little porcelain plaque bearing the word PRIVATE, before knocking.

'Yes?' Her voice sounded startled.

'It's only me,' he said and pushed the door open. The room was warm from an electric fire; too warm, he thought. Olivia was sitting in her faded chintz armchair in front of the television. Her feet were resting on the tapestry footstool she had uphol-stered herself. A cup of tea was at her elbow, and her hands were full of pale pink silk.

'Hello,' said James. He glanced at the screen where a black and white Bette Davis was talking frostily to a man with a square jaw. 'I didn't mean to disturb you.'

'Don't worry,' said Olivia. She picked up the remote control and reduced Bette Davis's voice to an almost inaudible murmur. 'What do you think?'

'What do you mean?' said James, taken aback.

'Isobel's dress!' said Olivia, holding up the pink silk. 'I thought it looked a little plain, so I'm just trimming it with some roses.'

'Lovely,' said James, still gazing at the screen. He couldn't quite make out what Bette Davis was saying. She had unbuttoned her gloves; was she about to challenge the square-jawed man to a fight? He looked up. 'I wanted to talk to you.'

'And I wanted to talk to you,' said Olivia. She picked up a red exercise book lying near her chair and consulted it. 'First, have you checked the route to the church with the council?'

'I know the route,' said James. Olivia sighed exasperatedly.

'Of course you do. But do you know if any road-works or demonstrations are going to spring up on Saturday? No! That's why we have to ring the council. Don't you remember?' She began to write in the exercise book. 'Don't worry. I'll do it myself.'

James said nothing. He looked around for somewhere to sit, but there were no other chairs. After a pause he sat down on the edge of the bed. Olivia's duvet was soft and smelt faintly of her perfume. It was spread evenly over her bed and anchored down with lacy cushions, neat and sexless as though she never slept in it. For all he knew, she didn't. James had not seen the underside of Olivia's duvet for six years.

'The other thing,' said Olivia, 'is about presents for the guests.'

'Presents *for* the guests?'

'Yes, James,' said Olivia impatiently. 'Presents for the guests. Everyone gives their guests a present these days.'

'I thought it was the other way around.'

'It's both. The guests give presents to Milly and Simon, and we give presents to the guests.'

'And who gives presents to us?' asked James. Olivia rolled her eyes.

'You're not helping, James. Milly and I have already organized for each guest to receive a champagne flute.'

'Well then, that's fine.' James took a deep breath. 'Olivia—'

'But I was wondering, wouldn't a flowering rose bush be more original? Look.' She gestured to an open magazine on the floor. 'Isn't that pretty?'

'A flowering rose bush for each guest? The place will be a bloody forest.'

'A *mini* rose bush,' said Olivia impatiently. 'Purse-sized, they call it.'

'Olivia, haven't you got enough to do without organizing last-minute purse-sized rose bushes?'

'Maybe you're right,' said Olivia regretfully. She reached for her pen and scored out an entry in her exercise book. 'Now, what else was there?'

'Olivia, listen for a moment,' said James. He cleared his throat.

'I wanted to talk about—' He broke off. 'About what's going to happen. After the wedding.'

'For goodness' sake, James! Let's just get the wedding safely over before we start talking about what happens next. As if I haven't got enough to think about!'

'Just hear me out.' James closed his eyes and took a deep breath. 'I think we both realize that things will be different when Milly's gone, don't we? When it's just the two of us in this house.'

'Fees for the choir . . .' murmured Olivia, ticking off on her fingers. 'Buttonholes . . .'

'There's no point pretending things are the same as they were.'

'Cake stand . . .'

'We've been drifting apart for years, now. You've got your life, I've got mine . . .'

'Speech!' said Olivia, looking up triumphantly. 'Have you composed your speech?'

'Yes,' said James, staring at her. 'But no one seems to be listening.'

'Because what I suggest is that you write *two* sets of notes. Then I can keep one, just in case.' She smiled brightly at him.

'Olivia . . .'

'And I'm going to suggest the same to Simon. Let me just write that down.'

She began to scribble and James's eyes drifted towards the television screen. Bette Davis was falling into the arms of the square-jawed man; tears glistened on her lashes.

'Right,' said Olivia. 'Well, that's it.' She looked at her watch and stood up. 'And now I must pop along to see the choirmaster. Was there anything else?'

'Well—'

'Because I am running a little late. Excuse me.' She gestured to James to stand up, and laid the pink silk carefully on the bed. 'See you later!'

'Yes,' said James. 'See you later.'

The door closed behind him and he found himself staring again at Olivia's little plaque.

'So what I'm saying,' he said to the door, 'is that after the wedding, I want to move out. I want a new life. Do you understand?'

There was silence. James shrugged, turned on his heel and walked away.

CHAPTER FIVE

As Milly arrived at the offices where Simon worked, there was a small shriek from the reception desk.

'She's here!' cried Pearl, one of the middle-aged receptionists. 'Milly's here!' She beamed as Milly approached the desk. 'How are you, dear? Not too nervous about Saturday?'

'There's nothing to be nervous about,' exclaimed another of the receptionists, a woman in a pale blue cardigan and matching eye shadow. 'Just make sure you enjoy the day, darling. It'll go by so fast!'

'It'll be a blur,' said Pearl, nodding seriously. 'What you need to do is, every so often, stop still and look around, and say to yourself: this is my wedding day. Just say it. This is my wedding day. And then you'll enjoy yourself!' She smiled at Milly. 'I'll buzz Simon for you, then I'll take you up.'

'It's all right,' said Milly. 'I know the way.'

'No trouble!' exclaimed Pearl. She tapped at her keyboard. 'Margaret, keep trying Simon, will you? And tell him I'm on my way up with Milly.'

To a chorus of good lucks, the two of them walked across the reception area to the lifts.

'We're coming to watch you on Saturday,' said Pearl, as the lift doors closed behind them. 'Outside the church. You don't mind, do you, dear?'

'Of course not,' said Milly confusedly. 'You mean you're just going to stand there and watch?'

'Beryl's bringing camp-chairs!' said Pearl triumphantly. 'And we'll have a thermos of coffee. We want to see everyone arrive. All the VIPs. It'll be just like a royal wedding!'

'Well,' said Milly, embarrassed. 'I don't know about—'

'Or that lovely wedding on the television,' said Pearl. 'On *East-Enders* the other day. Did you see it?'

'Oh, yes!' said Milly enthusiastically. 'Wasn't it romantic?'

'Those two little bridesmaids,' Pearl sighed fondly. 'Weren't they a picture?'

'Gorgeous,' agreed Milly. 'Not,' she added quickly, as the lift approached Simon's floor, 'that I really knew who any of the characters were. I don't normally watch *EastEnders*. I prefer . . . documentaries.'

'Do you, dear? I couldn't live without my soaps,' said Pearl comfortably. 'Your Simon teases me about them. Quizzes me on all the plots.' She smiled at Milly. 'He's a lovely boy really. So down-to-earth. You wouldn't think he was who he is. If you know what I mean.' The lift pinged. 'Here we are.' She peered down the carpeted corridor. 'Now, where's he got to?'

'Here I am,' said Simon, suddenly appearing round the corner. He held out a bottle of wine and some plastic cups to Pearl. 'Take these down for everyone on reception.'

'That's very kind!' said Pearl. 'And make sure you come down and show us your present.' She took one of Milly's hands and pressed it hard. 'Good luck, my dear,' she said. 'You deserve nothing but happiness.'

'Thank you,' said Milly, feeling tears prick the backs of her eyes. 'You're very kind.'

The lift doors closed, and Simon grinned at Milly. 'Come on,' he said. 'They're all waiting for you.'

'Don't say that!' said Milly. 'You're making me nervous.'

'Nervous?' Simon laughed. 'There's nothing to be nervous about!'

'I know,' said Milly. 'I'm just . . . a bit on edge at the moment.'

'Wedding jitters,' said Simon.

'Yes,' said Milly. She smiled at him. 'That must be it.'

Simon's department had clustered self-consciously in the office he shared with four other advertising salespeople. As they arrived, bottles of fizzy wine were being passed around in plastic cups, and a woman in a red jacket was hastily collecting some last-minute signatures on an outsize card.

'What shall I put?' a girl was wailing as Milly passed. 'Everyone else has been really witty.'

'Just put your name!' snapped the woman in the red jacket. 'And hurry up.'

Milly clutched her plastic cup and fixed a smile to her face.

She felt vulnerable under the gaze of so many people, so many strangers. She sipped at the fizzy wine and took a crisp from the plate offered to her by one of Simon's cheery colleagues.

'Aha!' A deep voice interrupted the general chatter, and she looked up. A man in a brown suit with receding hair and a moustache was bearing down on her. 'You must be Simon's fiancée.' He grasped her hand. 'Mark Taylor. Head of publications. Very pleased to meet you.'

'Hello,' said Milly politely.

'Now, where's he got to? We've got to get this presentation done. Simon! Over here!'

'Have you two met?' said Simon, coming up. 'Sorry, I should have introduced you properly.'

Mark Taylor was clapping his hands.

'All right, everyone. Hush up, hush up. On behalf of us all here at Pendulum, I'd like to wish Simon and Mandy all the very best for their future together.' He raised his glass.

'Milly!' shouted someone.

'What?' said Mark Taylor, screwing up his face puzzledly.

'It's Milly, not Mandy!'

'It doesn't matter,' said Milly, going red.

'What are they saying?' said Mark Taylor.

'Nothing,' said Milly. 'Carry on.'

'To Mandy and Simon! May they have a long, happy and prosperous life together.' A telephone began to ring in the corner of the room. 'Get that, somebody, would you?'

'Where's the present?' shouted someone.

'Yes,' said Mark Taylor. 'Where is the present?'

'It's being delivered,' said a woman to Milly's left. 'It's off the list. A covered vegetable dish. I've got a picture of it.'

'Very nice,' said Mark Taylor. He raised his voice. 'The present is a covered vegetable dish off the list! Sally's got a picture, if anyone's interested.'

'But there should be a card,' said Sally. 'Where's the card?'

'Here it is!' said the woman in the red jacket.

There was a small silence as Simon ripped open the huge envelope and opened a large card with two teddy bears on the front. He scanned the signatures, laughing every so often; looking up and nodding to people as he read their messages. Milly looked over his shoulder. Most of the jokes were about targets and quarter-pages and, bewilderingly, something called Powerlink.

'Great,' said Simon eventually. 'I'm really touched.'

'Speech!' yelled someone.

'I'm not going to make a speech,' said Simon.

'Thank the Lord!' interjected someone else.

Simon took a sip of fizzy wine.

'But I just wanted to say,' he said, 'for those of you who thought the most important thing in my life was beating Eric's insane monthly targets'—there was a small laugh—'or demolishing Andy at darts . . .'

There was a bigger laugh, and Simon smiled.

'For all of you,' he said, 'I've got some news. You're wrong.' He paused. 'The most important thing in my life is standing next to me.' He took Milly's hand, and there was a small sigh from some of the girls. 'This woman,' he said, 'for those of you who don't know her, is the most beautiful, sweet-natured, open and giving woman in the world—and I'm truly honoured that, on Saturday, she will become my wife. I feel very lucky.'

There was a short silence, then in muted tones someone said, 'To Milly and Simon.'

'To Milly and Simon,' chorused the others obediently. Milly looked up at Simon's happy, unaware face and felt a sudden misery come over her.

'I'll see you all in the pub!' added Simon. The crowd began to disperse and he smiled down at Milly.

'Did I embarrass you?'

'Just a bit,' said Milly, trying to smile back. Her skin was prickling with guilt and her insides felt clenched by a strong, bony hand.

'I just had to tell everyone how I feel,' said Simon. He stroked her hair tenderly. 'Sometimes I can't believe how much I love you.' A sudden rush of tears came to Milly's eyes.

'Don't,' she said. 'Don't.'

'Look at you!' said Simon, tracing her tears with his thumb. 'Oh, sweetheart. Do you want a hanky?'

'Thanks,' gulped Milly. She mopped at her face and took a couple of deep breaths.

'Simon!' A cheerful voice interrupted them. 'Your round, I believe!'

'OK!' said Simon, grinning. 'Give me a minute.'

'Simon,' said Milly quickly. 'Would you mind if I didn't come to the pub?'

'Oh,' said Simon. His face fell.

'I'm just feeling a bit tired,' said Milly. 'I don't really feel up to'—she gestured—'all of this.'

'Simon!' yelled someone. 'You coming or what?'

'Hang on!' called Simon. He touched Milly's face gently. 'Would you rather we went off somewhere, just the two of us?'

Milly looked at him and had a sudden vision of the two of

them in a secluded restaurant. They would sit tucked away at a corner table. They would eat risotto and drink mellow red wine. And slowly, quietly, she would tell him the truth.

'No,' she said. 'You go and have fun. I'll have an early night.'

'You're sure?'

'Yes.' She pulled his face down and kissed it. 'Go on. I'll talk to you tomorrow.'

She arrived home wanting to go straight to bed. As she took off her coat she heard voices in the kitchen, and winced as it occurred to her that Aunt Jean might have arrived early. But when she pushed open the door, it was Isobel she saw, standing on a kitchen chair, wearing a pink bridesmaid's dress and with a garland of dried flowers in her hair.

'Isobel!' she exclaimed, feeling sudden, almost tearful relief. 'When did you get back?' Isobel looked up and grinned.

'This afternoon. I got back home, and what do I find? My bloody pipes have gone.'

'Pipes?'

'Water pipes,' said Isobel. 'What did you think I meant? Bagpipes?'

'Isobel's going to stay here until the wedding,' said Olivia, with a mouthful of kirby grips. 'Although of course we'll be a bit squashed when Aunt Jean and the cousins arrive . . .'

'Get rid of Alexander,' said Milly. She sat down at the table and began to fiddle with a stray rosebud. 'Then there'll be room.'

'Don't be silly, darling,' said Olivia. 'He's got to stay here.'

She shoved another kirby grip into Isobel's hair and poked at the garland. 'There. That's better.'

'If you say so,' said Isobel. She grinned at Milly. 'What do you think?'

Milly looked up and for the first time registered what Isobel was wearing.

'What happened to your dress?' she asked, trying not to sound appalled.

'I added some silk roses,' said Olivia. 'Aren't they pretty?' Milly met Isobel's eye.

'Beautiful,' she said. Isobel grinned.

'Be honest. Do I look like an idiot?'

'No,' said Milly. She looked at Isobel and frowned. 'You look . . . tired.'

'That's what I said!' exclaimed Olivia triumphantly. 'She looks washed-out and peaky.'

'I don't look washed-out and peaky,' said Isobel impatiently. Milly gazed at her sister. Isobel's skin was almost grey; her fair, straight hair was lank. The flowers in her hair only emphasized the lack of bloom in her cheeks.

'You'll look fine on the day,' she said uncertainly. 'Once you're wearing some make-up.'

'She's lost weight, too,' said Olivia disapprovingly. 'We could almost do with taking this dress in.'

'I haven't lost that much,' said Isobel. 'Anyway, it doesn't matter what I look like. It's Milly's day, not mine.' She looked at Milly. 'How are you doing?'

'I'm OK,' said Milly. She met her sister's eyes. 'You know.'

'Yup,' said Isobel. She began to slip the pink dress off. 'Well, I might go upstairs and get sorted out.'

'I'll come and help you,' said Milly at once.

'That's right,' said Olivia. 'Good little girl.'

Isobel's room was next door to Milly's, at the top of the house. Now that she had left home it was occasionally used by bed and breakfast guests, but more often than not remained empty, clean and neat, waiting for her return.

'Jesus!' said Isobel, as she opened the door. 'What's all this?'

'Wedding presents,' said Milly. 'And this is just a few of them.'

They both looked silently around the room. Every spare piece of floor was piled high with boxes. A few had been opened: they spilled shredded paper and bubble wrap; glimpses of glass and china.

'What's this?' said Isobel, prodding one of them.

'I don't know,' said Milly. 'I think it's a soup tureen.'

'A soup tureen,' echoed Isobel disbelievingly. 'Are you planning to cook soup when you're married?'

'I suppose so,' said Milly.

'You'll have to, now you've got a special tureen to put it in.' Isobel caught Milly's eye and she began to giggle, in spite of herself. 'You'll have to sit in every night, and ladle soup out of your soup tureen.'

'Shut up!' said Milly.

'And drink sherry out of your eight sherry glasses,' said Isobel, reading the label on another parcel. 'Married life is going to be a riot.'

'Don't!' said Milly. She was shaking with giggles; her eyes were bright.

'Electric breadmaker. Now, I wouldn't mind one of those.' Isobel looked up. 'Milly, are you OK?'

'I'm fine,' said Milly. 'I'm fine.' But her giggles were turning into sobs; suddenly a pair of tears landed on her cheeks.

'Milly! I knew there was something.' Isobel came over and put her hands on Milly's shoulders. 'What's wrong? What did you want to talk to me about in Paris?'

'Oh God, Isobel!' More tears landed on Milly's face. 'It's all gone wrong!'

'What?'

'I'm in real trouble!'

'What do you mean?' Isobel's voice rose in alarm. 'Milly, tell me! What's happened?'

Milly looked at her for a long time.

'Come here,' she said at last. She went back into her own room, waited until Isobel had followed her inside, and closed the door. Then, as Isobel watched silently, she reached up inside the chimney, scrabbled for a bit, and pulled down an old school shoe-bag, drawn tightly at the neck.

'What—'

'Wait,' said Milly, groping inside. She pulled out a smaller bag—then, from that, produced a box tied tightly with string. She tugged at the string and wrenched it off, taking the lid off with it. For a few moments she stared at the open box. Then she held it out to Isobel.

'OK,' she said. 'This is what's happened.'

'Blimey,' said Isobel. Staring up at them from inside the box was a photograph of Milly in a wedding dress, beaming through a cloud of confetti. Isobel picked it up and stared at it more closely. Glancing at Milly, she put it down, and picked up the photograph underneath. It was a picture of two men standing side by side, one dark-haired, the other fair. Beneath that was a shot of the dark-haired man kissing Milly's hand. Milly was simpering at the camera. Her veil was tossed over her shoulder; she looked wildly happy.

Without speaking, Isobel leafed through to the end of the pile of pictures. Underneath the photographs were some old faded confetti and a little flowered card.

'Can I?' said Isobel, touching the card.

'Go ahead.'

Silently, Isobel opened the card and read the inscription: 'To the best bride in the world. Yours ever, Allan.' She looked up.

'Who the hell is Allan?'

'Who do you think he is, Isobel?' said Milly in a ragged voice. 'He's my husband.'

As Milly came to the end of her faltering story, Isobel exhaled sharply. She got up, strode to the fireplace and stood for a moment, saying nothing. Milly, who was sitting in an armchair, hugging a cushion to her chest, watched her apprehensively.

'I can't quite get my head round this,' said Isobel eventually.

'I know,' said Milly.

'You really married a guy to keep him in the country?'

'Yes,' said Milly. She glanced at the wedding pictures, still spread over the floor; at herself, young and vibrant and happy. As she had told the story, all the romance and adventure of what she'd done had flooded back into her, and for the first time in years she'd felt a nostalgia for those heady, magical Oxford days.

'Those bastards!' Isobel was shaking her head. 'They must have seen you coming!' Milly stared at her sister.

'It wasn't like that,' she said. Isobel looked up.

'What do you mean, it wasn't like that? Milly, they used you!'

'They didn't!' said Milly defensively. 'I helped them because I wanted to. They were my friends.'

'Friends,' echoed Isobel scathingly. 'Is that what you think? Well, if they were such great friends, how come I never met them? Or even heard about them?'

'We lost touch.'

'When did you lose touch? As soon as you'd signed on the dotted line?'

Milly was silent.

'Oh, Milly,' said Isobel. She sighed. 'Did they pay you?'

'No,' said Milly. 'They gave me a necklace.' Her hands reached for the little pearls.

'Well, that's a lot of compensation,' said Isobel sarcastically. 'Bearing in mind you broke the law for them. Bearing in mind you could have been prosecuted. The Home Office investigates phoney marriages, you know! Or didn't you know?'

'Don't go on about it, Isobel,' said Milly in a trembling voice. 'It's done, OK? And there's nothing I can do about it.'

'OK,' said Isobel. 'Look, I'm sorry. This must be awful for you.' She picked up one of the pictures and stared at it for a few moments. 'I have to say, I'm surprised you risked keeping these.'

'I know,' said Milly. 'It was stupid. But I couldn't bear to throw them out. They're all I've got left of the whole thing.' Isobel sighed, and put the photograph down.

'And you've never told Simon about it.'

Milly shook her head, lips clamped together tightly.

'Well, you've got to,' said Isobel. 'You do know that?'

'I can't,' said Milly, closing her eyes. 'I can't tell him. I just can't.'

'You're going to have to!' said Isobel. 'Before this Alexander character decides to say something to him.'

'He might not say anything,' said Milly in a small voice.

'But he might!' retorted Isobel. 'And it's not worth the risk.' She sighed. 'Look, just tell him. He won't mind! Plenty of people are divorced these days.'

'I know they are,' said Milly.

'There's no shame in it! So you're divorced.' She shrugged. 'It could be worse.'

'But I'm not,' said Milly tightly.

'What?' Isobel stared at her.

'I'm not divorced,' said Milly. 'I'm still married.'

There was a still silence.

'You're still married?' said Isobel in a whisper. 'You're still *married*? But Milly, your wedding's on Saturday!'

'I know!' cried Milly. 'Don't you think I know that?' And as Isobel gazed at her in horror, she buried her head in the cushion and sank into blinding tears.

The brandy was in the kitchen. As Isobel opened the door, hoping no one was about, Olivia raised her head from the phone.

'Isobel!' she said in a stage whisper. 'The most ghastly thing's happened!'

'What?' said Isobel, feeling a beat of fear.

'There aren't enough orders of service. People are going to have to share!'

'Oh,' said Isobel. She felt a sudden, terrible desire to cackle. 'Well, never mind.'

'Never mind?' hissed Olivia. 'The whole event will look shoddy!' Her eyes narrowed as she watched Isobel pour out a glass of brandy. 'Why are you drinking brandy?'

'It's for Milly,' said Isobel. 'She's a bit tense.'

'Is everything all right?'

'Yes,' said Isobel, backing away. 'Everything's just fine.'

She went back up to the bedroom, closed the door and tapped Milly on the shoulder.

'Drink this,' she said. 'And calm down. It'll be OK.'

'How can it be OK?' sobbed Milly. 'It's all going to come out! Everything's going to be ruined.'

'Come on,' said Isobel. She put an arm round Milly's shoulders. 'Come on. We'll sort it out. Don't worry.'

'I don't see how we can,' said Milly, looking up with a tear-stained face. She took a sip of brandy. 'I've completely messed things up, haven't I?'

'No,' said Isobel. 'Of course you haven't.' Milly gave a shaky laugh.

'Nice try, Isobel.' She took another sip of brandy. 'God, I need a cigarette. Do you want one?'

'No thanks,' said Isobel.

'Come on,' said Milly, pushing open the sash window with shaking hands. 'One cigarette won't give you bloody lung cancer.'

'No,' said Isobel after a pause. 'No, I suppose one cigarette can't hurt.' She sat down on the windowsill. Milly passed her a cigarette and they both inhaled deeply. As the smoke hit her lungs, Milly felt her whole body expand and relax.

'I needed that,' she said with a sigh. She blew out a cloud of smoke and wafted it with her hand out of the window. 'Oh God. What a mess.'

'What I don't understand,' said Isobel carefully, 'is why you didn't get a divorce.'

'We were always going to,' said Milly, biting her lip. 'Allan was going to sort it out. I even got some papers from his lawyers. But then it all fizzled out and I didn't hear any more. I never went to court, nothing.'

'And you never chased it up?'

Milly was silent.

'Not even when Simon asked you to marry him?' Isobel's voice sharpened. 'Not even when you started planning the wedding?'

'I didn't know how to! Allan left Oxford, I didn't know where he was, I lost all the papers . . .'

'You could have gone to a lawyer, couldn't you? Or the Citizens' Advice Bureau?'

'I know.'

'So why—'

'Because I didn't dare, OK? I didn't dare rock the boat.' Milly puffed quickly on her cigarette. 'I knew what I'd done was dodgy. People might have started poking around and asking questions. I couldn't risk it!'

'But Milly . . .'

'I just didn't want anyone else to know. Not a single person. While no one else knew, I felt . . . safe.'

'Safe!'

'Yes, safe!' said Milly defensively. 'No one in the world knew about it. No one asked any questions; no one suspected any-thing!' She raised her eyes to Isobel's. 'I mean, did *you* suspect anything?'

'I suppose not,' said Isobel reluctantly.

'Of course you didn't. No one did.' Milly took another shaky drag. 'And the more time went on, the more it was as though the whole thing had never happened. A few years went by, and still nobody knew about it, and gradually it just . . . stopped existing.'

'What do you mean, it stopped existing?' said Isobel impatiently. 'Milly, you married the man! You can't change that.'

'It was three minutes in a registry office,' said Milly. 'One tiny signature, ten years ago. Buried on some legal document which no one's ever going to see again. That's not a marriage, Isobel. It's a piece of dust. A nothing!'

'And what about when Simon asked you to marry him?'

There was a sharp silence.

'I thought about telling him,' said Milly at last. 'I really did. But in the end, I just couldn't see the point. It's got nothing to do with us. It would just have complicated things. He didn't need to know.'

'So what were you going to do?' said Isobel incredulously. 'Commit *bigamy*?'

'The first one wasn't a proper marriage,' said Milly, looking away. 'It wouldn't have counted.'

'What do you mean?' exclaimed Isobel. 'Of course it would have counted! Jesus, Milly, how can you be such a moron? I don't believe you sometimes!'

'Oh shut up, Isobel!' cried Milly furiously.

'Fine. I'll shut up.'

'Fine.'

There was silence for a while. Milly finished her cigarette, then stubbed it out on the windowsill.

'Aren't you going to smoke yours?' she said, not looking at Isobel.

'I don't think I want the rest of it. You can have it.'

'OK.' Milly took the half-burned cigarette, then glanced at her sister, momentarily distracted. 'Are you OK?' she said. 'Mummy's right, you look awful.'

'I'm fine,' said Isobel shortly.

'You're not anorexic, are you?'

'No!' Isobel laughed. 'Of course I'm not.'

'Well, you've been losing weight . . .'

'So have you.'

'Have I?' said Milly, plucking at her clothes. 'It's probably all this stress.'

'Well, don't stress,' said Isobel firmly. 'OK? Stressing is useless.' She pulled her knees up and hugged them. 'If only we knew how far your divorce had actually got.'

'It didn't get anywhere,' said Milly hopelessly. 'I told you, I never went to court.'

'So what? You don't have to go to court to get a divorce.'

'Yes you do.'

'No you don't.'

'Yes you do!' said Milly. 'They did in *Kramer versus Kramer*.'

'For God's sake, Milly!' exclaimed Isobel. 'Don't you know anything? That was for a custody battle.'

There was a little pause, then Milly said, 'Oh.'

'If it's just a divorce, your lawyer goes for you.'

'What lawyer? I didn't have a lawyer.'

Milly took a final drag on Isobel's cigarette, then stubbed it out. Isobel was silent, her brow wrinkled perplexedly. Then suddenly she looked up.

'Well, maybe you didn't need one. Maybe Allan did all the divorcing for you.'

Milly stared at her.

'Are you serious?'

'I don't know. It's possible.' Milly swallowed.

'So I might be divorced after all?'

'I don't see why not. In theory.'

'Well, how can I find out?' said Milly agitatedly. 'Why didn't I hear? Is there some official list of divorces somewhere? My God, if I found out I was actually divorced . . .'

'I'm sure there is,' said Isobel. 'But there's a quicker way.'

'What?'

'Do what you should have done bloody years ago. Phone your husband.'

'I can't,' said Milly at once. 'I don't know where he is.'

'Well then, find him!'

'I can't.'

'Of course you can!'

'I don't even know where to start! And anyway—' Milly broke off and looked away.

'What?' There was silence as Milly lit another cigarette with trembling hands. 'What?' repeated Isobel impatiently.

'I don't want to speak to him, OK?'

'Why not?' Isobel peered at Milly's downcast face. 'Why not, Milly?'

'Because you're right,' said Milly suddenly, tears springing to her eyes. 'You're right, Isobel! Those two were never my friends, were they? They just used me. They just took what they could get. All these years, I've thought of them as my friends. They loved each other so much, and I wanted to help them . . .'

'Milly . . .'

'You know, I wrote to them when I got back,' said Milly, staring into the darkness. 'Allan used to write back. I always planned to go back one day and surprise them. Then gradually we lost touch. But I still thought of them as friends.' She looked up at Isobel. 'You don't know what it was like in Oxford. It was like a whirlwind romance between the three of us. We went punting, and we had picnics, and we talked into the night . . .' She broke off. 'And they were probably just laughing at me the whole time, weren't they?'

'No,' said Isobel. 'I'm sure they weren't.'

'They saw me coming,' said Milly bitterly. 'A naive, gullible little fool who would do anything they asked.'

'Look, don't think about it,' said Isobel, putting her arm around Milly's shoulders. 'That was ten years ago. It's over. Finished with. You have to look ahead. You have to find out about your divorce.'

'I can't,' said Milly, shaking her head. 'I can't talk to him. He'll just be . . . laughing at me.' Isobel sighed.

'You're going to have to.'

'But he could be anywhere,' said Milly helplessly. 'He just vanished into thin air!'

'Milly, this is the age of information,' said Isobel. 'Thin air doesn't exist any more.' She took out a pen from her pocket and tore a piece of card off one of the wedding present boxes. 'Now come on,' she said briskly. 'Tell me where he used to live. And his parents. And Rupert, and Rupert's parents. And anyone else they used to know.'

An hour later, Milly looked up from the phone with triumph on her face.

'This could be it!' she exclaimed. 'They're giving me a number!'

'Hallelujah!' said Isobel. 'Let's hope this is him.' She gazed down at the road map in her lap, open at the index. It had taken Milly a while to remember that Rupert's father had been a head-master in Cornwall, and another while to narrow the village name down to something beginning with T. Since then they had been working down the index, asking Directory Enquiries each time for a Dr Carr.

'Well, here it is,' said Milly, putting down the receiver and staring at the row of digits.

'Great,' said Isobel. 'Well, get dialling!'

'OK,' said Milly, taking a deep breath. 'Let's see if we've got the right number.'

I should have done this before, she thought guiltily, as she picked up the phone. I could have done this any time. But even as she dialled, she felt a painful dismay at what she was being forced to do. She didn't want to speak to Rupert. She didn't want to speak to Allan. She wanted to forget the bastards had ever existed; wipe them out of her memory.

'Hello?' Suddenly a man's voice was speaking in her ear and Milly gave a jump of fright.

'Hello?' repeated the man. Milly dug her nails into the palm of her hand.

'Hello,' she said cautiously. 'Is that Dr Carr?'

'Yes, speaking.' He sounded agreeably surprised that she should know his name.

'Oh good,' said Milly, and cleared her throat. 'May I . . . may I talk to Rupert, please?'

'He's not here, I'm afraid,' said the man. 'Have you tried his London number?'

'No, I haven't got it,' said Milly, amazed at how natural her voice sounded. She glanced over at Isobel, who nodded approvingly. 'I'm an old friend from Oxford. Just catching up.'

'Ah, well he's in London now. Working as a barrister, you know, in Lincoln's Inn. But let me give you his home number.'

As Milly wrote down the number, she felt a bubble of astonishment expanding inside her. It was that simple. For years she'd thought of Rupert and Allan as people out of her life for ever; misty figures who might be anywhere in the world by now, whom she would never see again. And yet here she was, talking to Rupert's father, a phone call away from talking to Rupert himself. In a few minutes she would hear his voice. Oh God.

'Have I met you?' Rupert's father was saying. 'Were you at Corpus?'

'No, I wasn't,' said Milly hurriedly. 'Sorry, I must go. Thank you so much.'

She put the receiver down and stared at it for a few seconds. Then she took a deep breath, lifted it again and, before she could change her mind, tapped in Rupert's telephone number.

'Hello?' A girl's voice answered pleasantly.

'Hello,' said Milly, before she could chicken out. 'May I talk to Rupert, please? It's quite important.'

'Of course. Can I say who's calling?'

'It's Milly. Milly from Oxford.'

While the girl was gone, Milly twirled the telephone cord round her fingers and tried to keep her breathing steady. She didn't dare meet Isobel's eye in case she collapsed with nerves. Ten years was a long time. What was Rupert like now? What would he say to her? She could hear faint music in the background, and pictured him lying on the floor, smoking a joint, listening to jazz. Or perhaps he was sitting on an old velvet chair, playing cards, drinking whisky.

Perhaps he was playing cards with Allan. A dart of nerves went through Milly. Maybe, any moment, Allan would be on the line.

Suddenly the girl was speaking again.

'I'm sorry,' she said, 'but Rupert's a bit tied up at the moment. Can I take a message?'

'Not really,' said Milly. 'But maybe he could call me back?'

'Of course,' said the girl.

'The number's Bath 89406.'

'Got it.'

'Great,' said Milly. She looked down at the doodles on her notepad, feeling a sudden relief. She should have done all this years ago; it was easier than she'd thought. 'Are you Rupert's flatmate?' she added, conversationally. 'Or just a friend?'

'No, I'm neither,' said the girl. She sounded surprised. 'I'm Rupert's wife.'

CHAPTER SIX

Rupert Carr sat by the fire of his Fulham house, shaking with fear. As Francesca put down the phone she gave him a curious look, and Rupert felt his insides turn to liquid. What had Milly said to his wife? What exactly had she said?

'Who's Milly?' said Francesca, picking up her glass of wine and taking a sip. 'Why don't you want to talk to her?'

'Just a weird g-girl I once knew,' said Rupert, cursing himself for stammering. He tried to shrug casually, but his lips were shaking and his face was hot with panic. 'I've no idea what she wants. I'll call her tomorrow at the office.' He forced himself to look up and meet his wife's eyes steadily. 'But now I want to go over my reading.'

'OK,' she said, and smiled. She came over and sat down beside him on the sofa—a smart Colefax and Fowler sofa that had been a wedding present from one of her rich uncles. Opposite was a matching sofa which they'd bought themselves; on it sat Charlie and Sue Smith-Halliwell, their closest friends. The four of them were enjoying a quick glass of wine before leaving for the evening service at St Catherine's, at which Rupert would be reading. Now he avoided their eyes and stared down at his Bible. But the words swam before his eyes; his fingers sweated on the page.

'Sorry, Charlie,' said Francesca. She reached behind her and turned Kiri te Kanawa fractionally down. 'What were you saying?'

'Nothing very profound,' said Charlie, and laughed. 'I simply feel that it's up to people like us'—he gestured to the four of them—'to encourage young families into the church.'

'Instead of spending their Sunday mornings at Homestore,' said Francesca, then frowned. 'Do I mean Homestore?'

'After all,' said Charlie, 'families are the core structure of society.'

'Yes, but Charlie, the whole point is, they're not!' exclaimed Sue at once, in a way which suggested the argument was not new. 'Families are old news! It's all single parents and lesbians these days . . .'

'Did you read,' put in Francesca, 'about that new gay version of the New Testament? I have to say, I was quite shocked.'

'The whole thing makes me feel physically sick,' said Charlie, and gripped his wine glass tightly. 'These people are monsters.'

'Yes but you can't ignore them,' said Sue. 'Can you? You can't just discount a whole section of society. However misguided they are. What do you think, Rupert?'

Rupert looked up. His throat felt tight.

'Sorry,' he managed. 'I wasn't really listening.'

'Oh sorry,' said Sue. 'You want to concentrate, don't you?' She grinned at him. 'You'll be fine. You always are. And isn't it funny, you never stutter when you're reading!'

'I'd say you're one of the best readers in the church, Rupe,' said Charlie cheerfully. 'Must be that university education. We didn't get taught much elocution at Sandhurst.'

'That's no excuse!' said Sue. 'God gave us all mouths and brains, didn't he? What's the reading?'

'Matthew 26,' said Rupert. 'Peter's denial.' There was a short silence.

'Peter,' echoed Charlie soberly. 'What can it have been like, to be Peter?'

'Don't,' said Francesca, and shuddered. 'When I think how close I came to losing my faith altogether . . .'

'Yes, but you never denied Jesus, did you?' said Sue. She reached over and took Francesca's hand. 'Even the day after it happened, when I visited you in hospital.'

'I was so angry,' said Francesca. 'And ashamed. I felt as though I somehow didn't deserve a child.' She bit her lip.

'Yes but you do,' said Charlie. 'You both do. And you'll have one. Remember, God's on your side.'

'I know,' said Francesca. She looked at Rupert. 'He's on our side, isn't he, darling?'

'Yes,' said Rupert. He felt as though the word had been forced off his tongue with a razor. 'God's on our side.'

But God wasn't on his side. He knew God wasn't on his side. As they left the house and headed towards St Catherine's Church—ten minutes away in a little Chelsea square—Rupert found himself lagging behind the others. He felt like lagging so slowly that he would be left behind altogether. He wanted to be overlooked; to be forgotten about. But that was impossible. No one at St Catherine's was ever forgotten. Anyone who ventured through its portals immediately became part of the family. The most casual visitors were welcomed in with smiling enthusiasm, were made to feel important and loved, were exhorted to come again. Most did. Those who didn't reappear were cheerfully telephoned—'Just checking you're OK. You know, we care about you. We really care.' Sceptics were welcomed almost more keenly than believers. They were encouraged to stand up and express their reservations; the more convincing their arguments, the broader the smiles all around. The members of St Catherine's smiled a lot. They wore their happiness visibly; they walked around in a shiny halo of certainty.

It had been that certainty which had attracted Rupert to St Catherine's. During his first year in chambers, miserably riddled with self-doubt, he had met Tom Innes, another barrister. Tom was friendly and outgoing. He had a secure social life built around St Catherine's. He knew all the answers—and when he didn't know the answer, he knew where to look. He was the happiest man Rupert had ever met. And Rupert, who at that time had thought he would never be happy again, had fallen with an almost desperate eagerness into Tom's life; into Christianity; into marriage. Now his life had a regular pattern, a meaning to it which he relished. He'd been married to Francesca for three contented years, his house was comfortable, his career was going well.

No one knew about his past life. No one knew about Allan.

He had told nobody. Not Francesca, not Tom, not the vicar. He hadn't even told God.

Tom was waiting for them at the door as they arrived. He was dressed, like Rupert and Charlie, in work clothes—well-cut suit, Thomas Pink shirt, silk tie. All the men at St Catherine's had the same clothes, the same haircuts, the same heavy gold signet rings. At the weekends they all wore chinos and casual Ralph Lauren shirts, or else tweeds for shooting.

'Rupert! Good to see you. All set to read?'

'Absolutely!' said Rupert.

'Good man.' Tom smiled at Rupert and Rupert felt a tingle go up his spine. The same tingle he'd experienced when he met Tom for the first time. 'I'm hoping you'll read at the next chambers Bible study group, if that's OK?'

'Of course,' said Rupert. 'What do you want me to do?'

'We'll talk about it later,' said Tom. He smiled again and moved away—and ridiculously, Rupert felt a small dart of disappointment.

In front of him, Francesca and Sue were greeting friends with warm hugs; Charlie was vigorously shaking the hand of an old schoolfriend. Everywhere he looked, well-dressed professionals were thronging.

'I just asked Jesus,' a voice behind him said. 'I asked Jesus, and the next day I woke up with the answer fully formed in my head. So I went back to the client, and I said . . .'

'Why these people can't control themselves, I just don't know!' Francesca was exclaiming. Her voice was sharp and her eyes were shining slightly. 'All these single mothers, with no means to provide for themselves . . .'

'But then, think of the backgrounds they come from,' replied a blond woman in an Armani jacket. She smiled blandly at Francesca. 'They need our support and guidance. Not our condemnation.'

'I know,' muttered Francesca. 'But it's very difficult.' Unconsciously her hand stroked her flat stomach and Rupert felt a wave of compassion for her. He hurried forward and kissed the back of her neck.

'Don't worry,' he whispered in her ear. 'We'll have a baby. You just wait.'

'But what if God doesn't want me to have a baby?' said Francesca, turning round and meeting his eyes. 'What then?'

'He does,' said Rupert, trying to sound sure of himself. 'I'm sure he does.'

Francesca sighed and turned away again, and Rupert felt a stab of panic. He didn't know the answers. How could he? He'd been a born-again Christian for less time than Francesca, was less familiar with the Bible than she was, had achieved an inferior degree to hers, even earned less money than she did. And yet she deferred to him constantly. She had insisted on promising to obey him; she looked to him for guidance in everything.

Gradually the crowd dispersed, filing into pews. Some knelt, some sat looking expectantly ahead, some were still chatting. Many were holding crisp notes, ready for the collection. The amount of money generated by St Catherine's at each service was approximately the same as that gathered in a whole year at the small Cornish church Rupert had attended as a boy. The congregation here could afford to give extravagantly without their lifestyles being affected; they still drove expensive cars, ate good food, travelled abroad. They were a ready-made advertisers' dream audience, thought Rupert; if the church would only sell space on its walls, it would make a fortune. An unwilling grin passed over his face. That was the sort of remark Allan would have made.

'Rupert!' Tom's voice interrupted his thoughts. 'Come and sit at the front.'

'Right you are,' said Rupert. He sat down on his allotted chair and looked at the congregation facing him. Familiar faces looked back at him; there were a few friendly smiles. Rupert tried to smile back. But suddenly he felt conspicuous under the scrutiny of five hundred Christian eyes. What did they see? What did they think he was? A childish panic went through him. They all think I'm like them, he suddenly found himself thinking. But I'm not. I'm different.

Music struck up, and everybody got to their feet. Rupert stood up too, and looked obediently at his yellow sheet of paper. The tune of the hymn was jaunty; the words were happy and uplifting. But he didn't feel uplifted, he felt poisoned. He couldn't sing, couldn't free his thoughts from the same circular path. They all think I'm the same as them, he kept thinking. But I'm not. I'm different.

He had always been different. As a child in Cornwall he'd been the headmaster's son; had been set apart before he even had a chance. While other boys' fathers drove tractors and drank beer, his father read Greek poetry and gave Rupert's friends detention. Mr Carr had been a popular headmaster—the most popular the school had ever had—but that hadn't helped Rupert, who was by nature academic, poor at games and shy. The boys had scoffed at him, the girls had ignored him. Gradually Rupert had developed a defensive stutter and a taste for being on his own.

Then, at around the age of thirteen, his childish features had matured into golden good looks, and things had become even worse. Suddenly the girls were following him around, giggling and propositioning him; suddenly the other boys were gazing at him in envy. It was assumed, because he was so good-looking, that he could sleep with any girl he wanted to; that indeed he had already done so. Nearly every Saturday night Rupert would take some girl or other to the cinema, sit with her at the back and put his arm around her for all to see. The next Monday she would giggle hysterically with her friends, flutter her eyelashes and drop hints. His reputation grew and grew. To Rupert's astonishment, not one of the girls ever gave away the fact that his sexual prowess stopped at a goodnight kiss. By the time he was eighteen he had taken out all the girls in the school and was still a virgin.

He'd thought that at Oxford it would be different. That he would fit in. That he would meet another kind of girl; that everything would fall into place. He'd arrived tanned and fit after a summer on the beach, and immediately attracted attention. Girls had flocked round him; intelligent, charming girls. The sort of girls he'd always longed for.

Except that now he'd got them, he didn't want them. He couldn't desire the girls he met, with their high foreheads and flicking hair and intellectual gravitas. It was the men in Oxford who had fascinated him. The men. He'd stared at them surreptitiously in lectures, watched them in the street, edged closer to them in pubs. Foppish law students in waistcoats; crop-haired French students in Doc Martens. Members of the dramatic society piling into the pub after a show, wearing make-up and kissing each other playfully on the lips.

Occasionally one of these men would look up, notice Rupert

staring, and invite him to join the group. A few times he'd been openly propositioned. But each time he'd backed away, full of terror. He couldn't be attracted to these men. He couldn't be gay. He simply couldn't.

By the end of his first year at Oxford he was still a virgin and lonelier than ever before. He belonged to no particular set; he didn't have a girlfriend; he didn't have a boyfriend. Because he was so good-looking, others in his college read his shyness as aloofness. They imbued him with a self-confidence and arrogance he didn't have, assumed his social life was catered for out of college; left him alone. By the end of Trinity term, he was spending most nights drinking whisky alone in his rooms.

And then he'd been sent for an extra tutorial to Allan Kepinski, an American junior research fellow at Keble. They'd discussed *Paradise Lost*; had grown more and more intense as the afternoon wore on. By the end of the tutorial Rupert was flushed in the face, utterly caught up in the debate and the charged atmosphere between them. Allan was leaning forward in his chair, close to Rupert; their faces were almost touching.

Then, silently, Allan had leaned a little further and brushed his lips against Rupert's. Excitement had seared Rupert's body. He'd closed his eyes and willed Allan to kiss him again, to come even closer. And slowly, gently, Allan had put his arms around Rupert and pulled him down, off his armchair, onto the rug, into a new life.

Afterwards, Allan had explained to Rupert exactly how much of a risk he'd been taking by making the first move.

'You could have had me slung in jail,' he'd said in his dry voice, caressing Rupert's rumpled hair. 'Or at least sent home on the first plane. Coming on to undergraduates isn't exactly ethical.'

'Fuck ethical,' Rupert had said, and flopped backwards. He felt shaky with relief; with liberation. 'Christ, I feel incredible. I never knew—' He broke off.

'No,' Allan had said amusedly. 'I didn't think you did.'

That summer remained etched in Rupert's memory as a perfect bubble of intoxication. He'd subsumed himself entirely to Allan, had spent the entire summer vacation with him. He'd eaten with him, slept with him, respected and loved him. No one else had seemed to matter, or even exist.

The girl Milly had not interested him in the slightest. Allan had been quite taken with her—he'd thought her naively charming; had been amused by her innocent babble. But to Rupert, she had been just another shallow, silly girl. A waste of time, a waste of space, a rival for Allan's attention.

'Rupert?' The woman next to him nudged him and Rupert realized that the hymn was over. Quickly he sat down, and tried to compose his thoughts.

But the thought of Milly had unsettled him; now he couldn't think of anything else. 'Milly from Oxford,' she'd called herself tonight. A spasm of angry fear went through Rupert as he thought of her name on his wife's lips. What was she doing, ringing him after ten years? How had she got his number? Didn't she realize that everything had changed? That he wasn't gay? That it had all been a terrible mistake?

'Rupert! You're reading!' The woman was hissing at him, and abruptly Rupert came to. He carefully put down his yellow sheet of paper, picked up his Bible and stood up. He walked slowly to the lectern, placed his Bible on it and faced his audience.

'I am going to read from St Matthew's Gospel,' he said. 'The theme is denial. How can we live with ourselves if we deny the one we truly love?'

He opened the Bible with trembling hands, and took a deep breath. I'm reading this for God, he told himself—as all the readers at St Catherine's did. I'm reading this for Jesus. The picture of a grave, betrayed face filled his mind, and he felt a familiar stab of guilt. But it wasn't the face of Jesus he saw. It was the face of Allan.

CHAPTER SEVEN

The next morning, Milly and Isobel waited until a foursome of guests descended on the kitchen, then slipped out of the house before Olivia could ask them where they were going.

'OK,' said Isobel, as they reached the car. 'I think there's an eight-thirty fast to London. You should catch that.'

'What if he says something?' said Milly, looking up at Alexander's curtained window. Her lips began to shiver in the icy morning air. 'What if he says something to Simon while I'm away?'

'He won't,' said Isobel firmly. 'Simon will be at work all morning, won't he? Alexander won't even be able to get to him. And by that time, at least you'll know.' She opened the car door. 'Come on, get in.'

'I didn't sleep all night,' said Milly, as Isobel began to drive off. 'I was so tense.' She wound a strand of hair tightly round her finger, then released it. 'For ten years I've thought I was married. And now . . . maybe I'm not!'

'Milly, you don't know for sure,' said Isobel.

'I know,' said Milly. 'But it makes sense, doesn't it? Why would Allan begin divorce proceedings and not see them through? Of *course* he would have seen it all through.'

'Maybe.'

'Don't be so pessimistic, Isobel! You were the one who said—'

'I know I was. And I really hope you are divorced.' She glanced at Milly. 'But I wouldn't celebrate until you actually find out.'

'I'm not celebrating,' said Milly. 'Not yet. I'm just . . . hopeful.'

They paused at a traffic light and watched a crocodile of children in matching red duffel coats cross the road.

'Of course,' said Isobel, 'if your charming friend Rupert had bothered to call back, you might be in contact with Allan by now. You might know, one way or the other.'

'I know,' said Milly. 'Bastard. *Ignoring* me like that. He must know I'm in some kind of trouble. Why else would I ring him?' Her voice rose incredulously. 'How can someone be so selfish?'

'Most of the world is selfish,' said Isobel. 'Take it from me.'

'And how come he's suddenly got a wife?'

Isobel shrugged.

'There's your answer. That's why he didn't call back.'

Milly drew a circle on the fogged-up passenger window and looked out of it at the passing streets. Commuters were hurrying along the pavements, scuffing the new morning snow into slush; glancing at garish Sale signs in closed shop windows as they passed.

'So, what are you going to do?' said Isobel suddenly. 'If you find out you are divorced?'

'What do you mean?'

'Will you tell Simon?'

There was silence.

'I don't know,' said Milly slowly. 'Maybe it won't be necessary.'

'But Milly—'

'I know I should have told him in the first place,' interrupted Milly. 'I should have told him months ago, and sorted it all out.' She paused. 'But I didn't. And I can't change that. It's too late.'

'So? You could tell him now.'

'But everything's different now! Our wedding is in three days' time. Everything's perfect. Why ruin it all with . . . this?'

Isobel was silent and Milly looked round defensively. 'I suppose you think I should tell him anyway. I suppose you think you can't have secrets from someone you love.'

'No,' said Isobel. 'Actually, I don't think that.' Milly looked at her in surprise. Isobel's gaze was averted; her hands gripped the steering wheel tightly. 'You can easily love someone and still keep a secret from them,' she said.

'But—'

'If it's something that would trouble them needlessly. If it's something they don't need to know.' Isobel's voice grew slightly harsher. 'Some secrets are best left unsaid.'

'Like what?' Milly gazed at Isobel. 'What are you talking about?'

'Nothing.'

'Have you got a secret?'

Isobel was silent. For a few minutes Milly stared at her sister, scanning her face, trying to read her expression. Then suddenly it came to her. A thunderbolt of horrific realization.

'You're ill, aren't you?' she said shakily. 'God, it all makes sense. That's why you're so pale. You've got something terrible wrong with you—and you're not telling us!' Milly's voice rose. 'You think it's best left unsaid! What, until you *die*?'

'Milly!' Isobel's voice snapped curtly across the car. 'I'm not going to die. I'm not ill.'

'Well, what's your secret, then?'

'I never said I had one. I was talking theoretically.' Isobel pulled into the station car park. 'Here we are.' She opened the car door and, without looking at Milly, got out.

Reluctantly, Milly followed. As she reached the station concourse, a train pulled out from one of the platforms, and a trail of arriving passengers began to appear. Unconcerned, happy people, holding bags and waving to friends. People to whom the word 'wedding' meant happiness and celebration.

'Oh God,' she said, catching up with Isobel. 'I don't want to go. I don't want to find out. I want to forget about it.'

'You've got to go. You haven't got any choice.' Suddenly Isobel's face changed colour. 'Get your ticket,' she said in a gasp. 'I'll be back in a moment.' And to Milly's astonishment, she began running towards the Ladies. Milly gazed after her for a moment, then turned round.

'A day return to London, please,' she said to the girl behind the glass. What on earth was wrong with Isobel? She wasn't ill, but she wasn't normal, either. She couldn't be pregnant—she didn't have a boyfriend.

'Right,' said Isobel, reappearing by her side. 'Got everything?'

'You're pregnant!' hissed Milly. 'Aren't you?' Isobel took a step back. She looked as though she'd been slapped in the face.

'No,' she said.

'Yes you are. It's obvious!'

'The train goes in a minute,' said Isobel, looking at her watch. 'You'll miss it.'

'You're pregnant, and you didn't even tell me! Bloody hell, Isobel, you should have told me. I'm going to be an aunt!'

'No,' said Isobel tightly. 'You're not.'

Milly stared at her uncomprehendingly. Then, with a sudden shock, she realized what Isobel was saying.

'No! You can't do that! You can't! Isobel, you're not serious?'

'I don't know. I don't know, OK?' Isobel's voice rose savagely. She took a couple of paces towards Milly, clenched her hands, then took a couple of paces back, like a caged animal.

'Isobel—'

'You've got a train to catch,' said Isobel. 'Go on.' She looked up at Milly with glittering eyes. 'Go on!'

'I'll catch a later train,' said Milly.

'No! You haven't got time for that. Go on!'

Milly stared at her sister for a few silent seconds. She had never seen Isobel looking vulnerable before; it made her feel uneasy.

'OK,' she said. 'I'll go.'

'Good luck,' said Isobel.

'And we'll talk about . . . about it—when I get back.'

'Maybe,' said Isobel. When Milly looked back from the ticket barrier to wave goodbye, she had already gone.

Isobel arrived back home to find Olivia waiting for her in the kitchen.

'Where's Milly?' she demanded.

'She's gone to London for the day,' said Isobel.

'To London? What on earth for?'

'To get a present for Simon,' said Isobel, reaching for the biscuit tin. Olivia stared at her.

'Are you serious? All the way to London? She can get a perfectly good present for him in Bath!'

'She just felt like going to London,' said Isobel, ripping open a packet of digestives. 'Does it matter?'

'Yes,' said Olivia crossly. 'Of course it matters! Do you know what day it is today?'

'Yes, I do,' said Isobel, biting into a biscuit with relish. 'It's Thursday.'

'Exactly! Only two days to go! I've a thousand things to do, and Milly was supposed to be helping me. She's such a thoughtless girl.'

'Give her a break,' said Isobel. 'She's got a lot on her mind.'

'So have I, darling! I've got to organize extra orders of service, and check all the place settings—and to top it all, the marquee's just arrived. Who's going to come with me to see it?'

There was silence.

'Oh God,' said Isobel, stuffing another biscuit into her mouth. 'All right.'

Simon and Harry were walking along Parham Place. It was a wide road, civilized and expensive and, at this time in the morning, busy—as its residents left for their jobs in the professions and the law and the higher echelons of industry. A pretty brunette getting into her car smiled at Simon as they walked by; three doors down a group of builders sat on the doorstep and drank steaming cups of tea.

'Here we are,' said Harry as he stopped by a flight of stone steps leading to a glossy blue door. 'Have you got the keys?'

Silently, Simon walked up the steps and put the key in the lock. He stepped into a spacious hall and opened another door, to the left.

'Go on then,' said Harry. 'In you go.'

As he stepped inside, Simon immediately remembered why he and Milly had fallen in love with the flat. He was surrounded by space; by white walls and high, distant ceilings and acres of wooden floor. Nothing else they'd looked at had come close to this; nothing else had been so prohibitively expensive.

'Like it?' said Harry.

'It's great,' Simon said, wandering over to a mantelpiece and running his hand along it. 'It's great,' he repeated. He didn't trust himself to say any more. The flat was more than great. It was beautiful, perfect. Milly would adore it. But as he stood, looking around, all he could feel was resentful misery.

'Nice high ceilings,' said Harry. He opened an empty, panelled cupboard, looked inside, and closed it again. As he wandered over to a window, his steps echoed on the bare floor. 'Nice wooden shutters,' he said, tapping one appraisingly.

'The shutters are great,' said Simon. Everything was great. He couldn't locate a single fault.

'You'll have to get some decent furniture,' said Harry. He looked at Simon. 'Need any help with that?'

'No,' said Simon, 'thank you.'

'Well anyway, I hope you like it.' Harry gave a little shrug.

'It's a beautiful flat,' said Simon stiffly. 'Milly will love it.'

'Good,' said Harry. 'Where is she today?'

'In London. Some mysterious mission. I think she's buying me a present.'

'All these presents,' said Harry lightly. 'You'll be getting quite spoilt.'

'I'll bring her round this evening to see it,' said Simon, 'if that's OK?'

'Your flat. Do what you like.'

They wandered out of the main room into a light, wide corridor. The biggest bedroom overlooked the garden: long windows opened onto a tiny wrought-iron balcony.

'You don't need more than two bedrooms,' said Harry. There was a slight question mark in his voice. 'Not thinking of having children straight away.'

'Oh no,' said Simon. 'Plenty of time for that. Milly's only twenty-eight.'

'Still . . .' Harry turned a switch by the door and the bare bulb swinging from the ceiling suddenly came alive with light. 'You'll need lampshades. Or whatever.'

'Yes,' said Simon. He looked at his father. 'Why?' he said. 'Do you think we should have children straight away?'

'No,' said Harry emphatically. 'Definitely not.'

'Really? But you did.'

'I know. That was our mistake.'

Simon stiffened.

'I was a mistake, was I?' he said. 'A product of human error?'

'You know that's not what I meant,' said Harry irritably. 'Stop being so bloody touchy.'

'What do you expect? You're telling me I wasn't wanted.'

'Of course you were wanted!' Harry paused. 'You just weren't wanted right then.'

'Well, I'm sorry for gatecrashing the party,' said Simon furiously, 'but I didn't exactly have a choice about when I arrived, did I? It wasn't exactly up to me, was it?' Harry winced.

'Listen, Simon. All I meant was—'

'I know what you meant!' said Simon, striding to the window. He stared out at the snowy garden, trying to keep his voice under control. 'I was an inconvenience, wasn't I? I still am.'

'Simon—'

'Well, look, Dad. I won't inconvenience you any more, OK?' Simon wheeled round, his face trembling. 'Thanks very much, but you can keep your flat. Milly and I will make our own arrangements.' He tossed the keys onto the polished floor and walked quickly to the door.

'Simon!' said Harry angrily. 'Don't be so fucking stupid!'

'I'm sorry I've been in your way all these years,' said Simon at the door. 'But after Saturday, I'll be gone. You'll never have to see me again. Maybe that'll be a relief for both of us.'

And he slammed the door, leaving Harry alone, staring at the keys winking in the winter sunlight.

The Family Registry was large and light and softly carpeted in green. Rows and rows of indexes were stored on modern beech-wood shelves, divided into births, marriages and deaths. The marriage section was by far the busiest. As Milly self-consciously edged her way towards the shelves, people milled around her, clanking indexes in and out of the shelves, scribbling notes on pieces of paper, and talking to each other in low voices. On the wall was a notice headlined WE WILL HELP YOU TRACE YOUR FAMILY TREE. Two middle-aged ladies were poring over an index from the 1800s. 'Charles Forsyth!' one was exclaiming. 'But is that *our* Charles Forsyth?' Not one person looked anxious or guilty. For everybody else, thought Milly, this was a pleasurable morning's occupation.

Without daring to look anyone in the eye, she headed towards the more recent indexes, and pulled one down, scarcely daring to look inside. For a moment, she couldn't see it, and she was filled with ridiculous hope. But then, suddenly, it jumped up at her. HAVILL, MELISSA G——KEPINSKI. OXFORD.

Milly's heart sank. In spite of herself she'd harboured a secret, tiny belief that her marriage to Allan might have slipped through the legal net. But there it was, typed in black and white, for anyone to look up. A few thoughtless minutes in a registry office in Oxford had led to this lasting piece of evidence: an indelible record which would never, ever disappear. She stared down at the page, unable to tear herself away, until the words began to dance in front of her eyes.

'You can get a certificate, you know.' A cheery voice startled her and she jumped up in fright, covering her name with her hand. A friendly young man wearing a name badge was standing opposite her. 'We provide copies of marriage certificates. You can also have them framed. They make a very nice gift.'

'No thank you,' said Milly. The idea made her want to laugh hysterically. 'No thanks.' She looked at her name one last time, then slammed the book shut, as though trying to squash the entry and kill it. 'I was actually looking for the list of divorces.'

'Then you've come to the wrong place!' The young man grinned at her, triumphant at her ignorance. 'You want Somerset House.'

It was the biggest marquee Isobel had ever seen. It billowed magnificently in the wind, a huge white mushroom, dwarfing the cars and vans parked next to it.

'Bloody hell!' she said. 'How much is this costing?' Olivia winced.

'Quiet, darling!' she said. 'Someone might hear.'

'I'm sure they all know how much it costs,' said Isobel, staring at the stream of young men and women coming in and out of the marquee. They looked busy and purposeful; many were carrying crates or lengths of flex or pieces of wooden boarding.

'Over there we'll have a tube linking the marquee to the back of Pinnacle Hall,' said Olivia, gesturing. 'And cloakrooms.'

'Bloody hell,' said Isobel again. 'It looks like a circus.'

'Well, you know, we did think of having an elephant,' said Olivia. Isobel goggled at her.

'An elephant?'

'To take the happy couple away.'

'They wouldn't get very far on an elephant,' said Isobel, beginning to laugh.

'But they're having a helicopter instead,' said Olivia. 'Don't tell Milly. It's a surprise.'

'Wow,' said Isobel. 'A helicopter.'

'Have you ever been in a helicopter?' asked Olivia.

'Yes,' said Isobel. 'A few times. It's quite nerve-racking, actually.'

'I haven't,' said Olivia. 'Not once.' She gave a small sigh, and Isobel giggled.

'Do you want to take Milly's place? I'm sure Simon wouldn't mind.'

'Don't be silly,' snapped Olivia. 'Come on, let's look inside.'

The two of them picked their way over the snowy ground towards the marquee and lifted a flap.

'Blimey,' said Isobel slowly. 'It looks even more enormous on the inside.' They both gazed around the massive space. People were everywhere, carrying chairs, setting up heaters, fixing lights.

'It's not so big,' said Olivia uncertainly. 'Once the chairs and tables are all in, it'll be quite cosy.' She paused. 'Perhaps not cosy, exactly . . .'

'Well, I take my hat off to Harry!' said Isobel. 'This is something else.'

'We've contributed too!' exclaimed Olivia crossly. 'More than you might realize. And anyway, Harry can afford it.'

'I don't doubt that.'

'He's very fond of Milly, you know.'

'I know,' said Isobel. 'Gosh . . .' She looked around the marquee and bit her lip.

'What?' said Olivia suspiciously.

'Oh, I don't know,' said Isobel. 'All this preparation, all this money. All for one day.'

'What's wrong with that?'

'Nothing. I'm sure it'll all go swimmingly.'

Olivia stared at her.

'Isobel, what's wrong with you? You're not jealous of Milly, are you?'

'Probably,' said Isobel lightly.

'You could get married, you know! But you've chosen not to.'

'I've never been asked,' said Isobel.

'That's not the point!'

'I think it is,' said Isobel, 'very much the point.' And to her horror she suddenly felt tears pricking her eyes. What the hell was she crying for? She turned away before her mother could say anything else, and stalked off, towards the far end of the marquee. Olivia hurried obliviously after her.

'This is where the food will be,' she called excitedly. 'And that's where the swans will be.'

'The swans?' said Isobel, turning round.

'We're going to have swans made out of ice,' said Olivia. 'And each one will be filled with oysters.'

'No!' Isobel's laugh pealed around the marquee. 'Whose idea was that?'

'Harry's,' said Olivia defensively. 'What's wrong with it?'

'Nothing. It's just the tackiest thing I've ever heard of.'

'That's what I said,' said Olivia eagerly. 'But Harry said he thought weddings were such tacky affairs anyway, there was no point trying to be tasteful. So we decided to go for broke!'

'He will be broke,' said Isobel, 'by the time he's finished feeding all his guests oysters.'

'No he won't!' snapped Olivia. 'Stop saying things like that, Isobel.'

'All right,' said Isobel in mollifying tones. 'Truthfully, I think it's going to be a lovely wedding.' She looked around the vast tent and, for the hundredth time that day, wondered how Milly was getting on. 'Milly will have the time of her life.'

'She doesn't deserve the time of her life,' said Olivia crossly.

'Rushing off to London like this. There are only two days to go, you know! Two days!'

'I know,' said Isobel. She bit her lip. 'I know. And believe me, so does Milly.'

By the time Milly reached the Strand, a winter sun had begun to shine and she could feel an optimistic excitement rising through her. Within minutes she would know, one way or the other. And suddenly she felt sure she knew which way the answer would be. The burden which had been pressing down on her for the last ten years would be lifted. At last she would be free.

She sauntered along, feeling her hair lifted slightly by the breeze, enjoying the sun on her face.

'Excuse me,' said a girl suddenly, tapping her shoulder. Milly looked round. 'We're looking for hair models. I work for a salon in Covent Garden.' She smiled at Milly. 'Would you be interested?'

A sparkle of delight ran through Milly.

'I'm sorry,' she said regretfully, 'but I'm a bit busy.' She paused, and a faint smile came to her lips. 'I'm getting married on Saturday.'

'Are you?' exclaimed the girl. 'Are you really? Congratulations! You'll make a lovely bride.'

'Thanks,' said Milly, blushing. 'Sorry I can't stop. But I've just got some things to tidy up.'

'No, no,' said the girl, rolling her eyes sympathetically. 'I know what it's like! All those tiny things that you always leave till last!'

'Exactly,' said Milly, walking away. 'Just a few last-minute details.'

As she entered Somerset House and found the department she needed, her spirits were lifted further. The man in charge of divorce decrees was round and cheerful, with twinkling eyes and a quick computer.

'You're in luck,' he said, as he tapped in her details. 'All records since 1981 are on computer file. Before that, and we have to search by hand.' He winked at her. 'But you would have been just a baby then! Now, just bear with me, my dear . . .'

Milly beamed back at him. Already she was planning what she would do when she'd received confirmation of her divorce. She would take a taxi to Harvey Nichols and go straight up to the fifth floor, and buy herself a buck's fizz. And then she would call Isobel. And then she would—

Her thoughts were interrupted as the computer pinged. The man peered at the screen, then looked up.

'No,' he said in surprise. 'Not found.'

A stone dropped through Milly's stomach.

'What?' she said. Her lips felt suddenly dry. 'What do you mean?'

'There's no decree absolute listed,' said the man, tapping again. The computer pinged again and he frowned. 'Not in that period, for those names.'

'But there has to be,' said Milly. 'There *has* to be.'

'I've tried twice,' said the man. He looked up. 'Are you sure the spellings are correct?'

Milly swallowed.

'Quite sure.'

'And you're sure the petitioner applied for a decree absolute?' Milly looked at him numbly. She didn't know what he was talking about.

'No,' she said. 'I'm not sure.' The man nodded back at her, cheerful as a puppet.

'Six weeks after the decree nisi is issued, the petitioner has to apply for a decree absolute.'

'Yes,' said Milly, 'I see.'

'You were issued with a decree nisi, weren't you, dear?'

Milly looked up blankly and met the man's eyes, regarding her with a sudden curiosity. A quick stab of fear hit her in the chest.

'Yes,' she said quickly, before he could ask anything else. 'Of course I was. It was all in order. I'll . . . I'll go back and check up on what happened.'

'If you require any legal advice—'

'No thank you,' said Milly, backing away. 'You've been very kind. Thank you so much.'

As she turned to grasp the door handle, a voice hit the back of her head.

'Mrs Kepinski?'

She wheeled round with a white face.

'Or is it Ms Havill now?' said the man, smiling. He came round the counter. 'Here's a leaflet explaining the whole procedure.'

'Thank you,' said Milly desperately. 'That's lovely.'

She shot him an over-bright smile as she pocketed the leaflet and walked out of the room, feeling sick and panicky. She'd been right all along. Allan was a selfish, unscrupulous bastard. And he'd left her well and truly in the lurch.

She reached the street and began to walk blindly, aware of nothing but the seeds of panic already sprouting rapaciously inside her mind. She was only back where she'd been before—but somehow her position now seemed infinitely worse; infinitely more precarious. An image came to her of Alexander's malicious, gleaming smile, like the grin of a vulture. And Simon, waiting unsuspectingly in Bath. The very thought of the two of them in the same city made her feel sick. What was she to do? What *could* she do?

A pub sign caught her eye and without considering further, she slipped inside. She headed straight for the bar and ordered a gin and tonic. When that was gone, she ordered another, and then another. Gradually, as the alcohol dulled her nerves, the adrenalin pounding round her body began to slow, and her legs stopped shaking. Standing in this warm, beery atmosphere, downing gin, she was anonymous; the real world was far away. She could put everything from her mind except the sharp taste of the gin and the feeling of the alcohol as it hit her stomach, and the saltiness of the nuts which were provided on the bar in little metal bowls.

For half an hour she stood mindlessly, allowing the crush of people to ebb and flow around her. Girls gave her curious looks; men tried to catch her eye: she ignored them all. Then after a while, as she began to feel both hungry and slightly sick, she found herself putting down her glass, picking up her bag and walking out of the pub, onto the street. She stood, swaying slightly, and wondered where to go next. It was lunchtime, and the pavement was crammed with people hurrying briskly along, hailing taxis, crowding into shops and pubs and sandwich bars. Church bells began to peal in the distance, and as she heard the sound, she felt tears starting to her eyes. What was she going to do? She could barely bring herself to think about it.

She gazed at the blurry crowds of people, wishing with all her heart to be one of them, and not herself. She would have liked to be that cheerful-looking girl eating a croissant, or that calm-looking lady getting onto a bus, or . . .

Suddenly Milly froze. She blinked a few times, wiped the tears from her eyes, and looked again. But the face she'd glimpsed was already gone, swallowed up by the surging crowds. Filled with panic, she hurried forward, peering all around her. For a few moments she could see nothing but strangers: girls in brightly coloured coats, men in dark suits, lawyers still in their court-room wigs. They thronged past her, and she thrust her way impatiently through them, telling herself feverishly she must have been mistaken; she must have seen someone else. But then her heart stopped. There he was again, walking along the other side of the street, talking to another man. He looked older than she remembered, and fatter. But it was definitely him. It was Rupert.

A surge of white-hot hatred rose through Milly as she stared at him. How dared he saunter along the streets of London, so happy and at ease with himself? How dared he be so oblivious of all that she was going through? Her life was in disarray because of him. Because of him and Allan. And he wasn't even aware of it.

With a pounding heart, she began to run towards him, ignoring the beeps of angry taxis as she crossed the road; ignoring the curious looks of passers-by. Within a couple of minutes she'd caught up with the two men. She strode along behind him, gazed for a moment of loathing at Rupert's golden head, then poked his back hard.

'Rupert,' she said. 'Rupert!' He turned round and looked at her with friendly eyes devoid of recognition.

'I'm sorry,' he said. 'Do I . . .'

'It's me,' said Milly, summoning up the coldest, bitterest voice she possessed. 'It's Milly. From Oxford.'

'What?' Rupert's face drained of colour. He took a step back.

'Yes, that's right,' said Milly. 'It's me. I don't suppose you thought you'd ever see me again, did you, Rupert? You thought I'd vanished out of your life for good.'

'Don't be silly!' said Rupert in jocular tones. He glanced uneasily at his friend. 'How are things going, anyway?'

'Things,' said Milly, 'could not be going more badly, thanks for asking. Oh, and thanks for calling back last night. I really appreciated it.'

'I didn't have time,' said Rupert. His blue eyes flashed a quick look of hatred at her and Milly glared back. 'And now, I'm afraid I'm a bit busy.' He looked at his friend. 'Shall we go, Tom?'

'Don't you dare!' exclaimed Milly furiously. 'You're not going anywhere! You're going to listen to me!'

'I haven't got time—'

'Well then, make time!' shouted Milly. 'My life is in ruins, and it's all your fault. You and bloody Allan Kepinski. Jesus! Do you realize what the pair of you did to me? Do you realize the trouble I'm in, because of you?'

'Rupert,' said Tom. 'Maybe you and Milly should have a little talk?'

'I don't know what she's going on about,' said Rupert angrily. 'She's mad.'

'Even more reason,' said Tom quietly to Rupert. 'Here is a truly distressed soul. And perhaps you can help.' He smiled at Milly. 'Are you an old friend of Rupert's?'

'Yes,' said Milly curtly. 'We knew each other at Oxford. Didn't we, Rupert?'

'Well, look,' said Tom. 'Why don't I do your reading, Rupert? And you can catch up with Milly.' He smiled at her. 'Maybe next time, you could come along, too.'

'Yes,' said Milly, not having a clue what he was talking about. 'Why not.'

'Good to meet you, Milly,' said Tom, grasping Milly's hand. 'Perhaps we'll see you at St Catherine's.'

'Yes,' said Milly, 'I expect so.'

'Excellent! I'll give you a call, Rupert,' said Tom, and he was off, across the road.

Milly and Rupert looked at each other.

'You bitch,' hissed Rupert. 'Are you trying to ruin my life?'

'Ruin your life?' exclaimed Milly in disbelief. 'Ruin *your* life? Do you realize what you did to me? You used me!'

'It was your choice,' said Rupert brusquely, starting to walk away. 'If you didn't want to do it, you should have said no.'

'I was eighteen years old!' shrieked Milly. 'I didn't know anything about anything! I didn't know that one day I'd want to marry someone else, someone I really loved . . .'

'So what?' said Rupert tersely, turning back. 'You got a divorce, didn't you?'

'No!' sobbed Milly, 'I didn't! And I don't know where Allan is! And my wedding's on Saturday!'

'Well, what am I supposed to do about it?'

'I need to find Allan! Where is he?'

'I don't know,' said Rupert, beginning to walk off again. 'I can't help you. Now, leave me alone.' Milly gazed at him, anger rising through her like hot lava.

'You can't just walk away!' she shrieked. 'You've got to help me!' She began to run after him; he quickened his pace. 'You've got to help me, Rupert!' With a huge effort, she grabbed his jacket and managed to force him to a standstill.

'Get off me!' hissed Rupert.

'Listen,' said Milly fiercely, gazing up into his blue eyes. 'I did you and Allan a favour. I did you a huge, huge, enormous favour. And now it's time for you to do me a tiny little one. You owe it to me.'

She stared hard at him, watching as thoughts ran through his head; watching as his expression gradually changed. Eventually he sighed, and rubbed his forehead.

'OK,' he said. 'Come with me. We'd better talk.'

CHAPTER EIGHT

They went to an old pub on Fleet Street, full of winding stairs and dark wood and little, hidden nooks. Rupert bought a bottle of wine and two plates of bread and cheese and set them down on a tiny table in an alcove. He sat down heavily, took a deep slug of wine and leaned back. Milly looked at him. Her anger had subsided a little; she was able to study him calmly. And something, she thought, was wrong. He was still handsome, still striking— but his face was pinker and more fleshy than it had been at Oxford, and his hand shook when he put down his glass. Ten years ago, she thought, he had been a golden, glowing youth. Now he looked like a middle-aged man. And when his eyes met hers they held a residual, permanent unhappiness.

'I can't be long,' he said. 'I'm very busy. So—what exactly do you want me to do?'

'You look terrible, Rupert,' said Milly frankly. 'Are you happy?'

'I'm very happy. Thank you.' He took another deep slug of wine, practically draining the glass, and Milly raised her eyebrows.

'Are you sure?'

'Milly, we're here to talk about you,' said Rupert impatiently. 'Not me. What precisely is your problem?'

Milly looked at him for a silent moment, then sat back.

'My problem,' she said lightly, as though carefully considering the matter. 'What's my problem? My problem is that on Saturday I'm getting married to a man I love very much. My mother has organized the hugest wedding in the world. It's going to be beautiful and romantic and perfect in every single detail.' She looked up with bright eyes like daggers. 'Oh, except one. I'm still married to your friend Allan Kepinski.'

Rupert winced.

'I don't understand,' he said. 'Why aren't you divorced?'

'Ask Allan! He was supposed to be organizing it.'

'And he didn't?'

'He started to,' said Milly. 'I got some papers through the post. And I signed the slip and sent them back. But I never heard anything more.'

'And you never looked into it?'

'No one knew,' said Milly. 'No one ever asked any questions. It didn't seem to matter.'

'The fact that you were married didn't seem to matter?' said Rupert incredulously. Milly looked up and caught his expression.

'Don't start blaming *me* for this!' she said. 'This isn't my fault!'

'You leave it until a couple of days before your wedding to chase up your divorce and you say it's not your fault?'

'I didn't think I needed to chase it up,' said Milly furiously. 'I was fine. No one knew! No one suspected anything!'

'So what happened?' said Rupert. Milly picked up her wine glass and cradled it in both hands.

'Now someone knows,' she said. 'Someone saw us in Oxford. And he's threatening to say something.'

'I see.'

'Don't you dare look at me like that,' said Milly sharply. 'OK, I know I should have done something about it. But so should Allan. He said he would sort it all out and I trusted him! I trusted you both. I thought you were my friends.'

'We were,' said Rupert after a pause.

'Bullshit!' cried Milly. Her cheeks began to pinken. 'You were just a couple of users. You just used me for what you wanted—and then as soon as I was gone, you forgot about me. You never wrote, you never called . . .' She crashed her glass down on the table. 'Did you get all those letters I wrote to you?'

'Yes,' said Rupert, running a hand through his hair. 'I'm sorry. I should have replied. But . . . it was a difficult time.'

'At least Allan wrote. But you couldn't even be bothered to do that. And I still believed in you.' She shook her head. 'God, I was a little fool.'

'We were all fools,' said Rupert. 'Look, Milly, for what it's worth, I'm sorry. I honestly wish none of it had ever happened. None of it!'

Milly stared at him. His eyes were darting miserably about; fronds of golden hair were quivering above his brow.

'Rupert, what's going on?' she demanded. 'How come you're married?'

'I'm married,' said Rupert, giving a stiff little shrug. 'That's all there is to it.'

'But you were gay. You were in love with Allan.'

'No I wasn't. I was misguided. I was . . . it was a mistake.'

'But you two were perfect for one another!'

'We weren't!' snapped Rupert. 'It was all wrong. Can't you accept my word on it?'

'Well, of course I can,' said Milly. 'But you just seemed so right together.' She hesitated. 'When did you realize?'

'Realize what?'

'That you were straight?'

'Milly, I don't want to talk about it,' said Rupert. 'All right?' He reached for his glass with a trembling hand and took a gulp of wine.

Milly gave a little shrug and leaned back in her chair. Idly she allowed her eyes to roam around the alcove. To her left, on the rough plaster wall, was a game of noughts and crosses which someone had begun in pencil and then abandoned. A game already destined, she could see, to end in stalemate.

'You've changed a lot since Oxford, you know,' said Rupert abruptly. 'You've grown up. I wouldn't have recognized you.'

'I'm ten years older,' said Milly.

'It's not just that. It's . . . I don't know.' He gestured vaguely. 'Your hair. Your clothes. I wouldn't have expected you to turn out like this.'

'Like what?' said Milly defensively. 'What's wrong with me?'

'Nothing!' said Rupert. 'You just look more . . . groomed than I would have thought you'd be. More polished.'

'Well, this is what I am now, all right?' said Milly. She gave him a hard look. 'We're all allowed to change, Rupert.'

'I know,' said Rupert, flushing. 'And you look . . . great.' He leaned forward. 'Tell me about the guy you're marrying.'

'He's called Simon Pinnacle,' said Milly, and watched as Rupert's expression changed.

'No relation to—'

'His son,' said Milly. Rupert stared at her.

'Seriously? Harry Pinnacle's son?'

'Seriously.' She gave a half-smile. 'I told you. This is the wedding of the century.'

'And nobody has any idea.'

'Nobody.'

Rupert stared at Milly for a moment, then sighed. He pulled out a little black leather-bound notebook and a pen.

'OK. Tell me exactly how far your divorce got.'

'I don't know,' said Milly. 'I told you. I got some papers through the post and I signed something and sent it back.'

'And what precisely were these papers?'

'How should I know?' said Milly exasperatedly. 'Would you be able to tell one legal document from another?'

'I'm a lawyer,' said Rupert. 'But I get your point.' He put away his notebook and looked up. 'You need to speak to Allan.'

'I know that!' said Milly. 'But I don't know where he is. Do you?'

A look of pain flashed briefly across Rupert's face.

'No,' he said shortly. 'I don't.'

'But you can find out?'

Rupert was silent. Milly stared at him in disbelief.

'Rupert, you have to help me! You're my only link with him. Where did he go after Oxford?'

'Manchester,' said Rupert.

'Why did he leave Oxford? Didn't they want him any more?'

'Of course they wanted him,' said Rupert. He took a gulp of wine. 'Of course they *wanted* him.'

'Then why—'

'Because we split up,' said Rupert, his voice suddenly ragged. 'He left because we split up.'

'Oh,' said Milly, taken aback. 'I'm sorry.' She ran a finger lightly around the rim of her glass. 'Was that when you realized that you didn't . . . that you were . . .' She halted.

'Yes,' said Rupert, staring into his glass.

'And when was that?'

'At the end of that summer,' said Rupert in a low voice. 'September.' Milly stared at him in disbelief. Her heart began to thump.

'The summer I met you?' she said. 'The summer we got married?'

'Yes.'

'Two months after I married Allan, you split up?'

'Yes.' Rupert looked up. 'But I'd rather not—'

'You're telling me you were only together for two months?' cried Milly in anguish. 'I wrecked my life to keep you together for two months?' Her voice rose to a screech. 'Two *months?*'

'Yes!'

'Then fuck you!' With a sudden surge of fury, Milly threw her wine at Rupert. It hit him straight in the face, staining his skin like blood. 'Fuck you,' she said again, trembling, watching the dark red liquid drip down his gasping face onto his smart lawyer's shirt. 'I broke the law for you! Now I'm stuck with a first husband I don't want! And all so you could change your mind after two months.'

For a long while, neither of them spoke. Rupert sat motionless, staring at Milly through a wet mask of red.

'You're right,' he said finally. He sounded broken. 'I've fucked it all up. I've fucked up your life, I've fucked up my life. And Allan . . .'

Milly cleared her throat uncomfortably.

'Did he . . .'

'He loved me,' said Rupert, as though to himself. 'That's what I didn't get. He loved me.'

'Look, Rupert, I'm sorry,' said Milly awkwardly. 'About the wine. And—everything.'

'Don't apologize,' said Rupert fiercely. 'Don't apologize.' He looked up. 'Milly, I'll find Allan for you. And I'll clear up your divorce. But I can't do it in time for Saturday. It isn't physically possible.'

'I know.'

'What will you do?'

There was a long silence.

'I don't know,' said Milly eventually. She closed her eyes and massaged her brow. 'I can't cancel the wedding now,' she said slowly. 'I just can't do that to my mother. To everyone.'

'So you'll just go ahead?' said Rupert incredulously. Milly gave a tiny shrug. 'But what about whoever it is who's threatening to say something?'

'I'll . . . I'll keep him quiet,' said Milly. 'Somehow.'

'You do realize,' said Rupert, lowering his voice, 'that what you're proposing is bigamy. You would be breaking the law.'

'Thanks for the warning,' said Milly sarcastically. 'But I've been there before, remember?' She looked at him silently for a moment. 'What do you think? Would I get away with it?'

'I expect so,' said Rupert. 'Are you serious?'

'I don't know,' said Milly. 'I really don't know.'

A while later, when the wine was finished, Rupert went and collected two cups of noxious black coffee from the bar. As he returned, Milly looked up at him. His face was clean but his shirt and jacket were still spattered with red wine.

'You won't be able to go back to work this afternoon,' she said.

'I know,' said Rupert. 'It doesn't matter. Nothing's happening.' He handed Milly a cup of coffee and sat down. There was silence for a while.

'Rupert?' said Milly.

'Yes?'

'Does your wife know? About you and Allan?'

Rupert looked at her with bloodshot eyes. 'What do you think?'

'But why?' said Milly. 'Are you afraid she wouldn't understand?' Rupert gave a short little laugh.

'That's underestimating it.'

'But why not? If she loves you . . .'

'Would you understand?' Rupert glared at her. 'If your Simon turned round and told you he'd once had an affair with another man?'

'Yes,' said Milly uncertainly. 'I think I would. As long as we talked about it properly . . .'

'You wouldn't,' said Rupert scathingly. 'I can tell you that now. You wouldn't even begin to understand. And neither would Francesca.'

'You're not giving her a chance! Come on, Rupert, she's your wife! Be honest with her.'

'Be honest? You're telling *me* to be honest?'

'That's my whole point!' said Milly, leaning forward earnestly. 'I should have been honest with Simon from the start. I should have told him everything. We could have cleared up the divorce together; everything would be fine. But as it is . . .' She spread her hands helplessly on the table. 'As it is, I'm in a mess.' She paused and took a sip of coffee. 'What I'm saying is, if I had the chance to go back and tell Simon the truth, I would grab it. And you've got that chance, Rupert! You've got the chance to be honest with Francesca before . . . before it all starts going wrong.'

'It's different,' said Rupert stiffly.

'No it isn't. It's just another secret. All secrets come out in the end. If you don't tell her, she'll find out some other way.'

'She won't.'

'She might!' Milly's voice rose in conviction. 'She might easily! And do you want to risk that? Just tell her, Rupert! Tell her.'

'Tell me what?'

A girl's voice hit Milly's ears like a whiplash, and her head jerked round in shock. Standing at the entrance to the alcove was a pretty girl, with pale red hair and conventionally smart clothes. Next to her was Rupert's friend Tom.

'Tell me what?' the girl repeated in high, sharp tones, glancing from Rupert to Milly and back again. 'Rupert, what's happened to you?'

'Francesca,' said Rupert shakily. 'Don't worry, it's just wine.'

'Hi, Rupe!' said Tom easily. 'We thought we'd find you here.'

'So this is Milly,' said the girl. She looked at Rupert with gimlet eyes. 'Tom told me you'd met up with your old friend. Milly from Oxford.' She gave a strange little laugh. 'The funny thing is, Rupert, you told me you didn't want to talk to Milly from Oxford. You told me to ignore all her messages. You told me she was a nut.'

'A nut?' cried Milly indignantly.

'I didn't want to talk to her!' said Rupert. 'I don't.' He looked at Milly, blue eyes full of dismay.

'Look,' she said hurriedly. 'Maybe I'd better go.' She stood up and picked up her bag. 'Nice to meet you,' she said to Francesca. 'Honestly, I am just an old friend.'

'Is that right?' said Francesca. Her pale eyes bored into Rupert's. 'So what is it that you've got to tell me?'

'Bye, Rupert,' said Milly hastily. 'Bye, Francesca.'

'What have you got to tell me, Rupert? What is it? And you—' She turned to Milly. 'You stay here!'

'I've got a train to catch,' said Milly. 'Honestly, I've got to go. So sorry!'

Avoiding Rupert's eyes, she quickly made her way across the bar and bounded up the wooden steps to the street. As she stepped into the fresh air she realized that she'd left her cigarette lighter on the table. It seemed a small price to pay for her escape.

Isobel was sitting in the kitchen at 1 Bertram Street, stitching blue ribbon onto a lace garter. Olivia sat opposite her, folding bright pink silk into an elaborate bow. Every so often she looked up at Isobel with a dissatisfied expression, then looked down again. Eventually she put down the bow and stood up to fill the kettle.

'How's Paul?' she said brightly.

'Who?' said Isobel.

'Paul! Paul the doctor. Do you still see much of him?'

'Oh, him,' said Isobel. She screwed up her face. 'No, I haven't seen him for months. I only went out with him a few times.'

'What a shame,' said Olivia. 'He was so charming. And very good-looking, I thought.'

'He was OK,' said Isobel. 'It just didn't work out.'

'Oh, darling. I'm so sorry.'

'I'm not,' said Isobel. 'It was me who finished it.'

'But why?' Olivia's voice rose in irritation. 'What was wrong with him?'

'If you must know,' said Isobel, 'he turned out to be a bit weird.'

'Weird?' said Olivia suspiciously. 'What kind of weird?'

'Just weird,' said Isobel.

'Wacky?'

'No!' said Isobel. 'Not wacky. Weird! Honestly, Mummy, you don't want to know.'

'Well, I thought he was very nice,' said Olivia, pouring boiling water into the teapot. 'A very nice young man.'

Isobel said nothing, but her needle jerked savagely in and out of the fabric.

'I saw Brenda White the other day,' said Olivia, as though changing the subject. 'Her daughter's getting married in June.'

'Really?' Isobel looked up. 'Is she still working for Shell?'

'I've no idea,' said Olivia testily. Then she smiled at Isobel. 'What I was going to say was, she met her husband at an evening function organized for young professionals. In some smart London restaurant. They're very popular these days. Apparently the place was *packed* full of interesting men.'

'I'm sure.'

'Brenda said she could get the number if you're interested.'

'No thanks.'

'Darling, you're not giving yourself a chance!'

'No!' snapped Isobel. She put down her needle and looked up. '*You're* not giving me a chance! You're treating me as though I don't have any function in life except to find a husband. What about my work? What about my friends?'

'What about babies?' said Olivia sharply.

Colour flooded Isobel's face.

'Maybe I'll just have a baby without a husband,' she said after a pause. 'People do, you know.'

'Oh, now you're just being silly,' said Olivia crossly. 'A child needs a proper family.' She brought the teapot over to the table, sat down, and opened her red book. 'Right. What else needs doing?'

Isobel stared at the teapot without moving. It was large and decorated with painted ducks; they'd used it at family teas ever since she could remember. Ever since she and Milly had sat side by side in matching smocks, eating Marmite sandwiches. A child needs a proper family. What the hell was a proper family?

'Do you know?' said Olivia, looking up in surprise. 'I think I've done everything for today. I've ticked everything off my list.'

'Good,' said Isobel. 'You can have an evening off.'

'Maybe I should just check with Harry's assistant . . .'

'Don't check anything,' said Isobel firmly. 'You've checked everything a million times. Just have a nice cup of tea and relax.'

Olivia poured out the tea, took a sip and sighed.

'My goodness!' she said, leaning back in her chair. 'I have to say, there have been times when I thought we would never get this wedding organized in time.'

'Well, now it is organized,' said Isobel. 'So you should spend the evening doing something fun. Not hymn sheets. Not shoe trimmings. Fun!' She met Olivia's eyes sternly and, as the phone rang, they both began to giggle.

'I'll get that,' said Olivia.

'If it's Milly,' said Isobel quickly, 'I'll speak to her.'

'Hello, 1 Bertram Street,' said Olivia. She pulled a face at Isobel. 'Hello, Canon Lytton! How are you? Yes . . . Yes . . . No!'

Her voice suddenly changed, and Isobel looked up.

'No, I don't. I've no idea what you're talking about. Yes, perhaps you'd better. We'll see you then.'

Olivia put the phone down and looked perplexedly at Isobel.

'That was Canon Lytton,' she said.

'What did he want?'

'He's coming to see us.' Olivia sat down. 'I don't understand it.'

'Why?' said Isobel. 'Is something wrong?'

'Well, I don't know! He said he'd received some information, and he'd like to discuss it with us.'

'Information,' said Isobel. Her heart started to thump. 'What information?'

'I don't know,' said Olivia. She raised puzzled blue eyes to meet Isobel's. 'Something to do with Milly. He wouldn't say what.'

CHAPTER NINE

Rupert and Francesca sat silently in their drawing room, looking at each other. On Tom's suggestion, they had both phoned their offices to take the rest of the afternoon off. Neither had spoken in the taxi back to Fulham. Francesca had shot Rupert the occasional hurt, bewildered glance; he had sat, staring at his hands, wondering what he was going to say. Wondering whether to concoct a story or to tell her the truth about himself.

How would she react if he did? Would she be angry? Distraught? Revolted? Perhaps she would say she'd always known there was something different about him. Perhaps she would try to understand. But how could she understand what he didn't understand himself?

'Right,' said Francesca. 'Well, here we are.' She gazed at him expectantly and Rupert looked away. From outside he could hear birds singing, cars starting, the wailing of a toddler as it was thrust into its pushchair by its nanny. Mid-afternoon sounds that he wasn't used to hearing. He felt self-conscious, sitting at home in the winter daylight; self-conscious, facing his wife's taut, anxious gaze.

'I think,' said Francesca suddenly, 'we should pray.'

'What?' Rupert looked up, astounded.

'Before we talk.' Francesca gazed earnestly at him. 'If we said a prayer together it might help us.'

'I don't think it would help me,' said Rupert. He looked at the drinks cabinet, then looked away again.

'Rupert, what's wrong?' cried Francesca. 'Why are you so strange? Are you in love with Milly?'

'No!' exclaimed Rupert.

'But you had an affair with her when you were at Oxford.'

'No,' said Rupert.

'No?' Francesca stared at him. 'You never went out with her?'

'No.' He would have laughed if he hadn't felt so nervous. 'I never went out with Milly. Not in that sense.'

'Not in that sense,' she repeated. 'What does that mean?'

'Francesca, you're on the wrong track completely.' He tried a smile. 'Look, can't we just forget all this? Milly is an old friend. Full stop.'

'I wish I could believe you,' said Francesca. 'But it's obvious that something's going on.'

'Nothing's going on.'

'Then what was she talking about?' Francesca's voice rose in sudden passion. 'Rupert, I'm your wife! Your loyalty is to me. If you have a secret, then I deserve to know it.'

Rupert stared at his wife. Her pale eyes were shining slightly;

her hands were clasped tightly in her lap. Round her wrist was the expensive watch he'd bought her for her birthday. They'd chosen it together at Selfridges, then gone to see *An Inspector Calls*. It had been a happy day of safe, unambitious treats.

'I don't want to lose you,' he found himself saying. 'I love you. I love our marriage. I'll love our children, when we have them.' Francesca stared at him with anxious eyes.

'But?' she said. 'What's the but?'

Rupert gazed back at her silently. He didn't know how to reply, where to start.

'Are you in trouble?' said Francesca suddenly. 'Are you hiding something from me?' Her voice rose in alarm. 'Rupert?'

'No!' said Rupert. 'I'm not in trouble. I'm just . . .'

'What?' said Francesca impatiently. 'What are you?'

'Good question,' said Rupert. Tension was building up inside him like a coiled spring; he could feel a frown furrowing his forehead.

'What?' said Francesca. 'What do you mean?'

Rupert dug his nails into his palms and took a deep breath. There seemed no way but forward.

'When I was at Oxford,' he said, and stopped. 'There was a man.'

'A man?'

Rupert looked up and met Francesca's eyes. They were blank, unsuspecting, waiting for him to go on. She had no idea what he was leading up to.

'I had a relationship with him,' he said, still gazing at her. 'A close relationship.'

He paused, and waited, willing her brain to process what he

had said and make a deduction. For what seemed like hours, her eyes remained empty.

And then suddenly it happened. Her eyes snapped open and shut like a cat's. She had understood. She had understood what he was saying. Rupert gazed at her fearfully, trying to gauge her reaction.

'I don't understand,' she said at last, her voice suddenly truculent with alarm. 'Rupert, you're not making any sense! This is just a waste of time!'

She got up from the sofa and began to brush imaginary crumbs off her lap, avoiding his eye.

'Darling, I was wrong to doubt you,' she said. 'I'm sorry. I shouldn't mistrust you. Of course you have the right to see anybody you like. Shall we just forget this ever happened?'

Rupert stared at her in disbelief. Was she serious? Was she really willing to carry on as before? To pretend he'd said nothing; to ignore the huge questions that must already be gnawing at her brain? Was she really so afraid of the answers she might hear?

'I'll make some tea, shall I?' continued Francesca with a bright tautness. 'And get some scones out of the freezer. It'll be quite a treat!'

'Francesca,' said Rupert, 'stop it. You heard what I said. Don't you want to know any more?' He stood up and took her wrist. 'You heard what I said.'

'Rupert!' said Francesca, giving a little laugh. 'Let go! I—I don't know what you're talking about. I've already apologized for mistrusting you. What else do you want?'

'I want . . .' began Rupert. His grip tightened on her wrist; he felt a sudden certainty anchoring him. 'I want to tell you everything.'

'You've told me everything,' said Francesca quickly. 'I understand completely. It was a silly mix-up.'

'I've told you nothing.' He gazed at her, suddenly desperate to talk; desperate for relief. 'Francesca—'

'Why can't we just forget it?' said Francesca. Her voice held an edge of panic.

'Because it wouldn't be honest!'

'Well, maybe I don't want to be honest!' Her face was flushed; her eyes darted about. She looked like a trapped rabbit.

Leave her alone, Rupert told himself. Don't say any more; just leave her alone. But the urge to talk was unbearable; having begun, he could no longer contain himself.

'You don't want to be honest?' he said, despising himself. 'You want me to bear false witness? Is that what you want, Francesca?'

He watched as her face changed expression, as she struggled to reconcile her private fears with the law of God.

'You're right,' she said at last. 'I'm sorry.' She looked at him apprehensively, then bowed her head in submission. 'What do you want to tell me?'

Stop now, Rupert told himself. Stop now before you make her life utterly miserable.

'I had an affair with a man,' he said.

He paused, and waited for a reaction. A scream; a gasp. But Francesca's head remained bowed. She did not move.

'His name was Allan.' He swallowed. 'I loved him.'

He gazed at Francesca, hardly daring to breathe. Suddenly she looked up. 'You're making it up,' she said.

'What?'

'I can tell,' said Francesca quickly. 'You're feeling guilty about this girl Milly, so you've made up this silly story to distract me.'

'I haven't,' said Rupert. 'It's not a story. It's the truth.'

'No,' said Francesca, shaking her head. 'No.'

'Yes.'

'No!'

'Yes, Francesca!' shouted Rupert. 'Yes! It's true! I had an affair with a man. His name was Allan. Allan Kepinski.'

There was a long silence, then Francesca met his eyes. She looked ill.

'You really . . .'

'Yes.'

'Did you actually . . .'

'Yes,' said Rupert. 'Yes.' As he spoke he felt a mixture of pain and relief—as though heavy boulders were being ripped from his back, lightening his burden but leaving his skin sore and bleeding. 'I had sex with him.' He closed his eyes. 'We made love.' Suddenly memories flooded his mind. He was with Allan again in the darkness, feeling his skin, his hair, his tongue. Shivering with delight.

'I don't want to hear any more,' Francesca whispered. 'I don't feel very well.' Rupert opened his eyes to see her standing up; making uncertainly for the door. Her face was pale and her hands shook as they grasped the door handle. Guilt poured over him like hot water.

'I'm sorry,' he said. 'Francesca, I'm sorry.'

'Don't say sorry to me,' said Francesca in a jerky, scratchy voice. 'Don't say sorry to me. Say sorry to our Lord.'

'Francesca . . .'

'You must pray for forgiveness. I'm going—' She broke off and took a deep breath. 'I'm going to pray too.'

'Can't we talk?' said Rupert desperately. 'Can't we at least talk about it?' He got up and came towards her. 'Francesca?'

'Don't!' she shrieked as his hand neared her sleeve. 'Don't touch me!' She looked at him with glittering eyes in a sheet-white face.

'I wasn't—'

'Don't come near me!'

'But—'

'You made love to me!' she whispered. 'You touched me! You—' She broke off and retched.

'Francesca—'

'I'm going to be sick,' she said shakily, and ran out of the room.

Rupert remained by the door, listening as she ran up the stairs and locked the bathroom door. He was trembling all over; his legs felt weak. The revulsion he'd seen in Francesca's face made him want to crawl away and hide. She'd backed away from him as though he were contaminated; as though his evilness might seep out from his pores and infect her, too. As though he were an untouchable.

Suddenly he felt that he might break down and weep. But instead he made his way unsteadily to the drinks cabinet and took out a bottle of whisky. As he unscrewed the cap he caught sight of himself in the mirror. His eyes were veined with red, his cheeks were flushed, his face was full of miserable fear. He looked unhealthy inside and out.

Pray, Francesca had said. Pray for forgiveness. Rupert clutched the bottle tighter. Lord, he tried. Lord God, forgive me. But the words weren't there; the will wasn't there. He didn't want to repent. He didn't want to be redeemed. He was a miserable sinner and he didn't care.

God hates me, thought Rupert, staring at his own reflection. God doesn't exist. Both seemed equally likely.

A bit later on Francesca came downstairs again. She had brushed her hair and washed her face and changed into jeans and a jersey. Rupert looked up from the sofa, where he was still sitting with his bottle of whisky. It was half empty, and his head was spinning but he didn't feel any happier.

'I've spoken to Tom,' said Francesca. 'He's coming round later.' Rupert's head jerked up.

'Tom?'

'I've told him everything,' said Francesca, her voice trembling. 'He says not to worry. He's known other cases like yours.' Rupert's head began to thump hard.

'I don't want to see Tom,' he said.

'He wants to help!'

'I don't want him to know! This is private!' Rupert felt a note of panic edging into his voice. He could just imagine Tom's face, looking at him with a mixture of pity and disgust. Tom would be revolted by him. They would all be revolted by him.

'He wants to help,' repeated Francesca. 'And darling . . .' Her tone changed and Rupert looked up in surprise. 'I want to apologize. I was wrong to react so badly. I just panicked. Tom said that's perfectly normal. He said—' Francesca broke off and bit her lip. 'Anyway. We can get through this. With a lot of support and prayer . . .'

'Francesca—' began Rupert. She raised her hand.

'No, wait.' She came slowly forward, towards him. Rupert stared at her. 'Tom said I must try not to allow my own feelings to get in the way of our . . .' she paused '. . . of our physical love. I shouldn't have rejected you. I put my own selfish emotions first, and that was wrong of me.' She swallowed. 'I'm sorry. Please forgive me.'

She edged even closer until she was standing inches from him.

'It's not up to me to hold back from you,' she whispered. 'You have every right to touch me. You're my husband. I promised before God to love you and obey you and give myself to you.'

Rupert gazed at her. He felt too shocked to speak. Slowly he reached out a hand and put it gently on her sleeve. A look of repulsion passed over her face, but she continued staring at him steadily, as though she was determined to see this through; as though she had no other choice.

'No!' said Rupert suddenly and pulled his hand away. 'I won't do this. This is wrong! Francesca, you're not a sacrificial lamb! You're a human!'

'I want to heal our marriage,' said Francesca in a shaking voice. 'Tom said—'

'Tom said if we went to bed then everything would be sorted, did he?' Rupert's voice was harsh with sarcasm. 'Tom told you to lie back and think of Jesus.'

'Rupert!'

'I won't allow you to subjugate yourself like that. Francesca, I love you! I respect you!'

'Well, if you love me and respect me,' said Francesca in suddenly savage tones, 'then why did you lie to me!' Her voice cracked. 'Why did you marry me, knowing what you were?'

'Francesca, I'm still me! I'm still Rupert!'

'You're not! Not to me!' Her eyes filled with tears. 'I can't see you any more. All I can see is . . .' She gave a little shudder of disgust. 'It makes me sick to think about it.'

Rupert stared at her miserably.

'Tell me what you want me to do,' he said eventually. 'Do you want me to move out?'

'No,' said Francesca at once. 'No.' She hesitated. 'Tom suggested—'

'What?'

'He suggested,' she said, gulping slightly, 'a public confession. At the evening service. If you confess your sins aloud to the congregation and to God, then perhaps you'll be able to start afresh. With no more lies. No more sin.'

Rupert stared at her. Everything in his body resisted what she was proposing.

'Tom said you might not yet fully realize the wrong you'd done,' continued Francesca. 'But once you do, and once you've properly repented, then we'll be able to start again. It'll be a rebirth. For both of us.' She looked up and wiped the wetness from her eyes. 'What do you think? What do you think, Rupert?'

'I'm not going to repent,' Rupert found himself saying.

'What?' A look of shock came over Francesca's face.

'I'm not going to repent,' repeated Rupert shakily. He dug his nails into the palms of his hands. 'I'm not going to stand up in public and say that what I did was wicked.'

'But . . .'

'I loved Allan. And he loved me. And what we did wasn't evil or wicked. It was . . .' Tears suddenly smarted at Rupert's eyes. 'It was a beautiful, loving relationship. Whatever the Bible says.'

'Are you serious?'

'Yes,' said Rupert. He exhaled with a shudder. 'I wish, for both our sakes, that I wasn't. But I am.' He looked her straight in the eye. 'I don't regret what I did.'

'Well then, you're sick!' cried Francesca. A note of panic entered her voice. 'You're sick! You went with a man! How can that be beautiful? It's disgusting!'

'Francesca—'

'And what about me?' Her voice rose higher. 'What about when we were in bed together? All this time, have you been wishing you were with him?'

'No!' cried Rupert. 'Of course not.'

'But you said you loved him!'

'I did. But I didn't realize it at the time.' He stopped. 'Francesca, I'm so sorry.'

She stared at him for a silent, aching moment, then backed away, reaching blindly for a chair.

'I don't understand,' she said in a subdued voice. 'Are you really homosexual? Tom said you weren't. He said lots of young men went the wrong way at first.'

'What would Tom know about it?' snapped Rupert. He felt trapped; as though he were being pinned into a corner.

'Well—are you?' persisted Francesca. 'Are you homosexual?'

There was a long pause.

'I don't know,' said Rupert at last. He sank down heavily onto a sofa and buried his head in his hands. 'I don't know what I am.'

When, after a few minutes, he looked up again, Francesca had disappeared. The birds were still twittering outside the window;

cars were still roaring in the distance. Everything was the same. Nothing was the same.

Rupert stared down at his trembling hands. At the signet ring Francesca had given him for their wedding. With a sudden flash, he recalled the happiness he'd felt that day; the relief he'd experienced as, with a few simple words, he'd become part of the legitimate married masses. When he'd led Francesca out of the church, he'd felt as though he finally belonged; as though at last he was normal. Which was exactly what he wanted to be. He didn't want to be gay. He didn't want to be a minority. He just wanted to be like everybody else.

It had all happened just as Allan had predicted. Allan had understood; Allan had known exactly how Rupert felt. He'd watched as, over those late summer weeks, Rupert's feelings had gradually turned from ardour to embarrassment. He'd waited patiently as Rupert tried to abandon his company, ignoring him for days on end, only to succumb with more passion than ever before. He'd been sympathetic and supportive and understanding. And in return, Rupert had fled from him.

The seeds of his defection had been sown at the beginning of September. Rupert and Allan had been walking down Broad Street together, not quite holding hands, but brushing arms; talking closely, smiling the smiles of lovers. And then someone had called Rupert's name.

'Rupert! Hi!'

His head had jerked up. Standing on the other side of the road, grinning at him, was Ben Fisher, a boy from the year below him at school. Suddenly Rupert had remembered his father's letter of a few weeks before. The wistful hope that Rupert might come home for some of the vacation; the triumphant news that another boy from the little Cornish school would soon be joining him at Oxford.

'Ben!' Rupert had exclaimed, hurrying across the street. 'Welcome! I heard you were coming.'

'I'm hoping you'll show me around the place,' Ben had replied, his dark eyes twinkling. 'And introduce me to some girls. You must have the whole place after you. Stud!' Then his eyes had swivelled curiously towards Allan, still standing on the other side of the road. 'Who's that?' he'd asked. 'A friend?'

Rupert's heart had given a little jump. Suddenly, with a flurry of panic, he saw himself in the eyes of his friends at home. His teachers. His father.

'Oh him?' he'd said after a pause. 'That's no one. Just one of the tutors.'

The next night he'd gone to a bar with Ben, drunk tequila slammers and flirted furiously with a couple of pretty Italian girls. On his return, Allan had been waiting for him in his room.

'Good evening?' he'd said pleasantly.

'Yes,' Rupert had replied, unable to meet his gaze. 'Yes. I was with—with friends.' He'd stripped quickly, got into bed and closed his eyes as Allan came towards him; had emptied his mind of all thought or guilt as their physical delight had begun.

But the next night he'd gone out again with Ben, and this time had forced himself to kiss one of the pretty young girls who hung around him like kids round a sweet counter. She'd responded eagerly, encouraging his hands to roam over her soft, unfamiliar body. At the end of the evening she'd invited him back to the house she shared on the Cowley Road.

He'd undressed her slowly and clumsily, taking his cue from scenes in films, hoping her obvious experience would see him through. Somehow he'd managed to acquit himself successfully; whether her cries were real or false he didn't know and didn't care. The next morning he'd woken up in her bed, curled up against her smooth female skin, breathing in her feminine smell. He'd kissed her shoulder as he always kissed Allan's shoulder, reached out experimentally to touch her breast—and then realized with a sudden jolt of surprise that he felt aroused. He wanted to touch this girl's body. He wanted to kiss her. The thought of making love to her again excited him. He was normal. He could be normal.

'Are you running away from me?' Allan had said a few days later, as they ate pasta together. 'Do you need some space?'

'No!' Rupert had replied, too heartily. 'Everything's fine.' Allan had looked silently at him for a moment, then put down his fork.

'Don't panic,' he said, reaching for Rupert's hand, then flinching as Rupert moved it away. 'Don't give up something that could be wonderful, just because you're scared.'

'I'm not scared!'

'Of course you're scared. Everyone's scared. *I'm* scared.'

'You?' Rupert had said, trying not to sound truculent. 'Why on earth are you scared?'

'I'm scared,' Allan had said slowly, 'because I understand what you're doing, and I know what it means for me. You're trying to escape. You're trying to discard me. In a few weeks you'll walk past me in the street and look away. Am I right?'

He'd gazed at Rupert with dark eyes asking for an answer, a rebuttal. But Rupert had said nothing. He hadn't had to.

After that, things had deteriorated swiftly. They'd had one final conversation in a deserted Keble College bar, the week before the new term began.

'I just can't . . .' Rupert had muttered, stiff with self-consciousness, one eye on the incurious gaze of the barman. 'I'm not—' He'd broken off and taken a deep gulp of whisky. 'You do understand.' He'd looked up pleadingly at Allan, then looked quickly away again.

'No,' Allan had said quietly, 'I don't understand. We were happy together.'

'It was a mistake. I'm not gay.'

'You're not attracted to me?' Allan had said, and his eyes had fixed on Rupert's. 'Is that what you're saying? You're not attracted to me?'

Rupert had gazed back at him, feeling as though something inside him were being wrenched in two. Waiting in a pub were Ben and a pair of girls. Tonight he would almost certainly have sex with one of them. But he wanted Allan more than he wanted any girl.

'No,' he said at last. 'I'm not.'

'Fine,' Allan had said, his dry voice cracking with anger. 'Lie to me. Lie to yourself. Get married. Have a kid. Play at being straight. But you'll know you're not, and I'll know you're not.'

'I am,' Rupert had retorted feebly, then wished he hadn't as Allan's eyes flashed with contempt.

'Whatever.' He'd drained his glass and got to his feet.

'Will you be all right?' Rupert had said, watching him.

'Don't patronize me,' Allan had snapped back fiercely. 'No I won't be all right. But I'll get over it.'

'I'm sorry.'

Allan had said nothing more. Rupert had watched silently as he made his way out of the bar; for a minute or two he could feel nothing but raw pain. But after two more whiskies he'd felt a little better. He'd gone to meet Ben in the pub as arranged, and had drunk a few pints and a good deal more whisky. Later that night, after having had sex with the prettier of the two girls Ben had procured, he'd lain awake and told himself repeatedly that he was normal; he was back on course; he was happy. And for a while, he'd almost managed to believe himself.

'Tom'll be here in a few minutes.' Francesca's voice interrupted his thoughts. Rupert looked up. She was standing at the door, holding a tray. On it was the cream-coloured teapot they'd chosen for their wedding list, together with cups, saucers and a plate of chocolate biscuits.

'Francesca,' said Rupert wearily. 'We're not holding a bloody tea party.' A look of shocked hurt passed over her face; then she composed herself and nodded.

'Perhaps you're right,' she said. She set the tray down on a chair. 'Perhaps this is a bit inappropriate.'

'The whole thing is inappropriate.' Rupert stood up and walked slowly to the door. 'I'm not talking to Tom about my sexuality.'

'But he wants to help!'

'He doesn't.' Rupert looked at Francesca. 'He wants to channel. Not help.'

'I don't understand,' said Francesca, wrinkling her brow.

Rupert shrugged. For a few moments neither spoke. Then Francesca bit her lip.

'I was wondering,' she said hesitantly, 'if you should maybe see a doctor, as well. We could ask Dr Askew to recommend someone. What do you think?'

Rupert stared at her speechlessly. He felt as though she'd hit him in the face with a hammer.

'A doctor?' he echoed eventually, trying to sound calm. 'A *doctor?*'

'I thought—'

'You think there's something medically wrong with me?'

'No! I just meant . . .' Francesca flushed pink. 'Perhaps there's something they could give you.'

'An anti-gay pill?' He couldn't control his voice. Who was this girl he'd married? Who was she? 'Are you serious?'

'It's just an idea!'

For a few silent seconds, Rupert gazed at Francesca. Then, without speaking, he strode past her into the hall and snatched his jacket from the peg.

'Rupert!' she said. 'Where are you going?'

'I've got to get out of here.'

'But where!' cried Francesca. 'Where are you going?'

Rupert looked at his reflection in the hall mirror.

'I'm going,' he said slowly, 'to find Allan.'

CHAPTER TEN

Canon Lytton had asked for all the members of the family to be assembled in the drawing room, as though he were about to unmask a murderer in their midst.

'There are only the two of us,' Isobel had said scornfully. 'Would you like us to assemble? Or do you want to come back later?'

'Indeed no,' Canon Lytton had replied solemnly. 'Let us adjourn.'

Now he sat on the sofa, his cassock falling in dusty folds around him, his face stern and forbidding. I bet he practises that expression in the mirror, thought Isobel. To frighten Sunday school children with.

'I come here on a matter of some gravity,' he began. 'To be

brief, I wish to ascertain the truth or otherwise of a piece of information which I have been given.'

'By whom?' said Isobel. Canon Lytton ignored her.

'It is my duty,' he said, raising his voice slightly, 'as parish priest and official at the intended marriage of Milly and Simon, to check whether Milly, as she stated on the form she filled in, is a spinster of the parish of St Edward the Confessor, or whether—in fact—she is not. I will ask her myself when she returns. In the meantime, I would be grateful if you, as her mother, could answer on her behalf.' He stopped and looked impressively at Olivia, who wrinkled her brow.

'I don't understand,' she said. 'Are you asking if Milly and Simon live together? Because they don't, you know. They're quite old-fashioned like that.'

'That was not my question,' said Canon Lytton. 'My question, more simply, is: has Milly been married before?'

'Married before?' said Olivia. She gave a shocked little laugh. 'What are you talking about?'

'I have been given to believe—'

'What do you mean?' interrupted Olivia. 'Is someone saying Milly's been married before?' Canon Lytton inclined his head slightly. 'Well, they're lying! Of course Milly hasn't been married! How on earth can you believe such a thing?'

'It is my duty to follow up all such accusations.'

'What,' said Isobel, 'even if they come from complete crackpots?'

'I use my discretion,' said Canon Lytton, giving her a hard look. 'The person who told me this was quite insistent—and even claimed to have a copy of a marriage certificate.'

'Who was it?' said Isobel.

'That, I am not at liberty to say,' said Canon Lytton, rear-ranging his cassock carefully.

You love this, thought Isobel, gazing at him. You just love it.

'Jealousy!' said Olivia suddenly. 'That's what this is. Some-body's jealous of Milly, and they're trying to spoil her wedding. There must be a lot of disappointed girls out there. No wonder they're targeting poor Milly! Really, Canon Lytton, I'm surprised at you. Believing such scurrilous nonsense!'

'Scurrilous nonsense it may be,' said Canon Lytton. 'Neverthe-less, I wish to speak to Milly herself on her return. In case there are facts pertaining to this matter with which you'—he nodded at Olivia—'are not acquainted.'

'Canon Lytton,' said Olivia furiously. 'Are you seriously sug-gesting that my daughter might have got married without telling me? My daughter tells me everything!'

There was a small movement from the sofa, and both Olivia and Canon Lytton turned to look at Isobel.

'Would you like to say something, Isobel?' said Canon Lytton.

'No,' said Isobel quickly, and coughed. 'Nothing.'

'Who's she supposed to have married, anyway?' demanded Olivia. 'The postman?'

There was a short silence. Isobel glanced up, trying not to look too tense.

'A man named Kepinski,' said Canon Lytton, reading from a piece of paper. 'Allan Kepinski.'

Isobel's heart sank. Milly didn't have a hope.

'Allan Kepinski?' said Olivia incredulously. 'That's a made-up name, if ever I heard one! The whole thing's obviously a hoax.

Set up by some poor character, obsessed by Milly's good fortune. You read about this sort of thing all the time. Don't you, Isobel?'

'Yes,' said Isobel weakly. 'All the time.'

'And now,' said Olivia, standing up, 'if you'll excuse me, Canon Lytton, I've a thousand things to do, and they don't include listening to made-up lies about my daughter. We do have a wedding on Saturday, you know!'

'I am aware of that fact,' said Canon Lytton. 'Nevertheless, I will need to speak to Milly about this. Perhaps later this evening will be convenient.'

'You can speak to her all you like,' said Olivia. 'But you're wasting your time!'

'I will return,' said Canon Lytton portentously. 'Permit me to see myself out.'

As the front door slammed behind him, Olivia looked at Isobel.

'Do you know what he's talking about?'

'No!' said Isobel. 'Of course not.'

'Isobel,' said Olivia sharply. 'You may have fooled Canon Lytton, but you don't fool me! You know something about this, don't you? Is something going on?'

'Look, Mummy,' said Isobel, trying to sound calm. 'I think we should just wait until Milly gets back.'

'Wait for what?' Olivia stared at her in dismay. 'Isobel, what are you saying? There's no truth in what Canon Lytton said, is there?'

'I'm not saying anything,' said Isobel stoutly. 'Not until Milly gets back.'

'I won't have you girls keeping secrets from me,' said Olivia angrily. Isobel sighed.

'To be honest, Mummy,' she said, 'it's a bit late for that.'

Milly was trudging back from the station when a car pulled up alongside her.

'Hello, darling,' said James. 'Would you like a lift?'

'Oh,' said Milly. 'Thanks.'

Without meeting her father's eye, she got into the car and stared straight ahead at the darkening street, trying desperately to organize her thoughts. She had to decide what she was going to do. She had to come up with a plan. All the way back from London she had tried to think rationally; to form some sensible solution. But now here she was, back in Bath, minutes away from home, and she was still in a state of uncertainty. Could she really force Alexander to keep quiet? Already it was Thursday evening; the wedding was on Saturday. If she could just get through Friday . . .

'Did you have a good time in London?' said James. Milly jumped.

'Yes,' she said. 'Shopping. You know.'

'I do,' said James. 'Did you find anything nice?'

'Yes,' said Milly. There was a pause, and she realized that she didn't have any shopping bags. 'I bought . . . cuff links for Simon.'

'Very nice. He said he would call for you later, by the way. After work.'

A spasm of nerves hit Milly in the stomach.

'Oh good,' she said, feeling sick. How could she face Simon? How could she even look him in the eye?

As they got out of the car she felt a sudden desire to run away, down the street, and never see anybody ever again. Instead, she followed her father up the steps to the front door.

'She's back!' She heard her mother's voice cry as the door opened. Olivia appeared in the hall. 'Milly,' she said in clipped, furious tones. 'What's all this nonsense?'

'All what nonsense?' said Milly apprehensively.

'All this nonsense about you being married?'

Milly felt a hammer-blow to her heart.

'What do you mean?' she said shakily.

'What's going on?' said James, following Milly into the hall. 'Olivia, are you all right?'

'No, I'm not all right,' said Olivia jerkily. 'Canon Lytton came to see us this afternoon.' She glanced over her shoulder. 'Didn't he, Isobel?'

'Yes,' said Isobel, coming out of the drawing room. 'He came to see us.' She pulled a quick face at Milly, and Milly stared back at her, feeling fear rising inside her like choking gas.

'What did he—'

'He had some ridiculous story about Milly,' said Olivia. 'He said she'd been married before!'

Milly didn't move. Her eyes flickered to Isobel and back again.

'Only Isobel doesn't seem to think it is so ridiculous!' said Olivia.

'Oh, really?' said Milly, looking at Isobel with scorching eyes.

'Mummy!' exclaimed Isobel, scandalized. 'That's not fair! Milly, honestly, I didn't say anything. I said we should wait till you got back.'

'Yes,' said Olivia. 'And now she's back. So one of you had better tell us what this is all about.' Milly looked from face to face.

'All right,' she said shakily. 'Just let me take off my coat.'

There was silence as she unwrapped her scarf, took off her coat, and hung them both up. She turned round and surveyed her audience.

'Maybe we should all have a drink,' she said.

'I don't want a drink!' exclaimed Olivia. 'I want to know what's going on. Milly, is Canon Lytton right? Have you been married before?'

'Just . . . just give me a minute to sit down,' said Milly desperately.

'You don't need a minute!' cried Olivia. 'You don't need a minute! What's the answer? Have you been married before or not? Yes or no, Milly? Yes or no?'

'Yes!' screamed Milly. 'I'm married! I've been married for ten years!'

Her words resonated round the silent hall. Olivia took a small pace back and clutched the stair bannister.

'I got married when I was at Oxford,' Milly continued in a trembling voice. 'I was eighteen. It . . . it didn't mean anything. No one knew. *No one knew*. And I thought no one would ever find out. I thought . . .' She broke off. 'Oh, what's the point?'

There was silence. Isobel glanced apprehensively at Olivia. Her face was an ugly scarlet; she seemed to be having trouble breathing.

'Are you serious, Milly?' she said eventually.

'Yes.'

'You really got married when you were eighteen. And you really thought that no one would ever find out.'

There was a pause—then Milly nodded miserably.

'Then you're a stupid, stupid girl!' shrieked Olivia. Her voice lashed across the room like a whip, and Milly turned pale. 'You're a stupid, selfish girl! How could you have thought that no one would find out? How could you have been so stupid? You've ruined everything for all of us!'

'Stop it!' said James angrily. 'Stop it, Olivia.'

'I'm sorry,' whispered Milly. 'I really am.'

'It's no good being sorry!' screamed Olivia. 'It's too late for sorry! How could you have done this to me?'

'Olivia!'

'I suppose you thought it was clever, did you? Getting married and keeping it a secret. I suppose you thought you were being frightfully grown-up.'

'No,' said Milly miserably.

'Who was he? A student?'

'A research fellow.'

'Swept you off your feet, did he? Promised you all sorts of things?'

'No!' shouted Milly, suddenly snapping. 'I married him to help him! He needed to stay in the country!'

Olivia stared at Milly, her expression gradually changing as she worked out what Milly was saying.

'You married an illegal immigrant?' she whispered. Her voice rose to a shriek. 'An illegal *immigrant*?'

'Don't say it like that!' said Milly.

'What sort of illegal immigrant?' A note of hysteria entered Olivia's voice. 'Did he threaten you?'

'For God's sake, Mummy!' said Isobel.

'Olivia,' said James. 'Calm down. You're not helping.'

'Helping?' Olivia turned on James. 'Why should I want to

help? Do you realize what this means? We'll have to call the wedding off!'

'Postpone it, maybe,' said Isobel. 'Until the divorce comes through.' She pulled a sympathetic face at Milly.

'We can't!' cried Olivia desperately. 'It's all arranged! It's all organized!' She thought for a moment, then whipped round to Milly. 'Does Simon know about this?'

Milly shook her head. Olivia's eyes began to glitter.

'Well, then we can still go through with it,' she said quickly. Her eyes darted urgently from face to face. 'We'll fob Canon Lytton off! If none of us says a word, if we all hold our heads high . . .'

'Mummy!' exclaimed Isobel. 'You're talking about bigamy!'

'So what?'

'Olivia, you're mad,' said James in disgust. 'Obviously the wedding must be cancelled. And if you ask me, it's no bad thing.'

'What do you mean?' said Olivia hysterically. 'What do you mean, it's no bad thing? This is the most terrible thing that's ever happened to our family, and you're saying it's no bad thing!'

'Frankly, I think it would be good for us all to get back to normal!' exclaimed James angrily. 'This whole wedding has got out of hand. It's nothing but wedding, wedding, wedding! You talk of nothing else.'

'Well, someone has to organize it!' shrieked Olivia. 'Do you know how many things I've had to sort out?'

'Yes I do!' shouted James in exasperation. 'A thousand! Every day, you've got a thousand bloody things to do! You realize that's seven thousand things a week? What is this, Olivia? An expedition to the moon?'

'You just wouldn't understand,' said Olivia bitterly.

'The whole family's obsessed! I think it would be a very good thing for you, Milly, if you just got your feet back on the ground for a while.'

'What do you mean?' said Milly shakily. 'My feet are on the ground.'

'Milly, your feet are up with the birds! You've gone rushing into this marriage without considering what it means, without considering all the other options. I know Simon's a very attractive young man, I know his father's very rich . . .'

'That's got nothing to do with it!' Milly stared at James with an ashen face. 'I love Simon! I want to marry him because I love him.'

'You think you do,' said James. 'But perhaps this is a good chance for you to wait for a while. See if you can stand on your own two feet, for a change. Like Isobel.'

'Like Isobel,' echoed Milly, in a disbelieving voice. 'You always want me to be Isobel. Perfect bloody Isobel.'

'Of course I don't,' said James impatiently. 'That's not what I said.'

'You want me to do the things that Isobel does.'

'Maybe,' said James. 'Some of them.'

'Daddy——' began Isobel.

'Well, fine!' screamed Milly, feeling blood rush to her head. 'I'll be like Isobel! I won't get married! I'll get pregnant instead!'

There was a sharp silence.

'Pregnant?' said Olivia incredulously.

'Thanks a lot, Milly,' said Isobel shortly, stalking to the front door.

'Isobel——' began Milly. But Isobel slammed the door behind her without looking back.

'Pregnant,' repeated Olivia. She groped for a chair and sat down.

'I didn't mean to say that,' muttered Milly, appalled at herself. 'Can you just forget I said it?'

'You're married,' said Olivia shakily. 'And Isobel's pregnant.' She looked up. 'Is she really pregnant?'

'That's her business,' said Milly, staring at the floor. 'It's her business. I shouldn't have said anything.'

The doorbell rang, jolting them all.

'That'll be Isobel,' said James, getting up. He opened the door and took a step back.

'Ah,' he said. 'It's you, Simon.'

Isobel strode along the pavement, not stopping, not looking back, not knowing where she was going. Her heart was thumping hard, and her jaw was set and tense. The snow had turned to slush; a cold drizzle was coating her hair and dripping down her neck. But with every step she felt a little better. With every step she was further into anonymity; further away from the shocked faces of her family.

Her whole body still prickled with anger. She felt betrayed, misrepresented, too furious with Milly to speak . . . and yet too sorry for her to blame her. She'd never witnessed such an ugly family scene, with Milly defenceless in the middle of it. No wonder she'd lashed out with the first diversionary tactic she had to hand. It was understandable. But that didn't make it any easier.

Isobel closed her eyes. She felt raw and vulnerable; unready for this. On her return, her parents would surely expect her to talk to them. They would expect her to answer questions, to reassure them and help them digest this piece of startling information. But she had barely digested it herself. Her condition was a nebulous fact floating around her mind, unwanted and unformed, as yet unpresentable to the outside world. She couldn't articulate what she thought about it; could no longer distingiush between emotional and physical sensation. Energy and optimism alternated with tearfulness and the nausea made everything even worse. What does it feel like? Milly would no doubt ask. What does it feel like, to have a child inside you? But Isobel didn't want to answer that. She didn't want to think of herself as carrying a child.

She stopped at a corner and cautiously laid her hand over her stomach. When she imagined whatever was inside her, it was as a small shellfish, or a snail. Something coiled up and hardly human. Something indeterminate, whose life had not begun. Whose life might, if she chose, progress no further. A wave of strong feeling, half grief, half sickness, swept over her, and she began to tremble. The whole family, she thought, is concerned with whether Milly's wedding should go ahead or not. While I, all alone, am trying to decide whether another human's life should go ahead or not.

The thought transfixed her. She felt almost overcome by her burden, overwhelmed by the decision she was going to have to make, and for a moment she thought she might collapse, sobbing, on the hard pavement. But instead, with a slight impatient shake of the head, she thrust her hands deeper into her pockets and, teeth gritted, began once more to walk.

Simon and Milly sat, facing each other on armchairs in the drawing room, as though appearing on a television chat show.

'So,' said Simon finally. 'What is all this?'

Milly gazed at him silently. Her fingers shook as she pushed a frond of hair back from her face; her lips opened to speak, then closed again.

'You're making me nervous,' said Simon. 'Come on, sweetheart. Nothing's that bad. It's not life-threatening, is it?'

'No.'

'Well then.' He grinned at her, and Milly smiled back, feeling a sudden relief.

'You won't like it,' she said.

'I'll be brave,' said Simon. 'Come on, hit me with it.'

'OK,' said Milly. She took a deep breath. 'The thing is, we can't get married on Saturday. We're going to have to postpone the wedding.'

'Postpone?' said Simon slowly. 'Well, OK. But why?'

'There's something I haven't told you,' said Milly, meshing her hands together, twisting them around until her knuckles felt as though they might break. 'I did something very stupid when I was eighteen. I got married. It was a fake marriage. It didn't mean anything. But the divorce never went through. So I'm—I'm still married.'

She glanced at Simon. He looked bewildered but not angry, and she felt a sudden flood of reassurance. After her mother's hysterics, it was a relief to see Simon taking the news calmly. He wasn't freaking out; he wasn't yelling. But of course he wasn't. After all, this was nothing to do with their relationship, was it? This was nothing but a technical hitch.

'All it means is, I'll have to wait for the decree absolute before we can get married,' she said. She bit her lip. 'Simon, I'm really sorry.'

There was a long silence.

'I don't get it,' said Simon eventually. 'Is this a joke?'

'No,' said Milly. 'No! God, I wish it was! It's true. I'm married. Simon, I'm married!'

She gazed at him miserably. His dark eyes scanned her face; slowly a look of disbelief crept over his features.

'You're serious.'

'Yes.'

'You're really married.'

'Yes. But it wasn't a proper marriage,' said Milly quickly. She stared down at the floor, trying to keep her voice steady. 'He was gay. The whole thing was fake. To keep him in the country. It honestly meant nothing. Less than nothing! You do understand, don't you? You do understand?'

She looked up at his face. And as she saw his expression she realized, with a thud of dismay, that he didn't.

'It was a mistake,' she said, almost tripping over the words in her haste. 'A big mistake. I see that now. I should never have agreed to do it. But I was very young, and very stupid, and he was a friend. Or at least I thought he was a friend. And he needed my help. That's all it was!'

'That's all it was,' echoed Simon in a strange voice. 'So, what, did this guy pay you?'

'No!' said Milly. 'I just did it as a favour!'

'You got married . . . as a favour?' said Simon incredulously. Milly stared at him in alarm. Somehow this was coming out all wrong.

'It meant nothing,' she said. 'It was ten years ago! I was a child. I know I should have told you about it before. I know I should. But I just . . .' She broke off and looked at him desperately. 'Simon, say something!'

'What am I supposed to say?' said Simon. 'Congratulations?'
Milly winced.

'No! Just—I don't know. Tell me what you're thinking.'

'I don't know what to think,' said Simon. 'I don't even know
where to start. I can't believe it. You tell me you're married to
some other guy. What am I supposed to think?' His glance fell on
her left hand; on the finger wearing his engagement ring, and she
flushed.

'It didn't mean anything,' she said. 'You have to believe that.'

'It doesn't matter what it meant! You're still married, aren't
you?' Simon suddenly leapt up and stalked away to the window.
'Christ, Milly!' he exclaimed, his voice shaking slightly. 'Why
didn't you tell me?'

'I don't know. I didn't . . .' She swallowed. 'I didn't want to
spoil everything.'

'You didn't want to spoil everything,' echoed Simon. 'So you
leave it until two days before our wedding to tell me you're married.'

'I thought it wouldn't matter! I thought—'

'You thought you wouldn't bother to tell me at all?' He turned
round and gazed at her in sudden comprehension. 'You were never
going to tell me! Am I right?'

'I didn't—'

'You were going to keep it a secret from me!' His voice rose.
'From your own husband!'

'No! I *was* intending to tell you!'

'When? On our wedding night? When our first child was
born? On our golden anniversary?'

Milly opened her mouth to speak, then closed it again. She
felt a hot fear creeping over her. She had never seen Simon angry

like this before. She didn't know how to defuse him; which way to move.

'So, what other little secrets are you keeping from me? Any hidden children? Secret lovers?'

'No.'

'And how am I supposed to believe that?' His voice lashed across the room, and Milly flinched. 'How am I supposed to believe anything you say any more?'

'I don't know,' said Milly hopelessly. 'I don't know. You just have to trust me.'

'Trust you!'

'I know I should have told you,' she said desperately. 'I know that! But the fact that I didn't doesn't mean I'm keeping anything else secret from you. Simon—'

'It's not just that,' said Simon, cutting across her. 'It's not just the fact you kept it secret.' Milly's heart began to thump nervously.

'What is it, then?'

Simon sank into a chair and rubbed his face.

'Milly—you've already made the wedding vows to someone else. You've already promised to love someone else. Cherish someone else. Do you know what that feels like for me?'

'But I didn't mean a word of it! Not a word!'

'Exactly.' His voice chilled her. 'I thought you took those vows as seriously as I did.'

'I did,' said Milly in horror. 'I do.'

'How can you? You've spoiled them! You've tainted them.'

'Simon, don't look at me like that,' whispered Milly. 'I'm not evil! I made a mistake, but I'm still me. Nothing's changed!'

'Everything's changed,' said Simon flatly. There was a heavy silence. 'To be honest, I feel as if I don't know you any more.'

'Well, I feel as if I don't know *you* any more!' cried Milly in a sudden anguished burst. 'I don't know *you* any more! Simon, I know I've messed the wedding up. I know I've fucked things up completely. But you don't have to be so sanctimonious. You don't have to look at me as if I'm beneath contempt. I'm not a criminal!' She gulped. 'Well, maybe I am, technically. But only because I made a mistake. I made one mistake! And if you loved me, you'd forgive me!' She began to shake with sobs. 'If you really loved me, you would forgive me!'

'And if you really loved me,' shouted Simon, suddenly looking distraught, 'you would have told me you were married! You can say what you like, Milly, but if you'd really loved me, you would have told me!'

Milly stared at him, suddenly feeling unsure of herself.

'Not necessarily,' she faltered.

'Well, we must have different definitions of love,' said Simon. 'Perhaps we've been at cross purposes all along.' He stood up and reached for his coat. Milly stared at him, feeling a horrified disbelief creep over her.

'Are you saying'—she fought a desire to retch—'are you saying you don't want to marry me any more?'

'As I recall,' said Simon stiffly, 'you've already got a husband. So the question's academic really, isn't it?' He paused at the door. 'I hope the two of you will be very happy.'

'Bastard!' screamed Milly. Tears blurred her eyes as she tugged feverishly at her engagement ring. By the time she managed to throw it at him, the door was closed and he was gone.

CHAPTER ELEVEN

Isobel arrived back to find the house quiet. The lights in the hall were dim; there was no one in the drawing room. She pushed open the kitchen door and saw Olivia sitting at the table in the half-light. A bottle of wine was in front of her, nearly empty; music was playing quietly in the corner. As Olivia heard the sound of the door she looked up with a pale, puffy face.

'Well,' she said flatly. 'It's all over.'

'What do you mean?' said Isobel suspiciously.

'I mean,' said Olivia, 'that the engagement between Milly and Simon is off.'

'What?' said Isobel. She blinked at her mother, aghast. 'Do you mean off completely? Why?'

'They had some sort of row—and Simon called the whole thing off.' Olivia took a slug of wine.

'What about? Her first marriage?'

'I imagine so,' said Olivia. 'She wouldn't say.'

'Where is she?'

'She's gone to Esme's for the night. She said she had to get away from this house. From all of us.'

'I don't blame her,' said Isobel. She sat heavily down on a chair, her coat still on. 'God, poor Milly. I can't believe it! What exactly did Simon say?'

'Milly didn't tell me. She doesn't tell me anything these days.' Olivia took a deep swig of wine. 'Obviously, I'm no longer considered worthy of her confidence.'

Isobel rolled her eyes.

'Mummy, don't start.'

'For ten years she was married to that—that illegal immigrant! Ten years without telling me!'

'She couldn't tell you. How on earth could she tell you?'

'And then, when she was in trouble, she went to Esme.' Olivia raised bloodshot eyes to Isobel. 'To Esme Ormerod!'

'She always goes to Esme,' said Isobel.

'I know she does. She goes running off to that house and comes back thinking she's the Queen of Sheba!'

'Mummy—'

'And then she went to you.' Olivia's voice grew higher. 'Didn't it ever occur to her to come to me? Her own mother?'

'She couldn't!' exclaimed Isobel. 'She knew how you would react. And, frankly, she didn't need that. She needed calm, rational advice.'

'I'm incapable of being rational, am I?'

'When it comes to this wedding,' said Isobel, 'then yes. Yes, you are!'

'Well, there isn't going to be a wedding now,' said Olivia jerkily. 'There isn't going to be a wedding. So perhaps you'll all start to trust me again. Perhaps you'll start to treat me like a human being.'

'Oh, Mummy, stop feeling sorry for yourself!' shouted Isobel, suddenly exasperated. 'This wasn't your wedding. It was Milly's wedding!'

'I know that!' said Olivia indignantly.

'You don't,' said Isobel. 'You're not really thinking about Milly and Simon. You're not thinking about how they must be feeling. You don't even really care if they stay together or not. All you're thinking about is the wedding. The flowers that will have to be cancelled, and your lovely smart outfit that no one will see, and how you won't get to dance with Harry Pinnacle! Beyond that, you couldn't give a damn!'

'How dare you!' exclaimed Olivia, and two bright spots appeared on her cheeks.

'It's true though, isn't it? No wonder Daddy—'

'No wonder Daddy what?' snapped Olivia.

'Nothing,' said Isobel, aware she had stepped over a boundary. 'I just . . . I can see his point of view. That's all.'

There was a long silence. Isobel blinked a few times in the dim kitchen light. She suddenly felt drained, too tired for argument; too tired even to stand up.

'Right,' she said with an effort. 'Well, I think I'll go to bed.'

'Wait,' said Olivia, looking up. 'You haven't eaten anything.'

'It's all right,' said Isobel. 'I'm not hungry.'

'That's not the point,' said Olivia. 'You need to eat.'

Isobel gave a noncommittal shrug.

'You need to eat,' repeated Olivia. She met Isobel's eyes. 'In your condition.'

'Mummy—not now,' said Isobel wearily.

'We don't have to talk about it,' said Olivia in a voice tinged with hurt. 'You don't have to tell me anything if you don't want to. You can keep all the secrets you like.' Isobel looked away uncomfortably. 'Just let me make you some nice scrambled eggs.'

There was a pause.

'OK,' said Isobel at last. 'That would be nice.'

'And I'll pour you a nice glass of wine.'

'I can't,' said Isobel, taken unawares.

'Why not?'

Isobel was silent, trying to sort out the contrary strands of thought in her brain. She couldn't drink, just in case she decided to keep the baby. What kind of a twisted logic was that?

'All that phooey!' Olivia was saying. 'I was on three gins a day when I had you. And you turned out all right, didn't you? More or less?'

A reluctant smile spread over Isobel's face.

'OK,' she said. 'I could do with a drink.'

'So could I,' said Olivia. 'Let's open another bottle.' She closed her eyes. 'I've never known such a dreadful night.'

'Tell me about it.' Isobel sat down at the table. 'I hope Milly's OK.'

'I'm sure Esme will look after her,' said Olivia, and a touch of bitterness edged her voice.

Milly sat in Esme's drawing room, nestling a hot, creamy drink made from Belgian chocolate flakes and a splash of Cointreau. Esme had persuaded her to take a long, hot bath, scented with mysterious potions in unmarked bottles, then lent her a white waffle-weave bathrobe and some snug slippers. Now she was brushing Milly's hair with an old-fashioned bristle hairbrush. Milly stared ahead into the crackling fire, feeling the pull of the brush on her scalp, the heat of the fire on her face, the smoothness of her clean skin inside her robe. She'd arrived at Esme's an hour or so ago; had burst into tears as soon as the door was opened and again in her bath. But now she felt strangely calm. She took another sip of the hot, creamy chocolate and closed her eyes.

'Feeling better?' said Esme in a low voice.

'Yes. A lot better.'

'Good.'

There was a pause. One of the whippets rose from its place by the fire, came over to Milly and nestled its head in her lap.

'You were right,' said Milly, stroking the whippet's head. 'You were right. I don't know Simon. He doesn't know me.' Her voice trembled slightly. 'The whole thing's hopeless.'

Esme said nothing, but continued brushing.

'I know I'm to blame for all of this,' said Milly. 'I know that. It's me that got married, it's me that messed up. But he behaved as though I'd done it all on purpose. He didn't even *try* to see it from my point of view.'

'Such a masculine trait,' said Esme. 'Women twist themselves into loops to accommodate the views of others. Men turn their heads once, then look back and carry on as before.'

'Simon didn't even turn his head,' gulped Milly miserably. 'He didn't even listen.'

'Typical,' said Esme. 'Just another intractable man.'

'I feel so stupid,' said Milly. 'So bloody stupid.' A fresh stream of tears suddenly began to spill over onto her face. 'How could I have wanted to marry him? He said I'd tainted the wedding vows. He said he couldn't believe anything I said any more. He looked at me as if I was some kind of monster!'

'I know,' said Esme soothingly.

'All this time we've been together,' said Milly, wiping her eyes, 'we haven't really got to know each other, have we? Simon doesn't know me at all! And how can you marry someone if you don't know them? How can you? We should never even have got engaged. All along, it's just been—' She suddenly broke off, with a new thought. 'Do you remember when he asked me to marry him? He had it all planned, the way he wanted it. He led me to this bench in his father's garden, and he had a diamond ring all ready in his pocket, and he'd even put a bloody bottle of champagne in the tree stump!'

'Darling—'

'But none of that was to do with me, was it? It was all to do with him. He wasn't thinking about me, even then.'

'Just like his father,' said Esme, with a sudden edge to her voice. Milly turned slightly in surprise.

'Do you know Harry, then?'

'I used to,' said Esme, brushing more briskly. 'Not any more.'

'I always thought Harry was quite nice,' gulped Milly. 'But then, what the hell do I know? I was completely wrong about Simon, wasn't I?' Her shoulders began to shake with sobs, and Esme stopped brushing.

'Darling, why don't you go to bed,' she suggested. She gathered Milly's hair into a blond tassle and let it fall. 'You're overwrought, you're tired, you need a good night's sleep. Remember, you were up early; you've been to London and back. It's been quite a day.'

'I won't be able to sleep.' Milly looked up at Esme with tear-stained cheeks, like a child.

'You will,' replied Esme calmly. 'I put a little something into your drink. It should kick in soon.'

'Oh,' said Milly, in surprise. She stared into her mug for a moment, then drained it. 'Do you give drugs to all your guests?'

'Only the very special ones,' said Esme, and gave Milly a serene smile.

As she finished the last of her scrambled eggs, Isobel sighed and leaned back in her chair.

'That was delicious. Thank you.' There was no response. She looked up. Olivia was drooping forward over her wine glass, her eyes closed. 'Mummy?'

Olivia's eyes flicked open.

'You've finished,' she said in a dazed voice. 'Would you like some more?'

'No thanks,' said Isobel. 'Look, Mummy, why don't you go to bed? We'll have a lot to do in the morning.'

For a moment, Olivia stared at her blankly; then, as though suddenly jolted, she nodded.

'Yes,' she said. 'You're right.' She sighed. 'You know, just for a moment, I'd forgotten.'

'Go to bed,' repeated Isobel. 'I'll clear up.'

'But you—'

'I'm fine,' said Isobel firmly. 'And anyway, I want to make a cup of tea. Go on.'

'Well, goodnight then,' said Olivia.

'Goodnight.'

Isobel watched as her mother left the room, then got up and filled the kettle. She was leaning against the sink, looking out into the dark, silent street, when suddenly there was the sound of a key in the lock.

'Milly?' she said. 'Is that you?'

A moment later, the kitchen door opened and a strange young man came in. He was wearing a denim jacket and carrying a large bag and looked scruffier than most of the bed and breakfasters. Isobel stared at him curiously for an instant. Then, with a sudden start, she realized who he must be. A hot, molten fury began to rise inside her. So this was him. This was Alexander. The cause of it all.

'Well, hello,' he said, dumping his bag on the floor and grinning insouciantly. 'You must be multilingual, multitalented Isobel.'

'I don't know how you dare come back in here,' said Isobel softly, trying to control her voice. 'I don't know how you have the nerve.'

'I'm brave like that.' Alexander came close to her. 'They didn't tell me you were beautiful, too.'

'Get away from me,' spat Isobel.

'That's not very friendly.'

'Friendly! You expect me to be friendly? After everything you've done to my sister?' Alexander looked up and grinned.

'So you know her little secret, do you?'

'The whole world knows her little secret, thanks to you!'

'What do you mean?' said Alexander innocently. 'Has something happened?'

'Let me think,' said Isobel sarcastically. 'Has something happened? Oh yes. The wedding's been cancelled. But I expect you already knew that.'

Alexander stared at her.

'You're joking.'

'Of course I'm not bloody joking!' cried Isobel. 'The wedding's off. So congratulations, Alexander, you've achieved your aim. You've fucked up Milly's life completely. Not to mention the rest of us.'

'Jesus Christ!' Alexander ran a shaking hand through his hair. 'Look, I never meant—'

'No?' said Isobel furiously. 'No? Well, you should have thought of that before you opened your big mouth. I mean, what did you *think* would happen?'

'Not this! Not this, for Christ's sake! Why the hell did she call off the wedding?'

'She didn't,' said Isobel. 'Simon did.'

'What?' Alexander looked at her. 'Why?'

'I think that's their business, don't you?' said Isobel in a harsh voice. 'Let's just say that if no one had said anything about her first marriage, everything would still be OK. If you'd just kept quiet . . .' She broke off. 'Oh, what's the point? You're a fucking psychopath.'

'I'm not!' said Alexander. 'Jesus! I never wanted anyone to cancel any wedding. I just wanted to—'

'To what? What did you want?'

'Nothing!' said Alexander. 'I was just . . . stirring things a little.'

'God, you're pathetic!' said Isobel, staring at him. 'You're just a pathetic, inadequate bully!' She looked at his bag. 'You needn't think you're staying here tonight.'

'But my room's booked!'

'And now it's bloody well unbooked,' said Isobel, kicking his bag towards the door. 'Do you know what you've done to my family? My mother's in shock, my sister's in tears . . .'

'Look, I'm sorry, OK!' said Alexander, picking up his bag. 'I'm sorry your sister's wedding's off. But you can't blame me!'

'We can, and we do,' said Isobel, opening the front door. 'Now get out!'

'But I didn't do anything!' exclaimed Alexander angrily, stepping outside. 'I just made a few jokes!'

'You call telling the vicar a fucking *joke?*' said Isobel furiously, and as Alexander opened his mouth to reply, she slammed the door.

Olivia walked up the stairs slowly, feeling a flat, dull sadness creep over her. The adrenalin of the early evening was gone; she felt weary and disappointed and prone to tears. It was all over. The goal to which she'd been working all this time had suddenly been lifted away, leaving nothing in its place.

No one else would ever understand quite how much of herself she'd put into Milly's wedding. Perhaps that had been her mistake. Perhaps she should have stood back, let Harry's people take over with their cool efficiency, and merely turned up on the day, groomed and politely interested. Olivia sighed. She couldn't have done it. She couldn't have watched as someone else put together her daughter's wedding. So she'd gathered herself up and taken the job on and spent many hours planning and thinking and organizing. And now she would never see the fruits of all her labour.

Isobel's accusing voice rang in her ears and she winced. Somewhere along the line she had become at cross purposes with the rest of the family. Somehow she had become vilified for wanting everything to be just so. Perhaps James was right; perhaps it had become an obsession. But she had only wanted everything to be perfect for Milly. For all of them. And now no one would ever realize that. They wouldn't see the results. They wouldn't experience the joyous, lavish day she'd planned. They would just remember all the fuss.

She stopped at Milly's bedroom door, which was slightly ajar, and found herself walking in. Milly's wedding dress was still hanging up in its cotton cover on the wardrobe door. When she closed her eyes, Olivia could still see Milly's face as she tried it on for the first time. It had been the seventh dress she'd tried; both of them had known immediately that this was the one. They'd stared silently at the mirror, then, meeting Milly's eye, Olivia had said slowly, 'I think we'll have to have it. Don't you?'

Milly's measurements had been taken and somewhere in Nottingham the dress had carefully been made up again. Over the last few weeks it had been fitted again and again to Milly's figure. And now she would never wear it. Unable to stop herself, Olivia unzipped the wrapper, pulled out a little of the heavy satin and stared at it. From inside the cotton cover, a tiny iridescent pearl glinted at her. It was a truly beautiful dress. Olivia sighed, and before she could descend into maudlin grief, reached for the zip to close the wrapper again.

James, walking past the door, saw Olivia gazing mournfully at Milly's wedding dress and felt a stab of irritation. He stalked into Milly's room without pausing.

'For God's sake, Olivia,' he said brutally. 'The wedding's off! It's off! Haven't you got that into your head yet?'

Olivia's head jerked up in shock and her hands began to tremble as she stuffed the dress back into its cover.

'Of course I have,' she said. 'I was just—'

'Just wallowing in self-pity,' said James sarcastically. 'Just thinking about your perfectly organized wedding, which is now never going to happen.'

Olivia zipped up the cover and turned round.

'James, why are you behaving as though all this is my fault?' she said shakily. 'Why am I suddenly the villain? I didn't push Milly into marriage. I didn't force her to have a wedding! She wanted one! All I did was to organize it for her as best I could.'

'Organize it for yourself, you mean!'

'Maybe,' said Olivia. 'Partly. But what's so wrong with that?'

'Oh, I give up,' said James, his face white with anger. 'I can't get through to you!' Olivia stared at him.

'I don't understand you, James,' she said. 'I just don't understand. Weren't you ever happy that Milly was getting married?'

'I don't know,' said James. He walked stiffly over to the window. 'Marriage. What the hell has marriage got to offer a young girl like Milly?'

'Happiness,' said Olivia after a pause. 'A happy life with Simon.' James turned round and gave her a curious expression.

'You think marriage brings happiness, do you?'

'Of course I do!'

'Well, you must be a bigger optimist than I am.' He leaned back against the radiator, hunched his shoulders, and surveyed her with unreadable eyes.

'What do you mean?' said Olivia in a trembling voice. 'James, what are you talking about?'

'What do you think I'm talking about?' said James.

The room seemed to ring with a still silence.

'Just look at us, Olivia,' said James at last. 'An old married couple. Do we give each other happiness? Do we support each other? We haven't grown together over the years. We've grown apart.'

'No we haven't!' said Olivia in alarm. 'We've been very happy together!'

James shook his head.

'We've been happy separately. You have your life and I have mine. You have your friends and I have mine. That's not what marriage is about.'

'We don't have separate lives,' said Olivia, a throb of panic in her voice.

'Oh come on, Olivia!' exclaimed James. 'Admit it. You're more interested in your bed and breakfast guests than you are in me!'

'No I'm not,' said Olivia, flushing.

'Yes you are. They come first, I come second. Along with the rest of the family.'

'That's not fair!' cried Olivia at once. 'I run the bed and breakfast *for* our family! To give us holidays. Little luxuries. You know that!'

'Well, perhaps other things are more important,' said James. Olivia looked at him uncertainly.

'Are you saying you want me to give up the bed and breakfast?'

'No!' said James impatiently. 'I just . . .'

'What?'

There was a long pause. Eventually James sighed. 'I suppose,' he said slowly, 'I just want you to need me.'

'I do need you,' said Olivia in a small voice.

'Do you?' A half-smile came to James's lips. 'Olivia, when was the last time you confided in me? When was the last time you asked my advice?'

'You wouldn't be interested in anything I've got to say!' cried Olivia defensively. 'Whenever I tell you anything, you get bored. You start to look out of the window. Or you read the paper. You behave as though nothing I've got to say is of any importance. And anyway, what about you? You never confide in me, either!'

'I try to!' said James angrily. 'But you never bloody listen! You're always rabbiting on about the wedding. The wedding this, the wedding that. And before the wedding there was always something else. Rabbit, rabbit, rabbit! It drives me mad.'

There was silence.

'I know I run on a bit,' said Olivia at last. 'My friends tell me. They say "Pipe down, Olivia, let someone else speak." And I pipe down.' She gulped. 'But you've never said anything. You never seem to care one way or the other.'

James rubbed his face wearily. 'Perhaps I don't,' he said. 'Perhaps I've got beyond caring. All I know is . . .' He paused. 'I can't go on like this.'

The words resounded round the tiny room like gas from a canister. Olivia felt the colour drain from her cheeks and a slow, frightening thud begin like a death knell in her stomach.

'James,' she said, before he could continue. 'Please. Not tonight.'

James looked up and felt a jolt as he saw Olivia. Her cheeks were ashen, her lips were trembling, and her eyes were full of a deep dread.

'Olivia—' he began.

'If you have something you want to say to me—' Olivia swallowed '—then please don't say it tonight.' She began to back jerkily away, not looking him in the eye. 'Not tonight,' she whispered, and groped behind her for the door handle. 'I just . . . I just couldn't bear anything more tonight.'

Rupert sat at his desk in chambers, staring out of the window at the dark, silent night. On the desk in front of him was a list of phone numbers, some now crossed out or amended; some newly scribbled down. He'd spent the last two hours on the phone, talking to people he'd thought he would never speak to again. An old friend of Allan's from Keble, now at Christ Church. An old tutorial partner of his, now working in Birmingham. Half-remembered acquaintances, friends of friends, names he couldn't even put to faces. No one knew where Allan was.

But this last phone call had given him hope. He'd spoken to an English professor at Leeds, who had known Allan at Manchester.

'He left Manchester suddenly,' he'd said.

'So I gather,' said Rupert, who had already jotted this information down three or four times. 'Do you have any idea where he went?' There was a pause.

'Exeter,' the professor said eventually. 'That's right. Exeter. I know, because around a year later, he wrote to me and asked me to send him a book. The address was Exeter. I may even have typed it into my electronic organizer.'

'Could you . . .' Rupert had said, hardly daring to hope. 'Do you think . . .'

'Here we are,' the professor had said. 'St David's House.'

'What's that?' said Rupert, staring at the address. 'A college?'

'I haven't heard of it,' the professor had replied. 'Perhaps it's a new hall of residence.'

Rupert had put the phone down and immediately called Directory Enquiries. Now he looked at the telephone number written in front of him. Slowly he picked up the phone and tapped it in. Perhaps Allan would still be there. Perhaps he would answer the phone himself. A strong pounding began in Rupert's chest; his fingers felt slippery around the telephone receiver. He felt almost sick with apprehension.

'Hello?' A young male voice answered. 'St David's House.'

'Hello,' said Rupert, gripping the receiver tightly. 'I'd like to speak to Allan Kepinski, please.'

'Just a second, please.'

There was a long silence, then another young male voice came on the line.

'You wanted to speak to Allan.'

'Yes.'

'May I ask who's calling?'

'My name's Rupert.'

'Rupert Carr?'

'Yes,' said Rupert. His hand gripped the receiver tightly. 'Is Allan there?'

'Allan left St David's House five years ago,' said the young man. 'He went back to the States.'

'Oh,' said Rupert. 'Oh.' He gazed blankly at the phone. It had never even occurred to him that Allan would go back to the States.

'Rupert, are you in London?' the young man was saying. 'Could we meet up tomorrow by any chance? Allan left a letter for you.'

'Really?' said Rupert. 'For me?' His heart began to pound in sudden exhilaration. It wasn't too late. Allan still wanted him. He would call him up; he would fly to the States if need be. And then—

Suddenly his attention was distracted by a sound at the door, and his head jerked up. Standing in the doorway, watching him, was Tom. Rupert's cheeks began to flush red.

'Mangetout on Drury Lane. At twelve,' the young man was saying. 'I'll be wearing black jeans. My name's Martin, by the way.'

'OK,' said Rupert hurriedly. 'Bye, Martin.'

He put the phone down and looked at Tom. Humiliation began to creep slowly through him.

'Who's Martin?' said Tom pleasantly. 'A friend of yours?'

'Go away,' said Rupert. 'Leave me alone.'

'I've been with Francesca,' said Tom. 'She's very upset. As you can imagine.' He sat down casually on Rupert's desk and picked up a brass paperweight. 'This little outburst of yours has quite thrown her.'

'But it hasn't thrown you,' said Rupert aggressively.

'As a matter of fact,' said Tom, 'it hasn't. I've come across this kind of confusion before.' He smiled at Rupert. 'You're not alone. I'm with you. Francesca's willing to stand by you. We'll all help you.'

'Help me do what? Repent? Confess in public?'

'I understand your anger,' said Tom. 'It's a form of shame.'

'It's not! I'm not ashamed!'

'Whatever you've done in the past can be wiped clean,' said Tom. 'You can start again.'

Rupert stared at Tom. Into his mind came his house; his life with Francesca, his comfortable, happy existence. Everything he could have once more if he lied about just one thing.

'I can't,' he said. 'I just can't. I'm not who you all think I am. I was in love with a man. Not misguided, not led astray. In love.'

'Platonic love——'

'Not platonic love!' cried Rupert. 'Sexual love! Can't you understand that, Tom? I loved a man sexually.'

'You committed acts with him.'

'Yes.'

'Acts which you know to be abhorrent to the Lord.'

'We didn't do anybody any harm!' cried Rupert desperately. 'We did nothing wrong!'

'Rupert!' exclaimed Tom, standing up. 'Can you hear yourself? Of course you did yourself harm. You did yourself the gravest harm. You committed perhaps the most odious sin known to mankind! You can wipe it clean—but only if you repent. Only if you acknowledge the evil which you've done.'

'It wasn't evil,' said Rupert in a shaking voice. 'It was beautiful.'

'In the eyes of the Lord,' said Tom coldly, 'it was repugnant. Repugnant!'

'It was love!' cried Rupert. He stood up, so that his eyes were level with Tom's. 'Can't you understand that?'

'No,' snapped Tom. 'I'm afraid I can't.'

'You can't understand how two men could possibly love each other.'

'No!'

Slowly Rupert leaned forward. Fronds of his hair touched Tom's forehead.

'Are you really repulsed by the idea?' he whispered. 'Or just afraid of it?'

Like a cat, Tom leapt backwards.

'Get away from me!' he shouted, his face contorted with disgust. 'Get away!'

'Don't worry,' said Rupert. 'I'm going.'

'Where?'

'Do you care, Tom? Do you really care?'

There was silence. With trembling hands, Rupert picked up his papers and thrust them into his briefcase. Tom watched him without moving.

'You know you're damned,' he said, as Rupert picked up his coat. 'Damned to hell.'

'I know,' said Rupert. And without looking back he opened the door and walked out.

CHAPTER TWELVE

Isobel woke to a thumping headache and grey-green nausea. She lay perfectly still, trying to keep calm; trying to exercise mind over matter—until a sudden urge to throw up propelled her from her bed, out of her bedroom door and across the hall to the bathroom.

'It's a hangover,' she told the bathroom mirror. But her reflection looked unconvinced. She rinsed out her mouth, sat down on the side of the bath and rested her head on her hand. Another day older. Another day more developed. Perhaps it had features by now. Perhaps it had little hands, little toes. It was a boy. Or a girl. A little person. Growing inside her; looking forward to life.

Another wave of sickness swept through her and she clamped her hand to her mouth. She felt ill with indecision. She couldn't come to a conclusion, couldn't even shape the arguments within her mind. Rationality battled with urges she'd never known she had; with every day her mind seemed to weaken a little. The obvious decision now seemed less obvious; the logical views she'd once readily espoused seemed to be crumbling under a sea of foolish emotion.

She stood up, tottering slightly, and walked slowly back onto the landing. There were sounds coming from the kitchen and she decided to go down and make herself a cup of tea. James was standing by the Aga as she walked in, dressed in his work suit and reading the paper.

'Morning,' he said. 'Cup of tea?'

'I'd love one,' said Isobel. She sat down at the table and studied her fingers. James put a mug of tea in front of her and she took a sip, then frowned. 'I think I'll have some sugar in this.'

'You don't normally take sugar,' said James in surprise.

'No,' said Isobel. 'Well. Maybe I do now.' She heaped two spoons of sugar into her mug, then sipped pleasurably, feeling the hot sweetness seep slowly through her body.

'So,' said James. 'Milly was right.'

'Yes.' Isobel stared down into the milky brownness of her tea. 'Milly was right.'

'And the father?'

Isobel said nothing.

'I see.' James cleared his throat. 'Have you decided what you're going to do? I suppose it's early days, still.'

'Yes, it is early days. And no, I haven't decided.' Isobel looked up. 'I suppose you think I should get rid of it, don't you? Forget it ever happened and resume my glittering career.'

'Not necessarily,' said James, after a pause. 'Not unless—'

'My exciting career,' said Isobel bitterly. 'My wonderful life of aeroplanes and hotel rooms and foreign businessmen trying to chat me up because I'm always on my own.' James stared at her.

'Don't you enjoy your work? I thought—we all thought—you enjoyed it.'

'I do,' said Isobel, 'most of the time. But sometimes I get lonely and sometimes I get tired and sometimes I feel like giving up for ever. Just like most people.' She took a sip of tea. 'Sometimes I wish I'd just got married and had three kids and lived in divorced bliss.'

'I had no idea, darling,' said James, frowning. 'I thought you liked being a career girl.'

'I'm not a career girl,' said Isobel, putting down her mug loudly. 'I'm a person. With a career.'

'I didn't mean—'

'You did!' said Isobel exasperatedly. 'That's all you think I am, isn't it? My career and nothing else. You've forgotten all about the rest of me.'

'No!' said James. 'I wouldn't forget about the rest of you.'

'Yes you would,' said Isobel. 'Because I do. Frequently.'

There was a pause. Isobel reached for a packet of cornflakes, looked inside, sighed and put it down. James took a final sip of tea then reached for his briefcase.

'I must go, I'm afraid.'

'You're really going to work today?'

'I don't have much choice. There's a lot going on at the moment. If I don't show my face, I may find my job gone tomorrow.'

'Really?' Isobel looked up, shocked.

'Not really.' James gave her a half-grin. 'Nevertheless, I do have to go in.'

'I'm sorry,' said Isobel. 'I had no idea.'

'No,' said James. 'Well.' He paused. 'You weren't to know. I haven't been exactly forthcoming about it.'

'I suppose there's been enough going on at home.'

'You could say that,' said James. Isobel grinned at him.

'I bet you're glad to get away from it all, really.'

'I'm not getting away from anything,' said James. 'Harry Pinnacle's already been on the phone to me this morning, requesting a meeting at lunchtime. No doubt to talk about the costs of this whole fiasco.' He pulled a face. 'Harry Pinnacle snaps his fingers and the rest of the world has to jump.'

'Oh well,' said Isobel. 'Good luck.'

By the door, James paused.

'Who would you have married, anyway?' he said. 'And had your three kids with?'

'I dunno,' said Isobel. 'Who was I going out with? Dan Williams, I suppose.' James groaned.

'Darling, I think you made the right choice.' He suddenly stopped himself. 'I mean—the baby isn't . . .'

'No,' said Isobel, giggling in spite of herself. 'Don't worry. It's not his.'

Simon woke feeling shattered. His head ached, his eyes were sore, his chest felt heavy with misery. From behind the curtains was coming a sparkling shaft of winter sunlight; from downstairs wafted the mingled smells of the wood fire burning in the hall and freshly ground coffee in the breakfast room. But nothing could soothe his grief, his disappointment and, above all, his sharp sense of failure.

The angry words he had spat at Milly the night before still circled his mind with as much clarity as though he had uttered them only five minutes ago. Like a scene learned from a play. A scene which, it now seemed, he should in some way have predicted. A stab of mortified pain hit him in the chest, and he turned over, burying his head under the pillow. Why hadn't he seen this coming? Why had he ever let himself believe he could achieve a happy marriage? Why couldn't he just accept the fact that he was an all-round failure? He'd failed dismally at business and now he'd failed at marriage, too. At least, thought Simon bitterly, his father had actually made it to the altar. At least his father hadn't been let down, two nights before his bloody wedding day.

An image came to him of Milly's face the night before: red, tear-stained, desperate with unhappiness. And for a moment he felt himself weakening. For a moment he felt like calling her up. Telling her he still loved her, that he still wanted to marry her. He would kiss her poor swollen lips; take her to bed; try to forget all that was past. The temptation was there. If he was honest with himself, the temptation was huge.

But he couldn't do it. How could he marry Milly now? How could he listen to her making promises she'd made before to someone else; spend the rest of his life wondering what other secrets she might be concealing? This was no small rift that might be patched up and healed. This was a gaping, jagged chasm which changed the whole order of things; turned their relationship into something he no longer recognized.

Without meaning to, he recalled the summer evening when he'd asked her to marry him. She'd behaved impeccably: crying a little, laughing a little; exclaiming over the ring he'd given her. But what had she really been thinking? Had she been laughing at him? Had she ever taken their intended marriage seriously? Did she share any of his ideals at all?

For a few minutes he lay miserably still, tormenting himself with images of Milly, trying to reconcile what he now knew about her with his memories of her as his fiancée. She was beautiful, sweet, charming. She was untrustworthy, secretive, dishonest. The worst thing was, she hadn't even seemed to realize what she'd done. She'd dismissed it, as though being married to another man were a trifling matter, to be brushed over and ignored.

An angry hurt began to throb inside him, and he sat up, trying to clear his mind; trying to think of other things. He pulled open the curtains and, without seeing the beautiful view before him, quickly began to get dressed. He would throw himself into work, he told himself. He would start again, and he would get over this. It might take time, but he would get over it.

Briskly, he walked downstairs, and into the breakfast room. Harry was sitting at the table, hidden behind a newspaper.

'Morning,' he said.

'Morning,' said Simon. He looked up suspiciously, ready to detect a note of mocking or ridicule in his father's voice. But his father was looking up at him with what seemed genuine concern.

'So,' he said, as Simon sat down. 'Are you going to tell me what this is all about?'

'The wedding's off.'

'So I gather. But why? Or don't you want to tell me?'

Simon said nothing, but reached for the coffee pot. He had stormed in the night before, too angry and humiliated to talk to anyone. He was still humiliated; still angry; still inclined to keep Milly's betrayal to himself. On the other hand, misery was a lonely emotion.

'She's already married,' he said abruptly. There was a crackling sound as Harry thrust down his paper.

'Already married? To who, for God's sake?'

'Some gay American. She met him ten years ago. He wanted to stay in the country, so she married him as a favour. As a favour!'

'Well, thank God for that,' said Harry. 'I thought you meant really married.' He took a sip of coffee. 'So what's the problem? Can't she get a divorce?'

'The problem?' said Simon, gazing at his father incredulously. 'The problem is that she lied to me!' The problem is that I can't trust anything else she says! I thought she was one person—and now I've discovered she's someone else. She's not the Milly I knew.'

Harry stared at him in silence.

'Is that it?' he said at last. 'Is that the only reason it's all off? The fact that Milly married some dodgy guy, ten years ago?'

'Isn't that enough?'

'Of course it's not enough!' said Harry furiously. 'It's not nearly enough! I thought there was something really wrong between you.'

'There is! She lied to me!'

'I'm not surprised if this is the way you're reacting.'

'How do you expect me to react?' said Simon. 'We had a relationship built on trust. Now I can't trust her any more.' He closed his eyes. 'It's finished.'

'Simon, just who the fuck do you think you are?' exclaimed

Harry. 'The Archbishop of Canterbury? Why does it matter if she lied to you? She's told you the truth now, hasn't she?'

'Only because she had to.'

'So what?'

'So it was perfect before this happened!' shouted Simon desperately. 'Everything was perfect! And now it's ruined!'

'Oh grow up!' thundered Harry. Simon's chin jerked up in shock. 'Just grow up, Simon! And for once in your life stop behaving like a self-indulgent, spoilt brat. So your perfect relationship isn't as perfect as you thought. So what? Does that mean you have to chuck it away?'

'You don't understand.'

'I understand perfectly. You want to bask in your perfect marriage, with your perfect wife and kids, and gloat at the rest of the world! Don't you? And now you've found a flaw, you can't stand it. Well, stand it. Simon! Stand it! Because the world is full of flaws. And frankly, what you had with Milly was about as good as it gets.'

'And what the hell would you know about it?' said Simon savagely. He stood up. 'What the hell would you know about successful relationships? Why should I respect a single word you say?'

'Because I'm your fucking father!'

'Yes,' said Simon bitterly. 'And don't I know it.' He kicked back his chair, turned on his heel and stalked out of the room, leaving Harry staring after him, cursing under his breath.

At nine o'clock, there was a ring at the doorbell. Isobel, who had just come down into the kitchen, screwed up her face. She padded out into the hall and opened the front door. A large white van was parked outside the house and a man was standing on the doorstep, surrounded by white boxes.

'Wedding cake delivery,' he said. 'Name of Havill.'

'Oh God,' said Isobel, staring at the boxes. 'Oh God.' She bent down, lifted one of the cardboard lids, and caught a glimpse of smooth white icing; the edge of a sugar rose. 'Look,' she said, standing up again. 'Thank you very much. But there's been a slight change of plan.'

'Is this the wrong address?' said the man. He squinted at his piece of paper. 'One Bertram Street.'

'No, it's the right address,' said Isobel. 'It's the right address.' She gazed past him at the van, feeling suddenly depressed. Today should have been a happy day, full of excitement and anticipation and bustling, last-minute preparations. Not this.

'The thing is,' she said, 'we don't need a wedding cake any more. Can you take it away again?'

The man gave a sarcastic laugh.

'Carry this lot around in my van all day? I don't think so!'

'But we don't need it.'

'I'm afraid, my dear, that's not my problem. You ordered it— if you want to return it, that's between you and the company. Now, if you could just sign here'—he thrust a pen at her—'I'll get the rest of the boxes.' Isobel's head jerked up.

'The rest? How many are there, for God's sake?'

'Ten in all,' said the man, consulting his piece of paper. 'Including pillars and accessories.'

'Ten,' echoed Isobel disbelievingly.

'It's a lot of cake,' said the man.

'Yes,' said Isobel, as he disappeared back to the van. 'Especially between four of us.'

By the time Olivia appeared on the stairs, the white boxes had been neatly piled in a corner of the hall.

'I didn't know what else to do with them,' said Isobel, coming out of the kitchen.

She glanced at her mother and blanched. Olivia's face was a savage mix of bright paint and deathly white skin. She was clinging tightly to the banisters and looked as though she might keel over at any moment.

'Are you OK, Mummy?' she said.

'I'll be fine,' said Olivia with a strange brightness. 'I didn't get much sleep.'

'I shouldn't think any of us did,' said Isobel. 'We should all go back to bed.'

'Yes, well. We can't, can we?' said Olivia. She smiled tautly at Isobel. 'We've got a wedding to cancel. We've got phone calls to make. I've made a list!'

Isobel winced.

'Mummy, I know this is really hard for you,' she said.

'It's no harder for me than anyone else,' said Olivia, lifting her chin. 'Why should it be harder for me? After all, it's not the end of the world, is it? After all, it was just a wedding!'

'Just a wedding,' said Isobel. 'To be honest, I don't think such a thing exists.'

Mid-morning, there was a knock on Milly's door.

'Are you awake?' said Esme. 'Isobel's on the phone.'

'Oh,' said Milly dazedly, sitting up and pushing her hair back off her face. Her head felt heavy; her voice sounded like a stranger's. She looked at Esme and tried to smile. But her face felt dry and old and her brain felt as though it was missing a cog. What was going on, anyway? Why was she at Esme's house?

'I'll get the cordless phone,' said Esme, and disappeared.

Milly sank back on her pillow and stared at Esme's pistachio ceiling, wondering why she felt so lightheaded, so unreal. And then, with a dart of shock, she remembered. The wedding was off.

The wedding was off. She ran the idea experimentally round her head, waiting for a stab of grief, a renewed rush of tears. But this morning her eyes were dry. Her mind was calm; the sharp emotions of the night before had been rounded over by sleep. She felt more startled than upset; more disquieted than grief-stricken. She could scarcely believe it. The wedding—her huge, immovable wedding—wasn't going to happen. How could it not happen? How could the centre of her life simply disappear? She felt as though the peak to which she'd been climbing had suddenly vanished, and she'd been left, clinging to the rocks and peering disorientedly over the edge.

'Here you are,' said Esme, suddenly appearing by her bed. 'Would you like some coffee?'

Milly nodded, and took the phone.

'Hi,' she said in a scratchy voice.

'Hi,' came Isobel's voice down the line. 'Are you OK?'

'Yes,' said Milly. 'I suppose so.'

'You haven't heard from Simon?'

'No.' Milly's voice quickened. 'Why? Has he—'

'No,' said Isobel hurriedly. 'No, he hasn't. I just wondered. In case.'

'Oh,' said Milly. 'Well, no. I've been asleep. I haven't spoken to anyone.'

There was a pause. Milly watched as Esme pulled back the curtains and fastened them with thick braided tie-backs. The day was bright, sparkling with frost. Esme smiled at Milly, then walked softly out of the room.

'Isobel, I'm really sorry,' said Milly slowly. 'For landing you in it like that.'

'Oh, that,' said Isobel. 'Don't worry. That doesn't matter.'

'I just got rattled. I just—Well. You know what it was like.'

'Of course I do. I would have done exactly the same.'

'No you wouldn't,' said Milly, grinning faintly. 'You've got a zillion times more self-control than me.'

'Well, anyway, don't worry,' said Isobel. 'It hasn't been a problem.'

'Really? Hasn't Mummy been lecturing you all day?'

'She hasn't had time,' said Isobel. 'We're all too busy.'

'Oh,' said Milly, wrinkling her brow. 'Doing what?'

There was silence.

'Cancelling the wedding,' said Isobel eventually, her voice full of distress.

'Oh,' said Milly again. Something heavy sank inside her stomach. 'Oh, I see. Of course.'

'Oh God, Milly, I'm sorry,' said Isobel. 'I thought you would realize.'

'I did,' said Milly. 'I do. Of course you have to cancel it.'

'That's partly why I phoned,' said Isobel. 'I know this is a dreadful time to ask. But is there anyone else I need to call? Anyone who isn't in the red book?'

'I don't know,' said Milly. She swallowed. 'Who have you told already?'

'About half our guests,' said Isobel. 'Up to the Madisons. Harry's people are doing his lot.'

'Wow,' said Milly, feeling stupid, irrational tears coming to her eyes. 'You didn't hang about, did you?'

'We couldn't!' said Isobel. 'Some people would have been setting off already. We had to put them off.'

'I know,' said Milly. She took a deep breath. 'I know. I'm just being stupid. So. How are you doing it?'

'We're going down the list in the red book. Everybody— everybody's being really nice about it.'

'What are you telling them?' said Milly, winding the sheet round her fingers.

'We've said you're ill,' said Isobel. 'We didn't know what else to say.'

'Do they believe you?'

'I don't know. Some of them.'

There was silence.

'OK,' said Milly at last. 'Well, if I think of anyone I'll call you.'

'When are you coming back home?'

'I don't know,' said Milly. She closed her eyes and thought of her room at home. Presents and cards everywhere; her honeymoon case open on the floor; her wedding dress hanging up in the corner, shrouded like a ghost. 'Not yet,' she said. 'Not until—'

'No,' said Isobel after a pause. 'Fair enough. Well, look. I'll come round and see you. When I've finished.'

'Isobel—thanks. For doing all this.'

'No problem,' said Isobel. 'I expect you'll do the same for me one day.'

'Yes.' Milly managed a wan smile. 'I expect so.'

She put the phone down. When she looked up, she saw Esme at the door. She was holding a tray and looking thoughtfully at Milly.

'Coffee,' she said, putting the tray down. 'To celebrate.'

'Celebrate?' said Milly disbelievingly.

'Your escape.' Esme came forward, holding two porcelain mugs. 'Your escape from matrimony.'

'It doesn't feel like an escape,' said Milly.

'Of course it doesn't,' exclaimed Esme. 'Not yet. But it will. Just think, Milly—you're no longer tied down. You can do anything you choose. You're an independent woman!'

'I suppose,' said Milly. She stared miserably into her coffee. 'I suppose.'

'Don't brood, darling!' said Esme. 'Don't think about it. Drink your coffee and watch some nice television. And then we're going out for lunch.'

The restaurant was large and empty, save for a few single men, reading newspapers over their coffee. Rupert gazed about awkwardly, wondering which one was Martin. Black jeans, he'd said. But most of them were wearing black jeans. He felt over-smart in his own suit and expensive shirt.

After he'd left chambers the night before, he'd walked mindlessly for a while. Then, as morning began to approach, he had checked into a seedy Bayswater hotel. He had lain awake, staring up at the stained ceiling. After breakfast at a café he'd taken a taxi home and crept into the house, praying that Francesca would already have left. Feeling like a burglar, he'd taken a shower, shaved and changed his clothes. He'd made a cup of coffee and drunk it in the kitchen, staring out into the garden, then had put the mug in the dishwasher, looked at the clock and picked up his briefcase. Familiar actions; an automatic routine. He had felt, for an instant, almost as though his life were carrying on as before.

But his life was not the same as before. It would never be the same as before. His soul had been wrenched open and the truth had been pulled out, and now he had to decide what to do with it.

'Rupert?' A voice interrupted his thoughts and he looked up. Standing up at a nearby table was a young man dressed in black jeans. He had close cropped hair and a single ear-ring and looked very obviously homosexual. In spite of himself, a shiver of dismay went through Rupert and he cautiously advanced.

'Hello,' he said, aware that he sounded pompous. 'How do you do.'

'We spoke on the phone,' said the young man. His voice was soft and singsong. 'I'm Martin.'

'Yes,' said Rupert, clutching his briefcase tight. He felt suddenly petrified. Here was homosexuality. Here was his own hidden, unspoken side, duplicated in front of him for all to see.

He sat down, and shifted his chair slightly away from the table.

'It was good of you to come up to London,' he said stiffly.

'Not at all,' said Martin. 'I'm up at least once a week. And if it's important . . .' He spread his hands.

'Yes,' said Rupert. He began to study the menu intently. He

would take the letter and if possible a telephone number for Allan, then leave, as soon as possible.

'I think I'll have a cup of coffee,' he said, not looking up. 'A double espresso.'

'I've been waiting for your call,' Martin said. 'Allan told me a great deal about you. I always hoped that one day you might start to look for him.'

'What did he tell you?' Rupert raised his head slowly. Martin shrugged.

'Everything.'

A fiery red came to Rupert's cheeks and he put the menu down on the table. He looked at Martin, ready for a surge of humiliation. But Martin's eyes were kind; he looked as though he wanted to understand. Rupert cleared his throat.

'When did you meet him?'

'Six years ago,' said Martin.

'Did you . . . have a relationship with him?'

'Yes,' said Martin. 'We had a very close relationship.'

'I see.'

'I don't think you do.' Martin paused. 'We weren't lovers. I was his counsellor.'

'Oh,' said Rupert confusedly. 'Was he—'

'He was ill,' said Martin, and looked straight at Rupert.

A flash of deadly understanding passed through Rupert and he lowered his eyes. So here it was, without warning. His sentence; the end of the cycle. He had sinned, and now he was being punished. He had committed unspeakable acts. Now he was to suffer an unspeakable disease.

'AIDS,' he said calmly.

'No,' said Martin, the tiniest note of scorn creeping into his voice. 'Not AIDS. Leukaemia. He had leukaemia.'

Rupert's eyes jerked up, to see Martin staring sadly at him. He felt suddenly sick, as though he'd entered a nightmare. White stars began to dance around his field of vision.

'I'm afraid so,' said Martin. 'Allan died, four years ago.'

CHAPTER THIRTEEN

For a while there was silence. A waiter came up and Martin discreetly ordered, while Rupert stared ahead with glassy eyes, trying to contain his pain. He felt as though something inside him was splitting apart; as though his whole body was filling up with grief and guilt. Allan was dead. Allan was gone. He was too late.

'Are you OK?' said Martin in a low voice.

Rupert nodded, unable to speak.

'I can't tell you much about his death, I'm afraid. It happened in the States. His parents came over and took him home. I understand it was quite peaceful at the end.'

'His parents,' said Rupert in a cracked voice. 'He hated his parents.'

'They came to an understanding. Everything changed, of course, when Allan became ill. I met them when they came over.

They were decent, compassionate people.' He looked up at Rupert. 'Did you ever meet them?'

'No,' said Rupert. 'I never met them.'

He closed his eyes and imagined the two elderly people Allan had described to him; imagined Allan being carted back to a town he'd always hated, in order to die. A fresh pain swept over him and suddenly he felt as though he might break down.

'Don't think it,' said Martin.

'What?' Rupert opened his eyes.

'What you're thinking. What everybody thinks. If only I'd known he was going to die. Of course you would have done things differently. Of course you would. But you didn't know. You couldn't have known.'

'What . . .' Rupert licked his lips. 'What did he say about me?'

'He said he loved you. He said he thought you loved him. But he wasn't angry any more.' Martin leaned forward and took Rupert's hand. 'It's important you understand that, Rupert,' he said earnestly. 'He wasn't angry with you.'

A waiter suddenly appeared at the table, carrying two cups of coffee.

'Thank you,' said Martin, without taking his hand from Rupert's. Rupert saw the waiter's gaze run over the pair of them, and, in spite of it all, stiffened slightly.

'Will there be anything else?' said the waiter.

'No thank you,' said Rupert. He met the waiter's friendly eye and a painful embarrassment flooded him like hot water. He felt like running for cover; denying everything. But instead he forced himself to leave his hand calmly in Martin's. As though it were normal.

'I know this is hard for you,' said Martin as the waiter left. 'On all levels.'

'I'm married,' said Rupert roughly. 'That's how hard it is.' Martin nodded slowly.

'Allan thought you might be.'

'I suppose he despised me,' said Rupert, gazing into his cup of coffee. 'I suppose you despise me, too.'

'No,' said Martin. 'You don't understand. Allan *hoped* you were married. He hoped you were with a woman, rather than—' Rupert looked up.

'Rather than a man?' Martin nodded.

'He agonized over whether to contact you. He didn't want to rock the boat if you were happy with a woman. But equally, he couldn't face discovering that you were with some other man. What he wanted to believe was that if you had ever changed your mind, you would have come back to him first.'

'Of course I would,' said Rupert, his voice trembling slightly. 'He knew I would. He knew me like no other human being has ever known me.'

Martin shrugged diplomatically.

'Your wife—'

'My wife!' exclaimed Rupert. He looked at Martin with pained eyes. 'My wife doesn't know me! We met, we went out to dinner a few times, we took a holiday together, we got married. I see her for about an hour every day, if that. With Allan it was—'

'More intense.'

'It was all day and all night,' said Rupert. He closed his eyes. 'It was every hour and every minute and every single thought and fear and hope.'

There was silence. When Rupert opened his eyes, Martin was pulling a letter out of his bag.

'Allan left you this,' he said. 'In case you ever came looking.'

'Thank you,' said Rupert. He took the envelope and looked at it silently for a few moments. There was his name, written beautifully in Allan's handwriting. He could almost hear Allan's voice, speaking to him. He blinked a few times, then tucked the letter away in his jacket. 'Do you have a mobile phone?' he said.

'Sure,' said Martin, reaching into his pocket.

'There's someone else who needs to know about this,' said Rupert. He tapped in a number, listened for a moment, then switched the phone off. 'Busy,' he said.

'Who is it you're going to tell?' asked Martin.

'Milly,' said Rupert. 'The girl he married to stay in Britain.'

Martin frowned.

'Allan told me about Milly,' he said. 'But she ought to know. He wrote to her.'

'Well if he did, she never got the letter,' said Rupert. 'Because she doesn't know.' He tapped in the number again. 'And she needs to.'

Isobel put down the telephone and ran a hand through her hair. 'That was Aunt Jean,' she said. 'She wanted to know what we're going to do with the present she sent.'

She leaned back in her chair and surveyed the cluttered kitchen table. Lists of names, address books and telephone books were spread over the surface, each covered in a pattern of brown coffee cup rings and sandwich crumbs. Shoe boxes filled with wedding bumf, brochures and catalogues were stacked high on a kitchen chair: from one box protruded a glossy black and white print; from another had spilled a length of lace. Open in front of her was a sample bag of pastel-coloured sugared almonds.

'It takes so long to put a wedding together,' she said, reaching out for a handful. 'Months and months of time and effort. And then it takes about five seconds to dismantle it all. Like jumping on a sandcastle.' She crunched on the sugar almonds, and pulled a face. 'God, these things are disgusting. I'm going to break my teeth.'

'I'm very sorry, Andrea,' Olivia was saying into her mobile phone. 'Yes, I do realize that Derek bought a morning suit especially. Please give him my apologies . . . Yes, perhaps you're right. Perhaps a lounge suit would have done just as well.' There was a pause and her hand tensed around the phone. 'No, they haven't set a new date as yet. Yes, I'll let you know . . . Well, if he wants to take it back to the shop, then that's really up to him. Yes, dear, goodbye.'

She turned the phone off with a trembling hand, ticked off a name and reached for the red book. 'Right,' she said. 'Now, who's next?'

'Why don't you take a break?' said Isobel. 'You look whacked.'

'No, darling,' said Olivia. 'I'd rather carry on. After all, it's got to be done, hasn't it?' She smiled brightly at Isobel. 'We can't all just sit around feeling sorry for ourselves, can we?'

'No,' said Isobel. 'I suppose not.' She stretched her arms into the air. 'God, my neck's aching from all this phoning.'

As she spoke, the phone rang again. She pulled a face at Olivia and picked it up.

'Hello?' she said. 'Oh, hello. Yes, it is true, I'm afraid. Yes,

I'll give her your best wishes. OK then. Bye.' She slammed the phone down, then took it off the hook.

'Everyone has to ring back and gloat,' she said irritably. 'They all know she isn't ill.'

'Perhaps we should have given some other excuse,' said Olivia, rubbing her brow.

'It doesn't matter what excuse we give,' said Isobel. 'They'll all guess. Horrible people.' She pulled a face. 'Bloody Aunt Jean wants us to send her present back straight away. She's going to another wedding in two weeks' time and she wants to use it. I'm going to tell her we thought it was so hideous we threw it away.'

'No,' said Olivia. She closed her eyes. 'We must try to act with dignity and poise.'

'Must we?' Isobel peered at Olivia. 'Mummy, are you OK? You're acting very weirdly.'

'I'm fine,' whispered Olivia.

'Well, OK,' said Isobel doubtfully. She looked down at her list. 'I also had a call from the florist. She suggested that as Milly's bouquet is already made up, we might like to have it pressed and dried. As a memento.'

'A memento?'

'I know,' said Isobel, beginning to shake with giggles in spite of herself. 'Who are these people?'

'A memento! As if we'll ever forget! As if we'll ever forget today!'

Isobel glanced up sharply. Olivia's eyes were open and glittering with tears.

'Mummy!'

'I'm sorry, darling,' said Olivia. A tear landed on her nose and she smiled brightly. 'I don't mean to be silly.'

'I know how much you wanted this wedding,' said Isobel. She reached over and took her mother's hand. 'But there'll be another one. Honestly, there will.'

'It's not the wedding,' whispered Olivia. 'If it were just the wedding . . .' She broke off as the doorbell rang. They both looked up.

'Who the hell can that be?' said Isobel impatiently. 'Don't people realize we're not in the mood for visitors?' She put down her list. 'Don't worry, I'll go.'

'No, I'll go,' said Olivia.

'Let's both go.'

The couple on the front doorstep were strangers, dressed in shiny green Barbours and carrying matching Mulberry holdalls.

'Hello,' said the woman brightly. 'We'd like a room, please.'

'A what?' said Olivia blankly.

'A room,' said the woman. 'A bed and breakfast room.' She waved a copy of the *Heritage City* guidebook at Olivia.

'I'm afraid we're full at the moment,' said Isobel. 'Perhaps if you try the Tourist Board . . .'

'I was told we would be able to have a room,' said the woman.

'You can't have been,' said Isobel patiently, 'because there aren't any rooms.'

'I spoke to someone on the phone!' The woman's voice rose crossly. 'I specifically checked that we would be able to stay here! And I might add, you were recommended to us by our friends the Rendles.' She looked impressively at Isobel.

'What an honour,' said Isobel.

'Don't take that tone with me, young woman!' snapped the

woman. 'Is this the way you usually conduct business? The customer comes first, you know! Now, we were told we could have a room. You can't just turn people away at the door with no explanation.'

'Oh, for God's sake,' said Isobel.

'You want an explanation?' said Olivia in a trembling voice.

'Mummy, don't bother. Just—'

'You want an explanation?' Olivia took a deep breath. 'Well, where shall I start? Shall I start with my daughter's wedding? The wedding that was supposed to be taking place tomorrow?'

'Oh, a family wedding!' said the woman, disconcerted. 'Well that's different.'

'Or shall I start with her first wedding, ten years ago?' said Olivia, ignoring the woman. 'The wedding we didn't even know about?' Her voice began to rise dangerously. 'Or shall I start with the fact we're having to call the whole thing off, and that our entire family and all our friends are mocking us behind our backs?'

'Really, I didn't—' began the woman.

'But come in anyway!' cried Olivia, pulling the door open wide. 'We'll find you a room! Somewhere among all the wedding presents we're going to have to send back, and the wedding cake we're going to have to eat, and the clothes that will never be worn, and that beautiful wedding dress . . .'

'Come on, Rosemary,' said the man awkwardly, tugging his wife's sleeve. 'Very sorry to have disturbed you,' he said to Isobel. 'I always said we should have gone to Cheltenham.'

As the pair backed away, Isobel looked at Olivia. She was still gripping the door, her face streaked with tears.

'I really think you should have a break, Mummy,' she said. 'Keep the phone off the hook. Watch the telly. Or go to bed for a bit.'

'I can't,' said Olivia. 'We need to keep telephoning.'

'Rubbish,' said Isobel. 'Everyone I've spoken to has already heard. Gossip travels fast, you know. We've called the most important people. All the others will keep.'

'Well,' said Olivia after a pause. 'I do feel a little bit weary. Maybe I'll lie down for a bit.' She closed the front door and looked at Isobel. 'Are you going to have a rest, too?'

'No,' said Isobel. She reached for her coat. 'I'm going to go out. I'm going to go and see Milly.'

'That's a good idea,' said Olivia slowly. 'She'll be pleased to see you.' She paused. 'Be sure . . .'

'Yes?'

'Be sure to give her my love,' said Olivia. She looked down. 'That's all. Give her my love.'

Esme's drawing room was warm and tranquil; a haven of quiet civilization. As Isobel sat down on a pale, elegant sofa she looked about her pleasurably, admiring the collection of silver boxes heaped casually on a side table; the applewood dish filled with smooth grey pebbles.

'So,' said Milly, sitting down opposite her. 'Is Mummy still furious?'

'Not really,' said Isobel, screwing up her face. 'She's weird.'

'That probably means she's furious.'

'She isn't, honestly. She said to give you her love.'

'Really?' said Milly. She curled her feet underneath her and sipped at her coffee. Her hair was tied up in a dishevelled pony-tail and, under her jeans, she was wearing a pair of ancient ski socks.

'Here you are,' said Esme, handing a mug of coffee to Isobel.

'But I'm afraid I'll have to steal Milly in a little while. We're going out to lunch.'

'Good idea,' said Isobel. 'Where are you going?'

'A little place I know,' said Esme, smiling at them both. 'About ten minutes, Milly?'

'Fine,' said Milly. They both waited for Esme to close the door.

'So,' said Isobel, when she'd gone. 'How are you really?'

'I don't know,' said Milly slowly. 'Sometimes I feel fine—and sometimes I just want to burst into tears.' She took a shuddery breath. 'I keep thinking, what would I have been doing now . . . and what would I have been doing now?' She closed her eyes. 'I don't know how I'm going to get through tomorrow.'

'Get drunk.'

'I'm doing that tonight.' A flicker of a smile passed over Milly's face. 'Care to join me?'

'Maybe,' said Isobel. She sipped at her coffee. 'And Simon hasn't been in touch?'

'No.' Milly's face closed up.

'Is it really all over between you two?'

'Yes.'

'I can't believe it.' Isobel shook her head. 'Just because . . .'

'Because I deceived him about one thing,' said Milly in sharp, sarcastic tones. 'So obviously I'm a pathological liar. Obviously, no one can trust anything I say ever again.'

'Bastard. You're better off without him.'

'I know.' Milly looked up and gave the tight smile of someone battling with pain. 'It's for the best, really.' Isobel looked at her and suddenly felt like crying.

'Oh Milly,' she said. 'It's such a shame.'

'It doesn't matter,' said Milly lightly. 'Come on. It's not as if

I was pregnant. Now, that really would be a disaster.' She took a sip of coffee and gave Isobel a half-grin.

Isobel met her eyes and gave an unwilling smile. For a while there was silence.

'Do you know what you're going to do?' said Milly at last.

'No.'

'What about the father?'

'He doesn't want a baby. He's made that very plain.'

'Couldn't you persuade him?'

'No. And I don't want to! I don't want to push someone into fatherhood. What chance would our relationship have then?'

'Maybe the baby would bring you together.'

'Babies aren't glue,' said Isobel. She pushed her hands through her hair. 'If I had the baby, I would be on my own.'

'I would help you!' said Milly. 'And so would Mummy.'

'I know.' Isobel's shoulders twitched in a shrug. Milly stared at her.

'Isobel, you wouldn't really get rid of it.'

'I don't know!' Isobel's voice rose in distress. 'I'm only thirty, Milly! I could meet some fantastic guy tomorrow. I could be swept off my feet. But if I've already got a kid . . .'

'It wouldn't make any difference,' said Milly stoutly.

'It would! And you know, having a baby is no picnic. I've seen friends do it. They turn into zombies. And they're not even do-ing it on their own.'

'Well, I don't know,' said Milly, after a pause. 'It's your deci-sion.'

'I know it is,' said Isobel. 'That's exactly the problem.'

The door opened and they looked up. Esme smiled at them from under a huge fur hat.

'Ready to go, Milly? Isobel, sweetheart, do you want to come too?'

'No thanks,' said Isobel, getting up. 'I'd better get back home.'

She watched as Milly got into Esme's red Daimler and suddenly wished that her own godmother might suddenly appear and whisk her away, too. But Mavis Hindhead was a colourless woman living in the north of Scotland who had not acknowledged Isobel's existence since the eve of her confirmation, when she'd sent her a knobbly, ill-fitting jersey and a spidery, handwritten card of which Isobel had never managed to make sense. Not many godmothers, thought Isobel, were like Esme Ormerod.

When they'd roared off round the corner she began to walk away from Esme's house, telling herself to go straight home. But she couldn't quite face returning to the claustrophobic, sad atmosphere of the kitchen; couldn't face sitting down and making yet more awkward phone calls to curious strangers. Now that she was out in the fresh air, she wanted to stay out and stretch her legs and enjoy the sensation of not having a telephone clamped to her ear.

She began to walk briskly back towards town, feeling a mild sense of irresponsibility, as though she were bunking off school. At first she strode without considering where she was heading, merely enjoying the feel of her legs stretching out with every stride, the lightness of her arms swinging at her sides. Then, as a sudden thought struck her, she paused and, propelled by a curiosity she recognized as ghoulish, she turned off the main road, towards St Edward's Church.

As she stepped into the porch, she almost expected to hear bridal music playing on the organ. The church was filled with flowers; the pews were empty and waiting; the altar was shining brightly. Slowly she walked up the aisle, imagining the church filled with happy, expectant faces; imagining what it would have been like, parading behind Milly in a bridesmaid's dress, watching as her sister made the ancient vows that everyone knew and loved.

As she reached the front she stopped, and noticed a pile of white, redundant orders of service stacked at the end of a pew. With a stab of sadness, she reached for one—then, as she saw the two names printed on the cover, blinked in surprise. *Eleanor and Giles.* Printed in nasty, loopy silver lettering. Who the hell were Eleanor and Giles? How had they muscled in on the act?

'Bloody parasites!' she said aloud.

'I beg your pardon?' A man's voice came from behind her, and she whipped round. Walking up the aisle towards her was a young man in a cassock.

'Do you work here?' said Isobel.

'Yes,' said the young man.

'Well, hello,' said Isobel. 'I'm Milly Havill's sister.'

'Ah yes,' said the priest embarrassedly. 'What a shame. We were all very sorry to hear about that.'

'Were you?' said Isobel. 'So what happened? Did you think you might as well put Milly's expensive flowers to good use?'

'What do you mean?' Isobel gestured to the orders of service.

'Who's this bloody Eleanor and Giles? How come they've been given Milly's wedding day?'

'They haven't,' said the curate nervously. 'They're getting married in the afternoon. They booked it a year ago.'

'Oh,' said Isobel. She looked at the order of service, then put it down again. 'Well, all right then. I hope they have a happy day.'

'I'm really very sorry,' said the curate awkwardly. 'Maybe

your sister will be able to get married at some time in the future. When she's straightened everything out.'

'It would be nice,' said Isobel. 'But I doubt it.' She glanced once more round the church, then turned on her heel to leave.

'Actually, I was about to lock up,' said the curate, hurrying after her. 'It's a precaution we often take when there are flower arrangements in the church. You'd be surprised what people steal these days.'

'I'm sure,' said Isobel. She stopped by a pillar, plucked a single white lily from a twining arrangement, and breathed in the sweet aroma. 'It really would have been a beautiful wedding,' she said sadly. 'And now it's all destroyed. You people don't know what you've done.' The young curate bridled slightly.

'As I understand it,' he began, 'this was a case of attempted bigamy.'

'Yes,' said Isobel. 'But no one would have known. If your Canon Lytton had just turned a blind eye, and hadn't said anything—'

'The couple would have known!' said the curate. 'God would have known!'

'Yes, well,' said Isobel tersely. 'Maybe God wouldn't have minded.'

She strode out of the church with her head down, and walked straight into someone.

'Sorry,' she said, looked up, then stiffened. Harry Pinnacle was standing in front of her, wearing a navy blue cashmere over-coat and a bright red scarf.

'Hello, Isobel,' he said. He glanced over her shoulder at the curate, who had followed her out. 'Terrible business, all this.'

'Yes,' said Isobel. 'Terrible.'

'I'm on my way to meet your father for lunch.'

'Yes,' said Isobel. 'He mentioned it.'

There was a clanking sound as the curate pulled the church door closed; suddenly they were alone.

'Well, I must be off,' muttered Isobel. 'Nice to see you.'

'Wait a minute,' said Harry.

'I'm in a bit of a hurry,' said Isobel, and she began to walk away.

'I don't care.' Harry grabbed her arm and pulled her round to face him. 'Isobel, why have you been ignoring all my messages?'

'Leave me alone,' said Isobel, twisting her head away.

'Isobel! I want to talk to you!'

'I can't,' said Isobel, her face closing up. 'Harry, I just . . . can't.'

There was a long silence. Then Harry dropped her arm.

'Fine,' he said. 'If that's what you want.'

'Whatever,' said Isobel in a dead voice. And without meeting his gaze, she thrust her hands in her pockets and strode off down the street.

CHAPTER FOURTEEN

Harry was sitting by the bar, beer in hand, when James arrived at the Pear and Goose. It was a small pub in the centre of Bath, packed with cheerful, anonymous tourists.

'Good to see you, James,' he said, standing up to shake hands. 'Let me get you one of these.'

'Thanks,' said James. They both watched silently as the barman filled a pint glass with beer, and it occurred to James that this was the first time the two of them had ever met alone.

'Cheers,' said Harry, raising his glass.

'Cheers.'

'Let's sit down,' said Harry, gesturing to a table in the corner. 'It's more private over there.'

'Yes,' said James. He cleared his throat. 'I imagine you want to talk about the practicalities of the wedding.'

'Why?' said Harry, looking surprised. 'Is there a problem? I thought my people were sorting it all out with Olivia.'

'I meant the financial aspect,' said James stiffly. 'Milly's little revelation has cost you a small fortune.' Harry waved a hand.

'That's not important.'

'It is important,' said James. 'I'm afraid it's not within my means to pay you back fully. But if we can come to some arrangement—'

'James,' interrupted Harry. 'I didn't ask you here so we could talk about money. I just thought you might like a drink. OK?'

'Oh,' said James, taken aback. 'Yes. Of course.'

'So let's sit down and have a fucking drink.'

They sat down at the corner table. Harry opened a packet of crisps and offered it to James.

'How is Milly?' he said. 'Is she OK?'

'I'm not sure, to be honest,' said James. 'She's with her godmother. How's Simon?'

'Stupid kid,' said Harry, crunching on crisps. 'I told him he was a spoilt brat this morning.'

'Oh,' said James, unsure what to say.

'The first sign of trouble, he runs away. The first hitch, he gives up. No wonder his business failed.'

'Aren't you being a little harsh?' protested James. 'He's had a huge shock. We all have. It's hard enough for us to deal with, so what Simon must be feeling . . .' He shook his head.

'So you really had no idea she was married,' said Harry.

'None whatsoever.'

'She lied to you all.'

'Every single one of us,' said James soberly. He looked up, to see Harry half grinning. 'What? You think it's funny?'

'Oh come on,' said Harry. 'You've got to admire the girl's chutzpah! It takes a lot of guts to walk up the aisle knowing you've got a husband out there just waiting to trip you up.'

'That's one way of looking at it,' said James.

'But not your way.'

'No.' James shook his head. 'The way I see it, Milly's thoughtlessness has caused a lot of trouble and distress to a lot of people. Frankly, I'm ashamed to think she's my daughter.'

'Give the girl a break!'

'Then give Simon a break!' retorted James. 'He's the innocent one, remember. He's the wronged one.'

'He's a high-handed, moralistic little dictator. Life has to go a certain way, otherwise he's not interested.' Harry took a slug of beer. 'He's had it far too easy for far too long, that's his trouble.'

'You know, I'd say just the opposite,' said James. 'It can't be easy, walking in your shadow. I'm not sure I'd be able to do it myself.'

Harry shrugged silently. For a while neither of them spoke. Harry took a large gulp of beer, paused for a second, then looked up.

'How about Isobel?' he said casually. 'How's she reacted to all of this?'

'As usual,' said James. 'Gave very little away.' He drained his glass. 'Poor old Isobel's got enough on her plate as it is.'

'Work problems?' Harry leaned forward.

'Not just work.'

'Something else, then? Is she in some kind of trouble?' A flicker of a smile passed over James's face.

'You've hit the nail on the head,' he said.

'What do you mean?'

James stared into his empty beer glass.

'I don't suppose it's any great secret,' he said after a pause, and looked at Harry's frowning face. 'She's pregnant.'

'Pregnant?' A look of utter shock came over Harry's face. 'Isobel's pregnant?'

'I know,' said James. 'I can't quite believe it myself.'

'Are you sure about this?' said Harry. His hand gripped his beer glass tightly. 'Could it be a mistake?'

James smiled at him, touched by his concern.

'Don't worry,' he said. 'She'll be OK.'

'Has she spoken to you about it?'

'She's keeping her cards pretty close to her chest,' said James. 'We don't even know who the father is.'

'Ah,' said Harry, and finished his beer.

'All we can do is support her in whatever decision she makes.'

'Decision?' Harry looked up.

'Whether to keep the baby or . . . not.' James shrugged awkwardly and looked away. A strange expression passed over Harry's face.

'Oh, I see,' he said slowly. 'I see. Of course that would be an option.' He closed his eyes. 'Stupid of me.'

'What?'

'Nothing,' said Harry, opening his eyes again. 'Nothing.'

'Anyway,' said James. 'It isn't your problem.' He looked at Harry's empty glass. 'Let me get you another.'

'No,' said Harry. 'Let me get you one.'

'But you've already—'

'Please, James,' said Harry. He sounded suddenly dejected, James thought. Almost sad. 'Please, James. Let me.'

Isobel had walked as far as the Garden for the Blind. Now she sat on an iron bench, watching the fountain trickle endlessly into the little pond and trying to think calmly. Inside her mind, like a circular film, she saw Harry's expression as she'd left him; heard his voice again and again. The continuous repetition should, she thought, have dulled the pain inside her, should have left her numb and free to analyse her situation logically. But the pain would not be dulled; her mind would not still itself. She felt physically torn apart.

They had met for the first time only a few months before, at the party to celebrate Simon and Milly's engagement. As they'd shaken hands, a startled recognition had passed between them; both their voices had trembled slightly, and, like mirror images, they had each turned away quickly to talk to other people. But Harry's eyes had been on her every time she turned, and she had felt her entire body responding to his attention. The next week, they had met surreptitiously for dinner. He had smuggled her back into the house; the next morning, from his bedroom window, she had seen Milly in the drive waving goodbye to Simon. The month after that they had travelled to Paris on separate planes. Each encounter had been exquisite; a fleeting, hidden gem of experience. They had decided to tell no one; to keep things light and casual. Two adults enjoying themselves, nothing more.

But now nothing could be light; nothing could be casual. There was no longer any neutral. Whichever way she turned, she would be taking an action with huge consequences. One tiny, unwitnessed biological event meant that, whatever she chose to do, neither of their lives would be the same again.

Harry didn't want a baby. He'd made that perfectly clear to her. If she went ahead and had the child, she would be on her own. She would lose Harry. She would lose her freedom. She would be forced to rely on the help of her mother. Life would become an unbearable round of drudgery and coffee mornings and mind-numbing baby babble.

If, on the other hand, she got rid of the baby . . .

A slow pain rose through Isobel's chest. Who was she kidding? What was this so-called choice? Yes, she had a choice. Every modern woman had a choice. But the truth was, she had no choice. She was enslaved to herself—to the maternal emotions which she'd never known she possessed; to the tiny self growing within her; to the primal, overpowering desire for life.

Rupert sat on a bench in the National Portrait Gallery, staring at a picture of Philip II of Spain. It was a good two hours since Martin had said goodbye, clasping Rupert's hand and exhorting him to call whenever he felt like it. Since then, Rupert had wandered mindlessly, not noticing where he was going, not noticing the crowds of shoppers and tourists who kept bumping into him; unaware of anything except his own thoughts. From time to time he had stopped at a public phone and dialled Milly's number. But each time the line had been busy, and a secret relief had crept through him. He didn't want to share Allan's death with anyone else. Not yet.

The letter was still in his briefcase, unopened. He hadn't yet dared to read it. He had been too afraid—both that it wouldn't live up to his expectations and that it would. But now, under

Philip's stern, uncompromising stare, he reached down, fumbled with the clasps of his briefcase and brought the envelope out. A stab of grief hit him as, again, he saw his name written in Allan's handwriting. This was the last communication that would ever exist between them. Part of him wanted to bury the letter unopened; keep Allan's last words unread and unsullied. But even as the thought passed through his mind, his shaking hands were ripping at the paper, and he was pulling out the thick, creamy sheets, each covered on one side only with a black, even script.

Dear Rupert,

Fear not. Fear not, said the angel. I'm not writing to you just so that you'll feel bad. At least not consciously. Not much.

In truth, I'm not sure why I'm writing at all. Will you ever read this letter? Probably not. Probably you've forgotten who I am; probably you're happily married with triplets. My occasional fantasy is that any moment you'll appear through the door and sweep me into your arms while all the other terminally ill patients cheer and bang their walking sticks. In reality, this letter will probably end up, like so many other once-meaningful pieces of the world's fabric, in a garbage truck, to be recycled into somebody's breakfast. I rather like that idea. Allan flakes. With added optimism and a tinge of bitterness.

And yet I keep writing—as though I'm sure that one day you'll trace a path back towards me and read these words. Perhaps you will, perhaps you won't. Has my addled mind got it wrong? Have I elevated what we had to a significance it doesn't deserve? The proportions of my life have been curtailed so dramatically, I know my view of events has become somewhat skewed. And yet—against all the odds—I keep writing. *The truth is, Rupert, I cannot leave this country, let alone this world, without somewhere recording a farewell to you.*

When I close my eyes and think of you, it's as you were at Oxford—though you must have changed since then. Five years on, who and what is Rupert? I have my own ideas, but am unwilling to reveal them. I don't want to be the asshole who thought he knew you better than you know yourself. That was my mistake at Oxford. I confused anger with insight. I mistook my own desires for yours. What right did I have to be angry with you? Life is a far more complicated picture than either of us realized back then.

What I hope is that you're happy. What I fear is that if you're reading this letter you're probably not. Happy people don't trawl through the past looking for answers. What is the answer? I don't know. Perhaps we would have been happy if we'd stayed together. Perhaps life would have been sweet. But you can't count on it.

As it turns out, what we had might have been as good as it was ever going to get. So we broke up. But at least one of us had a choice about that, even if it wasn't me. If we'd left it until now, neither of us would have had a choice. Breaking up is one thing; dying is something else. Frankly, I'm not sure I could cope with both at once. It's going to take me long enough to get over my death as it is.

But I promised myself I wouldn't talk about dying. That's not what this is about. This isn't a guilt letter. It's a love letter. Just that. I still love you, Rupert. I still miss you. That's really all I wanted to say. I still love you. I still miss you. If I don't see you again then . . . I guess that's just life. But somehow I'm hoping I will.

Yours always

Allan

Some time later, a young teacher arrived at the door of the gallery, surrounded by her swarming class of cheerful children. They had intended to spend the afternoon sketching the portrait of Elizabeth I. But as she saw the young man sitting in the middle of the room, she swiftly turned the children round and shepherded them towards another painting.

Rupert, lost in silent tears, didn't even see them.

Harry arrived back that afternoon to find Simon's car parked in its usual place outside the house. He went straight up to Simon's room and knocked. When there was no answer, he pushed the door open slightly. The first thing he saw was Simon's morning suit, still hanging up on the door of the wardrobe. In the wastepaper basket was a copy of the wedding invitation. Harry winced, and pushed the door shut again. He paused for a moment, then retraced his steps down the stairs and along the corridor to the leisure complex.

The swimming pool was gleaming with underwater lighting, music was softly playing, but no one was swimming. In the far corner, the steam room door was misted up. Without pausing, Harry strode to the steam room and opened the door. Simon looked up, his face reddened and vulnerable with surprise.

'Dad?' he said, peering through the thick steam. 'What are you—'

'I need to talk to you,' said Harry, sitting down on the moulded plastic bench opposite Simon. 'I need to apologize.'

'Apologize?' said Simon in disbelief.

'I shouldn't have yelled at you this morning. I'm sorry.'

'Oh,' said Simon, looking away. 'Well. It doesn't matter.'

'It does matter,' said Harry. 'You've had a big shock. And I should have understood that. I'm your father.'

'I know you are,' said Simon without moving. Harry gazed at him steadily for a moment.

'Do you wish I weren't?'

Simon said nothing.

'I wouldn't blame you,' said Harry. 'Some fucking father I've been.' Simon shifted awkwardly on his seat.

'You—'

'Don't feel you have to be polite,' interrupted Harry. 'I know I screwed up with you. For sixteen years you never see me, then suddenly bam! I'm in your face all the time. No wonder things have been a bit tricky. If we were a married couple, we'd be divorced by now. Sorry,' he added after a pause. 'Sensitive subject.'

'It's OK.' Simon turned and gave him an unwilling grin, then, for the first time, registered his father's appearance. 'Dad, you know you're meant to take your clothes off?'

'That's for a steam bath,' said Harry. 'I came in here for a conversation.' He frowned. 'OK, so I've said my piece. Now you're supposed to tell me I've been a wonderful father, and I can rest easy.'

There was a long pause.

'I just wish . . .' began Simon at last, then stopped.

'What?'

'I just wish I didn't always feel like a failure,' said Simon in a rush. 'Everything I do goes wrong. And you . . . By the time you were my age, you were a millionaire!'

'No I wasn't.'

'It said in your biography . . .'

'That piece of shit. Simon, by the time I was your age, I *owed* a million. Fortunately, I found a way of paying it back.'

'And I didn't,' said Simon bitterly. 'I went bust.'

'OK,' said Harry, 'so you went bust. But at least you never sold out. At least you never came crying to me to bail you out. You stayed independent. Fiercely independent. And I'm proud of you for that.' He paused. 'I'm even proud you gave me back the keys to that flat. Pissed off—but proud.'

There was a long pause, punctuated only by the two of them breathing in the steamy air, and the odd spatter as a shower of warm drops fell to the floor.

'And if you have a go at working things out with Milly,' continued Harry slowly, 'instead of walking away—then I'll be even prouder. Because that's something I never did. And I should have done.'

There was silence for a while. Harry leaned back, stretched his legs out and winced. 'I have to say,' he said, 'this is not a nice experience. My underpants are sticking to my skin.'

'I told you,' said Simon.

'I know you did.' Harry looked at him through the steam. 'So, are you going to give Milly another chance?' Simon exhaled sharply.

'Of course I am. If she'll give me another chance.' He shook his head. 'I don't know what I was thinking of last night. I was stupid. I was unfair. I was just a . . .' He broke off. 'I tried calling her this afternoon.'

'And?'

'She must have gone out with Esme.'

'Esme?' said Harry.

'Her godmother, Esme Ormerod.'

Harry looked up with raised eyebrows.

'That's Milly's godmother? Esme Ormerod?'

'Yes,' said Simon. 'Why?' Harry pulled a face.

'Strange woman.'

'I didn't know you knew her.'

'Took her out to dinner a few times,' said Harry. 'Big mistake.'

'Why?' Harry shook his head.

'It doesn't matter. It was a long time ago.' He leaned back and closed his eyes. 'So she's Milly's godmother. That surprises me.'

'She's some cousin or something.'

'And they seemed such a nice family,' said Harry in half-jesting tones. Then he frowned. 'I'm serious, you know. They are a nice family. Milly's a lovely girl. James seems a very decent guy. I'd like to get to know him better. And Olivia . . .' He opened his eyes. 'Well, what can I say? She's a fine woman.'

'You said it.' Simon grinned at his father.

'I just wouldn't like to meet her on a dark night.'

'Or any night.'

There was a short silence. Water dripped onto Harry's head and he winced.

'The only one I'm not sure about,' said Simon thoughtfully, 'is Isobel. She's a bit of an enigma. I never know what she's thinking.'

'No,' said Harry after a pause. 'Neither do I.'

'She's nothing like Milly. But I still like her.'

'So do I,' said Harry in a low voice. 'I like her a lot.' He stared silently at the floor for a few moments, then abruptly stood up. 'I've had enough of this hell. I'm going to take a shower.'

'Try taking your clothes off this time,' said Simon.

'Yes,' said Harry. 'Clever.' And he gave Simon a friendly nod before closing the door.

By the time Rupert rose stiffly to his feet, put Allan's letter away and made his way out of the gallery, it was late afternoon. He stood in Trafalgar Square for a bit, watching the tourists and taxis and pigeons, then turned and began to walk slowly to the tube. Every step felt unsure and shaky; he seemed to have lost some vital part of himself that kept him balanced.

All he knew was that the one certainty he'd had in life was gone. The grounding force, to which his life had been nothing but counterpoint, had vanished. It now seemed to him that everything he'd done over the last ten years had been part of an internal battle against Allan. And now the battle was over and neither of them had won.

As he rode in the train back to Fulham he stared blankly ahead at his reflection in the dark glass, wondering with an almost academic curiosity what he might do next. He felt tired, ragged and washed up, as though a storm had deposited him on a strange shore with no clear way back. On the one hand there was his wife. There was his home and his old life and the compromises he'd come to take as second nature. Not quite happiness, but not quite misery either. On the other hand, there was honesty. Raw, painful honesty. And all the consequences that honesty brought.

Rupert passed a weary hand over his face and gazed at his blurred, uncertain features in the window. He didn't want to be honest. He didn't want to be dishonest. He wanted to be nothing. A person on a train, with nothing to decide, nothing to do but listen to its trundling sound and watch the unconcerned faces of other passengers reading books and magazines. Postponing life for as long as possible.

But eventually the train reached his stop. And, like an automaton, he reached for his briefcase, stood up, and stepped onto the platform. He followed all the other commuters up the steps and into the dark winter evening. A familiar procession moved down the main road, decreasing in size as people peeled off down side streets, and Rupert followed them, slowing down as he neared his street. When he reached his own corner he stopped altogether, and for a moment considered turning back. But where would he go? There was nowhere else for him to go.

The lights were off in his house, and he felt a tiny relief as he opened the gate. He would take a bath and have a couple of drinks and perhaps by the time Francesca arrived home, his mind would be clearer. Perhaps he would show her Allan's letter. Or perhaps not. He reached in his pocket for his key and put it in the lock, then stopped. It didn't fit. He took it out, looked at it, and tried again. But the lock was impervious, and when he looked more closely, he could see signs of handiwork around the keyhole. Francesca had changed the lock. She'd shut him out.

For a few seconds he could not move. He stared at the door, shaking with fury and a sharp humiliation. 'Bitch,' he heard himself saying in a strangled voice. 'Bitch.' A sudden stab of longing for Allan hit him in the chest and he started to back away from the door, his eyes clouding with tears.

'Are you OK?' A cheerful girl's voice came from across the road. 'Are you locked out? You can phone from here, if you like!'

'No thanks,' muttered Rupert. He glanced at the girl. She was young and attractive and looked sympathetic—and for a moment he felt like falling onto her shoulder and telling her everything. Then it occurred to him that Francesca might be watching him from inside the house, and he felt a shaft of panic. Quickly, clumsily, he began to walk away, down the street. He reached the corner and hailed a taxi without knowing where he was going.

'Yes?' said the driver as he got in. 'Where to?'

'To . . . to . . .' Rupert closed his eyes for a few moments, then opened them and looked at his watch. 'To Paddington station.'

At six o'clock there was a ring at the front door. Isobel opened it, to see Simon standing on the doorstep holding a large bunch of flowers.

'Oh it's you,' she said in unfriendly tones. 'What do you want?'

'To see Milly.'

'She isn't here.'

'I know,' said Simon. He looked anxious and strangely well scrubbed, thought Isobel, like an old-fashioned suitor. The sight almost made her want to smile. 'I wanted to check her godmother's address.'

'You could have telephoned,' said Isobel uncompromisingly. 'You didn't need to drag me to the door.'

'Your phone was engaged.'

'Oh,' said Isobel. She folded her arms and leaned against the door frame, unwilling to let him off. 'So. Have you come down off your mountainous horse yet?'

'Just shut up, Isobel, and give me the address,' said Simon irritably.

'I don't know,' said Isobel. 'Does Milly want to talk to you?'

'Oh, forget it,' said Simon, turning and going back down the steps. 'I'll find her myself.'

Isobel stared at him for a few seconds, then called, 'It's Walden Street. Number 10.' Simon stopped walking, and turned to look at her.

'Thanks,' he said. Isobel shrugged.

'That's OK. I hope . . .' She paused. 'You know.'

'Yup,' said Simon. 'So do I.'

The door was answered by Esme, wearing a long white bathrobe.

'Oh,' said Simon awkwardly. 'Sorry to disturb you. I wanted to speak to Milly.' Esme scanned his face, then said, 'She's asleep, I'm afraid. She drank quite a lot at lunchtime. I won't be able to wake her.'

'Oh,' said Simon. He shifted from one foot to the other. 'Well . . . just tell her I called round, would you? And give her these.' He handed the flowers to Esme and she looked at them with faint horror.

'I'll tell her,' she said. 'Goodbye.'

'Perhaps she could give me a ring. When she's up.'

'Perhaps,' said Esme. 'It's up to her.'

'Of course,' said Simon, flushing slightly. 'Well, thanks.'

'Goodbye,' said Esme, and closed the door. She looked at the flowers for a moment, then went into the kitchen and put them into the rubbish bin. She went upstairs and tapped on Milly's door.

'Who was that?' said Milly, looking up. She was lying on a massage table and Esme's beautician was rubbing a facial oil into her cheeks.

'A salesman,' said Esme smoothly. 'He tried to sell me some dusters.'

'Oh, we get those people, too,' said Milly, relaxing back onto the table. 'They always come at the worst time.' Esme smiled at her.

'How was your massage?'

'Wonderful,' said Milly.

'Good,' said Esme. She wandered over to the window, tapped her teeth for a few moments, then turned round.

'You know, I think we should go away,' she said. 'I should have thought of it before. You don't want to be in Bath tomorrow, do you?'

'Not really,' said Milly. 'But then . . . I don't really want to be anywhere.' Her face suddenly crumpled and tears began to ooze out of the sides of her eyes. 'I'm sorry,' she said huskily to the beautician.

'We'll drive into Wales,' said Esme. 'I know a little place in the mountains. Fabulous views and Welsh lamb every night. How does that sound?'

Milly was silent. The beautician dabbed tenderly at her tear stains with a yellow liquid from a gold embossed bottle.

'Tomorrow will be difficult,' said Esme gently. 'But we'll get through it. And after that . . .' She came forward and took Milly's hand. 'Just think, Milly. You've been given a chance which hardly any woman is given. You can start again. You can remould your life into whatever you want.'

'You're right,' said Milly, staring up at the ceiling. 'Anything I want.'

'The world is yours to reclaim! And to think you were about to settle for becoming a Mrs Pinnacle.' A note of scorn entered

Esme's voice. 'Darling, you've had such a narrow escape. When you look back on all of this, you'll be grateful to me, Milly. You really will!'

'I already am grateful,' said Milly, turning her head to look at Esme. 'I don't know what I would have done without you.'

'That's my girl!' said Esme. She patted Milly's hand. 'Now you just lie back and enjoy the rest of your facial—and I'll go and pack the car.'

CHAPTER FIFTEEN

As James arrived home that evening the lights were low and the house silent. He hung up his coat and grimaced at his reflection in the mirror, then noiselessly pushed open the door to the kitchen. The table was covered in forlorn wedding debris and coffee cups, and Olivia was sitting in the dim stillness, her head bent forward, her shoulders hunched and defeated.

For a few moments she didn't see him. Then, as though he'd spoken, she raised her head. Her eyes met his apprehensively and flickered quickly away; her hands rose defensively to her face. James stepped forward awkwardly, feeling like a schoolroom bully.

'So,' he said, putting his briefcase down on a chair. 'It's all done.' He looked around. 'You must have had a hell of a day, putting the world and his wife off.'

'Not so bad,' said Olivia huskily. 'Isobel was a great help. We both . . .' She broke off. 'What about *your* day? Isobel told me you've been having trouble at work. I . . . I didn't realize. I'm sorry.'

'You couldn't have realized,' said James. 'I didn't tell you.'

'Tell me now.'

'Not now,' said James wearily. 'Maybe later.'

'Yes, later,' said Olivia, her voice unsteady. 'Of course.' James raised his gaze to hers and felt a dart of shock as he saw the fear in her eyes. 'Let me make you some tea,' she said.

'Thank you,' said James. 'Olivia—'

'I won't be a moment!' She stood up hurriedly, catching her sleeve on the corner of the table, then wrenched it free as though desperate to turn away from him, towards the sink, the kettle; familiar inanimate objects. James sat down at the table and picked up the red book in front of him. He began to leaf idly through it. Page after page of lists, of ideas, self-reminders, even small sketches. The blueprint, he realized, for something quite spectacular.

'Swans,' he said, stopping at a starred item. 'You weren't really going to hire live swans for the occasion?'

'Swans made of ice,' said Olivia, brightening a little. 'They were going to be full of . . .' She halted. 'It doesn't matter.'

'Full of what?' said James. There was a pause.

'Oysters,' said Olivia.

'I like oysters,' said James.

'I know,' said Olivia. She picked up the teapot with fumbling hands, turned to put it on the table and slipped. The teapot crashed loudly onto the quarry tiles and Olivia gave a small cry of distress.

'Olivia!' exclaimed James, leaping to his feet. 'Are you all right?'

Pieces of broken china lay on the floor amid a puddle of hot tea; rivulets were running between the tiles towards his feet. The yellow-rimmed eye of a duck stared up at him reproachfully.

'It's broken!' said Olivia in anguish. 'We've had that teapot for thirty-two years!' She bent down, picked up a piece of the handle and stared at it disbelievingly.

'We'll get another one,' said James.

'I don't want another one,' said Olivia shakily. 'I want the old one. I want . . .' She suddenly broke off and turned round to face James. 'You're going to leave me, aren't you, James?'

'What?' James stared at her in shock.

'You're going to leave me,' repeated Olivia calmly. She looked down at the jagged piece of teapot and her hand tightened around it. 'For a new life. A new, exciting life.'

There was a still pause, then James exhaled in sudden comprehension.

'You heard me,' he said, trying to gather his thoughts. 'You *heard* me. I hadn't realized . . .'

'Yes, I heard you,' said Olivia, not looking up. 'Isn't that what you wanted?'

'Olivia, I didn't mean—'

'I assume you've been waiting until the wedding was over,' broke in Olivia, turning the piece of teapot over and over in her fingers. 'You probably didn't want to ruin the happy event. Well, the happy event's been ruined anyway. So you don't have to wait any longer. You can go.' James looked at her.

'You want me to go?'

'That's not what I said.' Olivia's voice roughened slightly; her head remained bowed. For a long while there was silence. On the other side of the room, the last brown rivulet of spilled tea slowly came to a standstill.

'The trouble at work,' said James suddenly, walking to the window. 'The trouble that Isobel was talking about. It's a restructuring of the company. They're relocating three departments to Edinburgh. They asked me if I'd like to move. And I said . . .' He turned round. 'I said I'd think about it.' Olivia looked up.

'You didn't mention it to me.'

'No,' said James defensively. 'I didn't. I knew what your answer would be.'

'Did you?' said Olivia. 'How clever of you.'

'You're rooted here, Olivia. You've got your business and your friends. I knew you wouldn't want to leave all of that. But I just felt as though I needed something new!' Pain flashed across James's face. 'Can you understand that? Have you never wanted to escape and start again? I felt trapped and guilty. I thought maybe a new city would be the answer to my malaise. A fresh view every morning. Different air to breathe.'

The kitchen was silent.

'I see,' said Olivia eventually, her voice clipped and brittle. 'Well then, off you go. Don't let me hold you up. I'll help you pack, shall I?'

'Olivia—'

'Make sure you send us a postcard.'

'Olivia, don't be like this!'

'Like what? How else do you expect me to react? You've been planning to leave me!'

'Well, what was I supposed to do?' said James furiously. 'Just say no on the spot? Settle down to another twenty years in Bath?'

'No!' cried Olivia, her eyes suddenly glittering with tears.

'You were supposed to ask me to come with you. I'm your wife, James. You were supposed to ask me.'

'What was the point? You would have said—'

'You don't know what I would have said!' Olivia's voice trembled and she lifted her chin high. 'You don't know what I would have said, James. And you couldn't even be bothered to find out.'

'I . . .' James stopped.

'You couldn't even be bothered to find out,' repeated Olivia, and a slight note of scorn entered her voice.

There was a long silence.

'What would you have said?' asked James finally. 'If I had asked you?' He tried to meet Olivia's eye, but she was staring down at the piece of teapot which she still held in her hands, and her face was unreadable.

The doorbell rang. Neither of them moved.

'What would you have said, Olivia?' said James.

'I don't know,' said Olivia at last. She put the piece of teapot down on the table and looked up. 'I probably would have asked you if you were really so unhappy with the life you have here. I would have asked if you really thought a new city would solve all your problems. And if you'd said yes—' The doorbell rang again, loud and insistent, and she broke off. 'You'd better get that,' she said. James gazed at her for a few seconds, then got to his feet.

He strode into the hall, opened the door and took a step back in surprise. Alexander was standing on the doorstep. His face was unshaven, he was surrounded by bags and his eyes were wary.

'Look,' he said, as soon as he saw James. 'I'm sorry. I really am. You've got to believe me. I didn't mean to set all this off.'

'It hardly matters any more, does it?' said James wearily. 'The damage is done. If I were you, I'd just turn round and go.'

'It matters to me,' said Alexander. 'Plus . . .' He paused. 'Plus, I've still got some stuff here. In my room. Your daughter chucked me out before I could get it.'

'I see,' said James. 'Well, you'd better come in, then.'

Cautiously, Alexander entered the house. He glanced at the wedding cake boxes and grimaced.

'Is Milly here?' he asked.

'No. She's with her godmother.'

'Is she all right?'

'What do you think?' said James, folding his arms. Alexander flinched.

'Look, it wasn't my fault!' he said.

'What do you mean, it wasn't your fault?' Olivia appeared at the kitchen door, her face indignant. 'Milly told us how you teased her. How you threatened her. You're nothing but a nasty little bully!'

'Give me a break,' said Alexander. 'She's hardly a saint herself!'

'Perhaps, Alexander, you thought you were doing the world a service by exposing her,' said James. 'Perhaps you thought you were doing your duty. But you could have come to us first, or Simon, before informing the vicar.'

'I didn't want to expose her, for God's sake,' said Alexander impatiently. 'I just wanted to wind her up.'

'Wind her up?'

'Tease her a bit. You know. And that's all I did. I didn't tell the vicar! Why should I tell the vicar?'

'Who knows how your nasty little mind might work,' said Olivia.

'I don't know why I'm bothering,' said Alexander. 'You're

never going to believe me. But I didn't do it, OK! Why should I wreck Milly's wedding? You were paying me to photograph the fucking thing! Why should I want to ruin it?'

There was silence. James glanced at Olivia.

'I don't even know the vicar's name,' said Alexander. He sighed. 'Listen, I tried to tell Isobel and she wouldn't listen, and now I'm trying to tell you, and you won't listen. But it's true. I didn't tell anyone about Milly. I really didn't. Jesus, she could have six husbands for all I care!'

'All right,' said James, exhaling sharply. 'All right. Well, if you didn't say anything, who did?'

'God knows. Who else knew about it?'

'No one,' said Olivia. 'She hadn't told anyone.'

There was silence.

'She told Esme,' said James eventually. He met Olivia's eyes. 'She told Esme.'

Isobel sat in a remote corner of the drive to Pinnacle Hall, looking through her car windscreen at Milly's marquee, just visible behind the corner of the house. She had been sitting there for half an hour, quietly composing her thoughts; honing her concentration as though for an exam. She would say what she had to say to Harry, brook as little objection as possible, then leave. She would be friendly, but businesslike. If he refused her proposal, she would . . . Isobel's thoughts faltered. He couldn't refuse such a reasonable plan. He simply couldn't.

She stared at her hands—already swollen, it seemed, with pregnancy. The very word sent teenage shivers down her back. Pregnancy, they had been instructed at school, was akin to a nuclear missile—destroying everything in its path and leaving its victims to struggle through a subsequent life hardly worth living. It destroyed careers, relationships, happiness. The risk was simply not worth it, the mistresses had opined, and at the back the lower sixth had sniggered and passed the telephone numbers of abortion clinics along the rows. Now Isobel closed her eyes. Perhaps the teachers had been right all along. Had this pregnancy not occurred, her relationship with Harry might have flowered into something more than occasional meetings. She had already begun to feel a longing to be with him more often; to share moments of pleasure and pain; to hear his voice when she woke up. She had wanted to tell him she loved him.

But now there was a baby. There was a new element, a new pace: a new pressure on both of them. To keep the baby would be to trample across Harry's wishes, to force their relationship into a new climate where, already, she knew it would not survive. To keep the baby would destroy their relationship. And yet to do anything else would destroy her.

Her heart aching a little, she reached inside her bag and gave her hair one final comb, then opened the car door and got out. The air was surprisingly mild and breezy, like a spring evening. Calmly she walked across the gravel towards the big front door, for once unafraid of observation by suspicious eyes. Today she had every reason to be at Pinnacle Hall.

She rang at the door and smiled at the red-haired girl who answered.

'I'd like to see Harry Pinnacle, please. It's Isobel Havill. The sister of Milly Havill.'

'I know who you are,' said the girl in less than friendly tones. 'I suppose it's about the wedding? Or the non-wedding, I should say.' She stared with bulging eyes at Isobel as though it were all her fault, and for the first time, Isobel wondered what people might be saying and thinking about Milly.

'That's right,' she said. 'If you could just say I'm here.'

'I'm not sure he's available,' said the girl.

'Perhaps you could ask,' said Isobel politely.

'Wait here.'

After a few minutes the girl returned.

'He can see you,' she said, as though bestowing a huge favour. 'But not for long.'

'Did he say that?' The girl was aggressively silent and Isobel found herself smiling inwardly.

They arrived at the door of Harry's study and the girl knocked.

'Yes!' came Harry's voice at once. The girl pushed open the door and Harry looked up from his desk.

'Isobel Havill,' she announced.

'Yes,' said Harry, meeting Isobel's eyes. 'I know.'

As the door closed behind the girl he put his pen down and looked at Isobel without saying anything. Isobel didn't move. She stood, trembling slightly, feeling his gaze on her skin like sunshine, then closed her eyes, trying to gather her thoughts. She heard him rise; heard him come towards her. His hand had grasped hers; his lips were pressed against the tender skin of her inner wrist, before she opened her eyes and said 'No.'

He looked up, her hand still in his, and she gazed desperately into his face, trying to convey all that she had to say in a single look. But there were too many conflicting desires and thoughts for him to read. A flash of something like disappointment passed over his face and he dropped her hand abruptly.

'A drink,' he said.

'I've got something to say to you,' said Isobel.

'I see,' said Harry. 'Do you want to sit down?'

'No,' said Isobel. 'I just want to say it.'

'OK, then say it!'

'Fine!' said Isobel. 'Here it is.' She paused, steeling herself to utter the words. 'I'm pregnant,' she said, then stopped, and the guilty word seemed to echo round the room. 'With your baby,' she added. Harry made a slight start. 'What?' said Isobel defensively. 'Don't you believe me?'

'Of course I fucking *believe* you,' said Harry. 'I was going to say . . .' He broke off. 'It doesn't matter. Carry on.'

'You don't seem surprised,' said Isobel.

'Is that part of your little speech?'

'Oh, shut up!' She took a deep breath and fixed her eyes on the corner of the mantelpiece, willing her voice to remain steady. 'I've thought about it very hard,' she said. 'I've considered all the options, and I've decided to keep it.' She paused. 'I've taken this decision knowing you don't want a child. So she'll have my name and I'll be responsible for her.'

'You know it's a girl?' interrupted Harry.

'No,' said Isobel shakily, put off her stride. 'I . . . I tend to use the feminine pronoun if the gender is unspecific.'

'I see,' said Harry. 'Carry on.'

'I'll be responsible for her,' said Isobel, speaking more quickly. 'Financially, as well as everything else. But I think every child needs a father if at all possible. I know you didn't choose for things to be this way—but neither did I, and neither did the baby.' She paused and clenched her fists tightly by her sides. 'And so I'd like to ask that you carry some parental responsibility and involvement. What

I propose is a regular meeting, perhaps once a month, so that this child grows up knowing who her father is. I'm not asking any more than that. But any child deserves that minimum. I'm just trying to be reasonable.' She looked up, with sudden tears in her eyes. 'I'm just trying to be reasonable, Harry!'

'Once a month,' said Harry, frowning.

'Yes!' said Isobel angrily. 'You can't expect a child to bond on twice-yearly meetings.'

'I suppose not.' Harry stalked to the window and Isobel watched him apprehensively. Suddenly he turned round.

'What about twice a month? Would that do?'

Isobel stared at him.

'Yes,' she said. 'Of course—'

'Or twice a week?'

'Yes. But . . .' Harry began to walk slowly towards her, his warm eyes locked onto hers.

'How about twice a day?'

'Harry—'

'How about every morning and every afternoon and all through the night?' He gently took hold of her hands; she made no effort to resist.

'I don't understand,' she said, trying to retain control of herself. 'I don't—'

'How about I love you?' said Harry. 'How about I want to be with you all the time? And be a better father to our child than I ever was with Simon.'

Isobel gazed up at him. Emotions were pushing up to the surface in an uncontrollable surge.

'But you can't! You said you didn't want a baby!' The words

came rushing out of her in a hurt, accusatory roar; tears suddenly spilled onto her cheeks and she pulled her hands away. 'You said—'

'When did I say that?' interrupted Harry. 'I never said that.'

'You didn't exactly say it,' said Isobel after a pause. 'But you pulled a face.'

'I did what?'

'A few months ago. I said a friend of mine was pregnant and you pulled this . . . this face.' Isobel swallowed. 'And I said, Oh don't you like babies? And you changed the subject.' She looked up, to see Harry staring at her incredulously.

'That's it?'

'Isn't it enough? I knew what you meant.'

'You nearly got rid of our baby because of that?'

'I didn't know what to do!' cried Isobel defensively. 'I thought—'

Harry shook his head.

'You think too much,' he said. 'That's your problem.'

'I don't!'

'You reckon I don't like babies. Have you ever seen me with a baby?'

'No,' gulped Isobel.

'No. Exactly.'

He put his arms firmly round her and she closed her eyes. After a while, she felt the tension start to sag out of her. A thousand questions were racing around her mind, but, for the moment, she let them race.

'I like babies,' Harry said comfortably. 'As long as they don't squawk.' Isobel tensed and her head jerked up.

'All babies squawk!' she said. 'You can't expect——' She broke off, seeing his face. 'Oh. You're joking.'

'Of course I'm joking,' said Harry. He raised his eyebrows. 'Are you this good at interpreting your foreign diplomats? No wonder the world's at war—Isobel Havill's been conducting the negotiations. She thought you didn't want peace because you pulled a nasty face.'

Isobel gave a shaky half-giggle half-sob, and nestled into his chest.

'You really want to have this baby?' she said. 'Seriously?'

'I seriously do,' said Harry. He paused, stroking her hair. 'And even if I didn't,' he added in a deadpan voice, 'you shouldn't get rid of it. You never know, this might be your only chance.'

'Thanks a lot.'

'You're welcome.'

They stood for a while saying nothing, then Isobel pulled reluctantly away.

'I've got to go,' she said.

'Why?'

'They might need me at home.'

'They don't need you,' said Harry. 'I need you. Stay here tonight.'

'Really?' Isobel tensed. 'But what if someone sees me?' Harry began to laugh.

'Isobel, haven't you got it into your head yet?' he said. 'I *want* everyone to see you! I love you! I want to——' He broke off and looked at her with a different expression. 'Try this for size. What would you think about . . . about giving the baby my name?'

'You don't mean . . .' Isobel stared up at him, feeling her skin begin to tingle.

'I don't know,' said Harry. 'It depends. Do you already have a husband I should know about?'

'Bastard!' said Isobel, kicking his shins.

'Is that a yes?' said Harry, starting to laugh. 'Or a no?'

'Bastard!'

James and Alexander sat at the kitchen table, drinking brandy and waiting for Olivia to come off the phone.

'I got these developed, by the way,' said Alexander suddenly, pulling out a stiff brown envelope from his bag. 'On the house.'

'What are they?' said James.

'Have a look.'

James put down his drink, opened the envelope and pulled out a sheaf of glossy black and white photographs. He stared at the top one silently, then leafed through slowly to the bottom. Milly stared up at him again and again, her eyes wide and luminous, the curves of her face falling into soft shadows, her engagement ring sparkling discreetly in the corner of the frame.

'These are incredible,' he said at last. 'Absolutely extraordinary.'

'Thanks,' said Alexander offhandedly. 'I was pleased with them.'

'She looks beautiful, of course,' said James. 'She always looks beautiful. But it's not just that.' He gazed again at the top print. 'You've captured a depth to Milly in these pictures that I've never seen before. She suddenly looks . . . intriguing.'

'She looks like a woman with a secret,' said Alexander. He took a swig of brandy. 'Which is exactly what she was.'

James looked up at him.

'Is that why you teased her? To get these pictures?'

'Partly,' said Alexander. 'And partly because . . .' he shrugged '. . . I'm an evil bastard, and that kind of thing gives me kicks.'

'And never mind the consequences?' said James.

'I didn't know there would be any consequences,' said Alexander. 'I certainly didn't realize she would panic. She seemed so . . .' He paused. 'On top of herself.'

'She may look strong,' said James, 'but she's fragile underneath.' He paused. 'Just like her mother.'

They both looked up as Olivia appeared in the kitchen.

'So,' said James grimly. 'Did you speak to Canon Lytton? Was it Esme who told him?'

'That silly young curate wouldn't tell me!' said Olivia, with a spark of her old vigour. 'Can you believe it? He said it wasn't up to him to break a confidence, and Canon Lytton was too busy to come to the phone. Too busy!'

'What's he doing?' asked James.

Olivia exhaled sharply and a curious flicker passed across her face.

'Conducting a wedding rehearsal,' she said. 'For the other couple getting married tomorrow.' There was a subdued little pause. 'I don't suppose there's much we can do about it,' she added, pouring herself a glass of brandy.

'Yes there is,' said James. 'We can go round there and we can get an answer.'

'What, and interrupt the wedding rehearsal?' Olivia stared at him. 'James, are you serious?'

'Yes,' said James. 'I am. If my cousin has betrayed Milly's confidence and deliberately ruined her wedding, then I want to know about it.' He put down his drink. 'Come on, Olivia! Where's your fighting spirit?'

'Are you serious?' repeated Olivia.

'Yes,' said James. 'And besides—' he glanced at Alexander '—it might be fun.'

Simon was sitting by the window of his bedroom, trying to read a book, as the doorbell rang. A spasm of nerves went through him and he quickly got to his feet, discarding the book. It was Milly. It had to be Milly.

He had driven back to Pinnacle Hall from Esme's house with a hopeful happiness bubbling through him like spring water. After the wounding shock and anger of last night, he felt as though life was once again on course. He'd made the first move towards a reconciliation with Milly; as soon as she responded, he would renew his apologies and try to heal the wound between them as best he could. They would wait patiently for her divorce to come through; organize another wedding; start life again.

And now here she was. He descended the wide stairs, a foolish grin spreading over his face, and briskly crossed the hall. But before he was halfway across, his father's study door opened and Harry appeared. He was laughing and gesturing to someone in his room; a whisky glass was in his hand.

'It's all right,' said Simon quickly. 'I'll get it.' Harry turned round in surprise.

'Oh, hello,' he said. 'Are you expecting someone?'

'I don't know,' said Simon awkwardly. 'Milly, maybe.'

'Ah,' said Harry. 'I'll get out of your way, then.'

Simon grinned at his father and, without thinking, allowed his eyes to roam inside the open study door. To his surprise he caught a glimpse of female leg by the fire. A mild curiosity began to rise through him and he glanced questioningly at his father. Harry seemed to think for a couple of seconds, then he flung the study door open.

Isobel Havill was sitting by the fire. Her head shot up, a shocked expression on her face, and Simon stared back at her in surprise.

'You know Isobel, don't you, Simon?' said Harry cheerfully.

'Yes, of course,' said Simon. 'Hi, Isobel. What are you doing here?'

'I'm here to talk about the wedding,' she said after a pause.

'No you're not,' said Harry. 'Don't lie to the boy.'

'Oh,' said Simon confusedly. 'Well, it doesn't—'

'We have something to tell you, Simon,' said Harry. 'Although this may not be quite the best time . . .'

'No, it's not,' interrupted Isobel firmly. 'Why doesn't one of you answer the door?'

'What have you got to tell me?' said Simon. His heart began to thud. 'Is it about Milly?'

Isobel sighed. 'No,' she said.

'Not directly,' said Harry.

'Harry!' said Isobel, a note of irritation entering her voice. 'Simon doesn't want to hear this now!'

'Hear what?' said Simon as the doorbell rang again. He looked from one to the other. Isobel was giving his father a private little frown; Harry was grinning back at her teasingly. Simon stared at the two of them, communicating in a silent, intimate language, and suddenly, with a lurch, he understood.

'Get the door,' said Isobel. 'Somebody.'

'I'll go,' said Simon in a strangled voice. Isobel shot his father an angry look.

'Simon, are you OK?' said Harry apologetically. 'Listen, I didn't mean to—'

'It's OK,' said Simon, not looking back. 'It's OK.'

He strode up to the front door and yanked it open with a shaking, clumsy hand. On the doorstep was a stranger. A tall, well-built man, with blond hair that shone under the lantern like a halo, and bloodshot blue eyes full of a miserable wariness.

Simon stared back at the stranger in disappointment, too nonplussed by events to speak. Thoughts were skittering round his mind like mad bowling balls, as his brain tried to link this new information to all the evidence that had been before him over the last few months. How many times had he seen his father and Isobel together? Hardly ever. But maybe that fact should have been a sign in itself. If he'd paid more attention, might he have noticed something? How long had their affair been going on, anyway? And where the hell was Milly?

'I'm looking for Simon Pinnacle,' said the stranger at last. His eyes shone entreatingly at Simon and there was a curious, preemptive defensiveness to his voice. 'Are you him, by any chance?'

'Yes,' said Simon, forcing himself to focus; to pull himself together. 'I am. How can I help you?'

'You won't know who I am,' said the man.

'I think I do,' interrupted Isobel, from behind Simon. 'I think

I know exactly who you are.' An incredulous note entered her voice as she gazed up at him. 'You're Rupert, aren't you?'

Giles Claybrook and Eleanor Smith were standing at the altar of St Edward's, gazing silently at one another.

'Now,' said Canon Lytton, smiling benevolently at the pair of them. 'Is it to be one ring or two?'

'One,' said Giles, looking up.

'Giles won't wear a wedding ring,' said Eleanor, a slight flush of annoyance coming to her features. 'I've tried to persuade him.'

'Ellie, love,' said Eleanor's uncle, filming behind on a video camera. 'Could you move slightly to the right? Lovely.'

'One ring,' said Canon Lytton, making a note on his service sheet. 'Well, in that case . . .'

There was a rattle at the doors at the back of the church, and he looked up in surprise. The door swung open, to reveal James, Olivia and Alexander.

'Forgive us,' said James, walking briskly up the aisle. 'We just need a moment with Canon Lytton.'

'We won't be long,' said Olivia.

'Sorry to interrupt,' added Alexander cheerfully.

'What's going on?' said Giles, peering down the aisle.

'Mrs Havill, I am busy!' thundered Canon Lytton. 'Kindly wait at the back!'

'It won't take a second,' said James. 'We just need to know— who told you about Milly's first wedding?'

'If you are trying to convince me, at this late stage, that the information is false . . .' began Canon Lytton.

'We're not!' said James impatiently. 'We just need to know.'

'Was it him?' demanded Olivia, pointing to Alexander.

'No,' said Canon Lytton, 'it wasn't. And now if you would kindly—'

'Was it my cousin, Esme Ormerod?' asked James.

There was silence.

'I was told in confidence,' said Canon Lytton at last, a slight stiffness entering his voice. 'And I'm afraid that—'

'I'll take that as confirmation that it was,' said James. He sank down onto a pew. 'I just don't believe it. How could she? She's supposed to be Milly's godmother! She's supposed to help and protect her!'

'Indeed,' said Canon Lytton sternly. 'And would it be helping your daughter to stand back as she deliberately entered a marriage based on lies and falseness?'

'What are you saying?' said Olivia incredulously. 'That Esme was trying to act in Milly's best interests?'

Canon Lytton made a small gesture of assent.

'Well then you're mad!' cried Olivia. 'She was acting out of spite and you know it! She's a spiteful, malicious troublemaker! You know, I never liked that woman. I saw through her, right from the start.' She nodded at James. 'Right from the start.'

Canon Lytton had turned to Giles and Eleanor.

'My apologies for this unseemly interruption,' he said. 'Now let us resume. The giving and receiving of the ring.'

'Hold on,' said Eleanor's uncle. 'I'll rewind the video, shall I? Or do you want me to keep all this?' He gestured to James and Olivia. 'We could send it in to a TV show.'

'No we bloody couldn't,' snapped Eleanor. 'Carry on, Canon Lytton.' She shot a malevolent look at Olivia. 'We'll ignore these rude people.'

'Very well,' said Canon Lytton. 'Now, Giles, you will place the ring on Eleanor's finger, and repeat after me.' He raised his voice: 'With this ring, I thee wed.'

There was a pause, then Giles said self-consciously, 'With this ring, I thee wed.'

'With my body, I thee worship.'

'With my body I thee worship.'

As the ancient words rose into the empty space of the church, everyone seemed to relax. Olivia raised her eyes to the vaulted ceiling, then looked down at James. A wistful look came over her face and she sat down next to him. They both watched Alexander as he crept forward and took a discreet picture of Canon Lytton trying to ignore the video camera.

'Do you remember our wedding?' she said quietly.

'Yes,' said James. He met her eyes cautiously. 'What about it?'

'Nothing,' said Olivia. 'I was just . . . remembering it. How nervous I was.'

'You, nervous?' said James, half smiling.

'Yes,' said Olivia. 'Nervous.' There was a long pause, then she said, without meeting his eye, 'Perhaps next week—if you felt like it—we could go up to Edinburgh. Just for a break. We could have a look around. Stay in a hotel. And . . . and talk about things.'

There was silence.

'I'd like that,' said James eventually. 'I'd like that very much.' He paused. 'What about the bed and breakfast?'

'I could close it for a bit,' said Olivia. She flushed slightly. 'It's not the most important thing in my life, you know.'

James stared at her silently. Cautiously, he moved his hand across towards hers. Olivia remained motionless. Then there was a sudden rattling at the door, and they jumped apart like scalded cats. The young curate of the church was striding up the aisle, cordless phone in hand.

'Canon Lytton,' he said, a note of excitement in his voice. 'You have a very urgent telephone call from Miss Havill. I wouldn't interrupt, normally, but—'

'From Milly?' said Olivia in surprise. 'Let me speak to her!'

'From Isobel Havill,' said the curate, ignoring Olivia. 'Speaking from Pinnacle Hall.' He handed the phone to Canon Lytton, his eyes gleaming. 'Apparently there's been a rather startling development.'

Isobel put down the telephone and looked at the others.

'I just spoke to Mummy at the church,' she said. 'You know, it wasn't Alexander who told the vicar about Milly.'

'Who was it?' said Simon.

'You won't believe this,' said Isobel. She paused for effect. 'It was Esme.'

'That doesn't surprise me,' said Harry.

'Do you know her?' said Isobel, staring at him in surprise.

'I used to,' said Harry. 'Not any more. Not for a long time,' he added hastily. Isobel gave him a briefly suspicious look, then frowned, tapping her nails on the phone.

'And Milly doesn't even realize! I must call her.'

'No wonder she wouldn't let me in the house,' said Simon, as Isobel picked up the phone again. 'The woman's a bloody weirdo!'

There was a tense silence as Isobel waited to be connected. Suddenly her face changed expression, and she motioned for the others to be quiet.

'Hi, Esme,' she said, her voice airily casual. 'Is Milly there by any chance? Oh, right. Could you maybe wake her up?' She pulled a face at Simon, who grimaced back. 'Oh, I see. OK, well, not to worry. Just give her my love!'

She put down the phone and looked at the others.

'You know, I really don't trust that woman,' she said. 'I'm going round there.'

CHAPTER SIXTEEN

As she reached the bottom of the stairs, Milly stopped and put her case down on the floor.

'I'm not sure,' she said.

'What do you mean, you're not sure?' said Esme briskly, coming into the hall. She was wearing her fur hat and holding a pair of black leather gloves and a road map. 'Come on! It's getting late.'

'I'm not sure about going away,' said Milly. She sat down on the stairs. 'I feel as if I'm running away from everything. Maybe it would be better to stay and be brave and face it out.' Esme shook her head.

'Darling, you're not running away—you're being sensible. If we stay here, you'll spend all of tomorrow with your face pressed against the window, brooding. If we go away, at least you'll have a different view to distract you.'

'But I should talk to my parents, at least.'

'They'll still be here on Monday. And they'll be too busy to talk at the moment.'

'Well then, maybe I should help them.'

'Milly,' said Esme impatiently, 'you're being ridiculous. The best place for you at the moment is somewhere far away, tranquil and discreet, where you can think about life properly for once. Take some time out, rebalance yourself, work out your priorities.'

Milly stared at the floor for a while.

'It's true,' she said at last. 'I do need a chance to think.'

'Of course you do!' said Esme. 'You need some unhurried peace and solitude. If you go home, you'll be surrounded by mayhem and distraction and emotional pressure. From your mother especially.'

'She was very upset,' said Milly. 'Mummy. She really wanted the wedding to happen.'

'Of course she did,' said Esme. 'We all did. But now that it's not going to happen, you're going to have to think about life in a different way. Aren't you?'

Milly sighed and stood up.

'Yes,' she said. 'You're right. A weekend in the countryside is exactly what I need.'

'You won't regret it,' said Esme, and smiled at her. 'Come on. Let's get on the road.'

Esme's Daimler was parked on the street outside, underneath a street light. As they got in, Milly turned round in her seat and peered curiously through the back window.

'That looks like Isobel's car,' she said.

'There are lots of these little Peugeots around the place,' murmured Esme. She turned on the ignition and a blast of Mozart filled the car.

'It *is* Isobel's car!' said Milly, peering harder. 'What's Isobel doing here?'

'Well, I'm afraid we can't hang around,' said Esme, swiftly putting the car into gear. 'You can give her a ring when we get there.'

'No, wait!' protested Milly. 'She's getting out. She's coming towards us. Esme, stop!' Esme put the car into gear and began to drive off, and Milly stared at her in astonishment. 'Esme, stop!' she said. 'Stop the car!'

Hurrying along the street, Isobel saw Esme's car pulling away from the kerb and felt a thrust of panic. She began to run after the car, panting in the winter air, desperate not to let Milly out of her sight. She could just see Milly's blond head incarcerated behind Esme's expensive Daimler windows; as she ran, she saw Milly turn and see her, then say something to Esme. But the car didn't stop. A surge of fury went through Isobel as she saw it disappearing away from her towards the end of the road. Who did this bitch think she was? Where the hell was she taking Milly? A furious adrenalin began to pump round her body and, with an almighty effort, she upped her pace to a sprint. She careered along the pavement, keeping the rear lights of the Daimler in sight, unsure what she would do when Esme turned the corner and zipped off down the main road.

But the traffic lights at the end of the road were red, and as Esme's car approached them it was forced to slow down. Feeling like a triumphant Olympic athlete, Isobel caught up with the car and began to bang on Milly's window. Inside, she could see Milly shouting animatedly at Esme, then struggling with the handbrake. Suddenly Milly's door opened and she spilled out, half falling, onto the pavement.

'What do you want?' she gasped to Isobel. 'I thought it must be important.'

'Too right it's important!' managed Isobel, red in the face and panting hard, almost unable to speak for anger. 'Too right it's important! My God!' She pushed her hair out of her eyes and forced herself to take a couple of deep breaths. 'For a start, you might like to know, it was this bitch who shopped you to the vicar.' She gestured scornfully at Esme, who stared back at her from the driver's seat with furious, glinting eyes.

'What do you mean?' said Milly. 'It was Alexander.'

'It wasn't Alexander, it was Esme! Wasn't it?' snapped Isobel at Esme.

'Really?' said Milly, looking at Esme with wide eyes. '*Really?*'

'Of course not!' said Esme tartly. 'Why would I do such a thing?'

'To get back at Harry, perhaps,' said Isobel, a new, scathing note entering her voice.

'You're talking nonsense!'

'I'm not,' said Isobel. 'He's told me all about you. Everything.'

'Has he now?' said Esme mockingly.

'Yes,' said Isobel coldly. 'He has.'

There was silence. Esme's glinting eyes ranged sharply over Isobel's face, then suddenly flickered in comprehension.

'I see,' she said slowly. 'So that's how it is.' She gave Isobel a tiny, contemptuous smile. 'I might have guessed as much. You Havill girls do have a penchant for money, don't you?'

'You're a bitch, Esme,' said Isobel.

'I don't understand,' said Milly, looking from Isobel to Esme. 'What are you talking about? Esme, did you really tell Canon Lytton about me being married?'

'Yes I did,' said Esme. 'And it was for your own good. You didn't want to marry that immature, sanctimonious little prig!'

'You betrayed me!' cried Milly. 'You're supposed to be my godmother! You're supposed to be on my side!'

'I am on your side,' retorted Esme.

Behind them, a line of cars was beginning to mount up. One of them sounded its horn and Isobel gestured impatiently back.

'Milly, listen,' said Esme. 'You're far too good for marriage to Simon Pinnacle! Your life hasn't begun yet. Don't you understand? I saved you from a life of tedium and mediocrity.'

'Is that what you think?' said Milly, her voice rising in disbelief. 'That you saved me?'

Several more cars began to sound their horns. Towards the back of the queue, a driver got out of his car and began to walk along the pavement.

'Darling, I know you very well,' began Esme. 'And I know that—'

'You don't!' interrupted Milly. 'You don't know me very well. You don't bloody know me at all! All of you think you know me— and none of you do! You haven't got any idea what I'm really like, underneath . . .'

'Underneath what?' challenged Esme.

Milly gazed silently at Esme, panting slightly, her face bathed green in the glow of the traffic light above, then looked away.

'Excuse me.' A truculent male voice interrupted them. 'Have you seen the light?'

'Yes,' said Milly dazedly. 'I think I probably have.'

'The lady was just leaving,' said Isobel, and slammed the passenger door of Esme's car viciously. 'Come on, Milly,' she said, taking her sister's arm. 'Let's go.'

As they sped away in Isobel's car, Milly sank back into her seat and massaged her brow with her fingertips. Isobel drove quickly and efficiently, glancing at Milly every so often but saying nothing. After a while, Milly sat up and smoothed back her hair.

'Thanks, Isobel,' she said.

'Any time.'

'How did you guess it was Esme?'

'It had to be,' said Isobel. 'No one else knew. If Alexander hadn't told anyone, it had to be her. And . . .' She paused. 'There were other things.'

'What things?' Milly swivelled her head towards Isobel. 'What was all that about getting back at Harry?'

'They had a liaison,' said Isobel shortly. 'Let's just say it didn't work.'

'How do you know?'

'He told Simon. And me. I was over there just now.' A tinge of pink came to Isobel's cheeks and she put her foot down rather hard on the accelerator. Milly stared at her sister.

'Is something wrong?'

'No,' said Isobel. But the pink in her cheeks was deepening to a red and she wouldn't look round. Milly's heart began to thump.

'Isobel, what's going on? What did Esme mean, you've got a penchant for money?'

Isobel said nothing, but changed gear with a crunch. She

signalled to turn left and turned the windscreen wipers on by mistake.

'Damn,' she said. 'This bloody car.'

'There's something you're not telling me, Isobel,' said Milly. 'You're hiding something.'

'I'm not,' said Isobel.

'What were you doing at Pinnacle Hall?' Milly's voice suddenly sharpened. 'Who were you seeing?'

'No one.'

'Don't play games with me! Have you and Simon been seeing each other behind my back?'

'No!' said Isobel, laughing. 'Don't be ridiculous.'

'How do I know? If my godmother can betray me, then why can't my own sister?'

Isobel glanced at Milly. Her face was white and tense and her hands were tightly gripping the seat.

'For God's sake, Milly,' she said quickly. 'We're not all Esme Ormerod! Of course I haven't been seeing Simon.'

'Well, what is it, then?' Milly's voice rose higher. 'Isobel, tell me what's going on!'

'OK!' Isobel said. 'OK. I'll tell you. I was going to break it to you gently but since you're so bloody suspicious . . .' She glanced at Milly and took a deep breath. 'It's Harry.'

'What's Harry?' said Milly.

'Who I was seeing. He's . . .' Isobel swallowed. 'The father.' She glanced at Milly's face, still blank and uncomprehending. 'Of my child, Milly! He's . . . he's the one I've been seeing.'

'What?' Milly's voice ripped through the car like the cry of a bird. 'You've been seeing Harry Pinnacle?'

'Yes.'

'He's the father of your child?'

'Yes.'

'You've been having an affair with Simon's *dad*?' Milly's voice was becoming higher and higher.

'Yes!' said Isobel defensively. 'But—' She stopped at the sound of Milly bursting into sobs. 'Milly, what's wrong?' She shot a quick look at Milly, who was doubled over in her seat, clasping her face in her hands. Tears suddenly sprang to her own eyes, blurring her view of the road. 'Milly, I'm really sorry,' she said. 'I know this is a terrible time to tell you. Oh Milly, don't cry!'

'I'm not crying,' managed Milly. 'I'm not crying!'

'What do you—'

'I'm laughing!' Milly gasped for breath, looked at Isobel, then erupted into hysterical giggles again. 'You and Harry! But he's so old!'

'He's not old!' said Isobel.

'He is! He's ancient! He's got grey hair!'

'Well I don't care. I love him. And I'm going to have his baby!'

Milly raised her head and looked at Isobel. She was staring ahead defiantly but her lips were trembling and tears had spilled onto her cheeks.

'Oh Isobel, I'm sorry!' Milly said in distress. 'I didn't mean it! He's not old really.' She paused. 'I'm sure you'll make a lovely couple.'

'Of fogies,' said Isobel, signalling to turn right.

'Don't!' said Milly. A tiny giggle erupted from her and she clamped her mouth shut. 'I can't believe it. My sister, having a secret affair with Harry Pinnacle. I knew you were up to something. But I never would have guessed in a million years.' She looked up. 'Does anyone else know?'

'Simon.'

'You told Simon before me?' said Milly, hurt. Isobel rolled her eyes exasperatedly.

'Milly, you sound just like Mummy!' she said. 'And no, I didn't. He came across us.'

'What, in bed?'

'No, not in bed!'

Milly giggled.

'Well, I don't know, do I? You might have been.' She glanced at Isobel's profile. 'You're very good at keeping secrets, you know.'

'Speak for yourself!' said Isobel.

'Yes, I suppose so,' said Milly, after a pause. 'I suppose so. But you know . . .' She stretched out her legs and put her feet up on the dashboard. 'I never thought of my marriage to Allan as a secret, exactly.'

'What was it, then?'

'I don't know,' said Milly vaguely. She thought for a moment. 'A secret is something which you have to keep hidden. But that was more like . . . something in a different world. Something which never really existed in this world.' She gazed out of the window, watching as the inky black hedgerow sped by. 'I still think of it a bit like that. If no one had found out about it, it wouldn't have existed.'

'You're mad,' said Isobel, signalling left.

'I'm not!' Milly pointed her feet, encased in pink suede, against the glass. 'Do you like my new shoes, by the way?'

'Very nice.'

'Twenty quid. Simon would *hate* them.' A tiny satisfaction entered her voice. 'I thought I might cut my hair, too.'

'Good idea,' said Isobel absently.

'Bleach it. And get a nose-ring.' She met Isobel's horrified eye and grinned. 'Or something.'

As they approached Pinnacle Hall, Milly's eyes suddenly focused on her surroundings, and she stiffened.

'Isobel, what's going on?' she said.

'We're going to Pinnacle Hall,' said Isobel.

'I can see that,' said Milly. 'But why?'

Isobel didn't reply for a while.

'I think we should wait until we get there,' she said at last.

'I don't want to see Simon,' said Milly, 'if that's your idea. If you've set up some meeting, you can forget it. I'm not going to see him.'

'You know, he came to apologize to you this afternoon,' said Isobel. 'He brought you flowers. But Esme wouldn't let him in.' She turned towards Milly. 'Now do you want to see him?'

'No,' said Milly after a pause. 'It's too late. He can't undo the things he said.'

'I think he's genuinely sorry,' said Isobel, as they approached the gates of Pinnacle Hall, 'for what that's worth.'

'I don't care,' said Milly. As the car crackled on the drive, she shrank down in her seat. 'I don't mind seeing Harry,' she said. 'But not Simon. I'm just not going to see him.'

'Fine,' said Isobel calmly. 'It's not him I've brought you to see, anyway. There's someone else who's come to see you.' She switched off the engine and looked at Milly. 'Brace yourself for a shock,' she added.

'What?' But Isobel was already out of the car and walking towards the house. Hesitantly, Milly got out and began to follow her, crunching on the gravel. Automatically her eyes rose to Simon's bedroom window, in the far left corner of the house. The curtains were drawn but she could see a chink of light. Perhaps he was behind the curtains, watching her. A dart of apprehension went through her and she began to walk more quickly, wondering what Isobel had been talking about. As she neared the front door, it suddenly opened and a tall figure appeared in the shadows.

'Simon!' said Milly, without thinking.

'No.' Rupert's subdued voice travelled easily through the evening air; as he moved forward his blond hair was visible under the light. 'Milly, it's me.' Milly stopped in astonishment.

'Rupert?' she said incredulously. 'What are you doing here? You were in London.'

'I came down by train,' said Rupert. 'I had to see you. There was no one at your house, so I came here.'

'I suppose you've heard, then,' said Milly, shifting her feet on the gravel. 'It all came out. The wedding's off.'

'I know. That's why I'm here.' He rubbed his face, then looked up. 'Milly, I tracked down Allan for you.'

'You've found him? Already?' Milly's voice rose in excitement. 'Where is he? Is he here?'

'No,' said Rupert. He walked slowly towards her across the gravel and took her hands. 'Milly, I've got some bad news. Allan's . . . Allan's dead. He died four years ago.'

Milly stared at him in stunned silence, feeling as though a bucket of icy cold water had hit her in the face. Allan dead. The idea circled her mind like some sort of foreign body, impossible to digest. It couldn't be true. Allan couldn't be dead. People his age didn't *die*. It was ludicrous.

As she gazed at Rupert, a sudden desire rose within her to giggle; to turn this into the joke it must surely be. But Rupert wasn't smiling or laughing. He was gazing at her with a strange desperation, as though waiting for a reaction; an answer. Milly blinked a few times, and swallowed, her throat suddenly dry like sandpaper.

'What . . . how?' she managed. Visions of car crashes ran through her mind. Aeroplane disasters; mangled wreckage on the television.

'Leukaemia,' said Rupert.

A fresh jolt hit Milly and the base of her spine began to tingle unpleasantly.

'He was ill?' she said, and licked her dry lips. 'All that time, he was ill?'

'Not while we knew him,' said Rupert. 'It was afterwards.'

'Did he . . . suffer much?'

'Apparently not,' said Rupert, a low, suppressed anguish in his voice. 'But I don't know. I wasn't there.'

Milly gazed at him for a few silent seconds.

'It's all wrong,' she said eventually. 'He shouldn't . . .' Something was constricting her throat. 'He shouldn't have died.' She shook her head violently. 'Allan didn't deserve to die.'

'No,' said Rupert in a trembling voice. 'He didn't.'

She stared at him for a moment and a thousand shared memories seemed to pass between them. Then, in a moment of pure instinct, she reached out her arms. Rupert half fell against her, stumbling on the gravel, and buried his head in her shoulder. Milly held on tightly to him and looked up at the inky sky, tears blurring her view of the stars. And as a cloud passed over the moon it occurred to her for the first time that she was a widow.

As Isobel entered the kitchen, Simon looked up warily from his seat at the huge refectory table. He was cradling a glass of wine and in front of him was the *Financial Times*, open but—Isobel suspected—unread.

'Hi,' he said.

'Hi,' said Isobel. She sat down opposite him and reached for the wine bottle. For a while there was silence. Isobel looked curiously at Simon. He was staring down, avoiding her eye, as though experiencing some kind of internal struggle.

'So,' he said at last. 'I gather you're pregnant. Congratulations.'

'Thanks,' said Isobel. She gave him a little smile. 'I'm really happy about it.'

'Good,' said Simon. 'That's great.' He reached for his glass of wine and took a deep swig.

'It'll be your half-brother,' added Isobel. 'Or sister.'

'I know,' said Simon shortly. Isobel looked at him sympathetically.

'Are you finding this difficult to deal with?'

'Well, to be honest, just a tad!' said Simon, putting down his glass. 'One minute you're going to be my sister-in-law. The next minute you're not going to be my sister-in-law. Then all of a sudden, you're going to be my stepmother, and you're having a baby!'

'I know,' said Isobel. 'It is all a bit sudden. I'm sorry. Truly.' She took a thoughtful sip of wine. 'What do you want to call me, by the way? "Stepmother" seems a bit of a mouthful. How about "Mum"?'

'Very funny,' said Simon irritably. He took a swig of wine,

picked up the newspaper and put it down again. 'Where the hell's Milly? They're taking a long time, aren't they?'

'Oh come on,' said Isobel. 'Give the girl a chance. She's just found out that her husband's dead.'

'I know,' said Simon, 'I know. But even so . . .' He stood up and walked to the window, then turned round. 'So—what do you think of this Rupert, then?'

'I don't know,' said Isobel. 'I have to say, I was expecting a complete bastard. But this guy just seems . . .' She thought for a moment. 'Very sad. He just seems very sad.'

'The truth is,' said Rupert, 'I should never have married her.' He was leaning forward, his head resting wearily on his knuckles. Next to him, Milly wrapped her arms more tightly around her knees. They were sitting on a low wall behind the office wing; above them, like a second moon, was the old stable clock. 'I knew what I was. I knew I was living a lie. But, you know, I thought I could do it.' He looked up miserably. 'I really thought I could do it!'

'Do what?' said Milly.

'Be a good husband! Be a normal, decent husband. Do all the things everybody else does. Have dinner parties and go to church and watch our children in a nativity play . . .' He broke off, staring into the darkness. 'We were trying for a baby, you know. Francesca was pregnant last year. It would have been due in March. But she lost it. Now everyone will be thanking God that she had that miscarriage, won't they?'

'No,' said Milly uncertainly.

'Of course they will. They'll be calling it a blessing.' He looked up with bloodshot blue eyes. 'Maybe I'm being selfish. But I wanted that baby. I desperately wanted that baby. And I—' He faltered slightly. 'I would have been a good father to it.'

'It would have been lucky to have you,' said Milly stoutly.

'That's sweet,' said Rupert, a faint smile coming to his face. 'Thanks.'

'But a baby isn't glue, is it?' said Milly. 'A baby doesn't keep a marriage together.'

'No,' said Rupert. 'It doesn't.' He thought for a moment. 'The odd thing is, I don't think we ever had a marriage. Not what I would call a marriage. We were like two trains, running side by side, barely aware of each other's existence. We never argued; we never clashed. To be honest, we hardly knew each other. It was all very civil and pleasant—but it wasn't real.'

'Were you happy?'

'I don't know,' said Rupert. 'I pretended to be. Some of the time I even fooled myself.'

There was silence. Somewhere in the distance a fox barked. Rupert sighed and stretched out his legs in front of him.

'Shall we go in?' he said.

'OK,' said Milly vaguely. Rupert looked at her curiously for a while.

'How about you?' he said at last.

'What about me?'

'You know Allan's death changes everything.'

'I know,' said Milly. She examined her hands intently for a moment, then stood up. 'Come on. I'm getting cold.'

At the sound of the front door opening, Simon stood up, as abruptly as though a small electric current had been passed through his body. He smoothed back his hair and began to make awkwardly for the kitchen door, checking his appearance as he passed the un-curtained window. Isobel looked at him with raised eyebrows.

'She probably won't want to talk to you,' she said. 'You really hurt her, you know.'

'I know,' said Simon, halting at the door. 'I know. But . . .' He reached for the door knob, hesitated for a few seconds, then pushed the door open.

'Good luck,' called Isobel after him.

Milly was standing just inside the front door, her hands deep in her pockets. At the sound of Simon's tread, she looked up. Si-mon stopped, and stared at her. She seemed suddenly different; as though the events of the last two days had remoulded her face, her entire person.

'Milly,' he said shakily. She gave a faint acknowledgement. 'Milly, I'm sorry. I'm so sorry. I didn't mean any of the things I said.' His words came tumbling out like apples from a tree. 'I had no right to speak to you like that. I had no right to say those things.'

'No,' said Milly in a low voice. 'You didn't.'

'I was hurt, and I was shocked. And I lashed out without think-ing. But if you give me another chance, I'll . . . I'll make it up to you.' Simon's eyes suddenly shone with tears. 'Milly, I don't care if you've been married before. I don't care if you've got six chil-dren. I just want to be with you.' He took a step towards her. 'And so I'm asking you to forgive me and give me another chance.'

There was a long pause.

'I forgive you,' said Milly at last, staring at the floor. 'I forgive you, Simon.'

'Really?' Simon stared at her. 'Really?' She gave a tiny shrug.

'It was understandable, the way you reacted. I should have told you about Allan in the first place.'

There was an uncertain silence. Simon moved forward and tried to take Milly's hands but she flinched. He dropped his hands and cleared his throat.

'I heard what happened to him,' he said. 'I'm really sorry.'

'Yes,' said Milly.

'You must be—'

'Yes.'

'But . . .' He hesitated. 'You know what it means for us?' Milly looked at him as though he were speaking a foreign language.

'What?' she said.

'Well,' said Simon. 'It means we can get married.'

'No, Simon,' said Milly. Simon paled slightly.

'What do you mean?' he said, keeping his voice light. Milly met his eyes briefly, then looked away.

'I mean, we can't get married.' And as he watched her in disbelief, she turned on her heel and walked out of the front door.

CHAPTER SEVENTEEN

Milly didn't stop walking until she reached Isobel's car. Then she leaned against the passenger door and scrabbled in her pocket for a cigarette, trying to ignore the burning ache in her chest; trying not to think of Simon's startled face. She had done the right thing, she told herself. She had been honest. Finally, she had been honest.

With shaky hands she put the cigarette in her mouth and flicked repeatedly at her lighter, but the evening breeze blew the flame out every time. Eventually, with a little cry of frustration, she threw the cigarette on the ground and stamped on it. She felt suddenly powerless and marooned. She couldn't go back into the house. She couldn't drive off without a car key. She didn't even have a mobile phone. Perhaps Isobel would come and find her in a moment.

There was a sudden crunching on the gravel and she looked up, then jumped as she saw Simon striding towards her, a look of serious intent on his face.

'Look, Simon, don't even bother,' she said, turning away. 'It's over, OK?'

'No, it's not OK!' exclaimed Simon. He reached the car, panting slightly. 'What do you mean, we can't get married? Is it because of the things I said? Milly, I'm just so sorry. I'll do anything I can to make it up. But don't give up on us just because of that!'

'It's not about that!' said Milly. 'Yes, you hurt me. But I told you, I forgive you.' Simon stared at her.

'Well, what, then?'

'It's more basic than that. It's . . . us. You and me as a couple, full stop.' She gave a small shrug and began to walk off.

'What's wrong with you and me as a couple?' said Simon, starting to follow her. 'Milly, talk to me! Don't just run away!'

'I'm not running away!' said Milly, wheeling round to face him. 'But there's no point talking about it. Take it from me, it just wouldn't work. So let's act with a little dignity, shall we? Goodbye, Simon.'

She paused, then began to walk quickly off again.

'Fuck dignity!' exclaimed Simon, hurrying after her. 'I'm not going to just let you walk out of my life like that! Milly, I love you. I want to marry you. Don't you love me? Have you stopped loving me? If you have, just tell me!'

'It's not that!' said Milly.

'Then what's wrong!' His voice jabbed at the back of her head. 'What's wrong?'

'OK!' said Milly, suddenly stopping. 'OK!' She closed her

eyes, then opened them and looked straight at him. 'What's wrong is that . . . I haven't been honest with you. Ever.'

'I told you, I don't care about that,' said Simon. 'You can have ten husbands for all I care!'

'I'm not talking about Allan,' said Milly desperately. 'I'm talking about all the other lies I've told you.' Her words rose into the evening air like birds escaping. 'Lies, lies, lies!'

Simon stared at her in discomposure. He swallowed, and pushed his hair back.

'What lies?'

'You see?' cried Milly. 'You have no idea! You have no idea who I really am! You don't know the real Milly Havill.'

'Kepinski,' said Simon.

Milly's eyes narrowed; she turned round and began to stride away.

'I'm sorry,' said Simon at once. 'I didn't mean it! Milly, come back!'

'It's no good!' said Milly, shaking her head. 'It won't work. I can't do it any more.'

'What are you talking about?' exclaimed Simon, hurrying after her.

'I can't be what you think I am! I can't be your perfect Barbie doll.'

'I don't treat you like a fucking Barbie doll!' said Simon in outrage. 'Jesus! I treat you like an intelligent, mature woman!'

'Yes!' cried Milly, turning with a spatter of gravel. 'And that's the trouble! You treat me like some thinking man's version of a Barbie doll. You want an attractive intelligent woman who wears expensive shoes and thinks soap operas are trivial and knows all about the effect of the exchange rate on European imports.

Well, I can't be her! I thought I could turn into her, but I can't! I just can't!'

'What?' said Simon, staring at her in astonishment. 'What the hell are you talking about?'

'Simon, I can't live up to your expectations any more.' Tears sprang to Milly's eyes and she brushed them away impatiently. 'I can't play a part all my life. I can't be something I'm not. Rupert tried to do that, and look where it got him!'

'Milly, I don't want you to be something you're not. I want you to be you.'

'You can't want that. You don't even know me.'

'Of course I know you!'

'You don't,' said Milly despairingly. 'Simon, I keep trying to tell you. I've been lying to you ever since we first met.'

'About what?'

'About everything!'

'You've been lying to me about *everything*?'

'Yes.'

'Like what, for Christ's sake?'

'Everything!'

'Name one thing.'

'OK.' Milly paused, and ran a shaky hand through her hair. 'I don't like sushi.'

There was a stupefied silence.

'Is that it?' said Simon eventually. 'You don't like sushi?'

'Of course that's not it,' said Milly quickly. 'Bad example. I . . . I never read the newspapers. I only pretend to.'

'So what?' said Simon.

'And I don't understand modern art. And I watch terrible TV.'

'Like what?' said Simon, laughing.

'Things you've never even heard of! Like . . . like *Family Fortunes!*'

'Milly—' Simon began to walk towards her.

'And I . . . I buy cheap shoes and don't show you them.'

'So what?'

'What do you mean, so what?' Angry tears started to Milly's eyes. 'All this time, I've been pretending to be something that I'm not. At that party, where we first met, I didn't really know about vivisection! I saw it on *Blue Peter!*'

Simon stopped still. There was a long silence.

'You saw it on *Blue Peter,*' he said at last.

'Yes,' said Milly tearfully. 'A *Blue Peter* special.'

With a sudden roar, Simon threw back his head, and began to laugh.

'It's not funny!' said Milly indignantly.

'Yes it is!' said Simon through his laughter. 'It's very funny!'

'No it's not!' cried Milly. 'All this time, I've been feeling guilty about it. Don't you understand? I've been pretending to be mature and intelligent. And I fooled you. But I'm not intelligent. I'm just not!'

Simon abruptly stopped laughing.

'Milly, are you serious?'

'Of course I am,' said Milly, in tears. 'I'm not clever! I'm not bright!'

'Yes you are.'

'No I'm not! Not like Isobel.'

'Like *Isobel*?' echoed Simon incredulously. 'You think Isobel's bright? How bright is it to get knocked up by your boyfriend?' He raised his eyebrows at Milly and suddenly she gave a little giggle.

'Isobel may be intellectual,' said Simon. 'But you're the brightest star of your family.'

'Really?' said Milly in a little voice.

'Really. And even if you weren't—even if you had only one brain cell to call your own—I'd still love you. I love *you*, Milly. Not your IQ.'

'You can't possibly love me,' said Milly jerkily. 'You don't . . .'

'Know you?' said Simon. 'Of course I know you.' He sighed. 'Milly, knowing a person isn't like knowing a string of facts. It's more like . . . a feeling.' He lifted his hand and gently pushed back a strand of her hair. 'I can feel when you're going to laugh and when you're going to cry. I can feel your kindness and your warmth and your sense of humour. I feel all that inside me. And that's what matters. Not sushi. Not modern art. Not *Family Fortunes*.' He paused, then said in a deadpan voice, ' "Our survey said . . ." '

Milly gaped at him.

'Do you *watch* it?'

'I catch it occasionally.' He grinned. 'Come on, Milly, I'm allowed to be human, too. Aren't I?'

There was silence. In the distance a clock chimed. Milly exhaled shakily and said, almost to herself, 'I could do with—'

'A cigarette?' interrupted Simon. Milly raised her head to look at him, then gave a tiny shrug.

'Maybe,' she said.

'Come on,' said Simon, grinning. 'Did I get that right? Doesn't that prove I know you?'

'Maybe.'

'Admit it! I know you! I know when you want a cigarette. That's got to be true love. Hasn't it?'

There was a pause, then Milly said again, 'Maybe.' She reached in her pocket for her cigarette packet and allowed Simon to cradle the flame of her lighter from the wind.

'So,' he said, as she inhaled her first drag.

'So,' said Milly.

There was a still, tense silence. Milly took another drag, not meeting Simon's eyes.

'I was thinking,' said Simon.

'What?'

'If you'd like to, we could go and get some pizza. And maybe . . .' He paused. 'You could tell me a little bit about yourself.'

'OK,' said Milly. She blew out a cloud of smoke and gave him half a smile. 'That would be nice.'

'You do like pizza,' added Simon.

'Yes,' said Milly. 'I do.'

'You're not just pretending, to impress me.'

'Simon,' said Milly. 'Shut up.'

'I'll go and get the car,' he said, feeling in his pocket for his keys.

'No, wait,' said Milly, waving her cigarette at him. 'Let's walk. I feel like walking. And . . . talking.' Simon stared at her.

'All the way into Bath?'

'Why not?'

'It's three miles!'

'You see, that just shows,' said Milly. 'You don't know me. I can walk three miles. At school I was in the cross-country team.'

'But it's bloody freezing!'

'We'll warm up as we walk. Come on, Simon.' She put her hand on his arm. 'I really want to.'

'OK,' said Simon, putting away his car keys. 'Fine. Let's walk.'

'They're going into the garden,' said Isobel. 'Together.' She turned back from the window. 'But they haven't kissed yet.'

'Maybe they don't want an audience,' said Harry. 'Especially a nosy older sister.'

'They don't know I'm watching!' retorted Isobel. 'I've been very careful. Oh. They've gone now.' She bit her lip and sat back on the window-seat. 'I hope . . . you know.'

'Relax,' said Harry from his seat by the fire. 'Everything will be fine.' Isobel looked at him. He had a piece of paper in his hand and a pen.

'What are you doing?' she asked. Harry glanced up and saw her gazing at him.

'Nothing,' he said, and quickly folded the piece of paper in two.

'Show me!' said Isobel.

'It's nothing important,' said Harry, and began to put the paper in his pocket. But Isobel was across the room in a moment, and whipped it out of his grasp.

'It's just a few names that sprang to mind,' said Harry stiffly, as she uncrumpled it. 'I thought I'd jot them down.'

Isobel stared down at the page and started to laugh.

'Harry, you're mad!' she said. 'We've got seven months to think about it!' She looked down the list, smiling at some of the names and pulling faces at others. Then she turned over the paper. 'And what's all this?'

'Oh that,' said Harry. A slightly shamefaced look came to his face. 'That was just in case we have twins.'

Milly and Simon were walking slowly through the gardens of Pinnacle Hall, towards a wrought-iron gate which opened onto the main road.

'This isn't at all what I was supposed to be doing tonight,' said Milly, gazing up into the starry sky. 'Tonight, I was supposed to be having a quiet supper at home and packing my honeymoon case.'

'I was supposed to be smoking a cigar with Dad and having second thoughts,' said Simon.

'And are you?' said Milly. 'Having second thoughts?'

'Are you?' rejoined Simon.

Milly said nothing, but continued to stare at the sky. They carried on walking silently, past the rose garden, past the frozen fountain and into the orchard.

'There it is,' said Simon, suddenly stopping. 'The bench. Where I proposed to you.' He glanced at her. 'Remember?' Milly stiffened slightly.

'Yes,' she said. 'Of course I remember. You had the ring in your pocket. And the champagne ready in the tree stump.'

'I spent days planning it,' said Simon reminiscently. He went over and patted the stump. 'I wanted it to be perfect.'

Milly stared at him, clenching her fists by her sides. Honesty, she told herself furiously. Be honest.

'It was too perfect,' she said bluntly.

'What?' Simon's head jerked up in shock and Milly felt a stab of guilt.

'Simon, I'm sorry,' she said at once. 'I didn't mean it.' She walked a little way away from him and looked into the trees. 'It was lovely.'

'Milly, don't pretend,' said Simon, his voice stiff with hurt. 'Tell me the truth. What did you really think?'

There was a pause.

'Well, OK,' said Milly at last. 'If I'm really going to be honest, it was beautiful—but . . .' She turned round to face him. 'Just a bit too planned. You had the ring on my finger before I could take a breath. The next minute, you're cracking open the champagne and we're officially engaged. I never . . .' She broke off and rubbed her face. 'I never had time to think about it.'

There was silence.

'I see,' said Simon at last. 'And if you'd had time to think, what would you have said?' Milly looked at him for a few long seconds, then turned away.

'Come on,' she said. 'Let's go and get that pizza.'

'OK,' said Simon, his voice tinged with disappointment. 'OK.' He took a few steps, then stopped. 'And you're quite sure you want to walk.'

'Yes,' said Milly. 'Walking always clears my head.' She held out her hand. 'Come on.'

Half an hour later, in the middle of the dark road, Milly stopped.

'Simon?' she said in a little voice. 'I'm cold.'

'Well, let's walk more quickly then.'

'And my feet hurt. My shoes are giving me blisters.'

Simon stopped, and looked at her. She had wrapped her hands in the ends of her jersey sleeves and buried them under her armpits; her lips were trembling and her teeth were chattering.

'Is your head clear?' he asked.

'No,' said Milly miserably. 'It's not. All I can think about is a nice hot bath.'

'Well, it's not long now,' said Simon cheerfully. Milly peered ahead at the black, unlit road.

'I can't go on any more. Are there any taxis?'

'I don't think so,' said Simon. 'But you can have my jacket.' He took it off and Milly grabbed it, snuggling into the warm lining. 'Won't you be cold?' she said vaguely.

'I'll be all right,' said Simon. 'Shall we go on?'

'OK,' said Milly, and began to hobble forward again. Simon stopped, and looked at her.

'Is that the best you can do?'

'My feet are *bleeding*,' wailed Milly. Simon's eyes fell on her feet.

'Are those new shoes?'

'Yes,' said Milly dolefully. 'And they were very cheap. And now I hate them.' She took another step forward and winced. Simon sighed.

'Come here,' he said. 'Put your feet on my feet. I'll walk you for a bit.'

'Really?'

'Come here. Put your shoes in your pocket.'

He grasped Milly firmly round the waist and began to stride awkwardly forward into the night, carrying her feet on his own.

'This is nice,' said Milly after a while.

'Yes,' grunted Simon. 'It's great.'

'You walk very quickly, don't you?'

'I do when I'm hungry.'

'I'm sorry about this,' said Milly in a subdued voice. 'It was a nice idea though, wasn't it?' There was a pause, and she turned round, nearly throwing Simon off balance altogether. 'Wasn't it, Simon?'

Simon began to laugh, his voice hoarse from the evening air.

'Yes, Milly,' he said at last, almost gasping with the effort of speaking. 'One of your best.'

When they finally arrived at the pizza restaurant, they were both nearly speechless with cold and effort. As they opened the door, the warmth of the air and the garlic-laden smell of food hit them in the face in an intoxicating blast. The place was full, buzzing with people and music; the cold dark road suddenly seemed a million miles away.

'A table for two, please,' said Simon, depositing Milly on the floor. 'And two large brandies.'

Milly smiled at him, rubbing her cold, reddened cheeks.

'You know, my feet feel a bit better now,' she said, trying them out experimentally on the marble floor. 'I think I'll be able to walk to the table.'

'Good,' said Simon, stretching his back. 'That's great.'

They were shown to a booth by a red-dressed waiter, who immediately returned with the two brandies.

'Cheers,' said Milly. She met Simon's eyes hesitantly. 'I don't quite know what we're toasting. Here's to . . . the wedding we never had?'

'Let's toast us,' said Simon, looking at her suddenly seriously.
'Let's toast us. Milly—'

'What?'

There was silence. Milly's heart began to thump. Nervously,
she began to shred her paper napkin.

'I haven't planned this,' said Simon. 'God knows I haven't
planned this. But I can't wait any longer.'

He put down his menu and sank to one knee on the floor beside the booth. There was a slight flurry around the restaurant as
people looked over and began to nudge each other.

'Milly, please,' said Simon. 'I'm asking you again. And I . . . I
hope beyond hope that you'll say yes. Will you marry me?'

There was a long silence. At last Milly looked up. Her cheeks
were tinged a rosy pink; her napkin was a red papery mess in her
fingers.

'Simon, I don't know,' she said. 'I . . . I need to think about it.'

As they came to the end of their pizzas, Milly cleared her throat
and looked nervously at Simon.

'How was your pizza?' she said in a dry voice.

'Fine,' said Simon. 'Yours?'

'Fine.' Their eyes met very briefly; then Simon looked away.

'Do you . . .' he began. 'Have you . . .'

'Yes,' said Milly, biting her lip. 'I've finished thinking.'

Her gaze ran over him—still kneeling on the floor beside the
table, as he had been throughout the meal, his food spread around
him like a picnic. A tiny smile came to her face.

'Would you like to get up now?' she said.

'Whatever for?' said Simon, taking a swig from his glass of wine. 'I'm very comfortable down here.'

'I'm sure you are,' said Milly, her lips trembling. 'I'm sure you are. I just thought . . . you might want to kiss me.'

There was a tense silence.

'Might I?' said Simon eventually. Slowly he put down his wine glass and raised his eyes to hers. For a few moments they just gazed at each other, unaware of the waiters nudging one another and calling into the kitchen; oblivious of anything but themselves. 'Might I really?'

'Yes,' said Milly, trying to control her shaking voice. 'You might.' She put down her napkin, slid down off her seat beside him onto the marble floor and wrapped her arms around his neck. As her lips met his, there was a small ripple of applause from around the restaurant. Tears began to stream down Milly's cheeks, onto Simon's neck and into their mingled mouths. She closed her eyes and leaned against his broad chest, inhaling the scent of his skin, suddenly too weak to move a muscle. She felt drained of all energy, emptied of all emotion; unable to cope with anything more.

'Just one question,' said Simon into her ear. 'Who's going to tell your mother?'

CHAPTER EIGHTEEN

At nine o'clock the next morning the air was bright and crisp. As Milly's little car pulled up outside 1 Bertram Street, the postman was about to push a bundle of letters through the letterbox.

'Morning!' he said, turning round. 'How's the bride?'

'Fine,' said Milly, giving him a tight little smile. She took the letters from him, reached inside her pocket for her key then paused. Her heart was beating in a mixture of anticipation and dread, and a thousand introductory phrases whirled around her mind. She stared for a few seconds at the shiny gloss of the front door, then put her key into the lock.

'Mummy?' she called as she entered, her voice high with nerves. 'Mummy?' She put the letters down on the hall stand and took off her coat, trying to stay calm. But suddenly excitement was bubbling through her like soda, and she could feel a wide grin licking across her face. She felt like laughing and singing and jumping up and down like a little girl. 'Mummy, guess what?'

She threw open the door of the kitchen joyfully and felt a sudden jerk of astonishment. Her mother and father were sitting companionably together at the kitchen table, both still in their dressing gowns, as though they were on holiday.

'Oh,' she said, not quite sure why she felt so surprised.

'Milly!' exclaimed Olivia, putting down her paper. 'Are you all right?'

'We assumed you stayed the night at Harry's,' said James.

'Have you had breakfast?' said Olivia. 'Let me get you some coffee—and how about some nice toast?'

'Yes,' said Milly. 'I mean, no. Look, listen!' She pushed a hand through her hair, and the smile returned to her face. 'I need to tell you some good news. Simon and I are going to get married!'

'Oh, darling!' cried Olivia. 'That's wonderful!'

'So you made up with him,' said James. 'I'm very glad to hear it. He's a good chap.'

'I know he is,' said Milly. A smile spread across her face. 'And I love him. And he loves me. And it's all lovely again.'

'This is simply marvellous!' said Olivia. She picked up her mug and took a sip of coffee. 'When were you thinking of having the wedding?'

'In two hours' time,' said Milly happily.

'What?' exclaimed Olivia, dropping her mug down on the table with a little crash.

'Milly, are you serious?' said James. 'This morning?'

'Yes! This morning!' said Milly. 'Why not?'

'Why not?' said Olivia, her voice rising in panic. 'Because nothing's arranged! Because we've cancelled everything! I'm very sorry, darling, but there isn't a wedding to have any more!'

'Mummy, we've got everything we need for a wedding,' said Milly. 'A bride and a groom. Someone to give me away'—she looked at James—'and someone to wear a big hat and cry. We've even got the wedding cake. We don't need any more than that.'

'But Canon Lytton—'

'We told him last night,' said Milly. 'In fact, it's all arranged. So come on!' She gestured to the pair of them. 'Get dressed! Get ready!'

'Wait!' called Olivia, as Milly disappeared out of the kitchen door. 'What about Simon? He hasn't got a best man!' The door opened and Milly's face appeared again.

'Yes he has,' she said. 'He's got a jolly fine best man.'

'It's all very easy,' said Simon, taking a gulp of coffee. 'Here are the rings. When the vicar asks you for them, you just hand them over. And that's it!'

'Right,' said Harry heavily. He took the two gold bands from Simon and stared at them for a couple of seconds as though trying to commit their form to memory. 'The vicar asks me for the rings, and I hand them over. Do I hold them out on the palm of my hand, or in my fingers, or what?'

'I don't know,' said Simon. 'Does it matter?'

'I don't know!' said Harry. 'You tell me! Jesus!'

'Dad, you're not nervous, are you?' said Simon.

'Of course I'm not fucking nervous!' said Harry. 'Now go on. Go and shine your shoes.'

'See you later,' said Simon at the kitchen door, and grinned back at Harry.

'*Are* you nervous?' said Isobel, from the window-seat, when Simon had gone.

'No,' said Harry, then looked up. 'Maybe a bit.' He pushed back his chair abruptly and strode over to the window. 'It's ridiculous. I shouldn't be Simon's best man, for Christ's sake!'

'Yes you should,' said Isobel. 'He wants you.'

'He hasn't got anyone else, you mean. So he asks his old dad.'

'No, that's not what I mean,' said Isobel patiently. 'He could easily phone up a friend from work. You know he could. But he wants you. You *are* his best man. And mine.' She reached for his hand and after a moment he squeezed hers. Then she glanced at her watch and pulled a face. 'And now I really must go. Mummy will be having kittens.'

'I'll see you there, then,' said Harry.

'See you there,' said Isobel. At the door, she turned back. 'Of course, you know what the perk of being the best man is.'

'What's that?'

'You get to sleep with the chief bridesmaid.'

'Is that so?' said Harry, brightening.

'It's in all the rule books,' said Isobel. 'Ask the vicar. He'll tell you.'

As she went into the hall, she saw Rupert coming down the stairs. Unaware that he was being watched, his face was full of an unformed grief; a raw misery that made Isobel's spine prickle unpleasantly. For a few moments she stood silently, saying nothing. Then, suddenly feeling like a voyeur, she forced herself to make a sound with her foot and pause for a moment before walking forward, giving him a chance to gather his thoughts before he saw her.

'Hello,' she said. 'We were wondering if you were all right. Did you sleep well?'

'Great, thanks,' said Rupert, nodding. 'Very kind of Harry to put me up.'

'Oh my God,' said Isobel. 'That was nothing! It was very kind of you to come all this way to tell Milly about . . .' She tailed off awkwardly. 'You know the wedding's back on?'

'No,' said Rupert. He gave her a strained smile. 'That's great news. Really great.' Isobel stared at him in compassion, wanting somehow to make everything right for him.

'You know, I'm sure Milly would want to you to come,' she said. 'It isn't going to be a big, smart wedding any more. Just the six of us, in fact. But if you'd like to, we'd all be delighted if you could come.'

'That's very kind,' said Rupert after a pause. 'Very kind indeed. But . . . I think I might go home instead. If you don't mind.'

'Of course not,' said Isobel. 'Absolutely. Whatever you want.' She looked around the empty hall. 'I'll find someone to drive you to the station. There's a fast London train every hour.'

'I'm not going to London,' said Rupert. A distant, almost peaceful expression came to his face. 'I'm going home. To Cornwall.'

By ten-thirty, Olivia was fully dressed and made up. She peered at her reflection in the mirror and gave a satisfied smile. Her bright pink suit fitted perfectly and the matching wide-brimmed hat cast a rosy glow over her face. Her blond hair shone brightly in the winter sunshine as she turned her face this way and that, checking for make-up imperfections and fluff on the black velvet collar of her jacket. Finally she turned away and picked up her bag, noticing with pleasure the handmade pink silk bows now decorating her patent leather shoes.

'You look stupendous!' said James, coming in.

'And you look very handsome,' said Olivia, running her eyes over his morning coat. 'Very distinguished. Father of the bride.'

'Mother of the bride,' rejoined James, grinning at her. 'Speaking of which, where is she?'

'Still getting ready,' said Olivia. 'Isobel's helping her.'

'Well then,' said James, 'I suggest we go and partake of a little pre-wedding champagne. Shall we?' He held out his arm and, after a moment's hesitation, Olivia took it. As they descended the stairs into the hall, a voice stopped them.

'Hold it. Just for a second. Don't look at me.'

They paused, smiling at each other while Alexander snapped away for a few seconds.

'OK,' he said. 'You can carry on now.' As Olivia passed him, he winked at her. 'Great hat, Olivia. Very sexy.'

'Thank you, Alexander,' said Olivia, a slight blush coming to her cheeks. James squeezed her arm and her blush deepened.

'Come on,' she said quickly. 'Let's have that champagne.'

They went into the drawing room, where a fire was crackling and James had laid out a champagne bottle and glasses. He handed her a glass and raised his own.

'Here's to the wedding,' he said.

'The wedding,' said Olivia. She sipped at her champagne, then sat down gingerly on the edge of a chair, being careful not to crease her skirt. 'Are we having speeches at the reception?'

'I don't know,' said James humorously. 'Are we having a reception?' Olivia shrugged and took a sip of champagne.

'Who knows? It's up to Milly. This is her day now.' A flicker of
emotion passed over her face. 'I'm just another guest.' James met
her eyes compassionately.

'Do you mind?' he said. 'Do you mind that we aren't having
the big lavish wedding that you planned? The ice swans and the
organist flown in from Geneva and the five thousand VIPs?'

'No,' said Olivia after a pause. 'I don't mind.' She smiled
brightly at James. 'They're getting married. That's the important
thing, isn't it? They're getting married.'

'Yes,' said James. 'That's the important thing.'

There was a pause. Olivia stared into the fire, cradling her
drink.

'And you know,' she said suddenly, 'in many ways, it's more
original to have a tiny, private wedding. Big weddings can become
rather vulgar if one isn't careful. Don't you think?'

'Absolutely,' said James, smiling.

'One might almost have planned this all along!' said Olivia,
happiness starting to edge her voice. 'After all, we don't want the
world and all its riff-raff at the wedding of our daughter, do we?
We want an intimate, exclusive wedding.'

'Well, it'll certainly be intimate,' said James, draining his glass.
'I'm not sure about exclusive.'

There was a sound at the door and he looked up. Isobel was
standing in the doorway, dressed in a long flowing column of pale
pink silk. Her hair was wreathed in flowers and her cheeks were
self-consciously flushed.

'I've come to announce the bride,' she said. 'She's ready.'

'You look wonderful, darling!' exclaimed James.

'Absolutely beautiful!' said Olivia. Isobel shrugged.

'I look all right,' she said. 'You should see Milly. Come and watch her walking down the stairs. Alexander is taking pictures.'

'Darling,' said Olivia sharply, as Isobel turned to go. 'What happened to the roses?'

'What roses?'

'The silk roses that were on your dress!'

'Oh, those,' said Isobel after a pause. 'They . . . fell off.'

'Fell off?'

'Yes,' said Isobel. 'You can't have sewn them on very well.' She looked at Olivia's perplexed face and grinned. 'Come on, Mummy. The roses don't matter. Come and see Milly. She's the main attraction.'

They all filed into the hall and looked up the stairs. Coming slowly down, smiling shyly through her veil, was Milly, wearing a starkly cut dress of ivory satin. The stiff, embroidered bodice was laced tightly around her figure; the long sleeves were edged at the wrist with fur; in her hair sparkled a diamond tiara.

'Milly!' said Olivia shakily. 'You look perfect. A perfect bride.' Tears suddenly filled her eyes and she turned away.

'What do you think?' said Milly tremulously, looking around at them all. 'Will I do?'

'Darling, you look exquisite,' said James. 'Simon Pinnacle can count himself a very lucky young man.'

'I can't believe it's really happening,' said Olivia, holding a tiny hanky to her eyes. 'Little Milly. Getting married.'

'How are we all going to get there?' said Alexander, taking a final picture. 'I want to take my tripod with me.'

'Milly?' said James, looking up at her. 'It's your show.'

'I don't know,' said Milly, a perturbed expression coming over her face. She descended a few steps, her train falling behind her. 'I hadn't thought about it.'

'Let's walk!' said Isobel, grinning at her.

'Shut up, Isobel,' said Milly. 'Oh God. What are we going to do?'

'If we take both cars,' said James, looking at Olivia, 'you could drive Alexander and Isobel, and I could come on with Milly . . .'

He was interrupted by a ring at the front door and they all looked up.

'Who on earth—' said James. He looked around, then silently went to open it. A man holding a peaked cap under his arm was standing on the steps. He bowed stiffly.

'Wedding cars for Havill,' he said.

'What?' James peered past him onto the street. 'But these were cancelled!'

'No they weren't,' said the man. James turned back.

'Olivia,' he said. 'Didn't you cancel the wedding cars?'

'Of course I did,' said Olivia crisply.

'Not according to my information,' said the man.

'Not according to your information,' echoed Olivia, shaking her head in exasperation. 'Does it ever occur to you people that your information might be wrong? I spoke to a young woman at your company only yesterday and she assured me that everything would be cancelled. So what I suggest is that you get back in your car, and speak to whoever mans the telephone, and sure enough, you will find—'

'Mummy!' interrupted Milly in agonized tones. 'Mummy!' She pulled a meaningful face at Olivia, who suddenly realized what she was saying.

'However,' she said, pulling herself up straight. 'By very good fortune, the situation has changed once again.'

'So you do want the cars,' said the man.

'We do,' said Olivia haughtily.

'Very good, madam,' said the man, and disappeared down the steps. As he reached the bottom, the words 'fucking nutter' travelled audibly back towards them.

'Right,' said James. 'Well, you lot go off . . . and Milly and I will follow. Isn't that the protocol?'

'See you there,' said Isobel, grinning at Milly. 'Good luck!'

As they descended the steps to the waiting cars, Alexander drew Isobel back slightly.

'You know, I'd really like to take some shots of you on your own some time,' he said. 'You've got fantastic cheekbones.'

'Oh really?' said Isobel, raising her eyebrows. 'Is that what you say to all the girls?'

'No,' said Alexander. 'Only the stunning ones.' He looked at her. 'I'm serious.'

Isobel stared at him.

'Alexander—'

'I don't know if this is out of order,' he said, hoisting his tripod on his shoulder. 'But maybe, when all this wedding business is over . . . you and I could go for a drink?'

'You've got a nerve!' said Isobel.

'I know,' said Alexander. 'Do you want to?'

Isobel began to laugh.

'I'm very flattered,' she said. 'I'm also pregnant.'

'Oh.' He shrugged. 'That doesn't matter.'

'And . . .' she added, a faint tinge coming to her cheeks, '. . . I'm going to get married.'

'What?' Ten yards ahead of them, Olivia wheeled round on the pavement, her eyes bright. 'Isobel! Are you serious?'

Isobel rolled her eyes at Alexander.

'It's just an idea, Mummy,' she said in a louder voice. 'It isn't definite.'

'But who is he, darling? Have I met him? Do I know his name?'

Isobel gazed dumbly at Olivia. She opened her mouth to speak, closed it again, looked away and shifted on the ground.

'He's . . . he's someone I'll introduce you to later,' she said at last. 'After the wedding's finished. Let's just get that over first. All right?'

'Whatever you say, darling,' said Olivia. 'Oh, I'm so thrilled!'

'Good!' said Isobel, smiling weakly. 'That's good.'

Harry and Simon arrived at the church at ten to eleven. They pushed open the door and looked silently around the huge, empty, decorated space. Simon glanced at his father, then walked a few paces up the broad aisle, his shoes echoing on the stones.

'Aha!' said Canon Lytton, appearing out of a side door. 'The bridegroom and his best man! Welcome!' He hurried down the aisle towards them, past the gleaming rows of empty mahogany pews, each adorned with flowers.

'Where do we sit?' said Harry, looking around. 'All the best seats are taken.'

'Very droll,' said Canon Lytton, beaming at him. 'The places for the groom and his best man are at the front, on the right-hand side.'

'This is very good of you,' said Simon, as they followed him towards the front of the church. 'To reinstate the service at such short notice. And with such small numbers. We're very grateful.'

'Numbers are immaterial,' said Canon Lytton. 'As our Lord said Himself, "Where two or three have met together in my name, I am there among them."' He paused. 'Of course, the collection plate may suffer a little as a result . . .' He broke off delicately, and Harry cleared his throat.

'Naturally, I'll make up the shortfall,' he said. 'If you give me some kind of estimate.'

'So kind,' murmured Canon Lytton. 'Ah, here comes Mrs Blenkins, our organist. You were very fortunate that she was free this morning!'

An elderly woman in a brown anorak was walking up the aisle towards them.

'I haven't practised anything up,' she said as soon as she reached them. 'There hasn't been the time, you see.'

'Of course not,' said Simon at once. 'We completely—'

'Will "Here Comes the Bride" do you?'

'Absolutely,' said Simon, glancing at Harry. 'Whatever. Thanks very much. We're very grateful.' The woman nodded, and marched off, and Canon Lytton disappeared in a rustle of linen.

Simon sat down on the front pew and stretched his legs out in front of him.

'I'm terrified,' he said.

'So am I,' said Harry, giving a little shudder. 'That priest gives me the creeps.'

'Will I be a good husband?' Simon threw back his head and looked up into the cavernous space of the church. 'Will I make Milly happy?'

'You already do make her happy,' said Harry. 'Just don't change anything. Don't think you have to act differently because you're married.' He met Simon's eye. 'You love her. That's enough for anyone.'

There was a noise at the back of the church and Olivia appeared, a vision in bright pink. She walked up the aisle, her heels clacking lightly on the floor.

'They'll be here in a minute,' she whispered.

'Come and sit beside me,' said Harry, patting the pew. For an instant, Olivia wavered.

'No,' she said regretfully. 'It wouldn't be right. I have to sit on the other side.' She lifted her chin slightly. 'Since I am the mother of the bride.'

She sat down, and there was a few minutes' silence. From out of nowhere the organ began to play quietly. Simon stretched out his fingers and stared hard at them. Harry looked at his watch. Olivia brought out a compact and checked her reflection.

Suddenly there was a rattling at the back of the church and they all jumped.

Simon took a deep breath, trying to steady his nerves. But his heart was pounding and his palms felt damp.

'Do you think we should stand up?' he whispered to his father.

'I don't know!' hissed back Harry. He looked equally agitated. 'How the fuck do I know?'

Olivia turned and peered towards the back of the church.

'I can see her!' she whispered. 'She's here!'

The organ music slowed down, then stopped altogether. Looking hesitantly at each other, the three of them stood up. There was an agonized silence; no one seemed to be breathing.

Then the familiar chords of Wagner's Wedding March swelled into the air. Simon felt a lump coming to his throat. Not daring to look round, he stared ahead, blinking furiously, until he felt Harry tugging his sleeve. Very slowly he swivelled his head round until he was looking down the aisle, and felt his heart stop. There was Milly on her father's arm, looking more beautiful than he'd ever seen her. Her lips were parted in a tremulous smile; her eyes were sparkling behind her veil; her skin glowed against the pale creaminess of her dress.

As she reached his side she stopped. She hesitated, then, with trembling hands, slowly lifted the gauzy veil from her face. As she did so, her fingers brushed the necklace of freshwater pearls she was wearing. She paused, holding one of the tiny pearls, and for a few moments her eyes dimmed.

Then she let go of it, took a deep breath and looked up.

'Ready?' said Simon.

'Yes,' said Milly, and smiled at him. 'I'm ready.'

As Rupert arrived at the little cottage perched on the cliffs, it was nearly midday. He glanced at his watch as he walked up the path, and thought to himself that Milly would be married by now. She and Simon would be drinking champagne, as happy as two people could ever be.

The door opened before he reached it, and his father looked out.

'Hello, my boy,' he said kindly. 'I've been expecting you.'

'Hello, Father,' said Rupert, and put down his briefcase to give his father a hug. As he met the older man's mild, unquestioning gaze, he felt his defences crumble completely, as though he might suddenly burst into unstoppable sobs. But his emotions were run dry; he was beyond tears now.

'Come and have a nice cup of tea,' said his father, leading the way into the tiny sitting room, overlooking the sea. He paused. 'Your wife called today, wondered if you were here. She said to tell you she was sorry. And she sends you her love and prayers.'

Rupert said nothing. He sat down by the window and looked out at the empty blue sea. It occurred to him that he'd almost completely forgotten about Francesca.

'You also had a call from another young woman a few days ago,' called his father from the tiny kitchen. There was a clatter of crockery. 'Milly, I think her name was. Did she manage to track you down?'

The flicker of something like a smile passed across Rupert's face.

'Yes,' he said. 'She tracked me down.'

'I hadn't heard of her before,' said his father, coming in with a teapot. 'Is she an old friend of yours?'

'Not really,' said Rupert. 'Just . . .' He paused. 'Just the wife of a friend of mine.'

And he leaned back in his chair and stared out of the window at the waves breaking on the rocks below.